W9-AQE-982

WITCHY WINTER

BAEN BOOKS by D.J. BUTLER

Witchy Eye
Witchy Winter

WITCHY WINTER

War Comes to the Serpent Kingdom

D.J. BUTLER

WITCHY WINTER

This is a work of fiction. All the characters and events portrayed in this book are fictional, and any resemblance to real people or incidents is purely coincidental.

A Baen Books Original

Baen Publishing Enterprises
P.O. Box 1403
Riverdale, NY 10471
www.baen.com

ISBN: 978-1-4814-8314-8

Cover art by Daniel Dos Santos
Map by Bryan G. McWhirter

First printing, April 2018

Distributed by Simon & Schuster
1230 Avenue of the Americas
New York, NY 10020

Library of Congress Cataloging-in-Publication Data

Names: Butler, D. J. (David John), 1973– author.
Title: Witchy winter / D.J. Butler.
Description: Riverdale, NY : Baen, [2018]
Identifiers: LCCN 2017054265 | ISBN 9781481483148 (hardcover)
Subjects: LCSH: Magic—Fiction. | BISAC: FICTION / Fantasy / Historical. |
   FICTION / Fantasy / Epic. | FICTION / Alternative History. | GSAFD:
   Fantasy fiction. | Epic fiction.
Classification: LCC PS3602.U8667 W59 2018 | DDC 813/.6—dc23 LC record
available at https://lccn.loc.gov/2017054265

10 9 8 7 6 5 4 3 2 1

Pages by Joy Freeman (www.pagesbyjoy.com)
Printed in the United States of America

Acknowledgements

Few books are written truly alone. Big thanks to
Jim Minz for joining me in the exploration of this
imaginary-and-yet-not-wholly-imaginary land that I
love and for providing great editorial guidance.

For all the reasons that I want to write this story, I want
to find people who will read it. I owe gratitude to the
entire Baen team (editors, writers, and readers) for their
efforts on this score, and especially to Corinda Carfora and
Christopher Ruocchio, for their advocacy, their time, their
enthusiasm, their wisdom, and their marketing mojo.

Thank you, my friends.

For my father, Dick Butler, who knows all the stars.

And for my friend John Lundwall,
who reminded me that I should know them, too.

"You didn't ask me to survive.
You asked me to show you how to find the healer."

————◆————

CHAPTER ONE

With one last push and a hiss of triumph, Waabigwan gave birth to their child. Ma'iingan's sister Miskomin scooped the baby up, cut and knotted its umbilical cord, dried its face, and as it emitted its first soft cries, began to swaddle it.

"Go." Waabigwan's eyes glittered in the dim light.

Ma'iingan yawned and stretched. "Fishing?" he asked his wife. "You hungry for walleye, again? Maybe lake trout? You know it isn't the season to harvest manoomin. At least I'm awake for your strange cravings this time."

"Go, my wolf." Waabigwan smiled, forgiving Ma'iingan his sense of humor again. "If you want this child to be one of the People, you must defend it."

Ma'iingan took his good German flintlock from where it leaned against the wall of the wiigiwaam. "If I'm to defend this child, I must alert the attackers, no? Good thing your brother is such a skinny, toothless pup. This baby will be a Loon baby, safe from whatever the Catfish might try."

He pushed aside the hide hanging in the wiigiwaam's doorway and stepped into the chill spring night. The bright fire burning at the center of the camp stole his vision for a moment, but Ma'iingan didn't need to see to perform his duty. He'd carefully loaded and primed his German rifle when Waabigwan had gone into labor early in the afternoon; now he raised it and fired his gun at the night sky, announcing the birth of their first child.

The shrill whoop of attack in his ear caught him by surprise, and then Ma'iingan hit the ground hard. He swung his elbow at the attacker's solar plexus but missed; the other man was already up and bounding into the door of the wiigiwaam while Ma'iingan still struggled to catch his breath.

Ma'iingan knew Waabigwan's brother Omagakiins by his skinny ribs and the long braids bouncing down his back. The Catfish weren't sleeping, then.

No matter.

Ma'iingan rolled to his feet, tossing his rifle against the stack of firewood beside the wiigiwaam. He settled into a crouch before the door, ready to snatch the baby from his wife's brother when the younger man emerged.

The women's cries from inside the wiigiwaam were full of energy, but no real distress. No one wished harm to the baby; Omagakiins was doing his sacred duty just as Ma'iingan was.

But then Miskomin's tone of mock-fear turned to real surprise. "You can't do that! This is Ma'iingan's wiigiwaam!"

Eyes still adjusting to the firelight, Ma'iingan nearly missed Omagakiins. The young Catfish sprinted out from behind the wiigiwaam. With one hand, he sank a tomahawk into a birch trunk as his passed. It was Ma'iingan's own tomahawk, made of steel and purchased from the same Dutch Ohio Company traders who had sold him the rifle. In his left hand, Omagakiins clutched a bundle against his chest.

He'd cut an exit out the back of the wiigiwaam, the clever snake.

And he had the child.

Ma'iingan sprinted after him. As he passed the wiigiwaam's corner, an old Catfish warrior stepped forward from the darkness and threw a bowlful of water into Ma'iingan's face. The water was cold—there was still ice on the lakes—and Ma'iingan shivered as he lowered his shoulder to knock the Catfish to the earth.

In return, the Catfish grabbed Ma'iingan's ankle and tripped him.

Ma'iingan bounded to his feet again and raced after Omagakiins, now visible only as glints of flesh occasionally showing between the trees. The younger man was running for his own wiigiwaam.

Would this baby be a Catfish after all? And would Ma'iingan be a laughingstock for that?

Leaning forward onto the balls of his feet, Ma'iingan ran faster.

Another Catfish stepped from the trees with a bowl in his hands. Ma'iingan swerved, but not far enough, and the hurled flour struck him squarely in the bare chest, exploding upward and down in a cloud that coated him with fine white grit and also blinded him momentarily.

Ma'iingan hit a tree.

"Wiinuk!" he cursed.

Hands grabbed Ma'iingan's shoulders. He didn't have to see to be able to wrestle; Ma'iingan stepped into the attack, ducked, and got his shoulder under the attacker's weight. Grabbing the other man's knees, he straightened and tossed the Catfish back over his shoulder.

Wiping soggy flour from his eyes, Ma'iingan turned toward Omagakiins's wiigiwaam and ran. "Father!" he yelled. Where were the warriors of his own doodem, the Loon? Where were his father, his brother, his two nephews?

As Omagakiins reached his own wiigiwaam, women beside the fire cheered. Omagakiins raised the little bundle over his head—and old Animkii barreled out of the wiigiwaam door.

Animkii was Ma'iingan's father and he was nearing sixty years old, but age hadn't slowed him a bit. He crashed into the much younger Catfish and sent him staggering backward until his calves struck a small boulder and Omagakiins sat down suddenly on the earth.

"The baby!" Ma'iingan shouted.

Animkii waved an empty blanket. "That's no baby, Moosh Koosh! You've been tricked!"

Two Catfish men stepped from the trees, hitting Animkii simultaneously with flour and water. Omagakiins fell back to the earth, laughing hysterically.

There were too many Catfish in the tribe. *Maybe I should have married a Marten instead.*

But then he thought of Waabigwan's open smile and her gentle hands and he turned to race back toward his own wiigiwaam.

Miskomin emerged from the wiigiwaam door as he reached it. "The baby?" Ma'iingan asked.

"Another Catfish came into the wiigiwaam as Omagakiins left it. He took the baby and ran that way." Miskomin pointed.

Clever Catfish. "Cheaters," he said. "Have you seen Waagosh? Giniw?"

She shook her head. "Ma'iingan..."

Was something wrong? "Waabigwan is well, no?"

"Heya," she agreed, "Waabigwan is well."

"Then I must get this baby, if it is to be a Loon."

Miskomin nodded quickly and retreated into the wiigiwaam. Something made her uncomfortable; after he rescued his child, Ma'iingan would find out what it was.

Ma'iingan ran in the direction indicated by Miskomin, and almost ran into his brother Waagosh. Waagosh was older by nearly ten years, and heavier. A wool blanket over his shoulder flapped behind him as he charged ponderously toward Ma'iingan. In his arms he cradled a bundle. His long black hair was white with flour.

"That's the baby, no?" Ma'iingan held his arms forward as he ran to meet his brother.

Battle whoops sounded in the trees.

Waagosh puffed. "I was hiding in the trees and I saw this Catfish run by with your son."

"Son?" Ma'iingan wanted to say something, but all he could do was grin stupidly.

"Henh, son. The swaddling is loose."

Water splashed Waagosh in the face, and Ma'iingan heard his son's clear cry again. The Catfish who had thrown the water stepped forward to grab the baby.

Ma'iingan stuck his leg between the attacker's feet and pushed him. The Catfish fell to the ground yelping.

"Take the baby," Waagosh grunted.

Ma'iingan needed no further encouragement. He grabbed the child from its uncle and turned left, racing in toward the camp's large fire. He filled his lungs with air, preparing to shout the victorious chant that would announce his son as one of the People and a Loon.

Two Catfish ran toward him, between Ma'iingan and the fire. Each held a wooden bowl, and Ma'iingan braced himself to get wet or powdered again, or both. The child would get wet too, but he would be mostly sheltered by Ma'iingan's body, and the shocks of cold water and flour now would prepare the boy to be a warrior later.

But then Giniw was there. Ma'iingan's nephew burst from behind him and charged the Catfish. Lowering his head and raising his arms, and boy struck both bowls at the same moment. Two fountains of water rose and fell, splashing the Catfish and Giniw as they all tumbled together in a tangle of adolescent knees and elbows in the dirt.

Ma'iingan rushed past. He reached the fire and raised his son over his head, whooping and howling like his namesake the wolf. Animkii joined him, bellowing like the thunder for which *he* was named, and Ma'iingan joyfully passed his son to the baby's grandfather.

"This boy," Animkii roared, "is a Loon!"

Giniw joined them, shoving himself under Ma'iingan's arm for a hug of approval. Ma'iingan gave the boy the embrace and tousled his hair as well. Giniw was a good shot with bow and rifle, and with the kind of courage he had shown tonight, he would be a productive hunter. Should the Free Horse People cross the river to attack, or should the Germans of Chicago call on their allies among the Anishinaabe to go to war, he would be a mighty warrior, as well.

Omagakiins threw himself onto Ma'iingan's back and laughed as the people of the Catfish doodem joined the dance. "My sister has a brave husband," the young Catfish said.

"My wife has a clever brother," Ma'iingan shot back. "The Catfish are a mighty people."

"We're no Loons," Omagakiins said, pointed up and north at the celestial Loon, hidden by the fire's light. "Keeping all the People pointed in the right direction."

"That's just stubbornness." Ma'iingan grinned. "If you don't know how to turn, it's very important to convince everyone else you're walking in the right direction."

The dancing and singing had become general. The baby boy had passed from Loon hands into Catfish and Marten hands and back again, but it didn't matter now. The boy was a Loon.

As, really, he had to be. As everyone had known he would be from the beginning.

And he was one of the Anishinaabe, the People.

Ma'iingan embraced Waagosh as his brother lumbered to the fire, grimacing. "I believe I've sprained an ankle," the older brother said.

"Henh." Ma'iingan nodded solemnly. "If only you had two."

Waagosh grunted his acknowledgement of the joke. "Where is

this nephew of mine? I want a closer look at the evidence before I'll admit you're really a man."

"You'll have to take the baby from his grandfather. He seems to think the boy is *his*." Ma'iingan pointed—Animkii turned around and around the fire, refusing to hand the child over until finally Ma'iingan's mother Niibin planted both feet squarely in front of him and scowled.

Shaken like a fruit tree in the autumn, Animkii dislodged the boy into the arms of his grandmother.

"Well done, little brother." Waagosh clapped a hand on Ma'iingan's shoulder.

"Henh." The racing of his heart, the adrenalin in his veins, the sweat and flour and cold water on his flesh, and the cool prickle of the night air together made Ma'iingan tremble. "Thank you for fighting to keep the boy in the doodem."

"My doodem is Loon." Waagosh chuckled. "My brother's son's doodem must also be Loon." He squeezed Ma'iingan's shoulder one more time and advanced toward the fire.

Ma'iingan found himself standing with Miskomin. She held her hands folded in front of her and she looked at the earth.

"Thank you, sister," he said. "The men of our doodem have fought for my son this night, and you have fought for my wife."

Miskomin said nothing.

"How is Waabigwan?" Ma'iingan asked. Again, something was not quite right. A small shadow of uncertainty crept into his pride- and joy-filled heart.

"She is well," Miskomin said. "As is your ... *son*."

"Son?" Ma'iingan looked over his shoulder at the crowd surging about the fire, passing his firstborn child from hand to hand. "You mean ... ?"

Miskomin shook her head no.

Ma'iingan spoke slowly. "You mean ... I have ... ?"

"I mean your *second* son."

Standing in the darkness outside the circle of the fire, Ma'iingan suddenly felt fear.

"The wiigiwaam is ready," Ma'iingan said.

"You're making too much of this, Animoosh." His father shook his head. *Ma'iingan* was the People's word for wolf, and it was the name given to Ma'iingan by old Zhiishiigwe, who was a member of the Midewiwin as well as a respected namer. Animkii was also in the Midewiwin, but Zhiishiigwe's dreams had power.

Animoosh was the People's word for dog, and it was what most people called Ma'iingan most of the time.

"Waabigwan has put fresh boughs in the wiigiwaam. It's clean. We've collected summer fruits and berries. I've slaughtered a deer."

"You brought the second boy out to the fire," Animkii said. "We danced with him, too. I felt joy in my heart for him, too. He is also my grandson. He is a Loon."

"Is he?" Ma'iingan looked closely at his father. "And tell me what you felt this summer as you met with the Midewiwin to play your drums and fill yourselves with spirit power. Surely, you thought of your little grandson then. What did you feel in your heart when you thought of him? What do you feel when you think of him now? Is he truly one of the Anishinaabe?"

Animkii looked away.

Ma'iingan nodded sadly. "Henh, you also feel it. Something is wrong. And the younger boy is sickly. He doesn't eat, he doesn't grow. Perhaps he can't eat the People's food because he isn't one of the People."

"The boy is my grandson!" Animkii snapped.

"Yes, and he's my son. And Waabigwan's. And so Zhiishiigwe has put asemaa in both the children's hands and has promised to dream for them. And today we will feast, with our two sons, and their grandparents of the Loon doodem, and their aunt Miskomin and their uncles Waagosh and Omagakiins, and our sons will learn what names have been dreamed for them. And perhaps the feeling you and I both have that something is wrong will be healed. And perhaps my younger son will be able to eat."

"Henh," Animkii agreed, hooking both thumbs into the leather cord holding up his breechcloth. "May it be so."

The two men stood at the edge of the lake, colored orange and gold by the rays of the setting sun on its other side. Having emerged from their sweat and bathed in the lake, they had then dressed in their best leggings, and both had feathers plaited into their bear-greased hair. Animkii wore a necklace of shells and the ring through his nose, the one he had taken off a Zhaaga-naashii war leader from Penn's people when he'd been a young man, and worn since on ceremonial and special occasions. He hadn't worn it the night of the twins' birth because a prudent man never goes to a wrestling match wearing jewelry that might be torn from his flesh. Ma'iingan wore a beaded armband he'd been given by Waabigwan's father. That old Catfish warrior and his wife had died two years earlier, but Ma'iingan would represent their presence at the naming with the band.

"Come, let's go," he said to his father.

They arrived only moments before the namer. "Boozhoo," Ma'iingan said to the dreamer. The word was a greeting the People had borrowed from the French, but it was more respect-ful than a relaxed *aniin*.

"Boozhoo, Ma'iingan." Zhiishiigwe had been a tall man once, but in age he was stooped. The medicine man was a full generation older than Animkii, had been an old man when he'd clutched the infant Ma'iingan to his chest and told Animkii and Niibin that he had dreamed that their son was a wolf. Zhiishi-igwe's nose jutted like a hawk's beak, but his smile still hinted at the smooth danger of the rattlesnake he'd been named after. He, too, was dressed in finery, including a blue Acadian naval officer's coat. Before Zhiishiigwe had begun to dream, he had killed many Frenchmen and Zhaaganaashii.

Ma'iingan didn't remember the day of his own naming—he had been a small child, not old enough yet to stand—but he had been told by his parents how it had gone, and he had seen the naming of his nephew Giniw; old Zhiishiigwe had dreamed that that child was an eagle, and not just any eagle, but a glorious golden eagle—a *giniw*.

Later, Ma'iingan had fasted in the wilderness for his vision, and received another name. But that was a name not to share.

"Come in, sit down," Ma'iingan said. He pulled aside the skin door-hanging and then followed after the dreamer and his father.

Waabigwan and Niibin sat opposite the small fire of embers within the wiigiwaam. Each sat on her right foot and each held one of the twins. Miskomin sat beside them on her right foot, and Waagosh and Omagakiins sat cross-legged.

"Please sit down," Ma'iingan said again. Animkii shushed him. Then both men sat, while Zhiishiigwe remained standing.

"Pass me the older child," Zhiishiigwe said. The infant was wrapped in a soft white rabbit-skin blanket, and though awake, made the journey around the fire and into the dreamer's arms calmly. Zhiishiigwe held the baby tightly to his chest and looked upward. "I have dreamed of the forest."

Animkii nodded sagely.

Ma'iingan smiled reassuringly at his wife. Waabigwan smiled back, a brief flash.

"The forest was here before the People arrived, and the forest will always be here. The forest gives us life; its birch trees build our wiigiwaams and our canoes, its creatures fill our bellies, its colors brighten our vision. In the forest, the wolf hunts, and the flower grows, but who is king of the forest?"

Ma'iingan meant wolf and *waabigwan* meant flower; Zhiishiigwe was connecting the name of Ma'iingan's son to Ma'iingan's own name, and the name of his wife.

"You'd better not say the king of the forest is the frog," Ma'iingan joked. Frog was *Omagakiins* in the language of the People.

Omagakiins snorted and Niibin glared at her son. Zhiishiigwe chuckled. "Well are you named Ma'iingan," he said. "The wolf is quick of wit, always the hunter. No, the frog is small, and sleeps too much to be king."

"The buck," Animkii said. "Ayaabe is king of the forest."

Zhiishiigwe nodded. "Just so. He's fast, he leads his family, he roams great distances, and in battle even the wolf must fear his antlers. And so I dreamed I ran with a herd of deer in the forest, and where we fed, and where we rutted, and where we did battle, were decided by this child, the buck."

"Ayaabe." Ma'iingan nodded. It was a good name.

"Ayaabe." Animkii handed Ma'iingan a smoking pipe.

Ma'iingan held the pipe in his hands and looked across the wiigiwaam to his wife. Waabigwan smiled and nodded; the boy would be Ayaabe.

Ma'iingan took a deep draw from the pipe. The sacred sweetness of the asemaa herb filled his lungs, and he handed the pipe back to his father. "The boy's name is Ayaabe," he said.

"Ayaabe," the others said as they smoked.

"The child will be Ayaabe," Zhiishiigwe said as everyone had taken a turn at the pipe. He passed the child back to his Catfish uncle, who returned the baby to Niibin.

The wiigiwaam was large, but the fire and the pipe smoke and the bodies were beginning to make it feel close. Ma'iingan focused on keeping his breathing regular as he waited for the dreamer to proceed.

"Pass me the other," Zhiishiigwe said.

The *other*? Not the other child or the other baby, just the *other*? Ma'iingan held his tongue with effort. If this baby, too, could get a name from the Midewiwin dreamer, then the world would feel right again. The baby would be Loon and Anishinaabe, and not a stranger or a monster.

And maybe the child would eat. His face was pinched and fearful as Ma'iingan passed him around the circle.

The dreamer took this second bundle of white rabbit skins in his arms and looked deeply into the child's face. From where he sat, Ma'iingan couldn't tell whether the child's eyes were opened, but if not, the Midewiwin was staring a hole in the baby's forehead.

Then Zhiishiigwe clutched this child to his chest as he had done with the first, and Ma'iingan saw tears on the namer's cheeks.

He forced himself to breathe.

"I've fasted many days for this child," Zhiishiigwe said, his voice a reedy wail. "I've offered many pipes of asemaa to the earth and to the four winds. I have begged for a vision."

And then he said nothing.

Nothing.

"What are we to call this child?" Animkii asked. It was a gentle prompt, but Ma'iingan heard a note of desperation and surprise in it.

"It doesn't matter," Zhiishiigwe said. "You may call him what you wish. It is I who have dreamed nothing. It is I who have failed."

"Your failure does *not* matter!" Waagosh sprang to his feet. "This is my nephew! He is of me, and of my people! If Zhiishiigwe's dreams have failed him, then I will be namer to the child. *I* have dreamed, and in my dream I sat among the Midewiwin in their secret lodge and heard their secret talk and I laughed. I laughed in my dream, and this boy laughed with me. He is laughing still, though we cannot hear it. I name this child Giimoodaapi."

Giimoodaapi; he laughs in secret.

It was a strange name. Was it a bad one? Or was it a queer name, such as a hero might receive, a name that would send the boy on a quest into the dangerous world?

"It doesn't matter," Omagakiins repeated, but he looked into the fire.

It *did* matter. The world still felt wrong.

The boy didn't have a name. He wasn't Anishinaabe, he wasn't a Loon, he had no name.

"We will call him Giimoodaapi," Ma'iingan said. "At least for now."

"It's a good name." Animkii nodded fiercely across the fire at his son Waagosh.

"It's a name," Ma'iingan said. He nodded at Waagosh, a weary thanks.

"When he is older, he'll seek his own vision," Zhiishiigwe said. "Perhaps he'll receive his name then."

He passed the nameless baby back.

No one handed around the pipe.

Niibin burst into tears, squeezing the infant Ayaabe to her chest. Waabigwan took her other baby and then stared at Ma'iingan, and her eyes reflected his own heart back at him. *You're my wolf,* they said. *The wolf mates for life, the wolf is loyal, the wolf is a creature of family. You're my wolf and this is your cub.*

Fix this.

They ate squash and wild rice, deer and bear, and an abundance of berries.

It all tasted of ashes.

"The Midewiwin have met for the year," Animkii said. "I've been filled with power." He touched Ma'iingan lightly on the shoulder. "I give you my blessing."

And yet the world still felt wrong. Neither of them said it, but Ma'iingan knew his father must feel the same. If his father felt the world had been healed, wouldn't he tell his son?

"Very good," Ma'iingan said. "I'm counting on my family to protect both my sons while I'm gone. The younger may already be laughing secretly, but the buck is in no condition yet to lead his people to water."

"Giimoodaapi should have been *your* name, Animoosh."

"Henh," Ma'iingan agreed. "Except I've never been able to keep my laughs secret, have I?"

"Where will you go?" Animkii looked to the forested hills on the other side of the lake.

"Where I went when I was a young man in search of my vision," Ma'iingan said. "The only place where one can go."

"Where you're led," Animkii said.

"Where I'm led."

"And you'll seek a vision?"

"Zhiishiigwe couldn't help. The Midewiwin have given you power, but haven't helped my son."

"You could wait. The boy can seek his own name when he's older. He's eating a little now."

"But not much." Ma'iingan sighed. "The boy was born outside the People. You know it as well as I do. He isn't Anishinaabe, not a Loon. It isn't a *name* he needs, though I hoped the dreamer could help him. He needs to be part of his people, to eat and grow strong."

"They'll say that you are a juggler."

"They can say what they like. They can call me a wizard, call me Zhaaganaashii, call me mad. It doesn't matter. My son will have to seek a vision for himself before he can become a man. Now I will seek a vision for me—*and* for him."

"May Gichi-Manidoo be with you."

Ma'iingan nodded. "May the great spirit be with you, too, my father. May Gichi-Manidoo be with my son."

They said nothing more, and Ma'iingan walked into the forest. He had eaten nothing for two days.

He left his rifle and his steel tomahawk both in the wiigiwaam. He took a stone knife—a long obsidian flake with a leather grip bound around one end—a bow and arrows, the clothing he wore, and nothing else, and as he had done as a young man, he struck out into the woods, feeling his path.

He left the tomahawk and rifle behind because they were too new. He could not choose to go to the spirits, he could only invite them to come to him, and he worried that they would find the German rifle and the steel axe too strange and would stay away.

Alone and so lightly armed, he would be an easy target for a Sioux raider or an angry bear, so he walked quietly. His moccasins made that easy. He poured into his heart thoughts of the great divine force that filled the universe, Gichi-Manidoo, and before he noticed any ache in his long leg muscles, Ma'iingan was miles away from camp.

He knew the trade routes used by his tribe to deal with other tribes, with the Germans, with the French Acadians, and with the Dutch Ohio Company men, and he stayed away from them.

When night fell, he continued walking. He kept his eye on the Loon, fixed in the northern sky. As he had done those long years earlier, he followed his doodem into the wilderness. Ojiig, the Fisher, circled slowly about the Loon as Ma'iingan walked, and Mooz, the moose, rose behind his back. Noondeshin Bemaadizid, the man emerging from a good sweat, marched west across the sky, and as he touched the horizon and began to disappear, Ma'iingan stopped at a small torrent.

This is the right place. Tomorrow I'll build a sweat lodge in this place.

He lay on the ground in a small clearing and looked up at the open sky. Biboonikeonini, the Wintermaker, was just beginning to appear in the east when Ma'iingan closed his eyes and fell asleep.

In the morning, he found the spot for his sweat lodge; six birch saplings grew together nearly in a circle. He trimmed the saplings with his knife, bent them inward and wove their tops together.

He was weak from three days with no food. He rested often, drinking from a cool spring and feeling the weakness in his hands and arms. The fatigue was good; that meant that his own spirit was detaching itself from his body. Too strong an attachment to the flesh and the spirits wouldn't come. He needed, if anything, to feel weaker.

Ma'iingan cut withies from other trees and wove them into six saplings to make a small hut, totally enclosed but for a small entrance, and only big enough to accommodate one sitting person.

While the sun was high, he started a fire outside the sweat lodge. He built the fire around a stone that was large, yet small enough for him to heft, and he tended to the fire as he worked, adding wood and slowly heating the stone.

He thought about his sons, Giimoodaapi but also Ayaabe. What life would they lead as boys, as men? Would they one day hear the story of their father who had gone fasting into the wilderness, seeking a vision on their behalf?

And how would that story end?

He cut strips of bark from a birch tree and stitched the bark with thinner strips into a rough bowl. With pine sap he sealed the stitches, until he had a serviceable bowl that would hold water and not leak.

He ached from the work, which wasn't good—it reminded him more than he would like of his body. But he felt nearly faint, and light, and ready. He took a last drink from the spring.

Putting his hands inside his moccasins to protect them, he grabbed the hot stone from the center of the fire and placed it in the sweat lodge. The sun was again going down—he had spent all day building his lodge. Now he laid his blanket over the entrance like a door, tucking the blanket's corners into the lodge's weave of branches. He stripped to his breechcloth and stooped to enter, bringing the bowl full of cold water with him.

He moved carefully, not wishing to burn himself on the hot stone. When he was seated cross-legged with the bowl by his side, he reached out with a cupped hand and let water drip where the hot stone should be.

He was rewarded with a sudden hiss and the feeling of steam on his face.

He poured more water, and breathed deeply.

I am here. I am open.

He sat, closed his eyes—pointless in the total darkness, anyway—and breathed.

Sweat ran down his forehead, his chest and his arms. With the sweat, he felt pain and poison leave his body. His aches disappeared as he relaxed into the cross-legged sitting position in which he'd spent so many hours.

He thought of his sons sitting beside him, and his father. *What should I do?*

How do I bring my son Giimoodaapi within the doodem? How do I help him become one of the People?

And then suddenly, he knew he was not alone.

Ma'iingan opened his eyes. Sitting across from him was a man he had seen once before, in his youth. The man had ears like a wolf, and wings, and his clothing was made of stars.

"Waawoono," the man said. "You've returned."

The inside of the sweat lodge was not as Ma'iingan had built it. The saplings had thickened and grown farther apart, and the boughs woven between the saplings now bore white fruit that glimmered faintly, lighting the interior of the lodge. The lodge was bigger than it had been, too; though Ma'iingan had built it barely large enough to fit a single man, and placed the heated stone nearly against the lodge wall, the stone now sat in the center and opposite Ma'iingan, legs crossed, sat the same spirit Ma'iingan had met in his youth, the spirit that had named him *Waawoono*. Ma'iingan's manidoo.

For all that the sweat lodge was changed and alien, that didn't mean that it was less real than it had been before. If anything, it was *more* real. The leaves on the boughs were more crisp to Ma'iingan's sight, he could smell the sweet and tart juices of the glowing fruit right through its skin, he could smell the wolflike musk of his spirit visitor. He was in the realm of spirits, now. He had been brought here by his spirit-namer.

He was in the *real* world.

Waawoono meant *he howls* in the language of the People. It was a good name, and it fit neatly with old Zhiishiigwe's dreams of Ma'iingan the wolf, running free along the great rivers, running wild in the forest, wandering far but always coming home. The wolf, he howls.

Ma'iingan had told his new name to his parents, and he had told it to Waabigwan the day they had married. She had never had a vision—every young man of the People *must* seek a vision, but young women had the choice—and had no vision-name to share with him. Someday, Ma'iingan had always planned to tell the name Waawoono to his sons.

Could he share it if they had not had their own visions?

Could he share it with Giimoodaapi at all?

"I need guidance," he said to his spirit-namer.

"You know how to be a man," the spirit said. "That's all I have to show you."

Ma'iingan's heart fell. Had he come in vain?

But no, spirits didn't always speak the complete truth. They could even deliberately deceive.

"Why did you bring me here, then?" he asked. "If you can't help me, why speak with me at all?"

"Maybe I'm bored," the spirit said. "Maybe I've come only out of respect for the People with whom I am connected. Maybe I've come merely because you and I are friends."

"We are not friends," Ma'iingan said, "though we *are* bound together. And if you value that connection, I beg you to help me. Show me how to fix what is wrong with my son."

"Giimoodaapi."

"He was born late, and so I didn't capture him for my doodem as I should have. I didn't fight the Catfish for his spirit, so he's a person without a doodem. He's neither Loon nor Catfish. And if he has no doodem, he is not Anishinaabe. He can't eat Anishinaabe food, he won't drink from the breast of his mother, and he starves. Help me help him. Show me in vision what I must do to heal him."

"There *is* a healer," the spirit said slowly. "He is far from you, and is laid low by illness himself. If you raise him up, he can heal your son and make Giimoodaapi one of the People."

"Show me the way to this healer."

"What will you give me?"

"I'll give you everything I have."

"A wiigiwaam, a rifle, a bow? What will I do with these things?"

"I'll send my sons to you to be named," Ma'iingan said. What could this spirit want? What did *any* spirit want?

"When your sons become men, they will wander into the forest. There I will find them if I wish, whether you want it or not."

Ma'iingan hesitated, silent.

"You have nothing to give me. And you have nothing I want. Why should I do this thing?" The spirit smiled, and his teeth looked sharp and wolflike.

"I offer you no gift," Ma'iingan said. "Instead, I make a threat."

The spirit's wings snapped once, as if in surprise. Glitters of light like tiny falling stars shot from his wings as they did so. "What?"

"If you do *not* help me, I will give you *back* the name Waawoono. I'll cease to be the howling one, I'll tell everyone I meet of my visions of you."

The spirit's brow furrowed. "Is this truly the best you can do?"

"I'm flesh and bone, spirit. Do not doubt my resolve." Ma'iingan felt lightheaded, but he pushed forward. If he angered the spirit too much, the spirit might kill him and he would disappear forever from the world he knew. Or he might drive Ma'iingan mad, and Ma'iingan might return to his wife gibbering and senseless, a permanent burden.

On the other hand, he didn't know how else to help his son. And the spirit had said there was a healer. "I'll creep up to the long lodge when the Midewiwin are meeting," Ma'iingan continued, "and shout your name through the cracks along with obscenities! I'll name every dog I own Waawoono, and I'll beat them all. I'll write the name Waawoono on birchbark paper and I'll use that paper to wipe my backside, and then truly will I howl—"

"Enough!" Ma'iingan's manidoo rose to its full height, eyes flashing. Ma'iingan could now see that the spirit had wolf's paws to match its ears, rather than feet like a person. "You would do these deeds? You would tread on things the People hold so sacred?"

Ma'iingan shrugged. "I have nothing else. Show me another way, spirit, and I'll take it."

And then the spirit laughed. Its laughter was the sound of running waters, a thousand brooks bubbling downhill together at the same time and shaking the land as they went.

Ma'iingan prepared himself for his own destruction.

"Come." The spirit reached down for Ma'iingan's hand. "Come and see."

Even as Ma'iingan was still reaching out to take the offered hand, he and the spirit rose together. The land beneath them was the land he knew, only it wasn't. Spirits swam in the rivers and walked among the trees. Further north—not as much further north as Ma'iingan would have liked—the ice cannibal wiindigoo stalked the hills. As he and the spirit held hands and rose higher still, he saw his own tribe's camp, only rather than people, the camp was inhabited by calling loons, wiggling catfish, and martens creeping in the underbrush.

In the sky above them, Ma'iingan saw not the *shapes* of the Wintermaker and the Moose, but the great giant himself, and the mighty snorting beast.

"Will I survive this, spirit?" Ma'iingan asked.

"You didn't ask me to survive," his manidoo reminded him. "You asked me to show you how to find the healer."

Fear struck at Ma'iingan, but he forced it down. The spirit was right. He hadn't asked to survive. And if he didn't live through the night, but his son joined the People, he could accept that.

The spirit took Ma'iingan on a journey at lightning speed along the paths of the air. They raced down smaller tributaries through Anishinaabe lands to the Great River, the Michi-Zibii. At a fork far from Anishinaabe lands, where a river nearly as large flowed into the Great River, the spirit turned east. Up the new river, over mountains, down further rivers and onto a shelf of dark earth, thickly cultivated. Were they still in the Turtle Kingdom, this far from Ma'iingan's home? He thought so. A farm, around a boxy Zhaaganaashii palace and a cluster of smaller buildings; at the edge of the farm, a small outbuilding.

The spirit took them through the log walls of the outbuilding and into its cellar, where the two of them stood on a dirt floor.

There lay a young man. No older than Ma'iingan had been when he'd first met this spirit, and received the name Waawoono. Zhaaganaashii, by his narrow, pale face. Narrow plank beds lined the wall and a low fire burned at one end of the room. Each bed held at least one young man and several held more than one, all breathing deeply under wool coverings.

The boy slept, but poorly, tossing and turning on the bed, crying out occasionally and slapping his hand to his ear.

"This is the healer?" Ma'iingan asked.

"Yes."

Abruptly the young man sat up. He pawed at his ear again, and he looked directly at Ma'iingan. His face was pale and his hair dark, like one of the silver-cursed Moundbuilders. "The healer?" the boy asked in Zhaaganaashii. It wasn't the Pennslander accent Ma'iingan knew, or Appalachee.

And then the outbuilding was gone.

The spirit was gone.

Ma'iingan found himself in steamy darkness. He lurched forward reflexively, burning his hand on the hot stone.

Cursing, he found the entrance to the sweat lodge and stumbled out into cold air and the blue light just beginning to shade into green that announced a coming dawn. He fell to his knees and found that he was shaking. The strength of his limbs was completely drained, and for a time he knelt immobile.

When he could bring himself to move, he tore his blanket down from the sweat lodge and curled up beside the last embers of his fire. He needed whatever rest he could get.

As soon as he was able to travel, he had a long journey to make.

"No, Your Graces. A miracle."

—◆—

CHAPTER TWO

Maltres Korinn, Duke of Na'avu and Regent-Minister of the Serpent Throne, stood in the busy market square and stared upward. He looked not at the sky, but at the Great Mound that bore at its summit Cahokia's mighty Temple of the Sun. As always, the Temple Mound was thick with ravens.

Take this burden from me, my goddess. Choose one of them this year. Choose any of them as your Beloved. Choose Sharelas, and we shall have a warrior-queen to lead us into battle against the choking hand of Thomas Penn. Choose Voldrich, and we will have a cunning merchant-king who may lead us back to prosperity despite the Pacification. Choose Torias, and we may have a priestess-queen whose knowledge of your lore will bring us your favor.

But take the burden from me, and let me go home.

He sighed.

Not that Na'avu was free of challenges either, but they were challenges on a smaller scale. It was true, his neighbors to the north had taken to hanging and stabbing more sacrifices to their dark All-Father. One of these days, one of Korinn's servants would be in the wrong place at the wrong time and would be taken and slaughtered.

The thought of having to deal with that tragedy seemed light, compared to the grip of the Empire.

"Regent-Minister." A voice broke into his thoughts. It belonged to one of the city's gray-caped wardens, an officer, judging by the stripes on the man's sleeves. He stood a respectful distance away,

19

two more wardens standing behind him. With the interruption of his thoughts, Maltres Korinn heard again the clinking of iron coins, the dickering of the few traders willing to put up with Imperial interference and stamp duties, and the low drone of a ballad being picked out in Oranbegan mode on a three-stringed fretless Cahokian lute. And he smelled people, sour and tired and hungry, even over the mild miasma of boiling beans and squash.

"Yes?" he asked.

"Two emissaries have arrived and wish to speak to you. We've put them in the council chamber. In the Hall of Onandagos."

Korinn frowned. He wanted to avoid giving his people the impression that he relished ceremony as much as he wanted to avoid coming to love power. The throne wasn't his, he was only Regent-Minister. And he wanted, above all, to go home. "You could have brought them here."

"Yes, Regent-Minister." The officer nodded. "Only . . . these are unusual emissaries."

What kind of emissary would the wardens find unusual? "From one of the Brother Nations? From New Muscovy? From the Misaabe?"

The officer lowered his voice and leaned in closer. "They're beastkind, Regent-Minister. They say they've come with a message from the Heron King."

Marching ahead of the wardens to the Hall, Korinn thought furiously. The Heron King was a real person, or a real being, or at least he had been once. His kingdom was in the Great Green Wood, and the beastkind that stopped in Cahokia, like those in the Missouri and elsewhere, usually claimed they owed allegiance to him.

But other than that claim of allegiance, the Heron King had been quiet all Korinn's life. He'd become a character in fables and riddles, and the subject of ominous speculation. Was he silent because he had died? Was he silent because he was angry?

Maltres Korinn had invested many hours in learning the political landscape of the Empire, in seeking alliances, and in developing trade networks that might circumvent the grip of the Pacification. Suddenly, he wished he had spent a few of those hours learning his people's fairy tales.

Entering the Hall, he collected the horse-headed staff. It was his only regular concession to ceremony—he dressed at all times in simple black.

Two beastkind waited in the council room. They stood,

respectfully not seating themselves at the table. Club-wielding wardens also stood in each of the room's entrances, trying very hard not to look at the beastkind.

Both emissaries were tall men in monklike gray robes. One looked like any son of Adam, other than the fact that one hand emerging from his robe resembled the claw of a crab, and from the other sleeve, only occasionally, darted something that might have been the head of a snake. The second emissary looked like a seven-foot-tall badger, standing on its hind legs.

"Thou art the Regent-Minister," Badger growled.

"I am," Korinn agreed. "I have been told ye bear a message. May I hear it?"

"Peter Plowshare is dead," Crab Hand said.

"The Kingdom of Cahokia extends its condolences." Peter Plowshare was another name for the Heron King. Who would succeed him? "Will there be a state funeral?"

"Simon Sword demands your surrender," Badger continued. "He offers you generous terms."

"Is this a declaration of war?" Korinn wished he'd gathered the seven candidates. Especially General Sharelas and the artillerist Zorales.

And who was Simon Sword, if not another name for Peter Plowshare and the Heron King? Wasn't that the Heron King's title when he rode to war?

"If ye surrender without struggle," Badger snarled, "Simon Sword will take one life in ten as tribute. And a further tribute annually."

"Slaves?" Korinn frowned.

"Sacrifices," Crab Hand said. "And if ye surrender not, he will kill you all."

Etienne Ukwu rode to the crest of the dune and saw the summer palace of the Bishop of Miami.

As palaces went, it was modest. It was built of the adobe clay bricks favored by Ferdinandia's Hidalgos, two stories tall, and surrounded by an adobe wall. Both the palace and the wall had been plastered with a white stucco in which something glittering was embedded—shards of china, perhaps?—that caused the whole thing to shine in the afternoon July sun.

Men with steel bonnets and long lances walked the top of the wall.

Etienne inhaled deeply, the salt air of the sea mingling with the piquancy of the raw peppers he'd eaten for breakfast. Eating the chilies stoked the fires within him and gave him power.

"Je n'aime pas ça, patron," Armand said. He was one of Etienne's largest fighters, a barrel-chested Bantu who had spent years in the chevalier's service, fighting smugglers. After the third time he'd been passed over for promotion in favor of some Frenchman, Armand had taken offense and killed several of his fellow customs agents. Etienne had given him refuge to save his life, and Armand had found that the same skills that had once helped him stop crime now enabled him to prosper at it.

Once, deep in his cups, he said to Etienne: "if the chevalier won't pay me willingly, then I'll *make* him pay."

Armand wore three loaded pistols on his person and two long daggers.

Etienne turned to look back at the ship that had brought them. *La Verge Caníbal* was a notorious pirate cruiser, famed for its ability to slip through any blockade like water through a net. Its pirate-queen captain, the Catalan Montserrat Ferrer i Quintana, had brought Etienne discreetly to this beach, and now lay at anchor awaiting his return. She had even received Armand, a former antagonist, as a passenger with a gracious smile and a nod of recognition. Indeed, the rangy pirate queen with long copper-colored hair and hands as big as any man's had rarely stopped smiling, as if she knew a great secret at which the world could only guess. The pale, tangle-haired girl who never left her side—the captain's lover, perhaps? The rumors of her sapphism were persistent—had only stared at both Etienne and Armand without expression.

Etienne waved to the ship; it was too far away for him to see whether anyone waved back.

He reached into the pocket of his trousers and removed his mother's locket. Caressing it with his thumb, he listened and heard her voice: *don't fear, my son. These men can't harm you.*

He popped open the face of the locket, which swung on tiny hinges to reveal a painted miniature of his father's face. Not the face of the later bishop, but the face of the young married Chinwe Ukwu, who was then a shopkeeper who read theology by candlelight at night, and not yet even a deacon. Etienne's mother had given Etienne this locket on her deathbed, and made him swear oaths to her, and promised that she would return as his gede loa.

His guardian spirit. His own personal holy ghost. His mother. She had kept her promise.

"Don't worry, Armand," Etienne said, putting the locket away. "These men are priests. They would cut each others' throats for a sou, but you and I are only in danger of being preached to, or offered wine from the bishop's famous collection."

Armand chuckled and the two men walked toward the palace gate.

Etienne had dressed carefully for the occasion. He didn't wish to hide anything, so he had retained the red sash that marked him as a houngan—one of his promises to his mother had been that he would pursue her spiritual tradition, whether or not he also followed his father. Otherwise, though, he wore simple white cotton, a loose tunic and trousers. He had no illusions that he could convince the bishops he was an angel by merely dressing in white, but he wished to appear vaguely baptismal, like a catechumen or a supplicant.

He was unarmed.

The gate swung open at their approach, and two lance-bearing soldiers ushered them both in. Within the walls, the palace was surrounded by palmettos, and a well stood beside the stone-paved path leading to the front door.

"Su hombre puede esperar aquí," one of the soldiers said, pointing at a stone bench beside the well, shaded by palmettos. The soldiers wore the jade green of the Bishop of Miami in a tunic over their steel breastplates.

"Patron." Armand shifted from foot to foot and cracked the knuckles of one hand. He had worn the black waistcoat and trousers in which Etienne dressed all his men, and sweat ran in streams down his face and neck.

"Have a cool drink of water, Armand. Rest. I'm safe."

Armand sat. He looked like a cat perched above roiling flood-waters, but he kept his hands away from his weapons.

"Take me to His Grace, please." Etienne smiled at the soldiers, and then followed them into the palace.

The Bishops of Miami and Atlanta both pointedly remained sitting when Etienne entered. Each man rested on a reclining couch that would have made a Roman senator proud; between the couches stood a marble pedestal; a fountain burbled merrily in the center of the room; a wooden mashrabiya lattice shielded the exit into the garden from the sun, while allowing the gulf's breezes to enter.

Etienne bowed deeply. The two bishops looked at each other, and then Miami extended his ring-heavy hand.

Etienne kissed it, and then did the same with the offered episcopal ring of Atlanta.

He moved slowly, kept his motions humbly constrained and submissive.

"Your Graces," he said. "Thank you for seeing me."

"You believe," Atlanta grunted, "the bishopric of New Orleans is for sale."

The Bishop of Atlanta was a heavy man whose swarthy complexion hinted at his partly Memphite ancestry. His hair was cropped short and his bulk was draped in yellow silk; he stared at Etienne through slitted eyes.

"My father is the Bishop of New Orleans," Etienne said. There was a third couch in the room, but he remained humbly standing, and laced his fingers behind his back. "I have no wish to shorten his term of office. He's a good man, and he does good things for the city."

"While *you* are a *bad* man," Atlanta snorted. "You corrupt your city in the old de Bienville tradition, and you would bribe us with the hoard you thereby accumulate."

Etienne shrugged. "I don't wish anything from you."

"Not now, perhaps," Miami agreed. He was bone-thin, with a hooked nose, thick lips, and a mottled complexion. Thick eyebrows clung imperiously to the top of his forehead. "But when your father dies."

"All men die," Etienne agreed. "And when my father passes, the Synod will appoint a new bishop in his place. And who will that be? Some stranger? Some nominee of the emperor, or the despised chevalier? Some Geechee tent-worker, an aspiring Haudenosaunee prelate, or a Yonkerman savant? Or will you simply appoint the beloved son of the beloved departed bishop?"

It was a rehearsed speech.

"Ha!" Miami clapped his hands once. Behind his back, Etienne heard the padding feet of servants on the stone floor.

"What makes you think I can be bought?" Atlanta asked.

Because you took the money. Because you invited me here to discuss it. "I'm not trying to buy you, Your Grace. If I were to give the income of my gaming establishment, or my other businesses, directly to the poor, or to the Bishopric of New Orleans for distribution to the poor, would that be wicked?"

Atlanta chuckled. "You would merely give the money to me so that I can distribute it to the poor."

"Your wisdom and good judgment are famed throughout the Empire." Etienne smiled. "Didn't the Lord tell us 'ye have the poor with you always'? Did he make some exception for the people of Atlanta?"

The Bishop's chuckle broke into a loud guffaw.

"Vino!" the Bishop of Miami called to the servants at Etienne's shoulders. "Algo blanco!"

The feet padded away.

"On the whole, the Synod is quite happy with its choice in Bishop Ukwu," Atlanta said, shifting his bulk about in anticipation of the arrival of the wine. "It has been refreshing to have a genuinely righteous man serving the poor of New Orleans."

"Was that your desire? Righteousness?" Etienne asked. "I rather thought the goal was to take power away from the chevalier's family. The Le Moyne branch retained civil leadership, but removing the de Bienvilles from the cathedral was one way to curb the family's ambitions. And indeed, such an obvious one, I have to wonder whether the Synod alone desired the curbing, or if perhaps other powers in the Empire were also interested."

Atlanta cocked his head to one side like a parrot and stared. Miami licked his lips.

"And if such is the case, then I think in choosing a successor to my father, you should desire not righteousness, but *effectiveness*."

"Meaning," Miami said, "that you know how to get things done."

Etienne shrugged humbly. "I hope my contributions to the poor of Atlanta and Ferdinandia would help convince you of that fact."

Miami crooked a finger at Etienne's sash. "The de Bienville Bishops have long been usurers, corrupt simoniacs, and worse. But they have been Christians."

"Does my traffic with the loa discomfort you?" Etienne smiled. "I understand. You are not of New Orleans, you've heard terrible things. You fear witchcraft, Satanism, black magic."

Miami grunted his agreement; Atlanta shrugged.

"But didn't God place his host in heaven? And didn't that same host sing at the announcement of his birth? And isn't he the Lord of the host?" Etienne touched two fingers gently to his sash. "If I, then, pay special respect to Saint Peter or the Virgin among the host, how am I not Christian?"

"You slippery bastard." Etienne thought he heard admiration in Atlanta's voice. "You might indeed make an excellent cleric."

Etienne nodded his thanks. "Someday, perhaps. When the time has come. And if the other members of the Synod could be persuaded."

"If," Miami agreed.

Etienne heard padding feet behind him again. "I'm pleased, Your Graces, that you choose to take a little refreshment. It offers me the chance to demonstrate my . . . spiritual . . . efficacy to you."

"What do you mean?" Atlanta grunted.

The servant was a Hidalgo boy, maybe thirteen years old. He carefully carried a wooden tray on which he balanced a green bottle sealed with wax, a small knife, and three wineglasses.

"May I serve you, Your Graces?" Etienne rolled his tunic's sleeves up above his elbow as he asked, and without waiting for an answer, he took the tray, shooed the serving boy away, and set the bottle and glasses onto the pedestal.

"'I am among you as he that serveth,'" Miami quoted. "Luke. God knows, you can cite enough scripture to be bishop, but that's never been a requirement of the office. Men have become bishop who weren't previously priests. Knowing your gospels isn't a sign of spiritual efficacy."

"Agreed." Etienne nodded, scraping the wax off the bottle with the small blade. "And this isn't what I mean."

"Well, then?" Atlanta's eyes were so narrowly slitted they almost disappeared. "What are you up to?"

Etienne removed the bottle's cork. "Our Lord's first miracle, according to the Gospel of John, was at the wedding in Cana."

"Water into wine," Miami said.

"Very good." Etienne smiled and filled the three glasses. "I see that you also know enough scripture to be bishop."

"And?" Atlanta asked.

Etienne passed each man a glass, and then took one himself. "And today I perform the miracle in reverse." He sipped from his glass and tasted cool spring water.

The other men also drank.

And stared.

"Magic?" Miami asked. "A Vodun trick?"

Atlanta shook his heavy head. "Haven't the Polites warded this building for you? This is more subtle."

"If you were to descend into your excellent wine cellar, Your Grace," Etienne said, nodding to the Bishop of Miami, "you would find that *all* of the bottles of your justly famous collection have become mere water."

"The cunning little whelp is showing you he can get to you," Atlanta said to the other bishop. "Don't you see? If he can bribe or threaten someone into replacing all your wine with bottles of water, what's to stop him from corrupting one of your own servants into cutting your throat while you sleep?"

"A threat!" Miami gasped.

"No, Your Graces." Etienne smiled. "A miracle."

Setting down his own glass, he bowed a final time and left. As he reached the front door his breath was already coming quicker, and he heard the Brides calling.

Thomas Penn gulped cold wine and stared into the shadowed end of the hall. There, on a low stone dais, sat the Shackamaxon Throne. He'd had it carved from the wood of the elm tree under which William Penn had agreed to his first treaty with the Lenni Lenape. The wood was stained such a dark red it almost looked purple in the dim light, and the throne's upholstery was blue, bearing the Imperial ship, horses, and eagle stitched in gold thread.

As a seat, it was suitably modest, yet undeniably elegant.

As a symbol of Imperial rule, it would be powerful.

As it was, the Shackamaxon Throne sat unused in this empty hall, forbidden to Thomas Penn by a gaggle of squabbling upstarts who, together with the Lightning Bishop, had enslaved John Penn. Unused, except on such occasions as this.

"I've done it, grandfather!" Thomas called.

He knelt on the cold stone floor. By day, light would have filled the hall from its high windows, but instead the room was lit by a single torch Thomas had placed in one of the brackets beside the doors. He set his goblet on the floor beside himself, touched his forehead to the stone in the direction of the Shacka-maxon Throne, and called again.

"I've done your bidding!" He ached

The man he summoned was already present, at least in spirit and in image. On one high wall hung two paintings of William Penn: one portrayed him kneeling in a tray of earth, abovedecks on a sailing ship, praying for the vessel's safe arrival at the land in whose soil he knelt; the second show Penn marching alone through the forest, a fanciful representation of the Walking Purchase..

He rubbed his cold fingers together, caressing his rings. On his right hand he wore the ring of Jupiter, tin with a white chalcedony set into it, and inscribed into the stone a man riding an eagle and wielding a javelin. On his left was the ring of Mars, iron, engraved with the image of an armored warrior holding a naked sword in one hand and a severed head in the other. Together, the rings brought him the service of men, eagles, lions, and vultures, and assistance in all the works of those two great planets.

"I've done as you asked!"

And then the Presence filled the throne.

Thomas was allowed no closer than this, not yet. He could see that the Presence took the form of a man. He hoped that one day he would sit on the throne and the Presence would fill and strengthen him. The Presence was the shade of William Penn, his ancestor, the true founder of the empire that by rights should bear his name.

The shade wore plate armor, and Thomas couldn't see its face. Then it spoke, and a voice like bells being hammered against an anvil filled the Shackamaxon Hall.

"I was with thee in the Slate Roof House, my servant Thomas. Unseen, I consecrated the death of thy sister to the good of the Empire, as I consecrated her confinement. I heard thy command to our servant Ezekiel Angleton."

Thomas liked the sound of the words *our servant*. They made him feel he was a joint actor with William Penn in creating this bold new world. He forced his forehead to the stone again.

"I receive and bless thy work, my servant Thomas."

"Thank you, grandfather." Not his father's father, John Penn, but his ancestor several generations before that.

Then the Presence was gone.

Thomas rose to his feet, bringing the wine with him. The wine was essential. In truth, Thomas had lost his sister years earlier, when she had married the Ohioan princeling Elytharias. And any part of her or her relationship with Thomas that had survived that corruption had surely shattered after Thomas had arranged Elytharias's death—under the guidance of his grandfather's Presence, of course—and Hannah had subsequently gone mad.

Still, however much her spirit and sanity or their joint familial feeling might have been long gone, it had been a blow to see her body finally pass. Especially twisted, as it had been, by the rack.

Had *he* chosen the rack, or had the Presence dictated it? Thomas no longer remembered. He had done what he'd had to do, for the good of the Empire.

He took another bracing gulp of wine.

The announcement of her passing, if not the details, had been communicated to the news-papermen of Philadelphia the day before she actually succumbed. By that act, Thomas had committed himself and given himself strength to do the necessary thing.

Thomas walked back into the lit portions of Horse Hall. Men in his livery smiled and saluted as he passed. Thomas finished the wine and made a point of saluting back, with volume and cheer. He gripped the hilt of his saber and rattled it in its sheath. His servants responded with bigger grins.

Thomas dallied a moment in the main entrance of Horse Hall, admiring his own portrait. The painting was twelve feet tall, nearly twice his height, and it bore all the marks of Jupiter. Painted, Thomas stood upon the Seal of Jupiter, a circle quartered by a cross with small knobs at each of the cross's four tips, and the faintest suggestion of stylized zodiacal swirls surrounding the circle; his belt buckle was woven of two interlocking glyphs, the S-like sign of Jupiter's intelligence and the more angular symbol of the planet's spirit; the buckles of his painted shoes were zetas, for Zeus. The portrait's face was Jovian, radiating regnant cheer and benevolence, and his body was Jupiter's as well, corpulence reflecting physical health and prosperity, flushed pink skin a sure sign of virility. They were the face and body of Jupiter, who ruled over serpents. Thomas had stood for the painting, and the artist had executed his work, only at hours when Jupiter was strong, to capture all the planet's beneficent influence. This was Thomas as emperor, as ruler.

This was Thomas who bowed to no man.

"Your Imperial Majesty. Lord Thomas."

Your Imperial Majesty was a form of address prescribed by the Philadelphia Compact, though the Electors had exempted themselves from using it, and instead only had to call Thomas *Mr. Emperor*. What kind of god-damned form of address was *Mr. Emperor*, anyway? It was a travesty! Thomas's servants additionally used the form *Lord Thomas*, which reminded him of his days as a military man. It also reminded him that his servants were sycophants, but he was willing to accept a certain amount of flattery for the good he did his people.

"Gottlieb," Thomas said.

Gottlieb was Thomas's body servant, his valet. He helped Thomas dress for state occasions and he ran small errands for his master at all times. Gottlieb rose from his bow with a dull glow to his pasty block-shaped face and a foxlike glint in his jaundiced eyes. That expression meant Gottlieb knew something secret. At this late hour, he might have foregone the powdered perruque without occasioning any remark, but he hadn't—Gottlieb's dress was impeccable.

"Your Imperial Majesty has visitors in the library. Two separate parties."

The library was Thomas's private reception room. Thomas changed course to head upstairs toward the library and Gottlieb clung to his flank.

"Tell me more, Gottlieb."

"Signor Mocenigo has been waiting longer."

The Italian was an astrologer, exiled from his native Venice and more recently a refugee from the Caliphate. He had composed several charts for Thomas and clearly wished to compose more, though Thomas had never asked him for any. For what preferment did the Venetian hope? Land? A salary? "I will deal with Zuan Mocenigo tonight. And the other?"

"Schmidt has just arrived."

Thomas frowned. "Schmidt who operates the coal mines south of Pittsburgh? Has he had to close the mines again?"

"Schmidt the Ohio Company Director."

"Ah, yes." The Imperial Ohio Company had five Directors, and Notwithstanding Schmidt was one of them. Thomas had promoted her from within the Company's ranks two years earlier, and Schmidt had shown an admirable willingness to take his orders literally and fulfill them with imagination.

They reached the library doors. Thomas nodded to dismiss Gottlieb and let himself in.

The library was high-ceilinged, its walls lined with books. Divans and writing desks were arranged around the perimeter of the room with deliberate asymmetry. Against one wall was a cabinet containing liquor and planks of imported tea, and in the center of the room stood a single large table. At that table had been sitting the Venetian Mocenigo, who now stood. He was short and slight, and he held his shoulders thrust back and his eyes wide open, which gave him the appearance of perpetual surprise. He wore a blue and gold robe, the sort of theatrical apparel one might wear on a market day to announce one's status as a wizard or a palm-reader. With his balding head, he looked like a parody of a monk.

In the corner stood Notwithstanding Schmidt. Her strong cheek-bones and the mole on her right cheek might have been beautiful on another woman, but Schmidt had the solid physique of a baker, or a farmwife, or a blacksmith. She stood with her feet planted apart and her fists balled in front of her, as if ready to fight, and her short hair might have been worn with equal elegance by a man.

Thomas found that he felt irritated.

"Please sit, Madam Director," he called to Schmidt. "I'll be with you in a moment."

She sat.

Zuan Mocenigo bowed. "Mr. Emperor."

"That is a title permitted to Electors under the Compact." Thomas sighed. "Thou mayest address me as *Your Imperial Majesty.*"

"Forgive me. Your Imperial Majesty."

Thomas nodded. "Signor Mocenigo. I was not expecting thee."

Mocenigo bowed again and sat. Before him on the large table lay spread a nativity, thoroughly filled in. "I have heard that my services may be of use to you. To thee."

Thomas felt empty. "Speak thou clearly, Chaldean."

Mocenigo looked suspiciously at Schmidt in the corner and then back at Thomas. "Thou hast recently learned of the birth of children to . . . thy sister Hannah." The astrologer whispered slowly, as if the Jacobean pronouns of Court Speech were a challenge.

Thomas kept his voice low as well, and dropped into Penn's English to speed up the interview. "I had imagined you were here to tell me of an auspicious day to move against the Cahokians."

Mocenigo shook his head. "I have taken what data the Empress . . . that is, Mad Hannah was able to give you, and I am attempting to construct a nativity."

"Of the three children." Thomas gripped the hilt of his saber. "And who passed this data on to you, stargazer?" It wouldn't have been Ezekiel Angleton; the Covenant Tract man hated astrology and everything that resembled it. Curious, given what a star-enthusiast old John Winthrop had been. And the famous Covenant with the

House of Spencer had been the repudiation of Oliver Cromwell and his works, not any of the other arcane arts. Angleton himself was something of an accomplished gramarist.

"Your valet de chambre." Mocenigo's voice was a thin whine, and he bent his face low over the table, until his forehead almost touched the wood.

Gottlieb. Wishing to ingratiate himself further to Thomas, no doubt. But was there more? Thomas resolved to investigate whether his valet had taken money in exchange for arranging this audience. "So my valet told you what little he knew, having heard it from me. And you have transposed these fixed pieces of information into a natal chart for these three children."

"And extrapolated everything therefrom that I could, yes. I believe you will find that we possess quite a lot of information."

"To what end?" Thomas drew his saber slowly, then reached forward with its tip to ruffle the corner of the star chart.

Mocenigo's eyes opened even wider and he swayed back from the blade. "I understood you were sophisticated in star lore."

"And I thought *you* were. Explain yourself."

"If we know the sky at the moment these children were born, Your Imperial Majesty, we will know their strengths. We will know their weaknesses. We will know when we should strike against them, and when to keep our distance."

"*Our. We.* You mean *me*, of course. You mean that *I* will know when I should act, and what I should do."

"Yes. Of course."

"You mean that I should let my choices be dictated to me by the stars."

Mocenigo hesitated. "A wise man does, Mister Emperor."

Thomas nodded slowly. He raised the saber's blade and rested it on his own shoulder, composing his thoughts.

"Signor Mocenigo, I have two great concerns with what you are telling me."

"Yes, Your Imperial Majesty?"

Thomas looked at Director Schmidt in the corner. She sat still as a statue, gazing upon a wall of books.

"First, I'm troubled by your incompetence."

"What? No!" Mocenigo leaped to his feet, but Thomas swung his sword around and pointed it at the astrologer's sternum, fixing the man in place. "I protest, Mr. . . . Your Imperial Majesty."

"Tell me, Signor Mocenigo, how many constellations lie along the path of the zodiac."

"Twelve, of course."

"Wrong. This is what comes, you see, of learning your stars from charts only, without ever looking up at the night sky."

The Venetian stared.

"If you had bivouacked, as I have, in the deserts of Texia, and looked up at the heavens as they revolved—if, in other words, you had to play your own stakes in this game of life, rather than simply gambling the fates of other men—you would know that there are not twelve, but *thirteen* constellations lying along the path of the zodiac, the ecliptic."

"But, Your Imperial—"

"The twelve you know. Aries, Sagittarius, Leo...to list them is child's play. The thirteenth is Ophiuchus. Is there an Ophiuchus in your tables?"

"You know that there is not." Mocenigo was trembling.

"I know that there is not. And yet there is an Ophiuchus upon the zodiac. And what I also know, what my sister knew and yet chose to ignore, is that *all* the children of Adam's cursed first wife are born under the sign of Ophiuchus. Ophiuchus is the serpent bearer and he is the star-sign of all Ophidians. He bears them, if you will, in their escape from the flat plane of the ecliptic in which we children of Eve remain trapped."

"Sir, Venice does not have—"

"I understand." Thomas waved his free hand to silence the Italian. "You are from the Old World. You killed most of your Firstborn decades ago, or drove them out. You, Signor Mocenigo, have never considered what being Firstborn means to a nativity. Let me tell you now. Being Firstborn renders your natal chart meaningless."

"Sir—"

"Nativities have great value for the children of Eve. Only."

Mocenigo's shoulders slumped. "I did not know."

Thomas nodded. "I see you didn't. The second thing troubling me is of greater concern. Signor Mocenigo, I—*I, of all men*—do not allow myself to be ruled by the stars. I may seek their guidance, I will endeavor to capture and exploit their power, but I will not be ruled. *I will be the ruler.*"

Mocenigo stared down at the chart and nodded.

"Even worse than the possibility that I might be governed by the stars, Signor Mocenigo, is the risk that I might instead be directed by the mere men who devised the star charts. You see that, don't you? You see that if I let my decisions be determined by your casting, then some would ask, who is truly emperor in Philadelphia?"

"No . . ."

"And others would answer, why, Signor Mocenigo, who binds the Emperor's mind with his triplicities!"

"But no!"

"Shhh. I am certain you intended no such thing, Signor Mocenigo."

Mocenigo's expression showed gratified relief, and he nodded vigorously.

"Though it occurs to me, Signore, that I'm troubled by a third thing."

"Please tell me, Your Imperial Majesty, how I may relieve your worry."

"I'm troubled that you know too much, astrologer."

"But—"

Thomas stabbed the stargazer in the heart.

The sharpened and polished weapon slid between the man's ribs and he died with his mouth open, his face frozen in a fishlike expression of astonishment. When Thomas pulled out his blade, blood spilled both from the wound and from the dead man's open lips.

Mocenigo fell sideways to the floor.

"There," Thomas said. "My worry is relieved."

He dropped his blade onto the worthless nativity, spattering the astrologer's own blood over the circles, dots, and quarterings that were to have told him how to find and destroy his sister's secret children.

And indeed, he *did* feel better.

Thomas crossed the library, his steps light. Notwithstanding Schmidt stood to meet him, her eye keen but her face as sober as a priest's on Sunday. "My Lord President," she said.

That was the form of address for Thomas as President of the Imperial Ohio Company. It cheered Thomas to hear it.

"Madam Director," he said. "Please sit. Do you know why my empire is called the Empire of the New World East of the Mississippi?"

She sat. "I understand that was agreed in the Philadelphia Compact."

"Of course. But it's a terrible name. *Any* other name would have been better. The truest, most natural name for the empire, of course, would have been *Pennsylvania*. But *Columbia* would also have been a good name, even if it did mean naming my empire after a dream-addled Jew. Even one of the Italian cartographers' names—*Verrazzania* or *Vespuccia*—would have been acceptable, if somewhat uncouth. So why does my kingdom have such a mockery of a name, awkward in the mouth and resistant to poetry?"

Schmidt looked Thomas in the eyes and nodded. "Power."

"That's exactly right."

"If your empire had a glorious name—like Pennsylvania—then you would have been Emperor of Pennsylvania. 'The Empire of the New World East of the Mississippi' sounds like a purely technical designation, like a bureaucratic label, like one of Napoleon's Departments. The awkward name is a means to restrict your power."

Thomas nodded, feeling a mixture of satisfaction and fatigue. "Did you receive my instructions?"

"I did, my lord."

"Good." Thomas flung himself into an overstuffed divan facing the one in which Schmidt sat. "I don't have the Electors' approval to raise additional troops to tighten the Pacification as I would like, and if I raise more without their consent, I violate the Compact. I'm not prepared to do that ... yet. As a Director of the Imperial Ohio Company, you've come here to tell me what you need from me to carry out your orders—to redirect Company resources to the Pacification."

Schmidt nodded again. "I'm going to need a hell of a lot of boots. And feet to put in them."

"Harder," Nathaniel Chapel murmured.

Clang! Clang!

The banging of the smith's hammer on the bar of iron produced a dull, repetitive racket. It was almost enough to drown out the shrieking sound of the world in Nathaniel's bad ear.

He rubbed at it, but the whine didn't go away.

Nathaniel hid in the corner of the Earl of Johnsland's stables, just out of the blacksmith's sight. He didn't need the man's attention, didn't want a lecture on the virtues of Wayland Smith, England's god of the Furrow. Like many practitioners of his craft, Benson was an initiate of the Smith; his devotion showed not only in his lectures, but also in the anvil and horseshoe tattoos on his arms and in the miniature anvil that presided fixed to a beam above the working anvil.

Nathaniel just needed the noise.

~It burns! The fire burns!~

"Burns," he whispered.

Nathaniel resisted the temptation to touch his strange ear at the bodiless voice, and felt a tugging at his elbow.

"Jenny," he said.

Jenny Farewell was, like Nathaniel, an orphan and a ward of the Earl of Johnsland. She had one dress that she wore all the time, and at this moment she complemented it with a mischievous smile. The smile brought out the brightness of her green eyes.

"Old One Eye is here," she said.

Old One Eye didn't always humiliate George Isham. But sometimes he did, and that possibility made the godi's arrival interesting to Nathaniel and Jenny both.

Nathaniel heard a shriek like rusted metal shearing apart. Whimpering slightly, he followed Jenny away from the smithy, the stables, and the outbuilding where Nathaniel and other less-important men of the earl's company slept, and into the earl's hall.

Jenny skipped as they went, and sang. It was a song Nathaniel knew, a ballad about the Cavalier settlement:

> *I watched that Roundhead captain march his mus-*
> > *kets to our door*
> *My father cried, "God save the King!" and they cut*
> > *him to the floor*
> *I dragged that Roundhead down the moor and I*
> > *drowned him in the sea*
> *And then I heard Old Skull and Bones had set his*
> > *cap for me*
> *So it's down the Dart, into wooden walls, and over*
> > *the salt and foam*
> *How I miss my old West Country home*

Her song, clear and golden, almost drove away the voices and the whine that Nathaniel always heard. Almost.

The great hall of the Earl of Johnsland looked like a cave. Its walls were thick with moss like green fur and its floor was littered with the filth of the children of Adam, much of it the earl's own—in his lifetime, Nathaniel had never seen the hall cleaned.

~Abomination! The land is polluted!~

"Polluted," he murmured.

It wasn't a requirement that a godi, a sheep-sacrificing priest of Woden, be tall, but Old One Eye was. And like his god, he lacked one eye, or at least, he always wore an eyepatch. Though his dark hair began to go silver, his frame beneath his black wool cloak was heavily muscled, and he leaned on a rune-carved spear.

Two men in similar cloaks stood behind him. They were both godar, and a fourth godi, the man permanently attached to the earl's lands—a scowling old man named Wickens—skulked to one side, nearly hidden under a green fringe of moss.

The earl's throne was turned to face the rear of his hall. The earl himself crouched on the seat of the chair and hid behind its back, making soft birdlike cries. From the front of the hall, standing among the few bent and breaking servants who dared to stay for Old One Eye's appearance, Nathaniel could just make out the earl's gray hair and the little wooden box he never released from his grasp.

Two men stood beside the Earl of Johnsland, one to either side, both wearing the earl's purple. Charles Lee was a military officer in his service; George Isham was the earl's youngest legitimate son and, because he was the only legitimate son surviving, the earl's heir.

"I didn't summon you, godi." George's voice trembled slightly.

"I don't need your leave to stand here," Old One Eye said.

"This man is your earl!" Charles Lee barked.

"I see the amulet around your neck," Old One Eye said slowly, his voice full of gravel. "Is that the hammer of Thunor, or the mallet of the carpenter of Galilee?"

"Cuius dominium," Charles muttered.

"Eius deus," Old One Eye said, more loudly. "Yes, I acknowledge Byrd's Compromise. And if the earl, good servant of the Old Gods that he is, wishes to permit his tenants Christianity, that is his affair, as it is his dominion. For now."

"Forever!" George Isham snapped.

"Nothing is forever but the tree of life," Old One Eye responded. "Which brings me to the reason for my visit."

"I will burn the Yule log this year, godi," George said through gritted teeth. "Or if not I, my father."

"Your father is mad," Old One Eye said. "You are a child. If either of you attempts to burn a log this Yule, know this: I shall place Woden's curse on you. Your few remaining people will leave. Your lands will be blighted. Death itself will stalk at your heels. You have a godi, and he shall burn the log, at my direction."

"To all the hells with you." George sneered at the priest, but his lip trembled.

Old One Eye only laughed. "I shall leave men behind to ensure that the worship of Woden is not undertaken by the unfit."

At that, soldiers in black entered the hall. Black was the color of the College of Godar, but Nathaniel hadn't realized they had their own soldiers. These men carried muskets, pistols, and knives, and they formed two columns leading to the door.

Charles Lee continued to glare fiercely at the priest, but George's face fell. Old One Eye ignored them both as he and the two godar from the College passed through the two columns of soldiers—Nathaniel counted twelve of them—and left.

He turned to Jenny and saw a bitter smile on her lips. Nathaniel knew why *he* enjoyed seeing George bullied.

Why did it amuse Jenny Farewell?

Montse stepped from her flat boat onto the long dock. The wood of the dock groaned and she felt its supporting pylons shift under her weight, but the half-rotted construct held, probably kept together by the bayou's mud as much as by anything else. She took the line from her craft and looped it quickly about the strongest-looking of the pylons, then laid her pole in the boat.

"Qui va allà?" a man's voice called from the shadows.

"Jo sóc la Montse," Montserrat replied. "Montserrat Ferrer i Quintana. She expects me."

On this bayou, the mere ability to answer in Catalan likely would have saved a traveler's life, or at least extended it long enough for the sentry to get a better look at the speaker's face. As it happened, though, Montse *was* expected.

"Come, Margarida." She held out her hand; the girl took it and climbed onto the dock with her.

"Getting your fortune told again, tia Montse?" Margarida asked. Like Montse herself, the girl wore a long coat, a man's coat that would downplay her femininity. Where Montse wore a tricorn hat cocked at a jaunty angle over her long hair the color of a copper pot, Margarida's head was bare. In the dark, the high tangle of her hair made the silhouette of her head look enormous. Margarida's skin was so pale, it almost glowed in the darkness, as if she were the daughter of the moon itself, walking among the cypress trees.

Which perhaps she was.

"You are confused, neboda. My fortune is a thing already known to me. I'm a merchant at all times, a smuggler when the profit margins outweigh the danger, and a pirate on rare occasions for the sheer joy of the chase. This is a good fortune, and I would have traded any other fortune in the world for this one."

"Hola, Montse," the sentry said, stepping forward into a sliver of moonlight to reveal his face. He held a short carbine with both hands, and had a heavy cutlass hanging at his belt.

"Hola, Carles." She recognized the man. "New rings?"

Carles shrugged, pulling his hands back into shadow to hide them.

Montse patted him on the arm. "Don't be ashamed of success, Carles." She and the girl continued up the dock as Carles slipped back into shadow and disappeared. "Just be careful who notices."

"You have good fortune now," Margarida insisted. "But if one of the Imperial Foresters caught us with unstamped goods? Or if that gangster son of the bishop decided he wished to be rid of the witnesses to his journey to Ferdinandia? Or the chevalier's customs men ran across us by accident in the fog?"

"The customs men could *only* do that by accident." Montse chuckled. "They're far too stupid to do it on purpose."

"Still. Perhaps you *should* have your fortune told."

Montse hissed her disapproval. "No, neboda, my cake is baked. We are here, as always, to know *your* fortune."

"I have the fortune to have you for my tia. That means I'm fed and clothed and I sail with you both up the river and down the coast. I've seen the Igbo Free Cities and the Draft Men of Memphis, and if I'm not allowed to participate in your daring smuggling operations, at least I'm allowed to listen to the stories."

Montse laughed.

The dock climbed over the bent knees of cypress trees and onto the land. There it became a path raised two feet off the ground, keeping walkers out of the mud and reducing the chances of stepping on an unseen snake or alligator. Shifting patches of darkness below the walkway probably indicated just such hazards, if not worse things. Montse had *seen* only a few live basilisks in her time on the bayous, but they were reputed to live here. Fortunately, they were also reputed to sleep buried in mud except during the very hottest months of the year.

She led the young woman she called her *neboda*, her niece, past the first few wooden shacks. They were all dark. It must be later than she had realized.

"I find it strange how superstitious you are," Margarida said. "You of all women, who have made your own luck in the world. And it's stranger still that what you are superstitious about is not *your* life, but *mine*."

"You'll find, Margarida, that there are some charges you may bear that are more important than your own life."

Montse found the door she sought, a door she'd known for many years. She could almost imagine that the indentation at her shoulder height had been pounded into the wood by her knuckles alone, over time, but that wasn't really true. Still, she threw her fist against the worn spot now, thumping out the announcement of her arrival.

"Jo sóc la Montse!" she called again, though of all the people she might visit in the bayou, this one likely did not need to be told her name.

"Endavant!" an old woman's voice cried from within.

Montse hesitated. Something in the tone of the voice; something in the way Carles hadn't wanted her to see his hands.

She pointed to a shadowed corner between two nearby huts. "Allà," she whispered. Just in case.

Margarida was quick enough to sense there might be a problem. She raised her eyebrows in question at her aunt, but did as she was bid.

"And stay calm, no matter what happens."

The pirate stepped off the walkway. The ground was muddy, but firmer with the October chill in the air than it would have been in July. Please, Mother Maria, do not let me step on a sleeping basilisk.

The mud was why she wore her tall, thigh-high leather boots. She couldn't run as fast, but her legs were the most protected part of her body. This was important for a woman who made her living jumping in and out of bayous at night.

She thought she was far enough away that Carles wouldn't see her. She hoped her intuition about him was wrong, but she'd start with the most pessimistic assumption possible. She began creeping around the outside of the hut.

"Endavant!" the old woman's voice called again. The voice belonged to Cega Sofía, the seeress Montse had come to see, as she did every month. She came to learn whether her lady and friend Hannah yet lived, and whether she had been restored, so that Montse could return to her her child.

But Cega Sofía was choking as she called. Whoever was forcing her to call Montse was relaxing a grip around her throat only enough to let her yell *endavant*.

Montse looked back to Margarida or, as her mother had named her, Margaret. The girl held still where she had been told and peered out from her hiding place with large eyes.

Montse finally got to a large enough crack in the shack's wall that she could place an eye to it and peer through. Within she saw the fortuneteller in her brightly colored silks, seated. Two men in blue uniforms stood beside her, one at each shoulder. One held a pistol to Sofía's head.

From a nail on the opposite wall hung an oil lantern, lit and full.

Montse looked closer at the uniforms; their blue was not the Imperial blue, but the blue with gold fleurs-de-lis of the Chevalier of New Orleans.

Customs men? Gendarmes?

They must be here for Montse.

Montse looked back toward Carles and saw no movement. She waved an arm in Margarida's direction and was pleased the girl promptly slipped across the walkway and into the mud to join her.

"I don't know what's going to happen," Montse whispered to her neboda. "But you're about to have an adventure. When I shoot, you run that way—" she pointed, "and you'll find moored boats. Not our boat, but others. Take one, and wait for me only for a minute. If I don't join you within a minute, flee. You know where to go."

"Back to *La Verge Caníbal*."

Montse nodded.

"Montserrat!" Cega Sofía howled. "On ets?"

Montse drew one pistol from her coat pocket and sighted along the barrel through the crack. She squeezed the trigger—

bang!—

Margarida ran—

somewhere in the darkness, Carles cursed—

and the lantern exploded as her bullet struck it, throwing flaming oil up and down the wooden wall on which it hung.

Montse replaced the empty pistol in her pocket and drew her second. Pressing her eye to the crack again, she saw the larger of the chevalier's two men dragging Cega Sofía to her feet and pressing a pistol to the old woman's temple. The smaller man turned to face Montse, and was staring at the wall...looking for her.

She cocked her pistol and shot the larger man, immediately afterward throwing herself to the side. She heard his cry of pain and the muffled crash as he fell, and then the sound of answering gunfire from within the seeress's hut. She heard the *snaps* of the wall's wood giving way to two bullets that would have hit her had she not dodged.

Then she ran into the trees after Margarida.

The fire would force the chevalier's men out, and it might give Cega Sofía a chance to flee. Maybe someone else in the village would help her run.

The thought made her stride falter. Where was everyone else in the village? Sofía didn't live alone. This wasn't a prosperous place, but there was an inn and there were several family homes. Other than in Sofía's shack, Montse hadn't seen a light.

She redoubled her pace, and when she caught up with Margarida, she almost knocked the girl down.

Margaret Elytharias Penn, known to herself and to the world as Margarida, stood at the edge of the bayou and wept. The wooden walkway here also ended in a rickety dock extending out into the water, but there were no boats.

Instead, there were bodies.

In the darkness, Montse couldn't see faces. She was grateful, because that meant the girl couldn't see faces either, and the faces of the dead can haunt one's dreams.

As Montserrat had reason to know.

"No time to weep!" Montse grabbed her ward by the elbow and dragged her away from Cega Sofía's cabin and deeper into the woods. "Breathe deeply!"

The seeress's shack burned like a hundred torches, throwing light out into the swamp. The chevalier's men—four of them now, no, five, surrounded Sofía herself on the walkway. Montse dragged Margarida behind a large cypress, shushing her with a finger over the girl's mouth, and crouched to watch.

Clearly visible now in the light of the fire, Carles swaggered up the walkway toward the chevalier's men. His thumbs were hooked in his broad leather belt, and his unshaven face cracked into a lopsided grin.

Carles said something Montse couldn't hear.

Sofía spit at him, and he laughed.

Then one of the chevalier's men pointed a pistol at Carles's head and fired. The Catalan sentry dropped, hit the walkway, and bounced off into the mud.

"Montserrat!" Cega Sofía wailed. "Mata-me!"

Margarida looked at Montse, startled. "What, she asks to be killed?"

"Yes," Montse muttered. She pulled her powder horns and other tools from her pockets and began to reload both her pistols.

"Are you going to do it?"

The fortuneteller clawed at one of the chevalier's men. He held her off with a hand to her forehead, laughing.

Montse sighed. "If I were alone, yes. With you . . . I don't know yet, let me think."

"Why does my presence make a difference?" Margarida's face looked angry in the dim light.

Montse did not want Margarida to get angry.

"It does, neboda. Shh. And be calm."

Bang!

Montse looked up, caught by surprise, just in time to see Cega Sofía fall to the ground, dead. She felt ill at the sight. Monthly at least, for the last fifteen years, the old witch had given Montse the best news she could get about her friend and lady Hannah. Sofía had been her strongest connection to the Imperial household, and now the seeress was gone.

Margarida's hair was beginning to twitch, switching back and forth like the tail of an agitated horse.

"Shh," Montse whispered. "Calm."

"I'm trying." The girl took a deep breath.

"Come." Montse pocketed her pistols, took Margarida by the elbow, and stood—

facing into a thicket of heavy pistols.

Four men stood with their guns trained on her and on her ward. There was nowhere to run.

"Nous nous rendons," she said. "We surrender. Don't shoot."

*"Call no man harmless until he is dead. My education
ended early, but I believe I remember that much of Aristotle."*

———⟶•⟵———

CHAPTER THREE

"Fire!" Bill yelled.

Chikaak, the scout with the head of a coyote, discharged
his Paget carbine immediately. Several of the others fired with
him. Then, in a ragged volley, the rest did the same, until every
beastkind warrior capable of holding a firearm—eighteen, slightly
more than half—had shot.

Of the row of bark targets Jacob Hop had propped up on
the log at the far end of the meadow, only two had fallen.

Jake thought he'd have done better than the beastfolk, but he
was very careful in how he handled guns around Bill. Captain
Sir William Johnston Lee, as his full name and titles would call
him, had agreed that Jake could be his aide, or squire, or sergeant. On the other hand, Jake knew from the sidelong glances
Bill still threw at him that the Cavalier was not fully convinced
Jake was now free of possession by the Heron King.

"Bill, dat is better than before, hey?" he called from where
he stood to the side of the drilling warriors.

Chikaak yipped his enthusiasm.

Calvin Calhoun the Appalachee was cleaning up the pots
from their bacon breakfast (the beastkind generally preferred to
forage for themselves in the woods, though Chikaak had happily
eaten several lightly cooked strips) and packing the horses. As
he had promised Queen Sarah he would, Bill was taking this
opportunity to train her troop of soldiers.

44

"Reload!" Bill removed his floppy black hat and slapped it against his thigh. Again, Chikaak and a few others promptly began reloading. When he saw the look of exasperation on Bill's face, Chikaak barked—two high-pitched yips and a long, low yodeling sound—and the other beastkind carabineers grabbed their powderhorns.

The remaining beastfolk warriors, the ones who lacked the fingers or the proper eye placement to be able to effectively use firearms, crouched in a row in front of their fellows. They held carbines too, but they had bayonets fixed to their weapons, and they pointed the blades toward the mostly unharmed plates of bark.

Each of the beastkind wore a shoulder strap from which hung one of the cartridge boxes taken from the Imperial House Light Dragoons Sarah and her company had defeated two days earlier on Wisdom's Bluff. The boxes were wooden blocks with holes drilled in them, and in each hole rested a paper cartridge containing powder and shot. Bill's idea, which he had explained with delight to Jake the evening before, was that each beastkind carabineer could empty first the cartridge box of the fighter in front of him and then his own, giving each shooter access to a large supply of ammunition. The shooters now reached forward to snatch cartridges from the boxes in front of them, mostly successfully.

"Pikemen, stand!" Bill shouted.

Nothing.

Chikaak barked again, this time a tone in the middle of his range that peaked sharply in pitch at the end. Without meaning to, Jake found himself imitating the sound in his head, and humming it slightly under his breath.

Jake had been born deaf and mute in the Hudson River metropolis of New Amsterdam. His parents hadn't wanted him, so he'd knocked about with a merchant uncle on voyages up and down the Empire's shores until a bad night in New Orleans and a run-in with the gendarmerie had left him half-prisoner, half-employee on the chevalier's prison hulks on the Pontchartrain Sea. He had some ability to read lips, if the speaker used Dutch or French—both languages he could puzzle out a bit in writing—but mostly Jacob Hop responded to gestures and kicks.

At least, that was the life Jake thought he remembered. If he focused on it, the threads of his past disappeared into chaos, but if he relaxed and thought about nothing, he remembered snatches of experience. Stitching those rags together over time, he more or less remembered his youth.

He also remembered fragments of a life that was clearly not the life of Jacob Hop. He remembered racing at the head of a horde of animal warriors to shatter walls and bring kingdoms to their knees. He remembered the blood sacrifice of thousands of men on an altar raised to him, and he remembered marriages—not one, but several, over millennia—to glittering serpentine goddesses. He remembered the births of sons, and the humiliation of having to either defeat or be routed by his own spawn.

Because, for a few weeks, Jake had had a god in his body.

Simon Sword, the wrecking and reaving incarnation of the Heron King of the Mississippi and Ohio Rivers, had filled Jake's body with his enormous soul. The soul had been too big for Jake's frame, and the sheer spiritual pressure had burst out Jake's nostrils, his ears, and his mouth—he had no better way to describe it—giving him the sense of hearing and the gift of speech he'd never had.

Washed by a flood of new sounds, Jake had found himself imitating them. When birds sang, he whistled back to them. He groaned softly to imitate the creak of harness. As he heard others speak, he subvocalized their words, even when he didn't know their meaning.

And then he found that, very quickly, he *did* know their meaning. The god in his body had spoken lots of English, with Bill and with Sarah and with others, and upon the god's departure, Jake was able to speak. Within minutes, he had found he could construct simple English sentences, too.

De gave van tongen, his preacher cousin Ambroos would have called it. The gift of tongues.

Though Ambroos might not have approved of the source of Jake's gift.

Even Jake's companions seemed to shift in and out of his memory, so that there were moments when he looked at Bill and couldn't remember who the man was. The sole exception was Sarah. She was fixed and permanent, and she shone for Jacob Hop like a star.

Unevenly, the front row of beastkind lumbered to their feet.

"Hell's Bells!" Bill roared. "Dismissed! We march in ten minutes!"

Most of the beastkind stood dully until Chikaak barked again.

Jake looked back to their camp in a stand of trees to see what Bill must have already seen; Sarah, Catherine, and Calvin were all mounted. Calvin led a string of horses—they couldn't be entrusted to beastkind, either as mounts or to be led, because the presence of the beastfolk made the horses skittish. All the children of Adam in the party now wore blue coats, cloaks, and hats taken from the Imperial House Light Dragoons, other than Bill; Bill still wore red.

Bill stomped to join Jake, Chikaak slouching at his side.

"I'm sorry for our bad aim," Chikaak yipped.

"But it's improved, hey?" Jake pointed out.

"The aim is not my great concern." Bill ground his teeth. "Naturally, I would be pleased as Punch if our soldiers were able to hit a man-sized target from twenty paces. Indeed, that is not an unreasonable requirement to impose on a musketeer. But even more pressing is the problem that only one of my warriors in five is even able to understand my commands when I give them. If we fight like barbarians, we lose half our strength!"

Chikaak growled low in his throat. "I could repeat your orders."

"Yes, that's what we are doing presently. And we may have to formalize that arrangement, if we can do no better. But if our soldiers cannot obey their captain's shouted order until one of their number has shouted it a second time, we lose precious seconds at every step."

"Ja," Jake agreed. "And what if Chikaak is killed?"

"God forbid." Bill nodded. "Or Peter Plowshare forbid, or whoever." He rested one hand on the butt of a pistol tucked into his belt, and the other on Simon Sword's horn, hanging at his waist from a shoulder strap.

"Peter Plowshare was a good god." Chikaak bobbed his head and shoulders up and down enthusiastically. "I follow Sarah Elytharias Penn now."

Bill sighed. "Well, Queen Sarah forbid, then. But now you'd better go find our trail. We ride in five minutes."

"I found the trail this morning." Chikaak grinned, exposing a row of yellow coyote teeth. "I don't sleep much. Others are preparing to travel ahead."

Jake abruptly remembered a massacre of Elfkind, under a star-bright sky, and an unrestrained dance of victory during which a thousand prisoners had been killed. He thought the memories were of the Ohio, which lay ahead of them on their journey.

They weren't the memories of the deaf-mute Dutchman.

"I suppose," Bill said, "I had better make you a sergeant as well. Jake, do you object?"

Jake shook his head.

"Very well, although I believe we are not quite following Freiherr von Steuben's scheme, lacking both an officer and corporals. Allow me to consult Her Majesty as to the appointment. I think it's unlikely she will disagree, but she is well-versed in a surprising range of subjects, and it is possible she has read the Freiherr's blue book and has a view on the matter. Chikaak, please invite the...*men* to form up."

Chikaak bounded away, tongue lolling out of his mouth, to carry out his instruction. He had a coyote's head, and though he would have been a taller man than average if he stood straight, Chikaak never stood straight. He hunched forward, and every step was a leap, shoulders first. The reddish fur on his coyote head spread out along both shoulder and tapered down his back in a V-shape, before blooming again to cover his legs, which were also the (oversized) hind legs of a coyote. Bill sometimes described Chikaak as *coyote-headed*, but that wasn't complete. Chikaak was a big, muscular coyote-satyr, but he had ten fingers, a quick wit, and the ability to speak English.

He'd be a good sergeant.

"May I join the scouts, Captain?" Jake asked Bill.

"You look contemplative, Jake," Bill said. "I know you are a pond of much deeper water than I, and I'd be pleased to know what you're thinking."

Jake rubbed his chin. Bill's jaw took only a day to go from clean-shaven to a full beard supporting his drooping mustaches, and even Calvin, who much younger than Jake, had stubble on his face. Jake was beardless. He always had been. "I'm not sure. Maybe my waters are deeper than even I know."

Bill frowned and arched an eyebrow at him. "Keep an eye on those waters, Jake. We don't want to be surprised."

By a return of Simon Sword. Though Queen Sarah had said

she could see when Simon Sword was present in another. Still, Jake nodded, then took to his horse.

He quickly found the scouts Chikaak had referred to, standing in trees to the side of the faint path they followed a few hundred yards ahead. One was a short man, with a man's face but a bear's arms. His paws didn't let him squeeze a trigger effectively, so he was a pikeman, and his name was Oriot.

Sliitch was the other's name, and he was one of the stranger warriors in Queen Sarah's retinue. Sliitch's head looked like a horse's, only covered with long fur. The beastman had a hand but only a single arm, so he couldn't use a carbine effectively, either as a pike or as a musket. Sliitch wore a pair of bandoliers crossed over his chest, from which hung four pistols. His eyes being set on opposite sides of his head, though, meant that Sliitch had poor depth perception, and rarely hit the mark unless it was practically within reach. Also, he reloaded slowly. Beneath the bandoliers, his body branched into three legs, which caused him to run in an off-balanced fashion that was nevertheless very fast.

Sliitch and Oriot grunted back and forth to each other as Jake approached. Unconsciously, Jake found himself once again imitating the hoots and whistles of the beastkind. They came in short bursts, and no matter what the method of vocalization—growl, bark, whine, roar, whistle—the sounds were melodic. They changed in pitch. The beastkind were singing short melodies back and forth to each other.

Jake's horse—acquired from the Imperial dragoons—had a carbine and a pair of long pistols holstered along its saddle. It had also come with a deck of cards in one of its saddlebags, and Jake now took these out to look at them.

"Go on," he said in answer to Oriot's questioning look and short whimper. "I'll follow."

The two beastmen jogged ahead, branches slapping them as they ran. Jake examined the cards. They were a Tarock deck; Jake had seen fortunetellers use such decks before, in many of the seaside towns he'd visited. He knew there was a Marseille Tarock some of the French liked, and a New World Tarock devised by old Bishop Franklin, and other decks. Jake had never handled any of them. Ambroos wasn't the only preacher in the Hop family, and divinatory cards had been banned from his childhood home. This deck appeared to be Franklin's Tarock, because the first card he turned over was Simon Sword. The Simon Sword in the miniature painting looked a little like Jake, young and blond, and he swung an enormous sword to behead three men simultaneously.

Simon Sword was definitely a creature of the New World, and wouldn't belong in a French deck.

Jake hesitated at turning over the second card, fearing for a moment—unreasonably—that it too would bear the image of Simon Sword. It didn't. On the face of the second card, Jake saw lightning bolts in the corners, a forest of saplings, and a man in a leather coat riding toward a sunrise.

He quickly counted the cards. There were four suits: cups, lightning bolts, swords, and coins, and in each suit a sequence of cards numbered one through ten, with a king, queen, knight, and page. Fourteen cards multiplied by four suits made fifty-six. These were the Minor Arcana, and each card had its own unique painting on it.

Beyond that there were twenty additional cards: the Major Arcana. These did not have suits, and around their edges the Major Arcana had interlocking cursive patterns almost like knots, each card with a unique motif. These cards had their own paintings too, and they were named at the bottom. Simon Sword was one of them. So were Peter Plowshare, and the Serpent, and the Horseman, and the Lovers. The Major Arcana were not numbered, or ordered in any other apparent way. Seventy-six cards in total.

A whistle from ahead stopped Jake's exploration. He pocketed the cards and found Oriot running toward him. The bear-man was grunting melodically. Did that mean he was trying to say something?

When he reached Jake, he grabbed the Dutchman's horse by its saddle and made a pained, thoughtful face.

"Ja?" Jake asked.

"Traaaaap," Oriot finally said.

The queer little Dutchman galloped back toward Calvin, where he rode with Bill, Sarah, and Cathy Filmer. Jacob Hop wasn't much of a horseman, it turned out; he bounced up and down above the saddle holding on for dear life, his blond hair bouncing with him.

Bill drew and cocked one of the multiple pistols he kept on his body and on the horse, a big Andalusian gray.

Cal raised the Kentucky rifle he carried across the saddle

bow. The weapon was too long for the carbine scabbards all the dragoons' horses had come with, but Cal favored the hunting rifle over the shorter military weapon, for accuracy and for his own familiarity with it.

"Er is a problem!" Hop gasped as he reined in his animal.

"Air?" Cal asked.

"He means *there*," Bill said gruffly. "*There* is a problem."

"Natuurlijk," Hop said.

"Sir William," Cathy Filmer drawled. "You have become an able interpreter."

"Unwillingly, Mrs. Filmer, and only by necessity."

Sarah straightened in the saddle, but said nothing. Instead, she removed the dirty gray strip of cloth that covered her gifted eye. Then she pulled the plain iron sphere that was one of the regalia of Cahokia, her father's kingdom, from her shoulder bag, and looked into it.

Sarah had one normal eye, and one—so blue it was almost white—that had only opened recently. Through her witchy eye, she saw ... things. Cal wasn't even sure. She saw people's spirits, and she saw ley lines, and he didn't know what else.

Sarah sat proudly on her horse, and her jaw was set with determination. The strangeness of her witchy eye, the stubble growing on her skull—she'd shaved all her own hair off in an act of defensive magic only a few days earlier—and the orb in her hands gave her an unearthly look.

"A trap," she said.

Cal couldn't see what she was gazing at, and he wanted to know more. "What kinda trap?"

"Cahokians, Oriot says." Hop smiled. "Though it was hard for him to say it. It is much easier to speak with Chikaak."

As he said the coyote-headed beastman's name, Chikaak jogged to join them. "I have run ahead to look. It is a trap." He bounded from side to side with irrepressible energy as he spoke; Cal had half an idea that if he were standing instead of mounted, the beastman might throw himself on Cal's knee and dry-hump his leg.

"You told me you had scouted this morning." Bill frowned.

"The trap has been set since. Cahokians, Oriot is right."

Jacob Hop nodded. "Er is a woman there, in a ... carry-chair, what do you call it?"

"A sedan?" Bill asked.

"A sedan." Hop nodded again. "She doesn't touch the ground. And she has others with her, and they mostly look harmless."

"Call no man harmless until he is dead," Bill said. "My education ended early, but I believe I remember that much of Aristotle."

"Aristotle, or perhaps Attila the Hun." Cathy smiled and she leaned over to pat Bill's thigh. She was too old for Calvin—who was in love with Sarah, anyway—but she wasn't too old to notice, especially when she smiled.

"I'll take good advice where I can get it," Bill growled.

"In the trees, there are men hidden," Hop said. "Dat is the trap."

"How many?" Bill asked.

"They outnumber us." Chikaak yipped low, a mournful sound. "Spears, swords, longbows, guns."

"We can ride around," Hop suggested.

Sarah returned the orb to her shoulder bag. "We'll ride into the ambush," she announced.

Bill inclined his head deeply. "Your Majesty. Perhaps the snare is not intended for us, and we can merely ride through."

"Oh, this offer is meant for me," Sarah said. "Only the buyer has no idea how much she's going to get for her bargain."

"At least let us git around behind these men," Cal suggested. "Git the drop on 'em, iffen they feel like ambushin' you anyway."

Sarah nodded once, sharply. "Take some who can shoot with you. Sir William, I'll need you at my side."

"He's jest about the *only* body as can shoot." Cal laughed. "Jake, you want to come with me? I reckon you got a better chance of hitting anythin' than that feller with bull hooves."

"Agreed." Hop turned his horse around.

"I'll come, too." Chikaak pointed with his carbine at the end of a long, narrow meadow. "If we go that way, we should come up behind these ambushers unseen."

Cal followed Chikaak. The beastmen didn't seem any faster in a sprint than an ordinary man, most of them, but they could run all day and not look tired. Now Chikaak paced out ahead of Calvin and Jacob Hop, leading the way.

Cal took one last look back at Sarah before he plunged into the trees and was separated.

"You know how to load those pistols, Jake?" he asked.

"I keep the pistols and the carbine loaded and primed," Hop said. "I try to be discreet about it so as not to unsettle Bill's mind."

"He ain't yet o'er the fact that you were Simon Sword."

"I was *not* Simon Sword." Jake spat the words, but then looked thoughtful. "I was Simon Sword's prisoner."

"I reckon I don't quite understand what he wanted with you." Cal and Jacob Hop followed Chikaak up a rocky defile. Here the beastman sergeant ran doubled over, sniffing the ground.

"I think dat he wanted to free Bill. I think dat he wanted to help Sarah recover the Cahokian regalia. I think dat he wanted exactly what happened on top of that mountain to happen. And dat, Calvin Calhoun, should give you pause."

"Jerusalem, but it does," Cal admitted. "And how do you think that should make Bill feel about *you*?"

Hop laughed. "Ja, exactly. And so I do not touch my guns in his sight, and I give him respect and obedience. Also, he is a good teacher, even though he does not quite trust me."

"Well, I trust you," Cal offered.

"You trust *me*? Or you trust *Sarah*, and what she says about me?"

"Shhh!" Chikaak turned and urged the two men to silence. The sight of a man's finger shushing him in front of a coyote's mouth, twisted into an imitation that almost looked like pursed lips, struck Cal as hilarious.

He bit his tongue to keep from laughing.

They tied the two horses to a tree and followed Chikaak up the next slope on foot. Cal was by long habit a silent walker—he'd been a rustler by trade at home, and wore high moccasins—and he was impressed now how quietly Jacob Hop moved, though he wore hard-soled leather shoes. All three held their long guns in one hand and a pistol in the other, and near the crest of the slope, Chikaak motioned to them to lie on their bellies.

They inched forward a few feet on their elbows and looked down.

The path they had been riding for two days now passed beneath them through a bowl. The circular valley had stands of white oak on two sides; one stand was at the bottom of the slope beneath Cal and his companions, and the other stood opposite.

Among the trees beneath them, some twenty men lay on their bellies. Half of them had long rifles pointed out into the bowl, and the other half lay with palms pressed to the earth, as if ready to spring to their feet at a moment's notice. They wore small steel helmets and blue cloaks, and their spears, bows, and muskets lay on the ground beside them.

"Bit of an oversight of these soldiers not to post a guard up here on the ridge behind 'em," Cal muttered.

"They had a guard," Chikaak whispered.

Cal looked at the scout, whose only answer was a long, knowing grin.

If Chikaak had killed the guard he referred to, he'd hidden the body as well.

"More men under those other trees?" Cal whispered to the beastman.

Chikaak nodded, panting like a dog.

In the center of the bowl was a sedan chair, just as Chikaak had told them. It was in use, and held an occupant, though from here Calvin couldn't see any detail. Eight burly men held the sedan on their shoulders by two long poles, two bearers to each corner.

Two men and a woman stood beside the sedan.

"How much time we got?" Cal asked.

"Not long," Hop told him.

Cal sighted along the barrel of his rifle, first at the nearer trees and then at the farther stand. "How good are your eyes?"

"Not as good as my nose," Chikaak said.

"Ja, good," Hop said. "Better than when I was a boy, even."

That was an odd answer, but Cal didn't press it. "Am I right to think there are wasps' nests o'er in those trees?"

The morning sun was at their backs, but Hop shaded his eyes anyway and squinted. "Ja, I think you have it right, friend Calvin. Or bees, maybe."

"You can call me *Cal*."

"Ja, and you call me *Jake*. You have a plan, Cal?"

"Mebbe," Cal allowed.

"We're badly outnumbered," Chikaak said. "I didn't think you were the sort of man to crave a hero's death."

"I ain't, but Lord hates a man as ain't willin' to *risk* a hero's death. We do nothin', until the moment when we have to, to help Sarah. And when that time comes, I'll think about those fellers o'er on the far side, iffen you two can manage the ones here on our doorstep."

"Ja. You give me your pistol, and you can have my carbine."

✧　　✧　　✧

Sarah removed the bandage from her eldritch eye. She would ride into this meeting seeing everything, seeing more than the other side could see. And if she also discomfited the ambushing party with the sight of her one eye white as ice, so much the better.

Sarah was determined to take her father's kingdom, at almost any cost. She needed her father's kingdom and its power to rescue her sister and her brother, whom she had never met.

Acquainted or not, kin was kin.

She pushed her shoulders back and her chin up, conscious that no matter what she did, she'd still look like a scarecrow-filthy, twig-thin, dirt-faced ragamuffin, with all the hair scraped off her skull. So be it.

She fixed her face into a cold stare.

"Your Majesty," Cathy Filmer and Captain Sir William Johnston Lee said together.

"Ride beside me," Sarah said. "Sir William, I hope not to need your pistols."

"They are here in any case, Your Majesty, loaded and ready."

"As are mine," Cathy added.

"Please form my guard up behind us. I would like the beastmen to look potentially threatening, though not poised immediately to attack. I hope that's a reasonably clear distinction."

"I have read some philosophy, Your Majesty." Sir William turned to one of the beastkind, who now clustered around. "You, there. You understand me when I speak English? No? You? Nothing?"

One of the beastkind warriors, a seven-foot-tall woman with the head of a long-horned cow, raised a hand. The gesture was almost shy.

"Your name?" Sir William asked.

"Ferpa."

"Two abreast, double file!" he snapped.

The ox-woman looked lost. "Double what?"

"One, two," Sir William counted, pointing. "One, two. One, two. Yes?"

Ferpa nodded. "Muskets?" She faltered. "Pikes?"

Sir William shook his head. "Not today. If we fight, charge them like animals and give them hell. Understood?"

"Give them hell." Ferpa laughed, delighted. Then she let out a series of mooing and squealing noises, at which all the beastkind laughed.

"You have delighted them, Sir William," Cathy said.

"I wish I knew *how*," he muttered. "But perhaps I have found my corporal. Freiherr von Steuben would be so pleased."

Ferpa made further lowing noises and the beastkind lined up as Sir William had commanded.

"Two by two, Your Majesty," Sir William said.

"Like the ark." She smiled at him.

"Yes," he agreed, "if Noah entered the ark protected by his goats and hippopotamuses, prepared to fight off an ambush on two fronts."

"We'll be fine," she said.

"Your Majesty." Sir William nodded.

"I recognize the improvements you've already made, Sir William. Don't distress yourself for the progress you have yet to make."

"I am not distressed," he said. "A general goes to war with the army he has, not the army he hopes he may one day create."

"*That* is true philosophy. Let's hope that what we ride to isn't war." Sarah started her horse forward.

It might be war, though. She had gazed through the Orb of Etyles and along the ley line of the Mississippi. The river was out of sight now, but close enough that, with the Orb, she could touch it and use its power. She had seen what was waiting.

Firstborn.

The ambush was set by Cahokians, Chikaak had said. Cahokia was a kingdom, and any sort of person might wear its livery. What Sarah knew from gazing through the Mississippi was that the people waiting in hiding were her people, the Eldritch or Ophidian descendants of Adam and his first wife, sometimes called Wisdom.

She knew they were mostly men.

She knew they expected not a battle, but a lesser confrontation. An arrest, maybe, or something similar. They didn't have the will to die written across their souls; instead, they had a demand to make.

And she knew that the leaders they followed included a woman borne on a litter by eight slaves.

The color of that woman's aura, the timbre of it, if it had been music, the smell and feel of it, were familiar. The aura was close—not identical, but similar—to the aura that had once shone from the acorn that had fallen from Sarah's own eye. It was like the aura that shone from the tree atop Wisdom's Bluff that had sprouted from that acorn, close to the aura of the Orb of Etyles and the Sevenfold Crown.

Close to the aura of the father Sarah had never met.

Close to Sarah's own aura.

Somehow, the woman in the palanquin was family.

One of her siblings? Her sister, Margaret? She didn't think so. The woman felt too old to be Sarah's triplet. Did her father have a living sister? Sarah had no idea.

How could this Firstborn woman, whoever she was, know to expect Sarah? Or did she? Were she and her men waiting in ambush for someone else?

It took an effort of will to neither speed up nor turn and run.

Sarah passed through two small valleys at a stately pace and entered a broad natural bowl. Wild grass grew tall all through it, and sturdy oak trees sheltered it on the east and west.

She saw the ambush immediately, through her talented eye. She saw it as a luminescent line of blue trying hard to flatten itself to the ground beneath each stand of trees.

"Under the oaks," she said to her companions.

"I do not see the scoundrels," Sir William said. "But that's where *I* would hide my men."

"They cannot mean to kill us, Your Majesty," Cathy Filmer said. "They're so far away, if they sprang their ambush, we could ride from the valley before they reached us."

"I see our three friends, too," Sarah said. "Don't look, but they're on the hilltop to the east, behind that line of Cahokians."

"Perhaps the Cahokians are only here as bodyguards, Your Majesty," Sir William suggested. "The woman we approach appears to be someone of importance."

"Because she's rich?"

"Because the man beside her holds a banner. And because she isn't touching the ground, Your Majesty. I do not pretend to understand it, but there are members of Cahokia's priestly caste— forgive me for using the term if it is offensive, Your Majesty, but these are your people."

"My people—you mean Cahokians? The Firstborn?"

Sir William shook his head. "I mean the priests of Cahokia. The royal family is one line of a larger clan from which many of the hierophants, prognosticators, and entrail-gazers of the kingdom are drawn. And some of them, at certain times and for reasons I do not understand, insist upon not touching the ground."

"You know this because you rode with my father?"

"Yes, Your Majesty. And there were periods—whole weeks at a time, though not corresponding to any calendar I could recognize—when he would eat in the saddle and sleep in a tree."

"In a tree?" Sarah could hear the smile in Cathy Filmer's voice. "Somehow, this detail didn't make it into any of the songs about the Lion of Missouri."

"He was a pious man," Sir William said. "Though I did not understand his piety."

"That woman is a priestess?"

"Likely," Sir William said. "Or a very, very delicate flower, indeed."

Sarah slowed her horse further and gazed at the stands of oak, trying to appear casual. The blue auras of the soldiers were agitated, and she reminded herself that she rode with a pack of monstrous warriors at her heels.

Like Herne in English belief, whose Wild Hunt rode the night sky once a year and destroyed anyone who witnessed the event, either by tearing them to pieces or by driving them mad.

"These people are my subjects," she said gently, "let's *try* not to kill them."

"I can always *try*, Your Majesty," Sir William said.

"Shall I act the herald again, Your Majesty?" Cathy asked.

Sarah considered the possibility. "No. Let's meet them incognito."

Sarah brought her horse to a stop. The beast was a big, fearsome animal, a mount more fit for a soldier than for a young woman, but it was obedient. The litter fifty feet away was made of silk and filled inside with cushions. The eight men who carried it were muscular and brutish-looking; they wore wool trousers and cotton shirts, and all wore a thin band of iron around their necks. The slaves, by their auras, were children of Eve.

Standing on the ground to one side were two men and a woman; she could tell these three were Firstborn even without the gift of her witchy eye, from the pallor of their skin, their slender eyebrows, and their long fingers. They looked a bit like Thalanes. They looked like Sarah herself.

The older of the two men had a weathered face, deep-set eyes, and hair sprouting from his ears. He wore a long gray tunic and gray leggings under his blue cloak and he looked on Sarah and her party coolly, probably counting the beastfolk and noting their weapons. A military man, or a counselor, or a spy. He was the man holding the banner on a ten-foot pole—when the breeze unfurled it, Sarah saw a horizontal gray bar across a royal blue field, and in the very center of the banner, the black silhouette of a flower blossom.

Beside the standard-bearer stood a much shorter man in Polite red. A wizard, then, and honest enough to announce himself as such. She looked more closely at him and saw several sharp points of light about his body—those would be enchanted objects, mana reservoirs, or the like. The wizard smiled blandly and held his hands in front of himself, fingers laced together. He didn't seem young either, but he had the smooth-skinned look of a man who had aged indoors, rather than on the trail; his eyes were oddly far apart.

The third person was a woman. She wore a mail shirt of bronze scales that fell halfway down her thighs; a long scimitar hung at her belt, its scabbarded tip grazing the earth. Her black hair was cut nearly as short as Sarah's. Her thin lips were set into a frown that showed a hint of white teeth.

The woman inside the sedan chair drew aside the curtain to reveal herself. She was middle-aged—definitely not Margaret—and she looked taut and polished, like a well-used and well-maintained bow, with its string pulled back to shoot. Her eyes were large and her lips full, and when she spoke she leaned forward ear-first, as if she were hearing Sarah rather than looking at her. The woman wore a simple blue robe and her feet were bare.

"Travelers!" the woman called. "You come from the Serpent Mound!"

Sir William shifted uneasily in his saddle.

"We've come from farther than that," Sarah answered. She rode closer, prompting the mail-clad woman to put her hand on the hilt of her sword and hiss. From close up, she saw lines of age around the priestess's face. "We've come from Nashville, some of us. Though I was born in Pennsland. And now I'm coming home."

The priestess smiled. "A riddle?"

"If you will."

The priestess nodded. "Then riddle me *this*: three things lay buried with a dead king, and no one could unearth them. What power would bring those sacred objects to light again?"

"What power but the king's own?" Sarah was enjoying this veiled mutual provocation. In part, she liked it because she felt safe with Cathy and Sir William at her side. "But then what power would part those three objects?"

The priestess's eyes opened wide. "Who *are* you?"

"My name is Sarah."

"Are you a thief?"

"I only take what belongs to me."

"Are you carrying those objects now?"

"Who are you to ask me?" Sarah asked. The questions were getting a little too personal.

The priestess raised her chin, which made her seem to be looking down at Sarah, though the two were at about the same height. "I am Alzbieta Torias. I am Handmaid to Lady Wisdom, and the rightful Queen of Cahokia."

Sarah laughed once, from surprise. Then she thought about what the Firstborn woman had said and laughed again, this time at herself. Of course! Who else would be so interested in the regalia? Who else might have a sense of where they would be found, but Sarah's unknown Ophidian relatives...who might think they had claims to Sarah's father's throne. Sarah bit back more laughs.

"You're traveling pretty light, for a queen," she called.

Torias didn't answer.

"So," Sarah said, getting control of herself, "this Polite over here, somehow he hexed up Wisdom's Bluff in a way that would tell you when someone had found the...three objects, as you say. Two days ago, he comes running into your chapel, only you don't have a chapel, do you? What do you have, a treehouse? Platform on a pole, like old St. Simeon Stylites? Never mind, you can tell me later.

"Your pet Polite comes rushing in and he says 'Your Holiness,' or 'Your Worship,' or whatever it is he has to call you, 'someone has taken the...objects.' So you gather up the family retainers—that's who these people are, right, servants? I mean, some of them are flat-out wearing slave collars, and the ones hiding in the trees, well, they're a little too nervous to be real professionals, aren't they?

"But you figured it was all you'd need, or maybe it was all you could scrape together, so you gather them up and come rushing down here, to sit in this place and wait to meet me." Sarah threw back her head and laughed again. "So either you marched really fast, or you weren't in Cahokia, right? Because that must be, what, four days north? Family estates, is that it?"

The Polite looked disconcerted. The counselor held an expressionless look, but his eyes darted back and forth violently. The woman with the sword definitely wanted to attack Sarah.

"You look as if you might be Firstborn," the priestess said slowly.

"About time you scored a point, Alzbieta," Sarah said.

"Most people don't address me by that name."

"Yeah?" Sarah slipped into Appalachee before she could help it. "I ain't most people."

"You could be the right age," Alzbieta Torias said.

"I could be," Sarah agreed. "If that age was about fifteen-sixteen."

"Barely," the priestess said.

Sarah raised her eyebrows. "Barely means exactly right. The right age to be the daughter you never heard of, the daughter nobody ever heard of."

"Whose daughter?"

"Oh no you don't, Alzbieta." Sarah waggled a finger at the priestess. "You want a score another point, *you* have to tell *me*."

"The Lion," Alzbieta Torias said.

"Of Missouri," Sarah agreed.

"Not only of Missouri."

Curious. But Sarah wasn't about to ask a question now. "That make us cousins, Alzbieta?"

"Why?" Alzbieta's face broke into a self-satisfied grin. "Are you hoping to marry me, Nashville child?"

"Don't mistake my willingness to banter for the toothlessness of a cub, Alzbieta Torias," Sarah snarled. "I am every bit the lion my father was."

"Being the lion got your father killed."

"Being the lion got my father an empress for a bride, and fame that will not die."

"And yet his daughter is a vagrant and a thief."

"I found and took what was mine. And I found and took what you sought and failed to find. Are you ready to name the three objects you believe I have, Alzbieta Torias?"

The priestess lurched forward to the edge of her palanquin, catching herself on the pole but forcing her slave bearers to stagger sideways. "The Orb of Etyles! The Sevenfold Crown! And the Heronsword!"

Sarah chuckled slowly. "Close, Alzbieta, but wrong. Now are you and your servants—my family's servants—ready to accompany me and my guard to our family lands, so we can discuss preparations for my enthronement?"

"Take her!" the priestess gasped.

The warrior in scale mail drew her scimitar, but at the same moment two pistols jumped into Sir William's fists and she froze, sword raised over her head. Cathy Filmer pulled a pistol and pointed it at the counselor leaning on his standard. Sarah jammed her hand into the satchel hanging from her shoulder to grab the Orb of Etyles. Somewhat restored after two days of no gramarye, she shouted "*dormi!*" and channeled the green fire of the Mississippi River into the mind of the Polite—

knocking down several invisible wardings in the process—

and the wizard fell to the ground like a chopped tree, unconscious.

With a cry, the Firstborn lying in wait on either side of the clearing rose to their feet. They wore blue cloaks over gray tunics, like their standard-bearer. *Bang! Bang! Bang!* Sarah heard three gunshots off to her right, in the east, and then the warriors on the west side of the valley began to scream.

"I believe someone has dropped a bee's nest on your servants, Lady Torias," Cathy Filmer said. "That, or some sinister spell is causing them to slap themselves and run about in circles."

"Don't look at *me*," Sarah said. "Might a been your Polite."

"My cousin Kyres was a renowned magician." Alzbieta Torias lay back against her cushions, looking more like a snake coiling to strike a second time than a person resigned to her fate.

"I ain't renowned," Sarah said. "But I am my father's daughter, I'm the rightful Queen of Cahokia, and I'm determined as hell. Now you can make nice or we can be enemies, but whatever you decide to do, remember this...the bees are on *my* side."

"Tell me your full name," Alzbieta said.

"You know it. I'm Sarah Elytharias Penn. What you don't know is that I've been raised as a Calhoun these fifteen years, and I've got a streak of pure Appalachee piss-off-and-die that runs all the way down to the marrow of my bones."

"I can see that for myself." Alzbieta Torias sighed. "Very well, then. Someone wake up the wizard. Cousin Sarah, I don't think you know quite what you've gotten yourself into."

"The Company is going to extract an extraordinary dividend."

—➤●◄—

CHAPTER FOUR

Nathaniel pawed at his ear, trying to silence the riotous noises of the world. His horse sounded a plaintive whinny. Landon Chapel and Charles Lee, also mounted, hooted and cheered loudly.

The goose honked. Its legs were tied to the upper crossbar in a simple frame that stretched across one of the plantation's lanes and the bird flapped its wings in vain, trying to escape. The young men had greased it thoroughly, not to increase the chances of the goose's survival, which were nil, but to make the game more competitive, and the grease now gave the goose a surreally slick look, its feathers lying stubbornly flat against its body and neck.

Naked fields stretched to either side of the lane. Beyond the fields lay the log homes of Irish field-workers, and beyond those lay forested hills. The earl's manor stood out of sight on the other side of a low ridge. A thread of smoke rose from the site of the manor, suggesting that the house's ever-skulking godi Wickens was offering sheep to Woden.

George Randolph Isham galloped hard beneath the honking goose, made his grab, and missed.

"Herne's bloody horn!" The earl's son shook his hand. "I'm bit!"

"Careful, George!" Charles Lee called. Charles was the oldest of the young men, old enough to be married, though he wasn't, and old enough to have a commission in the earl's cavalry, which he did. He was a lieutenant, and on leave, and spending his time with the younger men of the plantation. His greater years showed in the superiority of his facial hair, which consisted of a long drooping mustache. Under his faded purple coat, he wore brown breeches and a white shirt.

~Cut the throat in one motion. Collect the blood in the stone's groove.~

"Collect the blood." Nathaniel shook his head. He had hoped George would pull off the goose's head. A victory by the earl's son was the best outcome for everyone. Nathaniel burrowed deeper into the old coat he wore, patched at the elbows, and pulled the oversized tricorner hat down tight. The coat and hat had both once belonged to one of the earl's footmen, a kind old man named Barlow who had taken special care of Nathaniel when he'd been a boy; on Barlow's death, Nathaniel had taken to wearing the footman's clothing, hat and coat both long since faded to a dull blue. No one had stopped him.

George, by contrast, wore a gloriously tailored coat dyed the earl's color purple. Gold stitching on the outside of both sleeves and up the front traced out branches of the great world-tree, Yggdrasil, and he wore a gold hammer of Thunor on a gold chain around his neck. When he wore a hat, which he didn't at the moment, it was of the same brilliance as his coat.

Landon wore old cast-offs once worn by George, faded to a duller violet, and the hammer on his breast was pewter.

"Still trying to nursemaid me, are you?" George laughed out loud. "Don't worry your pretty head, Miss Lee! Even if the goose bites off my thumb, I can still be earl after my father is gone!"

"True!" Charles stroked his long mustachios. They made him look Texian, or maybe Ferdinandian. "If you fall and break your neck in a ganderpull, though, I am less optimistic of your chances. And you should be pleased you still have your father with you, and do your best not to disappoint him."

"And therefore I am doing my best to plump up every serving maid in Johnsland with a baby Isham . . . or rather, *Chapel*." George sneered at his half-brother, who now swung into the saddle of his own horse to take his turn.

Foster children and orphans were given good-luck names when their true family name was unknown, or could not be admitted in public. *Chapel* was such a name, and it was Landon's name as well, though he and Nathaniel were no relations, as far as Nathaniel knew. *Temple* was another such name, as were *Godsbless, Wodensson, Christborne,* and *Farewell.* As such names went, *Chapel* was vaguely Christian, and it only made Landon and Nathaniel stick out more on the earl's lands.

"My name is Landon Chapel," Landon said, "but everyone knows who my father is."

"Just not your mother," George shot back.

"I heard a surprising Elector Song in a tavern in Raleigh this week," Landon said. He burst into sudden melody:

> *Johnsland has two Electors, my word*
> *One slaughters sheep and the other's a bird*

It was a parody of the Elector Song for Louisiana. Not a very good one.

"Say what you like about Old One Eye, but the earl is father to both of us," George growled, "and I'll gladly kill you for his honor's sake."

"Easy, George," Charles murmured.

Landon shrugged. "If you die pulling the gander, it won't be your get on poor Jenny Farewell who inherits. It'll be me."

~*His get on Jenny Farewell. Get on Jenny Farewell.*~ Nathaniel felt punched in the stomach.

"If I fall and break my neck," George shot back, "our father's twenty other bastards will come crawling out of the woods and swamps of Johnsland to make their claims. You'll be fighting duels the rest of your life." He took a swig from the bottle of wine. All four of them were slightly drunk. "Or maybe the Chief Godi will just take the earldom for the College."

~*Eat what you kill. Kill not, unless you eat.*~

The buzz in Nathaniel's head from the alcohol didn't make the voices go away. It also didn't dull the high-pitched whine he always heard in the background, behind the voices. His sudden understanding why Jenny was pleased to see George abused didn't help, either. He rubbed his ear and managed not to whimper. "Kill," he said.

Charles shot him a pitying look.

"Worse," the young lieutenant said. "You'll be fighting lawyers."

"Woden's nine nights, that's a fate worse than death." George finished the alcohol, belched deeply, and tossed the bottle beyond Charles into the now-bare tobacco field. "You'd better hope I survive, little Landy."

Landon was the shorter of the two, but was muscular. He'd inherited the fine brown hair of his mother, whoever she was, rather than the rich, dark curls worn by George and—in his youth, if the paintings were to be believed—the earl himself. "I'll protect you from the ferocious goose, George." He smiled, maliciously. "And then maybe Jenny Farewell will tuck *me* into bed at night."

"Shall Jenny be the prize, then?" George wobbled on his feet, then leaned against the fence.

"You might ask Jenny," Nathaniel said softly. None of the others heard him.

~No! It is murder! I beg you!~

"I beg you," Nathaniel finished in a murmur.

"The prize is the purse," Charles said. He dug the small leather bag from the pocket of his coat and shook it, clinking the coins inside together to remind the others of their agreed stakes.

Landon rode past the scaffold and turned his horse around, prepared to begin his run at the goose. The goose, perhaps sensing Landon's intention, honked loudly.

"Shall the prize be Jenny Farewell?" George laughed harshly. "So be it! I give her to you, my stubby little bastard brother, if you can pluck off the goose's head!"

"I won't raise your whelp, of course!" Landon called.

George shrugged. "We'll call him *Chapel* and throw him in with the rest!"

The shrug unbalanced the young nobleman and sent him lurching sideways. Charles reached over the fence and grabbed George's arm, holding him upright.

George pulled himself away and spat. "Hands off me!"

"Relax, George." But Charles inclined his head deferentially and released the earl's legitimate son.

George rolled from one foot to the other like a man standing on the deck of a ship, but didn't fall.

"Go on, then!" he bellowed. "For the purse, for the goose, and for Jenny!"

Nathaniel held his breath, hoping Landon killed the goose. He didn't want to take a turn.

~Kill me. Kill me.~

"Kill me," Nathaniel repeated. He felt dizzy. It wasn't the gander whispering in his deformed ear, but in a way, it was.

"Hee ya!" Landon spurred his mount into a charge. The horse was a long-legged hunter—Landon was a Chapel like Nathaniel, but he was the earl's bastard, so he dressed in better castoffs and rode an expensive horse. The horse leaped into a blinding sprint and crashed toward the scaffold.

At the last moment, Nathaniel looked away. When Landon's hunter passed him, slowing, Landon was rubbing his right hand with his left and muttering.

"Let me see that," Charles called.

"He'll be fine. Where's that other flask?" George rummaged through his horse's saddlebags.

Landon dismounted and showed Charles his hand. It was covered in blood.

"You'll lose this finger if you don't get it treated," Charles told him.

"Fine." Landon jerked his hand away. "Once I tear off this bird's head, and swive Jenny Farewell senseless, I'll have the cook stitch me up."

"Too late." George found the flask, unstoppered it, and took a long drink. "She's already senseless."

"She is if she puts up with you," Charles said.

It was a joke, but a joke with a point in it, and George was too drunk to take it well. "Shut up!" he roared.

"George," Charles pleaded.

"You're the son of a murderer!" George snapped. "You should have been cast out with him!"

Charles looked George in the eye. "My father was a man of honor. I am not ashamed of him."

"And don't you ever forget that I am your earl!"

Charles looked down.

"Will be," Landon said. "Unless the goose breaks your neck."

George swung and took a punch at his half-brother. Landon being too far away, George only ended up lurching uselessly forward several steps. When he swayed and looked as if he might fall, Charles swung easily over the fence and caught him.

"Hands off!" George staggered away, leaned against the fence, and took another drink.

"My turn," Nathaniel offered. He wanted to stop the bickering, wanted peace. Even if the other young men had been completely silent, Nathaniel would still have been tormented by the voices he heard, but if he could reduce the noise in the world to only those voices, he thought he could feel calm. "I'll kill the bird, and happily take Jenny Farewell. She'd make a good wife for a fosterling like me."

He climbed onto his mount, which was a rugged hill pony of the sort the Irish ploughmen or house servants of Johnsland might ride. He hoped his words would disarm the others, but George and Landon both looked furious.

~Kill me. Kill me.~

Was it the gander? The voice sounded like a gander's voice, half-honk. "Kill me," Nathaniel whispered, helpless not to repeat the words he heard.

All his life, Nathaniel's left ear had jutted out sideways from his head, a complete mismatch to his right ear. When he heard the voices, blood filled his strange ear, which heated up and itched. He reached up to massage the ear now, hoping the gesture was inconspicuous.

"Well spoken, Nathaniel," Charles said softly. "Jenny's a good girl, and would be a good wife for any decent man."

"Oh?" George spun about, almost falling. "*Any decent man?* But I will not have her, so I must not be decent, is that it?"

The earl's son dropped his hand to the hilt of the saber on his belt.

"Impudent," Landon muttered.

"That's not what I meant." Charles spoke slowly, and sounded tired. "We're all a little drunk, and my words didn't come out the way I intended them."

"Try again, then." George's voice was icy.

Charles thought for a moment before speaking. "I meant that Nathaniel is a decent lad for thinking kindly of Jenny. You also, I know, think kindly of Jenny. Clearly, Jenny Farewell is far beneath your station and would not be a suitable bride for the future Earl of Johnsland. But she works hard, she's bright enough to know her letters and a little Cherokee as well, and she's a comely lass. For Nathaniel, I agree, she would be an excellent wife."

"Or for you," George said.

"Certainly." Charles smiled. "Or for me. And I would try to do right by her, if she were mine."

"Because he's a bastard, and you may as well be."

Charles's breath hissed through his teeth. Nathaniel was afraid this confrontation was heading toward violence.

"My turn!" He pulled his old coat on tighter. Urging his pony into a canter, he turned at the elbow of the lane and rushed back toward the goose, reins in his left hand and right hand held high. The landscape rushed past him, but it also seemed to revolve around him, and his head felt light.

~*Kill me. Kill me. Kill me.*~

"Kill me!" he screamed, then bit his own tongue trying to force the words back into his throat.

He didn't want to kill the gander. But the bird seemed to be begging him. He rode hard, fighting to keep his eyes open against sudden tears that threatened to blind him.

The goose honked one last time—

it turned its neck to thrust its greased head into Nathaniel's outstretched palm—

crunch!

Nathaniel slowed and then stopped his horse, looking down in shock at the bird's head that lay twitching in his cupped hand.

"Woden's beard, I think he did it." George walked away from Charles toward Nathaniel, reaching up to pull down the other young man's hand to look inside.

~*Thank you.*~

"Thank you," Nathaniel repeated, feeling exhausted.

"Publish the banns." George snorted as he took the goose's head. "Jenny's yours, young Chapel."

"I guess I'll be having goose for dinner tomorrow night." Nathaniel tried to grin big, and affect the bravado the others seemed to feel. Charles smiled back at him. Nathaniel's ear tingled, so he rubbed it.

"You know, if you left your ear alone, it might not have swollen up to that ridiculous size," Landon said.

"It's not that young Nathaniel's ear is large." George grunted, climbing onto his own horse, where he swayed back and forth during the pause in his speech. "It's that it sticks out sideways. Poor bastard looks like a windmill on his left side."

"I'd have said an elephant," Landon suggested.

"Master Nathaniel, you should take up merchant sailing," George said. "If you were pursued by pirates and needed to acquire that extra bit of speed to escape, you could simply turn your nose aft and gather wind in your ear."

"I'll cut down the bird and have it sent to the kitchens," Charles offered. "Why don't you three retire for the evening?"

"To a cold, unjennied bed?" George harrumphed. "I suppose I could find another girl. Or there's one of our tenant's daughters who's beginning to look ripe enough. The man can hardly object, we've just given him ten extra acres to work."

The earl's two sons rode back toward the big house.

Nathaniel waited a moment before speaking. "Thank you," he said. "And I'm sorry."

"You've nothing to be sorry for." Charles grabbed Nathaniel by the shoulder and squeezed, a grip that made Nathaniel feel respected and trusted. "A man gets dealt good cards and bad in this life, and he doesn't get to choose which. All he gets to decide is how to play them. And tonight, Master Nathaniel Chapel, I believe you played your cards quite well."

Nathaniel rode alone to the servants' building where he slept, trying not to slap his ear every time he heard one of the voices.

In the middle of the night Nathaniel awoke. The fire was low and the unmarried male servants with whom he shared the room tossed and turned, each on his plank bed.

Jenny Farewell sat on the edge of Nathaniel's plank. She was wearing the dress she always wore, but she had tied a pink ribbon in her hair. She was crying, and her lip was split and puffy; nevertheless, she was a beautiful girl. *Charles Lee is right, I'll count myself lucky if I marry a girl this fine.* Jenny sat at such an angle to the fire that Nathaniel could see, and notice for the first time, the swell of her belly that hid her unborn child.

"Are you mad, Nathaniel?" she whispered.

~The wind here never stops.~

"Never stops," Nathaniel murmured. The ambient whine raised in pitch. His vision began dissolving into smears of white light.

Jenny caught her breath and her eyes grew wide. "I was... I was told you wished to see me."

Nathaniel shook his head slowly; the motion aggravated the lights and his oncoming vertigo. He took her hand in his and squeezed it. "I think there's been a mistake, Jenny," he whispered. "You should go to sleep. But thank you for looking in on me."

She nodded, silent tears in her eyes, and left.

As she stepped out of the room, his seizure began.

Luman Walters took his time and worked with a prayer in his heart. An efficacious himmelsbrief required not only the proper words, but beauty worthy of heaven in the execution, and the concentration of a focused soul in the crafting. He alternately looked over and through the round glass lenses perched on his nose, he held the pen firmly, and his hand was slow.

Really, an efficacious himmelsbrief could only be drawn by a *righteous* hexenmeister. Luman Walters wasn't perfect, but he was trying.

On the other side of the office they were sharing, Director Schmidt looked up from the post's book of accounts and snorted. "Another one, my Balaam?"

"You insist on traveling by boat, Madam Director."

"It's not a boat. It's a canoe."

"The *Joe Duncan* is far too large to be a mere canoe."

"Oh, yes? Is this one of the arcane facts you learned from that old braucher you cheated, the maximum permissible size of canoes? Or have you also done some apprenticeship among the Haudenosaunee? You didn't seem like you were an honored apprentice when I rescued you from the Seneca six months ago; you seemed more like a man fleeing justice."

"I didn't cheat the braucher. I paid him well, and I also paid his granddaughter. I only...played fast and loose with some of their tradition's rules."

Notwithstanding Schmidt laughed. "You damned sophist, that's why I like you."

The old man had been a great hexenmeister, a braucher in the Ohio German Christian tradition in a farming village outside Youngstown. Luman, then a young man, had been passing through and had asked to be taken as the hexenmeister's apprentice. He spoke enough German, and a little Latin, he'd said, and he knew scripture.

The old man had explained that he would only pass his knowledge down within his own family, and moreover that tradition required that his braucherei alternate sexes from one practitioner to the next. The old man had many daughters and granddaughters, and was waiting for one of them to feel the spirit and come to him.

Luman almost accepted the dismissal. But the old man's brusqueness had offended him, and besides, the braucher was blind and nearly deaf. It had been a simple task to help one of the old man's granddaughters, Helga, feel the spirit. She had been stitching coats in an Imperial factory in Youngstown, which was a long day's work that left her fingers pricked and bleeding, so the spirit required very little enticement to come to her.

Then it had been a matter of sitting by Helga's side during her months of lessons. The wooden-headed little fraülein had never been able to retain a single charm longer than an afternoon, but Luman had soaked up all the old man's craft.

He'd given Helga the money to pay her grandfather the purely optional but traditional honoraria, and paid her double what her wages had been in the factory. He earned the money at night, using his seeing stone or dowsing rods to help farmers place wells, and sometimes helping parties of money-diggers look for buried treasure. As often as not, the money-digging expeditions failed, generally because buried treasures are cursed by those who bury them, and tend to move away from the diggers. When they succeeded, it was because Luman had the wit to pin the treasure down within a circle of witch hazel withies, an astuteness for which he had not been praised. Once, he'd employed his arts to help a clan of German mystics find a cave within which to await the Second Coming of Christ. Despite his pointing out that his clients would have no need of money following the return of their Lord and may as well give it all to Luman, the mystics had insisted on paying him strictly by the hour.

Studying by day and working by night, Luman had drunk a lot of coffee.

The old man's heart had given out just as he finished the course of instruction, convinced his granddaughter Helga was a coffee addict, but at least she was on her way to becoming a skilled hexenmeistres, capable of passing on the family's tradition of god-fearing braucherei.

Since Helga so clearly wasn't developing magical abilities, Luman had offered her a deal: she could keep all her grandfather's money, and he would take the old man's grimoires and other tools.

Helga, bored and by then convinced that Luman was rich, countered with a different deal: Luman could run if he liked, and she would call the constabulary.

He'd run immediately, but he'd taken the old man's books with him. A man who moved as much as Luman couldn't carry a library with him, so he'd pored over the books and extracted all their best for his vademecum. Unable to lug the books around and unwilling to destroy them, Luman had deposited them with the doorkeeper of a masonic lodge in Pittsburgh. He'd avoided Youngstown for a decade thereafter.

The Haudenosaunee...well, that was another story.

"You speak as if you don't value my learning," he said, affecting an injured tone.

"It is as St. Adam says. The ploughman is not as efficient as the man who only makes pins, but he is a much more interesting person."

"St. Adam Weishaupt?" He was teasing her, of course. "Adam of the Garden? He was a ploughman."

She snorted. "St. Adam the philosopher."

"Someday I shall read his *Lives of Wealthy Men* and discover what excites you so."

She said nothing, not even rising to the bait of his deliberately mangling the book title.

"I'm not certain you've answered my question," he reminded her. "I've worked hard to learn from so many traditions. Don't you value my knowledge?" Luman valued his own knowledge very much.

He lived for its further acquisition.

"I don't mind you sleeping with a loaded pistol beside your pillow," she said.

"That discourages hostile spirits."

"So you've said. Though I believe you've also told me that hostile spirits can be driven out with a writ of divorce."

"That is an exorcism technique," Luman said patiently. "The loaded pistol keeps the spirits away in the first instance."

"I'm not bothered by any of the other odd things you do, because I value what you can *accomplish*, my Balaam," she continued. "In all its variety and macaronick glory. Inasmuch as your Faculty of Abrac comes by education, then yes, it is what I value *most* about you."

"I was a frail child," he answered. "The only way I have ever been able to get *anything* done has been by education."

"Frail and poor," she shot back. "If you'd had money, you'd have accomplished plenty."

"Is that what your Scotsman teaches you?"

Notwithstanding Schmidt harrumphed.

"You know," he said, "the men have all placed wagers as to where the name *Joe Duncan* comes from."

"The name of my canoe."

"Yes, fine, the name of your canoe."

"What's your wager?" Schmidt crawled through the book of accounts with a straight edge as they spoke, and Luman continued brushing out the written blessing onto the fine sheet of paper he'd brought from Philadelphia, one letter at a time.

"Will you tell me the truth if I tell you my bet?"

"Natürlich." Schmidt's father had been an Ohio German, one of the Ministerium's preachers. She claimed that her mother had been a Yankee, and that the two had resolved their inability to agree on a name for their only daughter by opening to a random page of the Bible and shoving in a finger. Exodus chapter twenty-one, twenty-first verse: *Notwithstanding, if he continue a day or two, he shall not be punished: for he is his money.* Both had been horrified, but also too pious, too committed, and too recalcitrant to back down.

He'd seen one of the factors reporting to her call her *Nottie*, once. The next day, there was a newly promoted former subfactor in his place.

"Very well. I bet six Philadelphia shillings—a grand sum, you will acknowledge, even if they were the old shillings, bearing Hannah's face and slightly worn at the edges—that *Joe Duncan* was the name of your first lover."

"A curious guess."

"I'm not betting on your sense of nostalgia, but on your will to vengeance. I think if you were ever jilted by a man, you would want him under your feet forever after."

"Ha!"

Luman waited. "Well?"

Schmidt set down the straight edge and looked up at him. "Joe Duncan was the name of my first...horse." She smiled, her cheekbones standing out and her face abruptly looking feminine.

"I lose."

"Sorry."

"But you realize, this doesn't resolve the mystery at all."

Schmidt returned to the book. "Now you and the men can bet on why I named my first horse *Joe Duncan*. Do you feel confident enough to repeat the same wager?"

Luman considered. "I shall think about it, after I have finished this himmelsbrief, rolled it into an oiled case, and pasted the case inside the *Joe Duncan*, to replace the one that was soaked as we came over the Ohio Forks."

"Is this the same text as the last one?"

"Of course. They're letters from heaven. Heaven dictated the text, and to change it would be to destroy the power of the thing. A *lumanwaltersbrief*, God knows, would do you no good."

"How much good did the last himmelsbrief do? It was destroyed by a little rain and being knocked about in some rapids, after all."

"Yes, the letter was destroyed." Luman stabbed the quill pen through the air at Director Schmidt. "But the *Joe Duncan* was not, eh? Your first horse the *Joe Duncan* was not."

"And a teufelsbrief?"

Luman hesitated. "Well, yes, there are letters from hell, too. But..."

There came a knock at the door.

"Enter!" Notwithstanding Schmidt called.

The door opened and one of the Ohio Company traders stepped inside, quickly shutting the door behind him to keep out the late October chill. He removed his coonskin cap and rubbed some of the heated office's air into his face. "There's an Imperial chaplain here, Madam Director. He wishes to see you."

"Chaplain? What do I need a chaplain for? I've got money, and I've got a wizard."

The trader hesitated, toying with the cap in his hand. "He says he was father confessor to the emperor."

Schmidt frowned. "Is his name Angleton? A Covenant Tract man?"

The trader nodded. "The two dragoons who came into the stockade yesterday confirm his story. He was chaplain to the Imperial House Light Dragoons, Madam Director."

"If the dragoons corroborate his story, why not send him directly? Why this shuffling notice? Am I some pasha, only to be approached by supplicants on their bellies?"

"He looks...strange, ma'am. He's filthy. He stinks of the graveyard."

"Give me a moment," Schmidt said. "Then send him in."

The trader stepped outside and Schmidt called out, "also, send in the post superintendent. I'm ready to reconcile accounts with him."

The trader nodded and shut the door.

Notwithstanding Schmidt picked up two pistols lying on the table near her and refreshed their firing pans. Pushing chairs under the table beside her to both her left and right, she laid a pistol on each chair. Out of sight, but within her reach.

Luman blew dry the last of the ink. "Madam Director, will you indulge me?"

"Not if you want to bring the canoe in here."

Luman laughed. He laid the heavenly letter out flat on the desk before the Director, then carefully laid two of the post's account books on top of it. The letter became invisible, but visibility was not necessary for such a letter. Indeed, himmelsbriefe were often nailed within the walls of houses, or above doors, to do their work *without* being seen.

Luman stepped to the side, near the fire, and crossed his arms.

The door opened abruptly and a tall man strode in, slamming the door shut again behind him. "Director Schmidt, yaas?" he said, in a nasal whine.

The newcomer was pale, with a hawkish nose between piercing, close-set blue eyes. He was thin and wore the black steepled hat favored by some of men of Boston and Hartford. At his waist hung a medieval-looking long sword. More strikingly, he wore a brown coat that looked on the verge of rotting entirely from his body, and his tongue and one ear were blackened, as if with charcoal. His eyes were sunken and dark.

And he *did* stink of the grave.

Something else bothered Luman, too, though he couldn't quite have said what.

"*Madam Director* is the usual form of address," she said. "*Ma'am*, if you know me well enough. But we're in the Ohio, and I won't stand on ceremony if you won't."

"Madam Director," he said.

"Right Reverend Father Ezekiel Angleton," she answered, "if I remember correctly."

"I'm gratified you remember me. We've met."

"In Horse Hall. You had just returned from an expedition to Acadia with the emperor. And again I think in Cambry. You were preaching a stirring Martinite exhortation not to accept employment with any Ophidian master."

"Yaas. The Celts are entirely too quick to imagine themselves as magical creatures; that makes them sympathize more than they should with the Eldritch. You have a good memory."

She smiled.

Luman realized what was bothering him about the chaplain; the man had burst in nearly at a run, and yet wasn't breathing hard.

In fact, despite the long conversation he was carrying on with the Director, he didn't seem to be breathing at all.

Luman reached into his coat and took his Homer amulet into his fist. It was a thin iron lamella hanging around his neck on a fine chain, and he knew the three lines of Greek inscribed onto it, between two tiny stylized crocodiles, by heart. *Hos eipon taphroio dielase monychas hippous.* Book Ten of the *Iliad*, all the ancient writers agreed, had special power. The amulet was good against enchantments and demons and ensured victory, the grimoire Luman had copied from his Memphite initiator even before his time in Youngstown assured.

"What can I do for you?" Schmidt asked, her smile dropping. "I'm actually quite busy, but I'm sympathetic to the needs of a fellow Imperial, especially one down on his luck."

"Down on my luck?"

"You may already know that a few of the dragoons from your company have straggled into this post in the last twelve hours or so. I haven't heard a full, coherent story yet from any of them, but I gather that the Imperial House Light Dragoons have come to misadventure. Happily, I believe you weren't accompanying the emperor at the time, and His Imperial Majesty is safe at home in Philadelphia."

"Yaas." Angleton straightened out and removed his hat, holding it to his breast as if in salute. "Yaas, Madam Director, you've heard true. I come to you because I need additional assistance for my errand. The emperor's errand."

Andras t'aspairontas en argaleesi phonesin.

"The emperor could assign you men to assist, if he wished. If he is sparing, it may be because he finds himself somewhat short on manpower."

Angleton rubbed his eyes. "Thomas doesn't know my present need."

"Thomas?" Schmidt arched her eyebrows. "Well, I'm afraid it's out of the question. I have orders myself, you see. I'm recruiting additional men into the ranks of the Company Regulars, and I also bear letters patent from the emperor allowing me to take management of Imperial Militia units, which I am doing. And I and my men are marching west. And I can't spare any of them. Not one."

"You're building an army."

"I'm reinforcing the Pacification of the Ohio. As ordered."

"I have orders, too." Angleton jammed his hat back onto his head.

"Yes, what are they? Perhaps our errands are compatible, and I can help you in some way."

"I'm bound for Johnsland," the chaplain said. "The emperor has sent me . . . that is, I seek to capture an enemy agent. An Ophidian, a traitor."

Autoi d'hydro pollon aponizonto thalasse.

The iron lamella tingled in Luman's grip.

"You know, many Ophidians are loyal subjects of the Empire," Schmidt said mildly. "They pay taxes, engage in trade. Some of them work for the Company. I know you Martinites did good work in the Serpentwars, but you might be well advised to moderate your rhetoric now."

Ezekiel Angleton sprang forward, hands reaching for the director—

she thrust her own hands under the table, but she was too slow—

Luman jumped to intervene, but he was too far away and much smaller than the Yankee—

and then Angleton reached the edge of the desk and fell back, as if he had struck a brick wall.

Notwithstanding Schmidt blinked like an owl. Luman arrested his charge and stared.

Roaring, the Yankee cleric hurled himself forward again, and again bounced back.

"What is this?" he shrieked.

"This," Schmidt said, producing two pistols from under the table, "is confirmation that I receive value for money from my hexenmeister."

Ezekiel Angleton froze, stared at the pistols for several long seconds, and then retired to the door. He wrapped his coat about himself, adjusted his hat, and drew himself up to his full height. "Forgive me, Madam Director. I haven't slept these two nights, and I'm not myself."

"Forgiven. I still can't spare you the men. Good luck in Johnsland. Watch out for your Celts, while you're there. I hear the Cavaliers' Irish servants still sink the children of Adam into the bogs and sing their druidic chants. For that matter, who can say what sacrifices the earl's own godar really offer on those bloody rock-heaps?"

"None of my affair," Angleton said. "I follow St. Martin Luther."

"And lust for Firstborn blood."

Angleton nodded sharply and exited, leaving the door open.

Director Schmidt laid down her pistols, moved aside the account books, and examined the himmelsbrief lying on the table. "This is indeed a beautiful piece," she observed. "I rather think I'd like you to make another one...one I could wear, say, in the lining of my coat."

"One for you, Madam Director," Luman Walters said. "And a second for me."

The post superintendent, a big-nosed man named Weber, stepped into the office.

"Ah, Herr Superintendent," Schmidt said, pronouncing the S like a Z, in German fashion. "I have reviewed your journal accounts and recalculated the post's capital surplus. I must say, your mathematics were very nearly exact. That tends to suggest that you are an honest man, and even competent."

Weber looked at Luman and chuckled nervously.

Luman smiled back and checked his stock of fine Philadelphia-bought paper. He had himmelsbriefe to produce.

"Also, your working capital seems to be tightly managed. Now get the post's cash, please," Director Schmidt continued. "We will need to reconcile the accounts to cash on hand. The Company is going to extract an extraordinary dividend."

"Don't worry, though," Luman added. "In return, I'll hex the trading post to drive additional business here. I have all the orange wax I need to cast the spell, but I'd appreciate it if you could procure a rooster—the bird will die, you understand—and a copper coin earned by the post in ordinary trade. And please show me a spot where you don't mind me hiding something in the wall."

✧　　✧　　✧

Ma'iingan left his canoe buried under a drift of autumn leaves high above the river the Zhaaganaashii and the Haudenosaunee called the Ohio. He marked the location discreetly in the bark of nearby trees, but he wasn't too concerned; he had made the canoe himself, in a few hours' work, and he could make another if he needed to.

He had spent most of his journey in solitude. He shared a pipe of asemaa with Sauk and Fox hunters when he encountered them, to assure them of his peaceful intentions. He spoke Zhaaganaashii and he made a point of saluting all travelers when he passed, but he didn't need to trade—with his bow, or occasionally with his German rifle, he killed deer and other game to feed himself. He also found his own water, and he built his own shelter when necessary. And he knew his path from the vision his spirit guide, his manidoo, had shown him.

Ma'iingan simply didn't need to speak to anyone else.

This left him time to think. His manidoo had told him that the healer he sought would need Ma'iingan's help. What help would he need? Was the room Ma'iingan had seen in vision a prison cell? Ma'iingan had never been in a prison, and the People didn't administer such things, but he had seen them from the outside, in Waukegan and Chicago. If the healer needed food, water, or shelter, Ma'iingan could help.

But the spirit had said the healer was laid low by illness. What would the healer need, that Ma'iingan could provide?

Ma'iingan climbed through mountains the inhabitants called the Appalachee. He saw Shawnee, and Zhaaganaashii, and when the Shawnee settlements gave way to the brick and wood houses of the Cherokee towns, Ma'iingan knew he was getting close.

On the day when he could finally smell—faint and far away— the great waters of the ocean, Ma'iingan found the healer.

He stumbled into a hunt. Only it wasn't a hunt such as Ma'iingan knew, with the quiet stalking of a herd of deer, the hunter taking a knee with his bow and waiting patiently for the right moment to receive the sacred gift of the earth and the for- est. Instead, it began as an avalanche of fur.

Rabbits passed Ma'iingan first, running uphill. Behind the rabbits came foxes and raccoons, but these weren't pursuing the rabbits; they too were pursued.

Ma'iingan heard the baying of dogs and Zhaaganaashii curses.

He didn't think he was the intended prey, but a distracted hunter might shoot him anyway, so he quickly scrambled up the nearest tree, a tall white pine. Perched high in the pine's branches with his legs wrapped around the trunk, he carefully maneuvered his bow into one hand and a single arrow into the other, hiding the arrow alongside the tree trunk.

The Zhaaganaashii were arranged like a chevron of flying geese, only they flew backward. The loose arms of the chevron consisted of men and boys in coarse cloth, holding sticks. They were the source of the yelling and they struck bushes and trees with their cudgels, driving the animals ahead of them.

Between the two arms came a group of four Zhaaganaashii men in more elaborate clothing, with longer hair. All four of them wore long purple coats, faded and worn to different degrees. At least one of them was scented with perfume Ma'iingan could smell from the top of the tree and over the pine sap.

"This is beneath me, really," one of the men said. He had curly dark hair and carried a musket, but carelessly. Of all of them, his coat was the brightest purple. "I should be hunting the stag."

"True, George," said the oldest of the group. He was younger than Ma'iingan and bigger, with a broad chest and shoulders that would make him a fierce fighter. "But Landon and Nathaniel could use the practice."

"As could you, Charles," George sniffed.

The boy with long brown hair laughed. Rudely, Ma'iingan thought.

"Yes," Charles agreed. His answer was slow and sounded good-natured, but Ma'iingan heard a note of anger in it. "Especially with the musket. All the shooting I do these days is with the pistol, you know."

"*Do* I know?" George snapped. "Do I?"

"Easy, George," Charles said. "I only mean that in the cavalry, I don't get to shoot long guns much. Carbines and horse pistols."

"Yes, you remind me that you're in the cavalry. That my father has been good enough to pay for your commission, while I have not yet got mine! Thank you, Charles, for that reminder!"

"You'll have it soon enough," Charles said.

"Yes," the brown-haired boy said. "And you shall be captain, at least. Maybe colonel. And Lieutenant Charles Lee here will run your messages back and forth to other important commanders and to your many mistresses, and see that your laundry is done to your liking."

Ma'iingan didn't follow all the words, but he understood that the young warriors were talking about rank and who took precedence over whom. This was a much more complicated question among the Zhaaganaashii than in the People's war bands.

"Don't *you* start, *Landon*," George snarled.

"What?" The brown-haired youth, Landon, staggered sideways under George's glare. "I am only pointing out that you're the important one here!"

"I'm important, so I won't see any real fighting, is that it? I'll be a coward, the kind of commander who has more mistresses in his camp than victories to his name?"

Ma'iingan now noticed that the fourth boy was continually worrying his left ear. He cringed at each new demand or accusation from George, as if he could only barely keep from running away at a full sprint. His left ear jutted out obliquely from his head, barely visible under a large three-cornered hat, and it burned a dark, angry red. The boy's coat was too large for him, and he seemed to be constantly shrinking into its folds, as if trying to hide.

"Run fast, run free!" Then the fourth boy turned and Ma'iingan saw his face; this was the healer. He was the youngest of the three, maybe as old as fifteen winters, and he looked as if he were about to burst into tears.

"George," Charles said. "We all love you and respect you. I, for one, will be happy to fight under your command, when the time comes. And though they are not stags, I see two rabbits running up that patch of sandy earth over there—would you like to take the first shot?"

"What are you saying, that you think George will miss?" Landon nearly shouted this, pushing so close to Charles they almost butted noses.

The healer struck his own ear repeatedly. "Don't let them shoot me!"

"I think George will hit the rabbit," Charles said. "And if he doesn't, he won't be the first excellent marksman to fail to take a target."

"I want Landon to take the shot." Even from the top of the tree, Ma'iingan could see George's vicious sneer.

"I can hit it," Landon said after a moment.

"Of course you can," Charles said.

"Of *course* you can." George was still sneering.

The healer, who must be named *Nathaniel*, fell slowly behind. He whimpered softly.

The rabbits in question had moved on, but there was another target. "I'll shoot that raccoon over there," Landon suggested. "The one trying to hide under the dogwood."

"That's a long shot," Charles said.

"He can hit it," George said.

"I'm sure you're right," Charles agreed. "I don't think *I* could, but you're both better shots than I am."

Ma'iingan listened to the three young men talk about their raccoon, but his eyes were on the healer. The young man—boy, really—stood thirty feet from his friends, bending over his own knees and breathing deeply.

What was wrong with him?

Landon raised his musket. The weapon was of high quality, perhaps not quite as high as Ma'iingan's German gun. Landon's aim wavered slightly, but the raccoon was not so very far away. Ma'iingan considered shooting the animal with his bow, and relished in his imagination the looks of surprise on the youths' faces as an Anishinaabe hunter stole their prey from under their noses, right out of the sky.

But he didn't do it. Mostly because, with all the tension among the three oldest, they might respond by shooting him instead.

Bang!

Landon's gun went off and the raccoon lived, scampering away beyond the dogwood tree and disappearing farther up the slope.

"Damn you!"

"Theology has never been my forte, but I believe neither my father's godar nor Parson Brown contemplate the possibility of either damnation or salvation for raccoons." George delivered this speech with a smirk that made Ma'iingan want to climb down out of the tree and punch the young man in the mouth. "They're vermin."

"No, I don't mean...not the raccoon!" Landon shook his gun in a vaguely threatening gesture.

"Oh?" George asked. "If the raccoon is not to be damned, then who is?"

Landon looked trapped, but then he swung his weapon like a club at Charles's head. "You!" he shouted. "Damn you, Charles Lee!"

Charles sidestepped the attack. "Hell's Bells, Landon, stop it, you're embarrassing yourself in front of the beaters."

Ma'iingan looked to the people who had been driving game from the bushes with sticks. They had indeed stopped, and were looking at the three young men with a mixture of fear, surprise, and amusement.

"It's your fault. You made me take that shot!" Landon swung his gun at Charles's head.

This time the older, bigger youth simply caught the weapon. He yanked it from Landon's hands and threw it aside, then pushed his attacker to the ground with a single shove.

"You are too old to give in to your temper like that, Landon Chapel," Charles said gravely. "And you do not have the station to protect you from the consequences when you do."

"No?" George said drily. "And who would have such station?"

Charles snorted. "Do you never grow tired of this game, George?" Without waiting for an answer, he took the healer under his arm and walked away downhill. Nathaniel pawed at his ear repeatedly as they went.

Giimoodaapi's healer was indeed laid low by illness, and Ma'iingan still had no idea how to help him.

"Why? Have you cheated a Hansard recently?"

⟞⟝◦⟞⟝

CHAPTER FIVE

"These are Tawa lands," Alzbieta said.

Cal knew the name *Tawa*. He sang:

> *Koweta, Tawa, Adena in the south*
> *Talamatan in the north looks like Germany*
> *Oranbega with its towers on the St. Lawrence mouth*
> *And Talega, full of Lenni Lenape*
> *One Elector each per Eldritch throne*
> *Seven is Cahokia, always alone*

Evening approached, and the shadows grew long. Ahead of them marched Alzbieta Torias's soldiers, with their blue cloaks, gray tunics, and the little steel head-gear Bill called *sallet helmets*, and at the rear came Sarah's beastkind. The scout Chikaak paced nimbly alongside the Firstborn warriors in the brush, watching the entire column intently with his glittering black eyes.

"The Elector Songs." Uris was the senior member of Alzbieta's party, an old soldier and now her advisor, he'd said. On the march, one of the soldiers carried the priestess's banner and Uris walked with his hands free. He and Alzbieta's other two free companions—Sherem the Polite wizard and the scale-mail-clad Yedera, who had introduced herself as "Unborn, an oathbound Podebradan"—insisted on walking, notwithstanding the long string of horses Calvin led. The wizard seemed dazed, occasionally wandering off the path and needing to be called back. "And why is Cahokia 'alone'?"

"I always reckoned it was because the words rhymed," Cal admitted. He'd sung the ditty as a way to show off his knowledge, and now instead risked exposing his utter ignorance. "Old Walter Fitzroy had to write a whole lotta songs, they can't all be works of genius."

"Mmmm," the counselor said noncommittally. "But unless Fitzroy meant something by it, I expect him to use meaningful words and good grammar."

"That ain't a grammar point at all," Cal said. "Grammar is knowin' to say 'how did my herd git stolen' and not 'how did it git stole.' That's jest you bein' grumpy about a perfectly decent Elector Song."

"I understood that Wisdom's Bluff was Cahokian land," Cathy said. "Was I misinformed?"

"You were not, ma'am," Bill said. "Cahokian land, if designated on a map of the Ohio, would present a rather calico appearance. When I remarked upon it to Kyres, I sometimes teased him for being the leopard of Missouri, spotted here and there as his inheritance was."

Alzbieta laughed. "That is true. Certain sites—sacred places—were retained by old Onandagos of Cahokia when he and his brother kings shared out the lands of the Ohio, according to the old songs."

"The St. Lawrence is the passage that runs past Acadia to the Atlantic Ocean," Jake said. "Is Oranbega land also spotted?"

Uris laughed.

"Not generally," Alzbieta said. "But the Oranbegans were given the task of keeping the seaways open as the Serpentwars began in the Old World. They purchased land from the Champlains of Acadia, and there at the mouth of the St. Lawrence they to this day maintain watch towers."

"Though jest about everybody's come across as is gonna come across," Cal said. "The way I heard it."

"Perhaps," Alzbieta admitted. "Still Oranbega watches."

"You can't always tell who's Firstborn, just by looking at them," Sarah said. "There may still be Children of Wisdom at the fringes of the Drowned Lands."

Alzbieta Torias and Uris the counselor both shot sharp looks at Sarah. "You know my people's history," the priestess said.

"I know *my* people's history," Sarah said firmly. "Though not as much as I'd like."

Alzbieta inclined her head respectfully. "At my home in the city I have an archive of old writings you might wish to consult. You must read Priestly Ophidian as well as Common, I take it?"

Sarah didn't bat an eye. "I look forward to reading those writings."

"Well, I don't know what the fringes of the Drowned Lands are," Cal said. "I mean, iffen anybody thinks it'd be interestin' to tell me about 'em, I'm listenin'."

"Thousands of years ago," Uris said in a gravelly voice, "the Children of Wisdom in the Old World lived in seven kingdoms, four of which lay on a watered plain called Irra-Antum, entirely between what are now the island of Britain and Denmark."

Calvin shook his head. "Iffen I ain't walked a land myself, I ain't much for its geography."

"That's a sea now," Cathy Filmer said. "The North Sea, the English call it."

Uris nodded. "It was a mighty river valley then, a land of cultivated fields, low hills, and broad lakes as blue as the sky. And then one day the rivers flooded their banks, the seas leaped over their restraining dikes, and those four kingdoms were smashed. Some of the remnant fled to the surviving kingdoms—many to Bohemia, where they prospered a long time—but others came west. They came to the new world before the English, the Dutch, the Germans, the French, the Spanish, and all the other peoples of Europe. They treated with the ancestors of the Haudenosaunee and the Algonks, and here, with Lenni Lenape and other peoples, they again formed the seven kingdoms. But messengers never ceased to travel between the children of Wisdom in the Old World and their cousins in the New, and when the Serpentwars broke out, as Her Holiness indicates, the Oranbegans—who have provided many of our people's explorers, traders, mapmakers, and wanderers—were tasked with keeping open the gate of the St. Lawrence. So it has been since."

"The Oranbegans must have received Wallenstein and his Germans, then, as well as the Bohemians fleeing the Old World," Bill suggested.

Uris nodded.

Sarah shifted in her saddle as if she had an itch she couldn't scratch. "I've never heard what caused the seas to rise."

Alzbieta looked at her coolly. "No? Perhaps the answer is in those scrolls."

Cathy Filmer shot Alzbieta an irritated look, but Sarah ignored it.

"All the more reason to look forward to reading them," she said.

"Ahead lies Chester." Yedera pointed.

Cal was mounted and taller than the Podebradan and still had trouble making out the buildings she was pointing out. "That don't sound like a Firstborn name to me."

"It's English," Uris said. "Though most of the residents are German-speakers, and call the town *Lager.*"

"I've always been more of a whisky man, myself," Bill murmured. "But a lager in a pinch."

"English?" Cal squinted past the line of Ophidian warriors marching ahead of them, making out the log stockade and the buildings inside, all perched atop a bluff. Below the town, to Calvin's left, rolled the Mississippi River. It reminded him of Natchez. "It ain't Hansa, is it?"

"I believe Chester *does* abide by the Trading League Charter." Uris smiled, leaning on his spear. "Why? Have you cheated a Hansard recently?"

"I never cheated a body in my life," Cal said. "I stole a cow or two, but only from folks as had too many to begin with. And I ain't stupid enough to steal from the Hansa."

"The Hansa towns are the safest towns on the river," Alzbieta said.

"Iffen you're Hansa," Cal muttered.

"We'll be fine, Calvin," Bill said. "Though I don't believe we'll find an inn to billet Her Majesty's entire guard. Nor Her Holiness's, I should think."

"No," Uris agreed. "The warriors will all have to camp outside of town. The people of Chester won't mind."

"And the Tawans?" Cal asked.

"My men wear my colors," Alzbieta said. "I hope yours aren't taken for vagrants or wild animals."

"Or worse," Uris added, "an incursion from the Great Green Wood. There are rumors from the Missouri, isolated tales that the feral beastkind are rampaging."

"Her Majesty has not yet proclaimed her livery." Bill's Cavalier drawl was unhurried, but to Calvin he sounded annoyed. "In the meantime, I suppose we shall have to rely on the natural ferocity and obvious martial prowess of her warriors to deter molestation."

"Quite." Uris chuckled.

Bill gave the order for the beastkind to make camp. This was repeated through Chikaak to the rest in a series of barks and yowls, to which Jake listened intently, his head cocked to one side. At one point in the process, he thumbed through a deck of Tarocks as he listened, occasionally staring at one of the cards.

Then Jake dismounted, handing his reins to Cal, and walked with the beastfolk warriors into the nearby trees. He emerged a few minutes later, just as the Cahokian warriors had found a site for their camp a quarter mile away.

"Look," Cal said to the Dutchman as he handed back the little man's reins, pointing at the two campsites. "Look at the difference."

Like any ordinary military unit, the Cahokians had located their camp around a central clearing, where some of them now began to build a fire and erect tents. The beastkind, on the other hand, had chosen a grove, and now they singly burrowed beneath bushes, lay between close-growing trees, hid within snarled brambles, and otherwise bedded down for the night like animals.

Bill, overhearing, snorted. "We have much work to do yet to shape them, Sergeant Hop."

Jake smiled at the mention of the rank. "Less than you think, Captain Lee."

Then he leaned in to say something discreet to Sarah, which Calvin didn't hear.

Chikaak followed them into Chester, where he drew curious looks, but no more than Alzbieta in her palanquin. When Sarah had chosen an inn—the *Wallenstein*, the biggest, sturdiest, oldest inn in the small Hansa community, and located very near to the stockade wall opposite the river—Chikaak loped back to join the beastfolk.

Cal tried not to look like he was staring, but he kept an eye on Alzbieta as they approached the front door of the *Wallenstein*. Would the sedan chair go inside?

But at the door, one of her slaves—who must have been designated in advance, because Calvin saw no communication pass among any of the Eldritch at the time—stood at the palanquin's curtain and took Alzbieta in his arms when she climbed out. He held her like a child before him, marching across the common room of the *Wallenstein*, up the back stairs to the landing, and then through the door into Alzbieta's room.

"You hopin' to catch a glimpse of Her Holiness hoppin' into bed?" Sarah needled Cal.

Cal chuckled. "Didn't mean to stare, I's jest...Jerusalem, it's odd, that's all."

They stood isolated from their companions for a moment. Uris had announced he would seek a physician for Sherem, who continued to wander from his path from time to time, and stepped out.

Sarah turned so no one else could see her face, and suddenly she looked very tired, and even scared. "It *is* odd, Calvin. It's odd and backward and very old, and I don't understand it. And no, I don't read any kind of Ophidian, so what in tarnation am I going to do about that? And...and worse." She leaned heavily on her horse-headed ashwood walking stick, then reached up with her free hand to touch Calvin's cheek. "I'm sad Thalanes isn't here. So I'm glad you *are*."

"You want me to carry you, jest say so. Might have to be pig-a-back, though—I ain't got that feller's arms."

After Calvin had finished negotiating and paying for rooms (one for Sarah and Cathy, with two beds, and two spots beside the common room hearth that he figured he, Bill, and Jake would share), Sarah and Cathy went upstairs, and Cal found himself standing at the bar in the inn's common room, waiting with Jacob Hop for a small beer.

Jake turned away from the bar to look at the common room while they waited. He smiled, and then he spoke to Cal sideways, out of the corner of his mouth, and almost entirely without moving his lips. "Two things are very important tonight, hey?"

"Sure," Cal said. "Let's talk about tonight. Shall I git Bill down here?"

"He is already standing outside the women's door," Jake said. "Dat is a good thing, let's leave him there. First, do not get drunk."

"I ain't the most blazin' New Lighter you'll e'er meet," Cal protested. "I ain't a Kissin' Campbell, nor a Swoonin' Stone, but I got the New Light, after my own fashion. You don't have to worry."

The Dutchman blinked at him. "Sober, begrip you me? I mean, you understand?"

"Yeah," Cal said. "Jest this small beer and that's all. I don't quite trust these Cahokians, despite 'em bein' Sarah's people and all." Or maybe, partly, *because* they were Sarah's people, in a way Calvin wasn't, and couldn't quite understand.

"Ja, don't trust them. And here's the second thing, it's a distress signal."

Cal sighed. "I thought you weren't a Freemason."

"I am not." Jake frowned. "Can you whistle?"

"Of course I can whistle. How else you supposed to signal your cousin you're in position and ready to make off with all them Donelsen cattle?" Cal grinned.

"Hey?" Jake grinned back. "This is the signal if you see anything...dangerous. A threat." He whistled three tones, high, low, and medium.

Cal whistled it back. "That it?"

Jake nodded. "But outside, begripped? Understood? You don't have to be especially loud, but you moet whistle it outside." He whistled the three tones again, and again, and then a third time but finally slipped into some improvised melody to disguise what he'd been doing, just as the beers arrived.

Cal took his small beer, handed the other to Jake, and turned to see that Uris had joined them.

"I don't know that melody," the counselor said.

"I moet be doing it wrong," Jake answered. "It's a folk song I knew as a boy in New Amsterdam, only I haven't heard it in many years."

The Dutchman was a pretty smooth liar, and Cal was impressed.

"You've been long in Sarah Penn's service?"

Cal flinched at the name *Sarah Penn*.

Jake sipped his beer. "No, I have joined Queen Sarah's retinue only in recent days. With the beastkind, you know. They needed somebody to keep the animals in line, and I have been a drover and a merchant and many other things. But Calvin here has long been her man, hey?"

Calvin managed not to hug the Dutchman, and took another sip of his beer to hide the grin he felt spreading across his face.

"She's a surprise to me, your Queen Sarah," Uris said. "I think she'll surprise many in Cahokia."

"You ain't yet seen the half of her surprises."

✧   ✧   ✧

Bill liked towns, and indeed cities, just fine. He especially liked inns—a good tavern meant a steady supply of whisky, and though he now drank strictly when drinking with Mrs. Filmer, to keep his consumption down, a steady supply was a good thing.

But having acquired a troop of warriors—however uncouth and barbaric—he was loath not to be surrounded by them. Was he truly worried about threats to his queen, or did he merely feel he'd been stripped of his command again?

Bill growled low in his throat, warning himself away from maudlin feelings.

The Cahokians were noble enough. And Queen Sarah and Her Holiness, Alzbieta Torias, seemed to have reached an accommodation, uneasy though it might be. The war leader, Uris, now sat below Bill at a table in the common room and drowsed over a half-finished stein of beer, hood of his cloak down over his face. The red-robed Polite, after scratching at his mistress's door—whether hexing it or as the ongoing effect of the mental blow Sarah had dealt him, Bill couldn't tell—had laid himself out on the corner of the common room floor like a plank and gone catatonic. Seven of the eight bearers had marched with the palanquin, predictably enough, to the stables, the eighth remaining with the priestess, perhaps to carry her to the outhouse, should the need arise. Calvin lay on a straw pallet beside the hearth. Jacob Hop was outside, and scheduled to sleep next; Bill would take his turn to take a few hours' rest before dawn.

Sarah must have worked her own defensive magic on the room where she and Cathy slept. Why did Bill feel uneasy?

Perhaps he just missed Mrs. Filmer. Though he had not slept *with* her, as the carnal euphemism went, he had been sleeping quite *near* her for several nights, and had grown accustomed to it. Her breathing was regular and deep and she didn't seem to come awake repeatedly in the night as Bill did. He attributed that to her easier conscience, or to the natural grace that made her float when she moved.

Perhaps Bill felt uneasy about the very fact that he loved Mrs. Filmer. He might be, after all, still married.

"Stop reflecting so much, you morose son of a bitch," he grumbled to himself. "Serve your queen and be patient."

Bill stood on the wide walkway in front of Sarah's door. He'd told the innkeeper, a pear-shaped man named Waldrick Dixie who wore an orange tunic over leather leggings, that he would do so, and that it was to protect Sarah, who was his niece. Dixie had accepted this obvious fabrication with good grace, so either he was used to significant persons traveling incognito, or Calvin had correctly judged how much the man needed to be paid.

Bill carried four pistols, loaded and primed: two long horse pistols in the much-darned pockets of his old red coat, and two smaller guns in his belt. He let the coat hang mostly shut, to try not to broadcast to other patrons of the inn that he was heavily armed and ready to fight, though his position and stance should make it clear to any observer at all that he was standing watch.

He'd briefly considered taking a less-worn coat from the loot they'd acquired from the dragoons and the chevalier's men, as the others all had, but only briefly; blue and gold were definitely not his colors now.

As soon as Sarah declared her livery, he'd have a new coat made.

Two drunks staggered in the front door, laughing. Roused from his sleep, the old man Uris shushed them fiercely, then slumped back. The drunk men giggled, shushed each other more quietly, and staggered toward the stairs.

Bill assessed the two men. They were underdressed for the autumn chill gripping the town outside, in shirtsleeves and trousers. One of them appeared to have misplaced his shoes and the other had a tattered slouch cap clinging to his head.

"You've got the key, Ed," the shoeless man said to his comrade as they reached the top of the stairs and bumped into his other.

"I have not." Ed belched. "Did you bet and lose the key, Jim?"

This was so hilarious that Jim collapsed into giggles against the wall. Ed helped him up and the two of them tottered toward Bill. Bill smelled cheap rum on them, and urine. He growled, stepped closer to Sarah's door, and let his coat part to show the pistols in his belt.

"Oh look," Jim said, "there's a Dago here who wants to shoot me. A big Dago with a Dago mustache. Don't shoot me, señor!"

Ed pulled off his cap and peered inside.

"I am no Dago, suh. Indeed, I—"

Ed threw a fistful of chalk into Bill's face.

Bill was immediately blinded. He was afraid to shoot and accidentally hit Cathy or Sarah, so he reached forward and grabbed his attackers. He got one of them by the throat and the other by the shirt front.

"Cal!" he tried to yell, but as he opened his mouth he inhaled chalk dust, and his voice came out in a dry croak.

"Stab the bastard!" Jim hissed. He didn't sound drunk anymore.

Bill felt a sharp pain in his side. One of the men had stuck him with a knife. He needed to wake up Calvin and get these two away from Sarah's door, so he did the logical thing.

Gripping Jim and Ed more tightly, he dragged them with him over the railing and fell.

Bill hit a tabletop and two of the table's legs collapsed, turning it into a ramp. He and his attackers bounced off the ramp and onto the floor, and the fall, the two impacts, and the flow of his own tears cleared one of Bill's eyes, at least enough to see.

He staggered to his feet, yanking the two men with him. He felt another stabbing pain in his side—it was Jim stabbing him, because Ed was the one Bill could see, and Ed's neck was kinked at such an improbable angle that he must be dead.

"Bill!" Calvin cried, unseen. "The door!"

Bill spun toward the tavern's door, hurling Ed. Ed struck the first of a wave of dirty men armed with clubs. From the back of the crowd surging into the inn, Bill thought he smelled tar. For good measure, he picked up Jim and hurled him into the onrushing crowd. Men at the front of the assault tripped and fell.

Bill heard running footsteps behind him. He gripped his horse pistols and turned, only to see Uris charging him, spear lowered—

and then Calvin Calhoun's rawhide lariat settled around the Firstborn's neck. His feet flew forward, his head stayed in his place, his eyes bulged, and then the old man crashed hard to the floor.

"Drop the guns!" Waldrick Dixie yelled. Blinking back tears, Bill saw that the innkeeper held a scattergun aimed at him.

Outside the inn, he heard a queer little three-note tune whistled, over and over.

"Of course, suh," Bill said.

Then he and the innkeeper fired at the same time.

Bill felts the nails and other metal scraps strike him in the thigh. That was bad, the thigh housed a large vein and a man could bleed to death quickly if wounded in just the wrong part of the thigh. But he had the satisfaction of seeing Waldrick Dixie take one bullet to the forehead and a second to the sternum. The innkeeper fell backward into a shelf full of bottles of cheap liquor.

Bill heard guttural chanting and spun about, grabbing for a

pistol in his belt with his left hand and pulling the long horse pistol from his pocket with his right. It was fired, but he could still swing it like a club.

The Polite Sherem, looking not at all dazed, held a paper cartridge over his head. Just as Bill turned to see him, the wizard hurled the cartridge—

bang!

A second shot hit Bill, this time in his other thigh. He buckled and fell backward, catching himself on the bar with his elbows. Before he could shoot, though, Calvin Calhoun swung his tomahawk down at the wizard's head.

Deliberately, no doubt, the Christian Appalachee had the head of his war axe turned. The blade would have split the sorcerer's skull like a ripe pumpkin, but even the side of the weapon knocked him to the floor and left him still.

"Sarah!" Cal shouted, and staggered toward the stairs.

Four men slammed into Bill. He fired the pistol in his left hand, hitting one in the center of his kneecap. The man fell screaming. Bill swung his horse pistol horizontally and felt a second assailant's windpipe crumple.

He saw the Cahokian Uris on the ground, choking and clawing at the leather lariat around his neck.

He heard the odd whistles again.

Two men threw Bill onto his back on the table. One held a long triangular blade to Bill's neck.

"We just want the witch!" the other barked. He stank of rotting fish.

Bill answered by kicking the knife-wielder in his crotch as hard as he could. The three fell together as this table also collapsed. In falling, Bill got an upside-down glance at Calvin, racing up the stairs with his tomahawk in his hand. At Sarah's door stood the woman warrior, still in her scale mail and with her scimitar held high, ready to slash downward at the young Appalachee.

Something hit Bill on the top of his head. Glass broke, he smelled rum, and the vision in his one working eye wobbled.

Then, to his surprise, he heard the barking of a dog.

Jacob Hop led Chikaak and twelve hand-selected beastkind warriors through the front of the *Wallenstein* like an ocean wave through a sandcastle. In light of the possibility that the fighting might be at close quarters, the twelve Jake had chosen were not necessarily those who had trigger fingers or had eyes in the right place so they could shoot; they were the biggest, smelliest, most terrifying warriors in Queen Sarah's company.

The hired Hansards didn't expect a charge of bison, sloths, coyotes, and mustangs at their rear, and they broke immediately. Some rushed out the back of the inn, others crashed through windows. Some threw themselves behind the bar looking for shelter, and a few lay still and played dead.

A Hansard stood over Bill, holding a triangular short sword to the Cavalier's eye. "I'll kill him," the Hansard warned.

Rohoakk, a fighter with bison shoulders and legs, though his face was that of a man, barreled the threatening swordsman aside with his shoulder and then trampled him to death before Jake could draw a pistol.

Bill was in bad shape. He bled from both legs, dark blood and lots of it, and he was covered in white powder. Jake checked his pulse—weak and thready, but still beating. He needed Cathy's help, or Sarah's, but Jake didn't see either woman. Hopefully they were still behind the closed door in their room and safe, though Jake couldn't be certain they hadn't also been attacked through the windows.

On the walkway outside Sarah's door, the Unborn and Calvin swung at each other. His axe bit a chunk out of the railing when he missed, and then her sword gouged the wall. Ferpa stood on the stairs behind Cal, ready to charge but unable to intervene until Cal was struck down, due to the narrowness of the passage.

"Sarah!" Jake shouted.

He knelt, tearing strips from his own shirt. He didn't have the art to save Bill, but he could at least slow the bleeding. Jake quickly knotted a tourniquet around each of Bill's legs, shoving a club dropped by a fleeing Hansard underneath each and then turning the clubs to tighten the bands. Too long, and Bill would lose his legs. But if Bill lost too much blood, he'd simply die.

"Sarah!" he called again. "Cathy!"

He heard a choking sound and saw the Cahokian Uris, gasping around a leather lariat tightened about his neck. "Take this!" Jake called to Chikaak, and the beastman took over the tourniquets, holding them steady.

Jake kicked a chair out of the way, flipped Uris over onto

his back, and loosened the lariat. As he pulled the Cahokian to his feet, he thrust a pistol into the man's nose. "You did this!"

"I serve my queen," the taller man said.

"Ik ook." Jake grabbed the Cahokian by the hair and spun him around to face the Podebradan, pressing his pistol now to the man's temple. "Drop your sword, Ophidian!" he yelled.

In answer, Yedera lunged at Calvin again, pressing her attack with a ferocious series of sweeping blows that backed the Appalachee almost into the arms of the beastwife Ferpa.

"Sarah!" Jake yelled.

"Stop!"

A door opened on the walkway, but not Sarah's. In Alzbieta Torias's open doorway stood her bearer, stooping, with the priestess in his arms.

"Stop, Yedera!" the priestess cried again. "Lay down your sword." She looked at Jake, meeting his gaze across the common room that now stank of blood. "We've failed."

Sarah dreamed of faces and hands, and far away and beyond her reach, a lost father.

Her arm burned, and she came to wakefulness, finding Cathy pressing a small silver blade—a letter opener, the gift of Chigozie Ukwu, the good son of the Bishop of New Orleans—to her forearm.

Cathy's hair was disheveled from sleep, but her eyes were alert and calm. "Your Majesty, you and I have been ensorcelled. I suspect that bitch Torias."

"Sarah," Calvin said. He stood in the doorway, bloodied and bruised, and he held his tomahawk in one hand. "Your Majesty. Bill needs you now."

Sarah had gone to sleep with her satchel tucked between her side and her elbow; she was relieved to find it still there. She stood quickly, slinging the bag over her shoulder, and pushed her way past Calvin.

She left the bandage on the bed.

"What happened here?" she asked him.

Looking down at the common room, she saw still bodies on the floor and all the windows shattered. Jacob Hop held guns on the Podebradan and Uris the counselor. Yedera stood with her arms crossed, staring hatred at Sarah; Uris knelt over William Lee, holding tight what appeared to be tourniquets.

"Treachery," Cal said. "Jake figured it out and pulled us out of the tar. But Bill's a-bleedin' out iffen you don't save him."

Cathy pushed past Calvin and the two women rushed down the stairs together. "There are arteries in the leg," Cathy said. "He's bleeding out of one of them. See how much blood there is on his left leg? Can you close that wound?"

Sarah nodded grimly. Returning Yedera's look with a hostile glare of her own, she removed the Orb of Eyles and held it in her cupped right hand, placing her left on Bill's leg. She might not need the energy of this Mississippi ley, and using it would hurt her, but she would take no chances with Bill's life.

"St. William Harvey," Cathy whispered, "guide now this woman's art. As I have faith and seek to follow thee, restore thou health to this suffering child of Adam. Amen."

"*Venam restauro,*" Sarah murmured. She chose the bandage on the leg, already soaked in Sir William's blood, as a conduit, and she willed energy through her own left arm and that bandage. She envisioned in her mind's eye the torn artery, and looked at the leg. She saw Sir William's large vein there as a thicker thread of white light pulsing within the general glow of his aura, but lying beside it were gray specks. "*Pallottolas extraho. Venam restauro. Vitam do.*"

With her cupped right hand, she reached through the Orb and into the deep burning flow of the Mississippi River. Her skin burned, but she drew that power up through one arm and sent it down the other.

Her breath came shallow.

A shard of metal popped from Sir William's leg and fell to the floor. Then a second. He breathed deeply and cried without a word. Then a third shard.

Then Sarah felt the artery close.

She staggered back, shutting off the flow of the ley and sucking in cold night air. Cathy leaped into her place with bandages, needle, and a bottle of whisky. Calvin, who had treated more injured cattle than children of Adam, knelt to help her.

"You said you didn't have the regalia. You lied."

Sarah took in the room again. The accusation came from Alzbieta Torias, who was cradled in the arms of one of her bearers. Sarah hadn't seen her before because the Eldritch priestess was beneath the walkway. The beastman Chikaak stood beside her, pointing two loaded pistols at her.

"May I shoot her?" Chikaak's tongue lolled out of his mouth and he hopped up and down like an excited child. It might have been a grin. "Or her beast of burden? It might be amusing to see what happens when she touches the floor."

Sarah shook her head at both of them. "I never said I didn't have the regalia."

Outside the *Wallenstein's* shattered windows, she saw the backs of her warriors. Some of her soldiers pointed carbines, some pikes, and some teeth, but they all faced out at the blue-cloaked Eldritch troops of Alzbieta Torias in the darkness beyond. A cold wind groaned through the shattered windows.

"You betrayed me, Alzbieta," she said.

"I did it," Uris said immediately. "I am the one who contacted the Hansa, and paid them to intervene."

"Was I to be killed?" Sarah asked.

"Yes," Uris said. His voice was gravelly, his face solemn. He had a bright red weal on his neck, as if he'd survived a hanging. "It's the best outcome for my mistress."

"I told him to," Alzbieta said. "If someone must bear the consequences, let it be me."

"Well, ain't you jest a bunch of self-sacrificin' sweethearts." Calvin spat on the floor.

"Shut your mouth, Cracker," the Podebradan muttered.

"Silence!" Sarah roared. She looked down at Cathy and her ministrations. "Will Sir William live?"

Cathy nodded. "He will not be walking great distances in the near future."

"I know where we can git a sedan chair," Cal muttered. "And eight big oafs to carry it."

Sarah turned to face her cousin and steadied herself with a deep breath. "Your wizard lives."

"I haven't been allowed to look." Uris's gaze was steady.

"You've become a living Tarock, Uris," Sarah said. "Did you know that?" She pointed to her own neck. "The Hanged Man. Curious. And yet, unless I missed some daring piece of wizardry indeed in my unwanted sleep, you have *not* become Alzbieta Torias."

"I only—"

"Stop! If you open your mouth again, I'll kill you myself." Sarah turned her attention again to Alzbieta. "Your wizard lives.

That is not a question, it's a statement. I can see his orenda now. He weakens. He's dying. But he isn't gone."

When he did die, the Polite Sherem would explode in a burst of mana-energy, as Thalanes had done, as Sarah had seen Firstborn travelers on the Natchez Trace do, murdered by the Imperial dragoons.

"Thank you," Alzbieta said. She looked skeptical.

"I believe I can kill you and your companions here, now, if I wish. I believe in a battle with your men, I would prevail. I'm certainly willing to try. Do you see it differently?"

The burning hatred in Alzbieta's eyes suggested she did not.

"Here's what I offer." Sarah took the Sevenfold Crown from her satchel and placed it on her own head, feeling the iron cold through the scant stubble that served her for hair. She knew it must give her a scarecrow appearance, dirty and thin, with mismatched eyes, and she embraced her own strangeness. "You will swear an oath of my devising on the Sevenfold Crown. Your companions will swear it with you. Then we'll revive your wizard, he too will swear, and we'll travel on to Cahokia together."

"You'd compel me to swear an oath to help you take the throne?" The priestess looked offended.

"Of course," Sarah said. "And not harm me or any of my companions."

She looked at her cousin and saw herself. Ambitious, willful, disbelieving.

"I might be willing to do that," Alzbieta said.

"Spoken with a lying heart." Sarah pointed at her own witchy eye. "I see you, Alzbieta, do you understand? I know you think I can't compel an oath from you. You believe you can make reservations in your mind, you can outwit me. Perhaps you think that if you make an oath you don't intend, the Sevenfold Crown won't enforce it."

Alzbieta grew paler but said nothing.

"You're mistaken. We'll stand here until you're ready. Your wizard Sherem will die first. He must have enjoyed the irony of putting me into enchanted sleep after I had done the same to him. That irony will be the last thing he enjoys. I'll consume his soul as it evaporates on his death."

Alzbieta shuddered. Sarah sharpened her stare.

"When Sherem has died, you'll weep for your loss. You'll

pretend then that you're ready, you'll swear you're prepared to fully mean your oath, but I'll know it's false. I'll personally slit the throat of your Hanged Man, Uris, and as his life's blood pours out onto this floor, I'll drink his soul as well, and my power will grow."

"That would be cold murder." Small tears formed in the corners of Alzbieta's eyes.

"Colder than your plan to assassinate *me*? At that point, your men outside, and the Unborn of Podebradas here, will make a desperate attempt. I won't even turn my back as my beastkind tear them limb from limb, but I will savor their mana and fuel the fire of my own sorcerous might. I'll enjoy your tears, too, which by then will be flowing. You'll beg to die, I'll refuse you, and finally, you'll truly mean it when you ask to swear your oath."

Alzbieta Torias trembled. "I will swear."

"Then kneel."

Alzbieta hesitated. Sarah stared at her.

"Set me down," the priestess said to her slave.

He complied.

"See?" Alzbieta knelt in the dirt and the blood. "You take my priesthood from me, and I let you."

Sarah shook her head. "If the gods wish you to have priesthood, I can't take it from you, no matter what taboos I force you to violate."

"Say the oath I must swear."

"The Unborn and the Hanged Man must join you."

"Your Holiness," Uris said roughly to his mistress, "I will die for you."

"I am asking you to live, instead." She smiled at him, and Sarah felt a small pang of guilt. She shoved it down deep inside.

Uris and Yedera both knelt.

Jacob Hop suddenly laughed out loud.

"What is it, Sergeant?" she asked.

"You said it yourself, Your Majesty." Hop pointed at the three kneeling Cahokians. "Tarocks. The Hanged Man and the Priest. With the Daughter of Podebradas as the Virgin, they make a casting."

Sarah permitted herself a soft chuckle. "And will you tell me how you read it?"

"Good things, Your Majesty. An unexpected birth after death.

Consecration to a higher life. Meaning and reorientation. Surprise insight."

"I'm ready," Alzbieta Torias said. "*We* are ready."

Sarah looked at them with her Second Sight, and saw that they were. "I," she began, "say your name."

"I, Alzbieta Torias..."

"I, Uris Byrenas..."

"I, Yedera, Unborn Daughter of St. Adela Podebradas..."

Sarah continued, "swear that I will provide every assistance I can, asked or unasked, to Sarah Elytharias Penn in her attempt to become crowned Queen of Cahokia."

She opened the Orb's conduit to the Mississippi. Light no one else could see flowed through her and the Crown and into the kneeling Cahokians as they took the oath.

"I further swear," she continued, "that I will neither seek nor permit any harm to any loyal servant of Sarah Elytharias Penn."

They swore.

"I swear that I shall be honest with her in all things. By my life and by the life of all my gods, amen."

They finished the oath, and the Crown released them.

"Hell's Bells, Your Majesty," Sir William drawled weakly, his eyes fluttering open. "You compose oaths like a lawyer."

Sarah smiled at Sir William to show her relief.

"Thank you, Your Majesty," Alzbieta said.

"Wait." Sarah wasn't quite sure how to accomplish what she wanted to do next, but ignorance and inexperience hadn't stopped her yet. She raised the Orb of Etyles over her head, drew power through it and through the Crown and focused it this time on herself.

She felt the burning crackle of fire flowing through her, and she felt something else, too. She felt extreme concentration. The world had fallen away, and all that existed was the cosmic chamber of her heart, a dark and warm space into which she spoke.

Reorientation. Unexpected insight.

"I, Sarah Elytharias Penn, swear that I shall reward your good faith with loyalty, with protection, and with every blessing I can bestow. By my life and by the life of all my gods, amen."

The words fell into her heart and stayed there.

The Crown released Sarah.

She replaced the Orb in her shoulder bag. Slowly, because her

skin was tender and her joints ached, she lowered herself to he.
knees facing the three oathtakers. Alzbieta, Uris, and especially
Yedera stared at her.

Careful not to let the crown slip, Sarah bowed slightly toward
the Cahokians.

"I need you to guide me," she said. "I need you to help me
find my way among my people, whom I do not know. I need
you to help me take back my father's throne."

"Yes, Your Majesty," they said.

You would turn our father's funeral into an act of black magic?"

———⟫•⟪———

CHAPTER SIX

The door was locked, but it was a door whose key Etienne had long ago copied. He let himself in, followed by Monsieur Bondí and Armand. Armand closed the door and waited beside it, hands crossed unthreateningly in front of his waist, and well away from his weapons. Armand's size was threat enough.

Etienne and Bondí sat.

August Planchet, the parish's beadle, looked up from his ledgers in surprise. "Vous êtes le...fils de l'évêque."

The beadle's office was plain, if not austere. That was as it should be. The tapers were inexpensive, the drapes of plain cloth, the desk and three chairs all sturdy but simple. The two paintings on the wall were of St. Matthew the tax collector and St. Bernardo de Pacioli with his two columns. August Planchet knew what image the beadle should project to any visiting worthy.

That would make this conversation easy.

"The word you have omitted," Etienne mused, continuing the conversation in French. "What would it have been...*notorious? Criminal? Gangster? Violent? Dangerous?*"

"*Enterprising,*" Bondí said. "*Industrious. Thrifty.*"

"*Merciful,*" Armand suggested. "*Needlessly generous.*"

"*Other.*" Planchet smiled. "You're the bishop's *other* son. I'm more accustomed to seeing Chigozie Ukwu in this office. I haven't seen *you* since you were a small boy; remind me of your name."

"Etienne." He smiled. "The name my mother wished me to have." Her locket tingled in his waistcoat pocket. "And these are two of my associates. Monsieur Bondí is an accomplished accountant." He indicated Bondí, a Creole whom he knew to be part Choctaw, part French, part Sicilian, and part Bantu. He didn't know the proportions or what else might lurk in Monsieur Bondí's family tree, but Bondí was an excellent accountant, both managerial and forensic. He was also an apparently bottomless source of perspiration, so his white shirts were generally stained a splotchy yellow and on his best days he smelled a little sour, even in winter. "At the door is Armand, who practices an entirely different sort of reckoning. May I smoke?"

The beadle said nothing, so Etienne struck a Lucifer match and lit a cigarette, savoring the taste and examining his quarry with cool eyes.

Planchet leaned back in his chair, slowly steepling his fingers before him. "I'm pleased to meet any associate of yours, Etienne." August Planchet was an old man, thin as Etienne's father, with a short spike of white beard on his chin, long teeth, and eyes so pale they looked as if they'd been drained. "You're aware I have no cash here."

Etienne laughed. "Ah, Monsieur Planchet, how I esteem a good sense of humor. What need have I to take a loan from the parish?" He savored a deep puff of cigarette smoke, carefully releasing it toward the corner of the beadle's office. "No, we're here because you'll be seeing more of my associates in the future, in particular Monsieur Bondí. I believe it behooves us to commence our working relationship on the best of all possible bases."

Planchet continued to smile blandly, but he had visibly paled. Etienne's father, the former Bishop of New Orleans, had been dead for two weeks. What must Planchet be thinking? Whether Etienne would now shake him down, no doubt. Or rob him at knife-point. Or simply have him killed.

"Oh?" Planchet said neutrally. "To what do I owe the pleasure of this future association?"

"The bishop's throne is vacant," Etienne said.

"The bishop doesn't sit on a throne," Planchet said immediately.

"Only in a figurative sense, of course. In Latin he sits upon a *cathedra*, a throne, and the church in which he presides is therefore a *cathedral*. Please feel free to correct me if I am mistaken...my knowledge of church governance is as rusty as my theology and my Latin." Etienne steepled his own fingers and mirrored the beadle's mild expression, cigarette tucked neatly into the corner of his mouth.

"Of course, you're correct. The church requires a new prince."

"And the Empire a new Elector. I know, as it happens, that the Synod has already acted. The vote wasn't unanimous, but a majority agreed on a candidate, and in accordance with its traditions the Synod will only announce the outcome of the discussions, and not the misgivings of the dissenters. I expect that you'll shortly be informed as to the identity of your new bishop."

The beadle's mild expression struggled against a look of terror. "Oh? They took months to appoint your father."

Etienne nodded. "I understand this time they felt some urgency to act."

"And . . . you also know whom they intend to anoint." It was not a question.

"As I said, you'll work a great deal with Monsieur Bondí here. And I felt it vital that we discuss one key issue ahead of time, before the new bishop is consecrated."

"How thoughtful."

"You've been stealing, Monsieur Planchet."

Etienne leaned forward and placed his hands on the desk between them, palms down. It was a deliberate move to make himself appear harmless. "You've been stealing from the parish, Monsieur Planchet. You've been picking the pockets of the poor of the church."

August Planchet looked back and forth between Armand and Etienne. His eyes jumped and his breathing became noticeably shallower, but he said nothing.

"Thank you for not denying it. Monsieur Bondí and I have taken the liberty of letting ourselves in at night to examine your books. And I have enough men in my employ to investigate the factual questions, which made it a simple matter to locate the false charity and the nonexistent widows."

The Creole cleared his throat. "I make it about one hundred fifty Louis d'or a year you've been taking, on top of your salary."

"The salary," Planchet said finally, "is a pittance unworthy of a man of my professional qualifications."

"Quite." Etienne relaxed back into his seat. "The parish expects you to contribute your time as an act of service. Worship, even. Your salary is merely intended to pay costs of living, and that at a rate I would characterize as... frugal."

"Your father expected me to live as humbly as *he* did."

"Yes, I know my father's expectations."

"I don't believe your father knew. About the theft."

Etienne laughed. "Of course not. He'd have called you to repentance."

August Planchet looked around again at the three men in his office. "So... where do we go from here?"

"I propose to pay you twenty Louis a month to continue to act as beadle," Etienne said.

Planchet frowned. "But the Synod..."

"Not, you understand, from the Bishopric's funds. The West-wego plantations, the bonds traded in New Amsterdam, the rents from the Esplanade properties, the income from the textile mills, the cotton holdings... you will from this day forward treat that money as utterly sacrosanct. Do you understand me? The parish must be managed in a way that is completely above reproach."

"But..." Planchet was clearly perplexed.

"You ask yourself two questions. I'll give you two answers," Etienne said. "First, your monthly twenty will come from my other businesses, which will continue to operate under the direction of Monsieur Bondí. You will have no contact with those businesses. Monsieur Bondí will examine the Bishopric's accounts monthly, and provided they are pristine—understand me, they must be so shiningly, spotlessly perfect that you could write them in good conscience on the consecrated host—he'll pay you twenty Louis."

"I see." Planchet finally allowed himself to smile again.

"The other question you ask yourself is: *but this Etienne Ukwu is a famed breaker of legs, a man of violence and one who profits from the addictions and dire straits of others. He is a gambler and a whoremaster and a moneylender. How can such a man possibly want an uncorrupted Bishopric?*"

Planchet swallowed. "I will confess, the question had occurred to me. There has been more than one... fallible... priest in the past, and many parishes' accounts show at least *some* sign of disorder. Why, even the Borgia—"

"The Borgia only saved himself from being forcibly unseated

by the Emperor Charles the Affable by preemptively turning Turk. Why do you think we've had no popes or cardinals since?"

"And yet..."

Etienne smiled. "My father was an incorruptible man. He was personally abstemious, he was charitable, he was patient, he was good. If an irregularity had been discovered in the Bishopric's accounts while he was bishop, everyone would have assumed he wasn't to blame. Indeed, he would have been the first to seek to remedy the breach."

"Truth." Monsieur Bondí nodded sagely.

"But the new bishop is a much more fallible person, a man known for certain... irregularities in his attempts to live a Christian life. For such a man to survive as bishop, the parish must be error-free. The books and bank accounts of the Bishopric of New Orleans must come to shine with such a pure light of holiness and honesty that the most jaded and dishonest assailants couldn't call into question the bishop's management. Does that help you see the complete picture?"

"You plan to do battle."

"As any prince must."

"You will have seen the broadsheets on the Place d'Armes; the chevalier is recruiting additional gendarmes and raising their pay. It's as if he, too, expects to do battle soon. And with physical arms."

"Is that so?" Etienne knew.

"Yes." August Planchet's sly grin gave away his knowing flattery. "I can build you the suit of armor you ask, Your Holiness."

Etienne chuckled. "Not yet, Monsieur Planchet. Not yet." He stood, took his mother's locket from his waistcoat, and looked at it.

Well done, my son. He felt the warmth of love and approbation from his mother, his gede loa since her death. This was the path onto which she had put him, following her death. Carry on her legacy, follow her spiritual path, protect his father.

Until Etienne failed at that.

And now: avenge his father's death.

Kill the chevalier, and take the city. End the power of the chevalier's family forever.

Etienne didn't feel the summons of the Brides. Perhaps it was the tobacco smoke, which tended to keep them in check; perhaps it was his failure to eat peppers earlier in the day. Their slumber, in any case, was fortunate. He had much to do before the day ended, and no time for their riotous ministrations.

He replaced the locket as Monsieur Bondí climbed to his feet, rather more ponderously than Etienne. "One more thing, Monsieur Planchet."

Planchet stood. His cautious smile had broken now into a broad, beaming, grin. "Yes . . . sir."

"If you were to fail," Etienne said slowly. "If you were to fall short of the impeccable standard of conduct I expect of you. If, say, you decided that twenty Louis a month were not enough, and that no one would detect a few extra coins given to untraceable orphans or fraternal organizations, rest assured that Monsieur Bondí would notice."

Bondí grinned. "I'm a great noticer of things."

"I've never yet known him to make a mistake in a matter of money," Etienne said. "Monsieur Bondí is punctilious to the sou."

Planchet nodded. "I believe he would notice."

"And I would be promptly informed."

"I'm as loyal as I am discreet," Bondí said.

Planchet nodded, shuffling back half a step.

Etienne took a final drag on his cigarette.

"And no one would ever find your body. Do we understand each other, Monsieur Planchet?"

"Don't worry," Montse whispered to Margaret. "And stay calm."

Not that the girl looked worried, despite the shackles on both their wrists. Perhaps because she felt she could walk out at any moment she wished. Perhaps because she trusted Montse. Mostly, she looked impressed. The Palais du Chevalier was enormous, and gleamed with art and silver. Even in what appeared to be the administrative portion of the building, the halls teemed with busy servants and rushing clerks.

"This is a rich man," Margaret whispered back.

"That's only to say, aquest criminal és més èxit que jo."

Margaret laughed quietly, her head bobbing up and down like an amused hyena's, but it was true. The Chevalier of New Orleans was only a more successful criminal, and Montserrat Ferrer i Quintana was not afraid of him.

Or at least, she wouldn't admit to fear in front of the girl. She owed Hannah better than that.

Once, she had pledged Hannah everything.

Two of the chevalier's gendarmes had dragged the smuggler and her charge into a room that looked one part office and one part audience chamber. It had a desk and padded seat at one end, and benches lined the walls. No chairs stood in front of the desk. The gendarmes had pushed the two women onto a bench against one wall and then stood silent, waiting.

The gendarmes might have understood Montse's joke in Catalan, but they gave no sign of it.

"We'll escape," Margaret whispered. "I'm sure of it."

Montse shrugged. "We'll buy our way out. A message to *La Verge Caníbal* and Josep will send bags of money to redeem us."

That was true, Josep was loyal even though Montse had rebuffed him as a lover. He was loyal because she was generous and fair, and really, where else would he go to take hauls as big as they'd made running stolen silver baked into thick clay dishes across the Pontchartrain Sea? So long as the chevalier was unaware of Margaret's identity, the bribe he'd require shouldn't even be very much. His people benefited from Catalan and Igbo smuggling, which provided the necessary market for those who couldn't afford stamped goods brought in by Castilian and Dutch traders.

The door opened and eight men entered. They were tall and all wore padded black pourpoints that covered them from mid-thigh to wrists to neck. Long beards emerged from faces swaddled in silk scarves. They had the poise and the measured step of warriors, though none seemed to be carrying weapons. They stood, feet apart and hands behind their backs, seven of them in a semicircle several steps from the desk and the eighth directly in front of it.

A section of the wooden paneling at the back of the room swung open. Four more gendarmes entered and stood beside the door. These men were armed with muskets and bayonets, but the last man to enter, who followed them through the panel, carried only a dagger at his belt. He was tall and thin, with a thin French aristocrat's face, and black hair beginning to be dusted with white about the neck and ears.

Gaspard Le Moyne, the Chevalier of New Orleans.

The door stayed open behind him. Through the open panel, Montse saw dim yellow light but no details; a passage of some sort. She heard muffled murmurs.

Le Moyne sat, then looked up at the man standing before him. "How is the Caliph?"

The men in the pourpoints placed right hands over hearts and bowed slightly. Then the one directly before the chevalier lowered his scarf to reveal a small mouth with thin, chapped lips. "Insha'allah, well. He was prosperous when I saw him last, and God continues to send him victory." Even his lips moved with such economy that he resembled a statue.

Both men spoke French, which was Montse's second language, and came as naturally to her as cheating.

"You've come about my letter," the chevalier said.

"I don't know anything about a letter. I've come to take possession of a prisoner."

"The Abbé de Talleyrand is an Elector." The chevalier said this as if he were thinking aloud and uncertain of what he would do.

The scarfed man stood silent.

"That means he's an important man in his native Acadia."

"He's an important man in France."

"I understood the Caliph had taken his family lands and confiscated his wealth. What importance could he have in the Caliphate now?"

"The Caliph wants him dead. That fact makes him important."

"And here, he's important because he's entitled to vote emperors in and out, as well as consent to taxes. And he is protected by wealth and power. So if I am to deliver this man to you, I think you realize, the price will be high."

The scarfed man considered. "I had been given to understand that you already had the Abbé in your custody. Perhaps this was what you wrote in your letter."

The chevalier arched his eyebrows and pursed his lips.

"I am Ahmed Abd al-Wahid. I am mameluke-born and mameluke-bred, and prince-capitaine of that order. If I have been summoned here with a lie, the Caliph Napoleon will regard this as a declaration of war. His expectation of me is that my first act will be to kill as many enemies as I can before my own inevitable destruction. Is this what you seek?"

The chevalier chuckled. "Bring him in!" he called over his shoulder.

Four more musket-bearing gendarmes came through the short passage. They dragged a prisoner, an ageing man with hair spilling down his shoulders in tight white curls and a broad forehead. The man's mouth was gagged, but he murmured loudly when the gendarmes threw him to the floor.

"Let us be clear." Gaspard Le Moyne stood and rested his hands on his belt. "This Abbé is highly inconvenient for your master. He writes letters of encouragement to French Christians, and shelters them as refugees when they flee to Acadia."

"Oui."

"He funds the partisans who seek to overthrow the Dhimmi Kings of Spain."

"Oui."

"Some say, indeed, that there is no Bourbon worthy to retake the throne. Some say that if a mussulman Napoleon can take it for himself and found a Caliphate, may not the Abbé de Talleyrand take it back, and return France to Christendom? Isn't this so, Prince-Capitaine Ahmed Abd al-Wahid?"

"Certes, some say these things." The mameluke's face had no expression.

Montse had never seen the Abbé de Talleyrand. He was one of the three great Electors of the Acadian north, benevolent and rich, though some said he was a manipulator behind the scenes. It was believed Franklin had personally invited Talleyrand to come to the New World after the Caliph's Grapeshot Massacres. The elector's hands were tied together and his mouth gagged, but he knelt now in a posture of prayer or supplication, and craned his neck, trying to catch the chevalier's gaze.

"Good," the chevalier said. "We've established his value. Now let's consider his cost. Men delivered him to me, men who ran great personal risks, men whom I had to pay good sums of gold."

The mameluke nodded.

"At some point, my deed will be discovered. This may result in war with Acadia, or a trial before the assembled Electors. Thomas Penn has reasons to be annoyed with me, and will certainly try to say that what I've done is treason."

"Yes."

"In addition, the Abbé is known to be a sainted man. It grieves me greatly to act against such a holy man."

"Indeed?" The mameluke's face was still as stone. "I had heard the opposite."

"What would that be?"

"That killing a holy man didn't trouble your conscience. That maybe you were even known for such acts."

The chevalier chuckled. "That's not quite right, though. I don't rejoice in the blood of priests, Prince-Capitaine. But I do what needs to be done."

"These are the costs of this man." The mameluke caught Talleyrand up with a sweep of his arm. "High, indeed. Now tell me the price that will make your trouble, expense, and risk worth while."

"I have my men counting the gold."

"Excellent. We brought it for you, of course."

"All thirteen chests?"

"The wealth of Italy and Egypt."

"I am pleased." The chevalier inclined his head slightly. "It's almost enough."

"What final feather in the scale would you require, O great chevalier?"

"Only one." The chevalier held up a finger. "As I have given you one Elector, O prince-capitaine, I require that you deliver an Elector to me."

"The poet tells us to seek, for search is the foundation of fortune." The mameluke nodded. "Tell me."

"He hasn't yet been appointed Bishop of New Orleans, but my agents tell me that he will be. The prior bishop's son. Unexpectedly, not the pious one."

"An Elector for an Elector would be an even trade, no?" The mameluke cocked his head to one side. "Shall I pack up the Caliph's gold for return shipment to Paris?"

"I think not," the chevalier said. "You see, the Elector I require you to capture for me is here in New Orleans. Indeed, he is not yet even an Elector. He is a criminal, and but for the fact that he is soon to be an Elector under the Compact, this would be a simple police action for my own gendarmes."

The mameluke was quiet for a moment, then nodded. "Agreed. Then the renegade Abbé is ours?"

Talleyrand squirmed.

The chevalier gestured with an open hand. "Please feel free to pack him up for return shipment to Paris."

"We won't be taking the entire Abbé back to Paris. Only his head."

Talleyrand leaped to his feet, and Ahmed Abd al-Wahid
caught him. The chevalier drew his dagger and handed it across
the desk, hilt-first. Montse saw all the chevalier's men grow tense.

The mameluke grabbed the Abbé's head with both hands,
and Montse got one last look at the terrified cleric. With a single
motion, the mameluke twisted at the waist and pulled through
with both hands—

snap!

Talleyrand's neck pulled into an unnatural angle and his
body went limp.

"You are my witnesses, with God, that this man's death was
merciful." The mameluke then took the dagger from the chevalier's unresisting hand—Le Moyne's face bore an expression of
surprise and maybe disgust—and promptly pushed the blade into
the dead man's throat.

Blood gushed onto the chevalier's stone floor. Several of his
men gripped their muskets as if to respond, but the chevalier
inhaled sharply and raised a hand to restrain them.

Abd al-Wahid sawed through Talleyrand's head in several long
strokes and then handed back the chevalier's blade politely. The
Abbé's body hit the stone floor with a thud. The chevalier laid
the dagger on a stack of papers, marring them with the Acadian's
blood. Then the mameluke reached under his pourpoint and
produced a red silk sack, pulling it over Talleyrand's once-white
locks. He handed the bagged head to one of his seven men, then
nodded to the chevalier. "And this new Elector?"

"I must consider." Le Moyne's voice was calm. "For the moment,
once you've shipped the Abbé off to your master, please feel free to
move your possessions into the Palais. I have a room in which you
may sleep, and a separate room in which you may pray."

"Your men have our weapons," the mameluke said. "There
is nothing else."

The chevalier snapped his fingers and pointed to one of his
men. "Their weapons, Bertrand," he said.

The mamelukes bowed slightly and left by the door by which
they'd entered.

The last to depart hesitated in the doorway. "L'Abbé," he said.
"The body."

"Leave it for now." The chevalier dismissed his man with a
wave. "Later, the river will do."

Montse was trembling. She touched the arm of her charge and found the girl was also shaking.

The chevalier left his bloody dagger where it lay. Crossing the audience chamber, he stepped over the headless corpse on his floor and seated himself on the bench on the far side of Margaret. Looking at the dead body, he sighed and shook his head.

Montse tried to find her equilibrium and couldn't. Would the chevalier now kill them as witnesses? But if that was the plan, why let them see anything at all?

She decided to gamble on silence.

"Vous êtes une contrebandière," he said.

"We're your prisoners," she answered, in French. It seemed safe because it was neutral, it only restated the obvious, without even admitting to the relatively harmless fact that yes, she was a smuggler.

She was also, after all, Catalan.

The chevalier smiled and turned to Margaret. "Mais vous," he said. "Vous êtes une princesse."

Montse forced herself to breathe. Margaret's hair swayed slightly, though there was no breeze, and Montse took her hand to calm her.

"What are you talking about?" she asked.

"There is no need to lie, Ferrer i Quintana," the chevalier said. "One of my most trusted servants recently died, and I discovered by fortunate accident that *he* had been lying to me since the day we met. I learned that he was a member of a conspiracy, and when I gathered up some of his fellow-conspirators, I found out astonishing things. The man was in league with Jackson!"

"I am Ferrer i Quintana," Montse admitted. "Not Jackson. This is my niece."

"No," he said. "This girl is a Penn. The conspiracy I speak of has been watching her for some time, but now *I* have use of her."

René must be dead.

They hadn't admitted as much to her at the Palais, turning her away with no answers. But he hadn't answered her messages either, including the letter in the secret drop, and though the chevalier had returned to New Orleans, his seneschal hadn't returned with him.

René only left New Orleans when his master did. His responsibility was to keep order and function in the Palais, this was why he was called its *intendant*, or in English, its *seneschal*; a seneschal held a castle for his lord. René oversaw cooks, maids, and butlers, but also the gendarmes who secured the Palais, the grooms who kept its horses, and the gardeners who carved its bushes into the shape of exotic beasts. He also ran certain discreet errands indicated by the Palais's great inhabitant, the chevalier.

He hadn't answered, so he must be dead.

René was dead and Simon Sword was active. Had the Heron King discovered him? Would the Heron King discover Kinta Jane? Was the Conventicle itself already revealed and broken?

Regardless, the combination of René's death and the return of the god left Kinta Jane Embry only one course of action—she was traveling to Philadelphia.

She packed nothing but a few clothes, and those into a single carpetbag she bought for the purpose, second-hand from a blind Portugee pushing his two-wheeled cart through the Vieux Carré. She wore her luck in the form of her cluster of beybey medallions, hanging around her neck. There was no point in telling Elbows Pritchard, her useless drunkard pander; he might beat her out of sheer spite, but even if he had any ability to help her, he wouldn't offer it. He would get angry about her disappearance and likely batter another girl, but she didn't see a way around that for certain, and decided that if she left without a message, he might assume she'd died.

All in all, that would be for the best.

Kinta Jane came up the Mississippi River the same way she'd gone everywhere in her life: working.

A keelboat full of Ohio Germans with crates of New Orleans-woven cotton fabric packed into their hold took her with them, favorable winds initially filling the narrow vessel's sails. The boat flew no banner aft. The keelboatmen were mostly married, several of them to more than one woman at the same time, each in a different port. Few of them turned Kinta Jane away. None of them turned their backs.

It wasn't painted on the side, but she thought the name of the keelboat was the *Stolze Marie*.

Of all the boatmen, Johannes was her favorite. He was young and shy, with bright blue eyes and long hair down to his shoulders. When they stopped at Natchez-under-the-Hill, Johannes disappeared for an hour, much to the agitation of his fellow-keelboatmen. When he returned, he had three apples, late and small but tartly delicious, and he gave them all to Kinta Jane. Johannes had a wooden box like a snuffbox in which he kept anis seed, and before seeing Kinta Jane he always chewed a handful of it to sweeten his breath.

Before they reached the Mississippi's junction with the Ohio, the tide of traffic turned, boats of all descriptions beginning to stream southward past them. Some of those boats looked unmolested, the ordinary agents of planters, manufacturers, and middlemen, moving goods up and down the watery highway that bounded the western edge of the Empire of the New World.

But other boats, or their passengers, had clearly been attacked.

The captain of one such vessel was willing to drop anchor and lay alongside the Ohio Germans' keelboat for half an hour to tell what he'd seen, why his vessel was stuffed with elegant furniture, and why his passengers were all bandaged and stared constantly upriver behind them, as if fearing pursuit.

Beastmen.

Beastkind were rampaging in the Missouri.

Before any of her Ohio Germans had even muttered *Simon Schwert*, Kinta Jane knew what was happening. This was Franklin's vision, this was why he had founded both the Conventicle and the Compact. It might even have something to do, she thought, with his construction of the Lightning Cathedral.

Because Peter Plowshare always dies, sooner or later.

And because Simon Sword is always a reaver.

The Germans muttered more prayers to their queer saints as they continued upriver, but they didn't stop requiring Kinta Jane's services. "Die Beruhigung des Ohio," Johannes tried to explain to her when she managed to communicate her curiosity. His breath was sweet, but Kinta Jane didn't understand German and he spoke virtually no English.

Maybe that made them a good match.

Though it meant he couldn't explain what *Stolze Marie* meant. *Marie* was Mary, but the hodge-podge of languages spoken daily in New Orleans included little German.

The Ohio Germans were picky about where they moored the boat at night, sometimes engaging in lengthy debates as they pointed alternately upriver and down to discuss possibilities. Kinta Jane followed all this only in part, but she noticed they tended to avoid the Imperial Ohio Company's trading posts. From time to time they also pulled into difficult-to-spot streams flowing into the river, even going so far as to cut branches off trees and bushes growing alongside the creek and use them to cover the riverward end of their keelboat.

And those posts were hives of activities. The fact that soldiers camped outside them in tents, though winter was fast coming on, suggested that the three trading posts Kinta Jane saw were all full beyond their capacity of Company militia.

And then one overcast night, having left the trading post behind them and moving up the Ohio River mostly by the power of poles and German back muscles, the boat was hailed by a voice out of the darkness.

"Halt, who goes there?" cried one voice.

"Halt, wer da?" called a second.

Baskets were raised, revealing torches on two immense canoes. Gold-painted insignia on their blue hulls marked them as Imperial Ohio Company vessels, and the Company's men wasted no time in leveling a row of guns, long and short, at the Germans. The Company soldiers looked like irregulars, without a consistent uniform or weapon, but the range was close enough that they couldn't miss.

"Are you Hansa?" demanded a Company officer with a sword from the bow of one vessel. "Dutch Ohio Company? Traders?"

"Nicht, nicht, nicht!" The Germans tried to explain in slow, accented English and rapid German that they were only locals moving from one town to the next, by night because their appointment was urgent. They were laborers, they had a school to build, or was it a church? They were smooth enough in their falsehoods, but the Company officer wasn't having any of it.

"No stamped passport? I'm afraid I have no way to tell you from customs-evading criminals. Don't you support the Pacification?"

"Ja, natürlich," Johannes said.

The Germans all grinned.

"Good. Then you'll be happy to pay the thirty percent tariff on all goods you're carrying. Prepare to be boarded."

Nathaniel ran across the earl's field, trying to get inside the outbuilding where he slept. Two scrawny Irish boys looked up from digging a ditch.

"Lookit Mad Chapel run!" the one squealed.

"He's got the fear of Herne on him, hasn't he?" squawked the other.

"Run, Chapel!" they cried together.

Nathaniel didn't fear Herne, not exactly. He knew that the men who rode across the earl's land and through the surrounding villages were only men, and their leader a man wearing a Herne mask. But he also knew that when night fell on All Hallows' Eve, the voices he heard—the voices no one else could hear, and with them the shrieking of the wheels of heaven—would explode.

Nathaniel had encountered an itinerant peddler, a book-cadger, crossing the earl's fields. He'd become distracted not by the few volumes the man carried on his back, but by the lengthy catalogs of books he claimed he could bring down from Richmond, upon order. Now Nathaniel raced against the sun.

~Kill the child! Kill the child!~

~Drink its blood!~

~Come to us! The water down here is so cold, so lovely. Sleeeeep!~

The heavenly squeal pierced his ear like a lance, and Nathaniel collapsed against the doorframe of the outbuilding, falling down into the dirt.

~Eat him! Eat him now, before he can stand!~

"Help me!" he gasped.

Then hands did help him, lifting him up and pushing him through the door. His vision held, though he couldn't decide whether that was a mercy or not. A seizure at this moment might spare him an evening of pain.

He collapsed onto his sleeping plank, and a blanket was thrown over him.

"Thank you, Charles," he mumbled.

"You're welcome, Nathaniel." It wasn't Charles. Nathaniel's head echoed too much with strange voices and the grinding howl of the world to be able to open his eyes, but he thought the voice might be Jenny Farewell's.

"Thank you," he said again, and burrowed deeper under the blanket.

He huddled in darkness, willing time to pass and trying to ignore the bloodthirsty howls, cries for mayhem, and threats that crowded into his cursed ear. He couldn't tell how much time at passed, or even if time was passing at all.

And then he heard a gunshot.

He was accustomed to phantom voices and shrieks. He'd never heard a phantom firearm.

It was enough to spur his curiosity and chase away the other noises. Nathaniel crawled from his plank, hearing a second gunshot. The fire in the outbuilding was down to embers—the other men and boys he shared it with would be out all evening on the Wild Hunt, or at a dance, or otherwise celebrating the mad god of the Weald.

Afraid to open the door, he crept to a chink in the logs that he'd stuffed with a rag to block the wind. Pulling out the rag, he pressed his face to the gap, looked past the smithy, and saw the earl's stables. There stood five men masked and cloaked in black; four of them had simple cowls hiding their faces, but the fifth wore Herne's head, the neck and muzzle of a stag that added two feet to the wearer's height, crowned with a regal spread of antlers. Each of the five members of the Wild Hunt held a torch—the other lights of the manor had been dimmed already.

Between the Hunt and the stables stood the godi Wickens, leaning on his spear of office and holding up a warning hand.

Had the gunshots been a warning?

"No Yule log!" the old sheep-killer cried. "No Wild Hunt!"

"You defy Herne!" the man in the Herne mask roared. The mask had something in its mouthpiece that amplified and distorted the voice, but Nathaniel still recognized George Isham.

"No." Wickens chuckled. "I defy the puke-child whelp of a pathetic madman. Your horses will not leave the stables tonight. The earl's lands will not know the Wild Hunt. You will console yourself as pleases you, boy."

George-Herne raised a hand to strike the godi, but one of his companions caught his wrist. They grappled briefly, and then George stepped away.

"Ill luck from killing a priest of Woden," George agreed. "But not, I think, from simply moving him."

With no ceremony, he knocked aside the godi's spear, then picked the man up and hoisted him over the rail fence into the horses' yard. The priest splashed into a trough of drinking water and came up coughing.

"Ing and Erce!" the godi shrieked.

The laughter of the Wild Hunt was cut short when the stable doors swung open. Standing within were the eight soldiers in Old One Eye's black uniform, muskets raised and pointed at George Isham.

Wickens cackled as he dragged himself up by the rails of the fence. "No Wild Ride tonight! And no log for Yule, boy!"

George's companions dragged him away, cursing.

~Ride, Herne! Ride!~

The shrieking returned and Nathaniel collapsed.

"This is too much, even from you."

Etienne turned from examining the preparations for mass and found his brother Chigozie. Chigozie, unsurprisingly, looked angry. The black and white of his priestly garb stripped away his individuality and reduced him to a mere face, which had the effect of magnifying that face's expression of rage.

Etienne resolved to remember that, for use on a later occasion.

They both stood within the cathedral's chancel.

"I have been anointed priest as well as bishop, brother," he said. "May a priest not officiate at the mass? I have been reading the books closely, but I would certainly be pleased to have your assistance."

"You were anointed both priest and bishop very quietly."

"The Synod thought it best."

"Liar. His Grace, the Bishop of Miami, felt obliged to tell me he was voting for you, after all the years of hinting he thought I would follow in Father's footsteps. He told me that you would be seated as bishop, and that you would be installed quickly and quietly, *as you directed*. That was his word, and it was striking: you *directed*."

"How could I direct the Synod?" Etienne shrugged. "I was not even a priest, much less a bishop, still less one of their number. I was a layman and, let us be honest, something of a scoundrel."

"Indeed. You were a Vodun houngan."

"I *am* a Vodun houngan. Whose mother was a mambo, and speaks to him still."

Chigozie raised his hand as if to strike his brother, but held back. "Do not defile her memory."

"I do not defile her memory, brother. I do as she bids, every day."

Chigozie staggered away from the just-mended rood screen where Etienne stood, raising his arms to the stained-glass image of God the Father above and roaring. "Why?"

"Love, I suppose," Etienne said softly. "A son's love."

"Oh? A son's love? And it must have been a son's love that made you steal the body of our father and bury it in the woods!"

"You are listening to what people in the Vieux Carré say. Good.

There is wisdom in rumor, properly sifted. The voice of the people whispers in the streets, all their hopes and fears."

"The rumor I have heard is that you buried our sainted father in a Vodun ceremony."

"He is not sainted yet," Etienne said. "Though I will seek that, too, eventually. But he was *saintly*."

"Answer the question!"

"I did not hear a question," Etienne said softly. "But yes, I gave him a Vodun funeral. Vodun was the spiritual tradition of our mother, who was the love of his life. And the ceremony I gave him kept his body out of the hands of foul necromancers, who might have defiled him in ways that would horrify you even more than you are horrified by what I have done, brother Chigozie. Instead, his limbs are burned and safely buried, and his soul is free. And now I will give him a good Christian service, my first service as a Christian priest, so that his many parishioners who were too Christian to mourn with me in the streets can come remember my father in his church."

"God's church," Chigozie said.

"Yes," Etienne agreed immediately.

"And in that casket there," Chigozie said, pointing at the simple but elegant wooden coffin resting on a low raised platform before the rood screen, "there is nothing of our father. Not his body, not his ashes. Did you even put any of his clothing in the coffin, any possession of his?"

"I did not."

"You will pray over and bury an empty casket."

Etienne hesitated.

Chigozie's brow furrowed. "Etienne, what is in the casket?"

Etienne looked up at the stained-glass windows, and specifically at St. Peter, with his key. St. Peter, who was also Papa Legba, the great loa of the crossroads Etienne served. "If I tell you, I fear it will be the final rupture between us."

Chigozie gripped his own head between his hands. "Etienne, what have you done?"

"I would like you to stay," Etienne told his brother. "Indeed, I would like you to serve with me in our father's memory. Perhaps as a suffragan bishop."

"One does not become a priest to serve a dead man!" Chigozie snapped. "One becomes a priest to serve the living God!"

"I am trying to find common ground with you, brother," Etienne said slowly. "I would not fight you. I would have you here at my side, in the battle that is coming. I need your wisdom, your priestly acumen."

"Etienne." Chigozie stared, eyes and nostrils bulging. "What is in the coffin?"

Etienne consulted his mother's locket. *Tell him the truth. All of it.*

He sighed. "A wax image of the Chevalier of New Orleans. It is dressed in clothing made from fabric cut from uniforms of the chevalier's gendarmes and it holds in its hand a copper coin stamped with his grandfather's likeness. Regrettably, the chevalier is a careful man, who has his hair clippings immediately burned and the contents of his bedpan poured into the Mississippi River, so it is an imperfect effigy at best. But it is all I can do at the moment."

Chigozie's stare, if anything, hardened. "You intend to perform a mass for the dead over this effigy?"

Etienne nodded, grateful at least for the fact that his brother had chosen to confront him alone, in this place, rather than in the street.

"You will tell the world that you are burying our father. In reality, you are burying an effigy of the Chevalier of New Orleans?"

Etienne sighed and nodded again.

"A mass for the dead, said for a living man. This is a curse, brother. You would turn our father's funeral into an act of black magic?"

"Against the man who murdered him!" Etienne meant only to speak his words, but they came out in a guttural yell. "Yes, Chigozie, I will use this mass as a chance to curse our enemy. That he murdered our father strengthens his connection to this mass, gives the spell power. That our father was murdered in this very spot only adds to the power of the liturgy. That the cathedral will be full of heartbroken worshippers, singing songs of death under my direction strengthens the spell, don't you see?"

Chigozie backed away a step. "I see."

"I am led by our mother, Chigozie. I always have been. And now, I will take vengeance on the man who killed our father. I will destroy him, any way I can. This is not our father's funeral. Our father is buried, and at rest, and with his wife. This is our father helping me take revenge."

Chigozie backed away further. "Our father would not take revenge."

"No," Etienne agreed, "he would not. But our mother would."

"And who are you, to be so certain the chevalier is guilty of our father's death?" Chigozie asked.

"Who am I?" Etienne asked, and then suddenly he found himself shouting. "I am a man with eyes, brother! The chevalier's gendarmes and his Imperial guests entered this cathedral by force! One of those men, an Imperial soldier who was sleeping at the Palais, shot our father! The murder was witnessed by many, and now our great chevalier, fearing retaliation, hires more soldiers! *This thing was not done in a corner, brother! It was shouted from the rooftops!*" He paused to catch his breath and felt the sudden surge of the Brides' power within him; they felt his need and they answered. "And yes, I directed the Synod to act quickly . . . so the chevalier would not stop them. Who am I, you ask? I am my father's son."

Chigozie turned, his faltering steps becoming a brisk walk.

"Stay with me, brother!" Etienne called. He breathed hard, fighting to resist the Brides. "I need you!"

Chigozie Ukwu didn't answer or look back.

Etienne's heart hurt, but he couldn't run after his brother; instead, he succumbed to the Brides.

Ezili Freda sang to him in lilting, lyrical French, though when he tried to focus on the individual words of her song they slipped through his hearing like water through the fingers of imperfectly cupped hands. Ezili Freda was an animal force as a Bride, and the sound of her voice told Etienne he was about to be ridden to exhaustion. Ezili Danto sang along at the same time, but her voice was a strangled staccato cry, the arrested song of a slave or a silenced woman. She was the maid, always watching Etienne through the eyes of every Virgin Mary he saw, and though she would come to the bed with her more riotous sister, she would come to oversee, to nurture, and to heal Etienne of his exertions when they were done.

He would have preferred to be in his bed, but there was no time. Etienne staggered down the stairs into the crypt beneath the St. Louis Cathedral. There, Ezili Freda seized him bodily and began to whip ecstasy from him in great lashings.

"My loves," Etienne murmured, sinking to the cold stone floor. "My loves."

"You get outside Appalachee, folks believe all kinds of nonsense."

⇒➤◆⇐

CHAPTER SEVEN

Cathy was enjoying a quiet ride with Bill. Though she had done her best with his injuries and Sarah had augmented his body's healing processes with gramarye, he couldn't walk without support. Cal had dutifully hacked him a sturdy crutch out of a dogwood branch, but Bill's injuries gave Cathy an additional reason to stay close.

Leaving Wisdom's Bluff and entering the Ohio proper had stirred up memories Cathy wasn't ready to face. The man—a husband, of sorts, an escort, a gaoler—dead at her hands had been a trauma at the time, but Cathy had seen so much death since, in New Orleans as an infrequent matter of course but especially on the trail with Sarah and her company, that the once-vivid memory of his pallid flesh and dying gasps, though it hadn't faded, had lost its power to impress.

But the young queen's quest to save her unknown siblings had dredged up other memories, more painful still, more riddled with guilt. A liaison with a powerful man—her first, and her greatest mistake. Telling that same man of the birth of their child—her second error. The child, as she had expected, would be cared for, because his father was wealthy and, after the fashion his culture expected, generous.

Her own banishment had been a surprise.

And the final act, after the murder, had played out in a beguine cloister not far from the path she rode now. When the local sheriff came to investigate, she had found herself faced with two unpleasant possibilities: that the beguines would believe her accusers and take action against her, or that they would believe Cathy's own defense, half-lies and half-shaded truths, and put themselves at risk for her sake.

She had chosen the third path, and fled.

That flight, years ago, had taken her downriver to New Orleans. She'd tried teaching, but there were too many schoolmarms whose native language was French. She'd tried the practice of medicine, until the first threat of legal action against her terrified her into stopping.

Finally, she'd drifted to rest at *Grissot's*.

They pulled to a stop beside a knee-high stone to the side of the path. By agreement, Alzbieta Torias's Firstborn spearmen marched at the front, followed by Alzbieta and her party, and then Sarah and hers—though, after the events of the night before in the *Wallenstein*, Alzbieta and her Firstborn companions might properly be said to comprise a portion of Sarah's party.

Not a portion that should be trusted. Cathy kept a close eye on the Handmaid of Lady Wisdom.

Sarah and her friends rode slowly, because the Firstborn went on foot.

The beastkind brought up the rear.

Uris leaned on the spear he had taken to using as a walking staff and nodded at the stone. Looking at it more closely, Cathy saw that it was vaguely humanoid in form. At least, the stone looked like the top half of a person, carved with very general features. It had a head, with a small protrusion where a nose should be and two shallow depressions representing eyes. It also had sloping shoulders, and possibly faintly incised lines distinguishing an arm on each side from a chest in the center.

"Stones such as these mark most boundaries in the seven kingdoms," Uris said. "You might have remarked them around the Serpent Mound."

Sarah nodded. "I see."

Despite her mutual oath with the Firstborn, then, she was following Cathy's advice to play her cards slowly and keep her own counsel. Good. She, like Cathy herself, had seen no such stones on Wisdom's Bluff.

"Looks like a little man," Calvin Calhoun said. Then he blushed. "Or woman, I reckon."

"You're right," oathbound Yedera said. She smiled at Calvin in a way that made him blush even more. Cathy thought she saw a flash of irritation in Sarah's unbandaged eye. "What it definitely doesn't resemble is beastkind. These are Adam-stones, and they mark the places of mankind."

"Are there Eve-stones as well?" Cathy asked.

"Shhh." Alzbieta looked slightly offended.

Cathy resisted the impulse to slap the other woman.

"Is the Adam-stones' purpose to mark the Ohio as different from the Great Green Wood, and the lands of the Heron King?" Sarah asked.

"If you mean to ask whether our people adopted these stones upon coming here," Alzbieta said, a breeze blowing the silk veil of her sedan as if the fabric was moved by her words, "or whether they brought them from the Old World . . . perhaps that isn't a question to be discussed in this place."

What was she hiding?

The Polite mage Sherem had recovered consciousness, but not his wits. He lay curled up at Alzbieta's feet, muttering to himself.

Sarah nodded and removed the bandage from her head, revealing her powerful eye. She scanned the Adam-stone at length, and the path on either side of it.

"What you seein', Sarah?" Cal blushed again, perhaps thinking he was speaking too familiarly.

"I see that the world is more complex and interesting then ever I knew." Sarah replaced her patch. "I take it we now enter Cahokia?"

Uris nodded.

"Thank you, Uris, Yedera, Alzbieta. Let us continue."

As they passed the Adam-stone, Jacob Hop brought his horse parallel to Bill's, opposite Cathy. Cal and the string of horses fell slightly behind; Sarah rode ahead, beside Alzbieta's palanquin.

"I have an observation, Captain," the blond man said. "It's of a military nature. I fear Mrs. Filmer may find it boring, but I think it's a good idea to discuss it as soon as possible."

"Fear not." Cathy kept an eye on Sarah as she spoke. "I am easily entertained."

Jacob Hop laughed. He was an odd one. He seemed perpetually delighted with the world, curious about everything, and imperturbable. Just a few days earlier he had been the flesh and blood vessel of a violent god, and all his life before that he'd been deaf and mute. What was going on in Jacob Hop's brain?

"It is to do with the beastkind, and how to talk to them," Jake said.

"Chikaak may interpret for us," Bill rumbled. "I suppose that is no worse than passing orders through any other sergeant."

"Until the day when Chikaak becomes unavailable," Jake said. "If he is dead, or badly wounded, or on an errand, we may find ourselves unable to communicate with many of our warriors."

"You're thinking we should choose an additional sergeant?"

"I'm thinking about your horn." Jake pointed at the instrument swinging at Bill's side. It was made of yellowing ivory, trimmed with bands of gold. "Why did Simon Sword give that to you?"

Bill growled. "The Heron King did a number of things I do not yet understand, Jake. I am not certain I ever *will* understand them. But what he *said* was: 'You are my friend, Bill, like it or not. These warriors are my Household Guard, and not ordinary soldiers. I rejoice at giving them to you because they have not had a more able commander. You will, however, want this.' Those aren't exactly the words, you understand, but that was the gist of it. And he handed me the horn."

"You remember his words quite distinctly," Cathy said.

"It isn't often one converses with a god," Bill said. "Or a twelve-foot-tall bird-headed monster, as the case may be."

Jake nodded vigorously. "The horn goes with the beastkind. Do you see? Because their language is purely tonal."

Bill sighed. "What?"

Jake considered. "I think I'm speaking good English, ja?"

"Try explaining a different way," Cathy suggested.

Jake cocked his head to one side. "Ja, I do that. Have you noticed that when the beastkind communicate with each other, they used different . . . kinds of sound? Voices? What I mean, Ferpa will make a sound like a cow lowing, and then Chikaak will answer with barks like a coyote, and they still understand each other?"

"This hardly helps me, Jake," Bill said, "since I understand neither of them, and if I place my hands into my armpits, flap my elbows like a bird's wings, and hoot like a baboon, *neither* of them will understand me."

"Yes, but it's the . . . toonhoogte."

"Bless you," Bill said. "Or rather, gesundheit, as they say among your people."

Jake shook his head. "No, listen, it's like this." He whistled two notes, one high and one low. "You hear the different toon-hoogten, yes?"

"He means *pitch*, Bill," Cathy said.

Bill turned in the saddle to stare at Jacob Hop, the movement making him wince. "Pitch? As in music?"

Jake nodded. "Ja, dat's what I mean. Music."

"I chose pistols over the parlor arts many years ago, Jake. You'll have to spell it out for me more clearly."

"Think of it this way. For you, this animal is a horse." Jake leaned forward to pat his mount's shoulder. "When you say it, it's like that, *horse*. When you write it, you write H-O-R-S-E."

"You mean *horsey*, Jake. *Horse* does not need an E on the end of it. Too many letters in writing are an extravagance, especially for a military man."

Cathy refrained from comment.

Jake persevered. "But maybe for Chikaak, if he wants to communicate *horse* to Ferpa, horse is this." He whistled, two high notes, then a note of lower pitch.

"Chikaak doesn't whistle," Bill said.

Cathy could no longer restrain herself. "Bill, you are being perverse. Jake's saying that if Chikaak wants to communicate the idea of a horse, he makes those notes by barking. And then if Ferpa wants to signify a horse, she does so by mooing *the same melody*. They understand each other, though they cannot produce the same sounds."

"Hell's Bells," Bill said. "You mean they are *singing* to each other, all the time."

"The ideas they share with each other this way must be simple," Jake said. "But ja, dat's exactly what I think."

Bill fairly bounced in his saddle. "Have you asked Chikaak to confirm this notion of yours?"

"No," Jake said. "But last night, when he and I worried there might be treachery planned, we agreed a signal. I suggested a whistle of three tones, because it was a sound any beastkind could hear and understand, even from far away, and he agreed."

"Heaven's curtain, friend Jake. What you're telling me is that not only have you discovered how to send military signals to the beastkind, but you've already put the new system into practice."

"I would not say it's a system, not yet."

Bill stared off into the woods ahead, eyes blazing. "We must make a list of all the commands we'll commonly need. The simpler the list, the better, friend Jake. Let's try to get it down to a dozen, to start with. Twenty at the absolute most. We'll drill them tonight."

"Ja," Jake agreed. "And we should involve Chikaak. He can help us choose words the beastkind already know."

"Melodies, friend Jake." Bill leaned over to clap the Dutchman across the back. "Melodies."

"Tell me how you came to have contacts among the Hansa." Jake had dismounted and now led his horse, so they could talk. He smiled amiably at the old man Uris. The Firstborn walked almost stepping on Jake's feet, he was so close. Jake didn't understand quite how the man's oath to Sarah worked, but he found he was extremely uncomfortable with the thought that Uris might be *compelled* to help him.

He'd rely on that in a pinch, for Sarah's sake.

For his own sake, he wanted to make friends with the man.

"You mean, how did I manage to hire a gang of Hansard dockworkers to attempt to kidnap Her Majesty?" For a moment, the Firstborn looked like a much younger man, holding a golden sword in both hands. Jake blinked and the image disappeared, and once again the man was...

What was his name?

Uris.

"I was trying to be more tactful than that, but ja." Jake nodded. "Are you a Hansard yourself? Is it secret lore, or can you share it?"

"There are League passwords and countersigns," Uris said. "I don't know them. But I have a great deal of experience working with the Hansa, as anyone must do who advises the nobles of the seven kingdoms."

"Ah," Jake said. "Tell me more. I sailed with my uncle as a boy, but only on the Atlantic coast and in the gulf." He thought, having puzzled through his shattered memory. Also, when he'd sailed as a young man, he'd been walled off from the rest of mankind by a combination of his being a deaf-mute with his uncle's bitter resentment toward him.

"Out of New Amsterdam?"

Jake nodded.

"The Hansa towns are scattered up and down the Mississippi and the Ohio Rivers," Uris said. "German Hansards on both rivers. Dutch Hansards on the Ohio, especially the upper Ohio and around the Forks, though you may know that already. That's Haudenosaunee territory, but you Dutch have always got along well with them. The odd English Hansa town here and there. Really, Hansa is a nickname, and it's borrowed from the Old World. The Hansa towns are the towns that join the Trading League by signing the Trading League Charter."

"The Charter has a longer name?"

"Yes, Hanseatic something. It probably has the names Mississippi and Ohio in it, as everything else does. I forget."

Jake considered this. "Members of this League agree to trade with each other on favorable terms."

Uris snorted. "Yes. Also, they share a list of League enemies, and banned persons, who may not stay the night in a Hansa town or trade with a Hansard. A true Hansard, of course, being a League Trader, and the Charter specifies qualifications for advancement to the status of League Trader. The requirements are onerous."

As he spoke, Uris seemed to grow taller, and then seat himself on a throne, and then assume the head of a bird. He was Jake's father, explaining the world to Jake and urging him to choose to renounce his nature and seek the paths of peace.

Only Jake knew that the man he was talking with was not his father, not Peter Plowshare, but Uris, counselor to Alzbieta Torias.

He was the Hanged Man.

As if looking through the card, Jake saw a frame of knots about Peter Plowshare, and then Peter was suddenly gone, transformed again into the man Uris.

Curious.

"A certain amount of wealth?" Jake asked. "Years of experience? Number of employees? Committed capital?"

Uris shot him a sidelong look. "You *are* Dutch. Yes, I suppose all those things. I don't know the details, not being a Hansard myself. I've been told that there are *unwritten* qualifications and traditions regarding admission as well, that are passed on verbally and memorized by League Traders."

"That sounds like a lot of work to maintain," Jake said.

"I suppose. But they band together for mutual defense, and the Hansa towns collectively are as strong as any of the seven kingdoms. Maybe as strong as any two, or as strong as the three or four weakest. And the trust between any two Hansards allows fast and quick trading, as well as the ability to move quickly and hide, when necessary."

"They send no Electors."

Uris broke into a grin. "Some would say that's only fair, given how little support they give the Empire. You've heard the saying, *paying taxes like a Hansard*?"

"Meaning, avoiding taxes entirely?" Jake guessed.

Uris touched his own nose, a gesture of understanding. As they walked, the counselor moved closer and closer to Jake, until they were practically standing in each others' shoes. Jake resisted the urge to jump away.

"But if their trading is successful, it can only be because they bring new trade goods, or higher-quality goods, or cheaper goods to those who buy from them," Jake said. "That benefits the people of the Empire."

"Ah, you Dutch," Uris groaned. "You're as bad the Scots. Who *doesn't* benefit from this trade is Thomas Penn, don't you see? Who cares that people in Chester have cheap shoes and people in Youngstown can afford to eat pecan pie?"

"You don't know any passwords," Jake said. "You just walked out and asked where you could hire kidnappers?"

"I walked to the docks," Uris said. "I'd have paid less were I Hansard myself, no doubt, or maybe I'd even have had the assistance for free. But the worst of it isn't the cash I paid."

"Your friend Sherem," Jake guessed.

Uris sighed heavily. "It's too much to call him my friend. But he is my fellow servant. He was the most brilliant of Her Holiness's servants, learned in history, geography, languages, and music, as well as in a wide range of arcane arts. And now he's an idiot."

"Calvin did not mean to, I'm certain."

"I am to blame."

"Surely not."

"Consider," Uris said. "This is what I do with my years of experience, the dust accumulated on my boots from all my travel, and the dried blood of men under my nails, is it not? I consider. I consider and I advise. Consider then with me. First, I said I had gone to seek a doctor for Sherem, who was still stunned from Her Majesty's sleep spell."

"I thought perhaps he was feigning his dizziness."

"He wasn't. Her Majesty, he told me, more than makes up in raw power what she may lack in finesse or training. But rather than seek the physician my friend needed, I hired men to attack you."

"Did you counsel with him first? Did he agree?" Jake imagined throwing the witless Polite across a wooden altar and ripping his heart out with his bare, feathered hand.

"Yes and yes, and irrelevant," Uris growled. "I should have known better. Second, my plan required the already dazed and wounded man to exert himself beyond the bounds of reason."

"*His* sleep spell. He must have felt he was getting a just revenge."

"Yes. But it was my idea. And I regret it. And third, after the Appalachee had—quite within in his rights—bludgeoned Sherem over the head, I delayed. I let my friend lie untreated while I tried to bluff, lie, and cajole our way out of the predicament in which my plan had landed us."

On an impulse, Jake put an arm around Uris's shoulder. They both stopped walking, and the older man didn't pull away. "Listen, counselor. You served your lady to the best of your ability. Your fellow-servant knew the risks, approved your plan, and had been injured. It could just as easily have been you who took a blow to the head, and you would now be lying in the palanquin, talking to yourself."

"Hard truths provide hard comfort," Uris said.

"Is that a saying as well?"

"It is now." Uris sighed.

"Hard comfort is better than no comfort," Jake said. "That can be a saying, too. And consider this: Sherem isn't dead, and may yet recover. Cathy Filmer is a healer of some skill, once a devotee of St. William Harvey. And my queen is a great magician."

"*Our* queen," Uris said.

Jake smiled and hugged the other man again.

Calvin tried to decline Bill's invitation to join the military discussions in the afternoon in order to be closer to Sarah—he told himself he didn't quite trust the Firstborn, but that wasn't really it. But Sarah was having none of it, and sent Calvin and Uris both down to participate in the planning. The two ended up watching from the trees, between the beastkind fighters on the one side and the tethered herd of horses on the other, a few paces away from each.

"We'll work out further signals over time," Bill said to Chikaak, whose tongue hung out of his head and dripped on the dark earth of the trail. "For now, we only want to experiment with three signals. Three tones each, three short melodies, if you understand my meaning."

"Three words," Jake explained.

"Given the weather," Uris said, "something not involving loading or firing muskets."

Late in the morning, it had begun to rain. The water was cold and came down in a miserly drizzle, but it was enough to confound marksmanship. Cal had been drafted into the effort to show the beastkind musketeers how to wrap the locks of their guns and plug the bores against the rain.

"We shall begin with *advance, retreat,* and *halt,*" Bill said.

Chikaak barked several times. "That will do for advance." Then he barked differently. "And that is halt, or nearly enough, as I would say it to my kind." A third time: "retreat."

It took multiple attempts, but Bill found a combination of notes on the Heron King's horn that came close to Chikaak's sounds for advance, retreat, and halt, and he did it using only three notes: high, middle, and low. Then he explained the sequences to Jacob Hop, who took the horn to try and got them right the first time.

Uris leaned to whisper to Cal. "Your Dutchman is quite the learner."

"Yeah," Cal agreed. "Remembers me of a baby in that way, starin' wide-eyed at the world and takin' it all in with no effort."

Uris raised his eyebrows in thought.

Then the beastfolk had to be taught. They stood gathered in a clearing a hundred yards from the trail, snorting and hooting and pawing at the moist earth, as Chikaak yipped and growled, then pointed to Bill, who hadn't dismounted, and said in English, "advance."

Bill blew the notes for *advance.*

The beastkind lumbered forward in a mob.

Bill blew *halt,* and they stopped.

"Again!" Bill cried. "Impress upon our men, Chikaak, the importance of moving in lockstep. Left foot together, then right, then left, you understand?"

Chikaak herded the beastmen back across the clearing, barking and snarling at them as he did so. The coyote-headed warrior pantomimed marching, then stepped aside. "They're ready to try again."

Bill blew *advance.*

Unevenly, jostling, but more or less together, the beastkind advanced. Bill laughed with glee astride his big gray horse, the beast prancing from side to side until the beastfolk were about to overtake him.

Then he blew *halt,* and the beastfolk warriors stopped.

"Hell Bells, Jake!" Bill roared. "You've done it! And Chikaak! I'd promote the both of you on the spot, only then we'd have two officers and no sergeant, and Freiherr von Steuben would have me whipped."

"By the Serpent's breath," Uris murmured. "He's learned to talk to the beasts."

"Yeah," Cal agreed. "His English is startin' to sound almost natural, too."

Through Chikaak, Bill dismissed the beastkind warriors to eat, and Cal found himself rushing after Uris to talk to Bill.

"You have accomplished the miraculous, Sir William!" the counselor cried.

"You mistake me, suh." Bill leaned forward and rested on his saddlehorn. He looked peaked after just the morning's ride. "I am no miracle-worker. I will admit, however, to having two surprising fellows in my employ."

Uris grabbed Bill's saddle like he wanted to climb up onto the horse with him. "But Sir William, please allow me to expand your vision even further."

"Further than walking forward and stopping? By all the gods, suh, you must resist the mad ambition that seeks to swallow you."

Uris laughed aloud. "You plan a combined force of pikes and muskets, yes? Or at present, muskets and bayonets?"

"It is what I have," Bill said. "I shall follow as best I can in the footsteps of old John Churchill, who taught us that infantry is the thing that advances to the enemy and shoots him to bits."

"Tonight, let us examine your warriors' gear and mine," Uris said, "and reapportion some of it. I can give you real spears, for instance, rather than short carbines fixed with bayonets."

Bill stroked his long mustache. "That would be an improvement."

"What about the horses?" Uris asked.

"Hey!" Cal objected.

The other two men turned to look at him quizzically, and he realized he didn't have a good reason to protest their use of the animals he'd been leading. "Only I reckoned we might could sell some of 'em, or trade 'em for food."

"Uris is right, Calvin." Bill's eyes gleamed. "If we can mix some of his men in with the beastkind, we can mount the others. That gives us pike, musket, and horse. The pike protects the musketry as it advances up to the enemy as close as it may, and as it retreats. The horsemen are held in reserve, either to quickly move to meet flanking attacks, or to drive forward when the enemy is in disarray, cutting him down with sword."

"A few weeks, Sir William," Uris said, "and you are ready to go to war."

Bill chuckled. "A very small war, suh. All together we may have seventy fighters."

"Gideon defeated the Midianites with only three hundred."

"Pray, suh, let us not test how our warriors drink. I would be afraid to be any fewer than we are."

"*Advance, retreat,* and *halt* were a good choice to start," Jacob Hop said. "What other commands do we need, Captain?"

"*Left face, right face. Double-time advance, full retreat, charge.*" Bill tugged at his own chin as he considered. "*Load muskets, fire. Cavalry charge* and *withdraw.* That should be enough to get us started, and we can devise more as we develop more complex movements. Ideally, I'd like to be able to communicate more precise commands in relation to the firearms: *poise, cock, half-cock, aim,* and separate commands for each step of reloading the weapon is how the blue book has it. Though naturally, we do not wish to become too elaborate. Discipline and victory are generally better served by simple commands that are hard to misconstrue. Please tell me, counselor, that your Firstborn warriors are not tone-deaf."

"On the contrary," Uris said. "We are a people with a great musical tradition. What we don't have long traditions of, though, is horsemanship."

"Tell me how it is you come to have a claim on the Cahokian throne." Sarah watched Alzbieta'a aura react as she heard the question, tightening, changing shade slightly, vibrating at a different frequency. Turmoil. Fear?

"Your Majesty." Alzbieta looked down at the ground. "I support your claim."

True.

"I don't question it. I only want to understand your right." Sarah laughed. "I want to understand *my* claim."

Alzbieta still hesitated, and now she looked past Sarah at Cathy Filmer.

Cathy looked back with hard eyes.

The three women, together with the Podebradan Yedera, waited on a low rise while Sir William put his beastkind through their three-commands-only paces a little more. Forward and back, forward and back they went. In the meantime, Jacob Hop went among the Firstborn spear- and swords-men defending the knoll and whistled short tunes to them.

Sarah's servants trained her warriors. Excellent. With seventy men she couldn't attack her uncle's legions in Philadelphia, but she might be able to take a town if she needed to, or a cadre of the chevalier's soldiers.

Or a pack of berserk beastmen in the service of Simon Sword?

The Polite Sherem hadn't recovered. Sarah looked at him now, curled at Alzbieta's feet inside the divan, counting his own fingers and toes. She saw clearly in his aura the absence of guile, the open reactions, the childlike curiosity, and the slow processing that marked him as an idiot.

Was it her fault? Any objective analysis would surely say yes, in part.

But also, her alternative had only ever been to surrender, to give up on her father's throne.

And on her sister and brother.

And where were *they* now? And were they in danger? And from whom?

So she refused the guilt her own mind offered her. The wizard had made his choices, and now he suffered for them. That was less morally offensive than Sarah's own suffering for the choices of her uncle, for instance, or for the choices of her more sinister enemy, the Necromancer Oliver Cromwell. It was less burdensome to Sarah, in the end, than the suffering she knew she was putting Calvin through by refusing to treat him as her lover.

Thinking even fleetingly of Cromwell reminded her of the Necromancer's servants for whom there had never been a proper accounting. Where had the Sorcerer Robert Hooke ended up? Sarah had last seen him through her witchy eye, torn away in the current of the Mississippi River, but not destroyed. And Ezekiel Angleton, the Covenant Tract preacher who had entered into some unholy pact with Cromwell that had become manifest on Wisdom's Bluff, had simply disappeared.

Sarah sat a horse with Cathy on another mount to one side of her, and Alzbieta in her sedan chair, carried by her eight uncomplaining slaves, to her left. Beyond Alzbieta, Yedera stood with feet apart, hand resting on her scimitar's hilt.

"You may speak in the presence of Mrs. Filmer," she said.

"No, Your Majesty. Some things I may not speak in the presence of Mrs. Filmer. Other things I may not speak in *your* presence, not *yet*. And other things still I simply may not speak *here*."

Cathy's eyes got even harder.

Sarah almost bawled the priestess out, but caught herself. "I had a counselor, too. He was also my mentor in the arcane arts. A Firstborn, like you and me." She peered through the palanquin's veil and saw the priestess's soul let slip a flash of indignation. So Alzbieta Torias didn't fully accept Sarah as one of her people. Not yet. "His name was Thalanes, and he was a monk of the Order of St. Cetes. One of the monastic orders particular to the Firstborn."

"I know well who St. Cetes is." Alzbieta's sentence began haughtily, but finished in self-imposed abnegation. "Of all the Firstborn saints, Cetes is very much on our minds these days."

"Of course you know him. Please have patience with me, cousin Alzbieta."

Alzbieta looked up in surprise.

"I am used to being the one who knows . . . well, if not everything, then an awful lot. And now I'm coming into a situation in which I know very, very little. I'll need your instruction, but I'm afraid I'm poorly suited to being a student. The only three people who have ever been able to teach me were a one-armed old man I thought was my father, who was stubborn enough to stare down the emperor himself, and this monk, Father Thalanes, and Cathy Filmer. I don't think any of them enjoyed it very much, but of the three, Mrs. Filmer has been the most gracious. I beg you to be gracious with her, in turn."

Cathy smiled, warmly but with steel in her teeth.

"Tell me more about Thalanes," Torias said.

"What I was going to say is that he told me once, late at night on a lonely road, after we'd been attacked by demonic emissaries of the Necromancer Oliver Cromwell—" she noted with satisfaction Alzbieta's shudder of fear, "that my father possessed something Thalanes called 'royal secrets.' Secrets that might, for instance, relate to the meaning and use of Cahokia's regalia. Whatever these secrets were, Thalanes couldn't know them, though he was my father's confessor. And he thought my father might have taught them to me, had he lived."

Alzbieta said nothing.

"So if you tell me you can't speak here, or you can't speak in the presence of my trusted companion, I assume that must be because the answer to my question is such a secret as those."

"Not all secrets are royal. Understand this." Alzbieta held a palm up, facing Sarah, and she drew a tight circle in its center with her finger. "Imagine that this ring contains the royal secrets. Secrets about succession. About regalia. About language. About the throne itself. About sacred spaces. About marriage."

Marriage?

"Go on," Sarah said.

Alzbieta drew a larger circle in her palm, completely surrounding the first. "This larger circle contains the secrets of the priesthood. Calendar secrets. Ritual secrets. Magical secrets, maybe, for those who are gifted in that way."

Which Alzbieta was not, Sarah could tell from her aura's tint as she said the words. A hint of disappointment. Self-loathing?

"All royal sacred knowledge is priestly, though not all priest-craft has to do with the throne."

"Kingship . . . or queenship . . . is a kind of priesthood. Not only do I know things I cannot tell you here, or now, or in the presence of others, because they are sacred, but there are things I do not know."

"Royal secrets."

Alzbieta looked down again. "Also, there are things I *should not* tell you, because I am not supposed to know them, though I do."

Intriguing. Was Alzbieta about to confess to a misdeed? "Part of your claim is that you are my father's kin."

"True. Another part of my claim is that I'm a priestess."

"The Handmaid of Lady Wisdom, you said."

Alzbieta nodded. "The Mother of All Living."

"Eve?" Sarah was puzzled.

Alzbieta said nothing.

Sarah decided to leave that one for later. "And it is part of your claim that you know secrets you are not supposed to know."

"I nursed your father once, in an illness. He was not yet married then, and his mother was conferring priesthoods and secrets upon him as fast as he could bear, priesthoods and secrets his father had tried to eradicate. Kyres was winning his fame already as the Lion of Missouri, bringing hope and justice to the battered farmers of that wild land, but a battle with a sloth had left him badly injured, and his wounds became infected."

"I hear the sloths get big in the Missouri." Sarah cracked a grin. The mere thought of enormous sloths was a relief from all this talk of throne secrets, priesthood secrets, and so on. And what exactly had her father's father been trying to eradicate?

"They've always been there," Alzbieta said thoughtfully. "I think maybe they once roamed widely over this continent, and have been reduced to a mere remnant, holding on in the woods of the Missouri."

"Because of...Peter Plowshare?" Sarah ventured.

"The Heron King?"

"The peaceful version of him, anyway. I don't see Simon Sword going out of his way to save giant sloths, unless he could turn around and use them to attack someone else."

"But Simon Sword and Peter Plowshare are the same person," Alzbieta said. "Simon Sword is merely the war title of the Heron King, as Peter Plowshare is his title in times of peace. No?"

Sarah laughed.

"Seems Sarah has something to teach you, too, Your Holiness." The look on Cathy Filmer's face bordered on smug.

Alzbieta hesitated.

"Trust me," Sarah said.

Alzbieta shrugged. "Maybe. Although maybe that land has some other special power. Maybe whatever it is that leads people to say that it is Eden has also preserved the giant sloths, the dire wolf, the aurochs, the large-toothed tiger, the tiny forest horses, and the others."

"Somebody says Missouri is Eden?" Sarah shook her head. "You get outside Appalachee, folks believe all kinds of nonsense."

"Others would say you carry your own Eden within you,"

Alzbieta said. "Is that less nonsensical? Or what of those who say that Eden can only lie where the land is plowed, that after all the garden lay *east* of Eden? But Missouri is a wild land, untamed despite the children of Adam who live there. It's a land of secrets, and of raw creation."

"You were telling me about my father."

"He was wounded, he was ill. My people found him and brought him to me, and so I nursed him. We were cousins, and friends from earliest childhood."

"First cousins?" Sarah asked.

"No, the connection is more distant. But we were friends. And...for a short while...a little more than friends. As my physicians applied unguents, balms, tonics, and poultices, as my chanters sang and my musicians played, and as my incense-priests sweetened the air about his bower, I stayed by his side. We talked when he was awake. When he was sleepy, I recited to him the lays about his ancestors who led our people here and founded the seven kingdoms. And in his sleep he dreamed, and sometimes talked."

"He told you royal secrets." Sarah was uncomfortable thinking that this distant cousin of hers had once been her father's lover, so she forced herself not to dwell on it.

"I didn't know it then. I took them for fables, or riddles, or sheer madness. He was near to death more than once, and delirious often. But then I saw that many of the queer things he told me matched images on the walls of the great sacred places in Cahokia, the Temple of the Sun and the Basilica, and I began to wonder."

"If you know secrets you're not supposed to know, are you forbidden to pronounce them?"

"I fear that I am. And of course, there are secrets I don't know. Secrets I fear may not even be written down."

"Is there a place and time in which you might be able to divulge what you heard from my father?"

"I hope so," Alzbieta said. "Though I fear that my people...our people may have lost the ability entirely to create such places. At least, we seem to have lost the ability to create the most powerful places. But perhaps, by allusion, by the artful posing of riddles, by the casual juxtaposition of two seemingly unrelated texts... I might be able to lead you to the answers."

"I could command you," Sarah said.

"I pray you don't."

"It'd be a shortcut. What you're describing sounds like it would take years of prancing about in a well-stocked library before I'd figure anything out."

"Your Majesty doesn't give herself enough credit."

"I give myself a hell of a lot of credit. But what you're talking about... it sounds pharaonic, palatine, Masonic, I don't know. Secrets inside secrets, times and places. I have no preparation for this."

"You have much more preparation than you realize."

"I can't even recite all the Electors." Sarah snorted. "If I command you, the blame's on me. The sin, whatever. It's not your fault, if I order you to do it. I'm carrying enough fault already, a little more won't hurt me."

"If you order me," Alzbieta said, "I only have to choose between two oaths. I am not certain what I would do in that moment."

Sarah knew the older woman was telling the truth. Or at least, she thought she was.

"We could find out," Sarah said. "Experiment, ain't that the way of the age?"

"I doubt you'd understand, anyway."

Sarah sucked in air, prepared to blast her cousin for the arrogance of her words, but checked herself. "What do you mean?" she grunted slowly.

"Forgive me, I've sounded arrogant, and that wasn't my intention. I mean that the nature of an initiatic secret is *not* to remain secret forever."

Sarah had no idea what her cousin was talking about. "Go on."

"The nature of an initiatic secret is to reveal itself, in the proper place and time, to a person who has been properly prepared. Like a flower opening. Like a riddle that suddenly answers itself. Like—"

"Enough similes." Sarah raised a hand to stop Alzbieta. "I... need time to think."

Alzbieta nodded. "And I have one last qualification for the throne that is very important, Your Majesty."

"If it's just the one thing, I expect I have enough stamina left to hear you out."

"I'm a woman," Alzbieta said. "That, of course, is essential."

———◆———

CHAPTER EIGHT

"I hear the Irish girls dance naked," Landon said, shooting a sidelong grin in George's direction.

~Dance with me!~

"What, all the time? Stop dreaming," Charles said.

"They dance naked when I tell them to, by the Hammer," George said.

"That's not because they're Irish," Charles said. "They do idiotic things, even things that they know are stupid, to please you. That's because they're poor, and you're rich and their master, and you're a bastard."

"Figuratively," George said.

"Thank you for reminding us." Charles looked away from the others, at the dark forest around them. The moon was in its dark phase, which left the stars brilliant, but the trail hard to follow, especially here where it picked its way through thick trees.

"At their druidic ceremonies, they dance naked," George said by way of clarification. "Those dirty old druids, they like to see everyone naked. Before they drown them in bogs or burn them in wicker men."

"I suppose they have that in common with the godar," Charles said. "And the Earls of Johnsland. And the earls' sons."

"You don't have to come along," George snorted.

"I rather think I do," Charles said. "You've picked the darkest

143

night you could to run around in the woods looking for young women. I expect you're much more likely to find a hungry highwayman, or a rabid beastwife, or just a big hole in the ground you'll fall into because you can't see it. If I let you go unaccompanied, the earl might not forgive me."

"He might not forgive you anyway," George said slyly. "Just for being Charles Lee."

"I know it." Charles sighed and patted the two horse pistol holsters alongside his saddle, confirming in the near-darkness they were still there and full.

"Hands away from your pistols, Lee," George growled.

"Do the druids dance in the dark to avoid being seen?" Nathaniel asked. The sound of his own voice rang with the aural halo of the background whine he always heard, and he cringed, hunkering down inside his coat.

"They use torches," Landon assured him. "You'll be able to see all the naked flesh you want."

"I don't want to see naked flesh. I'm curious. To understand, I mean." And he wanted to distract George and Charles from the argument that seemed to be perpetually building between them.

~Grow up, grow down, seek waters deep.~

"Seek," Nathaniel whimpered.

"Poor mad bastard," George muttered.

"They dance by the dark of the moon because they worship the moon," Landon said.

"Wouldn't they dance by the full moon instead, then?" Nathaniel was puzzled. "Or maybe they dance when the moon is new to summon it back?"

"Haven't you read your Caesar?" By the sound of his voice, George was probably sneering. "*Gallia est omnis divisa in partes tres?*"

Nathaniel didn't know what he was talking about.

"Have you ever seen these druids?" Charles asked. "Or their dancers, the famed nubile young ladies' druidic dancing troop?"

"You'll regret the scorn you show me." Landon sniffed.

"So, you haven't."

"I haven't. But George has."

"George?" Charles said.

"I have indeed seen druidic dances," George said. "But that's not why we're out here."

Charles stopped his horse. Nathaniel, who'd been following

behind him, barely avoided a collision. "You'd better explain why we're out here, then. I don't know this trail, but I'd have sworn based on the positions of Orion and the Bear relative to that hill, that we've nearly come in a circle. And with all due respect to whatever it is you might have seen somewhere and sometime, no Irish girls will be dancing naked in the woods tonight. It's November, for God's sake, and freezing."

"Say *by Woden*, rather," George said. "Or by Ing or Thunor, if you prefer. You're in Johnsland, after all."

"Are *you* allowed to curse by Woden?" Charles asked. "Without Old One Eye's permission, anyway?"

"He means the Yule log," Landon said. "And the Ride."

"I know what he means," George ground out through clenched teeth. "The Earl of Johnsland will be burning a Yule log at midwinter."

"Will he?" Nathaniel asked.

The darkness of the evening couldn't hide the look of wrath that leaped into George's face.

"Hmm. The dancing girls," Charles reminded the earl's son.

"Very well." From the shifting shadows ahead of him, Nathaniel guessed that George was leaning forward from his saddle. His voice dropped, as if he were sharing a secret. "There *are* dancing girls out here, but we've come out for something even better."

Charles sighed heavily.

~Help me, I'm buried here beside the road.~

"Help me," Nathaniel whispered.

Charles gripped him by the shoulder, and it helped. He straightened his back. The whining faded, slightly.

"Go on," Landon said.

"Whatever it is," Charles suggested. "Let's forget it. Let's go home and drink instead."

"The druids," George said, "these druid-chasing Irish we invite into our homes—"

"Plenty of them are Christian," Charles said.

"Yes, and plenty aren't. Plenty, especially the ones who pull plows and pick cotton, the ones on the fringes, follow the faith of their ancestors, a disgusting and immoral cult. None of them, of course, rides with Herne the Hunter on All Hallows' Eve, like the true men of Johnsland. None of them burns the Yule log. None knows the harmony of the Furrow and the Weald."

"Dancing girls." Landon's breath was shallow.

"Dancing girls are only the start of it. They have special priestesses they call moon-women."

"It stinks here," Nathaniel murmured. "Something smells really bad."

No one paid him any mind.

"Moon-women?" Charles snorted. "I *have* read my Caesar. Enough to know there are no moon-women. What in hell are you talking about, George?"

"Caesar didn't know everything. The druids have moon-women, whose role is not to worship the moon, but to *be* it."

Charles laughed out loud.

~Don't slaughter me!~

"Slaughter!" Nathaniel slapped at his ear, causing the others to turn and look at him, but only for a moment.

"What does a moon-woman do?" Landon asked.

"It's not what she *does*, it's what she *is*." George pointed at the sky, his arm a darker patch of black, silvered at the edges. "On the new moon, she goes to the moon-woman hut and waits there for men to come help her fulfill her destiny."

A short silence.

"What do you mean?" Landon asked. "Like ... ?"

"She is empty," George said. "She needs you to fill her."

Landon's shuddering intake of breath was loud. "With my ... ?"

"With a baby. With the baby of the waxing crescent moon, who will be born tomorrow night."

"Yes." Landon breathed out, still shaking.

"Stop this nonsense, George," Charles said. "You're making it hard for Landon to sit straight in his saddle. Look at him, the poor clod is turned nearly sideways, trying not to snap off his yard."

"It's not nonsense," George insisted. "The moon-hut is just beyond that tree."

"Moon-hut!" Charles hawked phlegm from deep in his throat and spat.

"And here's the best part of it. I've told old Murphy, he's a sort of connection to the moon-women, he organizes them ..."

"Murphy is the imaginary pimp of your imaginary brothel," Charles suggested. "Poor Murphy. I'd have expected better things of him."

"You do them dishonor!" Landon snapped. "Just because the ladies aren't Christian, doesn't mean their faith deserves no respect."

"I can practically *hear* the respect your erection is trying to give these legendary moon-women," Charles said.

"I told Murphy I had two young men here who had never called upon the moon-women before. He agreed he'd keep others away tonight, keep away the Irishmen and the secret druids of our own people, so Landon and Nathaniel could—"

"Could rut with a stranger in the fields," Charles said.

"—have a special experience," George finished.

"I'm first," Landon said quickly.

"I don't want to," Nathaniel said.

"Well, he can't go alone," George said. "If Landon is to have his special experience, he has to have a witness."

"What are you playing at?" Charles asked.

"Come on," Landon said to Nathaniel.

"I don't want to."

~Feed me, feed me.~

Nathaniel clamped his jaws shut tight and managed not to repeat the voice's words. The whine spiked to a sudden shriek and he gasped.

"All you have to do is stand in the corner. You can look at the wall if you like. Where's the moon-hut, George?"

George pointed, and Nathaniel could just make out the corner of a log-chink wall. "The entrance is on the other side. You'll have to hop that fence and turn the corner."

"What are we waiting for?" Landon snatched the reins of Nathaniel's horse and dragged him ahead several lengths.

"Wait!" George called. "This is no ordinary tryst. There are taboos."

"What does that mean?" Landon asked.

"Rules. You go in naked."

Landon laughed. "Well, of *course* you go in naked."

"No," George said. "I mean from here. You take your clothes off. Nathaniel, your witness, will carry your clothes and hold them for you in the moon-hut. You may hold his when it's his turn. I'll keep your horses."

"George," Charles protested.

"Shut up, Charles," George said. "You and I have no role here, but to wait and stand watch."

Landon slid from the saddle. He practically pulled Nathaniel from his horse and threw clothing into his arms: a coat, a tricorn hat, a greasy shirt, breeches that smelled sour, stockings that smelled worse. "Boots?"

"Best give them to Nathaniel, don't you think?" George said. "Just in case the moon-woman is particular."

"Just in case!" Landon shoved his boots on top of the pile teetering in Nathaniel's arms and then seized Nathaniel by the elbow. "Anything else I need to know?"

"The moon-hut is extremely primitive. That's part of the taboo, it's identical to huts the Irish lived in two thousand years ago. Dirt floor. No lights are allowed, that's part of the ritual. But she's expecting you, so just find her bed and do your sacred duty."

Landon dragged Nathaniel with him. In the starlight Nathaniel could see the other boy's pale shoulders and naked back; he was grateful he couldn't see more, and terrified of what he was about to see in the moon-hut.

The smell got worse as the two boys approached the hut. At the fence, Landon didn't wait, hurling himself over the split rails and landing on the other side with a soft squelching sound.

"You're mad, but your nose works," he whispered to Nathaniel. "It *does* stink. We must be near a pasture somewhere, or a bog. Don't let the druids grab you! Now come quick, if you're going to witness this heroism."

In that moment, Landon's face caught the light of the stars, and Nathaniel saw fear in the other boy's eyes.

"You know," Nathaniel said. "You know this is nonsense. What George is saying *can't* be true. Don't let George do this to you just to amuse him. Don't let George rule you like this."

He felt like the words should have come from Charles's mouth, rather than his.

Landon's face twisted from fear to indignation. "Shut up! Shut up and follow me!"

Nathaniel stumbled over the rail fence more awkwardly. Dropping most of Landon's clothing, he hesitated, and then decided simply to leave it. The other boy disappeared into a low square doorway darker than the silver-gray log-chink wall into which it was cut.

The stink was overwhelming. It was an animal stink, but Nathaniel couldn't identify quite what it was. The ground was muddy with November's rain and sucked at his boots as he followed Landon to the moon-hut. At least he had foot-gear on.

Nathaniel imagined he'd be whimpering from cold, if he were the one who was naked.

He stepped inside.

Within, the air was even closer. Nathaniel heard deep breathing sounds and realized there were several sets of lungs inhaling and exhaling slowly.

How many moon-women were there?

"I think she's in the corner," he heard Landon whisper. Then the other boy sang softly, "come to me, my lovely, let us make a child for the moon..."

Oink.

"What in seven hells?" Landon barked.

Oink, oink, oink.

Bang!

Outside, a gunshot. Then more: *bang! bang!*

"George!" Landon whispered. Then he yelled: "Nathaniel! Thunor's fist!"

Nathaniel crashed into the wall of the hut trying to get out and dropped the rest of Landon's clothes. Squishing his way across the muddy pigs' enclosure, he saw lights come on in the building on the far side.

~Come back, bring food!~

"Come back!" he shrieked. He had no idea where Charles and George were. He saw a length of split-rail fence and ran for it.

"You there! What are you doing! St. Anthony, Mary, get me gun, there's a naked man in among the pigs!" The shouting voice had an Irish accent, the accent of a servant or a tenant farmer.

Or a druid?

Nathaniel had almost reached the fence when Landon tackled him. They went down together in cold wet pig droppings, and everything Nathaniel had previously smelled was a rose by comparison. Pig feces on his face and in his mouth, he began to vomit.

"You bastard!" Landon dragged Nathaniel to his knees and punched him in the jaw. Nathaniel fell back into the muck. "You bastard, George!"

George?

But Landon kicked Nathaniel in the ribs several times. His shrieked words began with *you bastard, George, you bastard, Nathaniel,* but quickly decayed into incoherent screaming.

~Not the knife! No, I'm innocent!~

"Not the knife!" Lights flashed, and Nathaniel didn't know whether he was seeing real lights, or a falling fit was coming on.

"Get your hands off that man!" The Irish voice had a slight slur to it.

Landon paused a moment in administering his beating. Nathaniel cracked an eye and saw his tormentor, stark naked and smeared with pig droppings from head to foot, standing over him in the watery yellow light of a lantern.

A white light flashed, obscuring his view. It was a seizure. A seizure was coming on.

"Sean, that's one of the lordlings from the big house." A woman's voice. "One of the earl's sons?"

"George?" the man called. "What in hell would George Randolph Isham be doing, swiving one of me pigs in the middle of the night?"

"Hush with that sailor talk, Sean." The woman slapped the man's shoulder.

The man staggered sideways, lantern in one hand and blunderbuss in the other weaving chaotically. Landon cringed as the gun swung past him, and Nathaniel covered his ears. "I'm only saying, George Isham can do better than old Bess. Hell, she's just a sow. If he wants her, he can have her."

"Not him," the woman said. "One of the bastards. Landon."

Landon shrieked and threw his hands up to cover his face.

"Mr. Chapel!" the Irishman barked. "Good fecking hell, man, if ye want to cuddle old Bess, ye've only got to say it!"

Whatever humiliation Landon suffered, he would take it out in rage on Nathaniel. Nathaniel had to get away.

He kicked Landon hard behind his knee. The earl's bastard fell backward into the muck, feet flying skyward as he hit the ground hard. Nathaniel rolled directly away from the Irish couple and sprinted for the fence.

"And who's that, then?" Sean yelled.

"Has he hurt ye, Mr. Chapel?" Mary called.

"Shoot him!" Landon squealed.

Boom! The blunderbuss went off, but the shot missed. Nathaniel caught the top rail of the fence in his solar plexus and fell forward over it, landing again in mud that was cold and wet, but had the virtue of not being pig feces. He staggered to his feet, seeing his nude and mud-smeared fellow-bastard charging at him.

~Kill them! Kill them! Give them to the god!~

"Kill!"

Landon was humiliated. He was angry. Did he actually blame Nathaniel?

Nathaniel, who had tried to pull him back?

Nathaniel was afraid to find out. He crouched as Landon raced up to the fence, and then sprang up to smash his forehead into the other boy's nose.

Landon went down again.

Nathaniel ran. "Charles! Charles! George!"

No sign of them.

Far away, he thought he heard drums, and the roll of thunder. A dream? His own blood, sounding gigantic in his ears?

Then, definitely, he heard running feet in the autumn leaves behind him.

But Landon could never catch him. Landon's feet were bare, and the forest floor was jagged with sharp mountain pebbles, twigs, and splintered fallen branches. His vision wasn't as clear as he could want, but Nathaniel lengthened his stride to a run—

Nathaniel ran into a tree.

He smelled ash wood, and absurdly thought it was a nice change from the reek of pig droppings—and bounced backward, falling to wet earth again.

"Laugh at me, will you, George?" he heard Landon shriek. The other boy's voice sounded far away, but then suddenly hands grabbed Nathaniel, picked him up, and shook him. He saw Landon's face close up, smelling pig shit and anger.

He smelled blood, too. But Landon wasn't bleeding.

White light flashed.

"I'm not George," Nathaniel said weakly.

Landon hurled him to the ground again.

Nathaniel screamed. This was it. He was going to die.

"You will never!" Landon kicked Nathaniel in the ribs. He felt one of them break with a wet *crack*.

"Ever!" Another kick, this time to his face.

His limbs began to tremble.

"Please," Nathaniel murmured. "Please stop hurting me."

"Tell!"

Landon dragged Nathaniel to his feet again. Nathaniel tried to resist, tried to embrace Landon defensively, but he was weak from loss of blood. The other boy threw Nathaniel down again—

And this time, he kept falling. He rolled down a slope. Rocks battered him, branches tore at his flesh.

"Landon," he murmured as he tumbled end over end.

He came to a stop, unable to see anything.

"Charles," he murmured. "Charles."

Nathaniel's body shook uncontrollably.

The chevalier's yacht lay alongside one of the prison hulks and dropped anchor. The hulk stank of rotting flesh and bilgewater, but Montse's attention was drawn to the other side of the yacht, where a mass of blackened stones beneath the waterline and scorched timbers jutting up above the waves suggested a hulk had burnt to the waterline. In the clear waters of the Pontchartrain, she saw a sharp-toothed eel gnawing at skeletal remains that might be those of a man.

A recent event, then.

"The *Incroyable*," the chevalier said. "Who would believe it?" He smirked gently at his own pun, then invited Montse to walk up the gangplank to the hulk.

Montse wasn't tied or shackled. She didn't need to be, since the chevalier had Margaret back at his palace under guard. Montse was on her best behavior. She was also looking for a way to get a message out.

The gangplank was sturdy and had a handrail that Montse, river- and gulf-rat that she was, didn't need. She scampered up to the hulk, noting the name painted on the side in faded letters: *Puissant*.

No longer, she thought, but she kept her own pun to herself.

On the *Puissant*, she waited until the chevalier joined her. His gendarmes remained on the yacht, and the hulk's crew of jailers, who muttered and chirped like idiots, mostly kept their distance, skulking at the edges of the ship's deck.

"If you've brought me here to imprison me," she said, "you're taking very little care to prevent me from jumping into the Pontchartrain."

Gaspard Le Moyne smiled, like a fox. "Isn't the child's welfare enough?"

Montse shrugged, pretending a nonchalance she didn't feel. She and Margaret had both denied that the girl had any connection with the Penn family—Margaret sincerely and with growing bafflement, since Montse had, true to her charge, never told her. "My niece Margarida is a good hand, and I'd be sad to lose her."

The chevalier chuckled. "Good. You're not here to be imprisoned. You're here to meet someone. Follow me."

He descended a steep ladder belowdecks. Montse followed, wishing her weapons hadn't been taken away.

The hulk retained its individual cabins, though many of the doors were rotting on their hinges and some of the walls themselves had been eaten away by the salt water of the Pontchartrain. The holes in the hull and in the deck above let in enough light to see. The chevalier led the way aft, to a large cabin. Montse had never served in any navy, but she had captured enough naval vessels to guess that this cabin would once have belonged to the captain of the *Puissant*.

Perhaps a quarter of the windows retained their glass. Others retained their wooden shutters. Many were now simply gaping holes, and a breeze came through the cabin. In hot weather, those shattered windows would be a blessing to anyone in the cabin, but in a storm, they would let in all the Pontchartrain's fury.

The cabin's single occupant lay chained in the corner, sprawled on his back out of reach of the door and the windows alike. He was old and thin, and the faintest smear of rouge persisted under a crust of grime and salt. His breeches, once fine and black, were stained with gray spots by the sea, and his once-white shirt was mottled dark brown with old, dried blood. His face was built on fine, high bones. Wispy hair circled his skull like a tangled cloud.

"Don Luis Maria Salvador Sandoval de Burgos," the chevalier said. "Until recently, a prominent merchant in our international shipping trade. Silver and rum imported, and cotton taken away, mostly."

The Spaniard raised a single blue-veined eyelid and stared at the chevalier, a faint smile curling his lip. "Y ahora, gracias a Dios," he said, "a man who has again found his soul."

"Though not, as you might suppose, through monastic spiritual exercises aboard my ship," the chevalier said. "Rather, Don de Burgos regained his soul, if that's how you wish to describe his change of heart, by attempted murder."

The Spaniard spat, a tiny spray of spittle that settled on his own chest. "I should have killed your son myself. That would have been an honorable duel."

The chevalier nodded. "And we would be here, in exactly the same circumstance, no doubt."

"It's against the law to duel in New Orleans," Montse said. She wasn't a duelist herself, favoring poison or a knife in the kidneys to giving an enemy an open shot at her, face to face. "Shouldn't you hang this man?"

"Perhaps I will," the chevalier admitted. "But not yet. He has a nephew who claims he can raise a ransom, in which case I may yet free Don de Burgos to ply the waters of the Caribbean and the Atlantic, provided he no longer sets foot in my city."

"In case you and I are to become fellow-ascetics," Montse said to the old man, "I have something to confess."

"Something against me?" Don de Burgos smiled. "I forgive it, freely."

"I've stolen from you. I know your name, Don. Also, I've competed against you, and unfairly. I have . . . not fully cooperated with the chevalier's customs men."

De Burgos chuckled drily. "If not you, then your cousin. I hear Catalonia in your accent. I forgive you still."

"You aren't going to become a nun of the *Puissant*, Mademoiselle Ferrer i Quintana. At least, not unless by your own choice." The chevalier leaned against the wall and crossed his arms over his chest. "I've brought you here so you could see your choice clearly."

Over the cypress trees on the far side of the Pontchartrain Sea, storm clouds gathered.

"One possibility is to be chained in this wreck," Montse said. "You brought me to see Don de Burgos so I'd understand that you're willing to imprison even powerful and wealthy men aboard the hulks. If you'd do this to the worthy don, how much worse would you do to me, a common criminal?"

Lightning across the sea flashed in the chevalier's eyes. "But fortunately, you're not a common criminal. You are Montserrat Ferrer i Quintana, captain of *La Verge Caníbal*."

"Eh." Montse shrugged.

"Once companion and friend of Hannah Penn."

Thunder.

"That was a long time ago," Montse said. "I didn't very much improve the Empress's reputation by hanging about in her company. And if you're hoping I can win you some favor at the court in Philadelphia, then I think you misunderstand the relationship between Thomas and Hannah."

The Spaniard on the floor cackled, but the chevalier was untroubled.

"No, I'll send you to an entirely different court. I assume you know that Margarida, your *niece*, wasn't an only child."

"Oh?"

"She's a triplet, one of three children born living at the same time."

The chevalier knew. What was this conspiracy whose agents he had unmasked?

And how *much* did he know?

"Tell me what you'd like me to do."

"Margarida's sister, who speaks with an Appalachee accent as thickly as Margarida does with her *accent català*, is currently making a bid to regain their father's throne in Cahokia. You'll be my ambassador to *her* court."

Montse took a deep breath. "You have many servants already, My Lord Chevalier. Why not send one of them?"

The chevalier smiled faintly. "I think she'll take the message more seriously if it comes from you."

"And what missive am I to bear to this Appalachee Cahokian Penn?"

The Chevalier of New Orleans smiled. "A simple one. That you're the embassy I promised to send her, and that my wedding gift to her will be her sister's life."

The turnout for the vigil the night before had been impressive, but the crowd that came to participate in the funeral liturgy of their beloved Bishop of New Orleans was staggering. It flowed out all the doors and halfway across the Place d'Armes. Armand had told Etienne an hour before he began the ceremony that the dueling ground behind the cathedral was also full. Etienne had quickly posted men at each cathedral door, choosing those he knew to have large lungs and voices that carried.

A man who could bellow across the crowded floor of the casino on Saturday night and make himself heard was a man who could pass on the words spoken, sung, and prayed inside the cathedral on Sunday morning.

These were not, by and large, the same people who had

participated in the funeral procession Etienne had led earlier through the Vieux Carré and the Faubourg Marigny. These were churchgoers, the pious, and the citizenry of New Orleans too respectable to participate in a Vodun parade.

Etienne felt the power of the crowd in the air as he welcomed them from the pulpit. He felt it in his bones, like electricity, when he took his father's aspergillum and used it to sprinkle holy water on the coffin containing nothing to do with his father, and instead an effigy of his father's murderer. The aspergillum was a short rod with a perforated ball on its end, and he imagined it as a mace, crushing the chevalier's skull as he repeatedly struck it. This mental act was no idle fantasy, but part of the magical assault he was building. Etienne spoke such words of love and welcome as "I am the resurrection, and the life" and "blessed are they that mourn," and in his heart he gave free reign to hatred.

In his heart: *vengeance is mine.*

He felt the energy of the crowd during the Penitential Act, as they cried repeatedly for mercy. He had adjusted his houngan's sash to fit over the bishop's priestly vestments, wearing it now from right shoulder to left hip. The power that came to him through the crowd caught in the sash and spun around him, filling him, burning him, warding him, expanding him to gigantic stature.

The energy swelled nearly to the point of exploding when he led them in the *Kyrie Eleison* chant. The crowd must have felt it as well, and it distracted them from noticing that Etienne changed the words after the first iteration from *kyrie eleison*—Lord, have mercy—to *kyrie kteinon*—Lord, kill.

His gede loa had helped him with that; he was no Greek scholar, but apparently there were many Greek among the dead willing to help him in his quest for vengeance.

For the chant, Etienne held a wafer of the host, consecrated in a previous ceremony, in his mouth. It was an old houngan's trick to channel stolen powers of heaven into your magical deed, and it was a good one. He also held his mother's locket concealed in the palm of his left hand the entire time. Of that, neither his father nor even his judgment-prone brother Chigozie could disapprove.

He led the congregation in singing the ninety-fourth Psalm.

Lord, how long shall the wicked, how long shall the
  wicked triumph?
They slay the widow and the stranger, and murder
  the fatherless
But the Lord is my defense; and my God is the rock
  of my refuge
And he shall bring upon them their own iniquity
And shall cut them off in their own wickedness
Yea, the Lord our God shall cut them off

It was not the entire psalm, but Etienne's own selection of the psalm's words. A hired quartet of Igbo musicians had written an appropriately dirgelike melody for the words, and the quartet's singer and bandleader led the congregation.

Etienne preached his sermon on Genesis thirty-four. He kept it short and focused on the need for active response to acts of great evil. If anyone noticed that he failed to condemn Simeon and Levi for murdering the Shechemites who had raped their sister, or for abusing the rite of circumcision by using it to render the Shechemites vulnerable, they kept it to themselves.

If any gods objected, they didn't make their concerns known, either.

He shuddered with the power of the rite.

For the closing doxology, Etienne offered the Lord's Prayer from Matthew six, again with a slight amendment of his own. "Forgive us our debts," he cried, and then lowered his voice to mutter, "as we *pursue* our debtors."

The crowd duly asked for forgiveness.

"Amen."

The energy that had been building for the entire rite in Etienne and his vestments flowed through him and was gone.

Into the coffin? Into the Chevalier of New Orleans?

Was it done? Was the man now dead, or would Etienne's spell require time to play itself out?

Exhausted, Etienne leaned on the altar for support.

Throughout, Etienne's men stationed in the doorways did their best, calling out what they could hear to the multitudes outside, or describing what they were witnessing. No one objected at any point; they were not pious enough to know the proper rite, or not focused enough to notice Etienne's alterations. They were too grief-stricken still at the loss of their humble bishop to cavil if one of the funeral liturgy's ushers reordered a few words here and there or identified the *Kyrie* as "Carry Me, Elation."

And how did they feel about the bishop's replacement?

At the very least, for a debut appearance as a Christian cleric, Etienne had brought in a large crowd.

"Now let us give the kiss of peace." Etienne straightened up and steadied himself with a deep breath. His Brides, awoken and aroused by the rite and participating in it with all the concentrated venom of their will, wanted kisses. He kissed the deacons and old Père Tréville from the Faubourg Marigny, who had helped Etienne organize the funeral rite in innocent ignorance of Etienne's true intent, but these did not satiate the Brides.

He descended through the rood screen to kiss parishioners.

Etienne did not intend to seek specifically female mass-goers, but the Brides drove him to them. Or perhaps the Brides drove the women to their houngan husband by the *maryaj-loa*, but Etienne found himself kissing one woman after another. They were Igbo, Bantu, Catalan, German, Spaniards, Cavaliers, Cherokee—all the many-colored races of New Orleans, but especially French.

They were all beautiful.

Each kiss fed his loa brides. Each kiss restored a little of the energy he had lost.

Sweat poured down Etienne's skin beneath the heavy chasuble and stole. His nostrils filled with the spiced scent of women eager for him.

The Brides.

The Brides and, under their invisible and irresistible influence, the women of the congregation.

He felt lightheaded, and leaned against a pillar.

Far back in the nave of the St. Louis Cathedral, Etienne saw men coming for him.

Beware, my son.

At the tingle he felt in his mother's locket, Etienne became alert. He looked closer at the men. They were tall and lean, not with the underfed emaciation of beggars but with the fighting muscle of leopards. They dressed strangely, even for New Orleans, in padded pourpoints that covered them from neck to wrist, and then dropped halfway to their knees. They wore silk scarves wrapped around their heads, concealing their faces but for their eyes. Long beards emerged from the folds of the scarves to tumble down their quilted chests.

At their waists, they carried curved swords.

To go armed in New Orleans was no particular distinction. It was the unarmed person who was extraordinary. But these men looked foreign, like fighters of the Old World in centuries past. They looked like warriors of the Caliphate. What mussulman would come to pay respects at the funeral rites of a dead Christian bishop?

And what funeralgoer would walk with such a blaze of determination in his eyes?

He counted three of them, coming up the nave.

A quick look at the side chapel told Etienne that that door too was blocked by two such men.

There would be men in the back, too. He was trapped.

Etienne had brought his own men in only limited numbers. After all, they had the casino to operate and protect, for those who might choose to mourn the bishop's passing by playing a hand of faro. And Etienne didn't think he had enemies who would be so brazen as to strike at him here, in the crowd.

Disgruntled members of the Synod? Unlikely.

Chigozie? Impossible.

The Chevalier of New Orleans. It had to be him. Maybe the chevalier anticipated Etienne's arcane assassination attempt, or maybe he simply saw naked ambition in Etienne's anointing as bishop and moved to cut off a threat.

He dared not escape through the crypt—to do so with all these witnesses would give away the existence of that very useful passage.

He turned to the Brides. First, he put the gede loa locket into a pocket in the shirt beneath his chasuble, feeling its tingle transfer from his palm to his side; his mother had arranged his maryaj-loa, as a mambo herself and as his mother, but that was no reason for her to see the Brides in action.

Etienne's mother had raised him with a sense of good manners.

"Ezili Freda," Etienne murmured, leaning to kiss a parishioner. She was a short woman, stocky and blonde, possibly a cheese-paring Republican or a German. He kissed her cheek and didn't let her go, drawing her instead to his side.

He felt her heat against him, and it was comforting.

She smiled. "Pax vobiscum."

"Ezili Danto." Etienne kissed another woman, dark-haired

and well-dressed, perhaps an Italian or a Spaniard. Tears had burrowed long wet streaks in what had been elaborate make-up. He drew her to his other side, feeling the fire of her body, too.

She smiled and clung to him. "Pax vobiscum."

"Bring them to me, my Brides," Etienne whispered. "Bring them all to me."

A sound like a low moan rushed through the cathedral. Women who were already moving toward Etienne to give their new young bishop the kiss of peace moved faster. Women who had been grieving at the coffin, or whispering beneath the cathedral's stone pillars to share their loss, turned and joined the throng.

"Pax vobiscum, pax vobiscum."

Etienne felt the ecstatic charge of the Brides' action shiver through his limbs. He would know none of these women carnally; he was married to the Brides, and they were the most jealous of women. But every woman in the cathedral, he knew, wanted him at that moment. If he did not prevent it, they would fall in love with him. Some would go away convinced they *had* become his lovers, and carry secret smiles in the corners of their mouths for weeks.

They would all obey him, at least to a point.

The women surged toward him.

Etienne couldn't control the Brides. They weren't his to command, any more than his mother was. They were goddesses, and he was their exclusive husband. But as any husband could do, he was able to invite their presence. He was able to court them, flirt with them, tease them until they took him.

Already trembling from the funeral liturgy, they took him now.

Etienne sagged, quivering, into the arms of the two women holding him. Others joined them and he kissed every face he could see. Kisses on cheeks became kisses on lips, and Etienne had to wrap his chasuble tightly about him to keep it from hungry hands. The women surging around him from all sides pushed him to his feet again.

The four approaching men half-drew scimitars and then resheathed them as a river of women flowed past them. The women jostled the mussulman fighters, knocking two of them down and earning a shouted curse.

The women didn't slow down.

"Pax vobiscum! Pax vobiscum!"

"I'm weak," Etienne said, kissing a dark woman with long, curly hair. "Will you help me outside for a breath of fresh air?"

They carried him. He was strong and young, having come up in Bishop de Bienville's mob as a sticks and stones man—it had amused the pox-ridden old bishop that righteous Father Ukwu's son wanted to learn the criminal trades. It might have amused him less to know that Etienne would win the fight to succeed him as criminal underlord of the Vieux Carré.

It would have amused him *much* less to know that he would eventually also follow him as bishop, and would use that office to perform acts of Vodun magic. The bishop had been a cheerful sinner, but he'd been a cheerful Christian sinner.

Weaker muscles and looser joints than Etienne's might have been torn apart by the pack of women. Like a pride of lionesses with a wounded deer, they dragged him toward the side door of the cathedral, tossing men aside as they went.

The two scarf-wrapped warriors stood in the door, others having moved aside or been moved. Armand lay on the stone floor behind them, clutching his side to stanch a strong flow of blood and glowering furiously. Etienne had insisted that his men not wear pistols to the cathedral for this service, and Armand had paid the price. Both warriors had drawn scimitars.

They had bested Armand, unarmed as he was.

Against the women, they never stood a chance.

Accelerating and howling, the women struck the two swordsmen like a storm. Several took wounds, but then the scimitars were in the hands of the women, and the warriors lay on the floor, taking kick after kick to the face and stomach.

"Pax vobiscum! Pax vobiscum!"

The whirlwind of loa-maddened femininity swept Armand into its protective embrace, and then Etienne and his bodyguard were outside, standing on the cobbles in front of the Polites' palace. Running toward them from the dueling ground came a dozen of Etienne's men in white shirts and black waistcoats, holding knives and pistols.

In the doorway, the two battered mussulman fighters dragged themselves to their feet and stared. Four others joined them from behind. Two made as if to charge, but the tallest restrained them, a hand on the shoulder of each.

"Thank you, my daughters," Etienne said. He kissed each woman again, retreating into the arms of his men with the wounded Armand, and waving farewell to his stunned attackers.

"Pax vobiscum."

"I'm just a man who has seen his manidoo."

———◆———

CHAPTER NINE

In the darkness, Ma'iingan lost the healer.

He had followed the four young men easily at first; they were on horseback, after all, and had been drinking. The combination of horse and ordinary night noises with the dulling of their senses would have let twenty Anishinaabe walk behind them on the trail in single file.

One reasonably skilled hunter had it easy.

Ma'iingan carried his loaded German gun ready, just in case, but the four Zhaaganaashii never saw him.

He wasn't worried only about the Zhaaganaashii; there were also the Irish. The Irish were a new people to Ma'iingan. Most of them spoke English, but they had another tongue, an older language of their own, so they were a different people. They seemed to have come in under the feet of the Zhaaganaashii, but had never advanced far inland. Here, in what Ma'iingan had learned was called *Johnsland*, after an old Zhaaganaashii king in their original homeland named *John Churchill*, the Irish planted and harvested on land owned by the great Zhaaganaashii lords. Apparently, there were also Irish in the big cities of the Turtle Kingdom, such as New Orleans and New Amsterdam.

A Cherokee teamster had confided to Ma'iingan over a cup of coffee that in the cities the Irish had mostly become Anama'e, like the French, the Dutch, and most of the Zhaaganaashii. Here,

162

many of them were something else, something the muleskinner called *druid*. Ma'iingan had never heard of *druid* before, but he was far from home and learning many new things. But since *druid* apparently sacrificed people to their manidoo, Ma'iingan slept by his loaded gun.

When the young chief George had sent the healer Nathaniel and Landon, the unruly warrior who teased Nathaniel too much, toward the pig sty to sleep with a druid moon woman, though, Ma'iingan had immediately recognized a prank. A good teller of jokes could spot the jokes of others.

Even when those others' jokes were cruel and petty.

When George had fired his guns into the air, summoning the Irish farmers from their hut, Ma'iingan had crept deeper into the forest to hide. When he'd emerged, Nathaniel and Landon had disappeared.

"Wiinuk," Ma'iingan cursed.

He skirted the confusion of the two Irish farmers squabbling as they reloaded their gun and the two Zhaaganaashii, still on horseback and now arguing. Charles was angry, but he was holding back his rage because George was his chief.

"He'll make his way back to his sty," George said.

"He's just a boy," Charles said. "They're both just boys, George."

Abruptly, a naked man loomed up in the darkness. With no moon, for a moment he looked enormous, pale and covered in raw earth, and Ma'iingan almost took him for a manidoo of some sort, and raised his rifle—

but then smelled the sour reek of animal droppings.

The naked man was Landon, and he screamed.

"Stop, please." Ma'iingan lowered his rifle and spoke in his clearest Zhaaganaashii. "You surprised me, I am not at war with you. You see, na?" He held his arms wide to show peaceful intentions. "My name is Ma'iingan, and I'm a friend."

Landon screamed again and charged.

Ma'iingan just dodged. He didn't want to hurt the boy, and he also didn't want to touch him, given his foul reek. Landon clawed at Ma'iingan's face twice, and then tried to punch him, but finally gave up and ran away into the forest.

Leaving Ma'iingan alone.

He was a man whose family never went hungry for lack of game. On a night with no moon, though, he wasn't going to be able to see any indications on the ground. He stood silent and listened awhile, considering.

The sounds of the Zhaaganaashii exploded in yelling, and then faded away in three different directions. Landon: shamed and fleeing? George: returning to the big house in satisfied triumph? Charles: perhaps looking for Nathaniel?

But Charles had quickly gone too far, unless Nathaniel was running away from the pigsty at a full sprint and in a straight line.

Silence descended again. Had Nathaniel run so far away he couldn't be heard? Was he dead? With a heavy heart, Ma'iingan picked a crooked pine between two chest-high spikes of rock. It was distinctive enough to be a landmark, and he kept his eye on it.

Then he began slowly spiraling outward around it.

In daylight, he'd have looked at the ground, seeking tracks. Instead, he looked for hiding places and peered into them: beneath fallen logs, behind boulders, up trees, within thickets. Nathaniel may have escaped by concealing himself, but Ma'iingan was a keen-eyed finder of hidden things.

As it happened, he was so focused on peering into the shadows that he almost walked past Nathaniel.

The boy's incoherent moan gave away his location, at the base of a short, steep slope. When he heard the sound, Ma'iingan had to look twice to spot the boy, because he lay in the shadow of a thick pine tree. The starlight was enough to let Ma'iingan see his blood, oozing from multiple injuries.

Ma'iingan shuddered. His manidoo had understated the case; the boy Nathaniel didn't need to be raised from a sickbed, he needed his life saved.

By feel as much as by sight, Ma'iingan examined the young man. There was a lot of blood, but it flowed from many small wounds, rather than from a severed artery. Nathaniel's skull was intact, and although he had cuts on his chest and back, he wasn't pierced through the body. He had a broken rib. His breathing wasn't as regular as Ma'iingan would have liked.

Mercifully, the boy was unconscious.

Ma'iingan began by laying his wool blanket out beside Nathaniel, and then carefully dragging the boy onto it. The bleeding immediately got worse; he took the boy's shirt off, tearing it into strips. He bound Nathaniel's wounds with the cloth, slowing the bleeding and then watching in satisfaction as the worst of the wounds, in one of the boy's arms, finally clotted.

Ma'iingan started a fire.

He kept it small, drilling flame with a firebow into a dried piece of wood, then feeding it chips and twigs until it could breathe on its own. Finally, he took his axe and collected large dead branches from the nearby pines, feeding the limbs one at a time into the fire.

He found a stream nearby. With rolled strips of birch bark he fashioned a pot, filled it, and then boiled the water on his small fire. Deep in the night as dawn began to pale the sky in the east, he cleaned Nathaniel's injuries with boiled water. That started the blood flowing again in some of the wounds, but this time the flow stanched easier. Ma'iingan bound the wounds again with new strips of cloth.

As the sun rose, he helped Nathaniel into a sitting position for a few moments. The boy was only half-conscious, but he was lucid enough to sip at the edge of the birch-bark pot and drink the now-cooled water. Ma'iingan kept pouring water into his mouth until he turned his head away and coughed, and then he laid the boy down.

Nathaniel's forehead was hot, and he was beginning to sweat.

"Gichi-Manidoo," Ma'iingan muttered, dropping into an unintended prayer. "Help this boy. I need this boy to bring my son Giimoodaapi into the People. I need this boy to arise from his sickbed and become the great healer my manidoo promised me he would be, so that Giimoodaapi may eat and grow strong. Heal him, Gichi-Manidoo. Knit his flesh, restore his blood, revive his spirit. Give *me* the wisdom to help him heal himself."

If anything, Nathaniel's fever burned hotter.

Ma'iingan rose and began to search the hillside in the early morning light for anything he might make into a tea.

Nathaniel opened his eyes.

Overhead, he saw the skeletal branches of a dead and barkless ash tree, and beyond it, pale sky.

He hurt.

~The boy is not dead.~

~He is not dead yet.~

"Not dead yet."

His mouth tasted tangy, acidic. Like pine needles, or a nettle soup, or maybe wild berries.

He smelled fire. He smelled...the intimate smell of another person, as if he were wearing someone else's clothes. Not a bad smell, just the smell of a stranger.

Realizing he lay on his back, he tried to raise his head to look down at himself. A bolt of lightning split his skull and he collapsed backward again. His ears rang with high-pitched whining.

"You must feel great pain," a voice said. He didn't know the accent, but the person's speech was deliberate, slow. "The dogwood brought your fever down, but you've been seriously wounded."

~Release me, O thou earth!~

Nathaniel mouthed the words, but he was too weak to pronounce them.

He turned his head slowly to one side to look. An Indian sat cross-legged a few feet away, looking closely at him. The man didn't wear the trousers and coat of a Cherokee, or the colorful shirt of a Haudenosaunee. He was bare-chested, and wore leather leggings and moccasins, and he seemed to be unarmed. His broad face was handsome, with jet-black hair, strong jaw and cheekbones, a high forehead, and clear eyes. His mouth was set in a cryptic, expressionless line.

No—there, a few feet away, a bow and a rifle and an axe all lay against a fallen log. The man wasn't unarmed, but he was deliberately sitting away from his weapons.

~I itch, I burn!~

Nathaniel tried to scratch his ear and found he couldn't raise his arm. His head pounded.

"Do I still have my arms and legs?" he asked.

"Henh." The Indian nodded. "I just wrapped you up tight. It was cold."

"Thank you," Nathaniel said.

"We're pretty far out here in the forest, and I don't know if you're going to be walking anytime soon. We get hungry, we might have to eat one of your legs. Maybe I should just take it off now, hang it up and let it start drying, na?"

The casual tone of the Indian's voice and his completely straight face struck terror into Nathaniel's soul.

Then the man laughed, his face breaking into a crinkled grin. "I'm joking, Zhaaganaashii. Where's your sense of humor?"

Nathaniel's heart pounded. "Maybe it's tied up. Like the rest of me."

"You're not tied up, Zhaaganaashii. You're *wrapped* up, like a dakobinaawaswaan. Like a baby, na? Wrapped in a cradleboard, so it can't run away from its mother."

"You don't want me to run away?"

"Maybe I look like your mother, na?" The Indian laughed again. "No, I would be a very ugly mother and you're much too good-looking. I don't want you to hurt yourself. You knocked yourself pretty good falling down that hill, and you bled a lot. I wrapped you to help keep you from opening the wounds by moving too much."

"I didn't knock myself. And I didn't just fall down that hill." The whining in his ears grew more shrill, making it hard for Nathaniel to even produce words.

The Indian nodded. "No, it was your friend, Landon."

Nathaniel stared. "Who are you?"

The Indian ground at the dirt with his moccasin heel. "I'm going to stop calling you Zhaaganaashii, because I know your name. Your name is Nathaniel."

"What is Zhaaga . . . anyway?"

"It means English. English-speakers. Cavaliers and Yankees and Appalachee and Pennslanders, you're all Zhaaganaashii."

"In Lenni Lenape?" It was a guess.

"No, I'm not one of the grandfathers. I'm Ojibwe, or Anishinaabe. However you want to say it."

"One of the Algonk peoples? Like the Massachusett or the Natick?"

"Henh." The Indian laughed. "If I can lump all you Zhaaganaashii together, I guess you can lump together the Algonks."

Nathaniel felt the urge to sing. It was childish, but he was tied up like a baby, so he went ahead:

> *Look east, look west, look here, look there*
> *Algonk Electors come from everywhere*
> *Outside the empire, they're "wild" or "free"*
> *Those inside send Electors three:*
> *Wampanoag, Massachusett, Mi'kmaq, Sauk*
> *Nanticoke, Chickahominy, Shawnee, Fox*
> *Mohican, Chippewa*

Abenaki, Ottawa
Look north, look south, look up, look down
Thirty-six votes for the empire's crown

As the song ended, Nathaniel realized that the ringing in his ears had stopped. He held his breath and said nothing, hoping the din might have disappeared permanently.

"Henh." The Indian smiled. "That's me, Chippewa. Or Ojibwe, or Anishinaabe. Same thing. I guess Chippewa rhymed best."

"How do you know my name?" Nathaniel asked. The shrieking sound returned, but softer than it had been.

The Ojibwe's face grew serious. "I've come a long way to meet you, Nathaniel. I need you to help my child, and I'm supposed to help you first. You see, I've been told you can heal my son Giimoodaapi."

"Are you some sort of wizard?" Nathaniel asked. He had never imagined the magical college in Philadelphia teaching Algonk adepts, but what did he know? "Or a medicine man?"

"Oh, no," the Ojibwe said. "I'm no Midewiwin. I'm just a man who has seen his manidoo. My name is Ma'iingan. It means *wolf*, in Zhaaganaashii."

"My name means *god has given*. That's what the parson says, anyway, when he tries to get me to come to his church. In Greek, I suppose, or Latin."

"Maybe Gichi-Manidoo has given you a wolf then, na?"

Nathaniel grinned. "So far, it's better than everything else He's given me." He turned his head back to look up through the tree branches. "Where am I?"

"That's the hill Landon threw you down." Ma'iingan pointed. "That means you're in Johnsland. You're out in the forest, beyond where the earl's Irish farmers live and where his priests kill sheep."

"I feel very far from home."

"Not so far. But all distances look long to a baby in a cradle-board, na?"

"How did you find me, and how do you know my name?"

"I had a vision." From his smile, the Indian might have been telling a subtle joke. "I saw my manidoo. I went looking for him so he could help my son, and he showed me where to find you."

"On a map?"

"In the vision. I've traveled in the Turtle Kingdom before, so I know the biggest rivers and the big lakes."

"The Turtle Kingdom. Do you mean the Empire?"

"Henh. All this land is Turtle Island. On account of it's on the back of a very large turtle, which Nanaboozhoo piled high with dirt. Or a muskrat, some say. Or maybe Nanaboozhoo *is* a muskrat. It's hard to tell sometimes, with those old stories."

"We mostly call it the New World."

"Henh, you Zhaaganaashii would do that. But then, you got here late, so it's new to you. And I know your name because I heard you and your friends talking the other day. I saw you when you were hunting."

"They're not really my friends."

"Henh. Charles, maybe, na?"

"Yes, Charles. George is the earl's legitimate son. Landon is also the earl's son. He's not legitimate, but that doesn't really matter. They both don't like me and they don't have to respect me."

Ma'iingan's face looked sad. "Henh. Well, I heard them say your name. Nathaniel. God-Has-Given. And for today, I think you should conclude that Gichi-Manidoo has given you another chance, because if I hadn't come along on the path shown to me by my manidoo, you would have died a cold and lonely death."

Nathaniel nodded slowly. "I would have died. No one will look for me."

"No? Why not? You have friends. At least Charles. Maybe the earl, the man whose house you live in, na? It's a big house."

"The earl won't care. I'm just a foster child, just a mouth to feed. And Charles didn't look for me when he could have."

"I think he did. But he went the wrong way. Maybe he'll come back later and find us here, na? But for now, you lie still. I'm going to cook a rabbit. Don't get too hungry, though, Zhaaganaashii Nathaniel, today you only get the broth."

The broth of a boiled rabbit sounded very good to Nathaniel. Before he could say *thank you*, or ask whether the Ojibwe planned to return him to the earl's big house, he found himself drifting back to sleep.

~*Listen to him, listen to him, listen to him.*~

The *Joe Duncan* slid smoothly into place at the end of the pier. Two men working paddles up front—a German from Youngstown named Schäfer and a Haudenosaunee whose name sounded like Dadgayadoh and who wore fringed leather leggings, a red blanket over one shoulder, and a black top hat—leaped to the dock and steadied the craft.

The *Joe Duncan* was a big canoe, built of light wood and painted Imperial blue. As a nod to economy, the canoe did without gold trim or the Company's seal—two stags rampant standing in a single long canoe, holding between them a shield on which was painted an outline of the courses of the Mississippi and Ohio Rivers, with a pitchfork-holding farmer standing inside the junction beside his mule and plow, and a beaver on all fours atop the shield—painted on its hull. Ironically, as the company's only canoe of that size without trim, seal, or name, the economy made the craft instantly recognizable as the *Joe Duncan*.

It was a really big canoe; Luman had seen it hold at one time fifteen adults, along with bales of furs, personal gear for all fifteen, and the "cash box," which in fact held very little cash, but was a waterproofed chest kept inside an oiled leather bag, mostly holding papers of various sorts—trading post balances, log books, order books, and drafts for money. The drafts were negotiable, but weren't the sort of money a highwayman would generally think of as cash.

Very few robbers would be bold enough to walk into a bank or a goldsmith's shop and demand to redeem stolen certificates.

So water damage was a bigger worry than theft.

In a pinch, the *Joe Duncan* would probably hold more than twenty. Now its customary crew of eight made the director's canoe secure, and two men with long rifles sat in it, fore and aft, watching both banks of the river for any sign of a threat. Mostly, they watched the Parkersburg side of the water.

The Imperial Ohio Company made regular use of oversized canoes like the *Joe Duncan*; they were hard to sink and could be portaged, which made them useful craft for a region bounded by four great lakes and two enormous rivers, and fissured by innumerable smaller waterways. What made the *Joe Duncan* noteworthy was that it carried one of the Company's five directors. The other four, all of whom were men, were generally to be found in an office near the eastern end of the Ohio or even in Pennsland, or occasionally in an ornate carriage on one of the Imperial pikes.

Notwithstanding Schmidt, the only woman of their number, spent most of her time in the west. She generally traveled by this canoe; Luman couldn't decide whether that, too, was a matter of economy, or a gesture of solidarity with her traders, or a point of personal style, or whether perhaps she simply found it convenient to go by boat in a land of many waters.

He still had no idea why the canoe was called the *Joe Duncan*.

The eight men paddling the canoe made it secure and then waited. They were armed, as anyone not a fool traveling in the Ohio was, but they weren't soldiers. They were porters and traders, Imperial Ohio Company men, and they were doing their best to look as innocuous as possible.

Oldham, the man who was to remain behind, stayed with them. He whistled some Pennslander hymn Luman didn't recognize, and stared across the river at Adena forestland.

Luman Walters followed Notwithstanding Schmidt up the pier to Parkersburg. The afternoon air was cool and descending with the sun toward chilly; he smelled woodsmoke and roasting meat.

Luman knew the plan and was prepared. While Schmidt carried only a packet of papers in an oilskin envelope, Luman carried all the magical paraphernalia he could, as usual, stuffed into the many pockets of his long, custom-made travel coat.

In addition, he carried a small wooden box in one hand. The box had small air holes drilled in the top, and every few minutes it shuddered slightly in his grip.

Other than Luman's ritual dagger, the black-handled athame he'd had made for himself in the cellar of the *King of Prussia* tavern in Cambry, they were unarmed.

Parkersburg was a small town, a jumbled shrug of wooden buildings that started with a cluster of warehouses around the docks and then scattered out concentrically through inns and hostels and coffee shops until it became farmland. Schmidt knew just where she was going and made a beeline for the back door of a nondescript two-story warehouse.

A boardwalk ran along the side of the warehouse, turning the corner at the edge of the building in a three-way intersection. Luman looked and saw that if he lay on his belly, he could squeeze his way under the boardwalk, and that the ground beneath it looked like simple earth.

Perfect.

Schmidt knocked once, but didn't wait, opening the door and marching in. Luman followed.

Within, a plain office: shelves of ledgers, a desk, two chairs in front of the desk. Behind the desk sat a thick-necked man with receding hair, wearing a cotton shirt printed with a paisley pattern, the pattern very *à la mode* among traders wishing to show their international sophistication, but the fabric too thin for the weather, and cort-du-roi trousers. He stood and smiled.

"I don't think we have an appointment," he said.

Schmidt sat down.

Luman shut the door and did the same.

"My name is Notwithstanding Schmidt. I'm a director of the Imperial Ohio Company."

"Mrs. Schmidt."

"Madam Director."

"Yes, Madam Director." The thick-necked man swallowed but then relaxed back into his chair. "I'm Reuben Clay, I'm Foreman of the Stevedores Association in Parkersburg."

"To hell with the stevedores." Schmidt laid her oilskin packet on the desk.

Clay looked at the packet and smiled. "I thought maybe you had come because the Imperial Ohio wanted to conduct some business here."

"We do. To hell with the stevedores. I'm here because you're the first man among the Hansa of Parkersburg."

Clay smiled. "Director..."

"Don't waste your time denying anything. And don't cavil about titles, because I don't know your Hansard title and I don't care. Grand Mufti Hansard of Parkersburg, that's you. I knew your predecessor in this office and I know your game. You run this town and all the traders in it."

Clay spread his arms. "The Lord Mayor..."

Schmidt didn't budge. "You run this town, like Tup Jenkins did before you."

Clay dropped his arms, sucked at his lower lip, looked from Schmidt to Luman and back again, and finally nodded. "Yeah. I run this town."

"You and I know the truth," Schmidt said. "We trade in life."

The Hansard raised an eyebrow. "How do you mean?"

"Money," Schmidt said. "Wealth. It's a mere abstraction for power, and specifically the power to purchase. Others may think you and I trade in money, but in fact we trade in the power to have food when one is hungry, the power to shelter within four walls from winter's blast, the power to have shoes on our feet. The power to live."

"Director Schmidt, you are delightfully philosophical, but a little indirect."

"The Emperor's enemies in the Ohio, the Cahokian rebels and other Ophidian traitors, continue to thrive."

"I'm not a condottiere, Director. My men would fight to defend a cargo, or collect a tariff, but I can hardly go to war with Adena."

"The Emperor doesn't require it. As I was explaining, we'll strike at the lives of the Emperor's enemies in another way. From now on, Grand Mufti Hansard, you will not sell to any representative of any power in the seven kingdoms."

Clay squinted. "Would you like to know my actual title? As opposed to calling me that bit of pseudo-mussulman nonsense?"

Schmidt ignored the offer. "You won't sell to any Firstborn. You won't sell to any person you have any reason to believe *will* sell to any Ophidian."

"I can't decide to blacklist purchasers on my own. I'll be violating the Charter. The whole League will know it because Parkersburg will wither and die. I'll be removed, at least."

The box Luman carried thumped once, in sympathy.

"You will continue to sell," Schmidt said. "I will leave an Imperial Ohio Company Trader here, and he will buy any goods you cannot sell to children of Eve. These are the rates he'll pay, eighty percent in bank notes redeemable in Philadelphia and twenty percent in silver." Schmidt opened the string catch on the oilskin packet and removed the first document, a three-page list of prices.

Clay took the list and scanned it. "These prices are . . . a little low."

"Yes," Schmidt acknowledged, "but only a little. You can make it happen."

"True." Clay set down the list. "But I'd rather sell to the Firstborn."

Schmidt removed the second document from the packet. "You will sign this agreement. You see that there are two copies; I'll keep one. So long as my agent is satisfied that you are keeping the terms of our agreement, he'll remit to you a douceur of one percent of all purchases he makes, in specie."

"Remit to *me* . . . or to the Hansa?"

"That will be your decision," Schmidt said.

Clay looked to Luman. "And is this your agent, then?"

"No. My agent is Ira Oldham; you'll meet him. This is my wizard."

That was Luman's prompt. He carefully settled his spectacles on the bridge of his nose. Then he opened the box and reached in to grab the sleepy and confused bat inside.

"Your copy of the agreement is your insurance," Clay said. "It's a threat. You'll blackmail me."

"Only if you stop cooperating. And as long as you cooperate, you'll be paid."

The bat squeaked a strong objection at being gripped, but when Luman pressed the tip of his athame to its left eye and popped the eyeball out onto the table, the bat screamed. Its cry sounded almost like a child's.

"Gott in Himmel!" Clay cursed. "Must he do that in here?"

"Yes," Schmidt said. "He must. I trust the agent I'll leave in Parkersburg, but I also suspect you'll try to subvert him, or try to sneak around him at the margins. So I need a second mechanism to watch you."

Clay frowned in distaste. "What would that be, a blind bat?"

Luman popped out the bat's other eye. The creature trembled with pain and fear in his closed fist, and he indulged in a moment of sorrow for the innocent bat.

Then he broke its neck.

He reached forward to lay its corpse beside the oilskin. This was pure theater, and theater agreed with Director Schmidt in advance. It worked; Reuben Clay stared at the eyeless bat as if it were a murdered baby.

In truth, Luman himself felt a little ill. Was he really cut out to be a wizard? Did he really want to do this?

"Luman will enchant this town so that we can keep an eye on it. He'll know immediately if you cheat on our arrangement. He'll know immediately if you act to cancel his spell. He'll know immediately if any harm comes to my agent."

"This isn't a deal," Clay said. "It's a prison cell."

"In which you will personally get rich. So long as you can keep quiet. And if things go wrong for you here, you know that any friend of the Emperor can expect to find a warm welcome in Pennsland."

From a coat pocket, Luman extracted a lump of uncooked bread dough. He had mixed the dough himself two days earlier in an iron pan, swishing wheat flour, water, and a nubbin of old sourdough together with his bare fingers, then left it to rise in his lap. This or orange beeswax were the two basic modeling clays preferred by his Memphite spells. Sometimes the substances could be used interchangeably, but Hecate definitely preferred bread dough.

And the sacrifice of living creatures, damn her.

Luman began to stretch and shape the lump.

"What's he doing?" Clay asked Schmidt.

She shrugged. "He's a bit of a thief, as magicians go. Steals one thing from the brauchers, something else from Memphis, a third spell from some Haudenosaunee witch. I never know *exactly* what he's doing."

Luman had shaped the dough ball into the form of a tailless dog, and he now stood the little animal on the desktop. "*Thief* is such a harsh word. Couldn't we say that I *borrow* other people's craft?"

"You aren't *borrowing* if you don't give it back."

Luman snorted, digging in another pocket for a clump of black dog's hair. The hairs had cost him a bite and a minor infection, but it had been worth it to harvest as much hair as he had from that shaggy black hound in Pittsburgh. At least he hadn't had to kill the beast. "You can't give back knowledge, Director. Think of me as an explorer of the arcane world, a man willing to take on any initiation or pursue any course of study, no matter how dark the road or how recondite the learning." He stuck the hairs onto the dog's rump, twisting them to stick them into the dough and fashion of them a dog's tail.

"For the good of the company," Schmidt said.

"And our investor, the Emperor." Luman cut an open mouth into the dough dog's head. Then he gouged tiny eye sockets into the dog's face and inserted one bat eyeball into each.

Reuben Clay shuddered. "You two are unarmed. You're alone, except for your traders, and they're ten minutes away, by the river." He reached under his desk and came up with a polished flintlock pistol, which he rested on the table, pointing between the two of them. "If I simply shoot one of you now, within moments my men in the warehouse will be in here with clubs and knives to subdue the survivor."

"True," Schmidt agreed. "And then the five hundred Company

Regulars following us downriver will arrive tomorrow morning. Not finding my agent here to give them the signal to stand down, their orders are to raze Parkersburg to the ground."

"You would make war on the Hansa?" Clay frowned.

"Not at all. I would buy Hansa goods and pay you handsomely, Grand Mufti Hansard of Parkersburg, to allow me to do so. Some of your traders will make a little less money than they used to, but the Pacification is expensive, and I have to be careful how I allocate my funds. If you can't find it in your heart—or rather, your *interests*—to be enriched, then Parkersburg will be destroyed, and multiple eyewitnesses will swear up and down that it was Firstborn warriors in the livery of Adena who did it. My men will have to procure the corpses of a few Adena fighters for verisimilitude, but that's easily done." She leaned forward, over the desk. "In fact, I imagine my soldiers would be very happy to do it. They've all just been let out of Imperial prisons in Philadelphia, Trenton, and Baltimore in order to enlist. They may have some rage they'd like to express."

Clay took his hand away from his pistol and rubbed his face. "It seems I have no choice."

"The Hansa god is good to you, Grand Mufti. He makes you rich."

Luman took the dough dog in hand and stood. "I'll be outside."

He let himself out.

"If you would be so good as to produce a pen," he heard Notwithstanding Schmidt say as he closed the door behind him, "we can close this deal."

On the boardwalk, Luman looked left and right to be certain he wasn't observed. Parkersburg's crowds didn't much flood into this narrow side street, perhaps out of deference to Clay. Excellent.

Luman took one last object from a coat pocket; a never-used drinking vessel. It was a large shot glass, and to be certain of its virginity—and therefore its power—he had personally watched the glazier in Philadelphia blow this glass and its nine companions, packed in straw in a small box in the *Joe Duncan*. No need to fill *every* pocket of his coat with breakable glass; Luman Walters wasn't punched very often, but when it happened, he didn't want shards driven into his skin.

Luman dropped to his belly on the ground and dragged himself underneath the boardwalk. He craned his neck to look up over his shoulder, positioning himself as near the center of the three-way crossroads as he could, and beneath the overhanging second story of the warehouse. No need to set up his sentinel in a spot where the next rain would simply wash it away, if he could avoid it.

Luman dug a hole, six inches deep. The earth was damp from the river's humidity, but packed solid, so it took him several minutes with his athame to scrape out a pit. He pressed his Homer amulet against the dough dog's back, imprinting its three efficacious texts into the little model. Then he gently placed the dog inside the shot glass. He was careful not to deform the dough creature beyond recognition; a mere lump of dough wouldn't do. But by curling the dog's spine a bit and pulling its legs beneath it, he could nestle the construct down in the bottom of the glass without disturbing its hair tail or depriving it of its canine shape.

Then he spoke to the dog.

"I adjure you three times by Hecate, the Black Bitch of the Crossroads, *phorphorba baibo phorborba*, that Reuben Clay keep ever mindful his agreements with Notwithstanding Schmidt, and that he lie awake under every visible moon, thinking fearfully of punishments that await him if he breaches. I adjure you by Kore, who has become the Goddess of Three Roads, and who is the true mother of Reuben Clay, that you warn me in dream of any action Reuben takes to breach his agreement. *Phorbea brimo nereato damon brimon sedna dardar*, All-Seeing One, *iope*, make it so."

He placed the dog in the bottom of the small pit. With his athame, he cut his own palm and squeezed three drops of blood into the drinking vessel and its dog passenger. He covered the pit with his uninjured hand, to keep excess blood from the enchantment, and finally he pressed his Homer amulet into the disturbed earth.

He dragged himself out from under the boardwalk and dusted himself off. Another advantage of his many-pocketed wizard's coat was that it shed dirt and rain easily.

As he stepped back onto the wood of the boardwalk, he felt it hum beneath his feet. He was not especially sensitive to magic, to his regret; they'd rejected him in Philadelphia for that very reason, setting him on this path of learning magic one scrap at a time, like a hedge witch with a grudge. Any person who stood still and paid enough attention, or who knew what to look for, could feel the same things Luman Walters felt.

That knowledge was sour in his belly.

He made up for lack of talent by working hard. There was no coven he didn't desire to infiltrate, no esoteric lore he didn't covet.

And his magic worked. Hecate's dog would watch. The dog would warn him.

Notwithstanding Schmidt emerged from Reuben Clay's office with the oilskin packet under her arm and a tiny smile on her face. Luman stepped easily into her pace—he had longer legs but she walked with more energy, and it evened out. Schmidt turned back toward the docks.

"You disliked killing that bat, Luman," she said. "Don't deny it, I saw the expression on your face."

"I deny nothing. I prefer magic that doesn't require me to kill."

"It could be worse," Schmidt said. "One of the early Wallensteins, I think old Albrecht's grandson Helmut, went to war with Acadia. Only then they called it *La Nouvelle France*. And he was losing, so he swore an oath to his All-Father that if the All-Father brought him victory, Helmut would make the greatest sacrifice he could—he would sacrifice himself."

"And did he win?"

"He won the war, and it was obvious he'd won because the gods intervened—portents in the sky, Valkyries fighting his battles for him, the dead rising to march, and so on. So he duly proceeded with the sacrifice. Only his wife—his *best* wife, as I believe he had more than one—wanted to join him in Valhalla, so first he sacrificed her. At her request. Hanged her, then ran her through with a spear. Because the two gates to Valhalla are death in battle and death as a sacrifice to the All-Father, you see. Then he hanged himself and his son impaled him."

"People will do strange things to go to heaven," Luman said.

"That wasn't the moral I intended, Bishop Franklin."

"Was the moral that the Germans of Chicago are insane?" Luman asked. "As I recall, after Albrecht's death, they burned the flesh off his corpse and distributed his bones around to the German settlements to bring them good luck. At least, that's what they told me when they showed me the thigh bones sunk into the mortar of the eastern gate of Waukegan."

"The moral," Notwithstanding Schmidt said slowly, "was that you should feel relieved you don't have to kill anything bigger than the occasional bat. And also, next time, don't let your

reservations show on your face. That rather undermines the terrifying effect we're aiming at."

She was right.

They walked in silence for a few steps.

"I don't suppose you really intend to make that Hansard
rich," Luman said.

"I'll fill his pockets for a short while."

"Ah." Luman considered. "You'll keep him on the company's
black payroll for awhile, and then cut him off, and what will he
do? He'll have to keep cooperating, or you'll publish his contract
and the accounts, with signed witness statements from Oldham,
and he'll be kicked out of the League. Or stoned."

"You will also provide signed statements. But I believe they
prefer to stab their malefactors in the back, or poison them."

"You don't love the Hansa."

"On the contrary. Were I not so committed to the Ohio
Company, I might be trading as one of their number. They do
a great work, St. Adam's work, dispersing capital through trade
and driving down prices and profits for the benefit of all."

"Would that be St. Adam of Bremen?"

Schmidt snorted.

"But you subvert your precious saint's freedom of the market,"
Luman said. "Don't you feel guilty?"

"Means to ends," the director said. "Means to ends. A unified
empire at peace will be the greatest market the world has ever seen."

"I believe all their Grand Muftis are men," Luman pointed
out. "I'm not sure the Hansa would take you."

"I slit the throats I had to slit to get where I am in the
Imperial Ohio Company, my boy. I'd have done the same as
a Hansard. Very well, my wizard, you're thinking like a good
company man now, like a director must think. But let me add
nuance to your plan."

They emerged in a triangular dirt plaza surrounded by warehouses. Schmidt turned them unerringly toward the river.

"Tell me, Madam Director."

Schmidt chuckled. "Yes, all in all, I believe I like that title
more than anything the Hansa could hang around my neck.
Consider this, my Balaam: what if we first have Oldham, one
article at a time, little by little, drive down the prices we pay for
Parkersburg's surplus goods?"

"There will be discontent among the merchants," Luman said. "Slowly increasing."

"Until what?"

He considered. "Until Clay tries to get out of his contract. Until he tries to sell to the Ophidians again."

"And how do you handle that eventuality?"

"Kill him. Oldham's a good man with a knife, or he could hire someone."

"That is one road. Me, I prefer owning a man to killing him."

"In that case, you pay Reuben Clay more. And tell him it's his problem to solve."

"Excellent." When Notwithstanding Schmidt smiled, deep wrinkles formed at the corners of her eyes. "Of course, we more than make up for the extra we pay him with the cuts in what we pay the others. Repeat that several times."

"Parkersburg more desperate. Clay more complicit. The record looks worse and worse for him, because he's been getting richer and richer by betraying his own."

"How does he get out?"

"He could flee."

"He'd have to run pretty far, to get away from his own people."

"He could come clean, throw himself on the mercy of the League, tell them everything. Make restitution. Hope for mercy."

"The Hansa *can* be merciful. Do you think he's the kind of man who would do that?"

"No." Luman shook his head slowly. "But if he tries, my spell will alert us."

"And the last thing Reuben Clay could do is turn to us for help," Schmidt said, "which would be excellent."

"Is this what they mean when they say *business acumen*?" Luman asked.

Schmidt laughed. "Out here in the Ohio? Yes. Blackmail, threats, wheedling, and hard-knuckle ball, all played like chess, only if the loser of the chess match had to be put to death."

"Are you going to buy all the Hansa towns?" Luman asked.

"Not even the Emperor has that much money. But I'll buy some of them. And our soldiers aren't really following us to attack the Hansa."

Luman tried to think like the most calculating and bloodthirsty chess player he could imagine. "They'll raid Adena."

"And Tawa, and the others. But they won't waste their effort trying to capture castles."

"They'll burn food."

"And warehouses and docks."

"Plow salt into fields."

"I don't know whether that really works," Schmidt said.

"We should experiment."

One last turn brought them in sight of the docks. "It's not too late, my Balaam," Schmidt said. "This is an English Hansa town, but I'm pretty sure that cart over there is selling pork sausages."

Luman's stomach turned. "You know I can't."

"Such a curiosity you are, Luman Walters. You bribe, conjure, and backstab like a good Christian, but you eat like a Jew."

"It's not a religious scruple." Luman had explained this before; Schmidt was teasing him. "The Memphite grimoire from which I learned insisted that certain spells will not work for an eater of pork."

"Abstinence is hard."

"Abstinence is *easy*." Luman snorted. "Not drinking liquor and not eating pork are *nothing* compared to achieving a broken heart and a contrite spirit."

They strode along the dock. Her traders, seeing Schmidt coming, prepared the *Joe Duncan* to cast off. Ira Oldham stood on the planks beside his luggage, awaiting any last-minute instructions.

"Spells from old King Solomon?"

"So they claim." Luman shrugged. "They work. And that's all you can ask from magic, isn't it?"

"I suppose so. I suppose this explains why half the spells you know are love charms and the other half are cures for impotence. These are the things people actually want done for them."

"Madam Director, I'm wounded," Luman said. "Those techniques occupy no more than one third each of my repertoire. I also know how to remove warts."

"Shame about the pork, though," Schmidt said. "The pig is truly a tasty animal."

"Bigger shame about the wine." Luman grinned. "I do it for you, Madam Director."

The director laughed. "For your loyalty, then, my Balaam, I'll give you a hint."

"A hint?"

"I did indeed once know a man name Joe Duncan. He was not my lover, but my hireling."

"An employee of the company?"

"Not even close. I hired Joe Duncan...to commit a crime."

"What sort of crime?" Luman felt shocked.

Schmidt laughed. "Means to ends, my Balaam."

Luman Walters found himself deep in thought as he approached the mooring place of the *Joe Duncan*.

"This is the reign of Simon Sword."

———◆———

CHAPTER TEN

They rode north for two days. Frost came on the morning of the first.

Though off to the west, Cal occasionally saw birds—herons, for instance—that indicated the presence of the Mississippi, the river itself was far enough away he couldn't see or smell it. The track they were on became a road, and then, passing an Adam-stone standing watch discreetly inside a blackberry bramble, turned onto a highway.

The highway was paved, but unlike, say, the Charlotte Pike, or the other Imperial highways Calvin knew, this highway had not cobbles but perfectly flat, round stones. In fact, the paving stones reminded Cal not so much of the Imperial roads or the main streets of Nashville, as of the stones in the plaza atop Wisdom's Bluff.

The highway cut a straight path through tall forest, the land was flat, and the journeying was easy.

They passed Ohioan Firstborn more than any other kind of traveler, dressed in long tunics and wool cloaks that looked vaguely archaic. The more Firstborn Cal saw, the more he saw the Firstborn blood in Sarah. She never had much color to her skin, but with the little summer's shading she did have fading into winter's pallor, she was really starting to look Ophidian. She wore her purple shawl and the bandage over one eye, though;

she was still Sarah, and the more so as a soft fuzz of black hair again covered her skull. When it was cold she shrugged into the blue riding coat of one of the Philadelphia Blues.

They also passed Germans, who wore wool coats and hailed the party with great gusto. Three riders moving north overtook and passed them, and Bill pointed them out as Free Horse Peoples of the north, most likely Sioux. And they passed one Wandering Johnny who tried really hard to sell Uris a dictionary.

Uris declined.

Bill, Jake, and Chikaak drilled their troop of beastkind warriors morning, noon, and night. Even after only two days, the beastfolk learned to advance shoulder to shoulder, retreat the same way, and stand in a line.

Still, very few of them could actually hit anything with a musket.

Alzbieta's palanquin at night was strapped between trees and served her as a hammock. The Polite wizard Sherem slept on a bedroll near the fire, and Cal found himself waking every hour to be sure the damaged mage hadn't accidentally rolled himself onto the hot coals.

The farther north they went, and the closer to midwinter, the farther south the sun rose and set.

On the evening of the first day, Uris organized the Firstborn warriors to join in the military drill. At first, they stood timidly, looking from side to side at the multiform beast-creatures that surrounded them. After an hour, they learned to stand calmly, and to advance and retreat together.

The sheer strangeness of the mixed troop should count for something in battle.

On the afternoon of the second day, they entered a clearing. To the west, toward the river, stretched cornfields and a scattering of buildings that amounted to a village. The fields had been harvested, and a few black birds, grazing goats, and villagers in long tunics now picked over the forlorn stalks that remained.

To the east lay the forest, with tall trees mostly limbless on their lower trunks, leaving wide spaces to pass between them. Here and there thickets and smaller trees grew, but mostly the forest gave the impression of being manicured, if not recently, then for a long time in its past.

The trees almost looked like church pillars.

Between the highway and the forest, withdrawn from the road

a few hundred paces, stood the mound. At first glance, Cal took it for nothing but a grassy hill, growing in the center of a tall wooden palisade, with two lower mounds at the foot. Initially, the low mounds were more interesting, because they were clearly irregular, and appeared to have windows and doors.

But the second time Cal's head swung around and his eye landed on the mound, he realized that wind, water, and ice would never have made such a thing. There were no hills around it, for starters. The land was flat as a Hudson River pannenkoek, with this sole peak jabbing skyward.

Also, whatever force had built the mound had rendered it a nearly perfect cone. God might move in mysterious ways His wonders to perform, but that just wasn't how the good Lord made mountains.

To Cal's eye, the only flaw in the cone was that the top was flat, with a ring of stones on it that looked a bit like a crown.

"Jerusalem," he muttered. "You *live* in that?"

"Such ferocious cursing," Cathy Filmer said.

Cal hung his head. "Well, I know Jesus said not to swear by Jerusalem, for it is the city of the great king. But I reckon sometimes I git strong feelin's, and it's better I jest say 'Jerusalem' than some of the other choices."

Cal hadn't been addressing any of the Firstborn in particular, but Yedera answered. "We do *not* live in that," she said. "No more than Franklin lived in the rod-tower of the Lightning Cathedral. No more than *you* live in a preaching-tent."

"We got churches where I come from," Cal muttered. "Both kinds: regular *and* New Light."

Yedera snorted. "This mound is a monument, a temple. Our queens and kings build such mounds, and our prophets. They contain libraries, orreries, ossuaries, calendars, and thrones. But no bedrooms."

"So nothin' useful to ordinary folk." Lord hates a prideful man, but Cal didn't want to admit he had no idea what an *orrery* or an *ossuary* might be.

"Perhaps order, government, ritual, and a knowledge of the cosmos aren't useful to ordinary folk in Appalachee. We find it important to know our place in the world, and the proper way and time for doing all things." Yedera looked at Cal with challenge in her eyes.

"Yeah, that's all interestin', no doubt," Cal admitted. "But iffen my pa didn't teach me any of those things, I reckon I can find the answer in the Bible or a Franklin almanac, or jest by lickin' my finger and holdin' it to the wind. I don't expect I need an ossurery to know when to plant and when to thin out my neighbor's herd. I sure as *hell* don't need a *throne* for the purpose."

"Hmmm," Cathy said.

What was she *hmming* about? The throne comment, or the fact that Calvin had said *hell*?

He began to feel ganged up on. The heat he felt in his face suggested he was blushing.

Yedera's expression changed to one of amusement. "And yet you serve a queen."

"That's different," Cal mumbled. "Sarah's kin."

Though that was basically a lie.

"Welcome to Irra-Zostim," Alzbieta Torias said from her sedan chair. "This was built by your grandfathers, Your Majesty."

"You mean John Penn and Kyres Elytharias's father, working together?" Jacob Hop asked. He rode alongside the beastman warrior Chikaak, who was the only one of the beastkind who had dared learn to ride. Since he was studying under the Dutchman, who was himself no great rider, his horsemanship was an awkward proposition at best. Add to that the manifest panic of the horse at smelling a coyote on its back, and the result was a blond man and a dog-headed monster constantly reining in horses trying to bolt five directions at once. "It seems much too old for that, hey?"

"I believe she means your more remote ancestors, Your Majesty," Bill said.

"If Your Majesty will permit, I'll be happy to help her further her studies of our languages." Uris inclined his head deeply.

Sarah laughed out loud. "We know each other well enough we can stop some of the pretending. I don't know any Ophidian. What do you mean, *languages*? Are there seven different ones?"

"Not for the seven sister kingdoms, no. But Ophidian is an old tongue, and has a classical priestly dialect you may wish to learn for ritual purposes, as well as the language that we commonly speak among ourselves. Also, there is a trade patois some of our merchants and soldiers know, that has German and Algonk and French mixed into it. The Germans call it *Schlangegeschäftssprache*, the 'serpent business language.' You won't need that one, I think."

"*I* might could be interested, though," Cal said.

"Me too," Jake added.

"Hey," Cal said appreciatively. "A week ago you'd a said 'ook ik' or somethin' Dutchish. You come a long way, Jake. I met you now for the first time, I might not even guess you for the Hudson."

"There are also Old World dialects." Uris inclined his head again.

Alzbieta Torias pointed toward the top of the mound. "The princes who built the mound of Irra-Zostim lived and died over a thousand years ago. The great Onandagos himself is said to have met here with the Zomas schismatics, before their flight into the Missouri. You can find some of his deeds written on those stones, when you have mastered enough of our tongue."

"Is that what those columns are, then? Writin' tablets?" Cal snickered. "Here Yedera had me thinkin' they's somethin' important."

"They're a temple," Uris said. "And a calendar. Standing atop Irra-Zostim one stands among the stars themselves. The stones do record ancient stories and genealogies, but they also mark the passage of time."

"Our people followed the stars back to this place," Alzbieta said. "And they stopped here, Irra-Zostim tells us, because of all the stars. With a view like this—" she gestured broadly with her arm at the absolutely flat horizon, "one sees a truly full sky. As one saw, the annals say, in our ancient homeland."

"Though the stars fell when the river rose," Yedera murmured.

"Whatever that means," Uris said.

"The mound's name, Irra-Zostim, comes from the name of one of the mountains in the range that bounded the northern edge of our ancestors' plain. Now even those mountains' tops lie buried beneath the waves." As Alzbieta said this she waved, and men standing in the tower to one side of the palisade's gate waved back.

The gate began to swing open.

"They's a lot of good places folk could go to see stars," Cal said doubtfully. "You tellin' me your people came all this way to git a clear look at the Big Dipper?"

"And God made for Man a companion," Uris said, "of starlight and river rock and foam of the sea. And God named her

Wisdom, for she was more subtle than any beast of the field, and breathed upon her, and she arose and shone. And she bare unto Man daughters and sons, and the starlight was within them all the days of their lives."

"I know that one," Cal said. "Where have I heard it? It ain't Bible."

"It's from *The Song of Etyles the Preacher*." Sarah looked as if her words pained her. "Thalanes quoted us those same lines."

Cal squinted at the priestess. "So you're star-people, are you? There's somethin' nice in that, somethin' permanent. Like the stars ain't changin', you ain't a-changin' either."

"The stars fell when the rivers rose," Yedera said again. This time her voice had a darker edge to it.

"Stars are beautiful even when they fall," Cathy Filmer said.

"Come in," Alzbieta Torias said. "This is Your Majesty's land as much as mine."

"Perhaps I might make camp with the beastkind in these trees, Captain." Jake pointed to the forest to the east of the palisade. "We don't know how comfortable they'll feel inside walls, hey? And you have the horn if you need to communicate."

Bill turned to Sarah, who was already nodding.

"I commend you both on your work with our warriors," she said. "Please communicate my pleasure and confidence to them all."

Chikaak yipped and panted at the praise. Then Jake and the beastman scout turned and rode into the trees. The ragged, musky troop followed.

"You got a place for horses in there?" Cal asked Uris.

"Her Holiness would invite you to let them roam free within the palisade," Uris said. "It's what the villagers do, until the nights grow too cold for the beasts and they must be put into stables and sheds."

Cal followed the counselor through the gate, which creaked shut behind them. "Winter'll be here soon enough."

"Then we'll build more stables." Uris waved at the forest. "There is no shortage of wood."

"I's admirin' your trees, in fact," Cal admitted. "Those are some tall, straight timbers."

"Our earliest ancestors here learned to groom the trees," Uris said. "As they were taught to grow corn and potatoes."

"Were taught?" Cal swung off his horse's back and set about

liberating the string of animals he'd been leading. "Taught by whom?"

"The Lenni Lenape, some would say." Uris and Yedera both helped disconnect horses from the lead rope. "The most ancient of the children of Adam still living in the New World, the tribe the Algonks call *their* 'grandfathers.'"

"*Some* would say'?" Cal asked. "That sounds like you don't believe 'em."

"It's hard to know what to believe," Uris said. "I try to state carefully what I know. In this case, what I *know* is that *some say* the Lenni Lenape taught us to choose trees that bear nuts and fruit, and grow them tall and straight to make such a forest canopy."

"Nice as any trees I e'er saw. What do others say?" Cal asked.

Uris was silent.

The three of them shooed the horses away from the gate. Within the palisade walls, the grass grew tall and wild.

"Secret, huh?" Cal said.

Yedera pointed at the top of the conical mound. "The stories carved into those rocks up there tell of our coming to the Ohio," she said. "Those stories say it *wasn't* the Lenni Lenape who taught us corn, bean, and squash farming, or the potato, or how to turn the forest into a garden."

Cal's heart was heavy. "Don't keep me in suspense."

"The stories carved into those stones say it was the Heron King." Uris shrugged. "Stories. They also say that we brought sicknesses with us, and that it was the Heron King's magic that saved the Algonks from our diseases. Is it true? Is it nonsense? Is it an old way to remember something else entirely?"

"I don't much like that feller," Cal said.

"The Heron King? You sound as if you know him." Yedera looked at Calvin as if she were looking right through him.

Since Sarah had let down her guard some, Cal thought he might, too. "I met him," he allowed.

"And lived." Uris arched his eyebrows. "I imagine this has something to do with Queen Sarah leading around a platoon of beastmen."

"Yeah it does. Simon Sword's a real son of a bitch, but I lived. We all lived."

"The Heron King gives the great gifts of civilization, including, trade, stability, and peace."

"Yeah?" Cal asked. "That sounds like Peter Plowshare. And what does Simon Sword do?"

Uris and Yedera shot each other a guarded look. "They're the same," Uris said. "*Simon Sword* is the title under which the Heron King rides to war, which he hasn't done for generations."

"That ain't how I heard it," Cal said. "But iffen it's true, I can tell you he's a-ridin' to war now, and look out."

"I'd like to see the scrolls you were talking about," Sarah said as she dismounted. Bill and Cathy had turned to inspect the palisade walls together, leaving her alone with the priestess—and her eight bearers.

Alzbieta climbed down from her palanquin. Sarah's surprise at seeing the other woman touch earth with her feet must have shown.

"We're within a sanctified enclosure here," the priestess explained.

"So you can touch the earth."

Alzbieta shook her head. "Rather, this is no longer earth."

"I got book-learning from my foster father," Sarah said, "an education that was a wonder to all my Calhoun cousins. And yet I find my father's people baffling."

Alzbieta bowed. "The scrolls aren't here, Your Majesty. They're in my city home."

"I guess I was so dazzled I just assumed," Sarah said. "What's this place, then?"

"A former country shrine I'm too poor to maintain. I built the wall so the villagers, who are my tenants, can defend them-selves and pen in animals. Also, it prevents casual desecration of the site."

"The animals aren't a desecration?"

Alzbieta shrugged. "The presence of living things here does not offend the Mother of All Living. They don't climb the high mound. But this shrine once had a library."

"Will you show me the building?"

Sarah caught the other woman's hand. The Ophidian priestess shuddered as if she'd been poked, but didn't pull away.

"It ain't a command," Sarah said.

"I understand, Your Majesty."

"You and I are kin, Alzbieta. I know it. I *see* it. When I swore those beastkind out there into my service? I didn't make any oath back to them, nothing. I swore an oath to you, and it's just as binding as the one you swore to me."

"Is it?" Alzbieta looked into Sarah's mundane eye.

Sarah removed her eyepatch. "It is."

Alzbieta, natural face and aura both, looked reassured. "Would you care to see the library now? Empty as it is?"

"I would," Sarah said. "I'm fairly itchin'."

Alzbieta led the way into the smaller of the two stone buildings and Sarah followed. The slaves stayed outside, which Sarah found an improvement; the slaves never talked, and generally they followed Alzbieta around staring, watching for any indication that she wanted to be picked up.

It was a very non-Appalachee arrangement.

Was it a coincidence that Alzbieta's slaves were all children of Eve? Or did her father's people exclusively enslave her mother's?

She tried not to dwell on that question.

"The other building was where we slept and ate, when I was a child," Alzbieta explained. "This was the palace of life."

There was no doorway or curtain in the entrance, but with her witchy eye Sarah saw very clearly a hex over the building. She stopped and examined it closely.

"Your Majesty?" Alzbieta asked.

Sarah squinted, examined the corners of the enchanted space, and finally laughed. "Let me guess. The palace of life held scrolls for hundreds of years. By a miracle of the goddess, those scrolls never rotted or got mildew."

"The palace *did* hold scrolls for hundreds of years," Alzbieta agreed. "By virtue of a spell cast hundreds of years ago, the scrolls never rotted or got mildew. Now, I have moved all the scrolls to my palace in the city."

Sarah followed a thin line of pulsating green westward, and realized what could power a spell for hundreds of years. "This spell was cast by one of the Queens or Kings of Cahokia." She didn't say: *using the Orb of Etyles.* "It's powered by the Mississippi River itself. I expect it still works."

"That may well be," Alzbieta said. "The carvings on the temple stones suggest that the great Onandagos built this place. The mound and the stone buildings, I mean. The rulers of Cahokia have always been magicians, and could have protected the shrine against rot."

"Excellent." Sarah stepped into the palace of life.

"Of course, what would be the source of that magic, but the goddess?" Alzbieta turned and walked down a narrow hall that seemed to be the axis of the building.

"Tricky little Handmaid." Sarah followed. "So does Cahokia have many places like this?"

"Palaces of life?"

"Well, that's an interesting question too, but I really meant... places that don't count as earth, for purposes of your taboo."

"The Greek word was a *temenos*. It meant a place marked apart from ordinary space."

"You said you weren't a wizard."

"I'm a Handmaid of Lady Wisdom, a priestess. And as a priestess, there are many old books I want to read. The answers to your questions are, palaces of life: fairly common. Temples have them, and universities, and some monasteries and palaces. My own city home holds the scrolls that were once here, and is therefore a palace of life, of sorts. As to whether the others have magical protection like this one does, I don't know. I have no gramarye myself."

"So you told me before. And yet just now you said the rulers of Cahokia have always been magicians. How is it that you aspired to be queen?"

Alzbieta was briefly silent. "Your own native power as a magician certainly contributes to your claim. As for me, I had hoped that... some stage in the process of becoming the Queen of Cahokia would bestow magical power upon me."

Enthronement? Coronation? The act of becoming queen might bestow magical power? But Alzbieta looked at her feet and said no more on the subject.

"I understand," Sarah lied.

Alzbieta continued. "As to *temenoi*, to borrow from the Greeks: fewer all the time. We've lost the means of making them."

"You as a priestess can't make a... sacred place? A *temenos*?"

"I've simplified too much. There are holy places, and holier places. None in Cahokia can now make a holy place." Alzbieta shook her head. "That is a royal power."

"But with an empty throne, surely no one would mind if..."

"You misunderstand me. I didn't say it was a royal *prerogative*. I said it was a royal *power*. I *cannot* do it."

Again Alzbieta looked at her feet.

"And a *holier* place?" Sarah asked.

Alzbieta said nothing.

"And if I press you, you'll evade my questions, because here, and not for the first time, we have come up against that space where you have knowledge you aren't willing to discuss with me. Some of it, that is, not unless in the right time and place, but some of it, in no time and in no place. Some of this being knowledge you aren't supposed to have yourself, having learned it from my father, your beau."

Alzbieta hesitated. "Here, I will tell you, I simply lack knowledge. But our holier places are all very, very old."

Sarah sighed. "Show me the palace of life, then, cousin Alzbieta."

Alzbieta led and Sarah followed.

The palace of life's long central hallway, now that Sarah was inside and could see it better, passed through four rooms and ended in an open window, empty of glass or other covering. Opposite each other at regular intervals, three additional doorways pierced both sides of the hall. Sarah realized with a jolt that the air inside the palace of life was not only dry, but was significantly warmer than the autumn chill outside. She saw no sign of a fire; it must be the effect of the same magic.

The rooms to the side of the central hall connected with each other by doorways, and connected also diagonally with the rooms on the main passage. The whole thing felt like a honeycomb, or a lattice.

The honeycomb impression was strengthened by the interiors of the rooms. The walls of each room—and of all the hallways—where not cut into by doorways, were covered with diagonal wooden slabs crossing each other at regular intervals to create a lattice of diagonal cubbies, all painted white. Bookcases holding cubbies of the same diagonal lattice construction stood free in the middle of the floor of each room, running all the way up to the ceiling.

"These nooks," Sarah asked the priestess. "They would have held scrolls?"

Alzbieta nodded.

Carved repeating knots decorated the outward-facing surface of the diagonal slabs, making them look vaguely Arab. *Mashrabiya*, wasn't that what they called their wooden lattices? Only those were made to block the sun, not to hold writing.

Besides, these knots looked too repetitive to be writing. Sarah ran her finger along one line of knots.

There was, though, something familiar about them. Where had she seen them before? The knots were repeating circles of the same size, with a distinctive twist to the line running through them, first to one side and then to the other, the one side and then the other.

"Well, cousin," Sarah said. "Now I really want to see your city home."

Alzbieta bowed.

"Why on earth would you call this a palace of *life*?" Sarah asked. "Doesn't that sound like a more fitting name for, say, a Harvite convent? I don't see sickbeds, there's no food or water, in fact I don't see even symbols of those things. I don't see signs or writings of any kind, except what would have been on the scrolls. What does *life* have to do with it, or did our grandfathers just get tired of naming everything after wisdom?"

Alzbieta laughed. "That is such an excellent question."

"And yet, your answer leaves so much to be desired." Sarah snorted. "Ah, well. I tell you, though, it does my heart good to see a library, even if it's an empty one. Maybe that's why it's a palace of life. It's a metaphor for a great place to read."

Alzbieta only smiled.

"Anyway, it's as good a name as a 'library.'"

At that moment, Sarah heard gunshots.

Bill stood at the base of the mound, gazing up at the stones at the peak. A path of stone steps led up the front of the steep slope, zigging and zagging back and forth—Bill counted—to make seven angles.

One for each kingdom.

"I cannot conceive the engineering that would build such a thing," he said to Cathy Filmer, at his elbow. "I believe if you piled an identical heap of dirt beside this one, the rain would instantly destroy it."

"Perhaps it was built one layer at a time, and once grass had grown up the mound to anchor it, each next layer was added," Cathy suggested.

"Or perhaps there is some structure inside."

"Do you mean stone?"

"Perhaps. But a wood structure might do as well. As you say, once the grass had grown over it, the mound would retain its shape."

"Perhaps fills of different sorts?" Cathy ventured. "Different sorts of soil, or gravel, or layers of stone, to give the mound stability and allow water to drain. And consider that this is a mound of modest dimensions. But the Serpent Mound too, must be artificial, rising as it does from the plain. What massive amount of effort, what power and what resources, were employed to erect *that* mountain?"

Bill looked at Cathy sharply. "I shall remember these remarks when Her Majesty is looking to appoint a chief of her engineering corps."

"I should recommend Mr. Hop for that. He seems to have an astonishing capacity to learn."

"That is quite a gift," Bill agreed, "if not one, strictly speaking, acknowledged in the Gospel of Mark."

"Who knows in what strange gospel lie recorded the gifts that shall follow the disciples of Simon Sword?"

Cathy smiled, and Bill chuckled, but his mirth was forced.

"Mrs. Filmer—"

"Bill, you call me that to hold me at arm's length."

He hesitated. "Forgive me. Cathy." He hooked his thumbs into his belt and stared at the mound-top temple again. "We have come to Sarah's kingdom. We've found her allies, and even family."

"You are thinking she will soon send you to get her sibling where you concealed him."

"Her brother Nathaniel. It seems likely. And there will be . . . reckonings."

"Your wife may be alive."

"She would not be an old woman. And I believe we are still married."

"I know all this, Bill." Cathy took his hand. "Tell me what you are really thinking about."

Bill sighed. "If I ride east, I fear it might be the end for you and me. If that happens, I hope you will understand that . . . without you, I could not have lived this long. Without you, I'd have died in a New Orleans ditch years ago. A man needs meaning, he needs something to live for. For a long time, what I had to live for was you."

"And your wife." Cathy's voice held a sorrow as sharp as a blade. "And Charles, your son."

"Say rather the *memory* of my wife and the *hope* of my son. But long separation had rendered those faint, and insufficiently vivid to keep me on my feet."

A single tear crawled down each of Cathy's cheeks. "You are perilously close, Sir William, to telling me that *your wife* owes your survival to *me*."

That wasn't what he'd intended, but Bill felt his foot far down his own throat, and was unsure how to extract it.

The sound of a gunshot saved him.

Bill spun to look westward, the direction from which the shot had come. His legs, still healing from his injuries of three days earlier, buckled under his weight and the pressure of the sudden move, but they held. The blue smoke lying over the gatehouse and the Firstborn warrior waving his arm suggested that the shot wasn't from a hostile, but the eruption of more shooting from the gatehouse strongly indicated enemies' presence.

Then long-tunicked farmers and their children began to stream through the gate.

"Please excuse me, Mrs. . . . Cathy." Bill touched his battered hat and hobbled for the gate as fast as he could manage.

He nearly collided with the counselor Uris, who emerged from the larger of the low mounds. Uris ran with an unsheathed long sword, demonstrating an ease that only came with long practice, and though the Firstborn must be older by a decade or more, his strides were longer and smoother than Bill's.

"Suh," Bill said, "I believe there may be trouble. Would you mind—"

"Dammit, man!" Uris snapped. "They're not shooting at *game*. There must be unity of command, and you're the queen's choice. Don't ask me if I'd mind, give me an order!"

Bill nodded. He needed to propose to Sarah a formal chain of command and ranks that included all the Firstborn. And he needed to stop thinking of the Firstborn and the beastkind as *warriors*. Warriors were the fighters of a barbarian tribe, the Celts and the Saxons had *warriors*.

Bill needed *soldiers*.

"Saddle up the horses and prepare for a cavalry charge," Bill said. "But arm them with their longbows in the meantime."

Uris nodded and began shouting orders in a language Bill recognized as Ophidian. The Firstborn soldiers within the palisade scrambled to prepare their horses.

Bill staggered to the gatehouse, hearing a dull roar on the other side of the sharpened logs as he drew closer, the tumult punctuated by the staccato snap of gunfire. A final handful of Firstborn villagers skipped in through the gate and then it slammed shut. He dragged himself up the iron ladder to the gatehouse platform at a ragged sprint, drawing two pistols as he reached the top.

His leg wounds stabbed him with pain.

Four Firstborn warriors crouched leaning into the shelter of the log wall. Bill squatted beside them, lowering his head just in time to avoid being hit by a javelin that came over the wall and fell into the enclosure, sinking its sharpened tip six inches into the hard earth.

Beastkind.

Bill's sense of how many beastfolk charged across the picked-over fields was uncertain, probably because some of what he saw looked like steeds charging and some looked like warriors, though more likely than not they were all beastmen. Dozens, certainly. A hundred?

"Tell me your name," he said to the Firstborn crouching nearest to him.

The man had thin lips and eyebrows and a scar across his forehead, almost hidden by the visorless steel sallet protecting his skull. "Olanthes," he said. "The men sometimes call me Ole."

"I'm not much of an expert in the longbow, Ole," Bill said. "Am I right to think our archers within the palisade should be able to shoot a hundred yards usefully, arcing their shots so as not to hit you and me?"

Ole nodded and pointed. "A hundred yards from our archers would put the arrows right about at that ditch."

The beastkind were crossing the ditch already.

"Colonel Uris!" Bill shouted, inventing a rank on the spot. It was not well done, and he knew he'd have to revisit it later. "Prepare to fire three volleys! Aim for the large irrigation ditch parallel to the highway. On my command!"

Uris had his thirty men lined up with bows ready, and saluted his agreement.

Bill was in over his head. He would readily have admitted

it, had his queen or his lady—as he knew Cathy truly to be—asked, but the truth was that the only other possible candidate for command in this battle was Uris, who had already deferred to Bill. But Bill was a dragoon and a pistoleer, a man who had led a single unit for a time, years earlier, and who had never had strategic responsibility for a field of action larger than a meadow, a mountain ridge, or a single wall.

Now his field of battle was the Kingdom of Cahokia, and House Elytharias was at stake.

The beastkind were nearly to the wall. Bill looked down along the palisade and saw roughly twenty men. They crouched behind the wooden wall to shield themselves from hurled spears and rocks, but they were armed with long spears and swords, and they wore helmets and mail.

It was medieval.

"Sergeant Olanthes," Bill commanded. "Prepare to repel the beastkind."

Olanthes shouted in Ophidian.

"Fire when ready!" Bill called to Uris.

The first volley of arrows launched overhead, striking in the middle of the beastkind horde. Bill took the Heron King's horn in his hand and blew. *Double-time advance.* It was not a perfect summons, but it was clear.

From the woods to the east of the palisade, he heard the same short melody repeated in a coyote's howl.

A second volley of arrows went overhead, falling into the back half of the bestial mob.

"Closer!" Bill roared. He could barely hear himself over the thunder of hoofs on the growling of beasts, but Uris nodded as if he'd understood, and shouted to his men.

The third volley fell at sixty yards, again in the middle of the pack.

Beastmen at the rear howled in pain and puzzlement. A few of them tore at each other. The late afternoon autumn sun was weak and behind his attackers, but nevertheless Bill thought he saw foaming muzzles.

The beastkind assault was not organized, it was madness.

Bill's beastkind marched from their forest camp. Pikemen led out, long spears borrowed from Alzbieta Torias's Firstborn warriors pointed forward and ready. Behind them came musketeers, including Jacob Hop and the coyote-headed Chikaak, marching on foot to one side of the column and holding carbines.

Not *Bill's* beastfolk. *Sarah's.*

The assault struck the wall with such force that the timbers shook. A sound that combined barking, snarling, baying, and guttural shouts washed over Bill. Ole and the other Firstborn stood and jammed down into the attackers with their long spears, drawing angry cries of rage in return.

"Mount up!" Bill waved to Uris. "Prepare to charge!"

Uris waved back.

Bill rose up to discharge one pistol and then the other into the attackers. He struck a crocodile with a man's head between the eyes, and put a bullet into the chest of a cobra-headed man who was at least eight feet tall.

Suddenly, Cathy was beside him, holding a pair of pistols. She fired her guns as well into the oncoming mass.

Sarah's beastfolk regiment was getting closer.

Bill crouched again to switch pistols, almost falling. Cathy caught him, and he gripped her fiercely. Lightning bolts of pain shot through both legs.

Uris's men were mounted, and had long swords drawn and raised. Good—a cavalryman who impaled a foe had to drop his lance, but a mounted swordsman could chop a target in half, propelled forward by all the muscle of his mount, and keep going.

The wall shook as another wave of the beastmen slammed into it. To his left, two Firstborn men screamed as they were dragged off the wall.

The palisade shook a third time, and it felt as if the center of the shockwave was directly beneath Bill's legs. He rose with two loaded guns, lurched forward—

a man with a rhinoceros head, who was very nearly the size of a rhinoceros himself, pawed the earth with bare feet and charged the wall again, slamming into the logs and shaking them—

Bill fired. *Bang! Bang!*

One shot struck the rhino-man between the shoulders. The other hit him in the top of his head. He backed away two steps and threw himself at the wall again.

A hurled stone the size of Bill's head struck him below the waist. The rock came at him from an oblique angle, and it managed to strike both his thighs. Bill screamed and collapsed to the wooden walkway, bouncing and nearly falling off, but for Cathy's tight grip on the front of his coat.

"Bill!" she gasped.

He nodded to indicate that he was fine, which was a lie; he could feel that both his legs were broken. Putting the Heron King's horn to his lips, he blew *firing position.* That would have his front row of soldiers arraying themselves into a defensive wall, bayonets forward. The wall shuddered. Then Bill blew again.

Fire.

BANG!

To Bill's immediate satisfaction, the carbines fired together, at the signal. Together, they sounded much louder than they did singly. The shuddering of the palisade wall suddenly stopped.

Cathy peered over the wall, and Bill dragged her back down. "I'd rather lose both my legs than your head, my lady."

She smiled at him through tears.

Reload, Bill blew again, and then he let the horn drop to his side and reloaded himself. He was much faster at this than any of his soldiers, so he reloaded two pistols and then dragged himself, wincing from the pain, to the edge of the palisade to look.

He got there in time to see the last of his carabineers snap his swivel ramrod back into place. That was a gratifying sight, but much better was the sight of what was happening in front of the shooters.

The pikemen were holding the line.

Their fellow beastkind threw themselves with ferocity and shocking courage into the spears, but though Sarah's beastfolk fighters snarled and roared in response, they held their pikes in disciplined fashion, creating a bristling wall of steel that kept the other, more feral, beastkind back.

The troop's right flank was protected by the palisade wall. One or two of the rampagers tried to creep around the left flank, but there Chikaak or Jake, each carrying a carbine and several pistols, shot them as they came.

"Ready!" Bill waved to Uris.

Uris waved back.

"Open the gate!" Bill shouted to Sergeant Olanthes. The gate began to swing.

Fire, Bill blew.

BANG!

Bill with his two loaded pistols shot the rhinoceros-headed beastman, who was looking with entirely too much enthusiasm at the opening gate. Wild beastkind dropped in the carbine volley.

"Charge!" Bill waved to Uris.

Charge! he blew.

Sarah's beastkind surged forward with a roar. The pikemen spread apart as they raced forward, creating a wider broom of mayhem with which to sweep the enemy. The musketeers raced in between them, with jaws wide or weapons swinging.

The few wild beastkind who turned to look at the palisade gate, or worse, tried to enter, were run down. Uris's men were enthusiastic and disciplined, and if they weren't great horsemen, they were good enough to remember that the lethal things were the weight and velocity of the horse, together with the blades of their long swords. They churned the beastmen underhoof and mowed them down like scythes cutting down dry hay.

The sound of death shrieks and squeals of pain behind them made some of the beastkind charging Sarah's warriors hesitate, and a few even turned around. Their uncertainty and division were their doom—Chikaak and his fellows tore them to pieces.

Numerically, the beastkind attackers still outnumbered the palisade's defenders. But they had been surprised and hurt, and they had lost their momentum. They fled now like leaderless men.

Or like wounded animals, not cornered and with no cubs to defend.

With more disciplined cavalry, he'd have wanted to pursue. With more archers, he could have launched a few more volleys into the retreating, shuddering mass of semi-bestial flesh. As it was, the Ophidians with him on the wall fired a few desultory shots at their retreating attackers. Jake, from where he stood on the ground, did the same, and then the beastkind horde was gone.

Bill slid down the ladder to the ground, bearing his weight entirely on his arms. Cathy followed, anxiety in her face. Reaching the earth, Bill collapsed before Chikaak and Jake, just as Sarah and Alzbieta Torias reached them.

"Sir William," Sarah said, "you're injured."

He nodded his acknowledgement. "Jake, Chikaak," he grunted up at his sergeants, "organize patrols. We need advance warning of any attempt to return, and especially of any indication that we are to be placed under siege."

"We won't be besieged," the priestess said. "That isn't a beast-kind art. This wasn't an organized attack or part of any plan."

"No?" Bill asked. "What was it, then, Your Holiness?"

"It was madness," the priestess said.

Sarah shook her head as if the answer were obvious. "This is the reign of Simon Sword. And this is only the beginning."

For the first time, Bill found he disliked Chikaak's lolling tongue and ever-present grin.

"Beelzebub's bedpan," he managed to gasp, and then he lost consciousness.

"Brother Onas, do you hear me?"

———◦———

CHAPTER ELEVEN

Kinta Jane rode a mule.

She'd worked for it—improbably, not as a prostitute, but as a seamstress, in the Ohio German hamlet whose name she never learned, where the *Stolze Marie* had come to dock, the morning after paying a negotiated bribe to the Imperial Ohio Company revenue enforcers somewhat lower than the thirty percent stated tariff, but high enough to send the Company men away in song.

Johannes had laboriously made it clear that the *Stolze Marie*, of which his uncle was one-fourth owner, was turning around and immediately going back downstream, hoping to get at least one more trip in before the winter made it impracticable. As it happened, there were no boats scheduled to head upstream for a couple of weeks.

Kinta Jane could station herself on the single rickety dock jutting out into the river and wave at passing boats, hoping one would pick her up, or she could find another way.

The Meekses at the *General Store & Dried Goods* hadn't exactly taken her in, but when Mrs. Meeks learned, through reciprocal pantomiming that Kinta Jane knew how to use a needle—it taking Mrs. Meeks several days to understand that Kinta Jane could hear perfectly, and was only unable to *speak*—she put the Choctaw to work making dresses to a pattern, giving her two meals a day and an old blanket on the floor beside the Franklin Stove. That device's presence, more than anything else, told Kinta Jane she was getting closer to Philadelphia.

The Meekses bathed every night in well-water heated on the Franklin Stove. Kinta Jane washed herself every morning in a torrent behind the store. Initially she thought Mr. Meeks had some grudge against the stream, until she overheard him giving directions to a traveling customer and realized that the body of water was in fact named the Goddamn River.

Kinta Jane considered the presence of the Franklin Stove a cheerful omen. It almost made up for the fact that she was awoken each morning by Mr. Meeks, unlocking the shop door and announcing his presence to his neighbors by shouting "Meeks shall inherit the earth!" at the top of his lungs.

The squirrel-faced shopmistress had also promised three pennies a day, payable at the end of a week, by which time Kinta Jane would have stitched enough dresses for herself and her four gangly daughters for a year. Kinta Jane accepted, planning to pay her eventual fare upstream with cash.

The town had a small subscription Bibliothek, a board-built building over stone foundations, in the style the locals referred to as *Klappholz*. Kinṭa Jane thought if she earned enough pennies, she might even spend one to borrow a little reading material, maybe a little poetry by that mad English godi, Blake.

Kinta Jane chose the Meekses' store because she understood spoken English, and because Mr. Meeks hadn't been aboard the *Stolze Marie*. The German keelboatmen generally didn't buy from the Meekses, but from German-speaking merchants in town.

Kinta Jane had felt immense pride when Mrs. Meeks had taken the first dress she'd sewn and hung it on her wall. She'd taken Kinta Jane by the hand and led her into the Meeks family's rectangular living space behind the store, a single large room under a loft. There, Kinta Jane had seen Mrs. Meeks's finest dresses, what she kept referring to as "Sunday best," as well as the Sunday best of her daughters, hanging on the wall as decoration. And telling Kinta Jane how pleased she was with her craft, Mrs. Meeks had taken down her old Sunday dress from where it hung pinned to the wall over the dining table, and carefully pinned into its place a new striped blue gingham frock.

The week was not yet up when one of the keelboatmen, Karl, had come into the store. Karl was broad-shouldered and also broad-bellied, a widower and a heavy drinker, and he'd had more than a beer or two before coming into the Meekses'. After purchasing several yards of cloth and a sack of dried beans, he'd seen Kinta Jane, sitting beside the Franklin Stove and stitching away. Karl had done as he would have aboard the *Stolze Marie*, pantomiming the services he would like from Kinta Jane.

Kinta Jane looked away as if she didn't know the German, but Mrs. Meeks and two of her daughters saw it all. When Mr. Meeks came roaring out of the back room demanding satisfaction from his ill-mannered customer, his rage quickly metamorphosed into a short conversation in German with Karl, after which Kinta Jane's time with the Meekses came to an abrupt end.

"We're New Light," Mrs. Meeks had said, pantomiming something wiggling over her head that might have been intended to be the sun. "New Light, you understand? We greet our brothers and sisters with the holy kiss. And besides, you know how it is . . . we got to maintain appearances. Be respectable, as the community sees us."

Kinta Jane shrugged and held out her hand, palm up, asking for payment.

Mrs. Meeks shook her head. "I don't understand, dear."

Kinta Jane showed three fingers and slapped them into her palm six times. *Three pennies times six days.*

"We couldn't possibly," Mrs. Meeks said. "For starters, I'm mighty concerned as to how the money would git used. Once a woman has fallen, you know, she takes to liquor and wild dance and worse. I couldn't in good conscience give you that money, dear. It might could make your life worse!"

"Meeks shall inherit the earth!" Mr. Meeks shouted by way of ratification.

So Kinta Jane had stolen the mule, along with a ham, the basket of sewing supplies she'd been using, and a short carbine Mr. Meeks had kept after his militia service as a young man. Whether it was shock at her brazen theft, lack of imagination to see that she'd been the perpetrator, or guilt at the knowledge they'd cheated her, the Meekses didn't follow, and sent no one in pursuit.

Maybe they just didn't care. The mule was old, and the gun older.

The ham was the most valuable thing she'd stolen. It would last her a week, if she was careful. There was more flesh on the ham than on the mule.

Kinta Jane rode north, asking for directions to Free Imperial

Youngstown. Though Youngstown lay more east than north, she kept north, and kept asking directions. She wanted to get away from German Ohio, which lay along the river, and away from Appalachee, which lay beyond it to the south. She feared getting caught, but more than that she enjoyed the feel of land she'd never seen before, unencumbered by the distasteful memories of life with the Meekses.

She soon crossed into one of the Moundbuilder kingdoms. No wall or even sign that Kinta Jane noticed marked the change—under the Compact, travel among the various powers of the Empire was supposed to be free, so other than those put up by the Imperials, there were generally no toll-gates or walls. But in the course of a single day's ride, the buildings moved from the high-peaked half-timber buildings the Germans favored, second and third stories cantilevered out to add floor space, giving the largest houses the appearance of being upside-down, to the simpler, older style the Ophidians built. Thatched and plastered stables and public houses. Wooden palisades on raised banks surrounded by ditches. Low mounds with doors and windows indicating that they were buildings, sometimes with more ordinary-looking buildings on top.

The people she passed changed, too. Each day she saw fewer Appalachee and Germans, and more Eldritch. The Firstborn wore long tunics and generally had long dark hair bound behind their heads. Spears and long swords replaced the long knives and sabers of the southern Empire, and the coins she saw veered sharply away from silver toward other metals, including iron as well as gold.

Kinta Jane made money as she could along the track, generally as she had done in New Orleans, and with a similarly grubby mob of clients. She made a great deal more copper than gold, but also a few coins of bronze and iron. She avoided plying her trade in public houses, where it would have been easiest to attract men, and instead eyed travelers on the road to assess them. A man who looked tired, travel-weary, rich, and not-too-dangerous, got an invitation from Kinta Jane Embry in the form of an outthrust hip slapped with her own hand.

Twice she found work as a seamstress, in roadside ordinaries.

She kept the carbine loaded and near to hand, just in case.

She'd lost track of the date, but knew it must be November. The evening wind was bitter, and she rode a broad track that had gone from a single rut to two ruts to covered with gravel, when she saw fire ahead.

Not a campfire. A town on fire.

Kinta Jane hid.

The mule was a placid old jenny she'd named *Mrs. Meeks*, and it was happy to plod after Kinta Jane into a grove of trees and lie down. Kinta Jane crept to a fin of cold rock and lay across it with the carbine, listening and looking for anything that would tell her what was happening.

The burning buildings illuminated a small town that squatted where two roads crossed at a river. The absence of a ferry suggested a ford instead, a stretch where the river's width made it shallow enough to cross on foot or on one's horse. The town had no ditch and bank and no mound, and its palisade wall was low enough that Kinta Jane thought she could probably scramble over it, if necessary.

The town looked peaceful, other than the fact that it was on fire.

Of the ten or so buildings Kinta Jane could see over the log curtain surrounding the town, at least two were burning.

Hands grabbed Kinta Jane from behind and hauled her to her feet. Surprised, she dropped the carbine, which landed on a bed of crisp autumn leaf-fall beneath her.

That left her the stiletto sheathed on her forearm. It wouldn't be enough, not against three men.

The fire behind Kinta Jane cast watery orange light on the man holding her and the two men at his shoulders. She saw their faces clearly; the fire must be closer than she realized. The men all wore some kind of Imperial uniform, blue and gold, but Kinta Jane didn't know it. She didn't think they were Foresters, because their shoes were heavy soldiers' shoes beneath painted canvas gaiters, rather than the lighter moccasins the Foresters had adopted from the Indians.

"I reckon," the man holding her said slowly, "we found ourselves another bit of contraband here." He smelled of cheap wine and old urine. Then he belched, adding in the pungent aroma of raw onion mixed with some kind of rotting meat.

"Naw, Joss," said the one on the right, "if it's contraband, we gotta burn it. That what you wanna do with this little morsel, light it on fire?"

Mrs. Meeks brayed a complaint.

"In a manner of speaking." Joss's voice was slurred.

"Henrik's right," said the man on the left. "But they ain't nothin' stoppin' us from enjoyin' a little friendly intercourse with the natives. Firstborn are fair game in every case, them's the orders."

"That's right, Pete," Henrik said. "And she looks like a Fairy to me."

Kinta Jane couldn't contradict them. She didn't think they would care, even if they believed her. She was the least Firstborn-looking person she knew.

Had she been standing, she would have cocked her hip to the side and slapped it; the gesture had never failed to communicate what she wanted it to. Hanging by two fists knotted in the front of her blouse, she had to try a different tactic.

She slowly licked her lips.

"She wants it," Pete said.

"She wants *me*." Joss dropped Kinta Jane.

She allowed herself to tumble all the way to the ground. The leaves padded her fall, and she bounced left, avoiding the gun on the ground.

"That's it," Henrik said.

Lying on her back with her knees up, Kinta Jane licked her lips again, looking from one brutish face to the next.

And spread her knees. Slowly. Teasingly.

As they stared where she knew they would, she snaked a hand through the leaf pile, unseen in the darkness, and found the gun.

"She wants all of us," Henrik said.

"She's gonna get me first." Joss grunted, fumbling with his hands to unknot the length of rope holding up his trousers. They hit the ground only a second before his knees did, and he thrust himself forward, prepared to assault Kinta Jane.

She let him begin, egging him on with soft moans of encouragement. Henrik and Pete similarly dropped their trousers, though Pete looked around as if fearing discovery. The stink of her rapist clogged Kinta Jane's nostrils; she breathed through her mouth and tried not to think about his stench. She'd smelled worse, in the Faubourg Marigny. When she thought Joss had gone far enough to be distracted, Kinta Jane swung the carbine up to rest it on his shoulder, right against his cheek, pulling back the hammer in the process. Fear gave her the strength to do it.

"What?" He grunted, rising up slightly on his knees, though not pulling back.

Bang!

Kinta Jane shot Henrik square in the center of his chest and he dropped without a word. Pete shrieked and rushed off into the darkness, nearly tripping over his breeches.

Mrs. Meeks yanked up her picket and bolted.

Joss bellowed, burned by the shower of sparks against his cheek. He punched Kinta Jane in the face and tried to back away, rising to his haunches—

but Kinta Jane locked her heels together behind his ponderous backside and held him.

"Ophidian cow!" Joss punched her again, missing her face this time in the dark and striking her repeatedly in the chest. He had rings on his fingers; Kinta Jane felt the skin of her shoulder tear as he struck it.

She answered by dropping the carbine and drawing the stiletto. She plunged the blade deep into Joss's head, entering neatly behind his ear. His hot blood poured down on her, he jerked spastically, and then he slumped over, dead.

Kinta Jane rolled Joss's body off and into the leaves. In the light of the burning village, she dug through the clothing of her attackers and found a pair of pistols.

She checked the priming on the guns.

Then she went looking for Pete.

Her surviving attacker had missed the track by which he'd come and run right into forest again. Kinta Jane heard him thrashing about in the trees and stopped on the trail. She held a pistol in each hand, pointed downward.

She wished she could call to him. Instead, she just stood in the track and tried to look innocuous.

She waited patiently.

Pete emerged. He shook; that might be the November night chill combined with his lack of trousers, or it might be fear.

"I didn't want to do it," he said. "I wouldn't hurt anyone."

That was clearly a lie. Kinta Jane nodded toward the burning town and shrugged, making a grunt that she hoped sounded like a question.

Pete frowned. "What do you care?"

Kinta Jane raised one pistol, not pointing it at Pete but making it clearly visible in the firelight. She repeated her grunt.

"I reckon you ain't much of a talker, are you? So I tell you, and you let me go?"

Kinta Jane nodded.

"Look, we're Ohio Company Regulars."

Kinta Jane frowned.

"Imperial Ohio Company soldiers." Pete spat. "Not Dutch. We was all prisoners, just weeks ago. I was in Pittsburgh, I think Joss there was in Philadelphia, Henrik might have been in a dungeon up in New Amsterdam. And we got let out."

Kinta shrugged and grunted.

"We didn't escape, if that's what you're thinking." Pete shook his head. "There's a word for it. Furloughed? Paroled? I don't remember. But some director of the Ohio Company cut a deal with the Emperor that he'd give us his pardon if we did a six-month tour of duty with the company."

Kinta Jane nodded at the fire. She could hear yelling from the town, and occasional gunshots.

"They ain't innocent villages, though, are they?" Pete grinned slyly. "If they've got anything as was supposed to be stamped by the Company and ain't, then they're smugglers. They got contraband, and our orders are to burn all contraband."

It was winter. They Imperial Ohio Company was burning the Adenans' food in the winter. Kinta Jane trembled with rage.

This wasn't her affair, though. The Conventicle didn't exist to thwart Thomas Penn in his struggle against the Electors of the Ohio. The Conventicle existed because of Benjamin Franklin and his Vision, and because of Simon Sword.

Kinta Jane should let Pete go and continue to Philadelphia.

"That's the Pacification of the Ohio, ain't it?" Pete continued. "If these Wigglies learn they're completely dependent on the Emperor for food, they're gonna calm right down and cooperate."

Kinta Jane Embry shot Pete in the chest.

He dropped, and for good measure she stepped closer and shot him in the head as well. Then she took her knife and stabbed it repeatedly into his neck, face, and belly.

When she finished, he was a disfigured wreck and she was sobbing.

Who had she really wanted to stab to death? Joss? Elbows Pritchard?

The weird-eyed beastwitch who had invaded her room in the Faubourg and taken her dignity?

René's murderer?

Kinta Jane took a deep breath. She could bury the bodies, but

there seemed to be little point. Anyone who found them would
think they'd been killed in the raid. Or maybe they'd killed each
other in the fight over raping priority of some Ophidian captive,
given that two of them had their trousers down.

That was just fine with Kinta Jane.

She tore the cluster of beybey medallions from around her
neck and threw them to the ground. The gods of New Orleans
had been no use to her. Kinta Jane Embry had saved herself.

She turned to find she was observed.

Six men stood in the road. They were shorter than the company men, and in the firelight Kinta Jane could see that their
foreheads were pale, their hair long and dark. Their mouths
were hidden by neckerchiefs, like outlaws might wear. Over their
shoulders they wore Ohioan cloaks, and in their hands they held
long, straight swords.

Firstborn. Eldritch, resisting the Ohio Company.

She nodded slowly, pointed at Pete's corpse. She wished she
could speak, but the Firstborn seemed to understand. They nodded back, turned, and disappeared into the night.

Kinta threw the two pistols deep into the woods, then retraced
her steps. As the adrenalin in her blood subsided, she realized
that her clavicle and her ribs on one side hurt acutely, especially
when she breathed.

Before she left, she took Joss's rings. To get all of them, she
had to cut off two of his fingers.

She never found the mule.

In the Walnut Street Theater lobby, just as he stepped onto
the bottom of the marble staircase that would take him up to
his private box, Thomas Penn got the message.

He entered last, so that the six dragoons accompanying him to
act as his bodyguard could cross the red-carpeted lobby without
forcing their way through a crowd. This was his deliberate habit,
as was the fact that, though he attended the theater often, he only
did so on evenings when the sky favored him. Nights when Jupiter
was strong, or Mars if he knew his men were fighting in the field.

Also, he wore his Town Coat, an elegant blue and gold coat
that had been much worried over in the weaving and the stitching
by a pair of Philadelphia gramarists. The Town Coat protected
Thomas at all times, including against threats he couldn't even see.

The dragoons were survivors of the destruction of his larger bodyguard unit, the Imperial House Light Dragoons, or Philadelphia Blues. Thomas needed to recruit additional men into their depleted ranks, and above all appoint a captain, before he could undertake any significant travel.

"Pardon me, Your Imperial Majesty." The messenger was the theater manager, a balding man in a threadbare black frock coat that had once been elegant but now looked like a costume worn in one production too many. Thomas made it a point to attend the theater regularly, though not because he was a lover of drama. It was a thing one did, when one was gentle. Also, it allowed him to meet Temple and gather information from him, in a place that was highly visible and therefore ironically more discreet than if Temple had crept to the back stairs of Horse Hall at midnight with a dark lantern. Thomas recognized the manager, though he couldn't recall the name. Throckmorton? Brockington? "I regret to inform you the Imperial Players are unable to perform tonight."

"I've come rather a long way to *not* see a play," Thomas complained. "And I suppose you have other theatergoers, as well. Members of the ticket-buying public, not to mention the meneers and the Cavaliers in the balconies? What do you plan to do, send us all home? Could you at least get a singer onto the stage?"

If he couldn't meet Temple in his theater box, the old debauchee would want to take him to less savory places.

Throckmorton, or whatever his name was, bowed deeply. "At significant additional expense, we have procured the services of another premier troupe of players."

"Oh, yes?" Thomas asked.

"Franklin's Players, Your Imperial Majesty."

Thomas frowned. "Shouldn't they be riding about in wagons, posing as Herod and throwing candies to children?"

"Yes, sir." The manager bowed again. "If it were Easter. But it isn't Easter, and Franklin's Players also do Shakespeare and Marlowe and other conventional works. They are, as I said, quite renowned."

Thomas snorted. Perhaps Temple would find the change amusing, or at least ironic. "Very well. I shall see this play, and, Throckmorton..."

The manager seemed puzzled by the name. "Yes?"

"I'll pay the additional expense. Have a bill sent up to the box, I'll sign it. And please don't make a public affair of it."

"Sir." Not-Throckmorton bowed one more time, the deepest bow yet. "Lord Thomas, you should be aware that Franklin's Players will be performing a different drama than what we had scheduled."

Thomas laughed and started up the stairs. "I have no idea what the other fellows were going to perform, anyway. I'm here, sir. That's the thing."

"The Imperial Players were to have performed *Henry the Fifth*, sir."

Thomas stopped. "Ah. Yes, well, that *is* a good one." His favorite Shakespeare, though he wouldn't have admitted it to Brockington. The plays featuring the younger Henry were also quite good. "And Franklin's Players?"

"I understand they'll be putting on a piece called *The Walking Purchase*."

"I don't know that one," Thomas said. "I assume from the title it is a history of my ancestors, in some fashion? A glorification of the vision and wise planning of William Penn?"

Brockington bowed almost to the floor. "I believe so. And I understand that it's a...mathematical...drama, sir."

"Love and conquest by the triplicities, eh?" Thomas resumed his climb. "Then these players have chosen their piece of a purpose. Perhaps they hope the Imperial coffers shall undertake to fund a second troupe."

"Your Imperial Majesty is known for his open hand."

Thomas had purchased a box at Walnut Street with a large cash contribution to the building's construction, shortly after Hannah's immurement. At the same time, he'd made a number of other civic contributions, as Emperor, as the Penn Landholder, and as Lord Thomas Penn. He'd funded a fire company the old Lightning Bishop had created, built a library for the Pennsland Philosophical Society, and put on an apron to become a Freemason—the last against his principles, since at least in theory it required him to swear binding oaths to other men. He already had to swear such oaths to the damned Electors, which was bad enough, but the Freemasons were a gaggle of Philadelphia merchants and doctors with scarcely a drop of good blood among them, so the oath galled.

But he did it.

His funding of the theater had bought him the box of his choice. The projectors had offered him a large box, directly facing the stage, and Thomas had declined in favor of a small one, high and in front. It meant that his view of the stage was oblique and Olympian, looking straight down onto the tops of the actors' heads—though he liked this latter fact, since it made him feel he was the reigning Thomas Jupiter of his portrait in Horse Hall. It also meant that he had a box that seated two comfortably, or four if the company was willing to squeeze in shoulder to shoulder.

But it also visibly demonstrated Thomas's generosity. He had paid for half the theater, and anyone in the audience could see his box was modest to the point of being monastic.

Modest, and highly visible.

And Thomas made it a point to go to the theater, and be seen.

Thomas's guards stayed at the foot of the staircase that led, with no other destination, to Thomas's balcony.

Temple Franklin was already in the box when Thomas arrived, parting the thick velvet curtain that served the box for a door and passing through. Franklin was older than Thomas, and heavy, like his episcopal grandfather. Temple was originally his surname, a bastard waif's name, given by the orphanage where he'd languished before his grandfather had found and acknowledged him, the bastard son of his own bastard. The man in between, William Franklin, had emigrated to England and wound up a sheep-slaughtering godi somewhere.

For all his saintliness and cunning, old Ben Franklin had been a man who recklessly generated reckless progeny.

"Today an old woman on the street offered to heal my gout by application of one of the new Philadelphia shillings," Temple said, looking up at his Emperor.

"An old shilling wouldn't work, would it?" Thomas said pointedly. "It isn't the coin that heals, but the image of the living Emperor. I'm pleased to know that in this one respect, at least, the Electors cannot stop me from blessing my realm."

"As I was pleased to see public feeling for the Emperor's power so strong."

"Thank you for having the decency not to be openly fondling an actress in my box when I arrived." Thomas was only slightly out of breath despite the climb; his insistence on staying in the saddle as much as possible and his light eating habits rewarded him with vigor and strong lungs.

William Temple Franklin, by contrast, positively sagged over the arms of his seat.

"You are not a man who scruples to fondle an actress when she presents herself, Lord Thomas," Temple said.

"In private, no. Indeed, an appropriate fondling may be seen as a beneficence, not to mention the fact that the ladies of Philadelphia have come to expect it. But the public scruples, Mr. Franklin. The public scruples."

Thomas stepped to the railing to look at the packed theater seats below. Deliberately below, rather than at the other boxes. The seating was full, and Thomas waved and smiled benevolently at the floor before turning a polite smile to the occupants of the balconies. The neat blond-headed cheese-parers visiting from New Amsterdam and the full mustachios of Baltimore planters wagged together as the playgoers in those boxes bowed deferentially.

"Ah, do I not know it! And therefore am I not a bishop, nor was my father before me, for an accident of birth beyond my control."

"Your father was so attached to the idea of priesthood that in the end he wasn't particular about which god he served. As for you, I could have you made a bishop," Thomas said. "I could *git you bishopped*, as they say in Appalachee. I have several bishoprics in my gift, and if they happen to be currently occupied, no matter: an inconvenient bishop can always be got out of the way. How do you feel about Newark? The challenge is less your bastardy than the aforementioned actresses."

"Because the public much prefers a bishop who fondles young *actors*."

Thomas suppressed a chuckle. "Discretion in either case, sir. Discretion in either case."

"Naturally, Lord Thomas. And therefore I wait for you here alone. Do you see an actress in your box?"

"I do not." Thomas sat. "And yet somehow, I detect the strong scent of an actress's perfume."

"Outrageous, Lord Thomas. That the actresses should wear so much perfume that you can scent it in their dressing room from here, three stories above."

"Interesting that you should know where their dressing room is located, sir."

"One supposes in the wings, for ready access to the boards. One only supposes. Although perhaps it is not their scent that is so extraordinary, but your faculties of scenting. Were you a tracker in the war with the Spanish, Lord Thomas?"

"I was a hero. Hadn't you heard? And therefore all the nubile ladies of Philadelphia, along with half its matrons, throw themselves under my feet. It is only Imperial decorum that restrains me."

"Or perhaps His Imperial Majesty is detecting my own toilet water. I have had it sent all the way from Cologne. However much the Caliphate has set back the art of painting in the Old World, it hasn't worsened their skills with scent."

"I understand that Napoleon doesn't permit plays in Paris."

"It's the mullahs, sir. Like portrait painting, drama is a wicked art inasmuch as it imperfectly and therefore sinfully represents God's greatest creation, man, so the more traditional of the mullahs persuaded Napoleon to end public displays. Also, French theater exposed actresses to the view of men."

"What, was all French theater nude? Heavens, why did I waste my youth on the frontier?"

"No, Lord Thomas, it exposed their *physiognomies*. But fear not! I have sufficient experience of Paris that if you should wish to travel there and see Molière performed in his original tongue and land, I know of several, ahem, *private* houses where such plays are still performed, and Lord Thomas might see actresses in all their bare-faced glory."

"Am I to understand from your throat-clearing that these *private houses* are *bordellos*?"

"In the right quarters, Lord Thomas, even the mussulmans of Napoleon's Paris scruple at very little."

A clatter of hard-soled shoes brought the theater manager onto the stage and under the proscenium arch. Ushers snuffed tapers, bringing darkness to the seating floor.

"Remind me of this fellow's name," Thomas said.

"Elias Brackenham," Temple Franklin answered immediately. "Laudanum addict. Twice a bankrupt, largely because of his fondness for the poppy."

"Safe?" Thomas asked, surprised.

"I supply his habit."

"Welcome, all!" Elias Brackenham flourished both hands as if summoning the audience up from the floorboards. "Two brief announcements before tonight's production begins. The first is that the Imperial Players have become unexpectedly unavailable. Therefore, Franklin's Players shall be performing tonight, an original stage play in prose and verse called *The Walking Purchase*."

The applause was polite, rather than enthusiastic. Perhaps Thomas wasn't the only one who had never heard of this play.

"And second, though he has strictly enjoined me to keep it a secret, the gods of the theater command me to tell you that the additional expense of hiring a second troupe has been entirely borne by His Imperial Majesty, the Emperor Thomas Penn."

The applause this time had energy to it. Thomas stood again and waved benevolently, especially at those seated on the floor below.

"Well done, Thomas," Temple murmured. "That's what money is for."

Brackenham scooted off the stage.

The curtain rose on the façade of a building, behind which hung a canvas painted with forest and a night sky. The façade was a reasonable simulacrum of the Slate Roof House, William Penn's original home and seat of government, until John Penn had begun construction on Horse Hall. The Slate Roof House still existed; Thomas had been born there, as had his sister Hannah. As his own children would be, once Thomas got around to finding a bride.

Hannah had been imprisoned there, and there she had died.

Thomas found he was gripping the arms of his chair with such force that his fingers hurt. He inhaled deeply and tried not to think of his sister's face, bloodied and twisted as she finally died.

Really, once Thomas brought peace to the empire, and appropriate glory to his own name, the right bride should be easy to find. She would come to him.

The night sky images were surprisingly accurate and showed the circumpolar region; the Big and Little Bear, the Dragon, the two Thrones.

A scene began to play out slowly on the stage, involving some actors dressed as Lenni Lenape and others as Englishmen. The one English character without a periwig would be William Penn, sometimes called Friend William or Simple Will, Thomas's ancestor and the first Landholder.

A man with painted face, skin dyed dark and head shaven,

wearing a feather headdress, stepped forward to address the audience.

"I believe I've seen that fellow before," Temple Franklin said. "Only he was dressed as John the Baptist and he stood munching carob beans on the back of a wagon filled with sand."

"What else should I be doing with my money?" Thomas asked mildly. "Since you have a view, that is."

"My comment wasn't sarcastic." Franklin looked at him sharply. "Use your money to buy loyalty. Buy guns, when you need them. And buy Electors, whenever you can get them."

Franklin didn't know about the payments Thomas made to the Chevalier of New Orleans, but the conversation was drifting perilously close to that point. Thomas changed the subject. "You haven't yet discovered the location of the other two children."

"My men work on it. It's only an assumption that one of the children was taken by Lee or went with that sapphic Catalan thief."

"Smuggler. But since the first was taken and hidden by Thalanes, it seems a good guess."

The actor dressed as an Indian droned on in blank verse, enthusing his way melodramatically through a prologue.

"The inference is probable. But remember, Thalanes didn't hide the first child with a Cetean monk, or among the Firstborn. He didn't take her to his own people. Instead, he put her with Andrew Calhoun."

"Irritating old bastard," Thomas muttered.

"You should have let me go after that one, rather than send the preacher."

"I didn't *send* the preacher. I was simply unable to *stop* him. I *sent* Berkeley and the Blues, and little help they were."

"For all we know now," Temple continued, picking up the earlier thread, "Ferrer i Quintana did take one of the children, and delivered it to a cloister of Acadian beguines."

"So what do you do?"

"We look. We have men on the gulf and on the Mississippi, searching for the smuggler. We have rewards posted for information about her. And of course, the Blues who survived the debacle on the Serpent Mound and were picked up by the company all report seeing William Lee. He's been in New Orleans for at least a decade, so we're looking there for evidence of one of the children."

"You should look in Johnsland," Thomas suggested. "His military adventures had made him quite a favorite there."

Temple nodded. "The fact that he'as been in New Orleans all these years rather than in the Chesapeake suggests possibly that he is unable to return to Johnsland...that he is outlawed or unwelcome. Or possibly it could suggest that he deliberately avoids the place in order not to draw attention to something that is there. In any case, I have agents in Johnsland looking now."

"You'll have heard the song, of course," Thomas said.

Temple raised his eyebrows.

Thomas sang:

Johnsland ladies have sharpened beaks
Say nothing but "caw!" when they're asked to speak
Johnsland ladies have sharpened beaks
Earl Isham sings coo coo, coo coo
Earl Isham sings coo coo

Johnsland ladies all sit on eggs
Naught but feathers to cover their legs
Johnsland ladies all sit on eggs
Earl Isham sings coo coo, coo coo
Earl Isham sings coo coo

"I didn't know that one," Temple admitted.

"So much for your intelligence network."

"He was a great falconer once, you know."

"In the chambers of his own mind, perhaps he is a falconer still. But I've been led to believe that instead he has become the falcon. In any case, these seem like easy questions," Thomas said. "And yet there are two children at large."

"Brother Onas!" the prologue called. "Brother Onas, do you hear me?"

Thomas wouldn't have noticed the line, except that he happened to turn his head at that moment and saw the actor standing at the edge of the stage, arms spread wide, visage upturned and facing...Thomas.

As was most of the crowd.

"Damn me if they aren't expecting you to answer," Franklin said softly.

"I'm not in the play," Thomas whispered.

"Lord Thomas," Temple chuckled. "You *are* the play."

"Brother Onas!"

Thomas stood. Brother Onas was an old name that sometimes referred to his ancestor William Penn. The actor playing Penn now knelt in front of the Indian, as if he were receiving communion, while the Indian faced up to Thomas.

As staging, as drama, it was satisfying. Mortal Penn knelt. Thomas was Penn Transcendent, invoked to participate in this scene, whatever it was.

He wished he'd been paying attention. Still, he assumed the Jupiter pose of his Horse Hall portrait, at the same time resting his hand on the hilt of his Mars-sealed saber to hint at his powers of conquest.

"I am here!" he called.

The audience applauded, but the actor didn't move.

"Brother Onas!" he called again. "Do you hear me?"

"I hear you!" Thomas cried. The feeling that all eyes were on him was beginning to fade from a sensation of merited love to the feeling that he was pinned to a card, as if by some spirits-stinking member of the Pennsland Philosophical Society.

"Brother Onas!" the actor declaimed again—

Bang!

Thomas felt punched in the chest. He stepped backward, struck the seat with the back of his knees, and fell to the floor.

"Lie still!" Temple Franklin dropped to the floor beside him with a thump that shook dust from the carpet. The spymaster looked over his shoulder at the theater's ceiling.

"Did you see who shot me?"

"No." Franklin didn't seem rushed or troubled.

"You're quite calm about this."

"No one will shoot you now. And I believe your bodyguard will apprehend the shooter momentarily, if they haven't already."

Thomas looked down at his chest. His ribs hurt where he'd been struck, but the fabric of the Town Coat was whole, and he wasn't bleeding. Probing at his ribs with his fingers, he winced, then found a hard lump in his coat pocket. He put his fingers into the pocket...and found the bullet.

"Clever trick, that," Temple grunted, dragging himself up to hands and knees.

"This is another thing I've been doing with my money. Protecting myself."

"I know. Keep doing it." Temple sniffed the air. "Do you smell fire?"

"With you practically lying on top of me, I mostly smell your toilet water. Which is definitely not the lady's perfume I smelled coming into the booth."

"Fire." Franklin frowned. "There's not supposed to be a fire."

Supposed to be?

Temple crawled to the box's curtain and poked his head through. Smoke billowed out.

"Fire!" Temple coughed.

"Fire!" someone yelled in the theater below.

Thomas heard the rattle of a sudden stampede of people. He crept to the low wall and banister separating him from the theater and peered over it. In a box opposite, he saw two of his dragoons wrestling a pale, thin man to the floor. Raising himself slightly, he saw the crowd fleeing for the exits.

"The dragoons have captured someone," he reported.

Franklin reemerged from the curtain. "The stairs are blocked. The dragoons are arresting Oloas Kalanites, a young Ophidian gentleman attached to the Prince of Tawa."

"You said you didn't see—" Thomas caught himself. "You *arranged* this."

"Of course I did. You weren't in danger."

"You're winning me sympathy."

"And resentment and suspicion for the Ophidians."

"Don't you think I would have preferred to know in advance?"

"Yes." Franklin looked Thomas in the eye, both of them on all fours. "But you are a terrible liar, Thomas. I planned on you getting shot, and then looking the impervious hero because you *are* the impervious hero. If you thought you had to *act* the part of the impervious hero ... well, just trust me."

"And the fire?"

Franklin dragged himself ponderously to his feet, coughing. "I didn't plan the fire. That troubles me."

The actor dressed like an Indian had a rope in hand and rushed across the stage. The far end of the rope was anchored somewhere out of sight above the stage, and the actor threw the rope over his shoulder, gripped the proscenium arch with both hands and began to climb. The arch was ornately carved, an explosion of galloping horses and clashing swordsmen, so there was plenty to grip.

"Lord Thomas!" the actor called. "Are you harmed?"

Smoke billowed out from behind Thomas, causing him to cough ferociously. "I'm fine, dammit. Just glad you've stopped calling me *Onas!*"

"Yes." The actor's eyes were fixed on picking hand- and foot-holds, but Thomas thought he smiled. "Well, that was the play. And I think tonight's performance has been canceled."

The actor was tall and thin, with the kind of long muscles that made a skinny man stronger than he appeared. He climbed easily, and within moments was stretching from the proscenium to grab the balustrade of Thomas's theater box.

Thomas heard dragoons shouting at the bottom of the stairs.

"Your Imperial Majesty, you must take this rope," the actor said.

"The hell I must!" Thomas dragged Temple Franklin forward. "This man goes down with the rope. I'll climb."

Franklin tried to argue, but his words collapsed into dry coughing each time. The actor threw a leg over the banister and sat astride it as on a horse, quickly knotting a bowline around Franklin's chest.

"Will it hold him?" Thomas asked.

"I protest," Temple said weakly.

The theater box's curtain burst into flame. Thomas seized Temple Franklin by one side of his coat and the actor seized him by the other, and together they threw Temple over the edge.

Franklin swung in a straight line for the center of the stage. Rushing with his feet just inches off the floor, he then crashed right into the center of the painted scenery representing Horse Hall. The wooden palace façade collapsed back into the stars and Franklin bounced back the other way, stopping when two actors in periwigs grabbed him by the shoulders, hanging on him and snapping the rope.

"Can you climb?" the actor asked, extending a hand.

"I can jump," Thomas said, and he did.

"I am a man of prejudices, I admit. But I'm learning."

———◆———

CHAPTER TWELVE

Cathy knew from the expression on Bill's face that he was plagued by the same two questions troubling her.

Must we include the Cahokians in this conversation?

And *must we hold this council here?*

As if she were reading their thoughts—and maybe, with her eyepatch off, she could—Sarah shook her head. "Thank you," she said, opening the discussion. "Thanks especially to Sir William, who came up here on two injured legs, and to Calvin and Jacob, who carried him."

"It was easy." Jacob didn't sound Dutch at all. "Two poles and some blankets make a simple travois, and we just dragged him up."

"I'm not certain my dignity requires this much discussion of how I arrived." The smile Bill directed at Cathy was rueful. He leaned on a pair of long crutches Calvin had made him. Despite Sarah's and Cathy's ministrations, his thighs—which *were healing*—were knitting together slightly *crooked*.

"It would a been easier iffen we could a used a horse." Cal shook his head. "I'm all for showin' respect, but that was a steep hill, and even with a travois it was longer'n I expected."

"This is a sacred site," Alzbieta Torias said. "Would you drag Sir William into a church on a travois?"

Calvin snorted. "Last time I stepped foot in a church, I had

223

a pistol in each hand. When I got inside, I's attacked by walkin' dead men straight outta a history book, watched a bishop git hisself murdered and then a monk, climbed on the altar with muddy moccasins, and eventually turned into a pigeon. So, yeah, I reckon I'd a drug Sir William into the same church on a travois without e'er a thought. Or up here."

Alzbieta only stared.

Cathy managed not to laugh out loud at the Handmaid's shock.

They stood within the ring of stones atop the mound Uris had called *Irra-Zostim*. What had appeared from the flat land below to be twelve rough-hewn columns were in fact thirteen, and each leaned inward slightly and came to a dull point, like an enormous canine tooth. A spiral groove climbed from the base to the tip of each stone, once deep but worn by centuries of weather, and crossed by hatch marks, loops, and branches on both sides. Occasionally the groove passed between simple carved pictures—a man with a snake's head, a mountain rising from the sea, stars in a configuration Cathy didn't recognize—but mostly they passed over age-mottled stone. Moss obscured the grooves on the lower halves of several of the pillars.

The Firstborn had said there were stories on the columns. Could the few and simple pictures record the tales? The Walam Olum of the Lenni Lenape was like that, a series of pictures illustrating that nation's history and prompting the memories of the storytellers who had learned the text. It was a picture book with the words taken away, in effect.

And the Lenni Lenape had ties with the Eldritch of the Ohio. The Elector song about the Seven Kingdoms claimed that Talega was half Lenni Lenape. She had never seen Talega herself, but hadn't the Ophidians said that one explanation for where their ancestors learned their civilized arts—the Three Sisters agriculture, the husbanding of the forests—was from the Lenni Lenape, whom they had met when they'd arrived?

All Sarah's companions who had survived the flight from New Orleans were in the circle: Cathy, Bill, Calvin, Jacob Hop. As well, she had brought up Uris, Yedera, Alzbieta, and even Sherem, whose wits hadn't recovered.

If anything, though Sarah ministered to him daily, he had gotten worse. Now he stood scratching one fingernail against a stone and mumbling.

Sarah hadn't invited any of the beastkind, though Chikaak was generally inseparable from Jacob Hop. Cathy hadn't asked why; she assumed that for Sarah, as for Cathy, the beastfolk warriors still carried a taint of the Heron King. Though they were bound by oath no less than the Ophidians, as far as Cathy knew, they still felt variable.

Wild.

Not that Cathy trusted the Ophidians.

"Thank you for the work, Calvin," Sarah said. "I think it's worth taking extra trouble to respect the holy things and spaces of my people. I didn't bring us up here *despite* the sacredness of this mound, but *because* of it."

Alzbieta Torias smiled. "You're thinking that perhaps up here I may tell you things I wouldn't tell you, if we were to hold this council on flat earth."

"I'm *hoping*," Sarah said quietly. "And there are other reasons."

Alzbieta nodded.

"I think the time has come for revelations," Sarah added. "I'll start. I haven't been fully forthcoming with you about what happened on Wisdom's Bluff."

"Your Majesty said she didn't recover the regalia of Cahokia. I know that to be at least partially false."

"I believe my words were 'close, but not quite,' in the riddle game you and I played. I'll tell you now, cousin Alzbieta, that I found where my father had hidden the Orb of Etyles, the Sevenfold Crown, and also the Heronsword."

Alzbieta held very still. "I thought I'd named those items."

"I found them because he meant me to find them. He hid them there for me. Though I don't know why he would carry such precious objects to the edge of the Empire."

"The ruler of Cahokia has ritual obligations," Alzbieta said. "Some of them can only be fulfilled in certain places. Some of them require the regalia to fulfill."

Sarah nodded. "I found the regalia, but I traded away the Heronsword, Alzbieta. I don't have it."

Alzbieta opened her mouth several times, but made no sound.

"Traded it?" Uris asked. "Your Majesty, it was yours to trade, if it was anyone's, but...to whom did you give it?"

"To the Heron King."

The Firstborn all looked shocked.

"It's worse than you think," Sarah said. "Whatever you may have heard in Cahokia, Simon Sword isn't just another name for Peter Plowshare. They are two different gods, or two different phases of the same god, maybe. Peter Plowshare is a giver and a builder. Simon Sword, well...he's the reason the beastkind are rampaging, I think. And I believe that's just the start."

Uris staggered and would have fallen if Jacob Hop hadn't caught him.

Sarah looked coolly at the Ophidians, not flinching or looking away. *Well done; show no fear.* "I did it reluctantly, and only because the alternatives seemed worse."

"What alternative could possibly have seemed worse?" Yedera asked. "You unleash the storm upon the Seven Kingdoms."

"Marriage." Sarah laughed out loud sharply, suddenly the fierce young woman again. "Not to just anybody, mind."

"The Heron King wished to marry you," Uris said.

"Yes." Sarah's Appalachee twang disappeared again. "And not the nice one."

Alzbieta sang:

> *I am the supplanter, the lion with prey*
> *I am the bridegroom, I am the bride*
> *I am the chosen, anointed of seven*
> *Breaker of horses, bane of the river*
> *Star-fallen wanderer, I lead the children sunward*
> *I am the secret, Beloved of the goddess*
> *Born of the tree, the city my mother*
> *Keeper of the crown of two kingdoms*

"Well, you sound like an interesting person indeed, then," Sarah said. "In fact, you sound like a *man*. Maybe even my father, who was Imperial Consort and King of Cahokia both—keeper of the crown of two kingdoms."

"Your father sang those words in delirium. He may have written them, though I could never ask. I'm translating out of Ophidian, of course. In fact, out of an older form of it." Alzbieta smiled, a thin, forced smile. "Your Majesty doesn't need to possess the Heronsword, sometimes called the Heronblade, in order to make a claim on the throne of Cahokia. Is that one of the questions you wished to ask me?"

Sarah nodded. "Thank you. And you fear for the consequences of Simon Sword being again in possession of his weapon, as do I. Or you *should*. Can you tell me what the sword does? He called it a 'Thing of Power.'"

"It's *his* power," Alzbieta said. "It's true, many of our kingdom believe that *Simon Sword* is just a different title of the Heron King. This is a deliberate half-truth they are told, to keep from them the darker truth, which is that the great ally and benefactor with whom we have built our civilization must every few generations be replaced by a ruthless destroyer. The kings and queens of Cahokia have held the Heronblade in custody for long generations. Perhaps since our arrival in the Ohio. Perhaps since the time of Onandagos himself. Our custody of the weapon weakens Simon Sword's power when he is born and shortens his reign. It has also given our queens and kings great martial prowess, and made us the foremost of the Seven Kingdoms." She met Cathy's gaze. "I knew, you see. We here, we all knew."

"Priestly lore," Sarah said.

"Cahokia, always alone," Cal muttered.

"War, death, change, judgment," Jacob Hop said.

The others turned to stare at him.

"What do you know, Jake?" Sarah asked.

"Nothing. Only what everyone knows about Simon Sword." Jake held up one of the Tarocks, the Simon Sword card. The illustration on its face looked a bit like Jake himself. "He's the great bringer of change."

Uris sighed. "And he's the great bringer of change even when Cahokia holds his sword. And now?" He shrugged. "Who can know what storm comes now?"

Sarah looked even paler than usual. "All the more important to retake my throne, then."

"Yes," Alzbieta agreed. "Your Majesty said you traded the Heronsword. You haven't yet said what you traded it *for*."

Sarah said nothing, but reached into her satchel and removed the Heronplow. It caught afternoon sunlight and flashed briefly. Her eyes dazzled, Cathy thought she saw plowed and drained fields, dotted with conical mounds rising from the earth and furred with rows of tassel-eared corn.

"I was rather hoping you might know what to do with it," she said.

Alzbieta shook her head.

"I had no idea such a thing existed," Uris said.

Sarah nodded and replaced the plow in her bag.

Jake followed the stare of the wit-stunned Sherem and began examining the grooves on the stones.

"Sir William," Sarah said. "We march with an army in the field. We've been tested in battle and emerged victorious. The time has come to tell me about my siblings."

"Siblings?" Alzbieta asked.

"We're triplets," Sarah said. "Raised separately and in hiding."

"Your Majesty is the oldest. I was told that by Thalanes, who attended the birth to pray by the midwife's side and ease her work with his gramarye." Bill broke into a grin. "Likely he also made Hannah coffee."

Sarah's laugh this time was soft and remorseful.

"When Thalanes bore you to Appalachee to hide you—at the time I did not know his destination—I took your brother Nathaniel. I rode to Johnsland."

"My brother," Sarah said haltingly. "What was . . . wrong with him?"

Bill straightened on his crutches, fire flashing in his eyes. "Nothing was *wrong* with him, Your Majesty. He was strong and slept well."

"You know what I mean."

Bill frowned. "Nathaniel Elytharias Penn had a very distinctive ear."

"Red?" Sarah asked. "Swollen?"

Bill nodded. "And pinned flat, forward against the side of his skull."

Sarah had lived her first fifteen years with an acorn in one eye socket, and when the acorn had come out, she had discovered a gift of sight. Sarah saw power, aura, emotion, dishonesty, fear.

What things could her brother Nathaniel *hear*?

Jake had taken a card from his coat pocket and was holding it up against the stone, squinting at it.

"Go on," Sarah said.

"I am a Cavalier of Johnsland, born and bred. The earl was my feudal lord—*is*, if my family's lands have not been taken away. He had also been a friend of Hannah and of her father. What I didn't know was that his mind had become weak."

"The earl is a passionate man," Cathy said, not meaning to. When Sarah looked at her quizzically, she explained herself. "His blood runs hot. He pursues what he wants, beyond reason."

Bill grunted. "His son and heir, Richard, was a friend of Thomas. I knew this, but I did not know how good a friend he was. The earl agreed to foster Nathaniel and took him into his house. For my part, I returned to my wife and children, thinking to develop farming skills and keep an eye on young Nathaniel from the vicinity.

"But Richard, wondering at my arrival and at the sudden appearance of a baby in his father's household, made inquiries. He confronted me with his suspicions, at a moment when I was... weak with whisky, shall we say?"

"Understood, Sir William." Sarah nodded.

"I inadvertently confirmed his guesses. He made to ride for Philadelphia immediately."

"So you did the loyal thing," Sarah said.

"I killed the man, Your Majesty." Bill took a deep breath. "I couldn't explain it to my wife. I had sworn an oath not to reveal the child except to the earl himself, and having broken the oath once in my cups, I was doubly resolved not to break it again. She got it into her mind that I had betrayed her. That my shooting of Richard was a duel over a woman. That the child was mine, perhaps. Since I wouldn't account for myself, she could see no other explanation."

This was more history than Sarah had intended to ask for, surely, but she didn't stop Bill. Cathy had heard the tale before, more than once. Still, it broke her heart.

Her heart broke on Bill's behalf, and her heart also broke for her own sake.

For her connection with the Earl of Johnsland, and for her son.

"I thought with time she would forgive me, and indeed, when she eventually learned the truth she might come to see me in a heroic light, or at least a tragic one. Alas, time was not to be given to me. On hearing of Richard's death, the earl's mind snapped. His men came to take me the very next day, and I fled, alone."

"Didn't you fear Nathaniel was in danger from a madman?" Sara asked.

"The earl is trapped in a maze of his own sorrow," Bill said. "But he keeps his word."

"My brother is in Johnsland."

"Likely. And likely attached to the earl's household still, and being raised with his own sons, legitimate and otherwise. Riding, shooting, and mastering the other manly arts of the Chesapeake."

Sarah was quiet, considering. "And the third?"

"I can tell you little," Bill said. "She's a girl. Margaret Elytharias Penn. I didn't notice any... *irregularities* about her person, though I saw her only momentarily, and swaddled. And she was taken by a friend and confidant of your mother named Montserrat Ferrer i Quintana."

"A Spaniard?" Cal asked.

"A Catalan," Sarah said. "They all carry two family names."

"A Catalan. On her mother's side, once noble, and Montse still gets treated as a kind of gentlewoman among some of the Catalans, despite her profession."

"Sir William has a grudge against certain occupations," Cathy murmured.

"I am a man of prejudices, I admit," Bill said. "But I'm learning."

"What was her trade?" Alzbieta asked.

"Montse is a smuggler and a pirate," Bill said. "Her ship, *La Verge Caníbal*, is the terror of customs men and small merchants from New Spain to Ferdinandia."

"She was a confidant of my mother?" Sarah smiled.

"To the scandal of some, it's true," Bill said. "Your mother was not a staid person, whatever you may see in the intaglios."

Sarah laughed. "And do you know where Margaret is?"

"I do not," Bill said. "*La Verge Caníbal* has always ranged over great distances. The girl could be in Miami as easily as in Memphis. Or just as easily in Barcelona, for that matter."

Jake had finished his examination of the stylized grooves and now piped up. "Will Your Majesty be sending *me* or *Mrs. Filmer* to recover your brother?"

"You or Mrs. Filmer?" Sarah asked. "Those are my choices?"

Jake shrugged. "Bill is needed to command the troops. Calvin wouldn't leave even if you ordered him to."

"I'm jest doin' like the Elector told me," Cal muttered.

"You need the help of the Cahokians to find your way to your throne. That leaves me and Mrs. Filmer."

"I cannot," Cathy said quickly. "Not in Johnsland."

She avoided Bill's questioning look.

"I wouldn't readily part Sir William and Mrs. Filmer." Sarah smiled warmly. "I suppose that means you have the job, Jake."

Jake bowed.

"But let's consider whether now is the right time." Sarah turned to Alzbieta, who looked unsettled. "Tell me how to prosecute my claim."

"Your Majesty," she said. "The goddess decides."

"I ain't e'er quite figured this part out," Cal said sourly. "Youins Christians, or ain't you?"

"We read the Bible," Uris said.

Cal scratched his head. "That don't exactly sort out the question for me. Jews read the Bible, and I b'lieve they read it in the Caliphate, too."

"Some of us read the Bible," Yedera said. "I am the daughter who never came into this world. Therefore, I am not subject to this world's rules."

Cal threw up his hands in disgust.

"How does the goddess decide?" Sarah asked.

Alzbieta looked about them, at the thirteen standing stones, and beyond, at the sea of green forest that stretched out at their feet, to the snaking brown Mississippi River in the west. "The goddess of light gives birth to her child at the turning of the seasons. At the moment of greatest darkness, the child of light, the Beloved, comes bringing new hope."

"You don't mean a physical birth," Sarah said.

Silence.

"The winter solstice," Sarah continued. "If the goddess chooses a queen, we expect it to be at the winter solstice. Late December, when the days are shortest."

Cal snorted. "You mean *Christmas*? Here we go again. Your child of light wouldn't be *Jesus*, would it? Malachi says the sun of righteousness'll arise with healin' in his wings. And that's Jesus, the beloved son."

"*Beloved* is a title," Alzbieta said softly.

Cal furrowed his brow. "Not as I ever heard."

"Just ask Elhanan the son of Jaare-oregim," Alzbieta shot back. "And Malachi really says the sun will have healing in *her* wings, in Hebrew. Are you so sure that's Jesus?"

"Ancient languages," Sarah murmured.

Calvin's jaw worked wordlessly a few times. "Well, I ain't able to match you Hebrew for Hebrew," he admitted finally, "but Isaiah says unto us a son is born, and the son shines light on those as walked in darkness. You tellin' me the Hebrew in Isaiah really says *daughter*?"

Alzbieta shook her head. "It says *son*. Though of course, it doesn't say that the son *is* the light."

Cal plowed ahead. "Not to mention old Zacharias in Luke calls Jesus the 'dayspring,' which I always reckoned had to mean the *dawn* in Hebrew."

"It means dawn," Alzbieta agreed. "In *Greek*."

"Greek." Cal threw up his arms, flustered. "Now are you tellin' me Malachi ain't talkin' about Jesus as the sun risin' with healin'?"

"I'm not telling you anything, Calvin," she said. "I'm only asking the question."

"Jerusalem." Cal retreated into silence.

"Be careful, Your Holiness," Bill drawled. "Calvin Calhoun may appear merely to be an enthusiastic New Light bible-thumper, but he's also a fighting man to be reckoned with, tomahawk in hand, and a crack shot with the Kentucky rifle."

"He is also a skilled hand with the lasso," Cathy added, "and no respecter of persons. I myself witnessed him capturing the Chevalier of New Orleans in a lariat and hog-tying the man. And he's my favorite cursing man east of the Mississippi."

Cal's flush of frustration became a blush of embarrassment. "I ain't none of those things. Hell, I ain't even much in the way of New Light, I can't generally quote you chapter and verse and I don't know my Hebrew from my home brew. I's jest . . . surprised, is all. Jerusalem, iffen one child in every three hundred and sixty-five can share Jesus' birthday, I don't see any reason why Sarah can't share it, too."

"Where does she choose?" Sarah asked. "I assume I can't just sit here and wait for Christmas."

"The Temple of the Sun," Alzbieta said.

"That sits upon Cahokia's largest and most prominent mound, Your Majesty," Bill explained.

"The *sun*?" Sarah asked. "Is she not rather the *moon*?"

Alzbieta Torias's answering smile was sly. "Build ye a temple to the greater light, and set therein a throne for the serpent. And let the throne have seven lights for those who would climb thereon."

"That ain't in the Bible," Cal muttered.

No one contradicted him.

"I'm no particular use to you in Cahokia," Jake said. "I know nothing about any of these Firstborn matters."

"You're proving to be of use to me wherever you go, Jake," Sarah told him. "But I agree, I would rather you go to Johnsland, to try to find my brother and bring him here."

"A young man fifteen years old, who *may* resemble you, *may* be named Nathaniel, and *likely* has a distinctive ear. Easy." Jake smiled. "But before I go, I'd like to be of use to you one more time here, if you will permit."

"Permit? I implore you, Jake. Be of use."

"In that case, let's descend. Despite my ignorance of the Ophidians...I have an idea about the library."

"It was the pillars that gave me the final key." Jacob Hop said. He was thrilled to present his guesses; the excitement almost took his mind off the alien memories that forced their way into his consciousness. "But my thinking started with the Tarock."

Alzbieta Torias, who had been smiling in rather too smug a fashion for a priestess, lost her grin.

"The Tarock?" Bill snorted. "Hell's Bells, Jake, next you will be saying your prayers in German."

Jake thought about that for a moment, then shook his head. "I don't think so."

"Lord hates a man as can't listen to a new idea, Bill," Calvin said. "Let's hear the little Dutchman out."

"I've been doing a lot of that lately," Bill said.

They stood outside the palace of life. The sun was sinking and the first torches were being lit by Alzbieta Torias's litter slaves against the night's darkness.

Jake held up one of the minor arcana, the three of lightning bolts. "Look," he said. "What do you see around the edges. The border, I mean."

"Circles," Cal said.

"Very good. And this one?" He held up the seven of swords.

"Circles," Cal said again. "This is a fun game. When do we git to squares?"

"In fact," Jake said, spreading out all the cards of the minor arcana, face toward his friends so they could see the borders, "all these cards have borders that are merely circles, touching at their edges."

"You ain't showin' us all the cards," Sarah said, dropping briefly into her Appalachee accent.

"Correct." Jake pocketed the minor arcana and pulled the major arcana from a different pocket. He showed the top card: the Priest. "What do you see on *this* card's border?"

"Circles again," Cal said.

"This time there's a line through the center of the circle, Cal," Cathy said, squinting. "And not just a line. A line with a squiggle."

"Very good." Jake handed Cathy the Priest. "You hold that one." Then he drew the next card and showed it: the Hanged Man.

"I know that card," Yedera said. "It's Uris."

Uris grunted and rubbed at the faint scar on his neck from Cal's lariat, which hadn't faded.

"Look at the border."

"Circle," Cal said. "Line. Same squiggle."

"Look closer," Jake suggested.

Cal did, stepping closer to peer at the card and then back to look at the Priest in Cathy's hand. "I take it back. The Priest has the squiggle above the line, and the Hanged Man has almost the same squiggle, only it's below the line."

"I had never noticed these before," Alzbieta Torias said. "But then, I'm no card reader."

"Nor I," Uris agreed. "May I see the rest of the cards?"

Jake handed over the major arcana and Uris thumbed through them. "These are letters, Your Majesty. Each of these cards is bordered with a single letter of the Ophidian writing system, repeated over and over within a circle. What Jake is showing you—is that the same mark may be made above the line, which makes it an Adam letter, or below, which makes it an Eve letter."

"Like consonants and vowels?" Sarah asked.

"No, they're all consonants. Adam and Eve letters of the same shape sometimes represent similar sounds, but not always. The vowels would be marked by indicators opposite the letter, not touching the line. These cards don't show the vowels."

"Ophidian has twenty consonants?" Sarah asked.

"Twenty symbols," Alzbieta said. "One of the letters has a null value. It indicates no consonant, but a vowel only."

Cal shook his head. "Jerusalem, iffen I ain't too old to do my A-B-Cs again."

Uris turned to Jake, looking impressed. "I know you're a fast learner of languages. Have you mastered our tongue, too?"

Jake shook his head. "I only realized a few minutes ago, up on Irra-Zostim, that these represent writing. I've been looking at the Tarocks for a week...thinking about the images on them and what they meant. I had noticed the differing borders, but assumed they were decorative. Then this morning, when I wandered through the library, I saw the letter markings, but didn't connect them with the Tarocks."

"The palace of life is a holy place," Alzbieta said. "You weren't invited in."

Jake shrugged. "There was no door stopping me."

"There is custom. And decency."

"I see," Jake said. "Invisible doors. Well, I missed those, and entered."

Sarah had her eyes closed. "The carved repeating knots. Letters. I thought they were ornamental. They reminded me of an Arab device."

"Yes," Jake agreed. "And you made nothing of them, and neither did I, Your Majesty. Only Uris and Yedera had both been emphatic that the stones atop Irra-Zostim recorded stories, so when I saw the repeating knots ascending in circles around those stones..." As he spoke, he looked up at the top of the mound, and saw files of chained prisoners being led up for sacrifice, one by one.

"You put two and two together and made four." Cal shook his head. "I'd ne'er a seen it, Jake."

"Or maybe I put three and three and four together and made seven."

Alzbieta gasped.

So he was right. He permitted himself a smile.

"That's a bit cryptic, Sergeant," Bill said.

Jake collected the cards from the others and pocketed them again. "I think you'll find that one key to the library's organization is simply writing. There are ten rooms, and ten characters representing consonants in Ophidian writing. Depending on which side of the line you place the letter, it belongs to Eve or to Adam. So my first guess would be that each room is marked by one of those characters, and is meant to contain writings whose title, or perhaps subject, begins with the Eve-Adam pair."

Uris laughed out loud. "Where did you find this fellow, Your Majesty? I'd like another dozen like him."

"I don't think there *are* a dozen like him," Sarah murmured.

"But there may be another organizational key," Jake said, "and it's suggested by the layout of the rooms."

"Three rows of rooms," Sarah said. "A row of three on each side, and a row of four in the middle."

"Which makes ten rooms," Jake said. "And that matches the alphabet. On the other hand, you will have noticed, as I have, that the Eldritch seem to like everything in sevens."

"Not everything," Cal said. "They count by twelve."

"They do?" Jake considered. "Hmmm."

"The Sevenfold Crown," Sarah said. "The Seven Kingdoms."

"And there were seven kingdoms in the Old World, Uris has told us," Jake added. "Before the stars fell and the waters rose."

"It ain't obvious to me how you make seven from ten," Sarah said. "Lessen you jest lop off one side of the buildin'."

"May I borrow one of your crutches, Bill?" Jake asked.

Bill handed over the stick. Cathy immediately moved to his side and took his free arm.

Near the library door was a patch of soft earth. Jake drew the long central row of rooms, four circles in a row. "Here is the trunk of the tree."

"Tree?" Sarah asked.

"Tree." He drew three rooms on each side of the central line. "If I draw in all the connecting doors and passages, you get a fairly complex lattice. But look what results if I only draw out the first passage connecting to each of these lateral rooms, beginning at the front door and proceeding toward the back."

He sketched in the six lines.

"A tree," Sarah said. "With a central trunk and three branches on each side. Seven branches."

"What does it *mean*?" Cal asked.

"That is the right question," Jake admitted, "and I don't know the answer. I can only tell you I'm absolutely certain that this pattern has some significance because of the look of shock at this moment on Alzbieta Torias's face."

Alzbieta stepped back as everyone looked at her, but the astonishment didn't fade. "I admit nothing."

Cathy laughed softly.

"Is he wrong?" Sarah asked.

"I also *deny* nothing." The Eldritch priestess stared at Jake. "How did you . . . what did . . . ?"

Jake shrugged. "I find that the quickest way to get useful answers is to ask exactly the right questions."

"You were going to drop hints and slowly lead me down the paths to secret knowledge, weren't you?" Sarah asked her Ophidian cousin. "Just think of Jake as my physically embodied, question-posing intuition."

"Whom you are sending to Johnsland to recover your brother?" Jake confirmed.

"Yes," she agreed.

"And Margaret?" Cathy reminded her.

"We'll see," Sarah said. "Perhaps you, when the times comes."

"We'll want some method for staying in touch," Jake said. "Perhaps something faster than letters entrusted to Dutch Ohio Company traders."

"I have an idea about that," Sarah said. "Alzbieta, do you have a writing slate? Such as a child might use to learn her school lessons?"

God in heaven, guide me.

Chigozie Ukwu shivered. The rain fell in drizzling sheets and had systematically soaked into his cloaking. The wool cloak stopped the wind, but it didn't cover his head or his hands.

Once, he'd imagined he'd labor in the vineyards of New Orleans his entire life, working at his father's side and—he admitted it to himself, though speaking it out loud felt impious—maybe even succeeding his father in the bishopric. The Synod's choice of Bishop Ukwu to replace the corrupt de Bienville who'd preceded him had been a great success. Might they not reinforce that success by appointing a second Ukwu after him? An Ukwu who had worked hard without aspiring, who had served humbly, who had showed devotion and commitment to his father and his parishioners?

And indeed, the Synod *had* chosen an Ukwu.

Only it had chosen the bad son.

"The *bad* son," Chigozie muttered out loud to reinforce the thought. Not the *prodigal*, for this was no parable in which Chigozie would play the part of the hard-working but proud older brother.

Etienne hadn't *wandered*, he had *fled* the path of Christian service. He had chosen the left-hand road, crime and Vodun, the inheritance of Bishop de Bienville that Bishop Ukwu had fought so hard to obliterate.

Could it be true, as Etienne insisted, that their mother spoke to him?

He dismissed the idea. She had grown up in a Vodun home, but had married for love a man who had left the seminary for her. And she had left Vodun for him... had she not? His choice to become a deacon during their marriage committed him to celibacy after she died and ultimately put him in the priesthood after all, but that was no betrayal.

Could *she* have betrayed *him* by continuing her Vodun, and becoming even a mambo, and after *her* death, the gede loa of her younger son?

Was it even possible that she was a mambo, and her husband had known?

Chigozie shook his head to clear it.

He could no longer bear the sight of New Orleans.

Once, the Bishop of Miami had been a mentor to him, a second bishop observing his pastoral progress and advocating for him in the Synod. But it was the Bishop of Miami who had told Chigozie that he, Miami, had voted in favor of Etienne's anointing, and that Etienne would succeed their father.

Chigozie doubted he could bear the sight of Miami, either.

He had burned his priestly garb and gone north.

He kept his cross.

A Memphite barge carried him, giving him passage and a small wage in exchange for work on the oar. He'd been tempted to identify himself as a priest, and offer to bless the vessel, its passengers and crew, and their food in exchange for his passage. It would have been easier work.

But if God had wanted Chigozie to do easy work, He would have made Chigozie bishop. And he hadn't. So God wanted something harder from the good son.

Chigozie had manned an oar.

His hands were blistered within hours. Before the end of the first day, they'd popped and he'd torn the skin beneath, leaving streaks of blood on the oar and hurting even when he lay in his narrow cot that night. But the pain in his hands, and the even greater ache of his back and shoulder muscles, had satisfied him.

Perhaps his shoulders simply ached so much that he didn't notice his heartache by comparison.

That evening, he'd been unable to pray.

The next day he'd rushed to his oar, urging the nighttime occupant to vacate the bench early. The scabs on his hands had cracked and bled, the ache in his muscles became a fire, he wolfed down his bread and beans at noon as fast as he could so he could return to rowing. If the tall, dark-skinned, red-headed oarmaster noticed Chigozie's wounds, he offered him no mercy on their account.

When night fell, Chigozie wished he were shackled to the oar.

That, too, he dared not say aloud.

The docks at Memphis were crowded with refugees rushing south. Mississippi Germans, farmers from Missouri, Hansa merchants. Chigozie had passed his small wages out among the refugees, choosing women who were traveling without men to share his copper coins with. The stories he heard from them were confused.

Had beastkind destroyed their settlement?

Had raiders, the children of Adam, ransacked their warehouses and burned their keelboats?

Was there an army on the march?

Were the princes of the Ohio mobilizing for war?

He heard a song there, with a familiar melody, but words he'd never heard before. The lyric he knew was that of a simple love song, but in its entirety, the ballad seemed to tell a tale of tragedy and loss, with names he mostly did not recognize.

> *The Hansa Towns shut me out homeless*
> *Away, you rolling river*
> *I toiled enslaved for bloody Zomas*
> *Away, I'm bound away, across the wide Missouri*
>
> *Beneath the towers of Etzanoa*
> *Away, you rolling river*
> *I spoke this prayer for Shenandoah*
> *Away, I'm bound away, across the wide Missouri*

In the hopeful eyes of a German woman to whom he'd given his last coin, Chigozie had found purpose. There was suffering in the north. What was a priest, if not one who sought to alleviate suffering? If he could not be a Levite, he could be a Samaritan, gathering up the wounded and binding their injuries.

He headed north and west on foot, directly into the Great Green Woods.

He had made his way by whatever tracks he could find, from small farm to small farm through the forest, avoiding the castles of the barons and the main roads. He chopped wood for food, or butchered livestock, and in one case carried a message from one homestead to the next, twenty miles through the forest, in exchange for a loaf of bread and a thick slice of pickled beef.

He'd hid more than once to let the strange creatures of the Great Green Wood pass. He'd seen aurochs, the nearly elephant-sized cattle with enormous horns, and sloths ten feet tall, loping between the trees, and even the elusive miniature ponies some called *dawn-horses*, which were the size of dogs and had four-toed feet. He'd approached the dawn-horses through the mud on his knees, hoping to touch one, but they'd fled at the sight of him.

Mercifully, he hadn't seen dire wolves, or basilisks, or any of the other deadlier inhabitants of the Wood and the Missouri.

Then he'd come across the burning wagon.

Three bodies lay face-down on the forest path. One horse lay near them, and all four bodies were savagely torn. The wagon, a cart almost too big to pass through the narrow track, had been smashed and its contents strewn into the trees: clothing, farm tools, some dried and salted foodstuffs.

He'd heard an animal snort behind him. Assuming it might be a second horse, Chigozie had turned slowly—

and found himself staring at half a dozen beastfolk.

God in heaven, guide me.

The thought was a prayer, the first prayer he'd said since his final conversation with Etienne. The sheer power of the act of commencing the prayer forced him to his knees.

The beastman at the front of the pack was heavy-shouldered, with tiny legs and a bison's head. He was naked and filthy. Despite the flat herbivore's teeth, he held in one hand what at first glance appeared to be a chicken wing, and as Chigozie stared up at the beastman, he took a large bite from the meat, spraying warm blood on Chigozie's face and hands. But the meat came from no bird.

It was a man's leg.

In his other hand, the bison-headed monster held an enormous club.

God, you want me to suffer, and I will suffer for you, Chigozie prayed silently. *You have put me in the hands of these beasts. Let me here do your will.*

In answer, Chigozie saw no angel, heard no ringing bell, smelled no frankincense. But a warm glow suffused him, and it was enough.

"Kill the son of Adam," rumbled another of the beastkind, moving forward. This one had a cat's hind legs and a face that resembled a lamprey's: a round mouth with rows of jagged teeth, and nothing Chigozie could identify as an eye.

"That's no son of Adam," growled a third. This beastman looked like a fish with legs. "It is too dark. Is it one of us?"

Behind them stood other beastkind who did not come forward: one with a rabbit's head, one with the upper body of a stag, one that looked like an octopus but dragged itself across dry land. Some of the beastkind lingering at the back seemed baffled by the English conversation, sniffing the air and pawing the earth.

"Are you one of us?" Bison Head asked. He took another bite, tearing away a mouthful of muscle and with it a sinew that dangled from his mouth like a stray noodle.

"I am one of you," Chigozie said. They were unplanned words, the phrase that sprang into his mind.

"Lies!" Lamprey-Cat shrieked. "It is a child of Adam! Kill it!"

"I'm not hungry," Bison Head growled. "Are you hungry?"

Lamprey-Cat skulked away.

"I am a child of Adam," Chigozie admitted.

"But you're brown." Fish blew a stream of thick spittle from its round lips in disbelief.

"You say you're one of us." Bison Head asked. He licked blood off the bone with a tongue the size of Chigozie's head and cast the bone aside. "How can that be?"

"I am a son of Adam," Chigozie said. "And so are you."

Fish and Lamprey-Cat both made sounds like giggling, but Bison Head responded by standing straighter, staring at Chigozie with inscrutable black eyes, and finally blinking slowly.

"I hadn't been told this," he said.

Chigozie began to recite. He found himself in Genesis. "And it came to pass, when men began to multiply on the face of the

earth, and daughters were born unto them, that the sons of God
saw the daughters of men that they were fair; and they took them
wives of all which they chose...There were giants in the earth
in those days; and also after that, when the sons of God came in
unto the daughters of men, and they bare children to them, the
same became mighty men which were of old, men of renown."

Chigozie hadn't planned that answer at all. Did that mean
it was inspired?

"What's that?" Bison Head asked.

"It is God's word," Chigozie said. "It is history. It is about the
birth of your people. You are the mighty men, the children of
the giants, who were born to the sons of God and the daughters
of Adam. Some might call you the *nephilim*, the fallen ones, but
you and I, we are all children of Adam. We are kin."

Bison Head stared.

Behind him, Lamprey-Cat hissed softly.

Then Bison Head leaned backward, placing both hands on his
hips, and began to laugh. It was a laugh that began in his belly
and rolled up and down until his entire body shook.

Once Bison Head was laughing, the other beastkind quickly
joined in. They closed ranks and came forward, forming a circle
around Chigozie, and he found himself staring up into a closed
net of animal faces with bloodied muscles, guffawing, snorting,
and hissing in mocking hilarity at his words.

Then Bison Head stopped laughing.

"I'm not hungry now," the beastkind leader said. "But I'll be
hungry later. Bring him along."

"Alive?" Lamprey-Cat asked.

"He'll be fresh when I wish to eat him."

God in heaven, make me thine instrument.

"I think you gravely overestimate the
appetite most people have for accounting."

———◆———

CHAPTER THIRTEEN

Nathaniel opened his eyes and he hurt.

~*The man-thing is not dead.*~

"The man-thing is not dead," he said, caught unawares.

"No, you are not. I wouldn't have called you a *thing*, though."

Nathaniel raised his head. He was still bound in a wool blanket and his mouth was dry. "Will you release me?"

Ma'iingan sat a few feet away, cross-legged on the earth, humming a tune Nathaniel didn't know. "You're not my prisoner, God-Has-Given. But I think it might be wise to lie still a little longer."

"I have to get back," he said.

"Don't worry," Ma'iingan said. "It's already too late. In your absence, the whole Turtle Kingdom collapsed. Just gave up. Without the boy Nathaniel, they said, can there be any point to any of this, na?"

"That's not it." Nathaniel lay back.

"Hmm. Well, my manidoo sent me to take care of you. I don't think I'd be doing a very good job if I let you reopen all your wounds."

"*My* manidoo said you should let me go." Nathaniel said it impulsively, but the Ojibwe seemed to consider it seriously.

"It's your manidoo that makes you scream strange things, na?" the Indian asked.

"Like what?"

"Like 'the man-thing is not dead.' Is that a message from your manidoo?"

The whine in his ear became a shriek. "I don't think I have a manidoo," Nathaniel said. "That was just a joke. My people don't get a manidoo. Except the New Light, they believe they get the Holy Ghost. But that's different. I think."

"Maybe this is the problem. I like jokes, but maybe you need a manidoo. Maybe all you Zhaaganaashii need a manidoo."

"I don't think that's the problem. Besides, did your manidoo tell you to help all the...English speakers, or just me?"

~Death! Death! Death!~

"Death!"

"*Zhaaganaashii* is the word you're looking for." Ma'iingan observed him closely. "Maybe you have a manidoo and you don't know it. Though if so, your manidoo seems to have a dark sense of humor."

Nathaniel only shook his head.

Ma'iingan shrugged. "Well, my manidoo said you're a great healer. It said you've been laid low, and if I can help you rise again, you can heal my son."

Nathaniel opened and closed his mouth several times before he found words. "That's...that doesn't make any sense. I can't heal anybody."

"Henh, not now," Ma'iingan agreed. "You are laid low."

"That's because I'm tied up in your blanket. If you want to raise me up, let me out of this...bundle board, or whatever you called it."

"Cradleboard. I think that's the Zhaaganaashii word. A dako-binaawaswaan, in the language of the People. Not one of the words you borrowed from us."

"We borrowed words from you?"

"Of course. Wiigiwaam. Makizin. Plus some animals: mooz, jidmoonh."

"What's a jidmoonh?"

"You know it. Like a small squirrel."

A chipmunk. "Well, isn't that how it goes? Languages borrow." Nathaniel cast about for an example. "What do you call your rifle over there, in Ojibwe?"

"Anwii-baashkizigan. I don't think we learned that word from the Zhaaganaashii. Or the Germans."

"What about money? What do you call a shilling?"

"Waabik." Ma'iingan scratched his chin. "It means *iron*, actually."

"You call a shilling *iron*? They're made of silver."

"Henh. But you know, the Moundbuilders make their money out of iron, and we've known them longer than we've known you."

"So you borrowed the term from them!"

"No, *waabik* is an Anishinaabe word. We just borrowed the idea."

"Close enough," Nathaniel muttered.

The Indian stood and stretched. "Very well, Nathaniel. Tell me why you're so anxious to get back. Before, you were certain no one would miss you. No one would even come look for you, except maybe Charles. Now you want to go back. Tell me the truth, you're just frightened of me, na?" He grinned, an expression that was fierce and comical at the same time.

Nathaniel laughed.

"Well, usually I only get that reaction from women and small children. But you *are* bound in a dakobinaawaswaan." He crossed his arms over his chest. "Too bad, God-Has-Given. You can learn to live with a little fear."

"I'll be blamed," Nathaniel said. "I know it."

"Blamed?" Ma'iingan frowned. "Blamed for what?"

"George played a joke on me and Landon. Mostly on Landon. And Landon was humiliated, and there were witnesses."

Ma'iingan cocked his head to one side. "Landon ran away naked in the night."

"People saw him. George will mock him. And Landon will do what he always does."

"Take his clothes off and roll around in pig shit, na?"

"No, that's...unusual. That only happened once. What happens all the time is he gets bitten by George, and he turns around and bites me."

"Good. You aren't there, he can't bite you."

"Yes he can. He can tell others his humiliation was my fault. He can say I played the joke, or..." Nathaniel searched his worst fears, "he can tell them I ran away. That I was scared of the farmer with the blunderbuss, and I ran. That I'm a coward."

"To be called a coward is a much less terrible thing than actually to be a coward, Nathaniel."

"But people will believe him." Nathaniel felt moisture in his eyes. It was the physical pain from the wounds in his arms and leg, he told himself.

~*Pain is life. Pain is life.*~

"Pain."

"Why will they believe him?" Ma'iingan looked skeptical. "Does Landon possess some great reputation for truthfulness?"

"He's...more important than me."

The Indian stared.

"He's the earl's son. A bastard, so he won't ever be earl himself, but he'll be set up with land someday, and when he's old enough he'll have a commission. Or he'll get easy admission to the College of Godar in Raleigh, if he wants to and Old One Eye will have him. I'm nobody, I'm just an orphan."

Ma'iingan considered. "Well, my manidoo made no mention of Landon or Old One Eye or any of the others. And it said *you* were a great healer. So that makes you more important than Landon to me, and to my son."

"But the earl..." Nathaniel groped. "Charles. Even George and Landon, and Jenny Farewell, and the others. They're my people."

"Ah." The Ojibwe nodded. "You fear separation from your people."

"Yes," Nathaniel said. "And from my world."

Ma'iingan knelt and began unwrapping the blanket. "You'll find the world is much bigger than your people, Zhaaganaashii God-Has-Given. If the manidoo of a simple man from the headwaters of the Michi-Zibii can send to have you summoned to heal a child, then you have journeys long and strange ahead of you."

"But you're unwrapping me."

"Henh. I would not have any person cut off from his people," the Ojibwe said. "But we'll travel slow, and you won't leave my sight. You understand, na?"

"I promise," Nathaniel said.

Ojibwe laughed. "Silly Zhaaganaashii."

"Why's that? Why am I silly?" Nathaniel sat up carefully, feeling pain lance into his wounded limbs and especially his rib. "Can I have some water, please?"

Ma'iingan threw the blanket back over his shoulders like a cape and fetched a birch-bark bowl full of cold water. Nathaniel sipped at it, feeling the shock as the chilled liquid soaked his tongue and the insides of his cheeks.

"You know that if you say 'I promise' when you want me really to believe you, that tells me that when you don't say 'I promise,' you don't really mean it, na? If you speak the truth all the time and keep all your obligations, you never have to say you promise."

Nathaniel reached out an arm and Ma'iingan helped him climb to his feet. "Do you think that's what I need, is to be taught a lesson in frank speaking?"

"No, I'm just a fountain of wisdom. I can't help it, I walk around with good advice and proverbs falling from my fingertips and getting tangled in my hair. Try not to trip on the good sense I accidentally fling into your path. That's what my name, Ma'iingan, means. Fountain of wisdom."

"You said it meant *wolf.*"

"Ah, caught in a lie, again."

Ahmed Abd al-Wahid, prince-capitaine of the order of mamelukes of the Caliphate of Egypt and the West, tried not to breathe in the fumes.

Even on his previous visit, he had found the smell of the chevalier's Palais off-putting. Under the best of conditions, it smelled like the Christian and Jewish quarters of Paris; of sweat, of unfreshened breath, and of the occasional hint of full chamberpot, wafting in from a bedchamber on an inopportune breeze. That latrine stench of Christendom never went away, and no amount of Cologne water (which the wealthy of New Orleans applied in cloyingly large amounts) and tobacco smoke (with which the inhabitants of this continent seemed determined to fumigate their entire land) could completely hide it.

All of Paris had once smelled thus, he knew. Abd al-Wahid was Egyptian, born a mameluke to a mameluke father and trained in Egypt's madrassas in the classical arts of language, literature, swordplay, strategy, herbalism, medicine, and the Qur'an. After the westerner Napoleon had first ingratiated himself into the mameluke brotherhood, then been initiated and finally exalted to its head, Abd al-Wahid had been part of the mameluke vanguard to return with him to conquer Paris.

The conquered parts had been scoured, irrigated, introduced to incense and spices. Those parts—the neighborhoods of Paris that were truly part of al-Islam, and not in name only—were now a garden of delights, the air breathable and the streets safe.

In their ghettoes, Christians dickered over the price of grain and Jews made sour faces over the interest rates of payable instruments in fetid clouds of mankindity of which New Orleans was a pungent reminder.

Now the Palais was full of smoke. Not the delightful citrus smell of frankincense burning, or the anointing fragrance of myrrh and cloves together in virgin olive oil, but thick, nose-shattering smoke made by burning a weed Abd al-Wahid did not recognize, green and fresh from the earth.

Clay pots stood at the corners of each room and at intervals in the halls. If he stooped, he knew he could get his head beneath the thick clouds and see more clearly, but Abd al-Wahid stayed erect.

A mameluke didn't stoop, except to pray.

And he liked that the thick, aromatic smoke tended to hide from his view the many idolatrous paintings with which the chevalier decorated his palace. Abd al-Wahid knew they were saints from the style of the paintings, with strange little icons—fish and books and weapons—attached to each figure, but he couldn't have identified any of them.

They were all idols to him.

The other five mamelukes in his party followed him: Ravi the Jew, who was an alchemist and astrologer; Zayyid al-Syri, who knew poisons and the care of beasts; Nabil al-Muhasib, who had memorized maps of this New World Empire and was the only member of the party other than Abd al-Wahid to speak its languages well; Tariq al-Farangi, who had been born *Gerard*, to Christian parents, and who was master of the intricacies of both ship and wagon; and Omar al-Talib, who claimed he had read every book in the al-Qayrawan mosque, but was such a liar that no one believed him. Still, Omar was a subtle torturer and a competent physician.

Abd al-Wahid had expected that he might be in this New World a long time, hunting the renegade Talleyrand across the filthy, freezing continent, and he had chosen his men carefully. They weren't loyal to him—al-Farangi and al-Muhasib had been known to Abd al-Wahid only by reputation before he'd selected them—but they were loyal to the order, to the Caliph, and to the prophet.

Peace be upon him.

They had come to the New World in eight, but two of those eight had returned to Paris with Talleyrand's head.

They climbed a staircase behind one of the chevalier's servants.

"The smoke," Abd al-Wahid asked, looking at Ravi and Omar each in turn. "What do you make of it?"

"I wish they were burning their furniture. This building has so many cabinets and bookcases!" Tariq laughed harshly. "A true man needs no furnishing but a mat."

"For prayer?" Al-Farangi asked. "Or for entertaining a woman?"

"By God," Tariq said, "I can't always tell the difference!"

Abd al-Wahid permitted himself a hidden smile.

"The smoke is against illness," Ravi said.

"Couldn't they spoil the air in the room only where the sick person lies, O stargazing son of Isaac?" Zayyid al-Syri coughed.

Tariq laughed again. "But it's the chevalier who is ill, and so his servants must suffer as well. It's the way of all great men."

Omar shook his head. "No, they fear contagion."

"What is it they burn?" al-Wahid asked.

"I know not, prince-capitaine," Omar said. "I know only that it stinks."

"Barbarians!" Ravi spat into the soil of a potted lemon tree.

"Christians!" Al-Farangi joined him in spitting.

"I believe I know the scent," al-Syri offered.

"A poison?" For a moment, Abd al-Wahid feared he had been lured into a trap to be murdered.

"Peppered camel's dung," al-Syri said. "Wet. Heavy on the pepper. With dried orange rind added for nuance."

"You have smelled such a compound before?" Abd al-Wahid asked.

"In Jerusalem," al-Syri said. "It was sold as a food."

"Only to children of Ishmael," Ravi fired back. "They're accustomed to eating camel's dung without any spices at all, and so regard the addition of the orange rind and the pepper as a great sophistication."

Abd al-Wahid laughed drily, and then the servant ushered them into a room.

This was the audience chamber where the chevalier had seen them before. The desk was gone, replaced with a bed such as the French kings before the Caliph had used to receive morning visitors. Bloated and pale, they had lain in their nightclothes in bed to demonstrate their power to force the nobility of their land to approach them in a ridiculous circumstance.

Now they all lay in muddy unmarked graves, downriver from Paris along the Seine.

But the chevalier lay in bed not to demonstrate his power, but as a sign of his illness. In the corners of this room stood not one smoking pot, but four, one per corner. A young girl sat on a stool to the chevalier's side, dabbing at his face with a damp cloth.

The Chevalier of New Orleans was skeletal. The flesh on his face, and his neck and hands, and around his collarbone where it was visible, had all sunk and turned gray. Here and there the ashen skin was marked with lesions, bleeding and oozing dark yellow liquid, leaving the chevalier's nightshirt a mottled orange and brown. The chevalier's beard had grown in along his jaw, thin and patchy. The orbs of his eyes were dark yellow and his teeth looked unnaturally long—his gums were receding.

"Va-t'en." His voice was sepulchral. The girl set down her rag and duly left.

Abd al-Wahid spoke to his fellows in Arabic. "When I am ill, it is God who heals me."

"Perhaps," al-Syri said drily, "the chevalier doesn't know the Qur'an as well as you do."

The chevalier exhaled, his breath rattling like the gasps of a dying man in his chest. He continued in French. "What experience do you have with curses?"

It was an unexpected question. "There is the evil eye," Abd al-Wahid said. "One does not compliment a mother too enthusiastically on the beauty of her child, for fear it may attract the envy of the djinn."

The chevalier waved his hand impatiently. "I mean *real* curses."

"By a magician?"

"Worse. A holy man."

Ahmed Abd al-Wahid considered. "Then you fear that it's God Himself who has cursed you, by the instrument of this holy man."

"Priest. Yes. He laid it upon me while living, and then the curse struck me the day the holy man was laid in his grave."

Abd al-Wahid consulted with Ravi. Everyone knew that for exorcism, you asked a Jew.

"Tell him, if God wanted the chevalier dead, the chevalier

would be dead," Ravi said. "This isn't the work of God, it's the work of a sorcerer. Or perhaps his humors are out of balance."

Abd al-Wahid passed on the message.

"Perhaps. The pain struck me first when I removed... certain defensive talismans. And when I tried to replace them, the talismans themselves burned." The chevalier ruminated. "The priest's son. The man you are to kill. He has a reputation for being a Vodun sorcerer."

The mameluke had little sense of what this word *Vodun* meant. "He's also a priest, like his father. And he is loved, if I'm to judge by the crowd that filled the cathedral."

"Ask him," Ravi said, "is the fumigation a magical defense against the curse?"

Abd al-Wahid turned to the chevalier. "Is the reason you're burning this camel's dung to protect you against the curse?"

The chevalier laughed, just a bit at first, and then enough that he vomited, leaning over to spit a yellow string of bile to the floor. "It's not camel's dung," he said. "I think. And yes."

Abd al-Wahid translated.

"Good." Ravi bobbed his head enthusiastically. "His defense is working, but it's not enough. So tell him, get his own sorcerer. Not to defend, you understand, but to go on the attack. Like a boxer, the chevalier must punch back until his enemy is compelled to pull away."

Abd al-Wahid translated. The chevalier's eyebrows rose slightly. "And you? What will you do?"

Abd al-Wahid sighed. "This man is difficult. He has many bodyguards, and for much of his day he's surrounded by them. The time when he's most exposed is when he's preaching in the cathedral."

"You attacked him there before."

"Yes."

"And failed."

"He's protected by some... power of fascination. He has djinn with him, or houris, and they are mighty to attract and command women."

The chevalier coughed. "If I have a choice, I'd rather he not be killed during an actual service. That would be two bishops in a row, and it might be too much for even the most jaded residents of New Orleans."

Abd al-Wahid bowed slightly, hand on his heart. "We'll find the right moment. Fear not, Chevalier; it is only a matter of time."

"Josep!" Montse called.

The man who poked his head up over the rail of *La Verge Caníbal* wasn't Josep, but Miquel. Miquel was Josep's younger cousin, too young to have seen war but old enough to have slipped through more blockades than he could remember.

Miquel waved. "Montserrat!"

Montse waved back and waited. She stood on a rocky arm of land that crawled out past jungle and bayou to create a small bay, unseen from any highway and out of the way of the sea-lanes. Two fires burned low beside her, two to make a coherent signal because a single fire might be laid by a casual traveler or a fisherman. *La Verge Caníbal* had sailed in in response to the fires and now dropped anchor.

She was a beautiful sloop, large enough to pose a threat to most commercial vehicles, but small enough to hide even on this busy coast, and with a sufficiently shallow draft that she could sail up the Mississippi at least as far as Shreveport. Her name was painted proudly on her prow, as if she were an Imperial cruiser—though a patch of black-painted sailcloth could be dropped over the name at a moment's notice to conceal it—and her Catalan crew now hastily threw two men overboard in a small boat to come retrieve their captain.

Josep was one of them. Once her would-be lover, his success was making him portly, but he was a deadly gunner with small arms as well as with cannons, and knew every spar and plank of *La Verge Caníbal* as if the ship, and not its mistress, was the woman he had wooed for years.

Josep sat in front. Miquel sat behind and plied the oars.

Montse had released the chevalier's horse to freedom miles away and walked here. Her route had taken her past alligator-infested creeks and muddy trickles squirming with venomous snakes.

Josep sprang to the earth and tweaked both mustachios before opening his arms. "Montse, meu amor!" he exclaimed.

"Josep, you fat bastard, you've been eating sugar candy non-stop since I left."

Josep nodded vigorously. "And washing it down with rum. How else shall I console myself for the absence of the light of my life?"

"If I die, you can have the ship," Montse said. "That's all I have for you, and you know it."

"You will no doubt live longer than I, Capità, and deprive me of my inheritance."

"That's certainly my plan."

They embraced briefly.

Miquel stepped into the shallow water and steadied the boat with his hands.

"The ship, I have taken good care of her in your absence, Capità," Josep said.

"You may as well tell me you have breathed in the time since I left, Josep. Of course you've taken excellent care of her." Montse stepped into the boat and sat down.

"In anxious anticipation that you would return to our ménage a trois." Josep leaped into the boat. Despite his bulk, he landed with perfect poise and the boat barely noticed his arrival.

"Why do you soil your manly Catalan lips with French words, Josep? They aren't worthy of your blood."

"In your absence, what else shall I soil them with? What but your skin would be worthy?"

"Never mind. If it keeps your sugar-stained lips away from me, speak all the French you like."

Josep and Miquel both hesitated, looking at the jungle at the end of the spur of earth.

"And Margarida?" Josep asked.

"Margarida has been taken," she said.

"Was she captured by the customs men?" Miquel's voice was proud. "The girl is old enough to spend a little time with the gendarmes, until we find the man to bribe."

"The girl isn't one of us," Montse said slowly.

"Why do you talk nonsense?" Josep cut her off sharply. "Of course she is one of us. *La Verge Caníbal* won't abandon any of her crew."

"Yes," Montse agreed. "*La Verge Caníbal* will abandon no one. But the girl has another heritage, and now I must tell it to you, if I'm to ask you to risk your lives."

"Well." Josep raised both his eyebrows several times in quick succession. "You could offer me other compensations besides knowledge."

"You'll die lonely waiting for me, Josep," she said.

"I'll die," he agreed. "But I'm not lonely."

"What's her heritage, then?" Miquel asked.

Montse stared at the jungle, and beyond it, the Pontchartrain and New Orleans. "She's the daughter of Hannah Penn, the greatest beauty ever to walk the woods and fields of Pennsland, and the King of Cahokia. She's a true princess born, and the Chevalier of New Orleans wishes to hold her hostage."

Miquel whistled low.

"I don't think so," Josep said immediately, a gleam in his eyes.

"No?"

"No. I think my friend Margarida is a Catalan to her bones, and the Chevalier of New Orleans is about to learn that no es fote mai amb els catalans."

The members of the City Council looked astonished.

There was the Dutch furniture merchant, Van Dijk, in a fine black frock coat and white cravat despite the hour; the weave of his waistcoat matched a popular style of upholstery he sold to the grandees of the city, a style called *Champlain*, for the great family of Acadia. Van Dijk was tall, thin, and beardless; white-haired, bespectacled, and baffled.

Van Dijk sat at the end of the table where the Council deliberated formally. The table rested on a broad dais at one end of a long room, which was filled with upholstered, wooden chairs on which an audience could sit.

The chairs were upholstered, naturally, in Champlain.

Beside him lounged Renan DuBois, a mixed French-Bantu plantation owner whose lands were on the border Louisiana shared with the Cotton Princedoms, but who preferred to spend his time in Etienne's casino, losing the Louis d'or his cotton earned at the gaming tables. Renan looked wary.

The third member of the City Council was Onyinye Diokpo. The heavy Igbo woman might have been Etienne's grandmother, for the lines around her eyes and the gray in her hair; she owned a constellation of elegant hotels along the Esplanade, and a galaxy of less elegant boarding rooms, hostels, and dives elsewhere throughout the city. Her dress was the colorful but simple garb you might see in any of the Igbo Free Cities, but her jewelry was gold and she wore a lot of it.

Beside Onyinye sat Eoin Kennedie. The Irishman's face looked younger than his years, and his keen eye was trained on Etienne. Kennedie owned a legitimate business, a tavern in the Faubourg Marigny, but what he really did was fence stolen and smuggled goods. His team of enforcers and leg-breakers almost amounted to a rival gang to Etienne. Eoin's jacket was made of costly black leather, but from the bulges at several corners, Etienne guessed the Irishman had metal plates sewed into the garment. Were the plates to deflect physical blows?

The final member of the City Council was Holahta Hopaii, a Choctaw tribal leader. Hopaii's plain white shirt and gray waistcoat and trousers made him look like a shopkeeper, but Etienne understood he was viewed in his tribe as a prophet. His people were numerous north of the city, and his membership on the Council was an attempt to keep the Choctaw from joining the Catalans and the Igbo in the lucrative smuggling trade.

Membership on the City Council had always been, in effect, a bribe. The chevalier neutralized potential rivals by paying them a stipend to do nothing. Those of the council members whose businesses were less than fully legitimate also gained a patina of respectability behind which to shelter their operations. The chevalier in turn gained a different veneer—a façade of democratic accountability. Since his was an inherited title, and inheritance alone made him a landowner and an Elector, a City Council voted into office, even if only taxpayers were allowed to vote, gave necessary vent to demands for elected government, such as the Hudson River Republicans boasted.

Most of the councilors ran unopposed. Candidates who ran against the chevalier inevitably lost, however enthusiastic the public might appear for them.

"Ladies and gentlemen," Etienne said, "I have come to give you purpose."

"We have purpose," Van Dijk sputtered. "We govern the city."

Onyinye laughed, a short, sharp bark. "There is someone in this city who will believe that ridiculous lie, Thijs. Not this man."

"I had the impression that one of my fellow councilors had called this meeting," Eoin said. "If I was mistaken, I'll just head back to the *Duke of Ormond*. I've customers to see to."

"How safe do you feel, Eoin?" Etienne asked.

To his left and behind him stood August Planchet, the beadle. To his right, Monsieur Bondí. Both were doing an admirable job of holding still. Armand at the door kept out several bodyguards, as well as any others who might come along. The deep scimitar-inflicted gash in Armand's side was healing nicely, but his facial expression hadn't varied from grim resolution since the day of the cathedral attack.

The meeting's timing—midnight—made a casual passerby unlikely.

"Fairly safe, I s'pose," Eoin said coolly. "I've lads enough, if ye mean to threaten me."

Etienne raised his empty hands in a show of peaceful intentions. "We're all threatened here."

"I was sorry to hear of your father's death," Van Dijk said. "He was a powerful preacher. And I attended your funeral mass; you're coming along nicely as a priest, yourself."

"Though you were a somewhat unexpected choice on the part of the Synod," Onyinye said.

Hopaii laughed. "An *unexpected* choice is not necessarily a *bad* choice."

"I could not agree more," Etienne said, "with both of you. And I've come today to propose another unexpected choice."

"I just don't see what I have to dread from the chevalier." Kennedie stood, his coat falling about him with a soft *clank*. "He pays me. He knows there'll be smugglin' and theft, and his people will need someone to sell those items. He leaves me in business, and we both prosper."

Etienne squinted. "If he would kill a defenseless old man, Eoin, why would he not kill you?"

"I s'pose because I'll avoid the mistake of standin' up in public to call him a thief and a murderer. I s'pose because I'll continue to provide his people a service they need, and support him as Chevalier of New Orleans."

Etienne considered. "You tell him what you buy. That's why he pays you. If you're the biggest fence in town, he keeps you on the payroll, and then he always knows what's happening in the black market."

"That's only a rumor," DuBois said.

"Also, not especially polite to say it in public," Onyinye added.

"This isn't public." Eoin Kennedie laughed. "And I'll admit it, yes, I tell his man what I buy. Most of it, anyway. Not everything. And I'm not the biggest fence in town, Etienne. That would be *you*."

Etienne dragged a sixth chair from the audience's space up to the dais and dropped himself into it. "I have been trying to master the Christian virtues, since taking orders. Humility is not the most natural of them to me, but you make it more difficult when you say such flattering things."

"They say the chevalier is ill," the Irishman continued. "Death's door, as I heard it. Was that your doin', Ukwu?"

Etienne kept a carefully composed straight face. "You wish to flatter me even more."

Eoin laughed and sat back down. He moved gingerly, like man with back trouble. Maybe it was the weight of the plates in his jacket, though Kennedie had fought Jackson alongside the Lafittes, and was known to have taken wounds.

Onyinye looked at Etienne out of the corners of her eyes. "The Christian virtue of chastity comes more naturally to you, I hear," she said. "Chastity of a sort."

"Of a sort." Etienne settled back into his chair and took a cigarette from his pocket. Striking a Lucifer match, he lit the tobacco and sucked through the first wisps of smoke. Tobacco tended to keep the Brides placated. "I would not appeal only to your fear, of course. You are all natural leaders of this city, and that is why the chevalier has bought you."

"Bought us?" Van Dijk snorted indignantly.

"Forgive me." Etienne nodded. "I mean, why he is happy to see you continue your tenure on the City Council."

"Van Dijk is correct," DuBois said. "I am not bought. I'm merely rented."

The quip landed in silence.

Hopaii laughed first, a long wheeze that shattered into short gasps. Onyinye followed, and then the rest couldn't resist.

"Very well," Van Dijk said. "Tell us what you have in mind."

"The quarterly tax returns will be before you for approval next week." Etienne took a long drag. The returns were a report generated by Louisiana's customs and tax authorities, and they summarized the revenue collected by the city's taxation apparatus. The money was already in the coffers of the chevalier, either in the form of coins in his Palais or in the form of credits at some of the larger counting houses in the city.

But the chevalier wasn't supposed to be able to *spend* the money until the Council had approved the returns.

Which it always did, without question.

"Ye cannot possibly mean we should disapprove of the returns," Kennedie said. "What would be the point? The man has the cash already."

"If you now disapprove the returns over questions having to do with the accounting, and other behavior of the city's secular ruler, later you can recommend that the tax and customs men stand down from collecting revenues due."

"Which they won't do," DuBois said, "since the chevalier pays them."

"But later still," Hopaii said, "we can invite the people of New Orleans to cease paying taxes."

"And when he cuts off our money?" Van Dijk asked. "Are we prepared to suffer that loss?"

Etienne gestured at August Planchet and Monsieur Bondí. "The parish will replace any lost sums, as a public act of support for our civil leaders in this dark time."

Planchet cleared his throat. "The parish is prepared to replace one hundred percent of your salaries the moment they are withdrawn."

"Over what are we to challenge the chevalier?" Onyinye asked. "If you think we should review the returns and declare some irregularity in the sums, I think you gravely overestimate the appetite most people have for accounting."

"The question," Etienne said slowly, "is what is being done with that money? What are the citizens of New Orleans to make of the fact that their chevalier uses the money he squeezes from them, on every bolt of cloth and every mouthful of rum, to murder their beloved bishop?"

He stood, removed a short stack of broadsheets from inside his coat, and set one in front of each councilor.

~ INNOCENT BLOOD CRIES FROM THE GROUND ~
Your bishop is dead! He did not ascend in a CHARIOT OF FIRE, as might be expected of a man of such sanctity, but was struck down by villains. VILLAINS, I cry, for can you doubt that a man willing to ASSASSINATE <u>a priest at the very altar</u>—though he be an Imperial officer—can you doubt that a scoundrel so foul-hearted and bold must rest upon the aid of accomplices?

We all know it, and none dares speak. WHO GAVE AID to this blackguard? Whose men <u>supported the murderers</u> at the scene of the crime at the heart of our city, as witnessed by many? None but THE CHEVALIER, Gaspard Le Moyne! People of New Orleans, is this the Lordship and Leadership you crave? Is this how you, as free people, expect to be treated? Is this the Elector you wish to choose our very Emperor?

<u>Every sou</u> you put into the hands of a customs officer became a <u>lead ball</u> in the bloodied body of our priest! Down with the house Le Moyne! Down with the Chevalier! The murdered innocent cries for justice from the grave!

—Publius—

"I can't say I like this much." Cal spat into the crisp autumn leaves, trying to eject the fear from his chest.

"None of us does," Bill agreed. "But Jake makes a terrific point."

Bill sat astride his horse, an Andalusian gray they had captured from the Philadelphia Blues. He couldn't walk without support, and they'd come a couple of miles west from Irra-Zostim, almost to the banks of the Mississippi.

Sarah rode a horse between Bill and Calvin. Cathy had remained at Irra-Zostim with the Firstborn—almost like a hostage, a token of good faith that Sarah and the rest of her party would return—and Jake himself, who had raised the issue they were about to test, had stayed with Uris and Sarah's mixed-species fighting force.

"Ferpa," Sarah said, "you deserve some explanation."

Ferpa, the seven-foot-tall woman with the head of a horned cow, including a massive spread of horns, snorted but held her position, arms at her side, club at the ready. Her drilling with Jake and Bill was showing.

"I know you're loyal," Sarah said. "I trust your word, and it doesn't need to be tested. What requires testing is the arcane binding of the oath. The spell by which you were bound, along with your own free will. We want to see what happens when we expose you to silver."

Ferpa made no response.

"She understands, right?" Cal asked.

"She understands," Bill said. "She is a soldier, and she is waiting for her orders."

"Am I right to believe that silver ordinarily has no special effect on beastfolk?" Sarah asked.

"That's correct," Ferpa said. She dragged out her last syllable in a basso rumble that sounded like the lowing of a cow. "I have often handled silver."

"Calvin is going to touch you with silver." As Sarah explained, she slipped the bandage from her witchy eye, revealing the piercing white iris. The orange sun, low in the west over the Great Green Wood, cast its light into that iris and gave it the appearance of gold. "He will touch you, and perhaps he'll even cut your skin, but he doesn't wish to harm you. He's doing my bidding. I'll watch your aura to see what happens."

Cal dismounted and drew two silver knives. One was a crude dagger the Chevalier of New Orleans armed some of his men with, when they faced magical foes. The other was a letter opener Chigozie Ukwu, son of the dead Bishop of New Orleans, had given Sarah and her friends as a gift.

Ferpa regarded Cal coolly, and he found himself wishing he knew how to read the expression on a cow's face.

"Whatever happens in the next few minutes," Bill said, "your oath as a soldier requires you to conceal it from the other members of your troop."

"Understood," Ferpa grunted. "I'm protecting Her Majesty on an important scouting mission, chosen because I'm valuable and a fierce warrior, and not because I'm disposable."

Ouch. "You ain't disposable," Cal said, conscious that he was nearly a foot shorter than the beastwife. "You speak English, for one thing."

"And it's true that you're protecting me on an important scouting mission," Sarah said. "It's a magical kind of scouting. We must know what may happen if we were to engage, for instance, with the chevalier and his silver-armed men again."

Ferpa nodded. "I'm ready. Do it, Calhoun."

"It'd be easier iffen you set down that club," Cal said. Also, that would reduce the chances that an enraged Ferpa immediately pounded him to paste.

Ferpa dropped her club into the leaves.

"Lord hates a man as won't poke a giant when pokin' is what's called for," Cal muttered. He crossed the two silver blades in a cruciform shape and pressed then both against Ferpa's upper breast.

The stink of burning flesh immediately filled his nostrils. Cal flinched and would have pulled away, but Ferpa grabbed his wrists and pulled him closer.

"For . . . Her Majesty," Ferpa grunted.

Sarah watched closely. Cal felt positively impaled by her gaze, pinned together with the beastwife warrior like two bugs on a card.

Beneath the silver blades, Cal saw red welts rise on the warrior's flesh. Skin chapped and split, and blood flowed. "This ain't supposed to happen."

"Jake was right," Bill said. "Hell's bells."

"It's the oath," Sarah said. "The silver burns away at its substance, but the magic of the oath repairs itself. The war between the blades and the oath burns at her mortal flesh."

"I b'lieve the oath is holdin'," Cal said.

"But if Ferpa were to be shot?" Bill asked. "If a bullet were to pierce her skin? Or a silver spearhead were to sink itself into her flesh to drink her blood?"

"We must know," Sarah agreed.

Cal hesitated.

"Do it." Ferpa dragged Calvin closer, and the blades dug into her skin in the same cruciform shape. Cal cringed, trying to turn the blades to avoiding cutting too deep, but Ferpa worked against him, drawing him closer and twisting the knives into her own body.

"Pull them out!" Sarah snapped.

Cal tugged, but the blades were stuck. He looked up into Ferpa's face—the impassive expression was gone, and in her eyes Cal saw fear, horror, and hatred.

"Now!" Sarah yelled.

Cal tugged, but could not pull the blades out.

"Calvin!"

Ferpa hurled Cal away. He crashed through a dogwood, narrowly managing to avoid the trunk but losing more skin than he'd have liked to the clawing leafless branches. He hit the ground hard. His ears ringing, he stared at his hands, finding that they were covered in blood and that he still held the letter opener.

But not the knife.

"Rrrrrraaaaoooooorggh!" Ferpa bellowed and staggered back,

slapping at her own torso. Blood flew from her fingers, and Cal saw the dagger's hilt protruding from her chest.

Bill pushed his horse forward, putting it between the injured beastwife and Sarah. Quicker than Cal's eye could follow, one of the Cavalier's horse pistols jumped into his hand, cocked and pointing at Ferpa.

"Ferpa!" Sarah called. "Ferpa!"

Ferpa wailed, finally ripping the silver dagger from her breast and slamming it to the ground. Bending quickly, she scooped up her club and raised it with both hands over her head, charging to smash Calvin—

"*Pax!*" Sarah shouted.

Ferpa paused. The silhouette of her enormous knotted club head hung over Calvin in the setting sun.

"Ferpa," Sarah said. "Your oath holds. I see it."

Bloody spittle fell from Ferpa's thick, rubbery lips. She swayed, eyes glaring at Cal. If she swung, his skull would crack like an eggshell.

"You're wounded," Sarah said, calling over Bill's shoulder. "You're surprised. So am I. But don't harm Calvin Calhoun, by your oath."

"*Rrrrrraaaooooooooorggh!*" Ferpa slammed the club to the ground. It struck beside Calvin's head, tearing out some of his hair. He raised his arms in a pointless attempt at defense—

and then Ferpa turned and fled, crashing through the brittle autumn trees.

Silence fell over the three left behind. Cal collapsed back onto the earth, heart pounding.

"Now we know," Bill said.

"Her oath held," Sarah said sadly. "But she very nearly killed Calvin, anyway."

"Thanks for noticin'." Cal climbed to his feet and dug through the leaves looking for the other silver blade.

"Jake was right."

"Do you feel better knowing?" Bill asked.

"In recent weeks, Sir William, I find that the more I know, the less happy I am. That doesn't mean I'd rather know less."

"I'd a said fifty times fifty is a passel."

———◆———

CHAPTER FOURTEEN

Bill sat uneasily in the saddle.

The problem wasn't his legs. They hurt, and after the blow they'd taken on the wall of Irra-Zostim, they might always hurt. Neither Sarah nor Cathy offered any promises to the contrary, and he asked for none.

He was a cripple.

Maybe, some day, he'd walk with a cane. For now, he rode or he leaned on a pair of crutches.

He told himself he wasn't troubled by Jake's departure, but that wasn't true. Jake had left that morning early on foot, carrying a sack of coffee beans over which Sarah had waved the Orb of Etyles and muttered her speed-and-endurance spell. She had also chanted Latin over a schoolboy's writing slate—procured by Uris from one of the village children for the price of an iron coin—then snapped it in half and given Jake one of the pieces.

Cathy had spoken private words with the Dutchman too, and Bill had the distinct feeling he wasn't intended to hear them. He had enough chivalric grace to permit Cathy the secret, though he burned with curiosity.

Jake was the right choice to go find Nathaniel Elytharias Penn, but Bill found he'd come to depend on the queer Dutchman. It was Jake who had connected the markings on the Tarocks and the stones of Irra-Zostim and the shelves of the palace of life. It was

Jake who had taught Bill to command the beastkind troop—and then the Firstborn, who took to the melodic commands quickly once Jake explained them.

Bill rested his hand on the Heron King's horn, hanging at his side.

The beastkind added to his sense of unrest. The experiment with Ferpa had demonstrated that the magical oaths binding the beastfolk to Sarah—and presumably also the oaths binding the Firstborn to her service—were damaged by contact with silver. Enough silver would likely destroy them.

That made Sarah's open treatment of the Firstborn seem more—Bill couldn't decide. Foolish? Maybe. If she revealed her secrets and weaknesses to someone who could be converted into an enemy by the mere application of silver, then yes. But if Sarah's revelations bound them beyond the duration of the oath?

Bill had many questions, and few answers.

Though if an oath bound by the Sevenfold Crown was an essential part of Cahokia's constitution, it seemed odd that the application of silver should be enough to dissolve the oath. Bill grimaced and filed the thought away for later consideration.

Sarah had spent a week in the palace of life, talking with the priestess. She hadn't told anyone—hadn't told *Bill*, at any rate—what she had learned from the experience. She seemed to be learning the Firstborn's language, and maybe other things. History? Ritual? Secrets?

Or Sarah was learning *one* of their languages, apparently. Bill had never realized there were several.

Languages were not his forte.

Cahokia itself didn't trouble Bill; he had been there before. But the thought that they would now ride into the moundbuilder capitol, aiming to participate in some Christmas Day ritual in which the Cahokian goddess Wisdom might, or might not, select Sarah as Queen of Cahokia made Bill uncomfortable.

It also left him puzzled. Why would she not simply become queen, being her father's eldest living child? Bill had always respected the kingship of his friend Kyres, but he was beginning to realize he had never truly understood it. The awareness of his own ignorance was unsettling.

Leaving the protective palisade walls of Irra-Zostim added to Bill's discomfort. He rode with a large troop of soldiers now, and their three-times-daily regimen of training was making them adept at forming up, marching forward and back, shooting, reloading, setting spears to receive an enemy attack, and more.

But something had caused a horde of beastkind to charge the palisade wall. Bill had ridden the Missouri as well as the Great Plains, he'd seen reptilian beastkind in the deserts of Texia and New Spain whose mere appearance strained a normal man's sanity. He'd never even heard of such a large group of them massed together, and he'd never seen such an attack. Feral beastkind were generally solitary. It was as if a pack of jaguars had charged the wall—such a thing was always possible in theory, but was simply not part of the ordinary behavior of the beasts.

Something was driving them. Something extraordinary.

Sarah was right. This was the beginning of the reign of Simon Sword.

Mercifully, beastkind had not again swarmed the palisade while they were at Irra-Zostim.

They traveled north toward Cahokia, two days' ride away. The priestess again rode in her palanquin with the idiot Polite, but Uris and Yedera were now persuaded to mount horses, along with those of the Firstborn warriors who were becoming cavalrymen. Cal had been as much help as Jake with that part of the project, teaching the Ophidian soldiers how to picket a horse, what to feed it, and how to extract a pebble from an animal's hoof, though Cal always demurred and stepped aside when it came time to talk about the mechanics of a charge, or how to fire a pistol while mounted.

Bill allowed each Ophidian soldier only three paper cartridges, keeping the blocky ammunition boxes strapped to the beastkind. He didn't want the Firstborn to panic and start shooting from afar on horseback; he wanted them to charge with saber and spear, after musket fire and the beastkind had softened up an enemy.

Bill had lost track of the days, but he thought November was growing long in the tooth the day they rode out. That first evening, he planned to provision in a small crossroads town whose English name was Wartburg, and make camp beyond it in the forest. As alien as he still found the Cahokians, he had ridden their land, and remembered where there was good water and a sheltered valley out of sight of the highway.

But they had come to a stop in Wartburg, finding it burned to the ground.

"Wisdom's name," Alzbieta Torias said, surveying the smoking wreckage from her sedan chair.

"The granaries." Uris seemed more interested in some smoldering wreckage at the edge of town than in the corpses strewn in front of him.

"Beastkind?" Sarah asked.

Bill was glad she considered the possibility, though he didn't think beastfolk had done this. "I doubt it, Your Majesty. Calvin, would you please look at the damage with me and give me your professional view?" He levered himself carefully down the side of the gray, taking his crutches and handing Cathy the animal's reins.

She looked lost in thought.

"As a cattle rustler?" Cal grinned.

"Yes," Bill said. "Or a tracker, as you please." He turned to Chikaak, who grinned disconcertingly, tongue hanging out his muzzle. The coyote-headed beastman had a coyote's sense of smell and would be able to tell him much more about the wreckage, but Bill first wanted to confirm his hunch that children of Adam were to blame for the devastation.

Wartburg had mounds. They weren't the conical stargazing ceremonial temples like Irra-Zostim and the Great Mound at Cahokia, but the lower mounds, multichambered, in which the Firstborn sometimes lived.

Bill had seen such a mound under construction once, in the Missouri but close into Cahokia where there were still passable roads. Kyres Elytharias had stayed in the region several weeks, riding after bandits and murderers and thieves by day and then presiding over their trials and punishments by torchlight. Over the weeks, a mound had come into being from nothing on the site of the court. The builders had begun by fabricating something that looked like a multichambered log home, single story, complete with peaked roof. Three long chambers connected by short hallways, and smaller chambers off the sides of each room. Three entrances, one at each end of the string of rooms and a third in the middle. The walls were tall, resulting in high ceilings with storage lofts above the ceilings and under the rooftops' peaks.

Then they had covered the entire thing in dirt. The peaks of the rooftops, from twelve feet off the ground, had been sunk beneath three feet of dirt. The next year, passing through, Bill had seen a mound with three doors in the sides, new grass climbing up its lower slopes, and beans, corns, and squash growing together in rows along the top.

What he saw now was mounds with their rooftop crops scorched by fire. Fire was why he doubted beastkind were the culprits—fire could be accidental, but as a weapon it was the weapon of ravagers who wished permanently to destroy, and not of wild animals.

The thatched wooden buildings of Wartburg were also burned. Bill could see little from the remains, and in his mind's eye he tried to associate each smoking pit with his memory of a whole building in a thriving market town. There at the crossroads itself—a hotel and a church. The brick building, which had lost its roof and its floors to fire and now sat as a charred and smoking shell, had been a bank. The fourth—Bill couldn't remember.

Bodies lay in the ruined buildings, and in the fields, and in the streets. From their clothing, many were Cahokian, clad in long tunics and winter cloaks. Others wore German embroidery. Bill saw a pair of dead men in Algonk-style leggings and blankets, their bodies perforated by multiple stab wounds.

Others appeared to have died by gunshot. Beastkind with muskets, like Sarah's?

"This weren't done by no beastkind," Cal said, stalking across a field toward the woods.

Bill hobbled after him on his crutches. "Tell me what you're seeing."

"Horses," Cal said. "The folks as done this rode away on horses. Lessen they's all beastkind as have the bottom halves of horses."

"Centaurs," Bill said.

"Only in my experience, beastkind ain't half that regular. They're all different from each other, and ain't none of 'em as straightforward as you'd think."

"No centaurs," Bill said. "Does the reign of Simon Sword bring madness to men, as well?"

Cal straightened and looked across the field, to where Sarah and Alzbieta conversed, horse by palanquin, surrounded by Sarah's troop. "Why in Jerusalem would you ask *me* that?" he asked. "Iffen you think I got any insight at all into Simon Sword, you've got me wrong, Bill."

Bill sighed. "I'm in over my head, too. And I'm only thinking out loud. We need more information about the men who did this."

"Like hell we do. We need to git Sarah behind walls where

she's safe. Iffen it ain't back to Irra-Zostim, it's on to Cahokia. We git some of the same coffee-magic Jake got and do it double-time through the night."

"Remember that this is Sarah's kingdom," Bill said. "This, right here. Wartburg. And it has been destroyed. Sarah has been wronged."

Cal ground his teeth and kicked at the earth. "Some days I jest reckon Sarah'd be happier iffen none of this had e'er happened. If we's still back in Nashville, growin' and sellin' tobacco, playin' stupid tricks on preachers when they come to town."

"We need more information. And you're the man to get it, Cal," Bill said.

"Am I?" Cal asked. "You sure you want to send away a workin' rifle jest now?"

It was a fair question; Bill ignored it. "Take Chikaak. Stay out of sight. Follow the tracks back, and come tell me whatever you learn about the people...the *men*...who did this."

His eyes and Cal's met, and he knew Cal understood. Chikaak could track as well as Calvin, no doubt better, and he was a fierce and competent fighter.

Only the experiment with Ferpa had left Bill uncertain whether he could trust any of the beastkind, if push truly came to shove.

"How long do I follow, afore I turn around?"

"If you don't catch them by dawn, come back. I would be sorry to lose your rifle." Bill grinned. "And your tomahawk."

"And the lariat." Cal nodded. "I'll keep my eyes open."

"And don't fight," Bill said. "If there's trouble, run. And if you have to choose between putting yourself in danger or giving the danger to Chikaak...don't be a fool."

"Right," Cal agreed. "That sure *sounds* easy."

"Alright, Chikaak," Cal said. "Tell me what you're seein'."

"Smelling, mostly." The beastman's voice could sound like a yip or a growl, but it was never very far from the sounds a real coyote might make.

"Yeah. That's what I meant."

They walked briskly, Cal leading his horse by its reins. He'd have preferred not to have the animal along, since it was big and its occasional snorts might attract attention of scouts or watchmen, but he wanted to be able to flee quickly, and at a moment's notice.

The marauders they were following left the obvious tracks of a large mounted party, earth shattered and branches torn off trees growing too close to the path. Cal could follow the tracks at a jogging pace even by the light of the sinking crescent moon, but he did want to know what the beastman detected.

"The warriors we're following aren't Ophidians," Chikaak said. "Also, not beastkind, but you already realize that, or you wouldn't have brought me along."

Cal didn't know whether to read that last comment as a shrewd guess, a wisecrack, or a pointed accusation, so he ignored. "How can you tell?"

"They smell of all the wrong foods. Also, they're probably not Germans."

"Food again?"

Chikaak yipped. "I smell liquor, but not beer."

"A German could drink whisky."

"Yes. But with this many men, I'd expect to smell more beer."

"Well, I'm thinkin' they ain't Indians."

"The boot prints," Chikaak said. "And the horses are shoed."

"Yeah, though that could be a trick."

They had come, by Cal's best guess, ten miles inland. They must catch up to the riders soon.

"You know a lot about the children of Adam," he said to Chikaak. He spoke in low tones, but he felt he had to speak—too much silence made him feel he was alone with a wild animal. "I guess you've traveled."

"I patrolled the Mississippi as a pup for my lord."

"Simon Sword?"

"The Heron King. At the time, he was Peter Plowshare."

"When you say *patrolled*..."

"I put down wild beastkind," Chikaak said. "Most of my people who make it to your big cities are civilized. And sometimes I dealt with outlaw sons of Adam."

"That sounds an awful lot like what they say about the King of Cahokia. The Lion of Missouri."

"I've heard of the Lion," Chikaak said. "Her Majesty's father. I didn't know him."

"And now he's Simon Sword, he ain't keepin' the wild beastkind in check anymore, is he?"

"Far from it."

"How's that make you feel?"

Chikaak looked into Cal's face with whiteless coyote eyes. "When I haven't eaten, I feel hungry. When I haven't slept, I feel tired. When I've been wounded, I feel pain. But I don't *feel* anything about the priorities of my former lord the Heron King, whether they be peaceful or warlike."

Cal swallowed, his mouth dry.

They continued in silence awhile.

"Peter Plowshare," Cal ventured. They neared the crest of a low ridge, bare of trees. "I always took him for a fairy tale, but it turns out he's a regular king, with border patrols and everythin'."

"The Heron King isn't regular." Chikaak laughed, a sharp bark. "Not in the sense you intend. Peter Plowshare builds. He trades with those who would trade with him, so there are merchants in the Ohio companies and among the Hansa who were well known at his court. But mostly, he builds walls."

"To keep out the children of Adam?"

"To keep in his *own* children, once the throne passes to his son."

"Simon Sword." Cal considered carefully. Maybe he had an opportunity to understand some of the larger issues that had troubled him. "And iffen I've grasped this aright, Simon Sword and Peter Plowshare are the same person."

"Yes," Chikaak said. "And no. And yes."

"Well, that sure clears things up."

Chikaak laughed again.

"Why ain't he part of the Empire, then?" Cal asked.

"You would have Simon Sword as an Elector under your Philadelphia Compact?"

Cal shrugged. "I ain't sure how big his kingdom is, but maybe it's big enough it could git more than one. Like Louisiana gits two, and it ain't that big. Acadia gits three. Or take Pennsland."

"Your Emperor's holdings."

"Yeah. The Pennslanders git seven, like this." Cal sang.

Indians, Eldritch, Christian men
All were welcomed by William Penn
Pittsburgh has Electors two
And three from Philadelphi-oo
Newark and the Delaware make it seven
And old Will Penn has gone to Heaven

"You would have the Heron King approach the Emperor and ask to be granted Electors."

"I b'lieve he'd have to approach the Electoral Assembly." Cal was himself a little unsure of the details. "But I reckon he'd git three or four votes, at least. Might depend on how much he's willin' to pay in taxes. Hisself an Elector, and mebbe his bishops, or priests."

"The Heron King has no priests," Chikaak said.

"I don't mean they gotta be Christian," Cal said. "The German duchies get votes, and they ain't Christian at all. The Crown Lands, too, and they're about half, I reckon. And the Eldritch... Sarah's folk... I ain't exactly figured out what they are, but some of them seem to be Christian, and some don't. Or it's a Christianity like I ain't e'er seen afore."

"The Heron King has no priests of any kind," Chikaak said. "You have no need of a priest when your god is present on his throne."

They reached the crest of the ridge and Cal crouched lower out of instinct. On the other side, in a broad valley, lay a camp. It was too dark to see individuals, so Cal quickly began counting campfires.

"Though he does bestow the gift of prophesy on his minions from time to time." Chikaak fell silent.

"I make it fifty fires," Cal said softly. "Hard to tell, it bein' so late, and lot of those fires've burned low. Iffen they's ten men to a fire, that's five hundred."

"And if there are fifty, then twenty-five hundred." Chikaak's tongue lolled out of a toothy grin. "You can tell I'm a civilized beastman. I can do arithmetic."

"Better'n I can," Cal cracked. "I'd a said fifty times fifty is a passel."

"To answer your question," Chikaak said, "I think neither Peter Plowshare nor Simon Sword would find membership in your Empire any use at all."

"Bein' an Elector means you git to vote on taxes. And you're gonna say the Heron King don't pay any taxes now and why should he want to, and that's right, but he'd git good roads and allies and a say in who the Emperor is."

"Does the rain want good roads?" Chikaak asked. "Does the rising sun need allies? Does the hurricano care who sits on the throne in Philadelphia?"

"So when you agreed to follow Sarah..."

"My god asked me to," Chikaak said. "And he warned me I may have to fight against him. And if that moment comes, I shall fight tooth and claw and do my futile best to strike down my god. As he commanded."

"Jerusalem." Cal's head spun. "I reckon that makes somethin' of a paradox, don't it? Can you git yourself into heaven by fightin' against God, if God commands you to do it?"

"There is no heaven," Chikaak said.

"You die, what happens to you?"

"I return to the river."

"As a fish?"

Chikaak shook his head. "I become one with the river."

"Fore'er?"

"Someday, I return to the dry land again."

"You had lives afore this one. You remember 'em?"

"There are few enough parts of *this* life that I remember, Calvin. But I know things that I cannot have learned here, knowledge deep down in my blood and under my nails. That is wisdom I earned in previous lives."

"And iffen you's good...righteous...I mean, let's say you mount an especially ferocious attack against Simon Sword, like he told you. What, you git to come back as a bigger beastman? Or a higher kind of animal? Or you come back as a giant sloth, or somethin'?"

"There is no reward for my actions in this life. There is only the river, and the dry land."

Cal scratched his scalp. Having stopped moving, he began to shiver from the cold, despite his long coat. "And what is it that makes you obey, then?" he asked. "What makes you willin' to go attack your god?"

"I fill the measure of my creation," Chikaak said. "I do it when my lord is Peter Plowshare. I do it when my lord is Simon Sword. I do it when my lady is Sarah Elytharias Penn."

"Calhoun," Cal muttered. He wanted to snatch Sarah back from this queer world of unthinking purpose and cosmic forces.

"I don't think so, Calvin. I don't think Sarah will ever again be a Calhoun."

"Jerusalem."

They were silent for a while.

"Your eyes are better than mine, Calvin," Chikaak said. "Do you see banners? Or anything that would tell you who this is?"

Cal pointed down at a dark line that meandered through the camp and beyond it. "That there is a crick. Big crick, or a small river. And in it, I reckon I see boats."

"I don't see that far," Chikaak said.

"Pretty sure they're boats," Cal said. "And it's dark, but I'm thinkin' they're the kind of boats the Imperial Ohio Company loves." He'd seen the company's enormous canoes in Nashville on many market days. "Iffen only we could git a little closer, I might be able to tell if they're blue or not."

"Blue?" Chikaak's eyes glinted. "Ah, the Imperial traders. But they come in much smaller numbers, twenty or fifty men to protect a trading post, or enforce a tariff."

"I reckon we can wait until mornin'," Cal said. "Then we'll be able to see even from where we are."

"You stay here, Calvin Calhoun," Chikaak said. "Stay hidden. I'll go look."

To his surprise, Cal felt he could trust the beastman scout. "Lord hates a man as gets shot for no purpose, Chikaak. At least *my* lord does. Keep your head down."

Chikaak chuckled. "Yes. Then the company men will mistake me for a stray dog."

Cal held out a hand, catching a tiny crystalline burr of ice in his palm. "Is that snow?"

"Doesn't it snow in your mountains, Calvin Calhoun?"

"It snows in Nashville," Cal said. "Only the snow don't generally stick."

The loss of Mrs. Meeks the mule hurt when the snow began to fall.

Kinta Jane had turned northeast, and was heading for Youngstown on foot. If the real Mrs. Meeks hadn't already sent a sheriff or a bounty hunter after her, she wasn't going to do so now. She'd hidden under a bridge when a marching company of Firstborn warriors passed her going the other direction. She thought they might be Adenans, but she'd never learned the heraldry of the Seven Kingdoms. She lay flat on her belly shivering in a knot of pine trees when ten marauders raced the other way on horseback, stopping only to hurl flaming oil into a barn and shatter the gate of a sheep pasture.

Her remaining coins went quickly. And with one arm in a sling, men who ordinarily might have thrown her a couple of shillings for a few quick minutes off the side of the trail now turned their noses up in disgust. As her wounded shoulder began to fester, the noses turned up all the quicker.

The loss of the mule meant the loss of the sewing needle and thread, as well.

She considered robbing a traveler, but couldn't bring herself to do it.

She did steal pumpkins from a bulging barn outside a village called Circleville, which had insane amounts of the squash stored in root cellars and warehouses. The name of the farmer she'd burgled was du Pont, and he had so many pumpkins he couldn't possibly miss the three she took.

She roasted the orange squash over small fires and ate them with her stiletto.

A band of traveling Sauk Algonks took pity on her and gave her a few handfuls of dried venison.

And she wasn't really dressed for winter. Even wearing a wool blanket she'd stolen from a drying line didn't protect her against the cold wet wind blowing against her knees and down her neck.

Cold wind and now snow. And every shock of cold summoned an answering stab of pain from her wounded shoulder and her cracked ribs. She checked her bandage when she could, but as she ran out of clean cloth and saw the bandage become clotted black and yellow with blood and pus, there was little she could do.

She carried the carbine under her blanket to keep it dry, but it became heavier with every mile that passed beneath her feet.

When the snow reached the height of her knees, her legs became numb. The air grew thick with flurries of fat flakes and she knew she was a day's walk, or maybe two, from Youngstown. Soldiers marched and countermarched in the snowstorm around her, and she took to smaller and smaller roads to stay out of their way. She was too afraid, after her assault in Adena, to try to seduce any of the marching men. Instead, she staggered along, freezing and half-blind, looking for a warm, dry place to sleep.

Until she tripped on a tree root and fell into a drift of snow.

Trees rose up all around her, blocking out the sky. Where had the path gone? Somehow, she had wandered from it. The numbness had engulfed her wounded shoulder and spread now to her neck and face.

She was going to die.

She could almost reconcile herself to the fact. It had been a hard life, marked by two great sources of happiness: her brother René and their joint service to Franklin's Vision. For those two goods, she'd willingly given up her tongue and ground out a dangerous and sometimes painful existence in the Faubourg Marigny. Now that René was dead, what did she have left?

Nothing.

Only... she knew that wasn't true.

She had Franklin's Vision.

She had the Conventicle.

She had a mission in life.

Kinta Jane needed to get to the dead drop in Philadelphia and tell the Conventicle what had happened, that René was dead, and that Simon Sword was active again on the Mississippi.

Wouldn't there be other messengers who would bring the same message?

Maybe, and maybe not. But Kinta Jane had agreed that she would bring it. And in her mind's eye she saw fire in the Ohio and the Kentuck, beasts of war unleashed upon the pyramids of Memphis and the fields of the Cotton League.

She rose to her feet, and then she saw the wall.

The trees grew so close to it, and the top of the wall was so jagged with the sharpened ends of its logs, that she almost took the barrier for part of the forest. But she blinked snow from her eyes and saw the palisade starkly, if not clearly, a dark patch against the white of the snow.

She stumbled forward and caught herself on the wall. The logs were still clad in scabby pine bark, and she scraped her hands. The sight of blood welling up from grated skin focused her mind.

If there was a wall, there must be a door.

It had to be a trading post. They built log palisades such as this, to protect the company's goods against theft.

She turned left, keeping a hand against the wall. Good, company merchants. Imperial or Dutch, it didn't matter. They'd have no reason to kill her, and indeed would be able to offer her a warm place to sleep and some food. Company traders must eat well enough, and Kinta Jane had things to offer them that they would want.

At the end of the wall she kept walking, not realizing that her fingers now trailed along empty air, and imagining her belly full of hot food.

But three steps later she caught herself. Turning, she ·found the corner of the palisade again and clung to it.

Stay lucid. Stay awake.

Her whole body was numb.

She found the door by its great iron hinge. Groping, nearly blind now, she found the center of the door and began hammering on it with her fist.

There was no answer.

She banged again.

Nothing.

She turned the carbine around and shifted the blanket out of the way so she could slam the weapon's butt against the gate. She lost count of the number of times she knocked.

No answer.

Kinta Jane shook her head, trying to clear it of the fog that crept in. She couldn't feel her feet. The carbine was loaded and primed—there was little point in carrying it unless she kept it ready to fire—so she turned it around again.

What if the trading post had been abandoned? What if the Adenans had driven the traders out in revenge for the burned town?

Lifting the carbine's muzzle from under her blanket-cloak, she aimed it away from the palisade wall and fired.

In her weakened state and with bad footing, the recoil of the weapon knocked her down. She let go of Mr. Meeks's old militia weapon and lost it somewhere in the wet snow.

No help would come.

She prepared herself to die.

Hands grabbed her suddenly, and she smelled smoke. And wine.

"Wobomagonda," she heard, "give me now the strength of the bear."

A person on each side lifted her to her feet and dragged her, toes barely touched the snow and earth, through a gate that was suddenly open.

I can pay, she mumbled. Or tried to mumble, having forgotten that she lacked a tongue.

The person on her right grunted with effort. Behind them, a loud thudding sound might have been the gate swinging shut.

Kinta Jane fumbled for her purse. It was empty, but at least she could show good faith by showing she had no money.

Her fingers numb, she dropped it.

A plank door in a stone wall loomed up before Kinta Jane Embry and then gave way, admitting her into a blaze of heat and light. She smelled smoke again, and with the smoke the greasy food-smells of bacon, butter, and bread. She saw a long wooden trestle table, a fire with a bubbling stewpot, a bread oven, and women.

Women in aprons making food. Women in coveralls cleaning the floor. Two tall women wearing bear and bison furs who had carried her in from the cold, and now lowered her gently onto a broad wooden chair near the fire. Women in white dresses who stripped away her cold things, pushing her into a plain linen shift and then piling a buffalo robe around her shoulders. Another woman in a white dress who began checking each of Kinta Jane's toes in turn—Kinta Jane could see what she was doing, though she felt nothing—and then looked at her wounded arm.

Elsewhere in the big room, women laughed. Were they laughing at her?

A warm mug of cider was pressed into her fingers by a woman who didn't let go of the mug herself, helping Kinta Jane hold onto it. Warmth spread into her chilled fingers, and then she was able to raise the liquor to her lips, smelling and tasting the cinnamon with which the cider had been spiced.

Kinta Jane groaned.

"Hush now, spare your voice." Kinta Jane couldn't see the speaker, but the voice was a woman's.

"You're wondering, are we nuns. Sometimes it seems like it," said the woman peeling away Kinta Jane's bandage. "Especially the way Sister Erikson runs things."

"This won't be a house for slatterns," called a different voice out of Kinta Jane's field of vision. "You want a man? Have a man. But you leave the cloister."

"We don't serve any saints," said one of the big women who had hauled Kinta Jane in. "Or rather, everyone chooses her own saints. I try to walk the forest path of Wobomagonda."

"I was almost a Circulator," said the woman tending Kinta Jane's wound. "I'm Sister Lamb." She leaned in close to whisper. "You can call me Elsie."

"We've got sisters who favor Reginald Pole and John Gutenberg, too," said the other woman who had carried Kinta Jane. She had a face like a meat slab, but delicate fingers. "Some of us who are godless. And some who won't say, or who follow none."

"And then there's Sister Lopez."

"Yes," the would-be Ranger said. "Georgia Jew, down from the silver mines."

Beguines. This was a beguine cloister.

Kinta Jane moaned, in relief and pain both.

"Shh," Elsie said. "You really need to sleep now."

So Kinta Jane did.

It wasn't a long walk to the big house of the Earl of Johnsland. The healer God-Has-Given limped most of the way under his own power, but near the end, as they came through a cluster of buildings on hard-packed dirt alleys and the first flakes of snow began to fall, he leaned on Ma'iingan.

Ma'iingan was happy to help. Had he raised the healer laid low? He hoped he had, and that this young man would turn about and join his son Giimoodaapi to the Loon doodem, to Ma'iingan's own family, to the People.

But looking at the young Zhaaganaashii, pale as snow from pain and blood loss despite all Ma'iingan and his simple medicinal arts could do, Ma'iingan doubted. What would this boy do?

Nothing. Nothing that Ma'iingan could imagine, at least.

Also, the young man continued with his strange outbursts and his scratching at his own ear. If he wasn't mad, he was plagued by something *like* madness.

What more remained to be done, to make the young man a healer? What *could* be done?

It was enough to make a man doubt his own manidoo.

Nathaniel and Ma'iingan made it through the village without attracting notice. Then they turned down a long straight lane that ran between a large field of asemaa plants on one side and a pasture for horses on the other. The lane ended in front of a wide house, boxy and three stories tall. It was the single largest building Ma'iingan had ever seen. Who could possibly use so many chambers? Did an entire clan live in that house?

The presence of the asemaa made Ma'iingan giddy. What a treasure trove of sacred and magical power these Zhaaganaashii sat upon! But to them, it was a mere filthy habit, a vice. He'd even heard it called *weed*, an astonishingly disrespectful name for the sacred herb.

Galloping hooves in the pasture made Ma'iingan and God-Has-Given both pivot to look. As they turned, a horse slowed to a walk just the other side of the rail fence enclosing the pasture, and Charles leaped down from the saddle.

"Nathaniel!" the older man cried. "I thought you were dead!"

Nathaniel slapped his ear and muttered. "Buried under turves. Sunk in the bog."

Ma'iingan kept his hand near his tomahawk, just in case. "I found him out in the forest, Zhaaganaashii." Best not to use the name *Charles* yet, and then have to explain how he knew it. "He was hurt, so I let him rest a few days."

"Downriver?" Charles asked.

"Uphill." Ma'iingan pointed, to be helpful. "Not too far from a pigsty."

Charles frowned. He embraced Nathaniel roughly, and when Nathaniel yelped, Charles held him out at arm's length, gripping his shoulder and examining him.

"You've been wounded," Charles said.

"He fell," Ma'iingan explained.

"Landon!" Nathaniel slapped his ear. "Landon did it!"

Ma'iingan was caught by surprise. He didn't think Nathaniel would come back here to his people just to accuse Landon. It didn't fit. And when he touched his ear, the boy said mad things.

Was he repeating words someone else said to him? Or some *thing* else?

Spirits?

Or just madness?

Hopefully, the boy heard spirits. A boy who heard spirits might indeed become the sort of healer who could connect Giimoodaapi to his people.

Charles caught Nathaniel's slapping hand. "Landon did it?" He looked at Ma'iingan with fierce eyes. "Landon...what? Dropped you? Made you fall? Did he beat you?"

"I..." Nathaniel looked down at his feet.

Charles spat. "Get on the horse."

Without waiting for any sign of agreement, Charles hoisted the younger man into the saddle. Nathaniel whimpered, but then clung to the saddle gratefully. Then the older man grabbed the beast's reins and took off toward the big house at a brisk pace.

Startled, Ma'iingan ran to keep up.

"Landon!" Charles roared as they reached the end of the pasture. The soldier opened a gate, brought the horse through, and kept going.

Ma'iingan leaped the fence to follow.

In front of the big house stood a pile of stones, each the size of a man's head. The pile stank of blood and flesh, and the rocks were stained almost black. Ever so slightly, Charles turned his path and walked *around* the rough altar.

Charles led the horse right up the front steps of the big house and through double-wide doors into the interior. Ma'iingan followed, flashing a broad grin and empty hands at the homespun-clad people in the door who stared.

The interior was dark, and stank. Long leaves on the floor and the lingering odor of decades of asemaa couldn't hide the fact that these people clearly urinated and defecated in the corners of their own home. Ma'iingan gagged.

"Landon Chapel!" Charles roared.

"Out back!" called one of the servants, and Charles pressed on, leading the horse straight out the back as he'd come in the front.

Nathaniel slapped at his ear and muttered.

Ma'iingan smiled and tried to look harmless.

On a broad stretch of green grass, a circle of boys yelled and waved their arms. In their center stood Landon, and he held a small bird in his mouth. The bird was alive, and Landon held its wing in his teeth. The bird—a sparrow—shrieked and scratched at its tormentor. Landon, meanwhile, tightly held a forearm-long rod behind his back with both hands, and slowly drew the bird into his mouth using his tongue and teeth. Blood ran down his chin.

Two men in black cloaks stood to one side, watching with

arms folded over their chests. One of them wore a black patch over one eye. Old One Eye? It seemed likely. And he was a godi, a chief priest among Nathaniel's people.

"Don't let go of the stick!"

"How does it taste?"

"Bite harder, Landon!"

Old One Eye grunted in approval.

Ma'iingan stopped in his tracks. Savages.

Charles dropped the reins and exploded into the circle of young men. He pushed Landon; the younger boy immediately dropped the rod and the bird fell to the ground, squealing.

Nathaniel looked too distracted or in too much pain to hold the reins. Ma'iingan took them in hand to keep the horse from wandering, and made shushing noises to the animal. How were you supposed to calm a horse?

"You filthy liar!" Charles roared. "You murderer!"

"What are you talking about?" Landon held his hands up in front of his face defensively, and then he looked past Charles and saw Nathaniel. His face paled immediately. "Whatever Nathaniel said, he's lying!"

"Charles, don't," Nathaniel murmured, but his voice didn't carry over the sound of the yelling boys, who were all now egging on Charles and Landon.

Nathaniel slapped his ear again. He shifted back and forth in the saddle and frowned, furrowing his brows.

"*You* said he fell into the river!" Charles pushed Landon again. "*You* had us searching down to the Roanoake trying to find him, when you knew all along exactly where he was, because *you left him to die!*"

Landon denied nothing. "You can't hurt me! My father's the earl, and your father is a traitor and a murderer!"

Charles drew back his hand and slapped Landon across the face with his knuckles. The smaller boy almost fell over with the force of the blow. "For two things, you will answer me with your body, Landon Chapel. You've attempted to murder my friend Nathaniel, and you've insulted my father!"

The two-eyed godi started forward, but Old One Eye caught him and held him back.

"I'm unarmed!" Landon squealed.

Ma'iingan almost felt bad for the younger man. He couldn't

possibly survive a fight with this soldier, who was bigger and a better shot.

Then he reminded himself that Landon had been perfectly willing to do away with God-Has-Given by secret murder, and his feelings of compassion greatly diminished.

"Please don't!" Nathaniel sounded as if he were having trouble breathing.

Ma'iingan touched the boy's thigh to reassure him.

"Right here!" Charles shouted. Behind Ma'iingan, the house was slowly exploding into noise and motion. He jerked one of the two pistols from his belt and shoved it into Landon Chapel's hands. "Right now! Ten paces, and if you want a second—"

Bang!

Charles sank to his knees in the gently falling snow. When he toppled over backward, Ma'iingan saw a small red hole punched neatly into his forehead.

Landon Chapel dropped the smoking pistol and ran.

Nathaniel shuddered uncontrollably. His eyes rolled back in his head, and he fell off the horse. Ma'iingan barely managed to catch him.

"I have filled the measure of my creation,
whether you show me mercy or not."

CHAPTER FIFTEEN

"Why are there Imperial soldiers guarding the gates?" Sarah asked. "Or do Cahokia's troops dress in blue? Everyone else seems to."

For days, Sarah has been watching the sun rise and set farther and farther south, feeling the pressure of the approach of the solstice, and at the same time seeing each day grow darker than the day before. The darkness had reminded her of the Sorcerer Robert Hooke, who'd been swept away in a trap of Sarah's devising, out of sight down the Mississippi, but never entirely out of mind. She ran her fingers through the short hair that had regrown to cover her scalp, giving her some scant protection against the cold.

It was a relief to have something else to think about.

The approach to Cahokia had been over flat land, dense with farms, creeks, and oxbow lakes and covered with forest. The Great Mound with its rectangular Temple of the Sun had appeared first in the distance—obviously a mound, and not a natural hill, because it was four-sided—as a knob over the treetops. Now it rose tall and angular, the largest of several mounds visible over Cahokia's palisade wall, and thick with black birds; another bore what looked like a cathedral, and was covered with flocks of white birds. A third might be a palace.

The wall was imposing. Its logs were enormous, both long and thick, so the wall towered over every palisade Sarah had ever seen. The timbers retained many of their natural branches, which were laced together, giving the upper portion of the wall a basketlike appearance. Cannon mouths and muskets peeked over the woven top of the barrier.

The timbers were also covered with the double-sided cursive flow that Sarah had learned was the Ophidian script, and which she was beginning to be able to decipher. For every Adam-letter on top of the script—or rather, as she had come to learn in light of the fact that the oldest scrolls in Alzbieta's collection were written in spirals, on the outside—there was a corresponding Eve-letter beneath, on the inside.

With her natural eye, Sarah wouldn't have seen the letters, but she rode into her father's kingdom with the patch off. She couldn't impress these Cahokians with silks and gold, but she had her unearthly eye, and she made sure those she met knew it, staring them in the face as if assessing them. In the Second Sight of her witchy eye, Sarah saw curving letters running up the front of each log, and lacing them together; the letters glowed an Ophidian blue.

The wall was enchanted.

Sarah had her unearthly eye, and her unearthly troop. They marched neatly to Sir William's command, cavalry skirmishers at the rear and pike- and musket-bearers in a compact mass in front, and they drew as many stares as Sarah herself did, riding beside the palanquin-borne priestess with her witchy eye naked to view.

But how far could she trust any of her warriors?

"The Treewall," Uris said.

A wooden gatehouse squatted over the front gate; the Imperials had beaten her here. The soldiers on the gatehouse wore imperial blue, with steel breastplates and bonnets, and worked beneath an Imperial banner, blue and gold and bearing the ship, eagle, and horses of her mother's family.

"This is the Pacification, Your Majesty," Uris said. "No gate is to be shut that isn't guarded by Thomas Penn's soldiers. No court is to be convened that isn't presided over by his judges. And no market is to be opened that isn't run by his traders and taxed by his revenue men."

"Jerusalem," Cal said.

"Yes," Sarah said instantly. "This *is* my *Jerusalem*, and I will have it back."

"Cahokia's own soldiers wore gray," Uris explained further, "when we had them. So do the city watch, who are called *wardens*."

Sarah spurred her horse forward, her entourage promptly matching her pace.

The foremost of the Imperials was a paunchy man wearing a broad gray hat rather than a helmet. The snow, beginning to fall more heavily now, had formed a crust of white around the crown and brim, which dislodged tiny avalanches as he moved.

"Business in Cahokia?" His voice was not the monotone of a clerk about routine business, but the crisp burr of a man who cared what he was doing.

Sarah hoped she wouldn't have to kill him, but she was conscious of a thousand eyes on her; her soldiers, the Imperials on the walls, Cahokians within the palisade and coming up behind her on the road.

This was her entrance into her kingdom, and it mattered.

She stared into the soldier's face until he flinched. "The Kingdom of Cahokia was old when *William* Penn laid the foundations of the Slate Roof House. By what authority does a servant of *Thomas* Penn ask any question of a subject of the Serpent Throne?"

"The Serpent Throne is empty," the soldier said.

"The Serpent Throne is never empty, whether you see its occupant or not." Sarah sharpened her voice. She was telling Ophidian theological ideas as fact, and they were moreover theological ideas on which she herself had at best a tenuous grip. "And you do not answer the question."

"By the authority of the Philadelphia Compact that makes Thomas Penn Emperor."

"Has the Electoral Assembly stripped Cahokia of its status as a voting power? Have the Electors authorized this outrage?"

The soldier hesitated. "I'm acting under orders from the Emperor. I've seen his signature myself, and I need to know your business."

"Apparently my business is teaching you a little lesson in civics."

Sarah rode through the gate, and the soldiers didn't try to stop her.

"Iffen I's a carpenter," Cal muttered as he emerged from the gatehouse at Sarah's shoulder, "that mound right there'd make me hang my head in pure shame."

By *carpenter* he was referring to the false name he and Sarah had given when they'd been in New Orleans a few weeks earlier, pretending they'd been married. Poor Calvin. Telling others he

was Sarah's husband might be as close as he ever got, she didn't
dare tell him otherwise and he knew it.

Though he'd be a good husband to someone, someday.

"Who you think you're kiddin', Cal?" she shot back, under
her breath so the crowd that grew along both sides of the avenue
wouldn't hear her. "You ain't a carpenter, you didn't build the
thing, and it still bothers you."

The mound he was talking about was low and rectangular, and
angled maybe thirty degrees off true. It lay just inside the gate in a
square of tall grass, at the edges of which stood stone and wooden
buildings, thatched Cahokian-style. Seven knobby boulders like
rotten teeth, like shorter, more worn cousins of the standing stones
atop Irra-Zostim, lay strewn in a loose oval about the old mound.

The other mounds, or at least all the tall ones Sarah could see,
were built on a single, consistent angle. The thatch-roofed buildings among the tall mounds, as well as some of the semi-interred
dwellings that were also called *mounds*, though they were really in
a different category from the earthwork pyramids, stood on roughly
the same orientation, though with some slouching by a few degrees
one way or the other.

"Oriented north-south?" Sarah asked Alzbieta, and knowing
the answer she pressed on immediately. "To the pole star, or to
the lodestone?"

"To neither, actually." Alzbieta nodded to the gathering crowds
to both sides of her palanquin, so Sarah took to doing the same,
deliberately making her nods just a little smaller than the priestess's. "The pole star changes over time."

"Now I know you're shittin' me," Cal said. "That's the one star
as *don't* move."

"As observed during your lifetime, Calvin, you're correct." Alzbieta looked skyward, as if imagining the motions she was describing. "But over thousands of years, you're wrong. The tree of life
points approximately at Polaris now, but it has pointed at different
stars in the past and it will point at still different stars in the future."

"The tree of life?" Cathy asked.

Alzbieta said nothing.

"Then how are the mounds oriented?" Sarah asked. "If they're
truly thousands of years old, they must be fixed on a north-south
line determined by some former pole."

"I saw a new heaven and a new earth," Alzbieta said. "For the first heaven and the first earth were passed away; and there was no more sea."

"There you go again," Cal muttered. "Soundin' half-Christian and half-crazy."

Alzbieta laughed out loud. "The mounds of Cahokia are oriented to the true celestial pole, the dark space in the night sky around which the transitional poles swing. *That* is the true eternity, the true fixed nail of heaven."

"Lord hates a showoff," Cal said.

"The mounds are thousands of years old," Sarah said. That must mean that Ophidian star lore, their knowledge of the movements of the heavens, was rooted thousands of years even earlier in ancient history.

"Yes," Alzbieta agreed. "Your ancestors and mine had been watching the northern sky revolve for millennia before ever they came here."

"From the sunken lands beneath the North Sea," Sarah said. "Another first earth that has passed away."

"Only in that case," Uris said, "there was more sea than ever before."

"And that mound?" Sarah nodded with her head at the low, weed-choked hill they were now leaving behind as they passed up Cahokia's main avenue. "Did someone else build it, then? Or does all Cahokia point at the true empty eternity of space, except for one itty bitty part, that points at the latrine instead?"

"The mound is sacred," Yedera said. "It's the grave of an early queen. She was known as the Sunrise Queen for the glory of her reign, though we've forgotten her proper name. That's the Sunrise Mound."

"*Those* are Eve-stones," Alzbieta said softly. Sarah caught the words and remembered that Alzbieta had once seemed offended at the mere question whether there *were* such a thing as Eve-stones, but the conversation had already moved on, and her chance to ask for more information had passed.

"Would Your Majesty like to meet the Regent-Minister?" Uris asked. "That low building in the west is his office."

"The regent can seek me out," Sarah said. "I come as supplicant to no man."

"The Great Mound," Alzbieta Torias said. "The Temple of the Sun."

The Great Mound. Sarah nodded.

The avenue was built of the smooth, round paving stones Sarah had seen elsewhere, including on the Serpent Mound. Snow lay piled high to each side of the avenue, and a dirty trench had been worn by feet and hooves down the center. As Sarah rode due north—toward the invisible dark hole in the sky above Cahokia—a buzz of voices ran ahead of her. She heard the questioning tones, and saw looks of doubt, fear, and surprise on the pale faces and clear eyes looking up at her.

She turned her head from side to side, nodding as she met the gaze of her people. They nodded back, and waved. The buzz faded to a deep hush.

Among the crowds, she saw from time to time pairs of Firstborn men in short gray capes, armed with clubs. The city's wardens, most likely. Jammed into every irregular corner were tents and lean-tos, and from them children of Adam in filthy wool blankets and furs stared at Sarah. They weren't slaves, and they were ragged and starving. Some were Firstborn, and some weren't.

Refugees from the Missouri and from the Pacification.

Having crossed half the distance to the Great Mound, Sarah entered a plaza. It took her a moment to realize that what she took at first for a circle had instead twelve sides. One thing obscuring the shape was the crowd of Cahokians thronging all its sides. They were not all dark-haired Ophidians—Sarah saw blond Germans, and Indians in fringed leather, and tricorn hats.

She saw slave collars too, in shocking numbers. Most of them were worn by children of Eve.

But not all.

Almost everyone in the plaza was on foot. Sarah halted in the center of the plaza and turned her horse in a slow circle, gazing on each face in turn and nodding from time to time. She made a point of making eye contact with the slaves in exactly the same fashion as she did with those who were free. She made eye contact with refugees, too—in some sense, they were her father's people.

Uris rode forward several steps and brought his horse to a snorting halt, apart from the rest of Sarah's entourage. "People of Cahokia!" he called. "Before you rides Sarah Elytharias, daughter of Kyres! Cry welcome to the daughter of the Lion of Missouri!"

For a moment, the hush deepened.

Then a deep-throated yell shot up from the crowd, echoed off the snow-laded clouds, and nearly left Sarah deaf.

Sarah's heart pounded. Blinking away tears—why should she weep?—she rode north again.

Cahokia's Great Mound was covered with moss, lichen, and grass. As she arrived at its foot, Sarah saw a staircase running up the front of the mound to its peak. "You may step on the mound," she said to Alzbieta. She did not intend it as a question.

The priestess nodded.

Sarah dismounted. "Please keep the horses, Cal," she said.

He looked disappointed, but he took her animal's reins and said nothing.

"Sir William, I doubt we're in any danger. If I'm mistaken, I'll require you to hold the base of the mound against any attack."

"Your Majesty." Bill doffed his hat and bowed.

"I'll stay with Sir William," Yedera said.

Sarah nodded.

She climbed the stairs. The rest—Cathy, Uris, and Alzbieta—followed.

Sarah wouldn't show weakness. This was her kingdom, and she would own it. Slipping a hand into her shoulder bag, she touched the Orb of Etyles. She didn't want her companions to see her casting a spell, so she merely willed strength and breath into her legs and lungs, and into the legs and lungs of her companions.

They marched to the peak without a stop.

The top of the mound was a platform. It was paved with the round stones, barely visible through a light skiff of snow, and dominated by a rectangular building, tall, narrow, and long, with a roofless porch. The building must be the Temple of the Sun, and black birds—ravens—squatted in a vast conspiracy atop it. The land around it appeared to be plowed and planted, though leafless in the winter's cold.

A warm breeze blew from the river. Sarah ignored the building, and instead turned to survey her land.

Cahokia sat in a bend of the Mississippi River. Though she and her friends had ridden several days through Tawa and Cahokia, she saw now that Cahokia sprawled at the base of a broad fan of fertile land. It guarded the riverine approach from the south to what must be a giant flood plain. The land was flat, and where it wasn't forested with the tall groves of nut and fruit trees of ancient and contested origins, it was farmed.

If the Mississippi flooded, what would happen to the land?

And what defenses were there against such a flood?

None that she could see.

West of the river was the Missouri, a tangled, river-fed land choked with the fringes of the Great Green Wood and hacked into patches by small farmers and petty barons. Somewhere just north of where she stood, the Missouri river must flow into the Mississippi. Thin tendrils of smoke rose from dozens of farmsteads in Sarah's sight. The Missouri rose in slow hills away from the river; somewhere out there in the dense forest was the Heron King's palace, where Sarah had rebuffed his advances but given him the sword he sought, the sword with which he now intended to run riot over the children of Adam. Beginning, no doubt, with the people of the Missouri.

As she looked, she realized that not all the tendrils came from chimneys.

Many of the farms burned.

And as she watched, a burning ship drifted down the river. Most of the wood above the waterline was already consumed, and as Sarah looked at it, the ship began to sink. Fore and aft, carved wooden dragon's heads slowly succumbed to the brown waters. "Is that a keelboat?" she asked.

"It's a German funeral ship," Uris said. "The nobility who follow the All-Father are buried thus."

"Some princeling of Chicago has died," Alzbieta said. "To judge by the flag."

They watched the ship sink in respectful silence.

"The people of the Missouri looked to my father for protection," Sarah said. "I will gather them under my cloak. If necessary, I will ride for them as the Lioness of Missouri. And if Chicago desires alliance with me against the same threats, I will grant it."

Uris knelt in the snow before her.

"I serve Her Majesty's interests," he said.

"Go on."

"I beg Her Majesty to remember she isn't queen yet. There are others who seek the throne."

"Not I," Alzbieta said.

"*Others*," Uris continued. "I would beg Her Majesty to be deliberate and thoughtful in her speech."

"Her Majesty is being quite deliberate," Cathy Filmer said. "And quite thoughtful."

"Indeed."

Uris opened his mouth as if he had more to add, but at that moment a tall Ophidian, clad from head to toe in black, swept to the top of the mound. He leaned on a black staff with a dull gray iron horse's head sculpted at its tip, and his cheeks were pocked with the scars of some childhood disease.

The newcomer looked around at the party atop the mound before meeting Sarah's gaze. "You're the Elytharian pretender."

"The hell you say."

He paused, mouth open. Then he smiled. "I mean *claimant*."

"The hell with that, too. I'm Sarah Elytharias Penn, and I've come to sit on my father's throne."

"I'm Maltres Korinn." The tall man stood upright and looked Sarah up and down critically. "I'm Duke of Na'avu and Regent-Minister of the Serpent Throne, and my sovereign is the Queen or King of Cahokia."

"Queen," Alzbieta Torias muttered.

"You don't bow to your sovereign," Sarah said.

"If I bowed to every child of Wisdom who said he was my liege lord, my head would long since have fallen off from the effort. So far, Wisdom Herself has not deigned to agree with any of the . . . claimants."

"I look forward to seeing the top of your head, Regent-Minister. When the goddess has chosen me, I may find use for you at my court."

Maltres Korinn laughed. "I could be persuaded that you're an Elytharias," he said. "You have the confidence. But you would convince me to stay at court with difficulty. I would much rather prune my cherry trees and dung my blackberry brambles, so I wish the goddess *would* choose you, and end my regency."

"Why wouldn't She?" Sarah asked. "I'm my father's daughter. She chose him, and our mothers and fathers before him."

"She will choose whom She will," Maltres Korinn said. "But Her grace hasn't descended your family tree in a straight line. Your father, for instance, was the younger prince, and something of a hellion, who was not expected to succeed. Perhaps now She will choose some cousin of yours. Perhaps Alzbieta Torias." He looked sidelong at the priestess. "She is, after all, slated to stand in the Presentation."

"I've accompanied Her Majesty for the purpose of demurring in her favor," Alzbieta said. She bowed in Sarah's direction. "Her Majesty may take my slot."

"Under the terms of my agreement with all the candidates, *I* decide who stands in the Presentation," Maltres said.

"Be very careful." Sarah willed ice into her voice.

"No, Sarah Elytharias," Maltres said, "if that *is* your name. *You* be careful. This city and kingdom are under my government until the goddess decides otherwise. Your bear-headed spearmen are ferocious to look at, but I think they would crumple before the might of the kingdom... especially with the Imperials also fighting against you. How much blood are you willing to spill?"

"I wouldn't spill *any* blood for my own sake," Sarah said. "For the sake of my kingdom, and my family, there is *no* blood I wouldn't shed."

The Regent-Minister of the Serpent Throne nodded. "As it happens, my discretion is irrelevant. The Presentation is full and withdrawal is not permitted. Seven candidates, including the Handmaid of Lady Wisdom Alzbieta Torias, will stand on the Great Mound on the shortest day of the year. If the goddess chooses one of them as her Beloved, we'll have a new queen or king, so long as she or he can keep what has been given from the hands of the Imperials and their bloody Pacification. And if she doesn't, then we face another year under the bumbling administration of our poor regent, who would rather make cherry wine and listen to the humming of the summer bees."

"You've performed this Presentation every year since my father died, and the goddess hasn't yet chosen a monarch?"

Korinn sighed. "Much of what you see around you is ancient, but the Presentation isn't one of those things. We've performed this rite only for six years. Before that, we had nearly a decade of assassinations, ambushes, and poisonings, encouraged by the Imperial diplomats and the Ohio Company traders alike. Eventually, the death toll became conspicuous enough that the various claimants came together and agreed on this process."

"The Presentation isn't part of the ancient kingly lore," Sarah said.

Alzbieta nodded, confirming against what she'd already told Sarah in the empty palace of life in Irra-Zostim.

"But there must be many alive who were adults when my father became king," Sarah said. "Don't they remember how it happened?"

"There came a dawn," Korinn said, "a winter solstice. Every child of Wisdom within the walls who awoke that day knew that

Kyres Elytharias was the goddess's Beloved, and that he was to be their king. I was one of them."

"And so you've constructed a rite of new vintage, and you hope the goddess will participate," Sarah said. "Couldn't you have cast the Tarocks instead?"

"Believe me," Maltres Korinn said, "you're not the first to have asked the question. And we hope that, this being the seventh year, our goddess will take pity on us and give us a king who can fight the Pacification." He looked westward, at the lingering smoke over the Missouri. "And a king to save the Missouri."

"Or a queen," Sarah said.

Chigozie didn't know why he still lived. Every time he heard the rumble of a stomach, he expected to be torn to shreds. He became so accustomed to living with the specter of his own impending death that he began to ignore it, and even to ignore the beastkind.

They defecated and rutted in his presence, and he prayed in theirs.

They came across evidence of armed resistance. Tangled with the corpses of men who wore lacquered wooden breastplates and carried short rifles, Chigozie saw a tattered red banner. The image on it was torn, but might once have been that of a bird, wearing a crown.

One night he awoke to find Lamprey-Cat, whose name was Aanik, crouching over him. Chigozie stretched out in full on his back and clasped his cross in both hands, interlacing his fingers, and looked over Aanik's shoulders at the twins, Castor and Pollux.

And what had come of his brother, the new bishop tainted with ancient corruption?

"If this is the purpose for which you have created me, God," he prayed aloud, "may I fill the belly of my brother Aanik well."

Aanik shifted from side to side, curling felinoid paws into long-taloned fists.

Chigozie heard a snort.

He and Aanik both looked to the source and saw Bison Head, whose name was Kort. Kort lay on his side as if sleeping, but his eyes were wide open and he looked at Aanik and Chigozie.

Hissing, Lamprey-Cat retreated into the shadows of the trees.

Bison Head blinked. "Son of Adam."

"We are all sons of Adam," Chigozie said.

"So you say. I believe I'm the son of a different god."

"Adam is not a god. I am Chigozie."

Bison Head snorted. "What do you think is the measure of your creation, son of Adam?"

Chigozie's heart pounded. "I do not know. I am trying to find it. But I believe my god has put me on your path for a reason."

"Perhaps to be my food."

"Perhaps." Chigozie took deep breaths. *If it be thy will.*

"But not to be food for Aanik."

"No."

"Adam doesn't will it. I don't will it. If you're to be eaten, you'll go into *my* belly. Understood?"

Chigozie said nothing. Bison Head closed his eyes again and soon made rumbling sounds that resembled snoring.

A week later, the beastkind band fell on a farmhouse.

Chigozie had little idea where they were. He'd staggered for days in Kort's wake, always through forest. Kort seemed to have a sense of direction, and they marched generally in a straight line. Chigozie had seen the great plains of the Free Horse Peoples, briefly. He'd seen an enormous river from time to time, which might be the Mississippi or the Missouri. He'd seen small baronial palaces, and walled towns, some on fire and some defended by bristling muskets, but always closely choked around by the forest.

During the day, constant movement kept Chigozie from getting too chilled. At night, he lay by Kort's side and slept in the beastman's warmth, reconciled to the possibility that his captor-patron might roll over and crush him to death.

He ate nuts when he found them, and killed a bird with a luckily thrown stone. He hadn't seen his own face in weeks, but his forearms were gaunt.

The farmhouse appeared suddenly in a flurry of snow, a constellation of yellow lights in the gray evening. With no planning, and not even any warning, Kort charged. He roared, and Aanik and the others followed him: Iiilit, who was a fish with legs; Brooft, the octopus; Yetch, whose upper body was a stag's and who ran faster than any of the rest; and Fsift, who looked like a completely normal son of Eve, but for his rabbit's head, which never stopped smiling and never made a sound.

The farmers never had a chance. A big-bellied man appeared in the door with a musket and a pistol; before he could even fire, Kort trampled him and smashed through the door, taking some of the frame and the surrounding wall with him.

The other beastmen hurled themselves through windows, or into the paddock full of cattle.

The screams of men began immediately and ended within seconds. So did the barking of the dogs.

The screaming of the women began and didn't end.

Chigozie raised his arms to heaven. "Great God in heaven," he began, but then he choked.

He couldn't pray above the screams. "God," he tried again, wanting to pray for the women's deaths, and faltered.

It wasn't the sound that stopped him. It was guilt.

Could he pray to heaven for mercy for the victims, if he would do nothing himself first?

He staggered toward the farmhouse, ears ringing with the shrieks and sobs. In the doorway, he stopped at the crushed body of the farmer and picked up both his firearms, tucking the pistol into his belt. He was no expert, but he knew basically how the weapons worked.

The inside of the cabin was a single room, with a loft overhead. Hand-tied rag rugs lay directly on a packed dirt floor, now soiled and wet with the blood of two men, a pig, and some number of dogs Chigozie couldn't count, for the fact that they had been torn limb from limb.

Kort and Aanik were in the cabin. Chigozie's eyes filled with tears, blinding him; each of the beastmen hunched over a live and screaming woman, and the violence with which the beasts were ravaging the Missouri women shattered Chigozie's heart.

He was ready to die.

Cocking the musket first, he approached Kort and aimed the gun—not at Kort, but at his victim.

"Please!" the woman screamed, locking eyes with Chigozie. She was young, barely an adult, perhaps the daughter of this farming family. "Kill me!"

Kort snuffled and roared in a rutting frenzy, not even noticing.

The woman was doomed. The beastkind would rape her and kill her and eventually eat her. All Chigozie could do was shorten her suffering.

Bang!

She fell back, her struggles suddenly stilled. His nose full of the stench of blood and lust, Chigozie couldn't even smell the gunpowder.

Kort hesitated, stared at the red hole welling with blood in the woman's forehead. Then he turned rage-filled eyes toward Chigozie.

Chigozie dropped the gun, expecting instant annihilation. Out of reflex, he raised his cross in his free hand. Warding off evil? Proclaiming his intent?

Kort snarled, but held still.

Drawing and cocking the pistol, Chigozie crossed the cabin to Aanik. Lamprey-Cat mounted a woman who should have been in mid-life. Her shoulders, breasts, and face were torn in bloody circular streaks by Aanik's teeth. Her eyes were already gone, and Aanik's lamprey mouth now settled onto her neck. She wasn't dead yet; with fingerless hands, she thumped against Aanik's shoulders, to no avail.

Aanik continued to bite and rut.

Chigozie almost shot Aanik.

But no. He wasn't killing from rage. He wasn't seeking revenge, or even justice. He couldn't save the woman from the wounds she'd already suffered, and he doubted he could kill Aanik in a single shot.

Chigozie killed as an act of mercy.

Bang!

The woman's arms straightened out, groping for the sky, and then fell to her sides.

Chigozie dropped the pistol. His arms, too, fell to his sides, and he faced Aanik.

Lamprey-Cat sprang back from the nude corpse, spraying blood across Chigozie's face and the cabin. He hissed, spraying more blood from his deep, fang-filled throat. He crouched, large feline legs gathering up energy—

Aanik sprang forward—

Kort slammed into Lamprey-Cat from the side. The great bison-headed beastman slammed into his fellow's throat with his own forehead, bowling Chigozie's attacker across the floor.

"Now you die!" Aanik rose, talons extended.

"Down!" Kort bellowed.

Aanik hissed. The long sides of his lamprey neck throbbed, and he opened his and closed his fists, his talons snicking along each other.

"Down," Kort rumbled slowly, "or I'll kill you."

Aanik lowered his head, then slunk toward the corpse of the woman he'd been assaulting.

"Leave the daughter of Adam," Kort growled.

"I'm needy," Aanik whined.

"I don't care."

Chigozie raised his cross again.

One last time, Aanik rose slightly on his hind legs, as if considering an attack, but then he dropped to all fours and loped out the door.

Kort pivoted and stared down at Chigozie. He smelled of blood and aroused animal and he towered over the priest.

I am going to die. If this was my purpose, Lord, I thank thee for the small mercy I was able to give these women.

"Tell me why." Kort's nostrils flared.

"Mercy," Chigozie said. "Those women suffered. Did you not hear their screams?"

"You ended their suffering."

Chigozie almost choked on the smell of blood, and tears flowed down his cheeks.

"It was a small thing."

"And do you think I'll show you such mercy?"

Chigozie shrugged. He was going to die. "I have filled the measure of my creation, whether you show me mercy or not."

A long silence.

"I leave the bodies of the children of Adam to you." Bison Head turned toward the door. "Do you feel you must show mercy to the cattle as well?"

Chigozie shook his head. "You are a child of Adam, too, Kort. I am more convinced of it than ever."

"And Aanik? Is Aanik a child of your god?"

"Yes." Chigozie blurted out the answer quickly, because he dared not hesitate.

In his heart, he was less certain.

Thomas knelt on the cold stone. He had been kneeling for a long time; an hour, he would guess, though by the direction of its ghostly occupant, Shackamaxon Hall contained no clocks. Gottlieb would intercept callers for His Imperial Majesty; it was a role at which he excelled, and a tiny power he loved to exercise.

Thomas had long since mastered the skill of kneeling for long periods of time.

He couldn't summon his grandfather, William Penn. Thomas

had occasionally consulted with wizards—his chaplain, Ezekiel Angleton, but also university professors, Polites, and others—as to how to do it, but the consultations were always indirect. He didn't want anyone to know he asked his grandfather's advice.

Thomas Penn must be his own man.

Powerful, benevolent, and free.

And yet, who wouldn't ask for the guidance of William Penn, if he could get it? For all that John Penn and Bishop Franklin had pieced together the Philadelphia Compact, the true founder of this Empire—of *Pennsylvania*—was William Penn, Penn who had treated with the Indians, the Dutch, and the Germans, Penn who had built the Slate Roof House, Penn who had founded the dynasty of which Thomas was now the scion.

So Thomas would kneel in Shackamaxon Hall and wait.

He pressed his forehead to the cold stone.

"Thomas, my servant."

The voice clanged through the hall, discordant and brutal. How William Penn had ever made so many treaties of peace and won so many men's hearts with such a voice, Thomas didn't know. He raised his eyes to the dais. He didn't look at the Shackamaxon Throne, but only at the mail-clad feet of the Presence sitting upon it.

"We tighten the noose upon the Ohio, grandfather."

"I have seen thy works, Thomas. They are mighty."

"The Ohio hasn't yet rebelled. Perhaps I grip it too tightly."

"Choke it tighter, Thomas. They will find the means to rise. A queen seeks to lead them."

Thomas's blood chilled. "One of the half-breeds." He couldn't bring himself to admit that Hannah's whelps were his kin.

"Sarah."

"Will the Ophidians accept her?"

"I cannot see that yet," the Presence said. "But she is determined, and she has arrived in her father's city. Christmas may tell. Are thy forces properly arrayed?"

"Yes," Thomas said. It was mostly true. "Our marauders are destroying their food supplies. What food they have, they buy from us, at prices that humble them and shatter their coffers."

"More, Thomas," the shade said. "Bring thou additional forces to bear."

"I have order to maintain elsewhere in thine Empire, grandfather."

"If the queen achieves her throne, thou must be prepared to crush her. In the field, and also in the Assembly."

"I shall publish a Summons."

"Excellent, my son."

Son?

Thomas raised his eyes. It was involuntary, a jerk of surprise, but his own brash blasphemy horrified him.

But the Presence was gone.

Thomas rose slowly, and found he was shaking.

His grandfather had called him *my son*. That recognition made it hard to think of anything else, but he forced himself.

If the Ohio rose, Thomas could publish a Summons, convene the Assembly of Electors, and authorize a Levy of Force. That would give him command of forces raised by all the powers of the Empire, an important step toward convincing the Assembly to grant him additional powers.

But Thomas didn't want to wait until Sarah Elytharias had taken her father's throne to begin raising a larger army. He wanted the army ready in time.

Christmas might tell, his grandfather had said.

Did Temple Franklin's planted assassin give him a pretext? He considered. Electors were unnecessary for a mere trial for murder, even if the murder was politically motivated. And as of yet, even under torture, the Ophidian hadn't implicated any of the Ohioan powers. The would-be murderer was Snakeborn, and that was all.

But taxes.

Electors always cared about taxes. He would publish a Summons, to propose an increase in Imperial tolls and tariffs. All the Electors would come.

By their greed, their unwillingness to fund their collective Empire of which he was at the head, he would have them.

He left Shackamaxon Hall physically drained, but with a light heart and a quick step.

His grandfather had called him *my son*!

Gottlieb met him beneath the Jupiter Thomas painting. Outside, the glittering darkness of Philadelphia peeped in through the tall windows; the shade of William Penn generally appeared at night, though there were exceptions.

This was often where Gottlieb waited for Thomas, to report

on any events that had occurred during his sequestered meetings, and Gottlieb waited now. At the front door to Horse Hall stood Imperial soldiers, blue-clad backs turned to Thomas, muskets at their sides.

All as should be, except that with Gottlieb waited a visitor.

It took Thomas a moment to recognize the man. "You're the actor," he said.

Stripped of his war paint and dressed in a long gray coat, the player looked like a Philadelphia burgher. He might be here to petition for the extension of some monopoly, or the waiver of a stamp duty. His long locks were curly but combed and oiled, his forehead was high, and his eyes were clear and gray, his hands clean, his boots fashionably knee-high.

And he was singing a lively tune.

> *I left my girl unhappily*
> *When she swore she'd never marry me*
> *I asked, she said she'd rather she*
> *Were handfast to a toad*
> *So I took my shilling from the King's army*
> *And I left for the hills, all the world to see*
> *My fifty new best mates and me*
> *All marching up the road*
>
> *And I'm over the hills and gone, boys*
> *Over the hills and gone*
> *The fire burns high, the devil drives*
> *I must be moving on*

For any other man, Thomas would have chased the fellow out of Horse Hall before he finished a verse. For the man who had climbed the Walnut Street Theater's proscenium arch to rescue him, and who had also rescued Temple Franklin, Thomas stood respectfully and listened to two more verses.

> *This basket hilt and an old Brown Bess*
> *Were the price of my soul in Inverness*
> *The sergeant swore it'd be my death*
> *If I fell out of line*
> *That line, it didn't hold too tight*

When those highland boys hove into sight
The Necromancer's Jacobites
All rushing down the pine

The earth is still but a cold wind blows
Down come the rooks and the carrion crows
Are those men or corpses? No one knows
An army forged in hell
So it's down with my blade and my old Brown Bess
And I'm over the hills, back to Inverness
On my heels comes the prince of death
Ring the funeral bell

"The Battle of Prestonpans," Thomas said, when the final chorus faded from the marble walls. He applauded gently. "The great return of the Necromancer, and his final victory before the House of Spencer could rally and defeat him on Culloden Moor. Is it from a piece you perform with the players?"

"I'm working this song into an opera." The actor's eyes sparkled. "To date, I have mostly performed the piece on street corners, to encourage as many shillings as possible to leap into my hat."

"The life of a player." Thomas took the hint and reached inside his waistcoat to dig out the small purse he carried around. "I have six Philadelphia guineas here," he said, weighing them in his hand and then holding them out. "It's not the reward you deserve, but perhaps you can sing a few fewer songs on street corners this winter. And labor at the opera instead. I take it the work will be heroic?"

"Tragic, I think." The actor took the coins and bowed. "In that the Necromancer, twice defeated by John Churchill and his descendants, has only ever fled, and hasn't been destroyed."

"A metaphor for death, surely. Undefeatable. Ever-present. Only pushed back by we free men who struggle to raise civilization from the mire, one brick at a time."

The actor smiled faintly. "I would give a great deal to be certain that's all the Necromancer is."

"Certainty is elusive in this life," Thomas said. "But I'll tell you this. Philadelphia is the city built by William Penn."

"Oh indeed," the actor agreed. "And Thomas. Don't forget Thomas."

, the maryaj-loa. Feel the Brides speak to you."

➤●◄═

CHAPTER SIXTEEN

"Is the houngan bishop still in his lair?"

"Really," Ravi said, "you must ask me questions I can answer."

Ahmed Abd al-Wahid glared at the Jew hard enough that he feared laying an evil eye on his astrologer. They were speaking Arabic. "I'll be more in a mood for word games, son of Isaac, when we've repaid the chevalier, a head for a head."

"When did precision become a game, son of Ishmael?"

They stood in a rented apartment in a cheap hotel al-Muhasib had scouted out and chosen for the view its windows gave of the garish gambling and drinking house owned by Etienne Ukwu. The hotel's name was the *Onu Nke Ihunanya*, a West Africk name such as you wouldn't see in Paris or in Cairo. Igbo? Abd al-Wahid didn't care. He had rented the hotel's entire floor, and the girl the chevalier had sent them was in the room next door.

The lights in both rooms were completely out, but for a single flickering taper—Abd al-Wahid hadn't asked of what unsavory fats the taper was made, but it sputtered and reeked as it burned—standing over a book of astrological charts through which Ravi pored. Though the sun had set outside, many people were taking advantage of the cool New Orleans winter to revel in and around the casino. The street below was lit by torches, and bonfires at the street corners.

"I must warn you, it's about to become a blood sport."

"Cool your rage, Slave of the One," Ravi said. "Here's another question you might have asked me: not *is he in his lair* but *have you seen him leave?*"

"Have you wondered, O picker of grammatical nits, why I am prince-capitaine, a leader of men, and you are a mere slave, engaged for his knowledge and skills?"

"Surely it's not because I am a Jew. I've served the order faithfully, along with many other followers of Musa the Lawgiver."

"It's not because you are a Jew."

"And it's not because of your staggeringly superior wit."

"I wouldn't entirely discount that possibility, O child of Judah. And yet, it wasn't the consideration I had in mind."

"Then it must be because you're tall. I've read the stories of the Nine Worthies, and the great warriors and kings of all ages, and I've noticed that either their height isn't mentioned, or they're identified as being tall. King Saul, for instance: 'from his shoulders and upward he was higher than any of the people.' Even Adam was said to be a giant."

"I am indeed tall. But my other great virtue, O Talmudical haggler over points of no relevance, is that I get things done."

"Indeed." Ravi nodded solemnly. "This is why the Caliph sent you to bring back Talleyrand."

"Talleyrand's head," Abd al-Wahid corrected the magician. "Which has been sent to him."

"You must feel anxious for the fact that we haven't yet killed the young bishop. And in the meantime, our ally-patron the Chevalier of New Orleans lies on his sickbed, pale and oozing from the curse of his enemy."

"*Anxiety* is not the precise word. I feel *shame.* The poet says what you seek is seeking you, and I hope that young Bishop Ukwu is seeking to place himself into my hands. Nevertheless, I will act as if he is in fact trying to elude me."

"I should point out that in what I said to the chevalier, I might be mistaken."

"Excuse me?"

"I said the curse wasn't from God. But of course, I could be wrong. The Torah tells of many curses from God. Infertility, plague, famine. Even hemorrhoids. Why not the sickness of the chevalier?"

"Organize the men," Abd al-Wahid said. "I'll check on the witch."

"Yes, Prince-Capitaine."

Abd al-Wahid hesitated in the door. "O Jew?"

"Yes?" Ravi looked up from his book again.

"Cease picking nits. The fact that you've been circumcised once already does not mean I cannot circumcise you again."

"Perhaps you're a leader of men because of your unparalleled ability to devise uncomfortable and shameful punishments, Prince-Capitaine."

Abd al-Wahid entered the room next door.

The girl's door wasn't locked; mamelukes stood watch at both staircases that accessed this top floor, and Abd al-Wahid had both paid and threatened the hotel manager into a promise of silence.

She knelt before an altar.

The girl was young, no older than fifteen. Her skin had the mellow caramel coloring of a person of mixed race, commonly called *Creoles* by the people of New Orleans. She wore a white scarf wrapped around her head like a turban, and a white shawl. Her eyes were dark and, when they looked at Abd al-Wahid, piercing. She might have fit in well in the Caliph's harem, or in the prince-capitaine's own seraglio, waiting for him in Cairo.

He chose not to think of his seraglio, or for that matter his garden, or his children.

What you seek is seeking you, the poet said.

The witch had arrived with a calling card from the chevalier, on which was printed simply *son nom est Marie*, and the initials *GLM*.

Now her eyelids fluttered, her eyes nearly shut. Her head lay back and she swayed in a circle like a top, humming a dronelike tune that never seemed to repeat itself.

Ahmed Abd al-Wahid was loath to interrupt any spiritual ceremony, even when it was the incantation of an infidel witch. He remained in the door to watch.

The altar before her was a table. When the mamelukes had taken the room, the table held only a lantern. Now the lantern stood on the balcony—unlit—and the table was stacked with bones, feathers, colored powders, bottles of strong liquor and vials of other liquids, two skulls, one a man's and the other an alligator's, chunks of a thick, dark, crumbling substance that looked like wax but tasted sweet. Abd al-Wahid knew, because he had accepted a brick of the substance from a coffeehouse owner in the Vieux Carré, who called it *shocolatl*. A word from New Spain, the coffeeist had explained. Aztec or Maya, he wasn't sure which.

In the center of the altar stood two two-foot-tall dolls, one of a man with jet-black skin and completely white eyes. He was wrapped in a white toga and his head was swathed in more white. In his hand, he held a golden rattle, as did the other doll, which was of a woman in similar garb and equally dark skin. Between them stood a small potted palm.

"Mmmmmm, Père Loko." Marie prostrated herself, placing palms and left cheek flat on the smooth wooden floor. Abd al-Wahid and his mamelukes had rolled up the carpet and removed it into the hall, along with the cot and upholstered chair that had once furnished this room. Marie now pushed her face against the floor in a circle of chalked markings. They weren't the astrological or kabbalistic signs Abd al-Wahid knew from Ravi's work. Instead, they were a pair of ornate Xs, touching at four of their eight collective extremities. The remaining four limbs of the glyph ended in curving flourishes. Between the Xs the ground was chalked with long straight lines. Six stars surrounded the diagram. "Mmmmmm, Mère Ayizan."

She slid forward until she lay entirely flat, turning her head to press her small nose against the wood, and lay still.

Ahmed Abd al-Wahid waited.

Had she fallen asleep? Perhaps the bishop's countermagic protected him.

Still he waited.

She rose back to her knees, bowed to the two idols on the table, and then stood. She crumbled shocolatl into a tiny porcelain bowl before each statue, then picked up a short burning candle that was marked with red and white horizontal stripes. "Loko and Ayizan are cool loa," she said. "For such an operation as you plan, cool loa are needed. They have subtle power, the power that lulls and soothes and brings eyelids down rather than the power that disembowels or shatters."

"I don't care, witch." Ahmed Abd al-Wahid arched an eyebrow. They spoke in French; he didn't know the word loa, but it must refer to her infidel idols.

"I'm no bokor, but a mambo. I'm an initiated priestess."

"I still don't care. Is it done?"

"As you have asked," she said, "and as the chevalier has commanded. They'll sleep no more than a quarter of an hour. A power there resists me, and I don't know what it is." She handed Ahmed the candle, and he took it. "Each of these stripes marks the passage of a quarter of an hour."

"Ravi!" Abd al-Wahid barked, switching back to Arabic. "We go!"

Al-Farangi stayed in the second-floor hallway, on a chair with loaded musket and two pistols and a bare tulwar across his knees. The French mameluke favored exaggerated Egyptian and Syrian styles, so even his musket was inlaid with fine filigree, a verse of the Holy Qur'an from the seventy-second sura: *we had sought the heaven but had found it filled with strong warders and meteors.* It was a reference to jinn struck down by God's shooting stars and al-Farangi would compare the fear the jinn felt of those meteors with the fear al-Islam's enemies felt of al-Farangi.

The *Onu Nke Ihunanya* had a guard, a dark-skinned man who stood in its lobby with his arms crossed over his chest and a long knife strapped to each leg.

The square surrounding the gaming palace, tumultuous only moments earlier, was now tranquil. The movements of traffic seemed slower and calmer. The torches and corner fires burned colder, and Abd al-Wahid would have sworn their smoke smelled of the drug *shocolatl*.

Within the gaming house, all slept. A chamber quartet and harpsichord player slumped at their instruments in white frock coats and leggings. Gamblers slept face down on their tables alongside the casino's staff, other than a black waistcoat-clad croupier who lay dozing on a roulette wheel, having narrowly missed impaling his head on the spike in the wheel's center. Two burly men with knuckledusters and clubs lay snoring in the open doorway.

The air of the room was chill.

Abd al-Wahid consulted the witch's candle; half the fifteen minutes had already elapsed.

Two quick turns took the five mamelukes up a narrow staircase toward the bishop's office. One of the bishop's own men had given them the layout, shortly after Omar al-Talib had removed the last skin of the man's left hand, plunging the hand into a bag of salt to stanch the flow of blood.

Once he'd given his information, al-Talib had slit the man's throat, stripped his uniform, and dropped him into the Mississippi.

"Do you feel that?" Ravi whispered, racing up the stairs.

"I believe the witch's spell has made it cold," Ahmed said.

"Not *that*." Ravi's face looked troubled.

The mamelukes burst through a heavy door with Abd al-Wahid at their head, swords drawn. Behind was an office, but an office that had been stripped of books. A desk remained, and chairs, and a painting on the wall of a man with a key at a crossroads.

Abd al-Wahid cursed. "You were wrong, Ravi."

Ravi spat on the floor. "I wasn't wrong. You see the importance of speaking precisely."

"And yet he isn't here." Ahmed looked at the witch's candle. "You have at most three minutes, and then you must be out of the building. Find the bishop!"

The other three men rushed back down the stairs, and then Abd al-Wahid *did* feel something. He stopped and controlled his breathing, trying to identify it.

And then trying not to be aroused.

"You feel it," Ravi said.

"What infernal power is that?" Abd al-Wahid asked. "Jinn? Houris?"

Ravi shook his head slowly. "Ishtar. Ashtoreth. Cybele. Aphrodite. Venus."

"That is five things, O word-multiplying Jew." Abd al-Wahid felt irritated.

"It may be five goddesses," Ravi said. "Or it may be a goddess with five names. This is an ancient fire."

"I feel its power," Abd al-Wahid said. "If you were a woman, I would take you now. What do I make of this?"

"If I were a woman, *I* would take *you*." Ravi considered, and sighed. "This man is no ordinary houngan. He's certainly no ordinary bishop."

Abd al-Wahid looked at the candle. "We must leave."

They rattled down the staircase and rejoined al-Talib, al-Muhasib, and al-Syri. Their blank looks and shaking heads answered Abd al-Wahid's question before he asked.

They crossed the plaza cursing. As they entered the hotel, the flush finally faded from Abd al-Wahid's cheeks and the ache of lust disappeared from his limbs. What did it mean, that the Bishop of New Orleans had such power?

In the lobby of the hotel, Abd al-Wahid stopped. The *Onu Nke Ihunanya*'s guard lay on the floor, throat slit. His knives were clenched in his hands, but unblooded, and the hotel's lobby was otherwise empty.

"The back stairs!" Abd al-Wahid drew his sword, but al-Talib and al-Muhasib were ahead of him, racing down the hall to the back stairs. Abd al-Wahid himself raced up the front stairs first—

and found al-Farangi dead.

The French mameluke sat exactly where Abd al-Wahid had left him, in the chair, with a curved sword across his knees. Like the hotel guard, his throat had been slit.

Ravi rushed up at Abd al-Wahid's elbow. "Sorcery? I see no sign of struggle, not here and not below."

Abd al-Wahid knocked open the doors of both the room he had used and the witch's room. No sign of the girl. Her altar was gone—the table was there, but it had been stripped, and the chalk markings wiped from the floor.

"By Musa's beard!" Ravi howled, elsewhere on the floor. "The witch is gone!"

Abd al-Wahid sheathed his sword and rejoined the Jew. "Sorcery?"

Ravi shrugged. "If anything, there is less sorcerous paraphernalia in these rooms than there was twenty minutes ago."

"The . . . Ishtar. Could the bishop's goddess have warned him?"

"Or protected him. Maybe. If so, it warned him in advance. He was prepared to exit his casino and strike at us in this hotel even as we were striking at him. And he did it under my gaze."

A new voice shattered Abd al-Wahid's eardrums with a screeching howl. It was a woman's voice, and though it started as a wordless shriek, it soon dropped into a babble of frantic questions. "Osinachi! Osinachi? What has happened here? Who has done this?"

The voice came from the lobby. Abd al-Wahid descended in a rush, and before stopping he crossed to the door to look across the plaza at the bishop's casino. The door guards there were awake and standing, and the sounds of music came from the doors and through the obscene stained-glass windows.

The witch's spell had ended.

Cursing under his breath, he turned to see the new speaker.

She was an Igbo woman, hair graying, with a simple green dress but large gold rings on fingers, forearms, and ears. Behind her stood half a dozen burly Igbo men with cudgels and pistols.

"You're the manager of the *Onu Nke Ihunanya*?" he asked in English.

"I am the *owner.*" Her fists clenched by her sides. "Onyinye Diokpo. Did you commit this murder? Did you witness it?"

"I am Ahmed Abd al-Wahid," he said, placing his hand over his heart and bowing slightly. "My companions and I are travelers from Paris. We returned moments ago to find your man dead."

"It was not your doing?" Diokpo's eyes narrowed.

"One of our own was also murdered. You'll find his body upstairs."

"A foul deed." The Igbo woman spat on the carpet.

"By God it was," the Egyptian agreed, and he stared at the hotel owner. "And the perpetrator shall pay."

Etienne led Armand and two other men down the stairs into the crypt beneath the St. Louis Cathedral. The two, Philippe and François, dragged between them the hooded and bound mambo, Marie.

Armand held a bloody knife in his hand and wore a satisfied snarl on his face.

Philippe and François were known to Etienne, and were trusted. Otherwise, after what they were about to see, he'd have had to kill them.

"What if they robbed you?" Armand asked.

"We left very little money in the casino." Etienne had a hard time speaking, given the ecstatic rush the Brides sent coursing through his veins. "Only enough to keep up the appearance. And we very carefully moved the Creole to different offices." He meant Monsieur Bondí, but he avoided saying the name in the hearing of the priestess. "If they've robbed us, they've taken the day's earnings, at most."

"They could kill the men we left behind," Armand said.

"That would be a loss." Etienne examined the walls and niches of the crypt; even in the light of strong lanterns, he couldn't tell the real ones from the false. "But it would be a loss I could bear. Worse would be the murder of tonight's *patrons*, but I think they won't go to that extreme. Not *this* time."

"You're very confident. Forgive me if I remind you that this is a man who murdered your father as he officiated at the altar. And he tried to do the same to you, while you were burying... while you performed your father's service."

Armand had been at the old bishop's true funeral, outside

the city, and at the end of a Vodun procession. "A brazen blow," Etienne agreed. "And the Chevalier of New Orleans will pay for what he has done... for *everything* he has done. But if he began to murder the great and good of his city, merely because they had an appetite for placing money on the throw of dice at my establishment, he would make many enemies, and principally of powerful people." Etienne reached back into the appropriate niche of the false wall and gripped the real skull that had been incorporated into the door's apparatus. Slipping his fingers through the eye sockets, he gripped the bone firmly and pulled it toward himself.

He felt the resisting tug of the wire on which the skull was mounted, and then heard the *click* as the wire reached its full extension and the mechanism engaged.

The false wall swung inward.

Etienne ushered his men and their captive through the door and shut it, pressing it back into place to rearm the opening mechanism. The passage in which they stood was still part of the original catacombs, though de Bienville had had it walled off, so shelves of bones glared down at them.

One skeleton had pride of place, fixed to the wall with iron nails just behind the door. It belonged to the architect, the mage-engineer who had built this passage for old Bishop de Bienville. A wizard had been necessary, because the construction had been undertaken in complete secrecy and had to be concealed from New Orleans at large even as it was happening. That magician, a man of great learning who had come all the way from Providence for the purpose, had made a vow of silence, and upon breaking that vow had died a sudden and very painful death.

De Bienville had nailed his body here as a warning to others. He'd repeatedly and in great detail told Etienne about the architect's death throes. With some glee, he never omitted the detail that the architect's untimely passing had allowed de Bienville to recover all the money he'd paid the man.

Etienne had always believed that de Bienville's obsession with secrecy would prevent him from telling his chevalier cousin about the passage. With no ambush waiting for him now, he seemed to have been proved correct.

They left behind the dead man and turned two bends in the passage, to where the catacomb gave way to a small brick-lined chamber. A table and three chairs sat on a rough rectangle of carpet. Two passages exited the room in addition to the one by which Etienne and his party had entered; one led to a secret entrance into the basement of Etienne's gambling den.

Etienne gestured, and his men sat the mambo on a chair and removed her hood.

Etienne sat opposite her. "Ma cherie," he said.

"Marie."

"Marie, alors. You're a sweet young girl. And you're a mambo, but you follow the cool loa. Ayizan, and Loko. What are you doing taking up a war with me?"

"I was asked to do it." The girl was beautiful, and though she had had her head in a sack for more than ten minutes, she gave no sign of discomposure, not so much as a blink. "I consulted the loa, and they said I could."

Etienne shook his head and tsked. "Like a cheap bokor. Like a mercenary."

She held her head high. "I'm a mambo-initiate. I do as my loa permit, and I don't take orders from any Christian priest."

"What makes you so sure I won't kill you right now?"

Marie shrugged. "I'm not sure of that at all. If you kill me, I join the gede loa with the clean conscience of one who has done as she was asked, and as she was permitted to do."

"And yet surely it has occurred to you that I could have killed you in the hotel."

"It has occurred to me."

"What do you know of the maryaj-loa, mambo?"

Her eyes widened. "If you think you can assault me to break my will, houngan, you're mistaken."

Etienne laughed. "I may in the course of your life do many terrible things to you, ma cherie. I may kill you. I may torture you. I may kill or torture your loved ones. I may take your possessions, I may drive away your flock. But I will never, ever assault you."

She raised her chin, pursing her lips as if to invite a kiss. "I'm desirable."

"Yes." He nodded.

She leaned forward slowly, exposing her breast, and her knees parted. "Very desirable." It was a girl's attempt at seduction, not a woman's. Too hasty. Too obvious.

"Far too young for a man my age, but yes, you're beautiful."

"Far too young... because you've become Christian?" She narrowed her eyes to examine his face. "Some have whispered that Etienne Ukwu, once the scourge of the Vieux Carré, has become a toothless lion, a mumbler of scripture. Perhaps it's true."

Etienne chuckled. "There's half a truth in there, Marie, at most. No, I'm not restrained by any Christian vow."

"Then it's this maryaj-loa?"

"Yes." Etienne stood and loosed the white cravat to let himself breathe better. He wanted a cigarette, but now wasn't the time. Instead, he unbuttoned his waistcoat and the front of his shirt, and then he removed his jacket and cufflinks, handing them to Armand.

Despite her earlier brave face, the girl shrank back in her seat.

"You don't have my consent," she said. "Not to any marriage, not to anything."

"I don't need it," Etienne said. Then he relaxed and let the goddesses Ezili Freda and Ezili Danto fill him.

Etienne was married to two goddesses. It was marriage, the *maryaj-loa*, between a man and a divine being. Because he was married to Ezili Freda and Ezili Danto, Etienne could have no mortal lover. It would shock most of the patrons of his casino to know that the famously debauched and thuggish owner of the gambling establishment was, in fact, a virgin.

Married to two goddesses, a crone and a maid.

And now a priest in two traditions.

Lust and power filled Etienne, and he felt as he always did his body's overwhelming need. But he knew, from his experience of the Brides and from the promises they whispered to him, that he didn't have to have recourse to a mortal partner. The fire welling up in him burned his skin, aroused all his senses—

and then passed through him—

into Marie.

Her eyes fell from a wide-open into a half-lidded gaze, the lizardlike wanton stare of a woman gazing upon her prey. She leaned forward, shoulders heaving as her breath quickened, but she remained tied.

"Feel it," Etienne said. His own body still tingled. "Feel the power of the maryaj-loa. Feel the Brides speak to you. They tremble with want. You're full of desire, too, Marie. You shudder with desire and you will obey me."

"I..." Marie hesitated.

"You will obey me," he said again.

"I will..."

"You will *obey* me."

"I will...*not*." The young mambo looked up, and her eyes were still a lizard's, but now instead of the half-lidded stare of a creature basking in the heat of a sun that gave it life and could also destroy it, her eyes were open, cold, unblinking. "Mère Ayizan help me, Père Loko give me strength, I will not give in to you, houngan of Papa Legba, invoker of Maitre Carrefour, bringer of war to New Orleans."

"I didn't bring war," Etienne said softly. He stepped away, wiping the sweat of lust from his forehead with the back of his sleeve.

"But you won't let it end."

That was true. *Well, mother?* He took his mother's locket from his waistcoat and looked at it. The metal tingled. *What do I do with this one, who helps your husband's murderer?*

Let her live.

Etienne hesitated. *She's dangerous, mother.*

She lives.

Etienne put away the locket. Would his mother always force him to pull back, when directly confronting a woman? She had done so with the Appalachee witch, even urging him to help the girl, and now she intervened with this mambo. Was it because his mother was a woman? Was it because of the maryaj-loa, did the goddesses require this restraint?

But his gede loa had spoken, and he was careful to show no weakness or hesitation.

"Hood her again."

Marie bared her teeth in fury as François dropped the sack over her head again.

His mother had told him to let her live, but she hadn't told him to be kind.

Etienne leaned in to whisper to Armand. "Put her back in the hotel. The same room, if possible."

"And if it's occupied?" Armand asked.

"As close as you can," Etienne said, "but I think the room will be vacant. Its purpose has failed, and I don't think the mamelukes are the sort to linger over failure."

"Shouldn't we kill the mambo?" Armand wasn't superstitious.

Etienne shook his head. "Not this time." Reaching forward, he cut a long lock of Marie's hair and tucked it into his pocket. She hissed and pulled away, but too late. "Not this time."

Ezekiel Angleton didn't feel the cold.

He knew that he should; snow fell on his tall hat, and on the moldering threadbare coat clinging to his shoulders. It wasn't the frozen snow and sleet of the Covenant Tract, not the ice that fell on Boston like marzipan upon an Italian cake, but thick, fluffy balls, like a host of caterpillars drifting down from heaven to caress Ezekiel's face.

Lovely snow, snow for marveling at with a lady by one's side.

Lucy.

But though the snow-caterpillars crawled down Ezekiel's cheeks and down the neck of his shirt, he didn't feel the cold.

It was nothing.

The coat didn't keep him warm. The coat guided him. Even in his sleep, he felt its gentle drag, and when he stood, it was as if an invisible hand had him by the collar. If he raised his foot off the ground without willing a direction, the coat chose the direction for him.

Always toward Johnsland.

Ezekiel didn't feel the miles, either, though he'd walked hundreds of them. One boot had split at the side, letting two toes protrude and poke lopsided dots into every snowpack. He didn't feel it.

He didn't sleep. For several days, he had lain awake at night, staring at the early winter sky. Did fear stop him from dreaming? Did he dread the triumph of the Witchy Eye? The failure of his errand for his master, Oliver Cromwell, the Painter who followed the Carpenter in order to perfect the great schemes of God?

Then he realized that his sleeplessness was a gift. He didn't become more delirious. He ate and drank but little. His own cheeks were cold. His master Cromwell had given Ezekiel a new gift, alongside the gifts from Ezekiel's first master, Christ. Fortitude. Stamina. Will. Heedlessness to the weakness of the flesh.

It was two weeks after his failed attempt on the Appalachee witch on the Serpent Mound, and after his attempt to press Imperial traders and militiamen to his master's cause, that he realized his heart wasn't beating.

Holding one cold hand to his cold breast within his cloak, and pressing cold fingers of the other hand to his neck, he fought down a wave of panic. His heart did not beat, but he did not die.

Experimentally, thinking of his rival and mentor Robert Hooke, he chose to stop breathing.

He didn't fall.

This was a gift indeed!

He ran, and found he didn't have to stop. The snow slowed him, but his progress across the Ohio and then up into the Kentuck and Appalachee, and then down the other side onto the slopes above the Chesapeake, was lightning-quick because he took no more rest.

Was this eternal life that Cromwell had given him? Was this what life with Lucy would be like after the great life-restoring and life-strengthening work of his master came to pass? Would he and Lucy cast aside their restraints and run free in the woods all year, like deer in God's Eden in the careless days before Eve's error?

Descending toward Johnsland, he came upon the body of a young deer and it gave him pause.

The creature was barely older than a fawn. It had been born late in the season, and caught away from its herd somehow, without the means or knowledge of its salvation, and it had starved or frozen to death. It lay stiff as wood where it had fallen, in a broad meadow bisected by an icy stream.

The sight of the fawn's frozen eye touched Ezekiel's heart. He looked into the sightless orb, seeing an icy reflection of himself. Would the deer, too, share in Cromwell's eternal life?

No, he didn't think so. Cromwell would slay the Firstborn to undo the Fall for the children of Eve. Deer were God's creatures, but not his children, and Ezekiel and his fellow-rejoicers in the millennial future would still need something to eat.

So the deer was dead.

Ezekiel felt pity for the deer. He knelt beside it and whispered into its ear. Strange words, words Cromwell had taught him—he wasn't sure quite when—words that felt unnatural on his tongue. Cutting his own tongue just at the tip, he kissed the beast, anointing it with his blood on its lips, on its brow, on its breast—

the deer jerked at his touch.

Ezekiel stood, tasting the tang of iron in his mouth. "Rise."

The animal obeyed with sudden, oversized movements, like

a marionette in the hands of an untrained puppeteer. It jammed its forelegs downward and then pushed itself onto all fours.

As it rose, the deer exposed portions its flesh that had been nibbled at by meat-eating creatures, and maggots.

The deer lunged for Ezekiel and shoved its muzzle into his hand.

The animal's lips were cold, and it did not breathe.

"Go!" Ezekiel flung his hands in a grand gesture of dismissal, urging the deer to take flight. It stared at him, and it seemed to Ezekiel that the reflection in the animal's eye was gone. "Go!"

The deer turned and moved away. It didn't spring, or gambol, or stride; it lurched away, it staggered, it thrust itself one direction and then the other into the snow until it disappeared from Ezekiel's sight.

He imagined it meeting Lucy in a snow drift, and putting its muzzle in *her* sainted hand, and receiving stroking and petting in return. Lucy had inherited all her family's gentleness, without their pulpit fire.

But if he could raise the deer, why not Lucy?

The thought sickened him the first time he had it.

But not the second.

And the third time it occurred to him, he lingered on the idea.

In the high hills above Johnsland, he resolved upon another experiment.

He'd come upon a town. It was little more than a crossroads, and he might have walked right through it without noticing it had the moon been dimmer or the sky overcast. But under a bright midnight moon, the hamlet's buildings bulked as large sheets of silver and gray, casting black shadows at their feet.

Near the crossroads itself, at the center of the little village, stood a church. It was wooden and rectangular, with a square tower culminating in a pointed roof. Surrounding it was a stone wall, low and crumbling, but two doors led through the wall—one into the church itself, and the second through a lych gate built of timber, and overgrown with climbing ivy frozen brown in the winter's chill.

Ezekiel stepped into the lych gate and felt resistance.

Was the church enchanted? What kind of town ensorcelled its churchyard?

Ezekiel looked about the village; all was dark.

At the other end of town, a dog barked its obscure objection.

Ezekiel pressed onward, and the resistance didn't stop him. Like pushing his finger into cold porridge, he found he could will himself forward and through the gate.

Curiously, the resistance struck him not so much as a physical impediment as it did a moral one. Standing in the lych gate, he felt *disapproved of.*

Standing in the churchyard, he looked up at three stained-glass windows of simple, blocky work, depicting frontier saints: Robert Rogers, John Gutenberg, and one Ezekiel didn't know, who leaned on a pitchfork and held the traces of a plow-pulling mule in his other hand.

The saints sneered at him.

He scowled back. "Yaas, show your disdain, but you gave what gifts you had to give and were only mortal in the end."

They said nothing, and Ezekiel found his way to the graves.

There were a dozen markers, all simple wood crosses or planks, with names and dates burned into them and the occasional simple piece of praise or admonition: *SHE WUZ A GOOD WOMYN* stood between *DRINK NOT* and *RISE EARLY SAYS HE WHO DIED YOUNG.*

Ezekiel knelt at the woman's grave.

Did he dare?

Cromwell dared. Cromwell dared redeem all mankind from the cross of death, and he had imparted of his power to Ezekiel Angleton. Could Ezekiel not dare to redeem a single woman?

And if this woman, then Lucy.

He could discharge his errand in the Crown Lands and then be in the Covenant Tract inside a week. He knew where Lucy was buried, he had wept into the earth a hundred times at least.

He stretched himself flat upon the earth of the woman's grave. As the Tishbite and the widow's son. He nicked the tip of his tongue and cast the knife into the snow beside him, pressing his face into the fluffy snow-blanket until he found thin grass and hard-packed earth beneath.

He anointed the grave with his bloody kiss. Then, with a second thought, he smeared the anointing into a cross. An upside-down cross.

Christ's defeat, His lesser redemption, would be Cromwell's victory.

He saw a horn lying beside the wooden plank. He had seen such affectations before; a loved one would press the small end of the horn to the earth as if to the ear of a person hard of hearing, and speak into the large open end. This would guarantee that the dead heard the words of the living, and so in cemeteries from Atlanta to Boston grave-speaking horns could be found lying beside the graves of the popular dead, and where there were no such horns—even in towns burning bright with the New Light, or towns with great zeal for the Covenant—some cunning woman could be found who would provide one.

Superstition. Silly nonsense to most, including, once, to Ezekiel. No longer.

Ezekiel took the horn and pushed its small end through the snow to impale the earth beneath. He twisted the horn, drilling it in as deep as he could. He ran the bloodied tip of his tongue around the large opening, binding it with his essence and with Cromwell's power.

He pressed his mouth to the horn, feeling the blood make a seal with his face. The horn was cold, but no colder than Ezekiel himself.

He was reminded, suddenly, of the double-bell-ended courting stick through which he and Lucy had whispered.

He didn't know the dead woman's name, and he felt that was a weakness. "Daughter of Adam." The voice coming from him rumbled low in his belly, darker and more guttural than Ezekiel's native high-pitched whine.

Beneath him, he felt something stir.

"You were a good woman," he told her. "You *are* a good woman. You're loved. Rise again, and feel the warm wind on your cheek and the sun on your brow."

Not in the dead of night and the dark of winter, of course. But if she rose to his call, one day she would feel those things again.

The horn pressed to his face vibrated.

Ezekiel pulled his mouth back, startled. The horn trembled again in his grip and he pressed his ear to it to listen.

A voice rose from the earth through the horn. "I...am... guilty..." Its tones were basso profundo and it croaked like a bullfrog, but Ezekiel knew it was the voice of the dead woman beneath him.

The corpse.

The woman waiting to rise.

"We're all guilty, yaas," Ezekiel agreed, pressing his face to the horn conduit again. "But you no more than any of us. There is a redemption and a rising." Then he spoke Cromwell's words again, words he didn't know or understand, and this time in a variation that came naturally to him, as if he were speaking sentences rather than spouting gibberish.

The woman's answer bubbled and buzzed as if through water. Ezekiel squinted with the moonlight into the horn and saw that blood from his tongue had nearly filled it. He pressed his ear harder to the smooth dry shell and listened more closely.

"I killed...my child," the dead woman groaned.

Ezekiel's heart hurt.

"Rise," he told her. "Rise and make amends."

"I made amends," she said slowly. "I drowned...myself."

Ezekiel shuddered. There was a tale here, and dark one. A suicide and a murderer, buried in hallowed ground? Her people must not know her crimes. Ezekiel could make this right. "Rise," he said. "Tell your husband, confess. Make amends."

"No...husband. Neighbor's...husband."

The compassion burning in his breast almost made Ezekiel feel warm. "Rise—"

No!

Ezekiel wasn't certain he had heard an actual word with his physical ear, and the sound certainly hadn't come from the horn. Still, the *no* had been shouted, and when he raised his eyes to look for the source, he was nearly blinded.

Light from the fullish moon rattled against the white side of the church and filled Ezekiel Angleton's eyes. In that light, one of the stained-glass images moved. It was the farmer-saint, the one Ezekiel didn't know, and it advanced.

Ezekiel blinked.

The farmer leaped off the window and onto the whitewashed wooden wall.

Ezekiel sprang back, rising onto his hands and knees. "By the Covenant!"

The other two saints, Robert Rogers and John Gutenberg, both the saints of pioneers and frontiersmen, stepped down from their windows and stood before Ezekiel. They rose twenty feet tall above him in chunky blocks of colored light.

The Lord Protector had spoken to Ezekiel once like this. Did he dare hope for another vision from his master?

The plow-chasing saint moved off the end of the church's wall and marched around the church's yard following his stained-glass mule. The plow cut a furrow in the snow and earth that tracked the stone wall, seemed to cut directly into it without disturbing its architecture.

"Leave her, foul thing!" Wobomagonda cried.

Foul thing?

The horn trembled, and Ezekiel heard a soft burbling within it, as the sound of a tiny brook.

A force gripped Ezekiel and pushed him. He resisted with all his strength, but when he looked down he saw a bloody furrow in the snow, fifty feet long, and knew he had been pushed all the way back to the lych gate.

"Leave!" St. John Gutenberg waved his book, the pane flashing in and out of Ezekiel's view as it turned in the light.

He heard a tinkling snort to his right and turned to see the mule coming toward him. He stepped, intending to step to the side—

and the same force pushed again, hurling him back out through the lych gate. He fell back into the snow as the plow-chasing glass saint rushed past, splitting the gate entirely without ruining it.

The saints loomed, if anything, taller.

Ezekiel stepped back in the snow. Would all churches repel him now? Had he become unholy, like a vampire? Or was this church wrong, somehow, not the kind of church conducive to the Lord Protector's work? This wasn't the place, nor the time, to experiment further. He would find another burial, one not protected by such saints.

He knew he could do it. He could speak with the dead, and he could raise them.

He would be with Lucy again.

Soon.

And for the first time in many days, Ezekiel felt hunger.

"Father, I do believe you are making even less sense than usual."

———— ⟫•⟪ ————

CHAPTER SEVENTEEN

"You're wrong." The rumbling snarl of Kort's ordinary speaking voice added an ominous note to everything he said. Chigozie flinched.

"I am weak as any child of Adam," he said. "I know I am wrong often. I pray God I am not wrong always, or in the most important things."

"The god in your belly." Kort harrumphed, a phlegm-filled snort that launched plumes of steam. They huddled against the cold with the other beastkind of Kort's pack in a thicket. Chigozie had stopped offering to make fires after several refusals, and instead wrapped himself in a combination of a wool blanket and a buffalo robe, both taken from a castle—really just a small stone tower in a clearing in the woods—the beastkind had destroyed and consumed.

Looted was the word Chigozie would have used for the depredations of mankind, but the beastkind didn't loot. They left behind banknotes, gold, firearms, tools, and many other things of value to the children of Adam. They ate and burned, like a plague of locusts.

They also raped. Since Chigozie's intervention, they didn't rape women, a fact for which Chigozie thanked God every time the marauders entered a goat pen or a cattle paddock and the startled and pained cries of livestock began to rise to the wounded sky. The beastkind didn't rape women, or men, or children, but they slaked their lust on any beasts that fell into their path, usually just before eating the same hapless creatures. Chigozie couldn't watch, and he couldn't stop them, so he cringed in the woods praying as the pack assaulted one farm after another.

The beastkind also didn't take prisoners. That meant that each farmhouse or Missouri stockade-enclosed town was left behind strewn with bodies, but it also meant that some of the Missourians escaped, fleeing into the woods past Chigozie, more likely than not headed toward their deaths from exposure.

Others fought, and Chigozie saw the bloody evidence of the battles in the snow. Again, he saw dead men wearing the curious wooden breastplates, and the red banner of the crowned bird.

Chigozie didn't flee. Was this not his lot, assigned him by God and the Synod? He knelt in the snow and begged for forgiveness and direction instead.

"What am I wrong about?" he asked Kort.

The bison-headed beastman raised his muzzle and gazed at the overcast sky of early evening. "We aren't giants."

"No?"

"We may be the children of your Cain. But the giants are another people."

Chigozie had been leaning back against a knotted tree trunk; now he sat up. "Do you mean the sloths? The giant cattle I have seen in the woods, the dire wolves? The strange and enormous beasts of the Missouri?"

Kort shook his head. "Before the Silver-Weak came, and long before the Germans, there were giants in this land."

Chigozie imagined men hundreds of feet tall, striding over the forest. He'd never heard of such a thing. "Where did they go?"

"Those who survived the judgment of Simon Sword?" Kort shrugged. "Some live in towns on the rivers in the far north and call themselves Talligewi. Others on the great inland seas, north and also east. Some survive among the Pueblo, where they are called Si-Te-Cah and are treated as kings and demi-gods. Their descendants among the Plains Horsemen are smaller now, but still have the red hair. Some live in the kingdom of stone pyramids, below the junction of the rivers."

"What did Simon Sword judge them of?" Chigozie asked. "What was their crime?"

"Everyone has committed some wrong." Kort shrugged. "Simon Sword judges everyone. It's his nature."

"These giants, then. The Si-Te-Cah. They must not have been mountain-sized, if they left descendants among the Free Horse People."

"The ones I have seen? Half again your height. I have heard of some who are twice the height of a man, but not more than that. Such a man as might give pause to other men, but no, not mountains."

"You have seen the giants."

Kort nodded. "In the north. The Talligewi. Their houses are on stilts standing above the water of lakes and marshes. Famous tellers of riddles."

"Red-haired?"

"Or fair, like the Germans. They're also great workers of copper. They herded us with spears of copper once, and our teeth were blunted against their copper breastplates. They drove all the snakes southward from their lands. But then Simon Sword judged them."

"Before the Firstborn?" The Moundbuilder kingdoms were thousands of years old, Chigozie had always heard.

Kort nodded. "But there *were* giants. You're right in this. There *are* giants, and they were here at the first, as my people were. The children of Cain. Tell me more about this Cain."

Chigozie hesitated.

"You fear I won't like what you say." Kort exhaled through his nostrils, a beastlike gesture. "But you should also fear to disobey me."

"I *do* fear you," Chigozie admitted. "But I fear God more."

"I've stood at the windows of your temples to watch your mysteries." The beastman snorted. "Your god is bread. Your god fills the belly, and nothing more."

"Cain was a son of Adam and Eve," Chigozie said.

"I know Adam and Eve."

"Cain was jealous because God loved his brother more," Chigozie said. "God accepted Abel's sacrifice of a lamb, and not Cain's sacrifice of crops, so Cain killed his brother and fled into the wilderness."

"Cain was a farmer."

"Or a priest, perhaps. In Hebrew, the Bible says he worked the land, but to work is also to serve God as a priest. And Cain denied being his brother's keeper, and in Hebrew to keep is to obey God's covenant." Was Chigozie mad to discuss subtleties of the Hebrew Bible with a rapist and pillager whose head was the head of a bison? He remembered a rainy evening in his father's study, digging with his father and the Bishop of Miami into the connections between Cain, offerer of firstfruits upon the altar and, Genesis and Eve claimed, fathered by the Lord Himself, and Melchizedek, with his feast of grain. God was bread, indeed. "Cain was a priest who carried out the liturgy, but who in the end failed to keep the covenant."

Really, Chigozie was talking to himself.

Kort snorted. "Your priest killed his brother and fled into the wilderness." His black eyes bored into Chigozie's soul.

Kort's choice of words gave Chigozie pause. Was he not the good son, then, but Cain? But that was ridiculous, he was guilty of no murder. "Cain fled God, who marked him with a mark of protection. Anyone who killed Cain was to be punished by God Himself."

"Judged by Simon Sword." Kort's voice sounded as if he approved. "So your god of bread is perhaps a real god after all."

Chigozie said nothing.

"And this face of mine that you find so terrifying, perhaps it's the mark of your Cain."

"Perhaps."

"Then isn't your Cain my Simon Sword? Isn't your story of a man fleeing murder really the tale of a god cast out for carrying out his nature, condemned for being, rather than for doing? My hands have often been reddened with my brothers' blood."

Chigozie shook his head, uncomfortable at the sudden turn this theological conversation had taken. He tried not to think of the pools of Missourian blood he'd seen reddening this winter's snow.

"And might not your god, then, be Peter Plowshare, my god's father and his son?" Kort continued. "Who casts out Simon Sword upon his return at every revolution of the wheel, every receding of the tide?"

"You sound like a theology student," Chigozie said. "The kind who is awarded his degree and takes to the practice of law, having decided he does not believe in God, after all."

Kort regarded him silently. "I believe in the gods," he said at last.

"God," Chigozie said.

"And Adam and Eve?"

"God," he insisted.

"And the one inside the bread?"

"God."

Kort chuckled slowly. "Be careful, priest. If everything is god, then nothing can be god."

Chigozie dragged himself to his feet using the tree trunk against which he was leaning. "And if there is no God," he answered, "then *everything* is god. Every shudder of your loins, every pang of your belly, every boiling rage becomes the creator of the universe."

Kort stared, then began to laugh. "I like this!" Other beastkind, dozing gently in the thicket about them, started up in surprise. "I'm glad I haven't eaten you, priest!"

Chigozie turned and stumbled away. *Is this what you want of me, Lord?*

"Yet!" Kort roared. "I'm glad I haven't eaten you *yet!*"

The myrrh ink Luman had made himself, grinding the chunks of resinous tree sap into powder over the course of days with his stone mortar and pestle, and then bottling it up in a small flask of brandy, as if he were mixing laudanum. The myrrh he'd acquired from a Venetian trader in New Amsterdam, who'd parted with it in exchange for a curse of wakefulness cast on a romantic rival for the affection of a fat meneer's daughter. Luman's curse hadn't been completely effective, but had deprived the man of so much sleep—reducing him to snatches of a few minutes' length at a time, twice or three times a day—that it had deprived him also of his wits. After a week, the rival had walked chattering in front of a team of horses pulling a wagonload of beer and had his skull staved in. Whether the Venetian had then managed to seduce the burgher's girl, Luman didn't know—he and the myrrh had promptly crossed the Hudson and into Pennsland.

He'd tried acquiring male eggs first by buying them from a chicken farmer, but the old Cherokee's guesses as to the sex of the chicks had been unreliable. So he'd cadged a spell that sexed eggs accurately from a gramarye student in lieu of a cash debt owed after a bad night at Philadelphia's gaming tables. The spell was simple enough, but collecting twenty-eight male eggs—even common chicken eggs, though some versions of the spell insisted on the use of doves' or ravens'—and carting them around in a straw-packed crate in the *Joe Duncan* until he found himself in a place he planned to remain for seven continuous days had been a significant labor.

Those seven days had finally come not at a trading post, but at a camp established only a few miles north of the confluence of the Mississippi and the Ohio. There raiding party captains had begun to come in to report the results of their marauding, and a war party that began the size of a bodyguard had swollen into a small army, fed mostly by depredating the communities of the Firstborn. Rumors of Ohioan armies of resistance scurried through camp, but no such forces actually appeared.

Luman had begun the spell the first sunset after he'd learned they'd be staying, walking to a meeting of three faint paths in a stand of oaks a mile from camp. During the course of the casting, the camp had expanded so much that its ragged edges were within a quarter mile of the site now.

He stood at the same crossroads, facing into an imminent sunrise, holding the last two eggs, one in each hand. Two eggs at sunset and two eggs at sunrise for seven days made twenty-eight, and he'd kept careful track of the passage of days as well as the number of eggs. He'd written his name in myrrh ink on each egg, as he had done on each of the previous twenty-six. Not the prosaic day-to-day exoteric name *Luman Walters*, but his secret name, the name bestowed on him by his Memphite initiator.

The disc of the sun cracked above the rim of the world.

Luman felt energy tremble within him, knocking his heartbeat into an irregular patter. This was by any reckoning the most powerful magic he had ever attempted, and he had felt the strength of it building in his bones over the seven days. Resuming his position at the place of casting with all the requisite tools, he felt as if he were on fire.

Luman deliberately licked the ink off the egg in his left hand. He brushed thoroughly with a flat tongue to be sure he got all the ink, but he didn't look at the egg, instead relying on patience and taste. When the tang of the brandy and the citrus curl of the myrrh had both given way to the porcelain blandness of eggshell, he threw the left-hand egg away into the forest without looking at it. He threw forcefully; the egg must crack.

Again without looking at it, keeping his eyes fixed on the sun and feeling its rays sear their image into the back of his skull, he raised the final egg over his head. He tilted his neck back, cracked the egg into his open mouth with his thumb, and swallowed white and yolk in a single gulp.

One reason to cast this spell with chickens' eggs was that the taste was simply better. In any case, the churning he felt within him was proof that the hens' eggs were efficacious.

"Hail, Tyche," he said, reciting words that were burned into his memory, "and you, daimon of this place, and you, the present hour, and you, the present day—and every day as well. Hail, Universe, that is, earth and heaven." He turned his face side to side to align with his greetings, and up and down, and returned to gaze again into the sun. "Hail, Helios, for you are the one who has established yourself in invisible light over the holy firmament, *orkorethara!*"

The magic words were the secret. They were the fragments of pharaonic lore passed down through Memphite magicians, and not written in the spell books, but only whispered into the ears of chosen initiates. The magic words were the names of dead gods and other powers nearly as ancient and awful as the gods, which had to be invoked to bring their power to bear and effectuate any spell.

And especially this spell. His shadow would give him power, but more importantly, it would teach him lore. Living on the other side as it did, it would have great secrets to impart, and Luman would thereby become the magician of his aspirations. He could stop stealing, and begin to truly learn.

And he could do it without killing any bats.

"You are the father of the reborn Aion Zarachtho; you are the father of awful nature Thortchophano; you are the one who has in yourself the mixture of universal nature and who begot the five wandering stars, which are the entrails of heaven, the guts of earth, the fountainhead of the waters, and the violence of fire, *azamachar anaphandao ereya anereya phenphenso igraa*; you are the youthful one, highborn, scion of the holy temple, kinsman to the holy mere called Abyss which is located beside the two pedestals Skiathi and Manto. And the earth's four basements were shaken, O master of all, holy scarab, *ao sathren abrasax iaoai aeo eoa oae iao ieo ey ae ey ie iaoai.*"

To an observer, he knew, he'd have sounded like a braying donkey. He didn't care.

His magician's coat was buttoned up the front, with all the protection it provided.

Closing his eyes and seeing nothing but the suddenly red crescent of the dawn leaping back and forth from one lid to the other, Luman turned away from the sun. Eyes tightly shut, he prostrated himself on his belly in the ancient gesture the Greeks called *proskynesis*, the gesture one made toward a king or a god, arms stretched forward in supplication, and he spoke the last part of the Memphite spell. The ground under his chest and face was frozen solid. Dry snow sifted down into the sleeves of his coat and promptly melted, trickling into his armpits in a cold stream.

The trembling within him reached a higher pitch, like a guitar string struck with a heavy plectrum. Something out of sight, but within the reach of his feelings . . . touched Luman.

Something was coming.

The spell was working. It didn't feel as his Memphite master had explained it would, a cutting that separated your shadow from your body. It felt, rather, as if a door inside Luman were opening, and something was coming through.

Something cold.

"Cause now my shadow to serve me, because I know your sacred names and your signs and your symbols, and who you are at each hour, and what your name is." He finished by crying out his secret name three times more.

He felt the invisible door shut, and footfalls he could neither see nor hear.

Then, eyes still shut and facing west, he rose to his feet, knowing—*feeling*—that he was no longer alone.

Luman opened his eyes.

From his feet, his shadow stretched out in the dawn's light down the faintest of the three paths and then rose against a snow-covered boulder. Luman wasn't certain in this moment what he had expected; perhaps that the shadow itself would now speak to him, or would rise and stand beside him as his companion and guide.

Instead, a man waited.

Luman blinked to clear his eyes, which still danced with the burning red crescents of the dawn. The man was pale and had red hair falling in rings around his shoulders. He was barefoot, and Luman saw with a cold shock to his heart that long yellow nails spiked from the tip of each white toe, as from the tip of each long, pallid finger.

The man's eyes were solid white, but black jelly wriggled in their corners.

Was this what the spell was intended to produce?

Not his shadow at all. "Lazar," he murmured.

Such a hopeful name. Might he learn from one raised as Lazarus?

The apparition strode forward. Luman looked down, and saw the Lazar's feet making imprints in the snow—this was no illusion, no figment. The Lazar's lips didn't move as he spoke, but his words crackled in Luman's mind with the sound of crunching dead leaves. *To call death's creature after the name Lazarus is to wish it hopefully to live, to try to coax the blasphemy of a moving corpse into the miraculous glow of the life-giving Shepherd of Galilee. Poignant.*

The thing coming through the door, coming to Luman, was a Lazar. And not just any Lazar.

"I know you," Luman said. "Hooke."

Learned, are we? A historian? A man of letters? We shall see how well thy learning aids thee in my service!

The Lazar marched closer in the snow.

"I didn't summon you to serve you," Luman ground out between his teeth. In fact, he hadn't intended to summon the Lazar at all. What had happened? Had the spell gone wrong? Had he been tricked? Had his master, and the author of the Memphite grimoire, all been deceived?

Or had he been told a half-truth, a story of a shadow concealing a deeper initiatic secret about a dead man?

He reached between buttons into his coat to grab his Homer amulet, clenching it deep in his left fist. Dropping the crushed eggshell, he gripped the handle of his athame in his right hand and waited.

No? A humorless grin curled the Lazar's lips like the rictus of a corpse. He stopped in his tracks within arm's reach of Luman. *Then why didst thou summon me, hedge wizard?*

Luman would show no weakness. Somehow, his spell had gone wrong, somehow it had produced this specter of Robert Hooke,

Sir Isaac Newton's Shadow and underling to the Necromancer. "I summoned you to serve me, Lazar. To be my guide and my tutor."

The Lazar's hand shot forward, nails curving inward like the teeth of an obscene shark, aiming for Luman's neck—

Luman managed to fumble the athame from his pocket, but not fast enough—

the Lazar's hand struck the front of Luman's coat, and all his nails shattered, like a church window with a stone hove through it.

Brittle fragments of nail snapped against Luman's chin as they flew away from his chest. He raised his athame, putting it between himself and the dead Sorcerer in a defensive gesture.

Hooke howled without sound and grabbed for Luman's arm with his other hand. On contact, all the nails of that hand, too, snapped off like sugar glazing and fell into the snow. The Lazar stumbled, and his arms dropped to his sides.

Luman grabbed Hooke by the front of his frock coat. The dead man smelled not of rotten flesh, but of river bottom. He stank as if he'd just climbed from the deepest trough of the Mississippi. Luman pressed the iron blade of the athame to the Lazar's white throat and stared into the Sorcerer's face.

Tiny black worms quivered in the corners of the Lazar's eyes and fell out, dropping onto Luman's coat sleeve.

"By the father of the reborn Aion Zarachtho," Luman began, attempting to ignite his spell by resuming the incantation midstream—

the world around him disappeared.

He found himself floating in a sea of amber fluid. Hooke was gone, the athame was gone, and a hedge of groping hands and staring eyes closed in on Luman. What sorcery was this?

Luman turned, as if treading water in a pond, and found that the hedge encircled him all around. Indeed, looking up and down, he found the hands and eyes in all directions. Only from one direction—up—filtered down to him a yellowish light, as if somewhere there was a sun he might see, if only he could swim far enough.

In the opposite direction—below—Luman saw darkness beyond the hands.

"Hooke!" he shouted.

Somewhere, an answering laugh.

"Lazar!"

There is no mercy for thee, hedge wizard. Spare me thy calls for it.

The first of the reaching hands arrived, and grabbed Luman by the front of his coat.

Luman's coat exploded in light. It flew open and light streamed forth as fire, as singing doves, and as beings Luman couldn't quite see except out of the corners of his eyes, beings with six wings and serpents' faces that appeared to be made entirely of lightning.

Seraphim?

The light and fire rang outward with a single chord Luman's ears couldn't resolve, as if each of the chord's notes contained within it the secret whisper of every other note of the audible scale, and notes above and below audibility but conceivable by Luman's mind in this state. The light above flashed bright, stars sang, the ring sprang away from Luman—

sweeping away the hedges of hands—

blasting away the amber sea.

Luman stood again in the snow, staring into the face of Robert Hooke. The Lazar stepped back, suspicion or fear visible in his face.

Luman laughed out loud, forcing a show of confidence he did not feel. "Who's the master now?" he bellowed. "Serve me!"

Hooke threw himself backward. Despite his demand for service and tutoring, Luman let him go, watching with relief as the Lazar turned and fled into the snow-covered skeletal trees.

His limbs were shaking. He unbuttoned his coat slowly and reached into its lining, pulling out the fine sheet of paper on which he'd inscribed the himmelsbrief matching the one he'd made for Director Schmidt.

The paper was sliced with long slash marks. And more: Luman blinked at first, not realizing what he was seeing, and then he leaned in closer to read the words, puzzling out the German with the sunspots still dazzling his eyes.

All the sacred words—every mention of God, or an angel, or faith—were gone. Disappeared. As if they'd been scraped from the page, leaving blank spots that might have been virgin paper, never touched by ink.

As if, Luman thought, the holy words had sprung from the page in the form of angels to defend him.

Taking a deep breath, Luman returned the himmelsbrief to

the lining of his coat. Most likely its potency was expended, but just in case...

He definitely needed to write another. Maybe several.

He staggered back into camp by the most direct route.

"This is the Earl of Johnsland's great hall," Nathaniel whispered.

Ma'iingan nodded. He couldn't imagine a possible use for a space this large; the room was three stories tall and ran the length of the building from front to back. Torches and candles on iron stands lit the room and choked its air with waxy smoke. If there were windows, they lay hidden behind long curtains or tapestries that were themselves buried in patches beneath a layer of moldering green fur. Two balconies ran the length of one side of the room on the second and third story level—they, too, sprouted moss and weeds like the mouth of a well. The moss hung draped like a long beard beneath the balustrades of the balconies, and where the rails within the banisters showed, they looked like teeth in a flat, humorless, or even threatening grin.

At the door stood eight armed men in black coats, and two in purple.

"This is a good room," he said, still nodding. "I have one like it at home. I keep my extra wives there."

"You do?" Nathaniel asked.

"No. Really, I let a herd of deer run in it. All my wives live in the same wiigiwaam."

"I can't tell when you're lying."

"Neither can I, God-Has-Given. Neither can I."

Nathaniel shook his head in confusion and rubbed his protruding ear. Ma'iingan felt a twinge of guilt for teasing the young man, but he couldn't help himself. Deadpan leg-pulling helped him deal with the sensation that he had entered a horrible realm, a place where only foul spirits and lost souls could possibly go, and he didn't really know the way back.

The old man on the chair was a lost soul. The chair was the sole furnishing on a low, raised platform at the end of the hall opposite the doors. It was heavy and solid-backed, and it had been turned around to face away from the doors and into the room's corner. The old man crouched on the chair, his bare toes curled in the tattered remains of what had once been an upholstered seat. He wore only a single garment, a filthy gray and brown rag that covered him from wrists to ankles, with a sagging hole out of which protruded the old man's bony neck. The old man gripped the top of the chair back with the filthy fingers of one hand, his elbows jutting out at right angles left and right, the gray stained fabric hanging down like the obscene loose skin of an aging turkey, stripped of its feathers. In his other hand, he clutched a small wooden box. He stared one direction and then the other, swinging his head sharply back and forth, and his lips moved in a constant motion that might have been produced by sucking on his teeth or clucking like a hen. Greasy hair sprouted in irregular patches from a flaking scalp and fell down to his neck, to his shoulders, and in some spots, farther.

"That's the earl," Ma'iingan said. It wasn't a question.

"He's mad," Nathaniel said.

"How do you know?" Ma'iingan asked.

Behind the earl stood a dark-bearded man in a black cloak and eyepatch. He leaned on a spear gnawed into intricate rune-patterns, such as Ma'iingan had seen used by the vitkis of Chicago.

"That's Old One Eye," Nathaniel said, following Ma'iingan's gaze. "He was at the...he was there when it happened."

"Henh, I remember," Ma'iingan said. "He isn't Anama'e, Christian. He's the most important priest of the non-Christian priests in this part of the Turtle Kingdom, na?"

Nathaniel nodded. "He's the Chief Godi of the College of Godar."

"Godi," Ma'iingan agreed, "this is the word. And why won't he allow the earl to burn a log?"

"It's a sign that he thinks the earl is mad. A madman shouldn't be burning Yule logs, any more than a child."

"The earl *is* mad."

"Yes. But it's disrespectful of the Chief Godi to notice."

Ma'iingan considered this. "You mean it takes away the earl's power."

"Yes," Nathaniel said.

The room was full of people standing in defensive clumps. A snakelike path wound from the door to the open floor before the earl and his perch, and in the open space stood the young man named George. The earl's son. He held a book under his arm, and he stood with his back straight and his head held high.

He cut an impressive figure, in a Zhaaganaashii way; he'd have looked good as a statue.

Nathaniel and Ma'iingan stood near the door, at Ma'iingan's urging. As the Ojibwe looked at George and wondered where this scene was leading, Landon Chapel entered the room with a clatter of hard leather shoe soles. He wasn't at liberty; a hinged and pierced wooden bar across his shoulders kept his hands raised to the height of his neck, and two men with rifles accompanied him, also wearing purple coats. From up close, Ma'iingan saw that the coats were frayed and old, fading like Nathaniel's coat.

They marched him up the snaking path and hurled him to his knees in front of the earl.

The earl opened his mouth wider and made a cooing sound, like a pigeon.

Ma'iingan turned to Nathaniel to make a wisecrack and discovered the young Zhaaganaashii had left him—

and was now drifting up the crooked aisle toward the earl.

"Wiinuk!" He shuffled after the boy, realized now that the path was crooked because the crowd of Zhaaganaashii stood as they did not to form ranks, but to avoid the worst filth on the floor. Ma'iingan tiptoed among slimy puddles whose acid tang suggested they were full of not-quite-evaporated urine, gnawed bones, and clods that might be raw earth or might be feces, rolled into balls by being kicked across the sagging wooden floor.

He gagged as he caught up to Nathaniel.

Suddenly, Old One Eye opened his mouth and bellowed. "This court is not proper!"

"Your Holiness treads on thin ice," George Isham growled.

"*I* am not the one who risks falling into frozen waters, Isham!" Old One Eye barked. "You are not the earl, and a madman has no right to summon the Thing and make rulings of law."

George's face was steely and he gestured about the room. "Does this appear to you to be to a regularly convened Thing?"

"That is my point," Old One Eye rumbled. "Where is Parks? Where are Byrd and Pruitt and Marshall? This is a farce!"

"My Lord Earl!" George called to the earl, ignoring the godi. He faced the crowd, and they faced forward, looking back and forth between vulture father and peacock son. "As supreme *chivalric* arbiter of Johnsland, a case comes before you for *knavery*, and for *violating the code duello*."

Ma'iingan had no idea what half the words meant, but they seemed to be an appeal to the madman's wisdom.

"Play at your court, then!" Old One Eye harrumphed. "It is only play!" He left, and the eight men in black coats fell in behind him.

The earl straightened his knees, rising two feet higher, and flapped his elbows like wings as he settled.

The crowd applauded, a faint smattering that ended in embarrassed silence.

The earl said something, but it was soft enough that Ma'iingan couldn't hear.

"My lord, I beg you to hear the evidence first!" George chuckled.

The earl repeated his phrase, and George ignored it.

"My lord, I offer my own eyewitness testimony. Landon Chapel, here before you as prisoner, did before myself and other witnesses, shoot and kill Charles Johnston Lee."

"Lee?" It was the first intelligible syllable Ma'iingan had heard from the Earl's mouth. He gripped his little wooden box with both hands. "William Lee?"

"Charles Lee," George said slowly. "The son."

"Lee!" the earl cried. His voice had a sharp note in it, like a bird of prey's. He spat on the floor, and then the lines of his face slumped into sorrow. "Lee... and the body?"

"We have buried him," George said. "He was a soldier."

"We're all soldiers," the earl answered. It sounded like the cry of a distant bird.

"The facts are these," George said. He still faced the crowd, and his raised one hand to the square. It was a theatrical gesture; Ma'iingan thought he was inviting the crowd to confirm or deny his testimony. "A duel had been agreed between the two men and was about to commence. Armed in preparation for the duel and on the field of honor, but before paces had been counted off and out of order, Landon Chapel shot Charles Lee dead without warning."

"Hang 'em!" the earl shrieked, flapping his arms again and rising so quickly he actually jumped off the seat, knocking a slat out of the chair when he landed on it. "Murderers hang! He killed my son!"

"Charles Lee," George said patiently. "He killed *Charles Lee*."

"Lee." The earl's head slumped.

Landon fell forward onto his face in the filth, weeping. "Please don't do this, George," the boy begged.

Ma'iingan took a close look at the Zhaaganaashii surrounding him. Other than George, they were all dressed in frayed clothing, old and stained. Their beards and hair were ragged, their shoes had visible holes. These couldn't be the notables of this Zhaaganaashii land—they were poor servants of a madman who had perhaps once been great, or at least sane. And they were standing here as the unwilling audience to a cruel act of humiliation.

He could kill the Zhaaganaashii George, and escape before anyone could stop him. Part of Ma'iingan wanted to do that, not because Landon Chapel was a worthy prisoner to rescue, but because George was a bully.

But Ma'iingan hadn't come to Johnsland to stop bullies. He leaned closer to Nathaniel and whispered, "Let's go, God-Has-Given."

Nathaniel shook his head mutely and continued to watch the farce trial.

"Please!" a voice called from the back of the room.

Ma'iingan turned with Nathaniel to see the newcomer. She was a young woman, dressed again like a servant, and she was pregnant.

"Please!" she cried again. "George, don't do this! Please spare him."

"Jenny Farewell." The cruel smile that had been playing about George's face disappeared instantly, his lips falling into a hard, flat line. "You have nothing to do with this trial."

"I don't." The girl came forward, her gait cautious with the tenderness of pregnancy. "But I have something to do with you, my lord."

Half the wicked smile returned. "I can't imagine what you could possibly mean, Jenny."

Rough masculine chuckles crossed the great hall one way and back.

The girl's face showed her wound. Ma'iingan reconsidered the possibility of simply killing George and running, dragging Nathaniel behind him. Nathaniel was still intent on the trial, though, so he shook off the impulse.

"I ask you to spare Landon Chapel," Jenny asked. She stood near Nathaniel now, and she knelt as she asked for mercy.

Nathaniel helped her, holding her hand and forearm as she levered herself down. "I beg you to end this misery. Release him, he only wants your approval. He'll do anything, no matter how stupid, for your friendship."

"My friendship?" George frowned. "And what else of mine does he want?"

"Nothing!" Landon sobbed from the floor. "Please!"

"Nothing," Jenny agreed softly.

"Jenny." George advanced on the serving girl, his voice chiding. "What are you not telling me?"

"Nothing, my lord. Please." The girl raised a brave face, with tears on both cheeks. "You are so generous and good. Please, spare Landon Chapel."

George stood before her, staring down into her tear-filled eyes. "Jenny," he said, his voice wheedling and sticky, "whose child are you carrying?"

Jenny swallowed. "My lord knows whose child I carry. Please, my lord. For the love I believe you bear me."

"Oh, Jenny." George shook his head slowly. "I bear you no love. How could I? How could the future Earl of Johnsland love a whore?"

"Whore!" the present Earl of Johnsland shouted, rising and flapping his wings. "Whore! Murderer! Hang 'em!"

"No!" Nathaniel hurled himself into the space between the young people begging for clemency.

Ma'iingan caught at his elbow and missed. "Wiinuk!"

"Nathaniel." George's smile broadened. "This is a court of chivalry. You don't belong here."

"He belongs!" the earl crowed, and then crouched, hiding himself behind the back of the chair. "Shh. Secret."

George frowned, then snorted a tiny laugh. "My lord the earl admits you to the court of chivalry, it seems. What would you, then? Do you have testimony to bear?"

Ma'iingan put his hand on the head of his tomahawk. If Nathaniel was so foolish as to contradict George in front of all these servants, what would the older boy do?

Nathaniel shook his head, then slowly settled down onto his knees. "I only want to ask for mercy."

"For yourself? But what have you done, my urchin foundling?"

"Secret!" the earl squawked.

"For everyone," Nathaniel said. "I hope for mercy for everyone. You are a great lord, and great lords can afford to show mercy."

"A great lord, am I?" George grinned. "Do you know how to show respect to a great lord?"

Nathaniel hesitated, then removed his tricorner hat, clutching to his head as he bowed.

George snickered. "How very Franklinesque of you, Nathaniel. No, to show respect to a great lord—as to the Caliph, or the Queen of England, for instance, or to the Inca—one lies flat on one's belly."

Nathaniel hesitated again, staring at the floor. If he refused to lie on his belly in the filth, what then?

"Did someone want mercy?" George asked. "I don't see the evidence of it, myself."

"Death!" Nathaniel yelped, slapping his outsized ear. Then he threw himself down, flat onto the floor. Landon joined him, face pressed onto the filthy wood by the heavy bar across his shoulders, and Jenny followed.

Ma'iingan wanted to kill George. He hid the feeling behind a relaxed smile, and took his hand away from his fighting axe.

"What do you say, My Lord Earl-Magistrate?" George asked. "Do we show 'em mercy?"

"Eh?" The earl peeped from behind his chair back. "Who?" Then, as if the question had triggered a mental connection, he hooted several times, like an owl, rapping his wooden box against his own forehead.

"The whore and the foundlings," George said, sneering. "Over Lee's death."

"Lee!" The earl stood abruptly, almost falling off the chair. He spread his arms wide as if he might leap from the chair and soar. "Lee?"

"Yes, Lee," George said. "Damn me, father, you'd think you'd never heard the name before."

"Exile!" the earl squealed. "Send them away! Lee! The whore! All of them!"

People in the crowd shifted from foot to foot.

George sighed. "I'm not sure I can really do that, father. This is, after all, only a court of chivalry, and not a regularly convened Thing."

"You must!"

"Could I have them whipped instead?"

"The whore goes!" the earl called. "Lee goes!"

"Lee is dead. Father, I do believe you are making even *less* sense than usual."

"Lee is dead?" An idiotic grin spread across the earl's face, and then he chuckled. "As he deserved, as he deserved."

George harrumphed. "Here is My Lord Earl's sentence, malefactors. First, the two thieves. Jenny!"

Jenny's answer was a muffled sob.

Ma'iingan took a step closer to Nathaniel and put his hand on his fighting axe. He coiled his leg muscles, preparing to leap forward if his intervention became necessary.

"Exile," George said grimly. "You never had my heart, girl, but I see you had pretensions. They end now. Find your comfort where you can, but do not come again to the great house."

Jenny whimpered.

"Nathaniel!"

Nathaniel dragged himself back up to his knees, but kept his face downcast. He was smeared with filth. "My lord?"

"You seem injured enough to me, boy. And you tried to speak up for Landon here, though God knows he's never been your friend. I'll do nothing to make you worse."

Ma'iingan exhaled slowly.

George gestured to the two men with rifles who'd brought Landon in. Ma'iingan had taken them for soldiers, but now he saw them for what they were: farmers, with old rifles and small knives at their belts, better suited for paring fruit than for stabbing a man. They bent now and dragged Landon to his feet.

"Release him," George said. "Take him outside and whip him. Ten stripes."

The farmers nodded. One took a ring of keys from his pocket and began to unlock Landon.

"George—" Landon began.

"Shut up, Landon," George said, cutting him off. "It's better than you deserve. You killed Charles Lee in cold blood. You're only lucky the man has no living family, or they'd come for you on the field of honor and I doubt you'd be so lucky this time. Frankly, if Old One Eye dragged you in front of the Thing, you'd be hanged. Maybe, just maybe, when he hears I've had you whipped, he'll consider that the end of the matter."

"But you...you made me..."

"I made you *what?*" George asked coldly. "Murder Charles Lee? I think not."

"The pig sty," Landon gasped, one arm falling to his side from his imprisoning plank. "The moon woman."

George shook his head. "Really, Landon. You must learn to take a joke."

Landon's other hand slipped from its restraint and fell to his side. He stared at George, mouth open.

"Ten stripes," George said to the farmers again. "Go ahead."

With a sudden roar, Landon grabbed the plank to which he'd been chained, ripping it from the farmers' hands. Spinning, he swung the plank in a long arc—

striking Nathaniel in the temple.

Ma'iingan leaped forward, and found the farmers suddenly in his way. They wrestled Landon Chapel to the ground and then dragged him away, shrieking.

Left behind, lying on the floor in a pool of his own blood, was the unconscious Nathaniel.

"I mostly jest want to look at the pictures."

———✦———

CHAPTER EIGHTEEN

"Look what you've done, Landon." George tsked and shook his head, standing over the unconscious Nathaniel.

Ma'iingan punched the earl's son in the mouth.

The young man went down like a buck with an arrow through the heart.

And then Ma'iingan realized his mistake.

The men and women standing around the room might be farmers and servants, but they served the Earl of Johnsland. And if they hadn't gotten rid of the crazy old man after behavior like what Ma'iingan had witnessed that day, they served him loyally.

And the men in purple coats had rifles.

And Charles Lee had been a soldier, so somewhere around here there must be more armed fighting men.

Ma'iingan stooped and grabbed George's hair. It came away in his hand, revealing much thinner, shorter hair beneath, tied in a club behind the young man's head.

"Wiinuk!"

George held his hands in front of his face, fingers splayed, mouth open in terror. Ma'iingan grabbed him by the collar of his coat with his left hand and dragged him to his feet, putting his stone knife to the Zhaaganaashii's throat with his right.

"Nobody move!" Ma'iingan swiveled to be sure his command was obeyed.

The people in the room all stared at him.

"Hang 'em!" The earl jumped in simulated flight and settled again.

"Good! You all keep standing there. I'm a crazy Indian, and you never know what I might do if you push me!" That was a pretty funny joke, except that Ma'iingan was indeed acting crazy, and didn't himself know what he would do.

"You're going to hang," George murmured.

"You two," Ma'iingan said. "And you two at the door. Drop your rifles."

The men complied.

"Get me a coach," he said. "Something fast."

"The Phaeton," Landon said. Ma'iingan was loath to believe the vicious young man, but then he saw the look of sheer resentment he shot in George's direction. Landon was giving Ma'iingan good advice, and he was doing it to spite George, who was going to have him whipped, and because Ma'iingan had struck the earl's heir.

"The Phaeton," Ma'iingan agreed. "We Comanche use a carriage much like the Phaeton, that will do."

As long as he was going to be a crazy Indian, he might as well not be Anishinaabe. He pressed his blade against George's throat.

"Do it," George muttered. The two purple-clad men at the door shuffled out.

But of course, Ma'iingan had no experience even with ridden horses, much less with chariots. "You, Landon Chapel," he said. "You'll come with us."

The look on Landon's face might have been relief, but it might also have been apprehension. "The Phaeton only rides two."

"Remember that, and stay on my good side. I may have to throw one of you Zhaaganaashii boys out of the coach in a mile or two."

"Send Lee away," the earl moaned on his perch. "He killed my son."

"I *am* your son, Father!" George snapped.

"Caw!"

Ma'iingan dragged George to the door of the hall in time to see the Phaeton roll up, beside the black-stained altar. He had seen wagons and coaches before, but nothing this slight, this minimal. A partly enclosed bench seat—Landon was right, it was wide enough for two—rode directly on a framework of iron bars, within four enormous wheels. The wheels had once been painted a bright red, but the red was now mostly flaked away, leaving exposed wood and an iron rim nailed to the outer edge.

Two horses pulled the Phaeton, whickering uneasily. Were they farm animals? The discomfort of the beasts made him nervous.

How to stop the farmers and servants from chasing him?

"Can you ride?" he asked Landon.

Landon rubbed his wrists and nodded grimly.

"Bring an extra horse," Ma'iingan told him. The boy headed for the long, low stables at the corner of the house.

"I hope you have an escape plan," George said.

"I do," Ma'iingan told him. "You drive."

"Damn me," George said. "You *are* a crazy Indian."

Ma'iingan shot one last look at the earl on his perch as he left the building. Was he mad? No. But his manidoo had told him to get this boy Nathaniel on his feet, so Nathaniel could heal Giimoodaapi, and every action Ma'iingan had taken since had been in furtherance of that end.

And Nathaniel was indeed a young man laid low, and in need of help.

But what help did he need, that Ma'iingan could give him?

"Shut up," he said to George, "and get in the Phaeton."

Sarah stood at the shoulder of Alzbieta Torias. Alzbieta sat at a table in a room she had described as the *council chamber*, in a building she'd called the *Hall of Onandagos*, on the third-highest mound in Cahokia. The only two mounds taller were home to the Temple of the Sun and the Basilica, Cahokia's royal chapel.

The Hall of Onandagos, apparently, was a holy place. Also, it had tunnel entrances hidden in the building around its base, and Sarah and Alzbieta had entered by one of those, climbing long stone stairs by lantern light.

Around the table sat six other people, all Firstborn, each with an advisor or bodyguard at his or her shoulder. This was the only solution Sarah had found for gaining access to this meeting of the claimants to the Cahokian throne—as the regent didn't recognize Sarah as a claimant, she was permitted only as Alzbieta's advisor.

At Alzbieta's request, Korinn had also agreed that the meeting could be conducted in English. Sarah's Ophidian was still rudimentary—she wished she had Jacob Hop's gift for accelerated learning.

Above the table arched a high ceiling, reaching a single point that was closer to a cone than to a dome. Seven tall stained-glass windows let in light; a green vine up the center of each window, and Sarah couldn't help noticing that the vines bore a resemblance to the seven-armed tree Jacob Hop had mapped out as the structure of Irra-Zostim's palace of life.

Everywhere she looked, the same motifs.

At the end of the table stood Maltres Korinn, the Duke of Na'avu. He wore simple black. Was that an affectation or a symbol? The effect it gave was on the one hand to depersonalize him, turning him into a kind of natural active force, and on the other hand to make him appear taller and more frightening than he otherwise was.

Surely, the fact that he was standing was a symbol. To one side of him, only two steps away, sat the most ornate chair in the room. It was carved of a wood so dark it looked like volcanic glass, with streaks of red through it as if the tree's rings had pumped blood. The regent stood where the queen would sit. He wasn't the king, he was only holding a place, and he acknowledged it.

Was the black clothing a similar acknowledgement?

Sarah found she was beginning to like Korinn.

On the other hand, Na'avu was north of Cahokia, closer to the German Duchies (they weren't really Duchies, but their rulers had German titles like *landgrave* and *waldgrave* and *margrave* and *landsknecht*, and the English speakers of the Empire generally called the area the Duchies). The Mississippi Germans and the Germans of the Great Lakes were pagan, and favored stark, often dramatic clothing, such as suits entirely of black. So maybe Korinn was just following the fashions of his neighbors.

Alzbieta sat immediately to the regent's right (at Sarah's insistence, following Cathy's whispered advice that she should arrive early, take advantage, and seat herself prominently). Act as if she were the queen now, already.

To Alzbieta's right sat a heavy woman with restless eyes. She wore a leather cape over a yellow tunic and had introduced herself as Jaleta Zorales, a retired captain in the Pitchers, the Imperial artillery corps. An Imperial officer, but also apparently a distant cousin of Sarah's, and a landowner with farms in three of the seven kingdoms. At her shoulder stood a swordsman in yellow.

Next was a dark-skinned man named Gazelem Zomas. Sarah thought he looked Bantu, but through her witchy eye (which she kept covered with her bandage for the meeting, but she peeked) she saw his aura was clearly that of a Firstborn. A person of mixed ancestry, like herself, then? Or were there dark-skinned Firstborn? In all the frenzied reading she'd undertaken among the scrolls now housed in Alzbieta's city house, she had yet to encounter such a reference.

But why not?

Zomas had served in the *Hall of Onandagos* when her father was King. Alzbieta was evasive about what Zomas's actual position had been, other than to deny that he'd been a priest. Just before the meeting began, then, Sarah had cornered the dark-skinned man.

"Folks are uncomfortable about what you used to do around here," she'd said.

"You're the Lion's cub." Zomas had smiled; his canine teeth were filed to points. "Tell me your best guess."

"Spy."

"Close. Poisoner." Zomas's smile widened further.

"My father employed a poisoner?"

"It's an ancient art, and we of the lost kinship have always excelled at it."

"The lost kinship?"

The smile hadn't faltered. "Are you sure you're prepared to be here, child? Perhaps you should indeed stand by the side of the priestess Torias and watch more experienced actors on the stage."

Zomas's companion, a thin man with straight black hair and yellow tobacco stains on his lips and fingers, snickered. Sarah exited the conversation with a cold bow.

At the foot of the table sat Lady Alena. She was tall and silver-haired, with wide eyes and colorless lips. Like Alzbieta Torias, she was a priestess. Unlike Alzbieta, her vows seemed to require silence, and she watched the proceedings without a twitch of the lip. Behind Lady Alena stood a narrow-shouldered and broad-hipped man whose face was painted in blue and red whorls. On a second glance, Sarah realized that each whorl was a colorful serpent, and the snakes converged with open mouths all pointing toward the painted man's own mouth.

Next was Voldrich, whose name sounded vaguely German, but who looked like the most Eldritch person Sarah could imagine;

pale, dark, slight, gray-eyed, thin fingers. He looked like a younger Thalanes, and Sarah flinched under a barrage of too many bittersweet memories. The Firstborn's long tunic was a dark red velvet and his low boots were of soft, fine leather. "I own Cahokia," he'd said to Sarah by way of introducing himself. It turned out that he meant he owned most of the land directly outside the city's walls.

The city itself, of course, belonged to the goddess.

And technically, the rest of the land was owned by the crown, but since Voldrich's only obligation to the crown in exchange for tenure of the land was a single pomegranate seed, four days of the year—a token, a symbol—he was the owner. Indeed, once the goddess chose to honor his claim and he sat on the throne, he was considering doing away with the archaic landowning ideas most Ohioans had and moving to freehold tenure...

Behind Voldrich lurked a fat man with an open ledger. He wrote at a furious pace.

After Voldrich was seated Eërthes. No second name, no companion, and apparently no land. Eërthes was a young, slender man, scarcely more than a boy. He acknowledged no occupation when Sarah questioned him, but Alzbieta had whispered that he was a poet.

"A good one?"

Alzbieta shrugged. "How can you tell? Also, he bears the offices of Royal Companion and Notary."

"You'll explain those to me at some point."

"Royal Companion means he has a stipend from the throne. He's far too young to have earned it, obviously; it was bestowed on his grandfather. The office passes to a child in each generation designated by the previous Royal Companion."

"Are there many Royal Companions?"

"Yes. The stipends are generally small, or sometimes symbolic."

"Pomegranate seeds."

"Or feathers, or naming rights, or the right to drink from a certain fountain. Notary means he may countersign written acts of the throne. Such written acts require three, or in some cases seven, signatures of Notaries."

"You're going to tell me there are lots of Notaries."

"Fewer. I know it seems a strange custom, but consider this, Sarah: it means the queen or king may not act without some amount of noble consent. When acting as queen or king."

"Constitutions are queer things," Sarah had muttered, dropping into an Appalachee accent in the near-privacy of her thoughts. "Mind, that ain't too different from the Compact. Ain't much the Emperor can really do on his own, without the consent of the Electors. What do you mean, 'when acting as queen'?"

Alzbieta had continued, ignoring the question. "The title of Notary is also inherited. In this case, Eërthes inherited the title from his mother."

"A Notary and a Royal Companion married," Sarah said. "Must have been the wedding of the year."

"It was, until the wedding of the Archivist and the Scribe."

The final claimant wore a shirt of mail over her heavy paunch. She looked like a veteran fighting bear, complete with short, grizzled hair and five long, thick scars on her face, three down one cheek and two running down the other. She was missing an ear, apparently torn off by the same assault that had left scars down her cheek, and half the fingers on her left hand were stubs ending at the second knuckle. She arrived last, sitting down just as Maltres Korinn stepped to the head of the table.

"General Sharelas. Valia, if you must know."

Behind General Sharelas, a burly soldier in matching chain hauberk stepped into place, heels clicking.

"Sarah Elytharias," Sarah said.

"Penn," the general added. "Or so you claim."

"Do you doubt me?"

The general shrugged, and looked to the regent before she'd even finished speaking. "It matters little. The goddess will choose whom She will choose . . . or She will choose none at all. And I will defend this land, regardless."

"Welcome, all," the Duke of Na'avu began, launching into a meeting with no preamble. "I remind you that this meeting is in direct violation of the terms of the Pacification, in that we have invited no Imperial representation. No minutes will be taken. Understood?"

The seated people all nodded and murmured their assent.

"Voldrich," Maltres Korinn said. "Your man puts the ledger on the floor right now or I'll have you both killed."

"He's only doing accounts!" Voldrich's voice was flustered, but his companion obeyed the duke directly.

Korinn continued. "I wish to share with you disturbing reports of a large force of Imperial Ohio Company forces gathering in Tawa lands. Adena tells us the depredation of its winter stores is nearly absolute, and it blames that fact on the Company. For unknown reasons, many of the Ohio Hansa towns are refusing to trade at any price, and the few that will sell food do so at prices that amount to extortion. Adena and Koweta starve, and take to raiding across the Ohio and into Pennsland and Oranbega. Gazelem, is there are any reason to doubt that the Emperor is behind these moves?"

Sarah was astonished by the efficiency of the conversation and its direction. She had expected ceremony, and that the subject would be the goddess's hoped-for decision, which would select one of these seven people to replace her father on the Cahokian throne. Instead, the subject seemed to be governance.

Curious. Expecting one of these seven people might succeed as queen or king, the regent involved them in his decision making. To make the transition from his interim rule to the chosen monarch's reign smoother?

"This is as predictable as winter snow," Gazelem said. "The Pacification tightens its grip. We are to be starved into submission."

"We should expect further raids on our own stores, then?" Maltres nodded.

"As at Wartburg," Sarah said aloud.

"Point of order!" the man with snake tattoos on his face bellowed. "Who is she?"

"Lady Alena is surely not so secluded in her sanctuary as to be unaware of the return to us of the daughter of Kyres Elytharias, our late king," Alzbieta said. "This is Sarah, Kyres's daughter by his wife the Empress Hannah."

"Mad Hannah," Snake Face rumbled.

"Slander!" Sarah tightened her grip on her ashwood staff, resisting the urge to step around the table and crack the pear-shaped man over the head with it.

"Hold your tongue!" Snake Face roared. "Whisper in the ear of your priestess, that's your place in this council, if you're not a claimant to the throne!"

"Are you a claimant, then, eunuch?" Eërthes asked, gently stroking his own fingernails. "Remind me of the substance of your claim!"

"I'm the Lady Alena's voice!" Snake Face waved his arms in rage. Was it *his* anger, or the Lady's? "As well you know!"

The Duke of Na'avu rapped the table with the knuckles of one hand. "I don't feel it is my place to silence my lord Elytharias's daughter, regardless. It would be an act of disrespect. An impiety."

Snake Face licked his lips and looked at Alzbieta with a sly expression. "And how is it that this whelp *returns* to us? Was she born here, in the City of the Goddess? Or was she conceived in the Slate Roof House? Or indeed, in the dungeons of Horse Hall, squired upon Mad Hannah by some obliging turnkey?"

"Silence, Lady!" the duke roared. It was a strange command to hurl into the face of the tattooed man, but in some way, the man was only speaking for Lady Alena, and now he and the Lady both stared down at the floor, fuming.

"A being who is eternal," Alzbieta Torias said, "is forever returning, and can never be truly gone."

"You missed your calling, priestess." Eërthes leaned forward, steepling his fingers together and resting his elbows on the table.

The general snorted and shook her head. "You babble in the language of holy writ and liturgy, Torias. Let us speak plainly. This woman is a claimant."

"No!" Maltres Korinn's voice had a sharp edge. "We agreed to the rules of this council and our supplication to the goddess, and I haven't broken them. Sarah Elytharias is admitted as body-guard, advisor, and witness of Alzbieta Torias only. But I won't bar her entry, and I won't insist upon her silence."

"I thank you, Regent-Minister." Sarah stepped back from the table, leaning on her staff and removing the patch from her witchy eye. "I see that you serve the kingdom well, that you carry out your office with wisdom and faithfulness."

Korinn bowed his head in silence.

"But know this. I will not be bound by rules that you agreed here in this council. You are people of wealth and office, but none of you is king. None of you is the goddess." She turned to look at Alzbieta. "I'll answer your riddle now."

Alzbieta's face was impassive. "What riddle is that?"

"Elhanan the son of Jaare-oregim slew the giant Goliath," Sarah said. "But Samuel chose *David* to become king."

"Yes?" Alzbieta smiled faintly.

"David means *beloved*. You are here as supplicants not asking the goddess to choose a ruler, but to choose a Beloved. A Beloved, a David, who may *become* your ruler. But you cannot command *Her*, and you do not bind *me*. I will follow the path my father has set for me, and I will do Her will."

Alzbieta beamed.

"Her will," the Regent-Minister of the Serpent Throne repeated, as if saying *amen* at the end of a prayer. He took up his staff with its iron horse's head at the tip, and tapped the tip, also bound in iron, against the stone floor. "And the rules of my office."

Sarah raised her own staff, carved at the tip into the shape of a horse's head by her foster father, the Appalachee Elector Iron Andy Calhoun, and slammed its tip against the stone floor with a resounding *thock!*

"*Signum quaeso!*" she shouted.

She didn't intend it as an act of gramarye, not exactly. She didn't truly intend it at all, she merely acted, caught up in the enthusiasm of her new understanding. But as she shouted, she slipped her hand into her satchel and touched the Orb of Etyles with three fingers. Immediately, the green fire of the Mississippi River ley line rushed through the Orb, across her chest, and into the staff—

which sprouted.

One leaf popped out first low on the staff, and then a second opposite it and slightly higher. A third and a fourth broke from the pale wood halfway up its length, nearly parallel, and finally a fifth and a sixth.

And then the tip of the staff exploded into flower. A riot of buds burst from and around the horse's head, adorning it and then concealing it, and at the same time a scent burst from the staff that Sarah seemed to vaguely remember.

Lemons, or oranges. But there were other notes mixed in, spices.

Where had she smelled it before?

Maltres Korinn bowed his head, but kept his grip on his staff.

"Theater." General Sharelas snorted.

"Perhaps this one, too, has missed her calling in life." Eërthes smiled coyly.

"My calling in life," Sarah said grimly, eyes fixed on the Duke of Na'avu, "is yet before me."

She didn't yet have a plan for how to intrude upon the Presentation, but she still had time to come up with one.

✧   ✧   ✧

Calvin climbed the mound alone.

He'd thought about inviting Cathy and Bill, Cathy because she was pleasant, and Bill because... well, because it felt awkward to invite Cathy without Bill... In the end, he'd left them at Alzbieta Torias's family house in Cahokia, Cathy coolly watching the mound-top palace into which Sarah had disappeared, and Bill describing his plans for the next stage of drilling with his mixed force of Firstborn and beastkind.

It felt right to climb this mound alone.

He'd spotted it when standing beside Sarah on the Great Mound. This other mound, one of the city's three largest, stood east of the Great Mound. And the building on its peak had to be a church.

It was cross-shaped, for one thing. The churches around Nashville, whether New Light or not, tended to be simple squares or rectangles, but older churches, and all the churches in some parts of the Empire, were cross-shaped buildings. Like the St. Louis Cathedral in New Orleans, for instance. The building was cross-shaped, and on its east-facing spire it bore a plain, tall cross.

Also, it had stained-glass windows. Tall ones, like the windows of a church. And it was hard to tell for certain from the outside, but Cal thought the images he'd seen from the Great Mound were images of the seven days of creation: light on the first day, the firmament on the second, and so forth.

He stood now on the highest steps of the stairs that climbed the eastern slope of the mound and looked up. The building was made of stone and it was covered with statuary. There were monsters, including many prominent half-man, half-beast creatures, but there were also women and men. Like any saints' representations, the statues were marked by icons, but Calvin didn't know any of them.

Was that because he was New Light, and a little wary of saints and their followers generally?

Or were these Ophidian saints?

The church was also covered with mourning doves. The gray and white birds were also called rain doves and turtle doves, though he was pretty sure it wasn't the same species mentioned in the Bible. The birds crowded every horizontal space outside the building, cooing softly and staring at him with their little round eyes.

The church's doors were recessed in a broad porch, and in front of the doors stood two stone columns. The pillars were carved, too, with climbing vines and leaves, and where the pillars reached the ceiling of the porch they branched out into boughs that seemed to hold up the front of the church. A carved vine hung across those boughs, connecting the two trees like the lintel above a door; even in the pale winter light, the vine glinted dully gold. He had only seen it from the foot of the slope, but Cal thought the building atop the Great Mound—the Temple of the Sun?—was fronted by a similar arrangement of two pillars and a vine.

One of the doors hung halfway open; Cal entered.

He stood a moment in the semi-darkness within, his eyes acclimating to the colored light through stained panes and his ears adjusting to the sounds bouncing off stone walls within, both muffled and amplified, when he heard a voice.

"What did you bring to trade?"

Cal turned and found a round-faced woman with short hair, dark brown with a hint of gray in it. She wore a gray robe with a crescent-moon shaped brooch pinned to her chest. "Ma'am, I ain't learned, but I've read enough Bible to know Jesus don't like you buyin' and sellin' things in a church."

The woman laughed. "I mean, you're a traveler, aren't you? You're Appalachee, and you look a little...road-worn. My guess is you've come here to trade. You might pick up beaver pelts from the Algonks or buffalo hides from the Sioux, or Cahokian crops. They call this the Cahokian Bottom, you know—it's a flat plain created by the Mississippi, and its soil is rich from centuries of flooding, and abounds in crops. Although I doubt there's surplus to sell, this year. What did you bring to trade? Not your neighbor's cattle, I hope?" Her eyes twinkled.

"No, ma'am. Iffen I e'er sold my neighbor's cow in the spring, it was because he sold mine in the fall." Cal felt his face flushing. "But not this trip, anyhow. I come on this trip for...well, Jerusalem, I come for love, iffen I'm honest about it. I can tell you that, can't I? You're a priest, or priestess? Nun? St. Cetes, ain't it?"

"We aren't exactly in the confessional booth. I'm Mother Hylia."

"Mother? Oh, as in *Father* Thalanes, *Mother* Hylia. I'm Calvin. Cal."

Hylia frowned. "Father Thalanes? Did you know someone of that name?"

Cal nodded. "I started this journey with him, seems like ten years ago, though it weren't but a few weeks."

"Started? Did you part ways?"

"In a manner of speakin'." To his surprise, tears sprang to Calvin's eyes. "He...died."

"I'm sorry to hear that. I knew Thalanes. He taught me rhetoric and heuristics."

"I have no idea what that means," Cal admitted, "but he was a hell of a teacher, so I believe it."

"I won't tell anyone you're in love," Mother Hylia promised.

"Aw, she knows, anyway." Cal scuffed the heel of his moccasin on the stone floor. "And I come for other reasons, too. I made a promise to my grandpa. And it's the right thing to do."

"I like to hear about people trying to do the right thing."

Cal shrugged. "And I saw this and figured it for a church. Only I'm a mite surprised to see you here, because St. Cetes and all. I mean, ain't you the ones as wander around and are all about freedom? I didn't take you for the kind as would run a church."

"We aren't." The nun bobbed her head. "This church...its proper title is *basilica*, by the way, meaning it's a royal chapel, and this is the Basilica Mound we stand on...has secular priests. That is to say, priests who aren't monks or nuns, and who perform services here. Some of them are away right now."

"You jest visitin', too?"

The nun shrugged. "Just visiting, and if someone needed any additional services, I'd help out the secular priests as I could. If a confession needed to be heard, for instance, or if there were call for an unscheduled Mass."

"How about a tour of the church?" Cal asked. "Iffen you got the time. I ain't e'er been in an Ophidian chapel, I reckon I might could use some explanation."

Hylia smiled. "Every true journey needs a psychopomp."

"I don't know why I'd need a pump," Cal said. "I mostly jest want to look at the pictures."

"I'll follow you," Hylia said. "When you want something explained, tell me, and I'll give it my best shot."

Cal nodded and ambled up the left side of the nave. He'd gone about halfway, nodding at every statue but not asking Hylia for more information about any of them, when he stopped with a sudden realization.

"Men," he said.

Hylia nodded.

"Every single one of these saints is a man. I don't know half of 'em—I mean, there's Elijah, and that's Paul, right? And the feller lookin' at his own skin on the door must be Cetes. But I don't know the one holding the basket, or the feller with the snake wrapped around his middle, or the one drivin' a mule, but they's no women."

"Arakles," she said. "Ophiuches. St. Peter of the Plow. Would you like to hear their stories?"

Cal considered. "I reckon not. Not at the moment, anyhow. But...I can't figure this. Where are the women?"

"Keep walking." Hylia smiled.

In the stained-glass windows around the center of the church, Cal read, moving backward through time, the story of the expulsion from Eden, the Fall, and the Creation. They were mostly told in images he knew—and here he found the first image of a woman in Eve—though those representations had a Cahokian twist. Adam and Eve, holding hands, fled the Garden before a fiery, sword-wielding angel, who stood across a line of what Alzbieta Torias had called Adam-stones. And when they built their home outside the Garden, it was a stone house perched on a conical mound.

At the rear left side of the chapel in stained glass, the first day of creation flowing from his lips, was a bearded giant, crowned and enthroned. "It ain't always you see God Hisself," Cal said. "Usually you jest see Jesus. I mean, not to fool around with God and Jesus bein' the same person, or the same substance but different persons, or howe'er it is you'd say it in betterick and holistics."

Hylia smiled and pointed back the way they'd come, over the church doors. There, always on the male-dominated side—the south side of the building—was a stained-glass image of Christ after the passion, wounds in his hands but smiling.

"I see," Cal said. "Well, mostly so far this is the same stuff I might could see in any chapel in Nashville or the Kentuck. Exceptin' you got some odd saints, but so do the Yankees and the French."

Hylia beckoned him to follow, and crossed through the center of the church. Looking to his left as he walked, Cal saw what must be the center of the stained-glass image dominating the apse: he recognized the circumpolar stars immediately, with Draco and the Bears. He cocked his head and thought; God the Father seemed to occupy the place of the enthroned King Cepheus, and he didn't see Cassiopeia—but he spotted a robe-covered arm that must belong to her.

Then he crossed to the north side of the nave, and saw that the Cassiopeia figure was a woman, crowned and enthroned like Cepheus-God the Father. From her flowed the same stories of Creation, Fall, Expulsion, and so forth, but the stories were different. On day one, the Father spoke and light came from his mouth; on day one, the... Mother?... spoke and angels flew from her lips, holding squares, compasses, trowels, garden spades, and other tools.

The stories were too much for Cal to absorb all at once. He noticed that in the Garden, there was no serpent—instead, Eve seemed to holding the apple out to Adam, having a reasoned conversation, while their free hands touched, fingers interlaced together. Rather than mound-top homes, after the Expulsion, this Adam and Eve built mound-top observatories like the one Cal had seen at Irra-Zostim. And at the end of the sequence of stories—bringing up the train of a parade of female saints—over the door in stained glass was a woman holding a baby.

"Mary," Cal said, relieved he finally recognized something.

"The Virgin," Hylia said. Smiling the same damned smile.

"Only your builders might could a used more models. All your women look the same—Eve, Mary, Cassiopeia—"

"Cassiopeia?"

Cal pointed at the great creatrix in stained glass.

"The Virgin," she said again.

"Right." And then Cal realized he'd walked right past something without noticing it. He retraced his steps into the center of the nave, where he'd passed through, eyes fixed on the circumpolar stars. This time he looked down.

There was an altar, such as he'd seen in the St. Louis Cathedral, and in other churches. But behind the altar, pointing up toward the stained-glass north (actually on the west side of the building), was a large golden candlestick. Its arms were irregular in size and height, giving it the appearance of a seven-branched tree, or an irregular ladder, climbing from the altar at the center of the church up into the center of the sky.

Was it in fact the trunk of a seven-armed tree, covered with gold?

Cal stared, feeling rooted into place.

He barely heard the hushed whisper of feet on stone approaching, but he felt the tug at his elbow and found Mother Hylia standing only inches from his shoulder, disconcertingly close, as Thalanes had liked to stand.

"I can't figure out," Cal said slowly, staring at the stars in the central window, "whether these pictures—and you, and Sarah, and all...*this*—are extremely familiar, or extremely foreign. Pretty sure it's one of the two."

"Do you feel like a man twenty years married, who looks on his wife one night and realizes he doesn't know her at all?"

"Jerusalem, I...mebbe. It's like they's a side to all these stories I ne'er knew, the right side, so to speak, or the left, dependin' on where you stand."

"Or the *inside*," Mother Hylia said.

"The inside. Jerusalem." Cal shook his head. "I don't understand this and I ain't about to understand it. I's New Light when I come through the doors and I reckon I'm New Light still, and that'll jest have to do for plain old Calvin Calhoun."

"The gods look on the heart, Calvin," Mother Hylia.

"*Gods.* Jerusalem." Cal thought of Simon Sword, the iridescent bird-headed giant king of the Mississippi, proposing marriage to Sarah. He rubbed his eyes, trying to wipe away the memory.

"Of course, gods. 'Let us make man in *our* image, after *our* likeness...*male and female* created he them.' Gods *and* goddesses."

"Jest tell me one thing."

"If I can."

"St. Peter of the Plow...that ain't some Firstborn way of talkin' about Simon Sword, is it? About Peter Plowshare?"

Mother Hylia laughed. "Of course not. But they sound similar, don't they? But then, the Vodun loa Papa Legba and St. Peter of the Rock both have a key, but they're very different beings. No, St. Peter of the Plow was a farmer who for his righteousness was given a plow by God."

Calvin's head hurt. "A magic plow?"

"A holy plow. And every furrow cut by that plow sprouted fruitful, with grain and squash and beans. And the farmer's neighbors urged him to become rich, but instead he gave all the food away to the poor, until there were no poor. *Then* the neighbors urged Peter to make himself rich, but still he refused. Instead, he gave the food to his immediate neighbors, and then all the people in the county, until the county was fabulously wealthy, famous for the abundance of its food."

"I'd be happy to own such a plow myself." Calvin tried not to think of the golden plow, the Heronplow, that Sarah now carried in the bottom of her shoulder bag.

"Still the plowed furrows grew food, and Peter traded the food for donkeys, and bundled the excess food on the donkeys and sent it over the mountains to people who were hungry there. And then he bought ships, and filled them with corn and squash and beans and sent them overseas to the poor around the world."

"Lord hates a man as lacks ambition."

"Finally, one night an angel appeared to Peter, and said 'Peter, God wishes you to be rich. Why won't you do as God commands?' And Peter trembled there beside his bed on his knees, and said 'God forgive me, but money is not the riches that I want.' The angel again: 'What riches do you wish, then? Ask, and Heaven itself cannot refuse.'"

"You mean *will* not," Cal said.

"Shh. 'Heaven itself *cannot* refuse.' And Peter, in the goodness of his heart, said, 'What I wish indeed is Heaven. I wish to live in Heaven, and my only regret is that I cannot live in Heaven and also do the works on earth God wishes me to do.' At his last word, the plow sprang from its place on the mantel and rushed outside on its own. With no hand guiding it and no beast pulling, that plow bit into the earth and carved a square all around Peter's house. From the moment it finished its work, the interior of the square it had marked became Heaven on earth. Angels descended to minister to Peter, and though he left his home to plow and reap, and to feed to the poor until the end of his days, every night he lay awake all night seeing visions of Heaven all around him, eating honeycomb and drinking wine with the angels, and then rising refreshed, though sleepless, every dawn."

Cal's temples throbbed. "Was he Firstborn, St. Peter of the Plow?"

"The stories don't say," Hylia told him. "But as you're familiar with my order, you know that we travel, and I can tell you that St. Peter of the Plow is famous throughout the Ohio and in Pennsland."

"Well, I ain't heard of him in Appalachee," Cal said. "On the other hand, I weren't e'er much of one for saints."

"You have a good heart, Calvin. Who knows? Perhaps one day a humble Cetean like me will stand here and tell passing visitors the story of St. Calvin."

"Patron of cattle rustlers and doomed love."

"No true love is doomed, Calvin. Love transforms and refreshes, whether it ever attains its object or not. Love is the great gift."

Cal laughed, his chest feeling hollow. "Is it? Or is it the great *curse*? Ain't that what the Eden story tells us, Adam and Eve fell in love and it led them to eat the forbidden fruit and then they got thrown out?"

Mother Hylia smiled. "As you've seen, there's more than one way to tell that story."

The Phaeton was fast, even carrying the three of them. It wasn't going to be able to leave the roads, though, and Ma'iingan was afraid that at the first sight of a soldier, George would cry for help.

He couldn't release George, for a similar reason.

He wasn't sure he could let Landon out of his sight, either. Ultimately, the ferocious envy and pecking order that connected the boys and defined their relationships meant he had to keep George and Landon with him until he was positive he could outrun them all.

He needed a canoe, and a long stretch of fast river to take him somewhere he could see to Nathaniel's injury.

Instead, he found a curing barn.

He found it as the sun had set, and he found it by sense of smell. The dried, aromatic curl of asemaa reached out to him across two harvested fields, and led him to turn the Phaeton across the trampled furrows, forcing George and Landon to remove and replace fence slats to let the coach through.

The barn was big enough to drive the Phaeton and four horses into, and shut the doors behind, even with the tall, airy drying racks for the asemaa taking up half the floor space. The horses snorted in protest—perhaps at the strong smell of asemaa—and Ma'iingan assigned Landon the task of calming them. The boy did this with reasonable success, and Ma'iingan set about tying George up.

He used the harness of the Phaeton, cutting up the leather into thin cord and then strapping George to the central pillar in the curing barn, sitting, with his hands behind him.

"My God, Old One Eye will eat you alive," George said. Then he looked away, as if he had humiliated himself.

"Henh. Your father might, too," Ma'iingan shot back. "Though I think vultures generally prefer carrion."

George bared his teeth and kicked his heels at the wooden floor of the barn, but said nothing.

With Landon's help, Ma'iingan lowered Nathaniel from the Phaeton. He looked bad. His wounds had reopened and he was pallid, but worse, he thrashed and shouted out the strange non sequiturs he generally did, only now he did so without pause. He slapped and clawed at his large ear as he did, until the ear was red and bled in many long scratches.

Ma'iingan would bind his wounds. Maybe he could save the boy's life. But that still left Ma'iingan with a healer laid low, it still left his son Giimoodaapi with no people and no doodem, not one of the Anishinaabe, and maybe doomed to starve to death. At best, it left Ma'iingan the father of one son, and one changeling, one spiritually outcast creature that must lurk forever in darkness, and never truly come forward into the light.

"Get water," he said to Landon. He didn't like trusting the boy, but he had no choice. He considered threatening him with another Crazy Indian act, but decided against it. "Quickly."

Landon took a bucket from the corner of the drying barn and slipped out the back door into the dark forest.

"Gichi-Manidoo," Ma'iingan said aloud. "Help me help this boy. Help me help my son."

On the wooden floor, surrounded by the thick scent of sacred asemaa, he began to build a sweat lodge.

"I see the lawyers have got at the Imperial College as well."

———— ⋙ ◦ ⋘ ————

CHAPTER NINETEEN

Ezekiel followed the smell of blood until he reached a clearing. His mouth watered as he ran through snow and between trees.

In the center of the clearing stood a pile of rough stones, uncut by chisel as the English tradition required. Standing on the other side of the pile of rock was a heavy-torsoed, bow-legged, bearded man in black breeches, shirt, and cloak. His head was bare and he looked up to the clouded heavens. A godi, by the long knife in his right hand and the horn in his left.

Blood ran down the knife and dripped onto the sheep carcass lying on the stones.

Ezekiel was hungry.

He hesitated, thinking he'd wait, and after the godi had finished, he'd take the sheep's carcass. In his mind's eye, he saw himself biting into the fresh throat of the sheep, savoring its blood.

No! No, that wasn't right. Roasting it, and then eating it.

"You!" the godi shouted. He met Ezekiel's gaze with anger in his eyes. "This is a sacred site, and you are trespassing. Did you not see the markers?"

He meant the horned skulls nailed to tree trunks, another well-known pagan practice. Ezekiel hadn't seen any such, but he'd been running fast, following the scent. He burned with hunger from the inside out. He needed flesh.

Cooked or raw, he didn't care.

"I am hungry, sir," he began meekly. "Could you spare..."

"Christian!" the godi snapped. "Get away! You are in Johnsland, and the College rules here!"

"I only want a bite," Ezekiel said, trying again.

The godi reversed the knife in his hand, pointing it at Ezekiel. "Leave now, Yankee, or I'll have you crucified like your effeminate god!"

Ezekiel was across the clearing in a single bound. His father's long sword sprang from its sheath into his hand, and swung down overhand at the pagan priest.

The godi raised his horn hand—

and Ezekiel sliced down, cleaving the horn in two, shearing off all the godi's fingers, and sinking his blade six inches into the priest's shoulder.

The godi screamed.

"So...effeminate," Ezekiel rumbled, his voice dropping an octave. He stepped forward.

Weaving back and forth on his feet, the godi stabbed Ezekiel. Ezekiel looked down at the blade sticking into his belly and noted dispassionately that the wound didn't bleed. Another divine gift.

He grabbed the other man by the knife arm and broke it, forcing the elbow to bend contrary to the natural direction until it snapped, and the godi's scream jumped up in pitch.

Ezekiel found he had no interest in the sheep.

The godi was still screaming when Ezekiel leaned forward and took a bite from the man's neck.

He thought he saw a man standing at the edge of the clearing as he ate. The man wore black plate mail and a white neck cloth like the Lord Protector, but when Ezekiel raised his head for a better look, the stranger was gone.

Ezekiel's coat tugged him onward.

"I admit I'd expected better pay than this." Josep stared down into the coins in his palm, shaking his hand slightly to make them clink together.

Montse looked yet again into the wooden crate bouncing beside her in the wagon. Onions. "It isn't your pay. Your pay is a share of all booty, and *La Verge* when I die. Now eat them."

Miquel did as Montse bid, slipping the tarnished silver coins between his lips and swallowing them, one at a time.

"Will there be much booty, then?"

"Not today."

"But I'm so fond of gold."

"Gold will do nothing for you in your belly, you fool. Eat."

"Or larger silver coins, at least? An English groat, for instance. Something larger than these Pennslander shillings."

"You would choke on a groat, you fat bastard."

"You could cut the groats into bits, and I could swallow the bits. If I'm going to swallow money, I would really like it to be a lot of money."

"Sharp-edged bits would perforate that gut of yours, already lacerated by years of cheap rum. I have no time today to stop and watch you bleed to death from your backside, Josep Portell i Boria."

"You say the sweetest things, Capità."

"Shut up and eat my money. We arrive."

Josep, having had his fill of flirtatious objection, threw the coins into his mouth and swallowed them in a mass. Montse had swallowed hers first; she imagined she could feel them, a solid lump of specie in her belly. Would an unborn child feel like that, growing with the berserker aim of expanding its mother's hips and dragging at her like a too-large anchor on a nine months' voyage until finally she could drop it overboard?

No, that was nonsense. And anyway, Montse was not the kind of woman who was ever likely to have a child.

The closest child to her own was Margarida—*Margaret*—Hannah's daughter. Whom the soulless, conniving, coin-grasping, murderous Chevalier of New Orleans had taken from her care.

Whom she was now coming to rescue.

"You know you shit your pants when you die," Josep said to Miquel.

Miquel shrugged. "At that point, I will no longer care."

Josep slapped his cousin on the shoulder. "But you should! We'll be legends, you and I! We'll be those two Catalan pirates who shat silver when bayoneted by the gendarmes."

"The gendarmes will bayonet no one." The wagon stopped, at a narrow rear gate piercing the outer wall of the Palais du Chevalier, and Montse hopped down. "Also, we're grocers. Think like a grocer."

"Like a grocer, trying to rescue a kidnap victim?" Miquel grinned, an easy, confident smile that hid no secrets. Someday soon, the boy would find out how attractive he could be to women, and then he would be dangerous. Would he stay with *La Verge*? Or would be give up sailing, robbery, and trade to do something safer in town?

Josep snorted. "You make us sound noble with all your rescuing talk, Miqui. We're pirates. We're here to spring our fellow pirate from prison."

"Our fellow grocer," Montse said. She dropped the back gate of the wagon and grabbed a crate. Peppers and garlic, by the smell of it. Say what you would of the chevalier, his table wasn't bland.

The driver of the wagon, having hitched his horses to a post, knocked at the door in the wall. Montse shuffled to his side, trying to walk with the prideless shuffle of a city dweller and an employee. She switched to French, but kept her voice low to deliver a final warning.

"Just get us inside," she said. "Your wife will live, and you'll have enough money to open a second grocery."

The grocer muttered through clenched teeth. "I'll have enough money to flee Louisiana. Which I will have to do, because I'll be blamed for whatever mischief you intend to accomplish inside the Palais."

"Your choice." Montse chuckled. She heard the grocery-laden footfalls of Josep and Miquel as the two men fell in behind her. "Only don't forget that you're also choosing for your family."

"Merde."

Montse and her crew had broken into the grocer's house before dawn. Several of her men were sitting with his wife and children while she, Josep, and Miquel accompanied him on this delivery. She hated threatening the grocer and his family, but Montse's own family—her daughter, in her heart—was in danger, and she saw no other way.

"Oui," Montse agreed. "Merde indeed. Merde for me as well, in this life. Merde for all of us."

The gate opened, revealing a thin man with large hands, knees, and feet, wearing a simple blue livery, with a short gray perruque covering his head. "Nouveaux employés?"

The wagon driver spat and answered, also in French. "The other lazy bastards quit."

The chevalier's man nodded. "We lost two footmen today. Drunkards."

"I wish I could hire drunkards, but I'm not so lucky. I'm stuck with these Dagoes I found practically begging on the Place d'Armes. Look at them, they barely fit their uniforms."

It was true. Josep only accommodated his belly in the white smock the grocer's employees wore by leaving the bottom three buttons undone, and Montse's height meant she had two inches of wrist showing at the end of her sleeves.

Montse had told the wagon driver they were Spaniards. Fortunately, he seemed not to have noticed any better.

"Let's unload this quickly," the chevalier's man said. "The butcher arrives in fifteen minutes."

Crossing the yard, Montse heard shouting to her left. She looked casually, and saw gendarmes drilling on the broad lawn that was part of the chevalier's garden. They had the sloppiness of recent recruits.

And there were hundreds of them.

"Un...deux...trois..." their drillmaster shouted as they advanced across the short-cropped grass, wooden training rifles over their shoulders.

Montse and her crewmen walked into the open door of the Palais. This was an extrance for tradesmen, and it led into a hall adjoining kitchens, pantries, and other working rooms. The swarm of servants barely gave Montse and Josep a second glance. This was the first part of Montse's gamble, and it paid off; in such a large house, the servants were used to vendors coming and going, and paid the Catalans no mind.

The three of them deposited their crates onto a table nodded at by a thin woman in chef's whites with scarred hands. When she turned her back, Miquel turned and duly trooped outside, while Josep and Montserrat scurried around the corner, found a narrow staircase, and climbed to an upper story.

In a nook bulging from the wall, two padded chairs sat illuminated by an arc of tall windows. A room only for what—sitting? On a small table between the two chairs, Montse spied a book and almost laughed out loud. What kind of insane wealth must a man have to build a room into his house—even if the house was a palace, and even if the room was small—whose sole purpose was to read in?

She and Josep both shrugged out of their grocer's clothing, shoving the smocks and baggy canvas pants underneath one of the two reading chairs. Then they squeezed into the corners of the nook, sheltered from the view of anyone passing in the hall behind them, and watched the yard.

Here came the second gamble. The chevalier's people mustn't suspect any of the grocer's staff had stayed behind.

Miquel sauntered into the yard and approached the chevalier's man watching the gate. He walked past the man in blue, pulling two hand-rolled cigarillos from his pocket as he did so. The chevalier's man turned, reaching out to take a cigarillo and as he did so turning his back to the gate.

"Look at that little fotut." Josep's tone was appreciative. "Even the men can't resist him."

"That sounds like envy. Would you like to be able to seduce men, Josep?"

"Only you, my light."

"Shhh."

Miquel grinned, shrugged, and talked as he and the chevalier's man lit their cigarillos and took a few puffs.

Miquel then nodded at the man in blue and passed through the gate—

just in time to pass two more of the crew of *La Verge Caníbal*, coming in with sacks of wheat over their shoulders.

The two additional crewmembers, who also wore whites stolen from the grocer, were Beatriu and Guifré. Guifré was a vicious fighter with a knife and had a reputation for cheating at dice, but he was fearless and, in approximate size, shape, and coloring, he could pass for Josep. Beatriu was not a consistent member of *La Verge*'s crew, but served as a guide and pilot when the ship sailed along the Igbo coast that she knew so well, or needed to contact a fence in Jackson or Montgomery. She was part Igbo herself, and her rich complexion was darker than Montse's, her hair more brown than red. Would the chevalier's man at the gate notice that Beatriu and Guifré had replaced Josep and Montse?

Anyone else might realize they were different, and simply assume there were six workers unloading groceries. The man at the gate had counted four entering, and must also count four leaving.

Beatriu and Guifré had arrived at the Palais hiding underneath piles of food. Now they walked right under the nose of the chevalier's man, and he didn't bat an eye.

"The chevalier spends too much money on his house," Josep muttered. "He should spend more on his servants, and employ people who can actually see."

"Better for us that he doesn't. But now we need a guide."

"The chevalier will know what he has done with the girl." Josep smiled and rested his hand on the dagger at his belt. "Let's ask *him*."

"But the chevalier won't be taking her food or emptying her chamber pots," Montse said. "What I really want is a maid."

"You're very saucy, do you know that? Talking about how much you want maids, right here in front of me."

"Josep, I can hit you with a throwing knife from here."

"Very well. You want a serving girl, I'll get one. Wait here."

Montse leaned against the window to watch. With the last of the cabbages and collard greens unloaded, Miquel stubbed out his cigarillo with his heel on the ground and tried to shake the hand of the chevalier's man. The chevalier's servant looked perplexed or perhaps offended, but bowed slightly, hands behind his back.

Miqui climbed into the wagon with Beatriu, Guifré, and the driver, and the four of them turned back toward the Vieux Carré from whence they'd come.

A truly ruthless pirate—like Anne Bonny, or Grace O'Malley before her—would have ordered Miquel to slit the grocer's throat. In more desperate straits, Montse liked to imagine she'd do the same. Instead, she'd instructed the boy to take him to a cheap hostel in the Vieux Carré and hold him there until Montse rejoined them.

The chevalier's man waved to another wagon rolling up to the gate, this one loaded with bloody paper parcels and a stack of hams.

"The maid you wanted." Josep reentered the reading room. With one arm casually around her throat and the other hand holding a knife pressed to her side, he held a young woman in a dress of white and the chevalier's blue, with just a hint of gold in a small bit of embroidery on her breast. "You see how I'm your slave."

"Easy, child," Montse said in French, smiling her most gentle smile. "Josep won't hurt you. Unless I tell him to, of course, in which case he'll kill you in a single painless instant."

"I don't have any gold," the young woman said. "My family has no money."

"We don't want your master's gold," Montse said. "We're looking for a friend of ours." *Une amie*, a friend who is a woman.

Ah, Hannah. You were ma grande amie. I miss you.

"Who is your friend?" The young woman's eyes were opened wide, and leaped back and forth between Josep and Montse.

"Young," Montse said. "And not a willing guest of the chevalier. Something closer to a prisoner."

"The witch," the serving girl said.

The chevalier had discovered something. How much did he know? What had Margaret done? Montse nodded. "Where is the witch now?"

"She rarely leaves her room," the girl said. "Other than in the company of those foreigners."

Montse's eyes narrowed. "What kind of foreigners? Pennslanders?"

The girl shook her head. "From France. The Old World. I think...the men are mussulman warriors. Assassins."

Montse frowned, weighing this information. "Where is her room?"

"I haven't been to it. It's down the west hallway. Only the senior maid knows the incantation that will let you pass. Otherwise, the Polite said, you die."

"The hall is ensorcelled?"

The girl answered with a nod.

"The senior maid." Josep sighed. "How many maids does she want from me, this buccaneer princess?"

"No," Montse told him. "You stay here, and hidden. You, child—tell me where this west hallway is."

"One floor up." The girl trembled. "Down the long hallway, and it is the final turn on the left."

Montse met Josep's gaze. "I can make myself vomit," her lieutenant said in Catalan. "You wouldn't want to swallow that silver again, but you could hold it in your hand."

Montse shook her head. "If I'm not back in half an hour, run."

Josep snorted. "If you're not back in half an hour, I'll kill the chevalier in revenge and then die tragically, cut down by his countless soldiers. This is what you do when a man kills the love of your life."

"I may yet be alive."

"Then you'd best return within the half hour, to avoid unfortunate misunderstandings."

Montse laughed out loud. The girl shrank from the laughter, terrified. "Give me an hour before you shed any blood."

Josep nodded and Montse left.

She moved quickly, averting her gaze from everyone she saw and taking measured, purposeful steps. In a household this large, who could be certain that a person moving alone through the building wasn't simply a guest who had lost her way, or a new servant?

She climbed to the floor above, nodding to a burly man in blue who passed her in descent, carrying a tray of fine china dishes. Having stripped off the stolen grocer's clothing, she wore a clean silk blouse and cort-du-roi trousers tucked into the tops of knee-high boots made of supple soft leather. The blouse was scarlet and the trousers were a pale brown; her only weapon was the knife at her belt.

Halfway down the long hallway on the floor above, a plump footman with a sallow complexion bowed to get her attention. "Et qui êtes-vous?"

"L'amie particuliére du chevalier!" she snapped, not slowing down. Let the man fret. Likely, he'd run to ask a more senior footman, or the butler, who the chevalier's special friend wandering the Palais unaccompanied was. That gave her time.

She found the left-hand turn the maid had described. The hallway looked utterly plain, its walls panels of dark wood, and had only a single door at the end. Montse stepped into the hall.

An invisible force punched her in the belly.

The silver! Sweet Virgin, if the lump of metal in her gut had felt like an unborn child, then this was a searing miscarriage, an abortion gone wrong, the stillbirth of a shaky grenado that was in the process of exploding in slow motion as it emerged.

She hit the wall with one shoulder and fell to her knees.

Pain shot across her body like a thousand needles simultaneously pushed into her skin from all directions. Her vision swam and her muscles trembled; sweat beaded suddenly under her arms and around her neck, staining her silk instantly.

The fist in her gut twisted. Montse ground her teeth, refusing to let out the scream boiling up within her.

The needles sank in deeper.

The fist opened. The knot in Montse's belly pushed out, and it felt as though all her innards were torn from their proper place, but then suddenly the knot of pain from the silver struck the penetrating needles—

and the needles disappeared.

"Mon dieu!" she heard behind her.

Montse rose deliberately, placing one hand against the wall but trying desperately to look strong. She turned, knowing that sweat poured down her skin, and stared at the plump footman, whose mouth hung open and whose eyes bugged wide.

"That's right," she said in French. "I'm *that* kind of friend."

He staggered back. She turned and opened the door.

Behind the small door she found the room she'd expected, with a cot and no windows. But instead of Margaret her ward, she found a dark-skinned girl in a white shift, kneeling at a colorfully cluttered Vodun altar and chanting.

"You're not Margarida," Montse said in French.

The sorceress stopped chanting. "I'm Marie. Margarida is the Penn girl? The Eldritch?"

"Where is she?" Montse snarled, whipping her dagger from its sheath and pointing it at the mambo.

"Ayizan told me you were coming." The girl's eyes were utterly calm.

"Margarida!" Montse demanded.

"I advised the Chevalier to send her away. I told him not to tell anyone where she was going, not even me."

"Why?" Montse stepped closer and pointed the dagger at the mambo's eye.

"Because otherwise, Ayizan told me, you would take her back."

Montse spat on the floor. "Did Ayizan tell you whether I would cut out your eyeball right now?"

Marie laughed softly. "She offered no guarantees, but she said most likely not."

"Fotuda!" The girl was telling the truth. Montse slammed the door behind her and headed back along the west hallway. She feared the defensive spell would assail her again, but it didn't; perhaps it was spent from its first attempt.

The footman stood at the end of the hall. Now he was the one sweating. "Madame, je vous prie..."

Montse swiped the blade of her dagger past her own throat, making the most terrifying face she could at the chubby servant. At the same time, she spread her index and pinky finger apart like a bull's horns and waved them in his direction in a wide circle. It was her best theatrical impression of a sorceress.

The footman shrieked and fell to the ground.

Into the larger hallway, Montse sheathed her knife. She turned and picked up her pace, heading to rejoin Josep. Margaret was gone, and she had no idea where she'd disappeared to. Short of interrogating the chevalier himself, she had no way to find out, either.

She had failed.

All she could do now was obey the chevalier and take his embassy north, to Hannah's other child.

Hannah, forgive me.

Montse broke into a run.

"The day's runners have returned. We near a quorum."

The Clerks of the Rolls stood in Thomas's office. His shoulders sagged permanently to one side, apparently from a Haudenosaunee arrow he'd taken as a young man at the Ohio Forks. The long tufts of completely white hair sprouting from his crown, his eyebrows, the back of his neck, and even the backs of his hands, along with stray threads rising from the loosening seams of his old black coat, made him look like a dandelion heavy with spores, bobbing in a breeze and about to throw its hopes of future progeny to the wind.

"Have you word from other Electors?" Thomas set down the letter he'd been reading, an encrypted account from Director Schmidt of her compromising of the Hansa towns, ordering of affairs at Company trading posts, and raiding of Ophidian stores across the Ohio.

"Two weeks, Mr. Emperor." The Clerk of the Rolls bowed.

Thomas gritted his teeth at the offensive title, but the Clerks—like the Electors—had the right to use it. He smiled and inclined his head, slightly. The Clerk was a small man, whose sole but essential task was to certify that enough Electors were present to constitute a valid Assembly, and in the event of a motion requiring any sort of supermajority, to again certify sufficient electoral presence. Under the Compact, no Assembly action was valid without his seal, so Thomas would put up with his scrupulous correctness, even when the scrupulosity offended.

"And will the quorum consist of Electors *in viva persona*?" He directed this question at both of the men standing before him in his study.

The second man was the Clerk of Proxies. His task, also

stipulated under the Compact, was to certify the validity of the proxy sent by any Elector. The Clerk of Proxies and the Clerk of the Rolls worked hand in hand at all times, and while the Assembly was not actually in session, they engaged in continual correspondence with the powers of the Empire so as to stay current as to who the Electors actually were at any given moment as well as to be informed as to the appropriate local judicial authorities who might notarize each proxy. Collectively called the Clerks of the Assembly (or sometime the *Electoral Clerks*, though that title didn't actually exist in the Compact), both men lived on pensions secured by a fund of bonds originally purchased by the combined powers. It was supposed to make them independent, as was the fact that the offices were hereditary.

The sheer number of Electors, along with the hodgepodge of local rules that determined who held any electoral seat, rendered the Electoral Clerks necessary. The result was always chaos, but chaos that gave Thomas some comfort—there were so many Electors, and from such different lands and peoples, that they had difficulty organizing to act against Thomas.

The Clerk of Proxies was young. His father, also a veteran of the Ohio Forks War, had passed away two years earlier. The new Clerk was tall and broad-shouldered, with a long, square beard that would have looked patriarchal on an older man but on him looked like an affectation or a mask. His bottle-green coat was new, and the coat and his breeches both seemed one size too small for him. His height was all in his torso and his legs were thin, so all in all he looked vaguely wrong-way-up and ill-balanced, like an upside-down wine bottle about to topple over.

"Approximately two-thirds of the currently present group consists of the actual Electors themselves," the Clerk of Proxies said. "Our correspondence suggests that those to arrive in the next two weeks will shift the balance further in favor of Electors *in viva persona* and away from Electors *per procurationem*."

Did the big-bearded dandy know any Latin other than those two professional phrases? Unlikely, but it didn't matter.

"Good." Thomas smiled to show his pleasure. "If they're coming in person, that suggests they're at least considering voting *yes*."

"There is grave concern about the Ohio." The Clerk of Proxies clasped his hands behind his back and thrust his chest forward. Trying to appear knowledgeable? Trying to drop some hint? He had no obligation under the Compact to share any intelligence with Thomas.

"You mean . . . some of them may wish to challenge me?" Thomas's smile dropped into a frown.

"Perhaps." The clerk nodded. "Or perhaps they're willing seriously to consider the possibility of voting additional funds to the Imperial Crown, in order to deal with the situation."

"In any case," the Clerk of the Rolls said, in a voice dry as dust and creaking like a rusted weathervane, "they wish to discuss."

Temple Franklin, reclining wholeheartedly in a soft chair across the office with his face hidden behind an upraised news-paper, snorted out loud. "Great god of heaven! It's almost as if this were a democracy!"

"Surely not," Thomas said drily. He dismissed the two clerks with a wave of his hand, then sagged back into his own slat-backed wooden chair as they trooped out. "Do you think they *want* democracy?"

"The Electors are wiser than that." Temple dropped the news-paper into his lap and gazed at the Emperor over the top of his lunette eye-glasses. "They know that a small democracy may burn brightly—as in Switzerland or Athens—and even for a long time—as in Venice—but that a large democracy must soon collapse under the weight of the rabble."

"*Do* they know that?" Thomas murmured, gazing at the door and reflecting.

"If they don't, then they know at least this: their positions as Elector, their ability to negotiate trade agreements and tariffs with the Imperial state, their common defense against the Free Horse Peoples, the Wild Algonks, pirates, bandits, beastkind, New Spanish lancers, and whatever other threats may arise—all depend on the Compact. They'll support the Compact that empowers you, because it also empowers them."

"Your grandfather didn't want me empowered very much."

"Nor did yours. John Penn signed the Compact, and sat through every discussion of its terms."

"I'd say *damn him*, but it wouldn't seem very gracious on my part." Thomas sighed. "Well, one step at a time."

"Or one death," Temple said, "a propos of your next appointment."

Two sharp knocks on the door only barely preceded its

swinging open. Gottlieb's powdered wig poked through first, followed by Gottlieb, followed closely by an unexpected visitor.

"Damn me," Temple said, giving voice to Thomas's thoughts. "The actor."

The visitor accompanying Gottlieb was indeed the actor from *The Walking Purchase*, the man who had saved Thomas's life at the Walnut Street Theater. He wore a kilt in some highland plaid Thomas didn't know, and slung over one shoulder he carried a long-necked instrument that was a member of the lute family. A cittern, maybe? His long, black locks were tied at his neck with a gray ribbon.

Gottlieb bowed low. "He was insistent, Your Majesty. He said you would admit him."

"He's right." Thomas waved Gottlieb back out the door again.

"Thank you." The actor bowed with one knee locked and one bent, a movement that looked almost like a curtsey.

"You've come in costume, this time." Thomas tried to look amused. "You were writing an opera about the Battle of Prestonpans, as I recall. From the point of view of a-not-entirely-willing recruit of the House of Spencer. Will you now perform the part of Cromwell's highlanders?"

"The opera is about the entire Forty-Five Resurgence, in fact."

"And you've come to sing me a song. How charming. I have come to move in rather artistic circles recently." Thomas liked thinking of himself as a patron and friend of performers. That, and the fact that he owed this man his life, made him willing to talk to the actor.

The Franklin's Player raised his fingers to the strings and began to play. The chords were slow and simple.

> I was born a free man
> And I thank the heavens still
> For giving me the bubbling brook
> And the heather-covered hill
> I had a wife and two braw boys
> What man could ask for more?
> I left them all for endless life
> Upon Culloden Moor
>
> Stinkin' Georgie Spencer
> Pursued us o'er the fen

With his filthy lies and his basket hilts
He slew three thousand men
Bonny Charlie Stewart, boys
To the Isle of Skye's bright shore
As Betty Burke, the spinning maid
Fled Culloden Moor

The King Across the Water
The king will ever be
The man who frees my soul from death
Is king enough for me
I lie here a free man
And I'll walk forever more
Head held high, and heart in hand
Across Culloden Moor

"The haunting of Culloden Moor," Thomas said as the last chord died away. "The naming of the Sweet George."

"Or the Stinking Georgie." A faint smile played about the actor's lips.

"You write with sympathy for the partisans of the Necromancer." Thomas pursed his lips.

"Don't you feel any sympathy for them, Brother Onas?"

He couldn't have said why, but the question made Thomas want to punch the actor in the face. He refrained. "That's the second time you've called me that name. What do you intend by it?"

The actor's eyes narrowed, in an expression that seemed sad. "Don't you know?"

Thomas sighed. "I'm not in the habit of asking things I *already know*. That's a lawyer's trick."

"Your grandfather knew the name. He bore it."

"You mean my ancestor, speaking poetically, I presume. William Penn was called Brother Onas by some."

"So were his descendants after him, including John."

Thomas was keenly aware of the fact that Temple Franklin was listening. "Well, I bear the name *Thomas*. Indeed, if you consult the birth registry in the flyleaf of the Slate Roof House Bible, I think you'll find that *Onas* made no part of my grandfather's name, either."

The actor studied Thomas with his gray eyes. "Your grandfather never told you."

"He never told me he was secretly called *Onas*, no. But in fact, this is the third time we've met, and you've never told me your name."

The actor's smile was faint. "Say rather that this is the third time we've met, and you've still never asked me my name."

Thomas nearly stood in indignation. "I'm your emperor, man. Tell me your name."

"I was baptized Isaiah."

"But you are called *Wobomagonda*, no doubt."

"In the right times and places, I am called *the Franklin*."

Temple harrumphed. The actor Isaiah took no notice.

"Head of Franklin's Players," Thomas said. "Clever."

Isaiah shrugged. "Your grandfather must have told Hannah."

"Told her what?" Now Thomas *did* stand, conscious of the fact that responding to provocation robbed him of a small margin of his dignity.

"Your grandfather bore the name *Onas*. With that name, he was in an alliance that he knew must stand, from time to time, against the rising tide of the Mississippi and Ohio. He gave that name to Hannah, perhaps, but he didn't give it to you."

"My patience is very close to gone," Thomas warned. "What do you want?"

"That isn't the question," the Franklin said. "The question is: what do you know? And another: given what you know, what are you willing to do?"

"Enough. Temple—ask Gottlieb to call the guard, if you will."

"You *could* simply impale him," Temple suggested, but he went to the door and poked his head out to talk to Gottlieb.

"Peter Plowshare is dead," Isaiah said. "Simon Sword is not *coming*, but is *already come*. You are Brother Onas, whether you know it or not. Where do you stand?"

"I stand with Pennsland!" Thomas thumped his fist on the desk, knocking a bottle of ink over onto the floor. "I stand with my family! With my office! With St. Martin, and against the blasphemers of the Ohio! With the Electors! I stand with the Empire and its peoples! I stand alone if I must, but by the bones of William Penn himself, *I will stand!*"

The Franklin shook his head sadly. "It is not enough."

"Go to hell!" Thomas bellowed. "Guards!"

"One more time, I will come," Isaiah said softly. And then

he slipped through the door, easily ducking Gottlieb's awkward attempt to grab him, and was gone.

Thomas yanked his sword from its scabbard, raised it over his head, and swung it down, biting into the wood of his desk.

"You'll harm the blade," Temple murmured. The spymaster set aside the news-paper, stood, and approached Thomas with his hands forward, palms up. It was a placatory stance, and it annoyed Thomas more.

"You'd rather I cut *you* with it?"

"I'd rather you took a deep breath and put the sword back." Temple smiled. "My grandfather was surrounded with this palatine nonsense his entire life. He swam in it, loved it, encouraged it... maybe even created some of it. It means nothing."

"You can't be sure."

"No one can ever be sure there aren't conspiracies. That's what makes imagining them so attractive. But I can tell you that I'm a brother of the ancient free and accepted order—"

"As am I." Thomas growled, but he lowered his sword.

"—and neither of us knows anything about this Brother Onas nonsense. It's invented, by a man who by his own account is a writer of operas."

Thomas growled.

"Really, the only less trustworthy voice you could choose to listen to would be a novelist."

Thomas slammed his sword back into its sheath. "Thank God I was raised without *that* particular vice."

Temple nodded soothingly. "Your next visitors are two junior faculty members from the Imperial College of Magic. They've done you a signal service, and they're here to collect their reward."

"Professors!" Thomas snorted. "And what signal service was that, then? Did they expound an exciting new theory of Pneumatology? Defend the Imperial honor in some Theurgistic debate? Raise graduation rates, for God's sake?"

Temple's face was grave. "They faked the assassination attempt at the Walnut Street Theater."

"What?"

"At my bidding. Their illusions convinced the crowd that an embittered Firstborn nobleman took a shot at you. The shot was also theirs, and you were never in any danger from the attack."

"There was the fire, though."

"Unrelated accident."

Thomas rubbed his eyes with the meaty parts of his palms. "Very well, then. What did you promise them from me?"

"Promotion. Tenure. Endowed chairs. Inclusion on the Imperial Honors List. Don't worry about the details. Only congratulate and thank them, and they will fall over themselves with gestures of gratitude and appreciation."

Thomas inhaled deeply, exhaled, then sat. Temple retreated to the corner of the room, where he busied himself at Thomas's liquor cabinet. The faint sound of clinking glass was vaguely soothing to the raging headache Thomas suddenly noticed he had.

The door opened, and Gottlieb ushered in two people. They wore matched orange frock coats, but there the resemblance ended: one was a square man with an elongated face and tiny nose who must have been sixty years old if he was a day, and the other was an attractive woman several decades younger, with bright red hair. On the breasts of their coats they wore the Imperial seal—it was the uniform for formal occasions of the faculty of the Imperial College.

"Welcome." Thomas smiled broadly, stood, and extended a hand. "And thank you."

"Your Imperial Majesty," they said with one voice. After a short bow, they shook Thomas's hand.

"Please, sit," he said, gesturing at the two chairs in front of his desk. Conscious of the fact that he'd met the actor Isaiah three times before learned the man's name, he added, "tell me your names."

Come to think of it, he still didn't know the actor's family name. Unless it was *Franklin*, but that didn't seem right.

The professors of magic sat.

"Magister-subordinate Lancaster," the woman said.

"Magister-ordinary Hurlbut," the man said.

Temple Franklin shuffled slowly to the space behind and between the two magicians and handed each of them a large glass tumbler. Thomas smelled the warm fruity aroma of a fine peach brandy, with maybe a hint of almond. The wizards scarcely noticed Temple at all, they were so fixated on Thomas; you'd have thought the glasses of alcohol had simply materialized, unaided.

Perhaps that was how they did it at the Imperial College.

Magister-subordinate Lancaster sipped her drink and smiled; Magister-ordinary Hurlbut swallowed two-thirds of his and gasped.

"Thank you so much for your service." Thomas also sat, and now Temple handed him a tumbler, too. "I appreciate that your actions must seem...extraordinary, but given the circumstances—"

"We understand completely!" Magister-subordinate Lancaster gulped the rest of her drink, eyes wide. "My own family, you may know, has long been aligned with Martinite doctrines and practices. You don't need to tell me about the threat the Firstborn pose to the Empire! Corrupting law and custom, and directly violating God's command that the children of Eve should have all dominion!"

"Nor me." Hurlbut grinned, a greasy smile that lacked two prominent teeth and made Thomas sick to his stomach. "Though mostly, I'm happy to serve Your Imperial Majesty against any foes, foreign or domestic, child of Eve or otherwise. Only I'd like a small share of that dominion, myself."

A fanatic and a climber. These were the wizards Temple had found to help him.

"If that particular Firstborn hadn't attacked you," Lancaster said, "and we have no way of knowing but that maybe he intended that very thing and indeed on that very evening, then some other Ophidian would have."

Hurlbut chuckled. "As when the preacher leavens a sermon with a story that isn't factually accurate, but tells an important spiritual truth. We've simply told a beautiful political truth... by means of fiction. An illusion that will point everyone in the right direction."

Thomas emptied the last of his tumbler for strength.

Hurlbut drained his.

Lancaster raised hers to her lips, found it empty, lowered it again to her lap, and smiled.

"I am thrilled to see loyal believers advance within the ranks of the Imperial College," Thomas said. "Forgive me, but never having attended myself, I forget some of the details. To what titles are we advancing you?"

"Magister-superior." Lancaster rubbed her temples.

"With tenure and a pension to continue to the end of one life within a life in being," Hurlbut added. "Meaning a child can inherit."

"I see the lawyers have got at the Imperial College as well."
Thomas laughed. "Theirs is the strongest magic."

"No!" Magister-superior-to-be Lancaster objected. "Your Imperial Majesty—" She stopped and pounded a fist against her own
sternum. "Your Imperial Majesty..." She coughed.

Hurlbut turned and stared at his colleague. "What is it, girl?"
Without warning, foam bubbled from his lips. Still staring at the
other wizard, he fell over sideways to the floor.

"Your Imperial Majesty!" Lancaster stood, alarm on her face.
"Poison!"

Thomas stared in surprise at his own glass. Poison? But that
would mean...

Lancaster raised her arms, fingers twisted into some arcane
gesture. "*Contra—*"

Temple Franklin slapped a hand to her shoulder and stabbed
her in the back of the neck. The knife was long and gleamed like
silver, and he pushed it in so deep it cut off her speech entirely
and the tip burst out the front of her throat in a shower of blood,
just above her Adam's apple.

She sank forward, her weight pulling her off the blade.

Thomas leaped to his feet. "Temple!"

Temple Franklin turned his left hand to reveal a silver medallion marked with the Franklin Seal. "From my grandfather. To
stop whatever spell she had been about to cast, and to force
down her defenses." He wiped off his blade with a white napkin
from the drinks cabinet. "Explain myself, you'll say. But you met
them, Lord Thomas. They would have talked. They would have
demanded more. Now they can't, and their illusion is complete."

Thomas found to his surprise that he had no more objections.
"I'll need another drink."

"The children of Adam are so fragile."

———◦———

CHAPTER TWENTY

The ground beneath Nathaniel shifted, and he opened his eyes.

Above him he saw the starry sky. He recognized the stars, though he was no sailor. But somehow, the stars of the ordinary night sky lay tangled and stretched into patterns he had never seen before.

A moose strode along in the path of the sun and moon. A loon drifted in the far north. A bather climbed into a sweat lodge. A crane soared, and a crouching hunter stalked a mountain lion.

Clouds obscured his vision.

"Rise, God-Has-Given. Time is short."

Nathaniel blinked. The clouds weren't rainclouds, but billows of sweet tobacco-smoke. He lay on the flat floor of a barn, beside a central pillar. Pine boughs were woven together to form an evergreen booth around the base of the pillar, and within the booth smoldered a small fire—the tobacco burned on that fire. Overhead were no shining stars, but the rafters of the barn and drying lofts that two months earlier would have been laden with dried leaf.

Ma'iingan knelt over Nathaniel and looked down into his face. The light of the small fire left the Indian's eyes dark pits, but the lines of his face were drawn into a tight mask of concern.

But the voice wasn't his.

Nathaniel blinked, and the floor beneath him shifted.

The strangely drawn stars reappeared. The path of the sun and moon circled around him like a level belt, and the ground he lay on, flat as a sheet of glass, lay at an angle to it.

Ma'iingan was gone. In his place crouched a wolf. The beast had long ears, a wide face, and an expression on its muzzle that on a man would have been a sly grin. It rested, watching Nathaniel with its tongue hanging out of its mouth.

"Rise, God-Has-Given. Your enemy is at the door."

The voice came from a personage standing behind the wolf. Nathaniel levered himself onto his elbows to see better. The personage shone and it stood several feet off the ground. The light coming from its body sounded the same as the light coming from the stars.

No, that wasn't right. The two light sources shone with the same *color*.

The personage wore only a breechclout. He had a wolf's paws, for hands and feet both, and a wolf's ears—long ears, like the ears of the wolf hunched over Nathaniel. And he had wings; the wings were in motion, and they seemed to Nathaniel to number more than two. Six wings, perhaps? So many?

A beastkind angel?

A devil?

"Help him, Waawoono," the personage said.

The wolf howled, and somehow the howl sounded supportive to Nathaniel, and maybe even nurturing. "Ma'iingan?"

Hadn't the Anishinaabe said his name meant *wolf*?

The wolf Waawoono howled again and pressed its muzzle against Nathaniel's side, wedging itself underneath his shoulder. The animal's nose was cold and wet, and tickled.

Nathaniel was naked. When had that happened? And where were Landon and George and the earl?

Someone had struck him, he remembered.

He climbed to his feet, leaning on the wolf. "Thank you."

The wolf pushed at the back of Nathaniel's bare calves with its forehead and nipped them gently with its teeth, pushing him toward a blazing fire a few yards away. Smoke rose from the fire in solid steps.

"What's that?" he asked the personage, who hovered beside the stairs.

"Asemaa is a sacred plant," the personage said. "It's the gift you children of earth make to the earth and to other powers. Today it builds the road you will climb into the sky."

Nathaniel took a deep breath and looked up again into the familiar-unfamiliar sky. "Yes."

"Waawoono," the personage said. "The healer needs horses to take him where he must go."

Nathaniel looked around and saw four horses. They stood as if at cardinal points around him, neighing softly with anticipation.

Waawoono the wolf leaped at the horse that stood beneath the moose. Was that east? The wolf tore out the horse's throat in a single motion, and the horse sank to the ground, emitting a single nicker that sounded joyous.

Nathaniel heard the sudden rush of blood and blinked.

He smelled blood, rich and sweet. The personage and the stars were gone and the barn was back; Ma'iingan eased a dying horse to the floor, whispering softly to it as it sank into a puddle of its own gore.

Landon stood against the wall, his arms crossed over his chest. George lay trussed beside him. Both stared, mouths open.

Ma'iingan crossed the barn toward where a second horse stood, whimpering nervously. In his hand, he held his stone knife, dripping blood onto the planks of the floor.

Nathaniel blinked, and watched as the wolf dispatched the second horse, in the west.

Then the horse of the south.

Then finally the horse of the north, beneath the hovering loon. The loon who, it seemed to Nathaniel, smiled down in approval.

But as each horse sank to the ground, each horse also stepped forward, moving to canter in a slow circle around the asemaa-fire and the heavenly stairs. As the horse of the east began its rotation, Nathaniel felt an inflow of strength. He straightened his back and brushed hair and blood from his face. The horse of the west brought more strength, and by the time the horse of the north joined them, Nathaniel had gone beyond vigorous and felt *mighty*, breath rushing in and out of his lungs like wind, blood coursing through his veins like a river, thoughts racing from his fingertips to the top of his head and back down to the ends of his toes like bolts of lightning.

"Come." The personage held out a hand of invitation.

Nathaniel stepped as close to the bonfire as he could bear. It smelled of incense, antiquity, other worlds, the soul.

He blinked, and found himself slumped over, balanced precariously on his own knees. His face dripped sweat downward into a tiny pile of burning tobacco leaves, and the sweet smells of tobacco and pine sap strove for attention.

He blinked, and saw the personage again.

"Who are you?" Nathaniel asked.

"I am Waawoono's manidoo," the personage said. "The great god of the sky has sent him and me to help you."

"Why?"

"Before you can heal anyone else, God-Has-Given, you must first be healed yourself."

Nathaniel had been struck on the head, been cut, and had broken ribs, but at the manidoo's words he touched none of those injuries. Instead, he put his hand on the one ear that protruded more than the other, on the ear through which he constantly heard voices, some of which were in so much distress that it reduced him to seizures.

He found there something small and hard. Plucking it from the side of his head, he looked at the object, and saw it was a glittering, star-blue acorn.

"An acorn!"

"Yes," the manidoo agreed.

"How can I be healed?" Nathaniel asked.

For answer, the manidoo looked up the stairs at the glittering sky.

"I'm ready," Nathaniel said.

"Bebezhigooganzhii of the rising sun, carry this man!" the manidoo cried.

One of the circling horses swerved without warning, and leaped into Nathaniel's arms—

where it became a drum.

The drum was a simple instrument, hide stretched over a wooden cylinder that bowed out in the center. Nathaniel turned it in his hands and saw that the drum was incomplete, consisting only of the wood and a single piece of hide covering one end.

"You must also ask the horse," the manidoo said softly.

Nathaniel raised the drum over its head and spoke to it. "Bebezhigooganzhii, I ask you to carry me!"

"I will carry you," said the drum.

"Bebezhigooganzhii of the setting sun, carry this man!"

A second horse leaped into Nathaniel's arms and became a hide that covered the other end of the drum.

Nathaniel turned the drum in his hands; at just the right angle, he saw a horse's head made of starlight reflected in each of the skins. "Bebezhigooganzhii, I ask you to carry me!"

"We will carry you."

"Bebezhigooganzhii of the underworld, carry this man!"

The third horse entered the drum, becoming hide lacing that connected the two skins and bound the entire drum together. Nathaniel plucked at one of the laces and heard the thunder of running hooves.

"Bebezhigooganzhii, I ask you to carry me!"

"We will carry you to the four corners of the world on which you stand."

"Bebezhigooganzhii of the loon in the north, ever watching, carry this man!" At this last invocation, the manidoo stepped aside.

The final horse hurled itself into Nathaniel's arms, nearly knocking him down with the force of its arrival. When he looked at the drum again, Nathaniel saw a leather shoulder strap that had been the fourth horse.

"Bebezhigooganzhii, I ask you to carry me!"

For a moment, the four horses raced in a circle around Nathaniel again. "We will carry you to worlds below, to worlds above, and to all the worlds that are." Then they sank again into the wood and skin of the drum.

"Come," Waawoono's manidoo said. "It is time."

Nathaniel slung the drum's strap over one shoulder. He placed his left hand on the top side and his right on the underside and began a slow rhythm. The rhythm was aimless at first, but then in the thicket of bass and baritone notes and tenor clicks Nathaniel found he could make with the instrument, he began to see the path of a song. He opened his mouth.

> *I ride upon four horses, to heaven I ride*
> *I ride the sacred smoke-path, horses by my side*
> *I walk the endless star-fields, my vision is wide*
> *I seek the land of spirits, to heaven I ride*

He knew not whence the words came; he opened his mouth, and they filled it. The melody was old and simple, scarcely more than a drone, and he thought he could hear a second voice harmonizing with him. The manidoo? Waawoono?

As he sang, Nathaniel raised his foot, found the lowest step nearly hidden in the brightness of the fire, placed his weight upon it, and climbed up.

The step held.

It was pure smoke, nothing but scented air and light, but beneath his bare foot it was unyielding. Nathaniel took a second step, and then a third.

> I call the stars to witness, I will not hide
> I call the winds to see me, as up I glide
> I call the sky to answer, and the gods beside
> I call the night to open, to heaven I ride

On the fourth step, Nathaniel hesitated. Looking up, he saw Waawoono's manidoo. The angelic being seemed now to stand among the stars, at the top of seven steps, and again held out a beckoning hand toward Nathaniel.

"Come," the manidoo said.

Nathaniel looked down.

Through a haze of smoke, he saw the lean-to of pine boughs, and the tiny fire within. He saw Ma'iingan at the edge of the circle of small light, stone knife in his hand, looking upward; Nathaniel couldn't see the Indian's face. He saw Landon and George, staring at him.

Nathaniel blinked.

Smoke filled his nostrils. He clung to the wooden column that held up the tobacco-curing barn. Wedges had been hacked from that column by an ax, as if in multiple spots someone had begun to fell the column, and each time decided not to; Nathaniel had the toes of each foot curled into one such divot, and the fingers of his left hand in a third.

Pain lanced through his side from his broken rib.

With his right hand he reached up, toward another carved wedge and, just beyond that, a crossbeam.

Nathaniel's hand slipped. He fell—

and blinked.

"Come," the manidoo said. "This is only the beginning of the road, and we must ride faster."

My drum is made of horses that never died
My bones I leave behind me, I'm iron inside
Spirits my father and mother, spirits my bride
I am a man of spirits, to heaven I ride

His own words meant nothing to him, but the words and the monotonous melody filled Nathaniel's breast with courage, and he took the remaining steps at a run, pounding louder and louder on his horse-drum as he did so.

At the height of the seven steps, Nathaniel sprang onto a shimmering path—

which suddenly vanished.

Nathaniel found himself standing in a space that was circular, and the confines of which were hard to see. Were those standing stones, irregularly spaced like the teeth in a dotard's mouth? Were they moss-covered trees? Beyond some sort of pierced and crumbling boundary, and high above him, lay the stars. He still saw the silver-golden path of the sun and moon, and on it the constellations—there was the Bather. The Sweat Lodge. But he glimpsed them as if through gaps now, as if he were watching a familiar scene, but through a keyhole.

The Loon was gone. The other constellations moved backward through the sky.

"Where am I?" he cried.

"You are in the place where all healing begins." The voice belonged to the manidoo, though Nathaniel couldn't see the spirit he thought was to be his guide. "The Pit of Heaven."

"What, a hole?" Nathaniel gripped his drum tighter. The trembling within it, and the faint distant echo of horses' hooves, comforted him a little.

No answer.

"Waawoono?" he cried. "Ma'iingan?"

No answer.

"Landon? George?"

He was abandoned.

But he wasn't alone. As he called George, he saw a shadow emerge from the serrated shadow wall encircling him and lurch forward.

"Bebezhigooganzhii, help me!" he called.

His drum shook as if something inside were trying to escape, but then fell still.

A second shadow detached itself from the circle. Then another, and another. He saw them mostly by the remote stars they blocked out. As they drew nearer, he grabbed for the knife he usually carried in his pocket, and remembered he was naked. He held his drum in both hands before him, as if it were a shield.

The drum trembled. From fear?

Scritch.

The rasp of a Lucifer being struck, and then a yellow light burst into being. It was so bright against the darkness, Nathaniel shielded his eyes behind the drum, but not before he noticed that the match appeared to be a long, thin bone, with burning ooze at one end.

A finger bone? But longer than the finger bone of any child of Adam.

"Well," a deep voice rumbled. "What have we here?"

The light grew brighter. Reluctantly, Nathaniel lowered the drum to see. The holder of the Lucifer match shook it to extinguish its flame, and then dropped it to the ground.

The earth was littered with bones. The bones of men, though many of them seemed far too large, and there were animal skulls and hooves lying among the tibias and femurs.

The stronger light came from a torch, in the other hand of the person who had struck the match. The torch—Nathaniel looked at it closely—appeared to be a thigh bone with a skull fixed on the end of it. The skull burned, and through the flame he saw two dark eye sockets, a triangular gap where a nose might once have been, and a grinning jaw that hung at an impossible angle.

The person holding the torch was a giant.

He was maybe half again as tall as Nathaniel, and he had bright orange hair. The giant's face shifted as if Nathaniel were seeing it through running water, but the twisting features seemed familiar.

He turned slowly and found himself surrounded by four of the creatures. Four to match the number of horses in his drum? Four for the four corners of the earth? Four because . . . some other reason?

He thought he knew the second face, similarly flowing. The third was a complete stranger. The fourth was the Earl of Johnsland, though gigantic, red-haired, and swinging fists the size of whole hams.

Nathaniel turned back to the first giant. "What is this place?"

"Ah, the riddle game." The giant grinned, a distorted, sloppy mockery of a smile. "Very well. This is an old place. It was old when the children of Adam found it, and had long been visited by people the children of Adam have now mostly forgotten. It's neither under the hill nor on its slopes, not quite in your heart and not fully in your nightmares. Few come. Fewer leave."

"I know you now." Nathaniel swallowed, his throat dry. "You're the Emperor, Thomas. And you ... I think you're the Necromancer, Oliver Cromwell." Naming the giants didn't give him any better sense of why he would encounter them, these men in particular, in giant form, here. He also left out the fact that one of the four completely baffled him.

"We are," the Giant Emperor agreed, "and also we are not."

"Your cryptic words reveal nothing."

"They reveal everything." The Giant Earl shrugged. "Though we never promised they would."

"Give the lad his third riddle," the Giant Necromancer said. "If nothing else, it will entertain us."

Thomas tried to find the song that had brought him here in his heart, and couldn't. He gripped his horse-drum tightly, but found it vibrating like a piano string.

"Why am I here?" he asked.

"That's an easy one." The Giant Earl grinned. "You're here to die."

Nathaniel took a step back from the Giant Earl—

and the Giant Stranger, the one whose face he didn't know, grabbed him by both arms, pinning him and raising him off the ground.

The Giant Necromancer stepped forward at the same time, batting with a cupped hand and knocking the drum from Nathaniel's grip. The drum fell with a distressed neigh, and rattled among the accumulated drift of bones.

"No!" Nathaniel cried.

The Giant Emperor seized Nathaniel by the throat and pulled. Nathaniel's head, still screaming, pulled away from his body. His spinal column came with it, plucked neatly out of his body as if the giants were deboning a fish.

Nathaniel's screaming stopped and he died.

✧   ✧   ✧

Dead, Nathaniel lay on the floor and watched.

The giants pulled his skull from the skin of his head, dropping brain, tongue, and eyeballs to the ground. Eyes no longer facing the same direction, dead Nathaniel continued to stare—unable now to blink—as the giants dismembered him.

They took surprising care not to damage his flesh and skin much. Having torn off one leg, the Giant Earl then peeled the meat and skin off the bone with great delicacy, as if he were peeling a grape. The Giant Necromancer worked more quickly, yanking the bones from Nathaniel's other leg in a single furious pull.

When they were done, Nathaniel's flesh and organs lay in a pile.

His bones lay intermingled with the bones of all the others who had died in this strange no-place. Nathaniel himself couldn't have picked out which bones were his.

Then the giants left.

He lay a long time, watching the new constellations appear through the windows in the darkness around him.

No sun ever rose.

Nathaniel noticed the passage of time by the movement of the stars through his windows of vision, but he didn't keep track. More than a year had passed, to judge by the movements of the Moose around the sunless and moonless path of the sun and moon. More than a hundred years.

A single giant returned. A giantess, in fact, eight feet tall and with bright orange hair to match her fellows. She wore a short skirt and a purple shawl with golden suns. She moved slowly with her gaze fixed on the floor, kicking aside bones that didn't suit her and stooping to pick up and examine a few. She apparently found these unsatisfactory too, tossing them back to the floor and cursing under her breath.

Nathaniel's eyes, disconnected and pointing separate directions, must be adjusting to the darkness.

When the giantess came to the pile of flesh parings and boneless meat that was Nathaniel, she stopped. Shaking her head, she clicked her tongue with disapproval. "This'll ne'er do." Her voice was the shrill whine of the highland Appalachee, but Nathaniel knew her face. Where had he seen her before? Why did she seem so familiar?

She left, and time passed again.

Vaguely, Nathaniel remembered that somewhere else he was

in a tobacco-drying barn. Had fallen, he thought. Had he died? He had been injured. Perhaps his wounds had taken his life.

The giantess returned, dragging a pot with one hand and clenching tucked under her other arm a sheaf of long, brown, dried leaves. She stuffed the leaves into several skulls, wrapped more leaves are long thigh bones, and carefully stacked the bones in layers of alternating directions, with the skulls in the center.

She struck a Lucifer match—definitely once a finger—and lit the bone fire.

Nathaniel tried to say something, but without bones to hold his flesh together, all he could do was make his lips tremble slightly, and add a thin stream of slobber to the puddle of gore in which he lay.

The giantess raised her cauldron onto a platform of bones and set it over the top of the fire. She dropped the last of her leaves inside the pot. Nathaniel smelled the sweet odor of burning tobacco. She wandered again across the landscape of bones, bending to collect a thigh bone here, a skull there, and bringing them back to drop them into the cauldron.

She approached Nathaniel again and squatted, bring her face down close to his. In the light of the tobacco-leaf fire, he now saw that her eyes were different colors. One of them was ice-white, a shocking color in an iris.

"Don't you worry your pretty little head none," the giantess said. "From here, it gits better."

Nathaniel wanted to thank her.

He also wanted to scream.

He could do neither, so he trembled like an aspic in a tornado.

The giantess left.

Time passed.

The four giants returned, shambling in through the star-windows and sniffing as they approached the fire.

"Fee!" shouted the Giant Earl.

"Fie!" cried the Giant Stranger.

"Foe!" roared the Giant Necromancer.

"Fum!" bellowed the Giant Emperor.

"I smell the blood of an Ophidian!" they howled together.

The Giant Earl reached into the pot, grimacing. He pulled a skull from the cauldron, and hanging below the skull a long, curving spinal column. Liquid smoke wisped from the bones and fell toward the floor like autumn leaves. The giant blew on the skull and spine to clear it of the last of the smoke and then strode toward the pile of Nathaniel.

The bones in his hand gleamed in the firelight, the dull, dark gleam of forged iron.

The Giant Earl scooped up Nathaniel's brain and stuffed it through the eye socket into the iron skull. Then he took Nathaniel's face-meat and the skin of his head, including his hair, and stretched it around the skull. Nathaniel's eyes, still lying on the ground, watched as his lips, once again wrapped around a skull, trembled in fear.

The Giant Earl reattached Nathaniel's tongue in its place and then lifted from the floor a mass of flesh that Nathaniel couldn't identify. The giant stabbed the iron spinal column down into the mass and tweaked the meat, and Nathaniel recognized it as his torso.

The giant left Nathaniel's eyes on the ground.

Also, one of Nathaniel's ears seemed to be missing.

The Giant Earl then held the torso and head like a scarecrow, or an enormous puppet, while the other giants took their turns. The Giant Stranger pulled iron arm bones from the cauldron, attached them to the meat puppet at the shoulders, and then pulled on the flesh of Nathaniel's arms like long gloves. The Giant Emperor similarly attached the legs, and stood working them awhile in delight, pumping Nathaniel's knees as if he were a dancing marionette. The Giant Necromancer attached the finer bones of fingers and toes, and then the Giant Earl held the reboned body draped over his arm as if it were a suit of clothes, and they all inspected their work.

The Giant Necromancer twisted one finger around to get it right, and quickly switched two misplaced toes.

The Giant Stranger disconnected and reconnected the elbow of one arm, so it would bend.

"Still isn't right, is it?" The Giant Earl scratched his chin thoughtfully.

"Eyes," the Giant Emperor muttered. "How do you expect him to go anywhere if he hasn't got eyes?"

"Do we *want* him to go anywhere?" the Giant Stranger asked. "He could stay right here."

The Earl, the Stranger, and the Necromancer nodded as if this were a sage suggestion.

"No," the Giant Emperor said. "This boy has work to do."

"What's his work, then?" the Giant Earl asked.

"He's a healer."

"He'll want his eyes." The Stranger bent and rummaged among the bones on the floor. Nathaniel watched him come closer and closer, until the enormous hands closed, each over one eyeball, blocking out his vision.

Soft, squishing sounds.

Then he could see again, and he was seeing from out of his own skull. He tried to raise a hand, and couldn't. He tried to speak, and couldn't.

"Still something missing," the Giant Earl said.

"The children of Adam have two ears, don't they?" the Giant Stranger asked.

The giants looked at each other.

"It's been such a long time," the Giant Necromancer said.

"I don't remember," the Giant Emperor said.

The Giant Earl shrugged.

"Yes," the Giant Stranger said. "He's missing an ear. Come on, then, let's find it."

Nathaniel found himself flung over the shoulder of the Giant Earl. He watched over the giant's rump as the four of them rummaged among the bones and carnage on the floor.

"Not here," said the Earl.

"Lost," the Emperor echoed.

"Might have eaten it," the Giant Necromancer suggested.

The Earl draped Nathaniel over his arm again and the giants stood looking at him and scratching their heads.

"Well, it just won't do," the Giant Stranger said.

"We could just throw him away," the Giant Emperor said. "I don't see that *we* need him at all."

"We could eat him," the Giant Necromancer added helpfully.

"Wait," the Giant Earl said. "I've got something here."

The giant grubbed about in his pocket and produced a stone. He held it up so they could all see it; in the firelight, the rock glinted white. It was a smooth piece of quartz, and it was in the shape of a perfect acorn.

"Ah, lightning," the Giant Emperor said.

"That'll make a good ear," the Giant Stranger added.

The Giant Necromancer crossed his arms and snorted, but eventually gave a curt nod.

"Right then," the Giant Earl said. "Here we go."

He slammed the stone against the side of Nathaniel's head.

The fist hurt.

The stone, penetrating into Nathaniel's new iron skull, hurt worse. He felt his brain splitting in two.

And suddenly, the bones began to speak.

He tried to turn his head to see the sources of the voices, but he still couldn't move. Still, he saw them with his ear—no, he heard them and knew what they were.

~I have only taken a small misstep off the road. Take me back, O spirit guide!~ This was the refrain of a giant wrapped in furs and wearing a bull's head for a mask. Nathaniel couldn't see the giant, or his bones, but he heard the giant's presence as well as his voice. He heard the lost, ancient sorcerer's mask as well as he heard his terror. ~Take me back!~

~I have devoured my own child.~ A giant sat heavy on a rough-hewn stone chair. He slumped forward, his crown of wildflowers not falling from his head only because the stems were plaited into his long, gray hair. ~I can certainly eat you.~

~We didn't ask to be a sacrifice!~ Two youths, covered in their own blood, holding hands.

Spirits. Spirits of the dead, or of forces perhaps that had never lived. But not voices in Nathaniel's own head.

Never just voices.

He wanted to weep, but couldn't.

"Does he hear?" This came from the Giant Earl, who held Nathaniel up and looked into his eyes. ~I think he hears.~

"Does he move?" the Giant Necromancer asked.

"Shake him," the Giant Stranger suggested.

The Earl shook Nathaniel. His limbs bounced and jiggled, but only as a puppet's would, shaken by its operator. His muscles regained no life.

"Another failure? How sad!" But the Giant Emperor didn't sound sad at all. He sounded gleeful.

"Not a failure at all. A great success!" The Giant Earl dropped Nathaniel to the ground. Nathaniel struck the side of the cauldron, narrowly avoided falling into the fire, and lay still. "The children of Adam are so fragile."

"I miss the Misaabe," the Giant Necromancer rumbled. All four giants shuffled away from the cauldron and into the shadows.

"Ah, we were mighty then," the Giant Stranger agreed.

"We'll be mighty again," the Giant Emperor said.

"We're always mighty," the Giant Earl said, and then the giants squeezed through one of the windows into the star-filled space beyond and were gone.

Time passed.

A cold, wet snout nuzzled Nathaniel awake.

"I'm not asleep," he said.

Out loud.

Had he been dreaming?

He lay on his back and gazed at the stars overhead. The crane, the loon, the moose, the other stars directly above the flat earth spun in a slow circle. If the cauldron was still nearby, its fire had gone out; Nathaniel lay in near-darkness again.

He tried to raise his arm and couldn't.

The cold nose again, in his ear.

"I'm awake," he said. "My eyes are open, and I can hear you. Who is that?"

The answer came again in the form of a wet animal nose, this time behind Nathaniel's ear. He flinched, but the beast didn't stop. It was big, whatever it was, and it worked methodically, slowly pushing its muzzle beneath Nathaniel's neck and then under his shoulders and then supporting his back.

Unseen in the darkness, the large beast pushed Nathaniel into a sitting position.

"Thank you," Nathaniel said.

~You're welcome.~

The beast trundled away from Nathaniel, momentarily blocking out the stars overhead. Nathaniel heard scratching sounds in the darkness.

"What are you doing?" he asked.

~Can you hear what I am?~ the beast called back.

Nathaniel listened. "You're a bear. I can hear the berries and salmon in your belly, and the long claws with which you caught the fish, and the sharp teeth with which you ate it."

~Well done, healer.~

"I can also hear the tender heart within your mighty chest, bear."

The bear laughed in the darkness. *~Call me Makwa. And*

don't be fooled by the tender heart. It's the tender heart of the healer that moves him to kill, when killing becomes necessary.~

Nathaniel considered. "I don't see how that can be so."

Scritch. A Lucifer match flared into life, and Nathaniel saw that the match was held by a large, brown bear.

"You can use a match," Nathaniel said. "But you don't have fingers."

Makwa leaned over the bone platform holding the cauldron and pushed together unburned leaf fragments and bone to make a pile of fresh fuel, then applied the match to it until the leaves caught, and a small fire again licked the underside of the cauldron. *~Yes I can.~*

"And light a fire. As if you were a man."

~Here I can. On the flat earth, no.~

"Who are you?"

The bear sat back on its haunches and looked at Nathaniel solemnly.

"You are me," Nathaniel said.

Makwa rose onto all fours and padded to within Nathaniel's reach. *~Rise, healer.~*

"I cannot move," Nathaniel said.

~You do not try.~

Nathaniel willed his arm to reach out and grab the bear by its neck, knowing he was paralyzed—

and his arm moved.

~Rise, healer,~ Makwa said again.

Nathaniel reached with his other arm and wrapped both of them around the bear's head. With an effort, he ground sideways and levered himself first onto one hip and then up onto both knees.

~Rise, healer.~ The bear stood.

Nathaniel stood with him. The weariness, the weakness of his muscles fell away and he stood with energy, almost leaping from the ground. He looked about and saw that the darkness surrounding him had gone. From the flat plain on which he stood all the way up to the peak of heaven's dome, the stars glittered without veil. He looked down at himself and saw his own naked body, but with more muscles than he was accustomed to seeing, and bearing no wounds.

"I'm healed."

~You're a new person.~

"*We* are a new person," Nathaniel said. He grabbed Makwa by the ears and scratched the bear's head. Patiently, the bear licked Nathaniel's face.

"A new person needs a new name." This voice, the voice of Ma'iingan's manidoo, came with a blaze of light. Nathaniel heard the light, and he also saw it, settling like blue-white fire on the dark fur and glittering eyes of the bear.

Or rather, of his bear-self.

Nathaniel faced the manidoo. "You left me here."

The manidoo nodded, its expression no less solemn for the fact of its wolf ears. "That was the only way it could be done."

Nathaniel cocked his head to one side. "You named Ma'iingan. Did you bring me here to name me, as well?"

"That's one reason for your coming to the Pit of Heaven. Mostly, you came here to be healed. But the bear is correct—in the healing, you've become a new person. A new person needs a new name. This is why kings and queens take throne names when they are crowned."

"Did Ma'iingan . . ." Nathaniel hesitated, then gestured at the plain of bones surrounding him. "Did Ma'iingan come to this place?"

The manidoo shook its head. "Ma'iingan's path is different from yours. He has never come here, and as far as my vision carries, he won't do so in the future. The trails of his people through the sky go elsewhere. But he needs you, as you needed him, so your paths crossed."

"And the god of the sky sent you to cross them."

The manidoo nodded.

But which god was that?

Nathaniel straightened his back, raised his chin, and took a deep breath. "You've brought me here to give me a name, manidoo. Give it to me now."

"You have it already. Can't you guess what it is?"

Nathaniel took his time to answer. "Makwa," he said eventually. "Our name is Makwa."

"Come." The manidoo turned and walked away.

Following, Nathaniel found himself suddenly on a shining path that passed between the stars.

"You have much to learn," the manidoo said, without looking back.

~*We will learn it.*~ Makwa growled from behind Nathaniel.

Abruptly, Nathaniel stood at the stop of the seven stairs. Looking down, he saw the interior of the barn, through a haze of tobacco smoke. He saw himself there, lying on the floor. Ma'iingan stood at the wall, peering through a crack between the boards. Landon stood with him.

Outside the barn, obscured by the smoke, men on foot approached.

Over Nathaniel's prone body crouched a black bear. The animal wasn't attacking Nathaniel, but protecting him.

Nathaniel spun to look behind himself, and Makwa wasn't there.

"On the flat earth," the manidoo said, "your nidji will light no fires. But he'll watch your body when you leave it."

"When I leave my body?"

"This is your first lesson."

"Will you teach me further lessons in the future?"

The manidoo shook its head. "I've done my work."

"Then how will I learn?"

The manidoo ignored the question. "You and your friends are surrounded by enemies. Are you ready to face them?"

"Do I have a choice?" Nathaniel asked.

"No."

Nathaniel descended the seven steps to reenter his body.

"If he would haggle over this, he would haggle over anything."

———⇒•⇐———

CHAPTER TWENTY-ONE

Sarah sat up in bed, her heart racing.

Sweat beaded on her forehead told her she'd had a dream. The sweat also meant that the dried sweet grasses that were piled on the stone slab to make her mattress stuck to her body. She peeled them off, rolling back her blanket and enjoying the early morning chill that set her thoughts racing and goose-pimpled her skin all over.

She slept in a room alone, in Alzbieta Torias's city home. The building was a low warren of a mound with half a dozen rooms burrowed into it, and then an above-ground structure of adobe brick, topped by a flat roof with crenellated edges that struck Sarah as Ferdinandian or Texian. Most of the neighboring houses had peaked and thatched roofs, and the buildings were generally of wood; when Sarah had asked about the roof, Alzbieta had said, "on certain nights, as Handmaid of Lady Wisdom, I am obligated to observe the heavens."

Sarah hadn't pressed for more information.

She had dreamed of two children. Her siblings?

But the dream hadn't been happy. She closed her eyes against the faint light of moon and stars filtering down through the slanted, barred light-shafts and tried to pierce the fog of waking.

She'd dreamed she was a witch. A witch with red hair, a detail that struck her as odd. And in cleaning her home, in a room of bones, she had come across a boy with no bones in his body at all, a boy who lay like a sack of skin with his eyeballs on the floor. She'd started a fire and she had begun to boil the boy's flesh.

No, his bones.

But why?

And when she'd stooped to look closer at him, she'd seen that he had her face, except that his two eyes matched in color, and in place of one ear he had a cluster of oak leaves sprouting out of the side of his head.

That could only be Nathaniel, her brother.

Was it the real Nathaniel, in some way? Was it only her own mind's image of the brother she'd never known?

She'd left her hut—in her dream, she realized with a start, she'd been a crone, living alone in a house made of baked goods in the forest—and in the yard had found a girl. A Hansel and a Gretel of sorts, then, like the story the Germans told, and the boy had gone into her cauldron as Hansel went into the oven of the witch in the story.

Why was Sarah the wicked witch?

The girl worked in the forest outside Sarah's cake-hut. Before Sarah saw her, she'd heard the *thud-thud-thud* of her labor, and when Sarah had come out into the yard, she'd found the child, knocking down trees.

With her bare hands.

This child, too, had had Sarah's face, but for hair she'd had a thicket of oak saplings sprouting from her head.

In her dream, Sarah wondered, sitting awake on her borrowed slab bed and scratching her scalp, what had her own eye looked like? An acorn? A scab of oak bark? A tree limb?

But that was a silly question. She was the dreamer, and not having looked into a puddle or a mirror in the dream, her eye didn't *look like* anything. Her eye *couldn't* look like anything unless other dreamers had shared her dream, which was plainly nonsense.

The girl with the hair forest had stopped her work and looked at Sarah with pleading eyes. "Help me." Then she swung one fist and knocked down a tree whose trunk was five times larger around than her own body. The tree cracked in half at the blow and toppled to the ground, but it fell atop previously chopped trees.

The girl had created a wide clearing, but every tree that fell had fallen into a circular wall that served to imprison the girl.

"Can you break the wall?" Sarah had asked.

And then she had awoken.

Left with the feeling that somehow, her dream had been real.

She touched her witchy eye. It smarted as if from strain, and it felt hot to the touch.

She heard a rapping at the entrance to the room. It wasn't a knock on the door, since it turned out that the Firstborn didn't so much like interior doors inside a house. Her privacy in this guest bedroom was only protected by strings of beads, mostly of black glass, though some were glazed and fired clay, hanging from the ceiling down to the height of her knees.

The rapping was made on the wall outside.

"I'm awake," she said. "But I woke up hard, so enter at your own risk."

"It's me." The voice was Calvin's. "Should I come back later?"

Sarah sighed. Calvin would sleep on hot coals without complaint rather than disturb Sarah, so there must be something he really thought needed her attention. "Confound it, Cal, I said come in."

Calvin entered, stooping slightly and brushing aside the beads with one hand. He was dressed and held a Kentucky rifle. It wasn't his grandpa's—he'd left that weapon behind in New Orleans, when they'd fled in the form of birds—but a very similar gun he'd found among the plundered equipment of the Imperial House Light Dragoons.

"You also allowed as it might be dangerous to enter," he said.

"I ne'er knew you for a coward, Calvin Calhoun." She looked him up and down. "You look like you's a-goin' somewhere."

Cal blushed. "I was. Only they's somethin' you oughtta see."

"Fixin' to leave, and you ain't planned on tellin' me first?"

"I'd a told you, Jerusalem. Lord hates a man as don't say his proper goodbyes. Only I's lettin' you sleep. You're so tired and thin these days, I figure you could use all the shut-eye you can git."

Sarah raised a hand in surrender. "Alright, Cal, I'll show mercy. You can tell me later why you's escapin'. First I reckon you better tell me why you're wakin' me up."

"They's Imperials come to town."

"They was Imperials afore we got here, Cal. Ohio is under

the Pacification, remember? All the Imperial troops my uncle can spare, plus the Ohio Company, and bounties posted, and worse."

"These Imperials are askin' to meet *you*. That regent feller said he's happy to arrange it. He said it in a way as made me think mebbe he already *had* arranged it."

Sarah sucked on her lower lip. "Dammit," she finally said.

Luman tried not to envy the Ophidians.

It wasn't their architecture, not as such. Luman had spent years in Memphis, where the pyramids as well as the mausolea were of stone, so even the tallest and most angular of Cahokia's conical dirt-piles left him cold. He didn't envy their land, either, though the Cahokian Bottom was supposed to be the most fertile land between Ferdinandia and New Muscovy, the place where the Mississippi and the Ohio had both dumped rich alluvial soil for millennia. Luman was happy there were farmers in the world, growing grain and raising hogs and cattle so Luman could eat, but he didn't care to think much about the details of their work.

It was the Cahokians' magic.

Something about old Adam's first wife, apparently, had left her children gifted. Not all of them, but a shockingly large number. And when they had the gift, they had it in spades.

He felt the gift for magic buzzing in the air around him as he rode through the gates on a horse stolen by the Emperor's raiders from some Cahokian rancher. He saw it in the palisade of trees surrounding the city—the palisade might be inert, but it was definitely the product of gramarye. He suspected it even in the tall mounds—they were primitive and garish, with grass on their steep slopes, but how else had they been built, if not by wizardry?

He bit back sour resentment of his own mediocrity.

"You're disappointed, my Balaam."

Notwithstanding Schmidt rode at Luman's side on another appropriated horse. The animals had been rebranded with a mark manufactured by a Company smith for the purpose, a mark that covered the original brand and hid the fact that they were stolen. The Cahokian crowds through which the two of them rode, preceded by an Ophidian herald and followed by ten Company men with rifles and pistols, were ragged and thin, slave and free. At a square where eight streets intersected—at perfect angles to each other, and to most of the city's mounds—and where food should have been for sale, Luman saw mostly piles of dirty snow.

Crude shanties and improvised tents crowded what must have been by design broad avenues. Dirty faces stared from them at the company's people—did they belong to Ohioans, refugees of the Pacification? But only some of them looked Firstborn.

"No, Madam Director. I'm only thinking."

"Tell me your conclusions."

"Observations, really. I was thinking that maybe St. Martin had a point, in being concerned about the Firstborn acquiring too much power."

"You'll find you don't encounter any Martinites here, my Balaam. Nor Mattheans."

Of course. "But doesn't the Compact protect belief? Can't a man revere any saint he wishes, and be permitted free access to any public place in the Empire?"

Notwithstanding Schmidt chuckled. "Welcome to Cahokia. Your religious beliefs and practices are protected by law here, but...if those beliefs happen to include too much respect for saints like Matthew Hopkins or Martin Luther, you are likely to receive a late-night visit from a vigilance committee."

"Tar and feathers," Luman said. "A one-way ride out of town on a rail."

"Illegal," Schmidt said. "Traditional. Common."

"Part of the justification of the Pacification."

"Say rather *pretext*."

Luman weighed the director's words. "I've chosen a name for my horse."

"Strictly speaking, of course, I should have insisted you ride upon an ass. A horse won't balk properly when it sees the angel, I fear. And who ever heard of a talking horse?"

"I'll call the horse *Joe Duncan*."

"Your horse is a mare, my Balaam."

"A mare named *Joe*. Does that offend your sense of propriety?"

"On the contrary. It amuses me so much, I'll give you another clue."

"I may not be able to place bets with a clean conscience, if you give me any more information than you already have."

"I care nothing for your conscience, my Balaam." Schmidt smiled, but then her smile fell flat and she rode in silence for a while. Finally, as if rising from sleep, she straightened in her saddle and took a deep breath. "Joe Duncan was the man I hired to kill my father."

Luman opened and shut his mouth without sound.

"Means to an end," Schmidt said. "Means to the *right* end."

They reached the base of the city's largest mound, the Great Mound, at the top of which stood the Temple of the Sun. The herald, a small man with shockingly bright teeth, dismounted. He handed his reins to one of several Cahokians who stood waiting there, apparently for the purpose. "This is sacred ground."

"Hmmm." Notwithstanding Schmidt raised her eyebrows briefly, then spurred her mount forward. The animal snorted in protest, but began the steep climb up the earth pyramid.

Luman nearly followed her, but then caught himself.

He had plundered what magic he could from the theurgists of Memphis, from the brauchers of German Pennsland, from the Haudenosaunee wise women at the headwaters of the Ohio River, and from elsewhere. What might he learn from the children of Wisdom?

But could he take any magic from them, if he began by offending their goddess?

Also, Notwithstanding Schmidt's comment about his conscience stung him. Luman *did* care about his conscience. He cared, and he had too much weighing it down already.

He dismounted and handed over his reins to the herald.

The ten Company agents hesitated, but then followed Luman's lead. The eleven men then marched, puffing and muttering, up the steep slope. Before they reached the peak, Luman was sweating heavily, notwithstanding the snow on the ground and the chill in the air.

At the top stood a rectangular building, tall, narrow, and long. The flat mound-top around it was gnarled with the leafless trees of a winter garden, and furrows that looked as if they'd sprout in the spring. The front of the rectangular building was a wide, roofless porch. A golden bough of gnarled ivy lay over the lintel of two enormous open doors; to each side of the doors stood a stylized pillar carved with intaglio leaves and branches as if it were a tree. Ravens huddled all over the structure, including on its golden tree branch, giving the structure the appearance of being dressed in funereal black.

The snorting noises of a nervous horse came from *inside* the building.

"This is the Temple of the Serpent," one of the agents muttered, checking the firing pans on his pistol. "Beware."

"Beware of what?" Luman was genuinely curious. "I had heard it was the Temple of the Sun."

The agent shrugged. "Just beware. They say dark things about the Serpent."

"They say dark things about the Imperial Ohio Company," grunted the agent to his side, who now followed his fellow's lead in checking his weapons.

"Yes." Luman laughed. "And we know those things are true. Rest easy, gentlemen. We aren't here to fight. Yet."

"Do we take our orders from you," growled the first agent, "or from the director?"

"Director Schmidt gives us all our orders," Luman acknowledged. "But *I'm* the one who can turn you into a *frog*."

He entered.

The interior looked like a church with its transepts shorn away. A long, straight nave ended in a wall that abruptly shot up, creating a cubical apse raised above the nave. A steep, narrow staircase climbed from the plain of the nave up to the apse. The apse was empty, but for a single spectacular piece of furniture.

It was a tree, whose boughs and branches ended in fine golden leaves. It was also a serpent, consisting of piles and piles of coiled reptile musculature, carved into the trunk and branches of the tree. It was a lamp; Luman saw seven bowls shaped from the branches in which oil could burn. And it was a throne, with a flat seat and back, just large enough for one person, cut into the heart of the trunk. The head of the serpent, as large as the head of an ox, rose and protruded above the back of the seat, so that a person sitting in the throne would almost appear to be wearing the serpent's head for a crown.

The throne was covered in hammered gold; its leaves were of gold foil. The walls and ceiling of the apse were covered with gold, as well. A curtain woven of multiple colors could conceal the apse, but clung instead gathered to either side of the opening by heavy purple cords.

"Disgusting," the irascible agent muttered. "They worship the serpent who made Adam fall."

"So did Moses," Luman murmured.

"The hell he did," the agent growled.

Luman shrugged. "He did if you believe the Bible. Be careful how you exercise judgment, my friend."

In the walls to Luman's left and right, and near him, curtained entryways suggested additional chambers. They'd have to be narrow, given the width of the nave. Perhaps storage rooms, for cult paraphernalia? Perhaps waiting alcoves, where liturgical actors could stand concealed until it was their turn to appear in the ritual? Stairs up to the roof—or down, to caverns below?

"My Balaam," Notwithstanding Schmidt called. "You've lost your horse."

"I didn't think Joe shared my interest in architecture," Luman said.

Schmidt stood, holding her own horse's reins and smiling. The smell of the animal filled the hall, which otherwise held little: a square altar, a table. The colored tiles of the nave's floor and walls suggested a landscape, with a desert near the doors separated from a garden at the deep end of the building by stylized blue waves. The upper walls and the ceiling were painted with an astral scene, which looked wrong to Luman—the northern stars were too high, by a handspan at least.

"No," Schmidt agreed, "neither does *my* beast. See how he objects." The horse pulled at the reins, its hooves clattering loud on the tile floor.

"Have you named him yet?"

"I'm considering calling him *Thomas*."

"I would be happy to accommodate Thomas in lodgings he might find more familiar." These words came from a tall, thin Elf, who might have been handsome but for the marks of acne or smallpox on his cheeks. He wore all black, and was unarmed, unless the staff he leaned on was a weapon. Judging by the iron horse's head affixed to the rod's tip, though, Luman took it for a badge of office. Two more of the Fey stood behind him, similarly dressed in black, though with no marks of rank.

"Thank you." Schmidt handed over her mount's reins to one of the two servants, who promptly walked the animal out of the doors. "You're Maltres Korinn, the so-called Regent-Minister of this city."

"Regent-Minister of the Serpent Throne, and therefore caretaker of the Serpent's realm." The Ophidian bowed. "In my capacity as regent, administering the throne and court until the goddess sees fit to give us a new monarch, I also administer the city."

Schmidt snorted. "Your people look poor and hungry, Regent-Minister. Inside the city walls as well as without. Your management seems to leave much to be desired."

Korinn raised an eyebrow. "The Emperor's tolls and taxes have been heavy. And someone has been stealing our stores. And we're also stretched thin, trying to gather in the refugees from the Missouri and from... elsewhere."

"Good of you."

"We do what we can. If the goddess finds my administration unsatisfactory, She hasn't yet told me so."

"Ah, you have a complicit priesthood. Convenient."

"If only that were true." Was Korinn himself a magician? Was his staff magical?

"And whom will your goddess choose, then?" Schmidt asked.

"Me."

The new voice spoke with a sharp, high-pitched tone, with just a hint of an Appalachee twang in it. Luman turned along with Schmidt and Korinn, but a look at their faces told him that, of the three, he was the only one who was really surprised.

Four newcomers stood in the open doors. Three were tall men, but Luman's eyes were immediately drawn to the fourth, who stood in front, and who had spoken. She was small and slight, pale of skin and dark of hair. Her hair was short as a boy's, but the really striking feature of her appearance was her eyes. They were mismatched, one a cloudy dark blue and the other a gray-blue so light it was almost white. It looked like an animal eye, and as it stared at Luman it seemed to pierce his soul. She wore trousers and a thin Appalachee shirt underneath a blue wool coat that looked as if it might more properly belong to an Imperial soldier.

She leaned on a staff, too, and hers came to a tip in a wooden carving of a horse's head. Two small blower buds gripped the wood of her staff, which was strange, since the wood appeared old and well-cured.

"You're Mad Hannah's illegitimate daughter," Schmidt said. "The rebel queen."

"The goddess hasn't chosen a queen," Korinn said again.

"Illegitimate, in a pig's eye," the young woman shot back. "My father was Kyres Elytharias, king of this land and Imperial Consort."

Schmidt shrugged, a chuckle escaping her lips. "Hannah is known to have played the whore."

One of the newcomers lunged forward. "Lies!" He was a large-framed man bordering on old who wore a red coat and a hat that had once been crisp and black, but was now faded and battered into shapelessness. His accent came from the Chesapeake. "Thomas is a usurper and a scoundrel! A man who would imprison his own sister should not be believed when he calumniates her as well."

Schmidt regarded the Cavalier coolly. "A man who would care for his sister through a decade and a half of her madness should be considered for sainthood, not to mention respected in his solemn secular calling."

Luman kept an eye on the other two men standing behind the witch, who both fidgeted as if they were anxious to start a fight. Perhaps they would already have done so, had Schmidt's party not outnumbered them two to one. One was a rangy, big-knuckled Cracker with long red hair; he stared at the Serpent Throne as if deep in thought. The final member of the group was a beastman, with the head and hindquarters of a coyote, whose eyes and ears darted back and forth alertly and who shifted from foot to foot.

"If you knew Kyres Elytharias," Maltres Korinn said, stepping in between the snarling parties, "you would only have to look at this girl to know the truth. She's his daughter, I have no doubt."

"Good," Schmidt said. "As it happens, I didn't know the King of Cahokia." She turned to the witch. "My name is Notwithstanding Schmidt, and I'm a Director of the Imperial Ohio Company. We conduct all the Ohio Valley trade for the Emperor in his capacity as our sole shareholder."

"Funny," the witch said. "I'd have said you looked more like an army than like a caravan of merchants. I've seen a few burned towns on the road this winter, and my best guess is the burning was done by your men."

Schmidt shrugged and waited.

"My name is Sarah Elytharias Penn," the witch said. "As the eldest child of Hannah Penn, I'm by legal right the Penn landowner, which I expect means by legal right I'm your sole shareholder. If you've come to make your report, I'm ready to hear it. In fact, I think I'm prepared to declare a big fat dividend."

"Show me a Philadelphia court judgment declaring you to be the Penn landowner, and we can talk," Schmidt said. "Until then, I serve His Imperial Majesty, Thomas Penn. And I haven't come to Cahokia to give you money, child, but to deliver a message."

"I ain't deaf," Sarah said, her accent cracking into full-blown Appalachee, "and I ain't gittin' any younger, either."

"He begs you to rebel."

"Hell's Bells," growled the ageing Cavalier. "What nonsense is this?"

"Does he recognize my rights?" Sarah asked, her face impassive.

"Absolutely not. None of them. Not a one. You're a pretender, a fake, or at best the bastard of a desperate madwoman tupped by her footman. And he earnestly hopes you'll rise against him in revolt.

"And when you do, he'll grind you into the dust from which you came."

"There's a man here to see you."

Kinta Jane looked up from her feet. She sat beneath one of the tall windows in the room that Sister Eliza Erikson insisted was the Solarium, though most of the other beguines followed the lead of the would-be Ranger Gerta von Humboldt and called it the Reflectory, with a mixture of affection and disdain. The Reflectory's windows, wide as well as tall and occupying most of the chamber's largest wall, faced south, so that even in a winter as cold as this one, as long as there was sun, the room heated up, and it did so without the wood- and-kerosene smoke that made breathing difficult in some of the other rooms.

This was Kinta Jane's first real winter, and she was still shocked by the three-foot drifts of snow outside. And she was appalled at the poor air quality inside the cloister.

She had lost three toes to frostbite, all on her left foot. It meant she walked with a slight limp now. She found if she swung her hips in the way she did when she aimed to attract a man, the limp was nearly invisible.

Of course, if she swung her hips like that in the cloister, Sister Erikson harrumphed if the First Sister was having a good day; if she was having a bad day, she might slap Kinta Jane.

Kinta Jane pulled on her stockings—beguine-knit, and woolen—and stood.

Gerta von Humboldt was broad-shouldered and bluff as any man, and after her husband had died she'd taken to the woods in what she herself described as a fit of madness. She'd ended up in the cloister, having walked hundreds of miles following no trail, and she alternated between periods of intense commitment to the cloister—building and repairing, planting, hunting to add to the stores, leading trading expeditions to Youngstown—and equally intense periods of wandering on her own in the woods, praying to St. Robert Rogers to descend as Wobomagonda and reveal the next stage of the forest path to her. Some of the sisters whispered that she had had children with her husband, and that in her initial madness, she had torn them limb from limb. They never said it louder than a whisper, and Gerta never said anything of the kind.

Now the would-be Ranger leaned in to whisper to Kinta Jane Embry. "I wouldn't say he's handsome, exactly, but neither would I turn up my nose. He's in the Library."

Kinta Jane smiled, squeezed her friend's hand, and made her way to the Library. She was glad now that she had insisted on keeping her stiletto; who, after all, could possibly be here to see her? Some Imperial officer, coming to arrest her for killing his men? A bounty hunter in the pay of Mrs. Meeks?

Some agent of Simon Sword?

She ascended the front stairs and entered the Library.

Each beguine cloister had its own personality, the sisters had told Kinta Jane, and this one was decidedly bookish. It had a flock, and fields, and an orchard, and an apiary, so it could feed itself; it also owned a woolen mill and a flour mill, both of which were shuttered for the winter, so it made goods for trade.

But what made the cloister stand out, for fifty miles around, was its books.

Kinta Jane entered the Library and looked immediately at the books, as she always did. She'd tried to count them one day, and lost track shortly after two thousand—five thousand, more or less, was her best estimate. Eliza Erikson's father had been a publisher and a bookseller, and when both her parents had died of the same bloody flux one spring, she had driven a wagon up to Palmyra in Haudenosaunee territory and brought back their entire stock.

Before that, this room had been an empty dormer.

"I know why you don't speak," said the man sitting at the Library's reading table.

He was slightly taller than average, lean with the sort of leanness that suggested lots of physical activity—a hunter's leanness, rather than a beggar's. Long black hair lay tied into a queue behind his neck with a black ribbon, and large gray eyes looked at her warmly.

She saw no sign of beastkind features. That didn't mean he couldn't be a servant of the Heron King, of course. And he didn't look like any kind of lawman she had ever seen before.

He appeared to be unarmed.

On the table in front of him lay a sheet of foolscap, an ink bottle, and a quill pen.

Kinta Jane tapped the side of her cheek and shrugged.

"Sit, please."

She sat and scooted in close to the table. That let her take the stiletto from its sheath on her forearm and hold the weapon ready, but out of sight.

He stood and shut the door behind her, closing the two of them in alone, then returned to the seat opposite her.

"You were born with a tongue." Before she could react, he raised a hand to cut her off. "Please, let me tell you what I know."

Kinta Jane nodded, keeping a straight face.

"You were born with a tongue. You had it removed, willingly, because you saw a vision. You were told the vision first, by your brother René, and then, having tasted a sacred herb in a secret room, you saw the vision yourself."

A vision of civilization destroyed, and forced to begin again.

Of the old world rolled up like a scroll, and its daughter born in fire and blood.

Franklin's Vision.

Kinta Jane nodded, ever so slightly.

"You found yourself here, traveling north into the teeth of the worst winter in twenty years, because you're going to Philadelphia. Because you have a message to deliver to a secret location, what Dr. Weishaupt taught us to call a *blind drop*. There is a seat in the Walnut Street Theater, on the floor, the right arm of which is deliberately loosened, allowing someone who knows it has been so modified to lift the arm, revealing a small cavity beneath. The seat is 17F."

Kinta Jane's heart beat faster. Her grip on the stiletto was slippery with her own sweat, so she wiped both her hands off on her skirt. She stared at the gray-eyed man and tried to keep her face expressionless. Who was he?

"You would attend a Saturday matinee performance. You would place your message in the dead drop in the arm of 17F. You must do this because your brother René is dead, and you know no one else in the Conventicle to which you have committed your life."

Kinta Jane nodded once and tightened her grip on the stiletto, bringing it to the edge of the table so as to be ready for action.

"My name is Isaiah Wilkes," the gray-eyed man said. "As a boy, I was an apprentice printer. When my master became a cleric, I didn't follow him, but instead left printing to become an actor under Walter Fitzroy's direction. I'm now the head of Philadelphia's second—or perhaps third—most famous troupe of players. We're best known for a series of plays we perform on wagonback at Easter, called the Philadelphia Mystery Cycle.

"But I never lost touch with my original master, nor ever left his service. And when he wrote his famous Compact, he and John Penn also founded their Conventicle, to protect what he had wrought from the apocalyptic flames he'd seen in his vision, and I was one of its first members.

"In some circles, at some times, I'm known as *the Franklin*." Isaiah Wilkes smiled, and the crooked crease broke his face from earnest anxiety into a relaxed warmth. "You couldn't reach the Walnut Street Theater, Kinta Jane, so the Walnut Street Theater has come to you. It was easy to find you."

He reached under his shirt and pulled out an irregular brown object, a tattered bit of leather. The object had a hole punched through it so it could hang on a leather thong—an amulet of some sort, then. She squinted at what initially appeared to be a line of astrological characters, and then pulled back.

The neatly inked characters spelled out KINTA JANE EMBRY.

The medallion was her tongue.

Kinta Jane dropped the knife to the floor. Its clatter rang loud in her ears, but if the Franklin noticed it, he said nothing. Instead, he reached across the table with both hands and wrapped them around her fingers.

"Will you write for me?" he asked. "Will you write what you would have put into the dead drop?"

With a trembling hand, Kinta Jane took up the pen. Dipping it into the ink, she drew two large circles, and then quickly sketched out the two sides of the Heron King's coin she had received aboard the chevalier's hulk *Incroyable*: the plow on one side, and the blade on the other.

She laid the pen on the paper.

She was crying.

Isaiah Wilkes looked solemnly at the drawing of the coin and nodded. Reaching into a pocket, he produced a gold coin and laid it on the table. It was identical to the one she had just drawn.

Kinta Jane gasped.

"I had this by a messenger from René," he said. "This coin is the reason I've come looking for you. The other members of René's cell are dead, discovered and killed by the Chevalier of New Orleans. You came as far as you could alone. We'll go the remainder together."

Kinta Jane was full of questions, and frustrated as never before by her muteness. She seized the pen again and gave herself a voice.

Where?

Isaiah Wilkes nodded. "To Philadelphia. On the way, we'll see a wise woman, who may be able to do something about your tongue. Whether she can or not, I need you to come with me as a witness."

Witness?

"The Franklin is a leader, of sorts, though mostly the parts of the Conventicle lead themselves. The Franklin gathers information and acts upon it, and principally what the Franklin does is bear witness. He's called to bear witness to power, and it turns out that my master was very far-seeing in establishing the Franklin for this role. Brother Onas has fallen asleep, you see, or perhaps he is corrupted, or both. He was to be one of the great bulwarks against the coming of Simon Sword, and instead he's about his own program, seeking his own power. He must be awoken, and if he cannot be, then other powers must be informed and aroused, who can take his place."

Brother Onas?

"The Emperor," Isaiah Wilkes said. "You and I must go to Philadelphia and try one last time to speak with Thomas Penn."

Ahmed Abd al-Wahid hurled the Dutchman to the floor.

Van Dijk bounced, rolled, and ended very nearly on his feet, an acrobatic maneuver belying his shock of white hair and the avuncular lines of his face.

"Why are you doing this?" Van Dijk snapped.

Abd al-Wahid was the only mameluke present. He and his surviving companions had tracked Van Dijk to the house of his daughter and her son, a shipping merchant who worked in precious metals and cloth. Van Dijk was the only member of the City Council they'd been able to find.

Now Abd al-Wahid delivered the Dutch furniture seller to the chevalier in the chevalier's office. This room was warded with burning herbs in pots in the corner, with yarn doodles stretched across the window-frames and the door-lintels, and with painted symbols on all the walls. At the far end of the chevalier's office stood paired Vodun altars, and the chevalier's pet mambo—or perhaps his captive?—came in at least once daily to offer rum, sugar, tobacco, and other delicacies to the idols worshipped there.

Thinking of the idolatry, Abd al-Wahid spat. He was careful to spit in the direction of the Dutchman, so as not to give the chevalier the idea that he was expressing contempt for the Vodun witch.

The chevalier himself appeared to be a Christian, rather than a worshipper of the dark Africk gods. He consulted the mambo as one who needed magic performed, rather than as a spiritual seeker.

Still, he consulted her.

It hadn't worked. The chevalier sat propped in his bed with large pillows, the skin of his face sallow, his pores larger than they should be, his hair thinner than it had been, his movements slow as those of a basking lizard. A spittoon at his feet collected the blood and bile he coughed into it. He worked and slept in the same room and he ate only food the mambo had blessed, which mostly seemed to consist of very bland, simple matter—baked sweet potato, boiled rice, stewed tomato, water. All of it without any spice at all.

It was a hard fall for a man who was famed for his palate as far away as Paris.

The chevalier clutched the writing board on his lap with both hands and glared at Van Dijk. "You voted not to approve the quarterly tax returns."

Van Dijk rose to a slouch and stared at his own feet. "I argued in favor of approval." Both men were speaking French.

The chevalier talked slowly, pausing to inhale with deep breaths that made a wet, rattling sound in his chest. "And yet the published... minutes do not reflect that... Indeed, the recorded vote was... unanimous."

Van Dijk shrugged and scratched behind his ear. "I didn't... I couldn't..." He was manifestly looking for an explanation of his own behavior that would seem innocent. "The Council votes are usually unanimous. I voted with the others to... to retain their good will. So I could stay on the Council, and maybe next time persuade them to a better outcome."

"You're on the Council because... I put you there."

"There are elections." The Dutchman looked embarrassed by his own words.

"The Council didn't do this alone." The chevalier adjusted his posture with a pained wince, leaning forward with elbows on his desk. "Who put... you up to this?"

Van Dijk looked out the window.

"I can think of... three possibilities," the chevalier said. "The Emperor."

Van Dijk snorted and looked confused. "What? No."

"The old... Bishop Ukwu. Before his death."

Van Dijk shook his head. "No, that man was as otherworldly as a saint. He'd sooner have swallowed live spiders than meddle in politics."

"A saint?" The chevalier arched his eyebrows, groaning with the effort. "Interesting. I think you'd be surprised at... how much the sainted former bishop... liked to meddle in politics. But of course... the third possibility is... his son Etienne, the criminal... and *new* bishop."

Van Dijk gulped. "He pressured us."

"With threats?" the Chevalier asked. "Arson? Kidnapping? Murder?"

"With... yes."

"And having announced... your disapproval of the returns... you are all now in hiding. He pressured you into this?"

Van Dijk hesitated. "He suggested it. And he... offered resources."

"Do you know where... the others are hiding?"

"No." Van Dijk looked up, a ray of light in his eyes. "But I could find out."

The chevalier considered this offer.

Abd al-Wahid rested his hand on his hip, near the hilt of his scimitar. He liked this man Gaston Le Moyne—the chevalier was ruthless. He'd be a worthy prince-capitaine of the order, should he accept the Prophet and say the Shahada. If he contributed his lands to the order, perhaps they could even be given back to him.

What value would it be to have an Elector of the Empire as prince-capitaine of the mamelukes?

"What did you hope...to accomplish?" the chevalier asked.

"You mean, what did *he* hope to do?"

The chevalier shook his head slowly. "I said *you*, and I meant it. Is this an attempt...to get power?"

"The other councilors...yes. Power. Independence. The death of the old bishop...some say that maybe you were involved. And if you could kill another Elector, you could surely kill a councilor."

"Kill a councilor?" The chevalier laughed softly.

"And therefore you needed to be restrained." Van Dijk looked up, sudden fear in his face. "This is what the other councilors have said, you understand."

"I understand." The chevalier's face was a mask. "*You* only went along with them...to stay in their good graces...so you could better serve my interests in the future."

The Dutchman gasped in relief. "Yes. Exactly."

"And the young bishop, then? What does he aim to do? I *have* the money already."

Van Dijk shrugged. "He has a fool's notions. He thinks people can be persuaded not to pay."

"He's right," the chevalier said. "Indeed, the people of New Orleans...have a grand tradition of evading...every stamp and tariff they possibly can. You Dutch, along with the Catalans...of the bayou and the Igbo of the gulf...keep my men very busy trying to... collect what is lawfully owed." It was a long speech, for a man who had such trouble breathing. "And I do have...need of the money."

"Not me," Van Dijk hastened to say. "I don't cheat. I'm an honest merchant."

"Which is as much as to say, a chaste harlot. So, the newly minted priest...wearing the mantle of his dead father...wishes to attack my legitimacy. I'm corrupt, a thief...an unjust taker of taxes...he says to those who already resent the...few and light taxes they pay. And if he can get them to pay less...he thinks he can starve me out."

Van Dijk shook his head. "It's a fool's plan. You're a richer man than he thinks."

The chevalier's eyes flashed. "I *am* richer than he thinks. What do *you* know about it?"

Van Dijk stepped back, off balance. "Only...only that, having built the furniture for this glorious Palais, I know your lands must bring you much more wealth than the city taxes could. I'm in your service, My Lord."

Abd al-Wahid could smell the merchant's fear.

"What would you do, in my service...Meneer Van Dijk? How far would you be willing to go?"

Van Dijk rubbed his hands together. "I'll vote how you like, of course. We can approve the next returns."

The chevalier showed no emotion.

"I can speak out now," the Dutchman added. "I'll speak publicly, and say it was a mistake, and that we should have approved the returns."

"What if instead I asked you to...continue to speak out against me, but to report...to me in secret on the doings...of the young bishop?" The faintest hint of a sly smile curled the corner of the chevalier's upper lip.

"A spy? A spy, yes!" Van Dijk rubbed his hands together as if they were cold. "I could do that."

"I'll have to punish the councilors, of course," the Chevalier said.

"You mean...the *other* councilors."

"All those appearing to be...in rebellion against me. I'll have to kill loved ones...burn down businesses. I must be respected... and so New Orleans must see the reprisals."

"But not me," Van Dijk said.

"I could spare your family," the Chevalier said slowly. "I could merely burn down a...warehouse or two. Perhaps even only a...half-full warehouse. But surely, you see that...I can't spare you...if you're to be my spy."

"But My Lord Chevalier...it seems harsh."

Abd al-Wahid saw where the interview was inexorably headed. He wrapped a fold of his scarf over the mouth of his scabbard to hide the rasp, and then slowly drew his scimitar.

"Does it?" The chevalier looked amused.

"Perhaps an empty warehouse, My Lord."

"Hmmm." The chevalier turned his head and looked out the window as if weighing his options. "Kill him."

"My Lord?" the Dutchman asked.

Ahmed Abd al-Wahid ran the merchant through the lungs, stabbing from the side and sinking his blade in all the way to the hilt. Van Dijk pivoted and stared upward in shock as he sank to the floor, dark blood suddenly bubbling from his lips and puddling around his white hair.

The mameluke withdrew his blade, wiping it clean on the merchant's carpetlike waistcoat.

"If he would haggle over this... he would haggle over anything." The chevalier looked down at the fresh corpse and shook his head. "I could never trust such a man. And his death is just as useful to me... as any information he might provide. I'll have him hung on the Place d'Armes. Jackson has been there long enough."

The chevalier leaned over his spittoon to hack a thick ball of bloody phlegm from his lungs and spit it into the brass container.

Abd al-Wahid said nothing.

"But for you and your men, Prince-Capitaine," the chevalier said, rising and wiping sputum on the back of his sleeve, "I have a more important task."

"The poet tells us that everyone has been made for a particular work," Abd al-Wahid said. "And the desire for that work has been put in every heart."

Young Bishop Ukwu must pay for the death of al-Farangi.

"What dog?"

———◦◦———

CHAPTER TWENTY-TWO

"Come," Ma'iingan whispered to the boy Landon.

"And what?" Landon stared, his face a slab of red in the glow from the asemaa fire.

"Whose men are those?" Ma'iingan nodded toward the other side of the wall.

Landon again pressed his eye to the thin crack between the boards and looked at the company of six soldiers in black coats, dismounting and hitching their horses to the fence surrounding the asemaa field.

Could the soldiers see the light inside the drying barn? Ma'iingan hoped not.

"They're the Chief Godi's men." Landon squirmed like a puppy in discomfort. "Black is the color of the College."

"You mean Old One Eye, na?"

"Yes. He's an Elector, like the earl." Landon looked at George hesitantly. "In the earl's madness, some say that Old One Eye rules alone in Johnsland. I'm not going to fight his men."

"I'm shocked you would pass up this opportunity to show what a warrior you are."

Landon's face registered confusion.

Ma'iingan sighed. "I'm joking, and this isn't the time for it." He crossed the barn floor and dragged George Randolph Isham to his feet. With a quick motion, he cut the rope tying George's

418

hands and began roughly dragging the young man out of his coat and hat. "Those men, you think they're interested in Landon Chapel, na?"

Landon hesitated. "No."

"They're looking for George, here," Ma'iingan continued. "And the Sioux raider who kidnapped him."

"You said you were Comanche."

"Did I?" Ma'iingan shook his head. "I have a hard time telling Indians apart, some days."

"I can never tell when you're being serious."

"Good. I think Old One Eye has caused too much trouble already, so you and I are going to stop him from causing any more." Ma'iingan tossed George's hat and coat to Landon. "Put these on."

George looked at Ma'iingan with curiosity in his face, and Ma'iingan winked at him.

He looked at Nathaniel. The boy moaned and stirred. He seemed stronger, louder than he had an hour earlier, but Ma'iingan was afraid to take any chances.

The shadow of the sweat lodge in which Nathaniel lay looked strikingly like a bear. Ma'iingan shifted left and right slightly, and the shadow still appeared to be a bear, moving as Ma'iingan moved, keeping its muzzle and powerful paws pointed at Ma'iingan.

What had happened after the boy had climbed the central beam and then fallen off? Ma'iingan had built the boy a sweat lodge because it was what he would have done for himself, and then he'd heard the voice of his manidoo, commanding him to slaughter the horses. He'd done so, and then the voice had gone silent.

Was this the sort of thing the Midewiwin did in their lodges? Ma'iingan wished his father were here, so he could at least ask. His father would say he couldn't reveal Midewiwin secrets, but he would drop a hint, or make a joke, or share a reassuring smile.

"Free me," George said in a hesitant voice. "If it's to undermine Old One Eye, I'll help."

Ma'iingan wanted the help, but he was afraid to take the offer. Not while Nathaniel was unconscious and wounded. If George and Landon decided to attack Ma'iingan together, he'd be in trouble.

"I want to trust you," he said to George. "You value your honor, na?"

George frowned. "Yes."

"So I won't bind your mouth while I deal with Old One Eye's men. You can call out for help, but I hope you won't. I value my honor too, and as soon as I can, I'll set you free."

He was counting on more than just George's honor; he was relying on his guess that George wouldn't want Old One Eye's men, of all people, to see him tied up and humiliated. And also on George's fear of the crazy Indian who had kidnapped him, tied him up, and then slaughtered four horses in front of him. He stood George against the center pole, tying his hands on the opposite side to lock him into a tight embrace with the wood.

Landon tossed aside his own coat and hat and shrugged into George's, which were much brighter purple and which glittered with ornate gold embroidery. They were near enough the same height and build; it would have to do.

George looked down into the tiny sweat lodge. Did he see the shadow-bear, as Ma'iingan did?

"Let me go," the Earl's son said.

"Henh. But not yet." Ma'iingan nodded at the approaching soldiers. "How close?" he asked Landon.

Landon ran to the wall and peered through again. "Closer," he said. "We have a minute."

"We go now." Ma'iingan grabbed his German rifle and checked the powder. "Landon, you must hold your fingers together, your fists as one."

"Like this?" Landon did as he was bid.

Ma'iingan nodded. "You're my prisoner, you're George Isham. We'll exit that way." He pointed north—the approaching soldiers came from the east.

"They'll run us down."

Ma'iingan nodded. "Henh. We must take their horses."

"It's too bad you killed the ones we had." Landon nodded at the corpse of one of the animals in the corner of the barn.

Ma'iingan didn't answer. He'd done as his manidoo had bid. The horses had filled the curing barn with the reek of drying blood. Had they also aided God-Has-Given in his flight into the heavens? *Had* he flown into the heavens?

What had really happened?

Ma'iingan wished he were Midewiwin, or at least a wiser

man than he was. A more spiritual man, so he could understand what was happening.

But right now, it was good that he was a man who could sneak and shoot. "Come."

He slipped through a small door on the north side and crept in the shadow of the building to a ditch a short distance away. He could see the six soldiers more clearly now, approaching the barn with their short rifles raised to the ready.

"Weapons on half-cock, men," said the only mounted man among them. Their leader, probably. "It could be vagrants."

They had seen the fire.

"If it's vagrants, we should shoot them anyway," one of the soldiers grumbled.

"It could be a picknicking gentleman, lighting a small fire to warm himself from this chill while resting from the hunt," the leader snarled. "You do not shoot until I tell you. And keep your voices *down*."

Ma'iingan pulled Landon behind him and crept down the ditch. They passed the soldiers going the other direction, and then came up behind the tethered horses.

"It's a pity we Haudenosaunee are not better horsemen," he murmured to Landon.

The boy shook his head. "You really need to decide what kind of Indian you are."

"We all do, na? Words of wisdom. You mount first, and I'll cover you."

Ma'iingan leaned against the rail fence with one elbow, pointing his German rifle toward the backs of the soldiers. He wouldn't shoot them from behind, but if they turned, he'd be ready.

Landon mounted easily.

Ma'iingan unhitched the remainder of the horses, then climbed onto one. He'd only ridden twice before, and his seat was awkward. The heavy leather saddle didn't help—he felt as if his hip bones were being stretched unnaturally far apart.

"I'm giving birth," he whispered. "And to my surprise, it's a horse."

"I guess I know now you're not Sioux," Landon said. "They leap onto their horses, and ride as if they were one with the beast."

"Na? Well, you should hear what they say about the people of Johnsland."

"What do they say?"

"Ride!" Ma'iingan said. Then he pointed his rifle at the sky, over the heads of the soldiers.

Bang!

The soldiers' leader fought to keep his own horse under control and his men wheeled around, throwing themselves under cover. Ma'iingan and Landon Chapel raced up a narrow lane toward the highway.

"It's the Indian!" one of the soldiers shouted.

"He's got Master Isham!" cried another.

Ma'iingan and Landon both hunched low over their mounts' shoulders, and then the bullets came. "Not too fast!" Ma'iingan called to Landon. "If we leave them behind entirely, they may go into the asemaa barn. We want them to follow us. Also, stay close to me. They won't want to shoot George...I think."

Landon mumbled something inaudible and slowed his pace.

They reached the end of the lane and turned onto the larger road. Ma'iingan risked a look back; the soldiers who had collected their horses were now mounting. Their leader had waited for them, and was spurring them on with curses and kicks. Two of the soldiers—those whose horses Ma'iingan and Landon had stolen—trotted ahead.

"Well done, George Isham," Ma'iingan said, and clapped Landon on the shoulder.

The boy slid and began to fall out of his saddle.

"Whoa, whoa!" Ma'iingan grabbed Chapel by the front of his borrowed coat and stopped his fall. "What's wrong?"

Then he saw the dark blood flowing down the boy's side.

"I can ride," Landon murmured. His face was pale.

Ma'iingan looked around. Snow carpeted the fields and forest around them. His experience with Zhaaganaashii was that almost none of them could track, but the snow would change that. They needed to outrun the soldiers, and they needed to do it on the road.

Only Landon was wounded, and Ma'iingan was a poor rider at best.

"Don't fall," he exhorted the boy.

He reloaded the German rifle.

It wasn't easy, doing the work on horseback. He kept his attention on the gun, the ramrod, and the powder horn as he worked, and that wasn't easy, either. He was tempted to look up at the approaching soldiers.

But he stayed focused, reloaded, and then raised the gun, sighting along it.

The leader rode in front now, having passed the two men running on foot. Three more men followed, further back.

"Mother earth and father sky forgive me," Ma'iingan murmured. They were the same words he'd said as he'd slaughtered the horses in the barn.

He shot the leader's mount in its breast.

The animal went down with a single scream, throwing its rider into the adjacent field. Ma'iingan's own horse objected, neighing loudly and leaping sideways, and Ma'iingan struggled to regain control.

He reloaded.

Bang! Bang! Bullets whizzed past him in the darkness, close enough that he could hear their trail through the air.

"Landon, you're still with me, na?"

No answer.

Ma'iingan spared a sideways glance and saw the boy slumped over the neck of his horse. The animal cantered away up the highway.

He held his fire until the second rider approached the spot where the first horse lay dead, and its rider struggled to get back over the fence and into the lane. Then he shot, again at the horse, and again dropping it. The second horse fell right on top of the first. Its rider tumbled to the ground and lay still, neck twisted at an unnatural angle.

The running soldiers reached the two horses' bodies and threw themselves to the ground behind the corpses, taking cover and loading their own rifles.

"Maajidook." Ma'iingan had slowed the soldiers, but he had also given them a wall behind which to shoot.

"Look at Master George!" One of the soldiers yelled. "The Indian's hurt him!"

Ma'iingan turned his horse, nearly knocking himself out of the saddle in the process, and caught up with Landon Chapel. The boy raised his head to grin weakly at Ma'iingan.

"Did we do it?"

"Henh, we did. Now hold on tight."

Ma'iingan snatched the reins of Landon's horse and pushed his animal forward. They had a long and circuitous ride ahead, to get back to the barn, and they couldn't afford to get too far ahead of their pursuers.

Bang! Bang!

"Mutter Hohman, guten abend." Wilkes bowed politely.

The old woman standing in the rectangle of warm yellow light that was her open doorway looked closely at Kinta Jane. Snow swirled down around Kinta Jane, obscuring the path at her feet and freezing her to her core. "You've brought her."

"It's time. May we come in, hexenmeistres?" Wilkes smiled.

"It's time. The meat you left for that dog of yours is almost gone. You may come in, but you mustn't be so formal with me."

"Mutti Hohman, then."

"Mutti Hohman." The old woman shrank to one side, and the shifting shadows of her face made her eyes look cavernous and the three thick hairs on her chin extraordinarily long. "It would make me feel young if you called me *Georgina*."

Isaiah Wilkes urged Kinta Jane through the door and then followed her, shutting the door behind them.

In the sudden warmth of the cottage, Kinta Jane took a deep breath. They had traveled two days from the cloister, riding horses that Wilkes had brought with him and leading two mules, laden with winter gear and food. The previous night, they'd slept in a farmer's barn a mile off the highway, having traded several pounds of dried beef for the privilege. Mother Hohman's cottage was somewhere near Youngstown, but this wasn't country Kinta Jane knew at all and it was mostly obscured from her view by a blizzard.

"I don't need a *young* woman, Mutti. I need a *powerful* one."

The crone nodded, smiling wistfully. "Ich weiss es, mein freund. Very well. I'm ready. Are you?"

"Give me a moment." Wilkes turned to Kinta Jane, gesturing at a sturdy wooden table beside a kitchen fire. "Please sit."

Kinta Jane sat, her limbs obeying her stiffly, and after a moment's delay. The house had only two rooms on the ground floor: a kitchen and a sitting room. The sitting room was full of books, and the kitchen was full of jars. At the back of the kitchen, steep wooden stairs climbed to a loft.

Wilkes disappeared out a back door of the cottage. Kinta Jane heard the growling of a dog.

The hexenmeistres opened a jar on a high shelf and removed a rolled sheet of yellow paper. Smoothing the paper out on the table between her and Kinta Jane, she sat. The paper bore a strange arrangement of letters:

SATOR
AREPO
TENET
OPERA
ROTAS

She noticed Kinta Jane looking at it. "This is an old charm. Older than the rest of the hexing I'll attempt for you today. This was around before there were Germans; it's Latin." She chuckled. "It's as close to gramarye as I come, and I hope my uncle Otto isn't disappointed with me for doing it. The Sator Arepo is older than our Lord."

The growling from behind the house became an urgent and angry bark.

Kinta Jane raised her eyebrows in question.

"The Sator Arepo is merely a defensive tool. I have letters inside the walls of the house, of course. But the Sator Arepo will give us additional protection. What we're asking for is delicate, and it may attract unwanted attention. We don't want it to go wrong."

The barking ended suddenly. The back door opened and Wilkes returned, holding one hand at shoulder height. In his other hand, he held a bloody knife. "Shall I put this in its place?"

"My boy, you're many things, but you're no braucher. Give it here."

Mutter Hohman cupped her hands; Wilkes leaned forward and deposited something in it, something pink and long.

A tongue.

A dog's tongue.

Kinta Jane felt ill.

The hexenmeistres held her cupped hands over the sheet of paper with its square acrostic. "Wrap your hands around mine, child," she said to Kinta Jane. "This is your magic, too."

Wilkes took one step away, but watched closely.

Kinta Jane wrapped her fingers around the outside of the

witch's hands. They were thin, bony hands, but they felt hot, as if they were full of blood. Or fire.

Or maybe it was just that Kinta Jane's own fingers felt like icicles.

"Have you spent the day in prayer and reflection, asking our Lord for forgiveness, strength, and success in all your endeavors?" the witch asked.

Kinta Jane shook her head, confused. She looked at Wilkes for support, but his face was impassive.

"Never mind, child, I *have*. And as sayers of prayer go, I'm a mighty woman. Now open your mouth."

Kinta Jane hesitated, but obeyed. The witch looked into her open mouth, and a single tear formed in the corner of each eye, sliding slowly down her parchmentlike cheeks. "Great God of heaven," she said, "forgive us for the things we feel we must do."

The witch shoved the dog's tongue into Kinta Jane's mouth.

Kinta Jane couldn't breathe. The tongue was hot and wet and tasted of blood. She gagged, but the hexenmeistres only pushed harder, forcing the tongue into place as if it were Kinta Jane's own.

Out of survival reflex, Kinta Jane raised her hands to her face.

The hexenmeistres snatched them both in her own, and slammed them down onto the table. Then she pulled Kinta Jane's face forward with her fingers gripping Kinta Jane's teeth. Kinta Jane looked down and saw that her face was over the Sator Arepo diagram.

"Gottes Wort und Jesu Muttermilch und Christ blut!" The witch's voice jumped an octave, into a shrill and unnatural tremolo. "Ist für alle Wunden und Brandschäden gut!"

The old woman released Kinta Jane's hands. "Hold the Sator Arepo," she murmured.

Kinta Jane's mind reeled, but she pressed both hands down on the sheet of paper, feeling it crinkle beneath her fingers. She felt as if she *was* the paper; something grabbed her.

The witch touched her thumb to Kinta Jane's left cheek, and with it made the sign of the cross.

Kinta Jane gagged. The alien tongue in her mouth twitched and she fought not to swallow it. It leaped and flopped like a fish on a riverbank, struggling to come out of her mouth.

"Amen!" the witch cried.

Then she pressed her thumb to Kinta Jane's right cheek and made the cross again.

Kinta Jane's stomach roiled. She pushed the table as if she were holding onto a life-raft with all her might. She struggled not to retch. A hand she couldn't see squeezed her throat.

Wilkes watched calmly.

"Amen!" the old woman cried again.

She pressed her thumb to the underside of Kinta Jane's jaw. The tongue rolled uncontrollably in her mouth, and the witch made a third cross.

"Und amen!"

The letters on the Sator Arepo burst into sudden flame.

Kinta Jane pulled away, her palms scorched, swallowed—

and the tongue pressed against the roof of her mouth naturally, as if it were her own. Kinta Jane swallowed, tasting blood.

Above each door, the wooden walls of the cottage burst into flame. These flames too were letter-shaped, though they weren't the Sator Arepo charm. Whatever they were, they were written in the ornate gothic lettering favored in the northern Duchies and in German Ohio.

The hexenmeistres released her patient and toppled backward. Stepping forward, Wilkes knelt in a smooth motion and caught the old woman in his arms.

"Is she alive?" Kinta Jane asked, and then clapped her burned hands over her own mouth.

She could talk.

She had a dog's tongue in her mouth, and she could speak.

"There was resistance. Even here, so far from the confluence of the rivers, the King's power is great. She's breathing." Wilkes stood, carrying the witch in his arms, and headed for the narrow stairs. "I'll put her to bed so she can rest. You and I will watch over her tonight, and in the morning, I think she will be well."

"And the dog?" Kinta Jane staggered to her feet, feeling the strangeness of having a working tongue in her mouth again. She found a kitchen rag, wrapped one hand in it, and began beating out the flames above the kitchen door.

Wilkes climbed the steps with his burden, which now seemed tiny and pitiable. "What dog?"

Cahokia had no Polite order.

It had no college of magic, not that Luman had ever heard of and not that he could find now, either.

It had wizards of some sort. Someone had built the mounds—could that all have been done by manual labor? Slaves too lightly dressed for the sudden avalanche of snow shivered past Luman in the central market square where he stood, and he shook his head.

The mounds, maybe.

But the wall was a work of magic, no doubt.

Cahokia's magicians could be underground, hidden away in some palatine network. Or perhaps they simply had no society, no tradition, and no way to pass on magical lore to other Cahokians. Perhaps every Cahokian magician was like Luman Walters, an arcane parasite swimming through the long intestine of the world, stealing nourishment when and where it could.

He didn't think so, though.

The open veil and the naked Serpent Throne unsettled him. Shouldn't the veil be shut, especially in the presence of an outsider, such as himself, such as Notwithstanding Schmidt and the Imperial Ohio Company's agents? Was it open because something had been lost, something that would let it shut? Was it open because the Cahokian regent Maltres Korinn simply knew no better—not being party to esoteric knowledge himself, he didn't know what to protect from the public view? Was the veil open as a symbol of non-resistance to Imperial occupation—was that why he and Schmidt had been invited into the Temple to see? Had the Emperor demanded that the veil remain open?

Was the veil open as an invitation?

The idea felt impious to Luman. He was accustomed to stealing secret knowledge, but such lore's value lay in the very fact that it was secret. Secret knowledge, sacred spaces offered to the whole world felt...wrong.

Was the open veil an invitation to him, to Luman Walters?

The director was conferring with the Imperial toll collectors and local agents, examining their accounts as she had examined the accounts of trading posts all along the Ohio River on their journey here. Left to his own devices, Luman toiled through the snow up another mound, one of the tallest, to look at what surely must be a Christian church.

The city's famous basilica, he thought, the chapel of her kings, as he stood outside and appraised it. Here, too, were two stone columns and an entwined vine; the front of the church matched the front of the Temple of the Sun, at least in its largest details.

What syncretistic semi-pagan nonsense this was, to nail together the incenses and hidden idols of the ancient Mediterranean and the austere heaven-reaching Christianity of the Old World behind a single façade? What ambition! What effrontery!

Luman laughed out loud.

The basilica was carpeted with birds just as the temple was, but these were whitish-gray creatures, a different breed. Fascinating.

A woman in the gray robe of a Cetean monk stood in the doorway of the church. "You're with the Imperial Ohio Company." She folded her hands placidly in front of her.

"And *your* accent sounds closer to Youngstown than to Memphis," Luman shot back. "You're not from here."

"My order is a traveling one. You must be a traveler, too, if you can hear the difference between eastern Ohio and western in so few words."

"I'm a wanderer." Luman squinted past her into the dim interior of the church. He heard the murmur of many voices inside. "In many ways, Mother."

"I'm Mother Hylia. May I show you around the building?"

"I'd rather look around on my own." Luman shot her his most disarming smile, touched his coat to feel the reassuring crinkle of his freshly written himmelsbrief, and stepped inside.

He put on his glasses and looked.

The sheer astrality of the place struck him instantly. Twelve recessed niches about the outer wall of the nave were each dedicated to a saint, mostly Ohioan saints Luman knew only vaguely. And each was also clearly marked with a pattern of stars identifying it with one of the twelve signs of the zodiac, as well as, carved discreetly into corners, the customary glyphs of the signs: the stylized ram's head for Aries, and so forth. Behind the altar rose a Cahokian Yggdrasil, climbing toward a depiction of the circumpolar sky. The transept on the right—which actually pointed north, but which, if aligned with the stars in the apse, would be the eastern transept—was carved with small disclike renditions of half a sun peeping above a flat plain; the corresponding image in the southern/western transept was half a sun peeping above wiggling lines, apparently representing water.

Cahokia lay on the eastern shore of the Mississippi River— the glyphs showed the sun rising in the east over the Cahokian Bottom, and setting in the west over the Mississippi.

The saints up the right side of the nave were women, and the constellations Virgo, nearest the altar, through Aries, nearest the front door. From the door to the altar up the left side of the nave ran a succession of six male saints bearing the signs from Pisces through Libra.

And one last star-sign: on the left, above the transept marked with the setting sun, descended the one asymmetrical feature Luman could see of the entire building's ornamentation, and here again the blasphemous will to miscegenate Biblical story, star-lore, and sheer pagan nonsense, struck Luman as cheerfully and gruesomely attractive. A woman and man descended, apparently from the circumpolar north, their arms wrapped about each other. They were naked, except that they wore a snake wrapped about their loins, a snake that managed to be at the same time modest and lascivious. And the right front foot of the woman just dipped into the ecliptic plane of zodiacal imagery tying together the long chamber's dozen saints.

Adam and Eve, fleeing the garden. Wearing the snake, their tempter, as clothing. Ophiuchus, invading the zodiac and breaking its eternal perfection into the audacious prime number of thirteen.

Luman envied the vision of the architect and the artists who had put *this* together.

Only after he'd taken all this in did Luman Walters notice the people.

There were masses of huddled Children of Adam in both transepts, and along both sides of the nave. They lay on furs and blankets, they slept piled in corners, they shared out loaves of oat bread and dried river-fish.

"You look with an experienced eye." Mother Hylia stood at Luman's shoulder, uninvited.

"The people," Luman said. "Who are they?"

"Refugees. The basilica takes them in."

"Under the regent's direction? Korinn?"

"He invited the priests to do so, but they had already begun, of their own initiative."

"Ohioan?" Luman hadn't realized the Pacification had grown this heavy. "But they don't look Eldritch . . . forgive me, Firstborn to me."

"They're mostly children of Eve," Mother Hylia said. "From the Missouri."

"Is the Missouri under the Pacification?" he asked.

"The beastkind rage," Mother Hylia said. "The Missouri burns, and the Mississippi has become dangerous."

Luman nodded, took a deep breath. Cahokia was besieged from east and west both. "My eyes have been opened," he said, pointed up at the astrological images in response to the Cetean's earlier remark. "More than once."

"But not here, I think."

Luman considered. "Not here. And I think you won't open them for me today."

"It isn't my role," she agreed. "Mine is a wandering order. We administer to the spiritually poor where we find them."

"In the church? What do you call this church, anyway?"

"It's the Basilica of St. Eve and St. Adam. Sometimes called Eve and Adam's."

"And it's . . . Christian?"

Hylia said nothing.

"And what's the difference between this church and the temple?" Luman asked. "The temple where the throne is, I mean. The Temple of the Sun."

"That's the very difference." Hylia spoke slowly. "The temple houses the Serpent Throne."

The Firstborn cleric didn't seem inclined to be forthcoming, but Luman wasn't discouraged. This was the way of the initiated everywhere, and in all traditions. Initiation required persistence. The door only opened to one who asked and knocked.

A man in a match coat and slouch hat approached slowly. He held dirty hands cupped before him, and two children drifted in his wake.

Luman obliged by handing over several coins. Would the Imperial money do them any good here? With Director Schmidt cracking down, surely there would be less and less to buy every day.

"You found me in this church," he said, resuming the conversation with the priestess. "You could minister here to me. Open my eyes."

"I'm a guest here, too, and I must take care not to overstep my invitation."

"Where's the homeowner, then?" Luman felt that somehow, he was asking this wandering priestess the same question he had been asking himself about the Serpent Throne earlier that day. "With whom can I speak? Whose favor must I beg, in order to know more?"

"Cahokia is today a land with no king." Hylia might not be Cahokian herself, but her voice filled with barely restrained tears as she discussed the kingdom's state. "It's a land whose queen doesn't today walk among her people."

"You're making a distinction I do not understand."

Hylia ignored his remark. "Even some of the city's priests are away. We who are here care for the city and the land until the queen comes."

"Not the king?" Luman pressed.

"Not yet the king. The queen first, and it's past time for her to come." The priestess looked up the left side of the nave; she was seeing some sign or meaning there that escaped Luman.

Luman frowned. "Because of us? Because of the Pacification of the Ohio?"

Mother Hylia sighed. "The emperor is the *least* of the goddess's foes."

He had to try one last time. "I have money."

She looked at him with a cold eye. "Simon Magus had money. Still, Peter would give him nothing."

"You mistake me, Mother." She didn't mistake him, of course, but he had to try. "I would make a contribution. I would put some of the emperor's money into the coffers of the goddess. To pay for this church, and for the temple. I would make a sacrifice at Her altar. Wouldn't that incline Her servants to share with me Her...wisdom?"

Hylia shook her head slowly. "Get thee behind me."

And Luman Walters felt abruptly very, very small. He was indeed a parasite, in the intestine of God Himself. He stole magic, he murdered God's tiniest creatures to cast mere magical spells, he was complicit in extortion, and in starving an entire people.

What purity did it give him, if he simply refrained from pork and from liquor?

Nodding silently to the Cetean, and again to the refugees, he let himself out.

Nathaniel opened his eyes to dim orange light, flickering against the deep green crosshatch of closely needled pine boughs.

A thick cloud of tobacco smoke enveloped him; somehow it managed to smell thick and close and at the same time sweet. Spiritual. Heavenly.

The voices were still there.

And yet everything had changed.

He now heard what the voices were, he could *hear* what they *looked like*, in life or in the world of stars and spirits.

Nathaniel heard the voice of the tobacco, the asemaa plant sacred to his Ojibwe friend. *~Taste the wisdom of my leaf, ride my smoke to all the heavens, O healer!~*

He heard the slow, creaking murmur of the wood of which the barn was built, slowly drying out over decades. *~Root and twig, bark and leaf, I miss the water that once coursed within me.~*

He heard the spirits of birds, tucked away in their nests. He heard the spirit of a field mouse, thrilling with victory at having scavenged two nuts from beneath the drying barn floor. He heard the dead spirits of four slain horses, whose neighing was a rhythmic drumbeat always in his ears.

He held a drum. A physical, tangible, real-world drum, clenched to his chest and strapped over his shoulder. He'd never seen it before in his life.

Nathaniel slowly rolled himself into a sitting position. Then he laughed out loud.

His wounds were gone.

He pressed the spots where his flesh had been cut, and found them suddenly whole. His broken rib was healed. He pressed his scalp, from which had flowed so much blood, and found it knitted clean.

Above all the other spirits, above his own laughter, above the equine thrum of his horse-drum, he heard a high-pitched, shivering chord. It reminded him of the glass harp he'd heard once, on a rare trip to Richmond, when a musician had wet her fingers and then touched the rims of variously filled glass tubes to produce notes.

Only the sound he heard now was bigger. Much bigger.

As if a glass harp the size of the world were being played constantly, and most people had no idea.

The perpetual whine he had heard the first fifteen years of his life was gone.

No, not gone. The whine had resolved itself *into* this musical chord, as if something had been distorting the sound all his life, and now that impediment was gone and Nathaniel could now hear the music that had surrounded him all the time.

He picked up his tricorn hat and put it on, one corner pointing forward. It felt wrong, to his surprise. As if it no longer fit his head. His drum neighed in protest. Experimentally, he rotated the hat, pulling it down toward his ears to try to find a good fit, and discovered that it fit quite well with two corners pointing out parallel to his shoulders and a third pointing behind his head.

In other words, backward. The hat he'd worn for years now fit him . . . but only backward.

The drum whickered in contentment.

He picked up his coat and shrugged into it. Despite the tobacco smoke and the closeness of the air, the barn two steps away from the fire and the tiny sweat lodge was chilly. The coat felt entirely wrong, hanging on his shoulders. He shifted, but it didn't become more comfortable. He pulled the coat down and tried to button it.

The buttons wouldn't stay closed. The drum objected with a discordant *thump.*

Nathaniel sighed, but then laughed.

Shrugging out of his coat, he pulled the sleeves through and turned the entire thing inside out. Then he put it on again.

It fit perfectly.

The drum rumbled its contentment.

The great invisible glass harp of the universe swelled its song to a sweet climactic chord of approval and then dropped again to a background whisper.

"Nathaniel," he heard.

It was no spirit, because when the spirits spoke to him now, he knew more. This was the sound of man, a man whose voice was muffled.

In the dim light, it took him a moment to find George Randolph Isham, strapped with leather belts to the central column of the barn.

Ma'iingan? And Landon?

Nowhere to be seen.

Nathaniel took the penknife from his coat pocket—

and found that mere contact with it hurt him. He didn't cut himself, he successfully grabbed the penknife by its handle, and still he felt it wound him deeply. He heard spirits of pain shrieking tiny objections from all along the blade, and his drum boomed out its support for their wrath.

He tossed the knife aside.

"I'm sorry," he said to George. "I can't use that. Not anymore."

"Why not?" George's voice was muffled slightly because he was tied so tightly to the column.

"I don't really know." Nathaniel set about untying the earl's son. The knots were tight and expert, but Nathaniel's fingers were strong and he was determined. With a couple of minutes' work, he had freed George.

George immediately flung his arms back, sucking in a deep breath and twisting his own neck around as if to relieve a cramp. The neck made a loud *crack!* and then George began to cough. He held on to the column because his ankles were still tied.

"Are you well?" Nathaniel asked.

George caught his breath and stared. "Am I well? Am *I* well? What about *you*, Chapel? What happened to you? Are you...are you mad?"

Though George trembled with energy, Nathaniel remained calm.

"There is madness in Johnsland," he said. "It may be *because* of me, at least in part. But it isn't *in* me. I know that now."

George raised an eyebrow. "I saw you climbing this pole, and then you fell. You were unconscious, and I would have sworn... it looked as if a bear was crouched over you. You talked a lot, but it made no sense. Were you dreaming?"

Nathaniel shook his head. "No dream."

George's laugh was bitter. "A vision, then."

"The Nathaniel Chapel you knew is dead. He was torn to pieces far from here. I'm a new person."

"You're a new person who doesn't know quite how to dress." George's smile was gentle, an expression Nathaniel wasn't used to seeing on the other young man's face.

Nathaniel chuckled. "Hasn't that always been true?"

"I owe you an apology," George said.

Nathaniel smiled. "I think Landon needs to hear it more."

George nodded. "I shall protect you," he said. "But my father may want you hanged."

Nathaniel stood still a moment, contemplating the young man who would one day be Earl. "No, I don't think so. I think in fact I might be the one who can heal him."

George's smile dropped into a flat, lipless line. "That's a cruel joke, Nathaniel Chapel."

"Look at me," Nathaniel said. "I was wounded, here, here, here, here . . . and here." He pointed out the spots he'd been cut and battered, and ended with the top of his head. "And now? Do I bleed? Is my bone crushed?"

George bit his lip.

"I'm not certain I can heal your father," Nathaniel said. "But I think *perhaps* I can. And I'll certainly *try*."

He knelt and untied his ankles. George stood silent while Nathaniel worked, and when Nathaniel had finished and rose to his feet again, they met each other's gaze.

Nathaniel smiled.

George's brow furrowed. "You aren't the Nathaniel I have known all his life."

"I'm a new man," Nathaniel said. "With iron bones and a stone from the vault of heaven in my ear. I've died and been remade. I ride the horses of song through all the worlds, and if I can heal your father, I will."

George shook his head slowly. "I can't tell whether you're mad or not."

The small rear door of the barn opened and Ma'iingan came in, propping up Landon under one shoulder.

"I see you've untied the Zhaaganaashii boy-chief." Ma'iingan knelt to lower Landon onto a bed of horse tackle. "That's just fine. If I need to, I'll tie him up again."

George raised a warning finger. "You—" But then he looked at Nathaniel, frowned, and lowered his arm. "I didn't cry out. I could have."

"True. You respect your honor, Zhaaganaashii. Well done."

"But you're a liar," George said.

"Yes," Ma'iingan agreed. "It's fun."

"You're no Comanche. *Zhaaganaashii* means a white man. That's an Ojibwe word."

"Really, it means an English speaker. We have other words for the French and the Germans." Ma'iingan gave no sign of being impressed at George's knowledge. Instead, he crept back to the door through which he'd entered and peered out. "I believe the soldiers will march the wrong direction for a long time before they realize we've lost them. I see you're well, God-Has-Given. I thank Gichi-Manidoo for that."

"What do you call a Frenchman?" George asked.

"French," Ma'iingan said. To George's look of irritation, he shrugged. "There are so many of you English speakers, we needed a word to describe you all. And it isn't *English*, since that means something else."

"I thank *you* for it," Nathaniel said. "You brought me to your manidoo, who showed me the way to be healed."

Ma'iingan's eyes fell, and then he raised them again to look Nathaniel in the face. "You know I've done it for reasons of my own. But I don't wish to ask for so great a thing."

"Your son," Nathaniel said.

"Giimoodaapi." Ma'iingan nodded. "My manidoo told me you were a healer, and would help."

"You have promised healing to many people," George muttered, rubbing chafed wrists.

"I will heal him," Nathaniel said, but then he heard low, rumbling words.

~Rest. Rest. Give me back my rest.~

He could hear what kind of creature was speaking, and it broke his heart immediately.

"May I take you to the People?" Ma'iingan asked.

"I'll heal your son," Nathaniel said. He looked at George. "I'll try my best, and if your manidoo thinks I am able, then he's no doubt right. But flight may be difficult. We're surrounded."

Ma'iingan shook his head. "I led the soldiers away."

"We're surrounded by others," Nathaniel said.

Ma'iingan raised his long rifle and grabbed his powder horn in his other hand. "To save my son, I'll kill any number of Zhaaganaashii soldiers."

"Too late," Nathaniel murmured, listening again to the rumble of the voices. "They're already dead."

"No worse than you, and I ain't got it in the face."

———◦———

CHAPTER TWENTY-THREE

The Duke of Na'avu leaned heavily on his ancient staff, shivering from the cold. The Earthshaker's Rod wasn't connected to his Dukedom, but to the throne of Cahokia and to the throne that had preceded it, in lost Irra-Antum, the land of many waters. The horse was the horse of the river and the sea, and the rod belonged to he who held back the waters by sacrifice from the royal herd.

Horses, rather than sons.

By rights, it should be the staff of the queen, not one of the sacred royal items the queen used in ritual and magic, but an external sign by which to recognize her. In the absence of the monarch, Maltres Korinn bore the Earthshaker's Rod as Regent-Minister of the Serpent Throne.

The appearance of the strange-eyed half-Appalachee witch leaning on a rough-hewn imitation of the Earthshaker's Rod had shaken Korinn.

Her choice to make her rod—and his—flower had shaken him further.

Should he take that arcane act, clearly a spell cast by the girl herself, as the divine hand of Wisdom, selecting Her candidate? The arrangement he and the other candidates had come to had been, after all, merely a mortal truce. Above all, the Presentation was a way to retain the loyalty of important Cahokians who believed they deserved the throne, and whose support Korinn needed, to help his land and people survive the tightening Imperial fist.

But he needed that truce.

He couldn't shake the feeling that perhaps he was choosing his own mortal device over the plain will of the goddess. It wasn't the girl's ability to make the staff flower—that was mere wizardry. What Maltres Korinn took for a sign was rather the girl's choice of the staff and the blossoms. It was too perfect, too right.

But he still needed the seven candidates. Since the arrival of Director Schmidt and her doubling of the imposts and duties, he needed them more than ever.

So he would choose his mortal device over what might be the action of the goddess, and he would do so deliberately. He was sinning against light and knowledge, but he did it to keep his oath of office.

If the goddess could lead the young witch to unwittingly mark herself as queen, She could straighten Maltres Korinn's course, notwithstanding the painful choice he made.

"There he is," he said to the wardens. "With the gray hair. It's important not to mark him."

Alzbieta Torias's counselor Uris had been a soldier of some renown in his youth. The man had taught Kyres Elytharias to use a sword, when the princeling had been a younger son with no other prospects than to become a soldier, before Kyres had stolen the Heronblade and run off to fight the Spanish with it. Korinn had expected Uris to be the advisor standing at Alzbieta's side, and the shocking appearance of the half-civilized girl with the Nashville twang instead was another reason he'd found her so unsettling.

The wardens of Cahokia carried clubs, but now, as previously ordered, they gave these to the regent. Instead, they held fishing nets. Cahokia didn't feed its folk with fish taken from the river, and those who did fish the Mississippi along the Cahokian Bottom generally did so with hook and line rather than by trawling with a net, so Korinn had had to buy these nets from the crew of a German keelboat, unloading cotton bales and telling wide-eyed dockworkers extravagant stories about the atrocities committed by the rampaging beastkind upriver and along the Missouri.

Korinn had heard the same stories from many of the refugees Cahokia had taken in, that it had housed in its public buildings and in the homes of the willing, until they were so numerous they began to spill into the streets. The duke's own house in the city was stuffed with the suffering poor of Missouri.

And with the city itself starving, why did they flee here? Why didn't they run for the Igbo Free Cities, or Texia, or anywhere east?

Faith in Cahokia's walls. Faith in its ancient monarchy.

The memory of the Lion, perhaps.

Uris stood dickering with a Dutch Ohio Company trader, offering way too many iron coins for way too little grain, but there were fewer and fewer options. The Dutch Ohio Company had effectively become smugglers, an outlaw operation along with the few Hansa traders who slipped through the Imperial cordon with merchandise for sale. This explained why Uris, a man of responsibility and prominence, stood huddled over a pile of grain sacks in a tiny square formed by the intersection of two alleys behind a third-rate tavern. Counselor Uris looked calm, but the two sword-armed warriors at his side shifted from one foot to the other and kept their hands on their hilts.

"Now," the regent said.

The four wardens charged out into the alley. At the same moment, four wardens charged from the opposite side. They ignored the swordsmen and tackled Uris, throwing nets over him from three directions and dragging him down into a thick snowbank under a pile of short gray capes. The swordsmen drew their weapons—

"Halt!" Maltres Korinn cried. He stepped forward into the square and raised his staff of office. "By virtue of the office of Regent-Minister, and in the name of the Serpent Throne, I order you to stand down."

"I've committed no crime!" Uris snarled.

"No," Korinn agreed sadly. He removed the heavy purse from his belt and pulled supple leather gloves over his hand. "Not yet."

One of the warriors stepped between Uris and the regent. "Even the Regent-Minister of the Serpent Throne can't arrest a man without cause." He held his sword in low guard position, ready to attack, and Korinn took care to watch the man's eyes rather than be distracted by the blade. "Do you have a writ, signed by three Notaries?"

Maltres Korinn sighed. "As you are loyal to your mistress, Alzbieta Torias, stand aside."

The warrior looked back and forth between Korinn and Uris, growled, and then stood down.

"What is this treachery?" Uris barked.

The Dutch trader, ignored now by all parties, pulled a canvas tarpaulin over his cart and quietly stole around to the driver's seat. Korinn let him go. His people needed smugglers right now, and if Uris didn't buy the man's grain, someone else would.

"This treachery is my best attempt to fulfill my oath." Korinn took a handful of German silver coins from the purse.

"I too have sworn oaths!" Uris shouted.

"Flat onto his back," Korinn directed the wardens.

The doubt showed on their faces, but they did as he told him. If the goddess came for their souls, he promised himself, he would stand in Her way and take all the blame.

He pressed the first handful of silver coins against Uris's chest. The pale, loose skin of the old man's sternum blistered immediately, and he let loose a howl. He writhed and buckled, pushing to escape, and Korinn leaned forward, pushing all his weight down on the other man's ribcage.

Then he poured the rest of the coins onto Uris's chest and neck.

Each coin that struck the man raised a welt. Where a coin struck flesh and rested, it raised a blister. Korinn was no magician, and he had no way to know when the magic that bound the counselor might be canceled, so he knelt on the old man and watched until blood flowed.

Then he relented and stood.

The wardens didn't need to be told. They dragged Uris to his feet and shook him. Most of the coins fell into the snow; with gloved fingers, Maltres Korinn tore out two last thalers that had sunk into marred flesh.

Uris hung between two wardens, panting with pain... but his eyes were clear, and the look he directed at Maltres Korinn was not a glare of rage.

It was a knowing look. And it contained a hint of gratitude.

Korinn picked up his staff and leaned on it, feeling heavier than ever. "Your oath. Tell me about it."

"I swore an oath to the witch," Uris said slowly.

"Sarah, daughter of Kyres Elytharias," Maltres said. "Who might, after all, be—or become—the chosen Beloved of our goddess."

"The same. It was taken under threat of violence. And it was bound upon me with the Sevenfold Crown."

"And Alzbieta Torias?"

"The same. And the Unborn Daughter of Podebradas, Yedera."

Korinn nodded. He'd thought as much. The use of the Sevenfold

Crown didn't itself make the oath illegal or unbinding; use of the crown was the prerogative of the King or Queen of Cahokia, used when necessary and not relied upon too much. If the goddess truly wanted this child as Her queen, it might be completely proper.

But Korinn knew that he might be going against the will of the goddess.

And he was resolved to do it, anyway.

Lightning flashed on the other side of the stained glass, and the images on it glowed dimly and briefly, like the fleeting infidel icons they were. *If you ever commit idol worship,* God had caused to be written, *all your works will be nullified.* Surely, if those words applied to anyone, they applied to Etienne Ukwu.

And also to the Chevalier of New Orleans, with his many saints.

"Do we wait for an actual bolt of lightning to strike the building?" Al-Muhasib asked.

"Bah." Ravi snorted. "What for?"

"To give countenance to the lie. I've placed gunpowder on the roof. I can ignite it when lightning strikes close enough."

"You imagine there will be witnesses."

"This is a large city, O son of Isaac. Perhaps you've noticed this. And it's a city accustomed to rain. Someone will notice that the fire appeared to begin inside the building."

"The Bishop of New Orleans is a man of many and strange resources, O son of Ishmael. Perhaps *you* have noticed *this.* Even if lightning were to strike the roof of this Christian temple and ignite it in truth, I have no doubt the bishop would suborn a mob of witnesses to perjure themselves and claim they had seen the chevalier himself lay a torch to the altar."

"And the chevalier would suborn a separate mob to claim that God Himself had rolled back the thundercloud, shouted aloud the sins of the bishop in evident displeasure, and then personally hurled the thunderbolt, being divinely disappointed only in the fact of having not in fact killed the bishop with the same throw."

"Here you're mistaken theologically, Nabil. I don't think even the Christian god would miss, once he started throwing lightning. Certainly, the God of Sinai would not."

"Nor would the Lord of Mecca."

"You're both correct, and therefore you should both shut your mouths in satisfaction at having won the argument." Abd al-Wahid rolled a casket of powder into place against one of the nave's columns. "Each man will blame the other, regardless. Each will have witnesses, each will have believers."

"I would be sad to believe that this rendered our actions pointless." Zayyid had placed a cask of powder on each of the four sides of the altar, and was now binding them together tightly with rope.

"You're fools if you imagine that this is a contest about right and wrong." Abd al-Wahid wiped sweat and humidity from his forehead as thunder rolled in the Place d'Armes outside. "This is a struggle between wrong and wrong. Between two wicked men, two idolaters, a corrupt governor and a racketeer. And most of the people of New Orleans see them clearly as such, and are perfectly content to have a corrupt man as their leader. This contest is simply to decide which corrupt man it will be."

"Because the people of New Orleans wish to see which corrupt man God will choose to anoint?" Al-Muhasib scratched the back of his neck.

Abd al-Wahid shook his head. "The people of New Orleans wish to see which corrupt man is more powerful. The more powerful their corrupt leader, the more he can do for them."

"Has it always been this way in New Orleans?" Ravi sloshed oil over several pews. "In the New World?"

"It has always been this way among the children of Adam. For this, thank God that you are a mameluke. Devotion brings clarity. Simplicity makes it easy to be honest."

This observation occasioned emphatic nods all around, curses of agreement, and spitting on the cathedral floor.

"If the chevalier burns down the cathedral," Zayyid asked, "and appoints his own bishop, what will Ukwu do to retaliate? Burn down the Palais?"

"I expect we'll find out." Abd al-Wahid took a deep breath. He wanted this contest between petty thieves and corrupt murderers to end, so he could return to the presence of the Caliph and reap his reward for having done away with the rebel Talleyrand.

"Shouldn't we just kill the priest?" Al-Muhasib asked.

"We've tried, fool," Ravi said.

"If he comes out tonight, we try again," Abd al-Wahid added. "For al-Farangi. For now...fire the gunpowder."

Al-Muhasib padded amiably to the staircase, where gunpowder fuses climbed up the steps to the rooftop and down into the crypt.

Zayyid laid a gunpowder fuse from the altar to the staircase and joined al-Muhasib. They both nodded at Abd al-Wahid.

"Give me a moment." Ravi smashed a jar of oil against the cathedral's rood screen, and then hurled one more against the wooden furnishings of a side chapel.

"Always the slow one, O Jew," al-Muhasib teased his friend. "Always last."

"The first shall be last." Ravi walked toward the other two. "By which we see that my tardiness is a true sign of the excellence and primogeniture of Abraham's son Isaac."

"Isaac by your own Jewish record was the second son."

"So was Jacob, who supplanted Esau." Ravi shrugged. "And neither was Joseph the eldest, and yet he rose to the throne of Egypt. If you were to read the words of Moses, O son of the desert, you would see that sometimes God favors one of the sons who is not the first. The last shall be first."

"The words of Moses are the words of a Jew." Al-Muhasib shrugged. "If I wish to hear the words of a Jew, I can go to any bazaar and haggle to buy an ass."

"Moses was a Levite, in fact." Ravi's cheerful smile was illuminated in many colors by another flash of lightning outside. "King David was a Jew."

"You make a Jew distinction. I understand it not, and neither do I care. In any case, we know from the Qur'an that the son who ascended Mount Moriah with his father Abraham was Ishmael, and not Isaac. Now get over here so you aren't blown to pieces when I ignite this fuse."

The four knelt together, facing four separate directions, each holding flint and steel in hand. "I shall count down," Ravi offered. "Shalosh, shtem, achat..."

The numbers were in Hebrew.

"Jew," al-Muhasib muttered.

"Ephes," Ravi said, finishing his count.

They struck fire.

Four gunpowder fuses ignited, burning quickly into the stairwell, toward the altar, toward the columns lining the nave, and in the direction of the pews. The sudden red flame threw tall shadows against the walls and ceiling of the cathedral, shadows that didn't illuminate any of the idolatrous art but instead made glorious patterns of light and darkness. For the first time, Abd al-Wahid found the interior of the building beautiful, and he stood to look at it.

"Call it the action of a Jew if you will," Ravi said, "but I'm leaving now."

The four of them exited the rear of the cathedral onto a dirt courtyard, the dirt packed so hard by a century of feet that even this torrential winter rain could not turn it into mud. Only a few lights shone in view of this tiny plaza, from the windows of the Polite monastery and from the City Council building. The mamelukes crossed the square and walked as far as they could down the street beyond and still keep the cathedral in view. Finding an open tavern with a boardwalk beneath a long balcony, they turned and waited in the shadow outside dimly lit windows.

They didn't wait long.

Ka-boom!

The first explosion was muffled. Abd al-Wahid felt it with his feet as much as he heard it with his ears. He saw no visible sign of it, and but for his own part in planting the explosive powder, he wouldn't have known the explosion had happened in the cathedral.

"The altar?" al-Muhasib asked.

Zayyid shook his head. "When the altar goes, you'll know it. That was your crypt."

Al-Muhasib frowned. "I had expected more."

"You did your work well," Ravi said. "It's a solid building. Wait."

KA-BOOM!

With a brilliant white flash, the powder on the roof blew. One of the pointed spires on the front of the cathedral vanished in the flash, either incinerated by the explosion or perhaps knocked off the front of the building. Abd al-Wahid nodded grimly, feeling no satisfaction other than in the fact of success.

"Indeed, I did my work well," al-Muhasib said. Ravi clapped him on the shoulder.

"Where is Omar?" Zayyid asked. "Shouldn't he have rejoined us by now?"

"He's watching," Abd al-Wahid said.

The cathedral roof sagged sharply.

"I fear the building will collapse before my true artistry can be seen," Zayyid murmured.

Ka-boom!

The explosion within the building was followed immediately by the shattering of a large stained-glass window at the rear of the building. The object that hurtled through the glass and wrecked it was large and blocky, and it wasn't until it thudded to rest, embedding itself several feet deep in the dueling ground behind the cathedral that Abd al-Wahid realized what it was.

The altar, or at least a significant chunk of it.

Zayyid beamed in the dim light. "Now *that* required the touch of an artist. The chevalier can say that God was so angry with this renegade bishop that He used His lightning to remove the altar from the cathedral."

"Only there is no lightning," Ravi pointed out.

At that moment, lightning flashed.

"A little bit late," Zayyid admitted, "but that will do."

"I *am* a little bit late," said a quiet voice behind them in New Orleans French. "But perhaps my arrival will do, nonetheless."

Abd al-Wahid turned, hoping to see the rebel bishop, and was disappointed to find instead the idolater's bodyguard. The large man held a pistol in either hand and his face was stony.

"Armand," he said, also in French. "Isn't that your name?"

"Oui." Armand nodded his head. "And you're the mussulman fanatics who serve the chevalier."

"We're the mussulman *warriors* who serve God, and God's deputy. We've agreed to perform a task for the chevalier."

"I can't kill all of you," Armand said to Abd al-Wahid. "But I think if I kill *you*, it will be enough. You're the leader, aren't you? The prince-capitaine? If I think if I kill you, the others will be discouraged, they'll lack direction, a sense of mission, perhaps they'll simply go home."

Abd al-Wahid nodded. "But before you kill me, I ask you to carry your master a message from the chevalier."

"Go to hell," the bodyguard grunted. "I will carry no message for you." He raised his pistols, cocking the hammers with his thumbs—

blood spilled from Armand's mouth suddenly, pouring down his chest as the tip of a knife protruded from his sternum—

Armand sank to the boardwalk, but his eyes glared hatred as he fell. Raising his pistols, he aimed first at Abd al-Wahid—

but his arm skewed sideways, his aim faltering—

bang!

Zayyid toppled backward and fell into the mud, instantly still.

Bang!

Armand's second shot struck Abd al-Wahid, but in the shoulder. Abd al-Wahid staggered sideways, keeping his footing with effort.

Armand fell to the wood of the boardwalk. Above him stood Omar al-Talib, who now pulled his blade from the dead man's back and wiped blood from the weapon on Armand's waistcoat.

"It's I who am too late," Omar said. "Forgive me, Prince-Capitaine."

"Zayyid is dead!" Ravi cried, his voice bitter.

"I take it the bishop himself hasn't emerged," Omar said.

"I haven't seen him. Perhaps he's too cunning to respond to this bait. Perhaps he's engaged in other tasks."

"Perhaps he doesn't care about the cathedral," Ravi suggested.

Abd al-Wahid turned to look at the church, just in time to see the roof collapse, and flames lick up the sagging walls.

"Perhaps." He leaned on Omar's shoulder, both to keep himself upright and to reassure al-Talib. "But you *will* carry a message, my friend," he said to Armand's corpse. "You will."

Sarah awoke to burning pain.

"Please don't resist," said the voice of Maltres Korinn in her ear. "The pain will end soon."

"Son of a bitch!" she snapped.

The darkness she saw out of her natural eye told her it was still night—in fact, that it was the wee hours of the morning, when all the city's fires had all been dimmed—and the sky was still overcast.

Through her unnatural eye, her father-gifted witchy eye, she saw the auras of men. Calvin, on the ground in the corner of the room, resentful and angry—tied up? Counselor Uris, who seemed conflicted; the satisfaction of revenge struggled within him against tendrils of doubt. Her gramarye-powered hold on him had disappeared. Warriors she didn't know, dutiful, confused, indifferent. Maltres Korinn leaning over her, trembling with fear.

Silver manacles on Sarah's wrists.

"Damn you!" she raged. "I'm your queen!"

Alzbieta Torias had betrayed her. It had to be the case—she and the Handmaid had agreed that Sarah would accompany her unseen to the Presentation, and now that the rite was imminent, her cousin had had second thoughts.

"I have no queen," Korinn said softly. "Not yet. And as regent, I'm taking the only course of action I may."

The men dragged her to her feet and along the tunnel toward the nearest exit. She kicked, but fighting not to scream in pain took most of her strength, and her kicks were feeble and inaccurate. Calvin staggered behind her, also prisoner and held by two men.

At the exit, Uris tugged Korinn's elbow. "Is it safe to leave the man Lee here? He and his beastkind rabble are dangerous."

"Safe?" Korinn's laugh was dry and mocking. "Safe, counselor Uris? When was the last time you did anything that was safe? When was the last time *I* did a safe thing?"

"Lee is dangerous." Uris's voice was sullen.

"By my count, I haven't done a safe thing in fifteen years. We leave Lee and the woman. And all the beastkind. We don't have enough cells to hold them all in the Hall of Onandagos, and I have no will to pay what it would cost to kill them now. Frankly, the beastkind within the walls of my city are much less of a threat than the beastkind without. Besides, they are surrounded."

"Be wary of him," Uris insisted.

"As I'm wary of everyone," Korinn agreed. "Come."

Maltres Korinn, Sarah now saw, carried the regalia. His own staff he had laid aside somewhere, and he carried Sarah's satchel holding the Sevenfold Crown, the Orb of Etyles, and the Heronplow in front of him with both hands. His erect posture, his stiff arms, and his bowed head made him look like a page, carrying out an official duty, or a priest carrying forward wafer and wine to the altar.

In the street, Cal made his move.

He threw himself sideways and into one of the men holding him. Wheeling and off-balance, he then slammed his own forehead into the face of the other man and lurched away. Sarah could only see his aura, but somehow Cal must have removed a gag from his mouth, because he staggered across the street shouting. "O Lord, is there no help for the widow's son?"

Two of the warriors tackled him, one kicking his legs out from under him and the other cracking the pommel of his sword into Calvin's skull several times.

"Cal," Sarah called. "Calvin, stop!"

"Is there no help?" Cal tried again, and got punched again in the temple. "Help for the widow's son...?"

"Cal!" Sarah cried.

He fell silent, and his captors dragged Calvin Calhoun to his feet.

"As it happens, Mr. Calhoun," Maltres Korinn said slowly. "I'm Grand Riverine Master of the Na'avu Lodge."

"Riverine...?" Cal's voice sounded groggy.

"Ohio Rite."

"You think you're actin' on the square with me, do you?" Cal demanded.

Korinn shook his head. "I would very much like to come to your aid, as I'd very much like to do anything other than what I find myself compelled to do. Gyntres, Kallyr... I know you."

Sarah looked at the two men he addressed. Their auras looked less conflicted than his did.

"We understand, Riverine Master," one of them said.

A patch of open star-filled sky and Sarah's normal eye adjusting to light allowed her to see as the soldiers pulled a gag back up over Cal's mouth, and then drag the two of them away. As Alzbieta Torias's house receded into the night, Sarah looked back with her witchy eye and saw squads of soldiers squatting behind protective barricades around all sides of the house. Within, through the windows, she saw hints of beastkind auras crouched defensively.

Someone had broken her magical hold over counselor Uris. Had Alzbieta done it?

Uris pulled a bag over Sarah's head, shutting off all her vision.

Her captors dragged her through snow and over stone. A bitterly cold wind scorched the skin of her neck and arms where it was exposed. She tried to count to be able to guess at the passage of time, but the shattering pain in her arms and the occasional thumps as she was knocked against a wall or bumped on steps distracted her and she gave up. Still, the time that passed was minutes, and not hours, and then she was dropped onto a wooden board. Her manacles were stripped away and she smelled greasy straw.

Another body struck the board beside her, and then she heard a loud *click*.

Sarah pulled the sack from her head.

She and Calvin lay on a broad plank bed, strewn only thinly with old straw. The bed hung by two chains from one stone wall of a windowless cell. Three walls of the chamber were stone, and the fourth consisted of iron bars, including an iron door, that was shut. Beyond the bars, in the other half of the stone chamber, stood Korinn, Uris, and the Cahokian warriors. Korinn held her satchel with reverence. A bracket in the wall clutched a single torch, and smoke drifted lazily up to a barred skylight Sarah could barely see, far overhead.

"*Dormite!*" she shouted, and felt the spell die within her.

"We Firstborn are a race that produces many wizards." Maltres Korinn seemed sad. "The Queens and Kings of Cahokia have long experience imprisoning upstart sorcerer cousins. The mortar that holds together the stones of this chamber is wound through with threads of silver filigree. It would take a mighty wizard to cast any kind of spell in here."

"*Dormite!*" Sarah shouted again, willing her soul into the spell, trying to knock her captors unconscious.

Instead, her mind hit a wall, and the sheer force of the rebound hurled her to the floor and took her breath away.

"Until the Presentation," Korinn said. "I have no legal cause to hold you, and I do this out of political necessity. But I must lock you away for now."

"When I become your queen, you'll regret this day."

"I regret it already." Korinn raised her shoulder bag slightly. "I'll take good care of these. I know what they are."

"And you, Uris," Sarah hissed. "Oathbreaker."

"You *forced* an oath upon me," Uris said. "I have older and greater oaths, to the lady Torias."

"Is she complicit in this?" Sarah asked. "She breaks her oath, too."

"I know the lady Torias to be compassionate," Uris said. "After the Presentation, when the goddess selects her, I know she'll show you as much mercy as you'll accept."

"*If* the goddess selects her," Korinn said pointedly.

Uris nodded his head in deference. As the front of his tunic opened with the nod, Sarah saw a constellation of blisters, welts, and boils across his chest. Looking down at her own wrists, she saw the same corruption.

"You made him do this," she accused Korinn.

"I freed him of your spell," the Regent-Minister admitted. "And I invited him to help me protect the Presentation from your interference."

"And when the Imperials find out what you've done, and ask you to turn me over to them?"

"I don't intend to tell them what I've done," Korinn said. "Indeed, I'm hiding you from them."

"But if they directly asked, you'd do it, wouldn't you? You'd talk about how sorry you feel, and how it's just your duty, and you don't really want to . . . but you'd hand me over in a heartbeat, if you thought you had to."

"With regret, yes. If you truly belong to the goddess, and I truly had to do so . . . I would trust in Her to save you."

"You'll pay for this," Sarah promised.

"I'm already paying."

Without another word, Maltres Korinn turned and left. His warriors followed him, leaving Uris behind.

"Want to gloat?" Sarah goaded the man, but she knew better. Storming through his aura was a mixture of emotions, only one of which was satisfaction. Mostly, she saw regret, uncertainty, hesitation, and sorrow.

"Maltres Korinn is a good man, doing the best he can by his lights. He won't turn you over to the Emperor."

Sarah snorted. "Every man does the best he can by his own lights. Somehow, half of 'em still end up murderers and thieves."

"I owed it to Sherem," Uris said. "I *had* to do this. I won't let Korinn turn you over to the Emperor Thomas."

"The hell you won't."

Uris took a deep breath.

"The hell you won't!" Sarah screamed again as he passed out a doorway and disappeared. "The hell you won't!"

"Mmmng," Calvin groaned from the bed.

It hurt her to use her hands, but Sarah pulled the gag off Calvin's mouth and then untied his wrists. He looked bad—dark bruises were quickly filling in his eye sockets, and the skin around both temples and along one side of his jaw was lacerated.

He noticed her staring. "Jerusalem, Sarah, I weren't e'er a *good*-lookin' man."

She shook her head. "Handsomer'n I am, Calvin Calhoun."

"That's a confounded lot of nonsense and you know it." Cal looked her right in the eyes as he spoke. "You're beautiful, Sarah. Most you can say about my face is it's got character. More character than e'er, right about now."

She found her vision blurred by a sudden upwelling of emotion. Thank goodness only Calvin was here to see her cry. "You're a good man, Calvin."

Cal shrugged, grinned, and then winced at the pain the grin cost him. "Lord hates a man as can't call a spade a spade."

"Then I reckon I better point out another spade. We're prisoners. Stuck here, and I got no idea what's comin' down the pike."

Cal groaned as he climbed to his feet. Shuffling across the cell, he tested the door, then each of the bars in turns—all firm. He tried and found he could pass his skinny arms between the bars, but to no purpose, as there was nothing within reach.

"I heard that about the silver," he mumbled. His lips were starting to puff up. "I reckon they's no hexin' us outta this jam."

She nodded. "Sir William might break free, but it don't look too good for him, either. I reckon he's outnumbered four or five to one, hunkered down in that house."

Cal saw her wrists for the first time and gasped. "What happened?"

"Silver," she said. "Stopped me from hexin' us free when they captured us."

"You're all torn up."

"No worse than you," she said, "and I ain't got it in the face."

He lowered himself heavily onto the planks. "Well, at least we're torn up together."

"In the name of mercy, do not do this!" Chigozie begged.

Kort looked at him with cold black eyes. "Mercy? Mercy isn't a quality of beasts. To rut, is a thing a beast does. To eat, yes. To battle for territory, for food or for a mate. To sleep. To show mercy? It is not of the beasts."

Chigozie stood on a boulder, raising his hands heavenward and imploring. In one hand, he held his cross. Below him stretched out a rocky, irregular slope that descended toward the Mississippi, strewn with chasms, boulders, and stunted trees; the worst of its irregularities hid beneath a thick blanket of snow, stained with mud and blood. A horde of beastkind descended the slope, slinking, creeping, or leaping as suited their respective limbs. On the other side of the river lay docks, from which now fled a motley assortment of galleys, yachts, and keelboats. Behind the docks rose walls that must belong to Cahokia—they looked like tree trunks, closely knit together by their limbs, and on the ramparts stood Ophidians with their rounded steel helmets and their longbows and rifles.

The beastkind were gathering on the western shore, gibbering and roaring challenges, and Cahokia battened down its hatches for an animal storm.

"I have known beastkind to read," Chigozie said. "I have known them to recite poetry."

"In the heart of the Heron King's palace, the beastkind learn to do many things to please their lord."

"You see? And may you not learn to show mercy to please the Lord?"

"*My* lord." Kort's eyes glittered. Behind him, the lamprey-headed, cat-limbed beastman Aanik hissed, a noise that sounded like laughter. "*My* lord, not yours. And what pleases *my* lord Simon Sword now is that we destroy the Firstborn. Zomas in the south, and Cahokia in the east."

"No!" Chigozie struggled to his feet, his weary muscles strengthened with the sudden conviction that this was his purpose. "No, it is not a question of *my* lord and *your* lord, but of *the* Lord, the god of heaven and earth and all who are in it."

"Your god is weak," Kort rumbled.

"Weak!" Aanik hissed again and moved closer to Chigozie, sidling past Kort's shoulder as his lamprey mouth full of teeth swung from side to side.

"There is only one god!" Chigozie cried.

"There is the Heron King," Kort said.

"He is a spirit," Chigozie insisted. "A creature. A monster."

Kort shrugged. "Call him what you will. I served the monster who was the father, who bade me roam the Great Green Wood in peace. Now I serve the monster who is the son, and he bids me rampage. We feed upon the Missouri, and then we feed upon Cahokia. If he is a monster, then the monster who is the Heron King is mightier than your god."

Chigozie pulled the cross from his neck and held it up to ward off Kort's words. "Take it back!"

A beastwife struggling up the slope against the tide of her kind, a giant with a cow's head, saw Chigozie's cross and stopped.

Kort shrugged. "My god leads me to crush his enemies. Your god led you to kill your own women. In your heart, you know it must be true."

"I killed those women to show them mercy!" Chigozie yelled, barely hearing himself or Kort above the tumult of the beasts.

Kort bellowed. "In that case, my god commands me to give mercy to the people of Cahokia! In the name of the mercy you adore so much, I'll kill every man, woman, and child in that place!"

Aanik hissed and lunged forward. The lamprey mouth splayed wide, revealing rows of teeth, and the creature hurtled toward Chigozie—

Kort caught Aanik by the tail and yanked, slamming the other beastman to the ground.

Aanik hissed in protest.

Kort laughed.

"What is it?" Chigozie asked.

The cow-headed beastwife moved closer. She dragged a club nearly as long as Chigozie was tall. Chigozie edged away from her, mistrustful of any beastkind he didn't know.

"I challenge him," Aanik hissed. "If his god is mighty, his god will protect him."

Kort looked to Chigozie.

Chigozie hesitated. "God can indeed do anything."

"Can your god save you, a weakling with a tender heart and no weapons, from this ferocious beast?" Kort sounded amused.

"God can do anything," Chigozie repeated.

"You understand that Aanik wishes to eat you."

Aanik hissed.

He couldn't win. Chigozie knew that. And Aanik *did* want to eat him.

But God *could* do anything. Had not God made the sun stand still for Joshua? Had not Samson slain the Philistines with the jawbone of an ass, by the power of God? Had not God brought down the walls of Jericho?

And if God had brought Chigozie here, it was for a reason. God would see him through.

But what if the reason God had brought Chigozie here was so that Aanik would eat him? What if Chigozie's value to God was as a martyr and a witness? What if God's plan *required* Chigozie to die? Maybe his death at the hands of a merciless beast would show Kort and the others the value of mercy. Maybe by his death, Chigozie could save lives.

To his surprise, the thought strengthened Chigozie's resolution.

"God can do anything." He brandished his cross. "If I fight Aanik and I live, then will you believe?"

"It would take an intervention of your god," Kort said.

"An act of God," Chigozie said. "A miracle. If I fight Aanik and live, it will be a miracle, and you will believe in God."

"I will believe in your god," Kort agreed, nodding his shaggy bison head. "And if you die, I'll tell every child of Adam I meet for the remainder of my life about the fool I once knew who believed his god would save him, and who instead was eaten by beastmen."

"Beast*men*?" Chigozie hesitated.

"I'll eat of your flesh myself," Kort added. "As you eat of the flesh of your strange, merciful, weakling god."

Chigozie's heart pounded like a blacksmith's hammer in his ears.

"Very well." He raised his cross. "A challenge."

Aanik hissed, long and low.

Kort stepped back, crossing muscular arms over his chest. Any faint and unexpressed hopes Chigozie might have had that Kort would act as his protector disappeared instantly.

Aanik leaped to the attack, his forelegs' cat-claws extended, his hind legs' claws rising as he jumped, his mouth open and teeth splayed. Aanik would land in a hurricano of tooth and talon that would reduce Chigozie to ribbons of flesh in an instant.

God of my father, help me.

A beastkind warrior sprang over the edge of Chigozie's boulder and rammed head-first into Aanik's side. The lamprey-cat spun sideways, yowling, and landed rump-first against a jagged tree stump.

The intervening beastwife was the cow-headed creature who had been watching Chigozie's earlier pleading. Now she stood perched in a crouch on the boulder, huffing and snorting and staring down at Aanik through slitted eyes.

Aanik hissed.

"Is this collusion?" Kort roared. "Who are you, cow?"

The cow bellowed back, with no words Chigozie could understand.

Chigozie raised his cross higher. "God of my father," he said aloud this time, "help me!"

Aanik sprang forward again, and the cow-headed warrior leaped at the same moment. They collided shoulder to shoulder in mid-air, then fell to the ground with a heavy thud. The cow head-butted the lamprey and then battered it with her club, but then the lamprey's hind legs slashed at the cow's belly, inflicting long red gashes.

The cow staggered away, and Aanik jumped at Chigozie again.

"I'd give a great deal just now to be
able to lob flaming beehives at the enemy."

⇒•⇐

CHAPTER TWENTY-FOUR

"Do you think His Holiness Bishop Planchet cuts a more striking figure than I do as bishop?" Etienne clenched his mother's locket in his fist and looked through the nearly shut blinds of the hotel room.

The building belonged to Onyinye Diokpo, though apparently through such a tangle of Philadelphia joint-stock companies and at least one partnership headquartered in New Amsterdam that it would take, Onyinye had cheerfully assured Etienne, Robespierre himself, the greatest legal luminary of the Old World, and a hundred hand-picked deputies, a century to find the true ownership.

Etienne had gratefully pointed out that he wouldn't need a century. On the other hand, if the chevalier once got it into his head that hotel owners in general were in opposition to him, or was in doubt as to which hotels might belong to Onyinye, he might take action by burning them all down.

Onyinye was a tough woman. She hadn't batted an eye at the loss of one of her employees, a distant relation, in the *Onu Nke Ihunanya*. She'd known about Etienne's planned raid to snatch the chevalier's mambo, and that thought gave Etienne even more pause: had Onyinye deliberately sacrificed one of her own cousins? How much must the Igbo hôtelière hate the Chevalier of New Orleans?

After the raid, she had summoned some large, cheerful cousins from Montgomery and Jackson. Eoin Kennedie had, without being asked, supplemented the Igbo fighters with a clan or two of bent-nosed, cursing Irishmen.

Add to that the rising number of gendarmes in the chevalier's service, and New Orleans felt on the verge of explosion.

August Planchet stood on the steps of what had been, until recently, the St. Louis Cathedral. Now it was a ruin that had only stopped smoking two days earlier. The Bishop of Miami, who had so nervously anointed Etienne himself not so long ago, now settled the episcopal mitre on the former beadle's head.

"I think you don't truly care," Monsieur Bondí said. "It amuses you to have people regard you as vain. Perhaps they take you less seriously when they believe you're a peacock. But I know you better than that."

"And still you stay with me."

Bondí grunted.

"Armand is dead. We don't even have his body, so there can be no decent funeral. And still you stay."

"You pay me. And where else would I have this much fun?"

"A lunatic asylum, perhaps?" Etienne suggested. "A whorehouse staffed by syphilitics? A sinking ship in a tropical storm?"

"No," Bondí answered. "This is more fun than any of those. For instance, the very minute I learned the cathedral was on fire, I knew what opportunities for graft there would be in the reconstruction, and how much you would want that contract. And to win that bid, I got to create two new joint-stock companies and have the legs of four men broken."

"You're a good man, Monsieur Bondí."

"Also, I have five other companies submitting fraudulent insurance claims for property damaged in the fire." Bondí grunted. "I'll say this one thing, since we're discussing how entertaining it is to be in your employ."

"Tell me."

"I think it's highly ironic that you made that petty criminal Planchet an honest man, and now the chevalier is using him to replace you."

"It makes a great deal of sense, if the chevalier is anxious to retain control over the money. Planchet knows where it all is, whereas if the chevalier brings a stranger into the parish, he risks being robbed blind. Indeed, the appointment makes so much sense, I wonder whether it was the chevalier who initiated that conversation, or Planchet. Also, this is New Orleans. The thief replaces the thief with a thief." Etienne shrugged and smiled. "I replaced Bishop de Bienville as criminal long before I replaced him as priest. So it goes, in this city at least."

Monsieur Bondí snorted.

The Bishop of Miami began to recite the words of one hundred and ninth Psalm: "*Dixit Dominus Domino meo sede a dextris meis donec ponam inimicos tuos scabilum pedum tuorum.*" *I will make thine enemies thy footstool.*

Would heaven do that for the new Bishop Planchet, and for his master, the Chevalier Le Moyne?

May it not be so, my son. Take this power yourself.

Etienne stepped out of his shoes and spread his feet.

"Boss?" Monsieur Bondí only looked perplexed.

The Bishop of Miami knelt to anoint Planchet's feet from a small cruse of sanctified oil. Etienne detected the presence of the Brides, unseen as always. Their power swelled within him and he felt their tears and hair upon his bare feet.

He sighed deeply.

Monsieur Bondí stepped back a few feet. "Etienne?"

"*Virgam fortitudinis tuae emittet Dominus ex Sion dominare in media inimicorum tuorum.*" Miami anointed the palms of Planchet's hands and pressed into them the episcopal scepter.

Etienne's Latin, like his Greek, was modest, but he knew enough.

Virga was the bishop's rod. And it was so close to *virgo*, a virgin.

He placed his mother's locket in his waistcoat pocket and stood with hands open, palms up. He felt the Brides, the Virgins, anoint his palms with their kisses. Then he filled his own hand with his mother's softly vibrating locket.

"*Populi tui spontanei erunt in due fortitudinis tuae in montibus sanctis quasi de vulva orietur tibi ros adulescentiae tuae.*" *Among sacred mountains, as if from the womb.*

Reborn. Delivered by his mother from the wombs of his own two Brides.

Etienne sucked air into his lungs like a newborn babe and squeezed it out again, stretching his back and shoulders and staring at the plastered white ceiling. He felt the weariness of his struggle leave him and new life enter.

The remaining words of the Bishop of Miami came to him on the wings of a melody with no source, and spoke truth directly to his soul. Etienne closed his eyes and listened.

Iuravit Dominus et not paenitebit eum
Tu es sacerdos in aeternum secundum ordindem
Melchisedech
Dominus ad dexteram tuam percussit in die furoris
sui reges
Iudicabit in gentibus implebit valles percutiet caput
in terra multa
De torrente in via bibet propterea exaltabit caput

"Monsieur Bondí," he said. The room looked lighter.

"Boss?" Monsieur Bondí's voice was tentative.

Etienne looked, and found his accountant cringing in the corner. "What's wrong?"

"Etienne...you're glowing."

Etienne laughed. "Then it's time."

Bondí appeared to relax, but not much. "For what?"

"Tonight." Etienne turned away from the window. "Tonight, I must address my people."

"Shall I send a message inviting...your people?"

"No. The Brides are summoning them already."

Jacob Hop lived on Sarah's enchanted coffee.

He found that it had more effect, the less food he ate. True, he became jittery and nervous, and more than once he found himself jumping at shadows or whipping around to fire his pistol at a branch swaying in the breeze. The woods around him seemed to ring sometimes with the shouts of Dutch children skating on the canals of New Amsterdam, and sometimes with the strangled cries of the murdered and the sacrificed.

But he also walked at a pace he would ordinarily have described as *running*.

He learned to ignore the hunger pains.

Eating very little, and stopping only to lie on his back and raise his feet in the air, leaning them against tree trunks to allow the blood to drain, Jacob also slept only one night in two. It added to the slippery feeling he had behind the eyes, as if increasingly the world he was looking at was not the real world, but the creation of his own shaky mind.

It also meant he covered great distances at very high speed. Wrapped against the bitter cold in furs over his blue Imperial coat, he must have looked from a distance like a monster.

When he lay on his back to rest, he checked the slate. From time to time, words appeared there, written by Sarah. With a lump of white chalk she'd given him, he wrote back to inform her of his progress by identifying town signboards he'd seen and highways he'd crossed.

The bricks from which his mind built the world were memories from two different lives, and the life of Simon Sword was much longer. He found that, being alone, he was immersed more and more in the memories of the violent manifestation of the Heron King, so much so that at times he was unsure where Jacob Hop ended and Simon Sword began. When words didn't appear on the slate, he took to thumbing through his Tarocks. The pasteboard, wetted multiple times by snow and worn from travel, was beginning to split and pull apart, but he couldn't stop playing with the cards. He did it to remember his friends: the Horseman was Bill, especially since his recent injures; the Hanged Man, Uris; the Serpent, Sarah, because he needed the Virgin to be Yedera; the Priest was Alzbieta and the Widow was Cathy and the Drunkard was the head-wounded Polite Sherem, but Jake could find no easy match for Calvin in the Major Arcana. Instead he assigned Calvin to be a character who appeared in numbered cards of the suits of Shields and Swords, a buckskinner in fringed leather garb with a long rifle. The hair was the wrong color, but the narrow, homely face was just about perfect.

Seeing his friends in the Tarock helped. It brought the Jacob Hop memories to the fore, and kept Simon Sword in the dark recesses.

There was a Beastkind card, but since it showed a creature like a minotaur, with a bull's head and tail, Jake had a hard time thinking of it as Chikaak.

First, he memorized the knots—the Ophidian *letters* entwined around the images of the Major Arcana. Later, he fixed into his mind the images on the cards themselves, Major and Minor Arcana both. The Major Arcana were more interesting at first sight, containing the more baroque and sometimes grotesque images, but he soon realized that the images of each of the four suits could be read to tell a story. Four separate stories, two about a man, the frontiersman who resembled Cal, and two about a woman.

And did the four stories intertwine?

Little details from the Major Arcana were sprinkled throughout the Minor Arcana, as well, as if the named cards wanted to intrude into the tales.

And then he found his mind trying to insert him into the stories.

And, perhaps because of the coffee and the sleep deprivation, he learned that he could in his mind insert facts—stations along his road, numbers of steps taken, number of days traveled, and more—into the images on the cards, and the images held the facts in place, and held them in order.

He filed that trick away for future use.

When he slept, he dreamed of running.

At all times, he marched holding the Franklin medallion, the one given to him by the chevalier's dying Seneschal atop the Serpent Mound. He was to give it to Franklin, the dying man had said. He'd said it after trying to get assistance from Jacob, as if Jacob were a Freemason, which he wasn't.

Should he become one?

And who was *Franklin*?

He avoided the forces of the Pacification. This was difficult because Imperial militia or Company men or occasionally Imperial soldiers held all the major crossroads. He eluded them by following old tracks, sometimes even animal trails. These paths were more deeply buried in snow, but only rarely traveled, except by the occasional Sauk or Shawnee.

Several times, at night, he saw masked parties of armed Firstborn racing through the forest. The Firstborn groups were small, and they looked always looked hungry, so when Jacob saw them carrying sacks of grain or squashes, or with weapons soiled with (presumably Imperial) blood, he cheered them silently, in his heart.

Without deviating from his course; Jacob Hop was bound for Johnsland.

Chigozie threw himself from the rock. It was awkward and off-balance, but he landed more or less on his feet and rolled away without injury.

Aanik's lunge missed, and the lamprey-cat sailed over the spot where Chigozie had stood, landing in a bramble of wild berries.

Chigozie rose and found himself beside a dead tree. Seizing a branch the size of his arm in both hands, he leaned against it with all his weight and snapped it off. The branch had a long smooth stretch that could accommodate both Chigozie's hands, and ended in a gnarled knot of wood where it had once sprouted from the tree's trunk. And it was heavy; it would make a serviceable club.

Aanik charged on all fours, shoulders down and lamprey-like head raised and hissing. Chigozie's club felt very tiny in his hands. "God of my father—" was all he had time for, and then Aanik was bearing down, all his teeth glistening moist and evil and the muscles beneath his pelt bunching and stretching as inexorably as a watermill.

Chigozie raised his club to swing it—

and the cow-headed beastwife jumped straight toward the lamprey-cat, knocking them both to the ground in a tangle of arms and legs.

She dropped her club.

Chigozie stepped in and swung, landing a single feeble blow on Aanik's shoulder before the tussling creatures crashed out of his reach.

He looked up and saw Kort. The bison-headed leader of the beastkind leaned on his own club and stared, snuffling and growling but not interfering.

Kort wasn't going to see the light and suddenly become Christian.

What insane challenge had Chigozie gotten himself into?

Aanik rose and fell again, diving against the cow-headed warrior to bite her ear and her forearm.

The beastkind howled and snarled, but they said no words.

Chigozie wasn't fighting to convert now, if he ever had been. He had been granted a miracle, in the form of this beastwife who had already saved his life twice, but now he was fighting simply for his life.

He ran forward and attacked again, bashing Aanik in the back of his long, sinewy neck.

Aanik's neck twisted back around and snapped, but in doing so, he exposed his neck to the cow. She rolled right, pulling Aanik left at the same time—

and rammed one horn deep into Aanik's throat.

Hot blood gushed from the wound, spattering the bovine

fighter in the face and sending up thin columns of steam in the crisp air.

Aanik's body convulsed, arms and legs flailing. The claws of all four limbs scratched at the beastwife, further tearing in the flesh of her belly and her thighs. She rolled over twice to one side, struggling to get both hands around Aanik's neck, but his blood made it more slippery, and her hands slid, failing to find purchase.

Then suddenly, made slick by his own blood, Aanik escaped. He staggered to his own feet and charged Chigozie. Blood from his wound spattered a wide swathe of snow, shockingly red against the virginal white, but also boiled back into his own throat, and his scream came at Chigozie with an obscene gargling edge to it and a fine mist of red that sprayed forth like a basilisk's venom.

The beastwife tumbled onto all fours and chased after Aanik.

"God of my father!" Chigozie shouted.

Aanik roared and leaped—

the beastwife gripped him by his heel with both hands—

Aanik's lamprey mouth opened wide and his neck extended, snapping and biting, but not quite far enough to reach Chigozie—

and Chigozie shoved his club down Aanik's open mouth.

Aanik tried to scream, but had no air. He scooted backward, trying to escape, and locked himself more tightly into the beast-wife's grip. She wrapped powerful arms around Aanik's upper limbs and leaned on him with her body, trapping his hind legs so he couldn't further scratch her.

Aanik swiveled his serpentine head this way and that looking for escape, and couldn't find it. Chigozie kept his grip on his club, his arms nearly pulling from their sockets with each new twist of the beastman's head, and he leaned forward, putting his weight onto the weapon.

Slowly, an inch at a time, Chigozie forced his club deeper down the lamprey-cat's unnatural throat.

He was grateful Aanik had no visible eyes. It meant he couldn't look into them and imagine a plea for compassion. Instead, killing the beastman was like killing a snake he'd found in the woodpile—it was simply the necessary thing to do so.

One minute, Chigozie was leaning and sweating, and the beastwife strained to hold Aanik in place.

The next, Aanik was still.

Bloody foam bubbled up at the corners of the lamprey mouth,

around the wood of Chigozie's club. Chigozie stepped back to catch his breath, but the beastwife didn't. She rose to her feet still clutching Aanik tightly in both arms, raised him over her head—

and brought him down swiftly, driving his back against her raised knee with a loud *crack!*

Aanik spasmed a final time, and the beastwife tossed him aside.

"Mercy," Kort said.

"I was attacked," Chigozie pointed out.

Kort shrugged. "Two on one is no miracle."

Chigozie's heart sank, despite the adrenalin still coursing through his veins at having faced and survived death. "The miracle is that help arrived."

"Miracle," Kort grunted. "Or coincidence."

"I'm Ferpa," the cow-headed warrior said. "My arrival here is no coincidence."

"No?" Kort's bison face expressed an impressive amount of disdain and skepticism. "Were you sent here by his god, then?"

Ferpa reached slowly for the neckline of her makeshift tunic, gripped it with bloodied fingers, and pulled it down.

Burned into her breast, just below incisions left by Aanik's savage teeth, was a cross.

Chigozie heard his own breathing, suddenly loud in the dead air. Far away, beasts in the shallows of the Mississippi howled and collided in rage.

"That is...that is..." Kort glared. He snorted.

Finally, he turned his muzzle toward the river and loped away, his pack following.

Chigozie found himself alone with Ferpa. Standing beside her, he felt tiny and frail. She was eight feet tall, heels to horns, and her body from the neck down was that of a voluptuous and dark-skinned woman, with one addition—she had a long black cow's tail, ending in a flourish of long hairs twisted together like a paintbrush. Her scent was not quite that of a person, though he wouldn't have called it *bovine*—she smelled musky, strong, animal. And from the neck up, she was a black and white, long-horned cow. Her eyes were liquid, long-lashed, and shy.

Aanik's blood painted one of her horns.

"Thank you," Chigozie said.

"I've heard that you preach a new god to the beastkind." Her tail switched.

"Not a new god." Chigozie nodded. "But perhaps a god that is new to some of them."

"And the scar I bear. It's in the shape of this new god's symbol."

"Yes," Chigozie said. "It is the shape of the instrument on which He sacrificed himself for others. Out of love."

"This is mercy?" Ferpa asked.

Chigozie nodded. "Mercy is to spare others. It is to act out of love. It is to risk and sacrifice self."

"I want to receive mercy," Ferpa said slowly.

"So do I."

"And also...I wish to *give* mercy."

Chigozie found his own cheeks wet with tears. Inexplicably, he was thinking of his brother. "So do I."

"Our situation makes a mockery of all good maxims of military strategy, ma'am. Our enemies outnumber us. They have access to more materiel—bullets and arrows, and so forth. Our larder is virtually empty, while theirs, practically speaking, is infinitely stocked."

"That does indeed sound dire, Sir William. Might we perhaps console ourselves with the fact that our men may take cover behind walls of solid wood and clay?"

Bill and Cathy lay beside Chikaak on their backs on the roof of Alzbieta Torias's city home. Bill had affixed a lady's toilet mirror to a long stick and held it up, angling it left and right to get an aerial view of the numbers and positioning of the soldiers who surrounded them. So far, none of them had noticed the mirror, or if they'd seen it, they had the discipline to avoid wasting bullets by firing at it.

Or arrows. So many of these damned Ophidians were armed with medieval weapons. Like the Spanish, only without horses.

Bill found he had a sudden strong desire for a drink. After a moment's impotent rage, he was grateful he was on the rooftop, and not in the wine cellar.

He had been awoken early in the morning by Chikaak, who had seen Uris and Alzbieta leave together with her palanquin, well before first light. Agreeing that this was suspicious behavior, Bill had awoken all the men with whistled commands—the same notes he would have blown on the Heron King's horn, only much softer—and within moments they were positioned at all the windows and doors of the building.

The beastkind, at least. The Firstborn were simply gone, soldier and civilian, free and slave alike. Bill wasn't sure, but he thought he spotted some of their faces on the men laying siege to the palace now.

Only later had he realized that Calvin and Sarah had also disappeared.

At dawn, a warrior bearing no weapons and carrying a white flag over his shoulder had come to the front door. There he had twice recited a short message in a loud voice, then turned and rejoined his comrades.

"By order of the Regent-Minister of the Serpent Throne, Maltres Korinn, you're detained in this house. None of you is to leave or attempt to leave until further notice. You're outnumbered and surrounded."

Thinking of the ease and beauty of the thirty-odd commands he could now give his beastkind soldiers by sheer tone reminded Bill of Jacob Hop. Not for the first time in recent weeks, he wondered how far the little Dutchman had got. As recently as two days earlier, Sarah had consulted her hexed slate and announced that he lived and was high in the hills of Appalachee, bound for Johnsland.

Johnsland... and Bill's wife and son.

He shook away the thought.

"Our cover is an advantage if they charge our position, ma'am. It is worthless if we charge theirs, and therefore useful only in buying us time. Sooner or later, if we do nothing, our food will run out. We must therefore do something, losing our advantage of cover. They know that, and therefore they will waste no lives charging our positions. They will wait for us to assault theirs, and then they will mow us down like spring hay."

"Why, Sir William, you have become poetic."

"I have become *old*," he said, "and rather wistful of my long-since-discarded career path of becoming a farmer."

Chikaak laughed. "No, Captain, a farmer doesn't need your instinct for the kill."

"I am a gunfighter," Bill complained. "Even *I* do not need instinct for the kill. I merely point and shoot, and so long as I am lucky enough that the other fellow takes it worse than I do, I can continue."

"You do not mean that," Cathy said. "I have heard you speak

often of honor, and loyalty. Now you speak of your life as if you made shoes for a living."

"Honor in defense of innocence." Bill really wanted a drink, and he sighed. "I don't mean it, Cathy. And I am discouraged but for a moment; in your presence, such gloom cannot long persist."

"That's better," she said. "Now how are we going to shoot those sons of bitches across the street without getting shot ourselves?"

"There you have it," Bill said. "That is the essence of every strategy discussion. Let us consider possibilities. I would give an arm and a leg for a secret passage that led from this house to a place of strength behind our attackers."

Cathy shook her head. "If there is such a passage, we don't know it."

"Well then, I would be pleased to have a flanking force that could attack our foes from the rear."

Cathy shook her head.

"The gift of flight? Superior firepower, positioned here on the roof?"

"Were Sarah here, we might have either of those, I think."

"Agreed. And she isn't. But I am not inclined to wait for her return to solve our problem. I would be pleased if we could get a large quantity of liquor into the hands of our enemies. Bored soldiers have often been their own ruin."

"The food has mostly been eaten by refugees, but Alzbieta has wine in her pantry."

"Yes, hmm." Bill considered. "But if we simply offer it to them, it will arouse their suspicions. Perhaps we could arrange for them to have false but terrifying news."

"Such as a plague," Cathy suggested. "Sudden death to thousands of their comrades by a mysterious falling sickness."

"That is quite Biblical of you. I was thinking about the approach of a greater force, coming to our aid."

"Do you have the means to get them either piece of false information?"

"I do not," Bill admitted. "Perhaps our best recourse is to lie still and see what develops, at least for the time being."

"And what would you expect that to be?" Cathy asked.

"If we are detained," Bill drawled, "it means Sarah is detained. Why would that be? Well, she came her to reclaim her father's crown and throne, and we've known all along she wouldn't be unopposed. Then again, I cannot regard it as coincidental that Alzbieta and Uris have also vanished."

"You don't think they might be accompanying Sarah?"

"Not as friends. I cannot believe that we are only politely being asked to wait a short while, after which we should expect to rejoin our companions. No, something is afoot, and I do not like being in a cage."

"Fire," Chikaak suggested, bouncing on all fours. "We could make firebombs of spirits or powder, and throw them over our enemies' heads."

"Then charge while they are distracted." Bill nodded grimly. "I like your train of thought, Sergeant. I doubt mere wine would be sufficiently flammable." He hesitated. "It's worth inspecting the pantry, though, to see whether Alzbieta might have something stronger."

Chikaak nodded. "If only there were beehives."

It struck Bill as a strange thought, but then finally amused him. "Yes. I'd give a great deal just now to be able to lob flaming beehives at the enemy."

A clattering of hooves brought Bill's attention back to the enemy. He resisted an urge to raise his head and look, and instead shifted the mirror. At the same time, he grabbed the Heron King's horn with his left hand, preparing to give orders if the moment seemed opportune.

New forces arrived, pouring in behind the Cahokians from multiple points. They were irregulars, wearing no uniform, and the large quantity of knives and pistols that hung from their belts and shoulder straps made them look more like pirates than like militiamen. They moved like skirmishers, jumping quickly upon the Firstborn soldiers and taking them by surprise. Wicked long knives and pistols pointed at the faces and bellies of the Ophidians put an instant end to resistance.

Should he blow a call to attack?

But even as Bill hesitated, the struggle was over.

A woman strode into view. Seeing her through a mirror and from across the street distorted what Bill saw, but she looked to be perhaps fifty years old, despite hair that was still dark. She was heavy, but her cheekbones were strong, marked with a single large mole that probably prevented her ever from being the belle of the county. She planted her feet shoulder-width apart with her hands behind her back, and called to the Ophidians with the voice of a drill-sergeant.

"I'm Director Schmidt of the Imperial Ohio Company. You may call me *Madam Director*. If you're asking yourself, *isn't that the same person who has been buying up grain in the countryside and raising all our tolls and taxes, inflicting a miserable winter upon us even as the beastkind of the Missouri rampage as they have not done in a century?*, the answer is: I am she.

"But I'm not your enemy. I'm here to capture a party of rebels, many of whom now lie inside the palace before you. They serve a pretender queen, who has been disallowed from the Serpent Throne by your own regent, and who also claims to have a right to the Penn land fortune.

"At my request, the Regent-Minister of the Serpent Throne has directed you to detain these rebels. You were told this morning to await further orders. I'm here to give you those."

"I cannot see the woman bellowing," Cathy murmured, "but I believe I would happily shoot her in the face."

Chikaak grinned. "I would hold her down for you."

"Before I issue you orders, though," Director Schmidt continued, "you would like some token that what I say is true, and here it is. You become as of this moment Imperial militia, acting as part of the Pacification to bring peace to the Ohio. Here, then, is your first day's pay."

Man after man, the skirmishers reached into belts and purses to produce a single gold coin each, which they immediately handed to the Ophidian nearest them.

"Hell's Bells," Bill whispered to Cathy and the coyote-headed beastman.

They rolled over onto all fours and the three of them scurried toward the rooftop trapdoor by which they'd come up. Bill brought the Heron King's horn to his lips and blew three notes that meant *defensive position*.

"Immediately?" Chikaak asked.

"I think so," Bill said.

The beastman bounded ahead, fast as an actual coyote, and threw himself down the trapdoor and into the palace.

"What comes immediately?" Cathy panted for breath.

"Attack!" Director Schmidt roared.

✧   ✧   ✧

The crowd was large despite the late hour, and growing larger by the minute. Monsieur Bondí hadn't summoned them, nor had Onyinye or Eoin, but they had come. Without knowing why, Etienne guessed, each simply feeling the pull of the Brides.

The faces of the men glowed with anticipation.

The faces of the women shone with appetite.

Etienne wore his full episcopal dress, mitre and chasuble and all. Armand would have led the way and made the crowd part like the Red Sea before the Israelites, but Armand was dead. The chevalier's men had killed him—eyewitnesses watching from the common room of the tavern outside which Armand had died all told the same tale, that the killers were the foreigners with headscarves and pourpoints who had been seen around the Vieux Carré in recent weeks.

The chevalier's mamelukes.

Poor Armand.

What had killed him? The former customs man had always been quick to desire vengeance and violence—had that been his downfall?

Etienne pushed the question aside. Armand wasn't needed. The waters parted of their own accord, and Etienne strode across the Place d'Armes with a self-consciously ceremonial pace, extending each foot out with dignity and stepping heel-first. He entered the Place d'Armes from the ruined cathedral, appearing from behind the jagged stump of a shattered column and crossing toward the three iron cages.

For years the cages had held the pretender Andrew Jackson and two of his lieutenants, killed in Jackson's 1810 attempt to carve a kingdom for himself out of the Mississippi. The lieutenants were still there, skeletal and moldering, but Jackson had been taken out, and his body replaced with the corpse of Thijs Van Dijk. The former city councilor was bloated with the recent rains, his flesh puckered and white, his eyes melting already into pools of worm-ridden corruption.

Standing beneath the fresh corpse, Etienne turned to face the crowd. He stood on their level, and that was important. The Brides would carry his words to all of them, and that was important, too.

The crowd hushed itself in anticipation.

"During his lifetime, the enemies of Our Lord included not

only the Romans who pounded in the nails," he began slowly, "but also the Pharisees who connived at the action. The priests and the choosers of priests."

He felt the thrill of the Brides, which had been humming a low basso within his body all day, begin to rise in pitch. Strangely, he couldn't tell whether he was speaking French or English.

The crowd nodded.

"And these priestly conspirators one day sent their disciples to try to trap Our Lord. How to 'entangle' him, the gospel tells us. And after some flattery designed to put Our Lord at ease, they asked: 'What thinkest thou? Is it lawful to give tribute unto Caesar, or not?'" He paused, letting them remember the story. "And what did Our Lord say to these betrayers?"

"Render under Caesar." The first to give the answer was a heavyset Creole man clutching a straw hat to his chest, but others quickly took up the phrase.

Etienne nodded. "'Render unto Caesar.' Not render unto Caesar *everything*, of course. 'Render therefore unto Caesar *the things which are Caesar's.*'"

"'And unto God the things that are God's,'" the Creole with the hat added.

Etienne rewarded him with a gesture of blessing. "But not the things that are God's." He paused again, giving the crowd time to think about the implications of his words and guess where he might be going with the sermon.

"In recent days," he continued, "our good City Council and the chevalier have had a disagreement. Perhaps you have heard of it." Nodding heads. "It was a disagreement such as often is had between the wealthy and powerful, a disagreement over taxes. I would not bore you with the details, even if I were master of them myself, and I am not. In its essence, the disagreement is this: the City Council said that the chevalier collected taxes to which he was not entitled. He took too much.

"How should the chevalier, a great man, a wealthy man and a man of power, an Elector under Franklin's compact, react to such a suggestion?" Etienne knitted his fingers together, a gesture intended to look contemplative and pious at the same time. "He could have argued. He could have tried to persuade the City Council of his view. He could have opened up his books to say 'look, here are the funds flowing in and what I have done with them, tell me if you would prefer me to have done something else!' Indeed, he too could have quoted the twenty-second chapter of Matthew. 'Render unto Caesar the things which are Caesar's,' he might have said. 'And as I, the Chevalier of New Orleans, am the Caesar of Louisiana, render unto me these tariffs and tolls, that I may have funds from which to care for the poor.'"

This last point was a deliberate jab; the bishopric cared for the poor, funding various hospitals, hospices, and workhouses. The chevalier's expenses in the public interest included such items as roads and docks, law enforcement, and defense.

"But he did none of those things." Etienne stopped and looked over his shoulder at the bloated, rotting corpse of Thijs Van Dijk. Poor stupid bastard. When Etienne had warned the councilors that he expected the chevalier to come for them, Van Dijk was the one who had refused to go underground. Etienne had offered him resources, places to stay. Van Dijk had been sure his station would protect him.

It hadn't.

Very well. Etienne would play the cards he had been dealt.

"Thijs Van Dijk was a good man. He was a family man. He built good furniture and he sold it for a fair price, and if he haggled a little more fiercely than some of his suppliers might like, well, that is the nature of a commercial society, is it not? But Thijs served the city as councilor for many years, and he gave to the poor." Etienne had no idea whether Thijs gave alms to the poor. He doubted it. "Meneer Van Dijk was a member of that very City Council that refused to approve the quarterly tax returns when ordered by the chevalier.

"Note: no indictment was filed. No assets of the chevalier were seized. The returns were not approved, a minor thing. A minor thing that might have been followed by negotiations, questions, the sharing of information, loving persuasion.

"In this case, though, it was followed by murder."

The congregation was rapt. He saw it in their faces. He felt it in the song of the Brides.

Etienne raised his voice. "I ask you this: was Thijs Van Dijk obligated to render his integrity unto Caesar? His soul? Was he required to give his life to the chevalier?"

"No!" cried a woman's voice from the crowd.

"No!" Etienne roared, shaking a clenched fist.

"No!" the crowd bellowed.

Etienne lowered his voice, barely above a whisper. The Brides would ensure he was still heard. "No. Thijs Van Dijk rendered unto Caesar that which was Caesar's. And when Caesar took too much, when Caesar became a mere robber, Thijs Van Dijk rendered his integrity and faith unto God, and told the truth about Caesar. And for that, Caesar murdered him."

Silence.

Etienne reached beneath his chasuble and removed a folded copy of the broadsheet he himself had written and distributed under the name Publius. He unfolded it and held it high over his head, showing it to the crowd. The Brides would make certain that people saw it clearly, even those who were too far away to see the paper well with their natural eyes.

"Someone has written about the chevalier's taxes. Someone who calls himself Publius, *the man of the people*. He suggests dark things about the Chevalier of New Orleans. He accuses our chevalier of murdering our former bishop. My father." To his surprise, his own words brought Etienne a flood of emotion and he struggled against tears.

Be strong, my son.

"I did not witness my father's death, and I do not know the truth of this matter. But should we not investigate the question? Should we not seek to know the truth?"

"The murderer was a guest of the chevalier!" This from an unseen face in the crowd.

"Was Thijs Van Dijk Publius?" Etienne shrugged. "How can we ever know, now? But should not this incident as well be investigated?" He paused. "Should we not cease to pay our tolls and our taxes to the chevalier until we know the truth?"

"Yes!" cried many in the crowd, with one voice. "No more taxes! Not one sou!"

"The cathedral." Etienne raised his arm and gestured across the Place d'Armes as the scorched stone husk. "We, the people of New Orleans, built that cathedral." In fact, the building had been built by the old corrupt bishops, the chevalier's de Bienville cousins. "We rendered our labor and our wealth unto God, and we built him a house, and a seat for his servant, the bishop.

"Did the chevalier murder the bishop? We should investigate. And we should also investigate the destruction of our cathedral.

Fire caused by lightning, say some of the news-papers. The *Pica-yune Gazette* says so. Of course, the *Picayune Gazette* is owned by the chevalier. The *Pontchartrain Herald* says there were explosions, and indeed, who ever heard of lightning causing a stone building to burn down? Those of us who live in the Vieux Carré heard explosions. We saw the explosion that broke the cathedral's back, we heard the explosion that shattered the foundations we so carefully laid and consecrated to God. We heard the explosion that hurled the altar itself from the cathedral and left it lying in the mud and the rain. Why would the *Picayune Gazette* try to hide these explosions? Why would the chevalier try to conceal the truth of the events?

"Is it because once again the chevalier's foreign visitors are responsible? An Imperial soldier visiting the chevalier in his Palais murdered the bishop. Mameluke envoys visiting the chevalier from France were seen entering the cathedral and then leaving it again, shortly before it was destroyed. Those who saw them enter report they carried casks and crates, gunpowder and oil lanterns." This was a bald lie; Etienne had been unable to find any witnesses who'd seen the mamelukes enter, and when they'd come out, they'd been empty-handed.

"Yes!" cried voices in the crowd.

"We rendered our bishop unto God, and the chevalier killed him. We rendered a cathedral unto God, and the chevalier in his envy caused it to be destroyed. The Chevalier of New Orleans, it seems, cannot abide that God should have anything. Caesar wishes all things to be rendered unto him."

"No more taxes!" shouted the Creole with the straw hat.

"After my father's death, I was pleased to serve in his place. God knows, as you all know, that I have not always been a righteous man." Etienne shrugged slightly, trying to look self-deprecating and humble without appearing too dismissive of his own wickedness. "But God looked into my heart and saw fit to call me, anyway." He smiled, again, a restrained expression. "Perhaps God thought that a city of sinners would be best served by a bishop with some experience of sin."

Warm laughter.

"And so, called by the Synod, I rendered my life to God. I would be his servant, I would walk among the poor to bless, to comfort, to distribute alms." This part was true. "And I did my best.

"Now the chevalier says I am to be removed. Why? Because I am not an honest man. Because I have stolen the bishopric's funds for my own purposes."

Murmurs of disbelief.

"But I ask the chevalier this: if the funds of the bishopric have been so badly used, how is it that the proper man to replace me is the parish beadle, the very man who manages those funds?"

Etienne shook his head in skepticism. "No, I tell you this, I did not steal from the bishopric, I did not steal from the poor. The beadle, August Planchet, is a good man, and he also did not steal from the parish. What we have here is a chevalier who is a jealous Caesar, and must have all things. He could not abide that the bishopric was honestly administered, and so he took it. He installed a new bishop, making false accusations against the old one...against me.

"Shall we render our bishop unto Caesar?"

"No!"

Etienne shook his head. "And yet, Caesar has taken two bishops from us. My father he killed. Me, he has pretended to remove from office."

Whimpering sounds, and the sniffing of held-back tears.

"Shall we render our house of God unto Caesar?"

"No!"

Etienne's shoulders sagged. "And yet, Caesar has destroyed it, leaving not one stone upon a stone."

Weeping.

Etienne turned slightly, gesturing at Van Dijk's corpse. "Shall we render our integrity unto Caesar? Shall we render unto him our souls? Shall we render unto him our lives, when he sees fit to murder us?"

"No!"

"The Bishop!" the Creole with the hat cried.

Etienne looked up at Van Dijk and staggered, falling to his knees. It was not a rehearsed gesture, not theatrics; the countenance of Thijs Van Dijk had changed. Perhaps it was the dim light of the evening, or the irregular shadows from the lights of the Place d'Armes, or a trick of the mind caused by Etienne's rhetoric, or the work of the Brides, but Van Dijk's face was gone.

In its place was the face of Etienne's father.

Taken by surprise, Etienne found himself weeping. The Brides wrapped their arms around him, warming him, loving him. It was not enough. He missed his father. He missed his brother Chigozie, who had never understood him, but who had always been the best of men and an honest priest. He wrapped his hand around his mother's locket, seeking comfort from his gede loa.

We love you, son.

Etienne struggled to rise to his feet, and found the Creole helping him, along with others from the crowd. Strangers. Parishioners. His flock.

"Caesar wants everything," he gasped. "He takes what is not offered to him. He takes the things we have offered to God, the things we can *only* offer to God. We must teach Caesar a lesson."

"No more taxes!" shouted the Creole.

"No more taxes," Etienne agreed. "No more tariffs. No more tolls. We must show Caesar that he can only have the things we choose to render unto him, only the things that are due to him. We must have a chastened Caesar, a Caesar who will enforce the laws fairly and justly, who will not murder or rob."

"No more taxes!" the crowd shouted together.

"Caesar will try to take his tariffs and tolls by force. We must help each other resist. When our sister is robbed by Caesar, we must help her feed her children. When our brother is beaten by Caesar's thugs, we must bind his wounds and nurse him back to health. Only together will we be strong enough to chasten Caesar, so that we may again render unto God the things that are God's."

Etienne collapsed into the arms of the man with the straw hat and Monsieur Bondí. The two men carried him through the crowd as the crowd took up the chant, passing it further and further back across the Place d'Armes and deep into the Vieux Carré.

"No more taxes! No more taxes! No more taxes!"

Fires had sprung up in two buildings along the periphery of the Place d'Armes. As Etienne looked, a third conflagration burst into life, shattering the storefront windows of a high-priced bakery.

The crowd was rioting.

Etienne struggled to look back and find again the image of his father, but it was gone. In its place was the ghoulish face of Thijs Van Dijk, grinning at Etienne with puffed lips and empty eye sockets.

"This is no ordinary wagon."

———⋙◦⋘———

CHAPTER TWENTY-FIVE

Philadelphia was larger than New Orleans. If possible, it was also more grand.

Kinta Jane was unfazed by the Babel of languages around her, though, which was more subdued than the linguistic storm on the Pontchartrain. Most people around her spoke English, though there was plenty of Dutch, French, and Haudenosaunee, and more than a smattering of other tongues. But her head spun at the blossoming of shops all around her and at the new construction. Philadelphia was New Orleans, but bigger, newer, and growing, whereas New Orleans was old, chipping, and slowly decaying into the bayou on which it sat. Philadelphia had just as much sweat and horse manure on the breeze as her sister on the Mississippi, but lacked the pervasive tang of salt and mud.

Horse Hall was vast, a block of stone on a stone plaza, intricately carved on the outside into the shapes of rearing horses, eagles with spread wings, and sailing ships, rather than with gargoyles. Kinta Jane recognized those icons from the Imperial seal. More subtly, she noticed that woven among those elements were others: some of the eagles clutched swords in their talons; some of the horses drank from cups, and others bore shields; many of the ships sailed underneath clouds from which fell long bolts of lightning.

The Franklin Seal, then, as well as the Imperial. The four

suits of his Tarock, corresponding to the four seal components: the sword that was the letter T that stood for Tarock; the cup that was an upended C that stood for the Compact and, for those who knew, the Conventicle; the B for bishopric that was also a shield; and the bolt of lightning.

This was a Franklin place. That thought allowed Kinta Jane Embry to relax.

Slightly.

"Why on earth would they allow me into a place so grand?" she asked Isaiah Wilkes. Now that she could speak again, she forced herself to think of him as Isaiah Wilkes, and not as *the Franklin*. If she thought *the Franklin*, the words might actually escape her lips at an inopportune moment.

"Because they know me as one of the Lightning Mummers." He smiled, his solemn and somewhat plain face becoming instantly lively and attractive.

"You mean the Franklin Players?"

"Yes. And as one of the Players, one day I saved the Emperor Thomas's life."

"Who from?"

"Why, from me, of course." Wilkes's grin disappeared. "I am, after all, a man of the theater."

Kinta Jane didn't understand, but she let it lie.

"And as a man of the theater, I have one small, final piece to perform for my friend Thomas."

"Do I have a role in that piece?"

"You have the most important role. You'll play the Teller of Truths."

"What must I do?"

"You've learned your speech. Be prepared to give it."

They approached the main entrance to Horse Hall across broad flagstones. At the front door stood four men in Imperial blue, with two short-haired mastiffs. When she was thirty steps away, both dogs rose to their feet and began to bark angrily at Kinta Jane.

When she was twenty feet away, their sound stopped.

They continued to open their jaws and snap them shut, as if they were barking. Their eyes continued to be screwed into fierce, hostile glares, foam dripped from their jaws to the stone, but the sound of their barking simply ceased.

"What is wrong with the dogs?" she whispered.

"It's an old, old spell." Wilkes smiled.

"What is? Are *you* casting the spell?"

"No, my friend, *you* are. Burglars take with them the tongue of a dog, often dried and placed within their shoe, but sometimes worn as an amulet about the neck or merely carried in a pocket."

"And that prevents the dogs from making a sound?"

Wilkes nodded. "After you have finished bearing witness to Brother Onas, you may have a career ahead of you as a second-story woman."

"I don't know whether I can do this," Kinta Jane said, but Wilkes said nothing, and they arrived at the door.

"It's the actor again," one of the men said. He wore a surly expression and his teeth were dark yellow behind blistered lips.

"Gottlieb said to let the actor in, and to let Gottlieb know of his arrival." The second guard's eyes were deeply bloodshot, as if from too much wine.

The third guard had a nose the size of an onion, pitted all over with tiny indentations. He stepped aside, belching, and Wilkes led Kinta Jane into Horse Hall.

The yellow-toothed guard followed them. "Wait here. I'll go find Miss Fussypants." He walked away.

The entryway into which they arrived was two stories tall and had passages branching left and right; presiding over the intersection was a painting of a man in very fine clothing, and from much less detailed woodcuts, Kinta Jane guessed the subject's identity immediately.

"That's Thomas Penn."

"The Emperor."

"Brother Onas."

"I didn't give him that name." Wilkes trotted up the stairs. Kinta Jane followed.

"You don't wish this person Gottlieb to find us."

"I think the Emperor hopes to trap me. I wore out my welcome the last time I was here."

"You *wish* to see Thomas."

Wilkes nodded. "But not in chains."

On the second story of Horse Hall, Isaiah Wilkes turned down an angular side passage that connected them with a smaller staircase in the corner of the building. He took this up another floor, crossed the central hall to a different staircase, and then descended.

Kinta Jane said nothing.

"My apologies for the route. I have spent some time here in disguise, finding the least obvious paths to the Emperor's offices."

"In disguise as what?"

Wilkes smiled. "Various things. A footman. A soldier. A cook. Even, once or twice, as an actor."

"But you *are* an actor."

"Oh, yes." He stopped at a door. "Here we are."

He entered without knocking and on tip-toe, and Kinta Jane found herself inside a library; the high walls were lined with a fortune of books, and writing tables and divans were scattered about the deeply carpeted floor.

Two men sat hunched over a news-paper. One was the emperor Thomas, dressed in Italian silk shirtsleeves. The other was a fat man, old, bald, and wrinkled, whose face seemed familiar.

The fat man tapped a particular paragraph on the news-paper with a pair of spectacles, pointing it out. "And if the Landgrave is able to attend Mrs. Hancock's soirée, we should absolutely expect his attendance at the Assembly."

"*Expect* it?" Thomas snorted. "Given his cousin's death, the landgrave may be the only Elector from Chicago who will attend in person. I should command it."

"Say rather *encourage* it. I'll have a man follow him the day before, and on the morning of, we'll send a footman bearing a signed personal invitation to appear."

"I don't know that he values my signature so highly. For that matter, I don't know that the Elector can read English."

"We'll have the invitation printed in German and English both. And for the footman's safety, of course, we'll send him accompanied by four armed guards. Philadelphia can be so dangerous these days."

"Indeed, it can," Isaiah Wilkes said, stepping into plainer view. He bowed to each man in turn. "Your Imperial Majesty. Mr. Franklin."

Kinta Jane bowed with him, mouthing the same titles and names. *Franklin? But of course!* The old man couldn't be the Lightning Bishop, who was dead, but he could be Ben Franklin's son. Or grandson, more likely.

"The player," Franklin said. "Has the Emperor summoned you?"

"Gottlieb let me in," Wilkes said. "He told me he believed you needed entertaining, and hoped I could do it in a sufficiently allegorical fashion to meet the Emperor's tastes."

"Allegorical fashion?" Thomas snorted. "Good heavens, you're thinking of another man."

"No, Brother Onas," Isaiah Wilkes said. "I'm thinking of you." He opened his arms wide, spread-eagling himself as if he were a living facsimile of the letter T.

"The man believes he is Jesus," Thomas muttered to Franklin. To Wilkes he said, "I've had enough. I've been more than expressive in my gratitude, and this *Brother Onas* business in particular has become tiresome. Now I suggest you run." The Emperor raised his voice to a shout. "Gottlieb!"

Kinta Jane drifted to the side. It was the habit of a New Orleans entertainer, positioning herself so as not to be between the combatants when violence was imminent.

"Behold!" Isaiah Wilkes cried. "The three wounds of William Penn!"

He slapped himself on the chest with his right hand. To Kinta Jane's surprise, a flower of bright red blood blossomed in his white shirt, right where'd struck himself, in the sternum.

"What in the hell?" Thomas Penn barked.

Wilkes slapped himself again, with his left hand this time, on the thigh. Blood appeared there, in a spatter-edged circle of dark red, and Wilkes swayed as though his knees were buckling from the pain.

"Gottlieb!" Franklin waddled past Wilkes to the door and opened it, shouting again. "Gottlieb!"

Wilkes struck himself again with his right hand, this time in the forehead. Blood exploded into his dark hair and ran down his forehead and face from his high hairline.

Thomas Penn stared, fascinated.

Wilkes returned to his spread-eagled position. "Brother Onas, hear my plea!" His voice dropped to such a groan, he sounded as though he were in a trance.

Franklin hobbled back. "Nonsense! Folk tales! Lies! Masonic higgledy-piggledy!"

"This is not masonic," Thomas murmured. "I know the stories the masons tell, about the murdered bricklayer and King

Solomon's magic. This is something else. Besides, for all their theater, the masons would never use such blood props. Their carpets are too costly."

"No, I didn't mean it literally." Franklin harrumphed. "But this is the *sort* of errant nonsense my grandfather loved to tell me, dandling me upon his knee and terrifying me with puppets of a monster with a heron's head."

Wilkes shot Kinta Jane a silent glance and raised his eyebrows.

This was her signal. She stepped forward and began to speak.

"Your Majesty, Mr. Franklin," she said again. "I've come a long way to bear witness to you."

"And I've come far too long a way to listen to the testimony of actors and strumpets," Thomas said. "If Gottlieb has lost his path, you'll find I can solve my problems without his assistance." He strode to the largest desk and took a sword belt and sword from where they had been hanging across the back of the chair. He gripped the sword's hilt and glared at Kinta Jane.

"He doesn't think he's an actor." Franklin laughed. "Look at him. He thinks he's a prophet, sleeping on one side for seven years, or—" he pointed at Kinta Jane "—marrying a harlot."

"The Heron King has crossed his bounds," Kinta Jane said. "It's Franklin's Vision made flesh. Peter Plowshare is dead. The emissaries of Simon Sword have been seen on the Mississippi. I found this in New Orleans." She held out the deaf-mute's gold coin, the gold disc with the plow on one side and the sword on the other.

Thomas took it, looked at both sides, and frowned at Franklin.

"Brother Onas!" Isaiah Wilkes dropped to his knees and reached toward the Emperor. "Will you help us?"

"The raging of the beastkind," Thomas said to Franklin. "Could it be? Could it be Simon Sword?"

"There's no such person." Franklin sniffed.

"There *is*," Kinta Jane assured him. "I've seen him perform magic. He made the mute speak." Suddenly, the tongue in her mouth felt enormous. "He freed the prisoners."

"And he gave balm to the afflicted." Franklin laughed. "Is this Simon Sword you speak of, or Jesus?"

Kinta Jane's face burned.

Tears streamed down Isaiah Wilkes's face. "Your ancestor William Penn stood against Simon Sword with his brothers.

Your grandfather John Penn founded the Conventicle with the Lightning Bishop, to stand as a bulwàrk against Simon Sword's return, which Franklin saw coming. They made those preparations against *this very day!* Can you do less than they, Your Majesty?"

"Good heavens," Franklin drawled. "It is *exactly* the same nonsense my grandfather used to tell me."

Thomas turned to his comrade, drawing his long saber from its scabbard and resting the naked blade on his own shoulder. "Then he may have told it to others. Such as this player here. Others may believe it. *Must* believe it."

"Others *do* believe it," Franklin assured him. "It's still nonsense."

"But it may be useful nonsense," Thomas said. "What if... *Electors* believed it?"

"You mean: what if a sufficient number of Electors believed it, that they would be moved to vote you additional power and money? What if the Pacification of the Ohio were not merely a question of suppressing some rebel Ophidians on the borders of the Empire, but were about the return of the legendary destroyer, Simon Sword?"

Kinta Jane was shocked at the cold calculation in Franklin's voice.

Thomas shrugged. "Yes. Well... what *if?*"

Franklin nodded. "We'll need more credible witnesses than these. Naturally, those can be hired. Shreveport and the Memphites and some of the others have been complaining about the beastkind, so they'll add credibility even if they say nothing about this Heron King fairy tale."

"Brother Onas," Isaiah Wilkes begged. "Will you rise? Will you take up your sword and shield?"

Franklin looked at Wilkes, and then back to Thomas. "We *do* have *one* problem."

"Noted." Thomas Penn's voice was dry and matter-of-fact, but Kinta Jane heard murder in its flat tone.

She threw herself toward the door, grabbing Isaiah Wilkes's long hair as she passed. "Run!"

She pulled the actor back and he fell from his knees onto his rump. The shift in stance saved his life; Thomas stepped forward and swung his saber in a long killing arc, which would have sliced Wilkes's head off. Instead, the sword's tip passed just before his nose and missed him.

Sliding backward, Wilkes from some unseen pocket produced a tiny hold-out pistol. One shot only, and small caliber; Kinta Jane knew the type, because she knew many ladies of the New Orleans boardwalks who carried them.

Thomas stepped forward and raised his sword again.

Pop!

Wilkes's shot was surprisingly quiet, but he hit Thomas in the shoulder and the Emperor stumbled, dropping his sword.

Wilkes scrambled forward as Kinta Jane grabbed the doorknobs to the entrance. He scooped up the Emperor's saber and leaped to his feet. With his free hand, he punched Thomas right where the blood stained the Emperor's sleeve, and Thomas fell back, yelping.

Then Wilkes turned on Franklin. The heavy man had a side drawer in one of the writing tables and was reaching into it. Wilkes rose up on one foot and with the other foot kicked the drawer shut.

Franklin screamed and fell to his knees.

Wilkes cracked the pommel of the saber down on the top of Franklin's head. Franklin sagged to the thick carpet; Wilkes grabbed Kinta Jane by the hand and they raced through the open door.

Outside the door stood a short man with a blocky face and a powdered white perruque. He held a pistol in each hand, pointed at the floor.

"Make it look good," he said.

Wilkes ran him through the leg.

The man with the perruque sank to the floor, crying out. "Too much!" he gasped, his perruque falling from his head into a puddle of his blood.

Wilkes snatched the pistols from his hands. "Thank you, Gottlieb," he whispered. Then he ran for the nearest stairs.

As they reached the bottom of the spiral staircase, Kinta Jane heard cursing behind them. She and Wilkes both whipped about, and Wilkes fired one shot at Franklin's emerging face. The shot rang out loud in Horse Hall, and the bullet lodged into the door of the wood just above Franklin's head.

Franklin withdrew behind the door, and Wilkes and Kinta Jane ran up the stairs.

"We're going the wrong way!" she gasped.

"I'm glad you think so!"

The upper floor seemed to be comprised of servants' lodgings. Wilkes led Kinta Jane down a short passage—

to a dead end. No windows, no doors. Only a trap-door in the wall.

"What is this?" she asked him.

"Laundry chute." Wilkes pulled open the trap-door and Kinta Jane saw a passage descending to lower floors. Ten feet down, the shaft disappeared in darkness.

A rope was tied to a steel hook bolted into the wall at the top of the chute. The rope descended into darkness, knotted every few feet.

"Go!" Wilkes snapped.

He held open the chute with one hand and with the other kept his borrowed pistol trained on the empty space at the end of the passage where pursuit might appear. Kinta Jane crawled into the chute feet-first, twisted herself around until she got her hands on the rope and its knots, and then began the descent.

Wilkes slid into the shaft as neatly as a snake and then shut the trap-door, closing them in darkness. "Count the knots out loud as you go," he whispered. "If I go too fast, I'll step on your hands."

She counted and climbed downward.

Muffled by the walls of Horse Hall, she heard the running of booted feet, and lots of shouting. The sound faded between floors, and then rose in volume as she passed trap-doors at some levels. In the cracks of light seeping in around the edges of those trap-doors, she looked at her hands; they ached from the climb, and in the dim occasional light, she saw that her fingers were swelling from the work, and the skin of her palms was torn and bleeding.

The shaft smelled vaguely of sweat, and the closeness of the tunnel made her feel she was choking. The stink got thicker as she dropped, and Kinta Jane began to wonder whether she might die of asphyxiation.

She'd just passed the count of two hundred—and the sounds of frantic search had significantly faded—when her feet found purchase in a soft pile of soiled laundry.

"I'm at the bottom," she whispered.

"I'm passing down the pistol," Wilkes murmured back. "Grip first. Don't shoot me."

She took the pistol, able to see it because here at the bottom there was a final trap door, larger than all the others. Wilkes remained over her head, a dark mass hovering above a dangling pair of boots.

"Open the door," he said.

She hesitated, but his unerring path through the building this far gave her confidence. Pressing her back against the wall of the shaft opposite the door, she aimed the pistol at the trap-door, cocked the hammer, and then kicked the door open.

The door opened into a laundry. Steam from boiling cauldrons brought forth an instant slick of sweat on Kinta Jane's skin. Pipes gathered the smoke from coal-fires below the cauldrons with large lead hoods and carried it away; other pipes brought in fresh water. The room smelled pungently of lye.

"Go!" Wilkes said again.

She climbed out into the laundry, pistol first, and he followed her. Once he had enough room to move, he stretched his back and neck, took the pistol, and resumed the lead again.

"Why aren't we seeing more servants?" she whispered.

"They're being kept out of the way," he said.

Next to the laundry was a coal room. An enormous pile of the chunky black mineral cascaded down the far wall beneath another chute, this one rising up and terminating quickly in a metal lid.

Wilkes scrambled up the pile, urging her on. At the top of the coal-heap he tucked the pistol into his belt and made a stirrup of his hands. "Foot here," he said. "Up you go. Knock on the plate on top."

She did as she was told. "You're filthy, you know. Dirty laundry, fake blood, sweat, and now coal dust?"

"Who says the blood was fake?"

Wilkes hoisted her up the coal-shaft. She slid on her belly, shooting quickly up the shaft and catching herself against the heavy metal trap on top. She rapped on the metal with sore fingers, and it lifted. Strong arms yanked her arm, and then a rope was dropped into the hole for Wilkes.

Kinta Jane didn't know the two men who dragged them up from the coal room, and she'd never be able to describe them; their faces were thoroughly smeared with coal-dust, and clouds of the dust rose from their coats as they moved. The vehicle was a heavy wagon pulled by two dray horses and piled high with chunks of black coal.

As he emerged from the coal-chute, Wilkes kicked it closed behind him and then dragged Kinta Jane by the arm underneath the coal-wagon. Lying on her back, she looked up in surprise and discovered that the bed of the wagon was much higher than she would have imagined, and beneath the wagon were two long shelves, each long and wide enough to accommodate a person, bolted into opposite sides of the wagon's frame.

"This is no ordinary wagon." She climbed onto one of the shelves as Wilkes climbed into the other.

"An ordinary wagon would be much less useful," Wilkes pointed out. "We'd have to bury ourselves in the coal and risk suffocating."

"Have we failed?" she asked him.

"*You* haven't failed," he said immediately. "You've succeeded spectacularly. I...I don't know about myself. *I* may have failed. But we together, we *all of us*, haven't failed yet. Now let's you and I both keep still while our friends take us to someplace quiet."

"Who's out there?" Ma'iingan asked.

Nathaniel shook his head. "I don't know a *who*. I know a *what*. There are spirits of the dead out there, and they aren't quiet."

"Wiinuk. I have no herbs, I have no charms." He wished his father had inducted him into the Midewiwin before he'd left on his journey. He wished he knew a reliable way to invoke his manidoo.

Nathaniel considered. "I may be able to do something. But it will take time."

Ma'iingan swung his axe through the air to emphasize his words. "I'll get you time, God-Has-Given."

Nathaniel crossed to the corner of the barn and collected a double handful of dried asemaa leaf. Ma'iingan watched him sit cross-legged beside the last tongues of the fire inside the tiny sweat lodge and lay leaves one at a time across it, blowing on the leaves as their crinkly edges ignited.

Nathaniel took his drum and began to pound out a rhythm and sing.

Ma'iingan tore his attention away and peered through the cracks. Beside him, he felt George Isham do the same.

"What do you mean, the spirits of the dead?" George asked.

"I see men walking out there. Surely, it's the Chief Godi's soldiers. They've realized their mistake and they've come back to get me. Or perhaps some of my father's own men."

"No," Ma'iingan said.

"Look, I will...I'll tell them to let you go. My father's men will listen to me. His men, and the Chief Godi's men, too. You can go. Nathaniel and Landon can go if they want, or they can come home."

"That is how you dress your soldiers, na?" Ma'iingan asked. "Or your godi, his men wear such clothing?"

"How I dress...what?" George pressed his face flatter against the barn wall to get a better look.

Behind them, Nathaniel's song rose to a crescendo.

The nearest of the approaching people crossed a stray puddle of starlight. He was dressed as no soldier of Johnsland dressed, Ma'iingan was certain. He wore simple white trousers and a white shirt; a long shroud was wrapped around his head and neck and trailed behind him. As Ma'iingan and George looked on, that strip of cloth caught on a branch, and the end of the cloth tore off. The fabric was rotten. It was falling off the body now, but it had once been wrapped around him to prepare his body for burial.

"Ing and Erce," George Isham muttered. "Herne's bloody horns."

"Henh," Ma'iingan agreed. "We need more fire."

They had minutes, but likely no more. Together, he and George rushed to snap off whatever dry wood they could find in the barn. The tobacco-curing racks were an obvious place to start.

Ma'iingan was hesitant to steal fire from Nathaniel, for fear he might disrupt the boy's ritual. "You can make fire, na?" he asked George Isham.

George snorted. "Of course."

"Torches," Ma'iingan told him. "Get torches lit."

He grabbed his axe and ran to the barn's small door. Leaping, he grabbed the top of a tall drying rack and pulled it down with all his weight, scattering a tangle of timbers in front of the opening and hopefully slowing the progress of anyone who tried to enter thereby.

He reached the barn's larger door just as two of the attackers did. They were both women, and the first looked lively—her skin pale but elastic, her step sure, her eyes clear. She was naked, but for a long white shroud wrapped around her from head to toe. For a moment Ma'iingan thought maybe she was someone who had been disturbed in her sleep by the noise of shots, and he hesitated.

That nearly cost him his life. The first woman jumped for him with mouth gaping, and the fetid stench that washed from her open maw into Ma'iingan's nostrils was the stink of decaying flesh. She was dead, walking dead, a horror his people had never had to deal with directly and for which they had no name of their own.

He'd heard of such things from traders who came from the mouth of the Michi-Zibii, though. *Zaambi*, they called them there. And the Germans of Chicago called them *draug*, and burned their dead on ships or sealed them in stone chambers underground to prevent them from returning in this fashion.

The first zaambi knocked Ma'iingan down. He raised a defensive arm, and she sank her teeth into it, midway between wrist and elbow. The pain was far worse than it should be, but Ma'iingan didn't scream. Instead, he straightened his arm and swung it left, hurling the draugar from him and slamming it to the ground flat on its back.

The teeth sank deeper into his flesh. This time, he screamed.

Behind him, within the barn, he smelled and heard gunpowder burning, and then the room became much more brightly lit.

The second zaambi lurched in through the door, and this one only bore a faint resemblance to a living person. Flesh hung in tatters from long bones, and flesh and clods of frozen earth fell to the ground in the creature's wake. Threads protruding from upper and lower lip, and a bit of the upper that had remained fixed to the lower, exposing bony gums and dull yellow teeth, showed that the woman's mouth had been sewn shut when she was buried. Similar torn threads pierced and clung to the zaambi's ankles. Had she been executed for a crime? Or was such stitching a defensive measure against hostile spirits or magic?

Perhaps a measure meant to prevent just such a case as what had actually happened, revival as a draugar.

Keeping the fresher zaambi pressed to the floor with his left arm, with his right Ma'iingan swung his axe. With one blow, he smashed through both the attacker's ankles, toppling her to the floor. Swinging the axe around, his second blow crashed downward through the zaambi's neck, completely severing its head and biting into the wood of the floor.

The draugar's head bounced three feet away and stopped,

eyeless sockets staring and nearly fleshless jaws working open and shut, as if anxious still to bite Ma'iingan.

Footless and headless, meanwhile, the zaambi's body dragged itself to its knees and groped toward Ma'iingan.

"George!" he yelled.

"Soon!" George Isham called. Ma'iingan hoped he could depend on the young man.

He swung his axe twice more in quick succession. The first blow snapped off one of the riper zaambi's arms at the shoulder, dropping it sternum-first to the floor. With the second, he chopped through the neck of the zaambi biting his arm.

He stood, a woman's head still gnawing on his forearm. He took a step toward George, to see how the fire-starting efforts were coming, and hands grabbed at his ankles. Looking down, he found the headless zaambi with both hands around his left foot, and the disembodied arm of the other draugar clutching his right.

Smash! Smash! Smash!

He chopped through the hands at the wrist, causing the finger bones to fall apart uselessly and freeing himself. Feeling woozy, he looked down at the head chewing on his arm and found the flesh of his arm, around the undead teeth sunk into it, marbled white and black.

He found Nathaniel; the boy lay prone and apparently unconscious on his back, drum clutched to his belly. Under his breath, the boy chanted a droning melody.

"George!" he cried, unable to see the young man, either because the drying barn was filling with smoke or because his vision was failing. "Where's your fire?"

As answer, a lattice of flame rushed toward Ma'iingan from the back of the barn. How could so much flaming wood move so fast?

The Phaeton! George Isham had turned the Phaeton into a flaming chariot.

Ma'iingan threw himself aside and could just make out George as the young man hurled a good portion of the frame of a tobacco drying rack, now on fire and piled onto the light coach, through the open doorway.

The frame burst apart as it hit, filling the doorway with fire and scattering flaming wood against the walls around it. The coach rolled on, forcing two more zaambi, about to step through and into the barn, back several steps. Scattering flaming brands as it went, the Phaeton struck a ditch or a fence at the end of its path and overturned, wheels spinning in the smoke.

Beside the Phaeton stood a man. Ma'iingan hesitated and took a long look; he was Zhaaganaashii, tall, and even in the firelight Ma'iingan could tell he was unnaturally pale. Dead? He wore a tall, peaked cap and dull colors, such as Ma'iingan had seen before on Zhaaganaashii travelers from Massachusett lands. And he wore a long cloak, so tattered that at its fringes it almost seemed to discompose itself into brown spider's web.

"Brother Ephraim sold his cow," George Isham sang, "and bought him a commission."

Ma'iingan didn't know the song, but he thought he'd heard the tune before. It was shockingly jaunty, given the scene.

The Zhaaganaashii raised something long and thin to his mouth and tore a piece out with his teeth.

It was a forearm.

The forearm of a child.

George stopped singing.

"Wiindigoo!" Ma'iingan shouted.

He staggered back from the door, shaken and cursing. He waved his arm, and the biting head didn't fall off. The dead woman's eyes stared up at him with hatred and she worked her jaws, digging deeper into his flesh. He felt the corpse's poison and corruption flowing through his veins.

"More fire," he murmured.

The zaambi head on his arm groaned.

The witch's child! the wiindigoo groaned through the doorway of fire. *The rest of you may live, but give me the witch's child!*

Ma'iingan heard the voice in his mind as well as in his ears.

He could only mean Nathaniel, God-Has-Given.

The healer whom Ma'iingan's own manidoo had given him in order to join Giimoodaapi to the People.

Ma'iingan stooped to pick up a flaming brand and shoved the burning end into the zaambi's eyes. He felt the searing heat on his own arm, but the draugar opened its mouth to shriek in rage and pain—

and fell off his arm, hitting the floor and rolling several feet toward the opening.

Ma'iingan felt lightheaded, but he wasn't incapacitated yet. Taking three steps, he kicked the woman's head like a ball, straight through the open door and into the night. The wiindigoo stepped to one side, but not fast enough, and the hurtling head struck him in the knee.

He growled.

"More fire!" Ma'iingan called again.

Cathy held the mirror-on-a-stick in her left hand, and a loaded, primed, and cocked pistol in her right. She reached out with the mirror and probed the shadows on the other side of the street through the large window.

She was rewarded with three powder flares, three *bangs* in quick succession, and three bullets whizzing narrowly over her head.

She answered with a shot of her own.

Bang!

"It is doubtful I hit anything," she said. "The Lafitte pistols may be consecrated, but they're not especially accurate."

"I rather fancy I saw your shot go home." Bill leaned against the earth wall of the mound. One advantage of their position had turned out to be that the dirt walls of the lower floor were so thick that they stopped all incoming bullets cold. Having repulsed two waves of attacks, Bill and his beastkind were beginning to run low on ammunition, and now they crouched behind solid dirt walls and waited for the dawn.

"I only wish it had gone home into the face of that liar Torias." Cathy reloaded. "I knew from the start she wasn't to be trusted."

Bill grunted.

"Does this window face east?" she asked.

"It does, ma'am. You should see dawn as a lightening of the horizon over there."

"The solstice morning."

"The shortest day of the year."

"Sir William, shall we live to see Christmas?"

Bill chuckled. "I would not wager a large sum on my own life at the moment, ma'am. This, however, is not the first moment in my life when I would have said that. You in any case shall live for all eternity, even if only in my heart."

"Your gallantry lightens my soul at this dark moment, my love."

She hadn't meant to say it, but there it was. *My love.* Suddenly, she felt more naked than she had ever felt in all her years in New Orleans.

He hesitated, but only for a moment.

"My lady," he said, his voice sounding more gravelly than ever. "I would that I were sufficiently gallant to remove your every care forever."

She rested a light hand on his forearm, feeling the hard muscled beneath the bristly hair. "You are my hero."

Time passed.

"Sir William," she began again, having cleared her head of the distraction. "Would you be so good as to tell me why the sun is rising in the west of the city? Have we entered some enchanted Firstborn space in which the directions are not what they seem, so that the sun rises in the west and sets in the south, while the Big Dipper revolves in a six-sided star-shaped movement around the celestial east pole?"

Bill chuckled. Then he gasped. "Hell's Bells, but you're right! That direction is west and the river!"

"Are you certain of it?" Cathy pressed him.

He hesitated. "I haven't seen the stars for some time, but I am quite sure."

"Then that light?" Cathy asked. "Is it possibly the indication of our arriving reinforcements?"

Bill laughed out loud. "Other than on the day on which I met you, my lady, I have *never* been that fortunate."

Chikaak sniffed the air. "Fire."

"The light is behind us, at least," Cathy said. "Is that not what a pistolero desires most?"

"Usually with respect to the sun, my lady, but yes. I suppose a large fire at my back would be nearly as useful."

"Let us make use of it, then." Cathy leaned out from cover just a moment, firing at a tight-capped skirmisher in a fur vest. She could see the man clearly with the western glow, now clearly an orange color, shining in his face, but he likely couldn't see her.

Her shot took him in the center of his chest, right where she'd aimed, and he crumpled forward.

She returned to cover and reloaded.

An answering volley came, which included two arrows that flew deep into the room and sank into the wood of a standing armoire belonging to Alzbieta Torias.

When the hostile volley had finished, Bill carefully laid five guns on the sill beneath his window. He then slipped in front of the window and filled his hands with a pistol each. Cathy held out her mirror-on-a-stick to watch. Taking careful aim with one gun, he shot through an upended table, and Cathy heard a grunt of pain and surprise.

Bill dropped the pistol and immediately took another... but didn't take cover.

Imperial Ohio Company men popped up from behind wagon beds and dead horses and low walls to fire back.

Bang! Bang!

Bill neatly dropped two before they could fire, one a big-shouldered German with a shiny long rifle, who fell with a sound like a sneeze, and the other some kind of Creole, part-Haudenosaunee, judging from the colorful shirt and feathers.

As bullets and arrows whizzed toward him, Bill pressed himself against the side of the window well and took two more pistols into his hands. With the volley finishing, but before the Imperials could take cover again, he shot two more. A man wearing a conical raccoon cap and a fringed leatherstocking suit dropped clutching his throat with blood pouring between his fingers; a Cahokian longbowman fell forward onto his own bow, snapping the stave as well as his arrow in his collapse.

Bill began to reload.

The smoke smelled thicker. Chikaak sniffed the air again.

Cathy heard a long howl, not far away.

"Wolf?" she asked.

"Wolflike," Chikaak said.

"Beastkind," she said.

Chikaak nodded. "They're within the walls."

"Very good. Thou knowest thy fairy-stories."

———————>○<———————

CHAPTER TWENTY-SIX

Nathaniel's horses caught him up easily this time, and bore him up the seven golden steps with a song on his lips.

> *I ride upon four horses, to heaven I ride*
> *I ride the sacred smoke-path, drum at my side*
> *I walk the endless star-fields, my vision is wide*
> *I seek the land of spirits, to heaven I ride*

At the top of the stairs waited no manidoo and no golden path. Instead, Nathaniel stood upon a dark and trackless prairie, and overhead again he saw the inverted bowl of star-signs in their new patterns.

New, but now familiar. Now right.

Cold winds blew across the plain, and Nathaniel stood for a time in thought, at a loss. Then he listened.

On the wind, voices.

And Nathaniel found that as he shifted his position, listening into the wind, listening down the wind, stepping along the prairie to find new winds to listen to, he heard voices.

~Wiindigoo!~

He heard this word shouted in Ma'iingan's voice, and it troubled him. Nathaniel didn't know who or what a *wiindigoo* was, but the word was monstrous in his ear. It reeked of loneliness, despair, power, and the eating of forbidden flesh.

495

Riding up that wind, Nathaniel found a thin trail. The trail led him down a steep hillside to a tobacco-curing barn, surrounded by picked fields, and under siege. The besiegers were women and men, but not entirely. Skeletons raged around the outside of the barn, banging on it with bony fists and feet. They moved with the rattle of iron, and Nathaniel quickly noticed that each was shackled at the ankle to a leather sack. From the sacks rose a mélange of vitriolic scents that nearly overpowered him.

Within the barn burned fire. Where the fire burned wood, it appeared to Nathaniel as a low orange flame, like a Lucifer match lying on the floor, about to be snuffed out. Where it devoured instead the sacred asemaa, it rose like a wall of white morning, shutting out the dark night with the trumpets of dawn.

Inside those rings of fire, Nathaniel saw Ma'iingan and George Isham, running about and throwing wood on the flames to feed them. Landon Chapel lay on the ground, sleeping. Something about Landon's appearance struck Nathaniel as odd, and it took him a moment to realize what—though Nathaniel knew that Landon was physically wounded, the sleeping young man in this place looked well.

Nathaniel approached and dismounted. One of the skeletons turned and groaned to him. "Help me!" He heard in her voice the physical beauty she'd possessed in life, and the lonely fears that had driven her to intimate betrayals and once, to hide those betrayals, to a tiny murder, a friend pushed down a well into darkness.

Those passions and memories roiled about in the leather sack. Nathaniel knelt to slip the shackle from the skeleton-woman's ankle, and hesitated.

The sack wasn't leather, but skin; the woman's features, a proud Irish face with bright yellow hair, stared up at him from the sack, with bile and gall oozing through the tightly shut eyelids.

His horses neighed sharply.

Something hit Nathaniel from behind.

He struck the skin-sack of the woman's grief and missteps and its bulk knocked him sideways. Nathaniel rolled across rocky ground, watching the stars overhead whirl, and struggled to his feet, drum held before him like a shield or a weapon.

"Wiindigoo!" he cried.

The wiindigoo looked like a man from the Covenant Tract. He was narrow-faced and tall beneath a black peaked hat. His cloak was a starless abyss that sucked in light, and his eyes were gaping tunnels that led to the same bottomless void.

Serpentspawn! the wiindigoo hissed back.

Nathaniel touched the skin of his drum, tapping a soft pattern like spring rain. He felt the horses beneath him and took courage.

"No," he said. "I'm no child of Wisdom."

Liar! The wiindigoo stood to his full height, and suddenly he was as tall as the world-axle, and the black of his cloak hid the stars. *You're the get of the half-cocked rider of the Missouri on his half-witted Penn slattern. You're mixed-blood Fey and child of Eve, an abomination, and I've come for you!*

Something in the rage-filled words rang true.

"No," Nathaniel said again. "What I was, I am no longer. I've died in the Pit of Heaven and been made anew. I owe you nothing, wiindigoo."

Stop calling me that! The wiindigoo swept an arm through his own cloak, gathering up infinite night, and slammed his black arm into Nathaniel.

Nathaniel felt his iron bones bend as all the breath was pummeled from his lungs. He fell back, knocked from his horse, and tumbled, not earthward, for earth wasn't beneath him, but toward the infinite void—

but caught himself at the last moment on the lip of his drum.

He drummed rain again, his horses neighed, and Nathaniel galloped away.

The wiindigoo roared behind him as Nathaniel rode back up the mountain to the windy plain, but couldn't follow. Before the curing barn disappeared entirely, Nathaniel saw the wiindigoo turn his attention back to the walls of white flame, hurtling the dark emptiness of his cloak against the light.

Nathaniel reached the starlit plain and thought.

The wiindigoo was too powerful for him.

What about the witch? The witch who'd had Nathaniel's own face, the red-haired cauldron-witch in the pit of giants where Nathaniel had been torn apart and rebuilt. Might she be an ally?

Nathaniel listened for the witch.

He heard many hungry voices on the winds. Voices filled with fear, and others with hatred.

Somewhere far away, at the beginning of an especially strong gust, he heard the cry of a heron that shook him to his iron bones.

Elsewhere, a shrill laugh that sounded like shattering glass, and brought with it the sound of moldering bones.

An eagle's cry with sad tones in it, and Nathaniel realized he was hearing the Earl of Johnsland.

Then he found the witch's voice. ~*Cal*,~ the witch said. ~*I reckon this is it for me. I tried, and I failed.*~

Nathaniel followed the wind that bore that voice. It took him across leagues of grassland and into a shallow depression through which flowed a trickle of a creek. When the stream dropped sharply downhill, Nathaniel knew he was close, and in a circle of short hills he found her.

The hills were hollow, with doorways and windows carved into their sides. Some had small buildings on their peaks. Most were squarish, and all but one were built upon a foundation of stars, and specifically upon the Loon.

The remaining hill was built upon the sun, and therefore pointed a different direction than the others. A gulf separated that hill from the others, a ravine from which rose a foul-smelling smoke. On that hill stood a woman beside a tree with a serpent wound around it and a spring bubbling from its roots. Somehow, the woman, the tree, the spring, and the snake were all the same being.

And She was ancient, and Her face radiated so much loneliness it hurt.

Nathaniel looked away.

The witch sat inside a hill, surrounded by a sheet of something that shone like glass. Nathaniel knew her face, which looked strikingly like the face he saw when he looked in the mirror, even though the witch's red hair was gone, replaced with short, black hair. She sat with a young man who did have long red locks, whose heart sang the most guileless song Nathaniel had ever heard, and whose face was glum.

~*What you mean, Sarah?*~ the young man asked.

"Today is the solstice. Today at dawn all the candidates gather and hope the goddess chooses one of 'em. I had a plan with Alzbieta to sneak in, but it looks like she changed her mind. I ain't sure quite how this is supposed to work, but I git the feelin' She ain't gonna choose me, locked up in here."

Nathaniel reached out to touch the surrounding sheet and it froze his fingertip, bringing up an instant blister.

The witch looked up and met his eyes. "Who are you?"

~*Who you talkin' to, Sarah? Ain't nobody here but you and me. Jerusalem, even when I finally git you alone, you go talkin' to specters.*~

"It ain't a specter, Calvin. Someone's here."

~*Well, I can't see him.*~

Nathaniel and the witch looked each other, and Nathaniel smiled.

"I think he's my brother."

"My name's Nathaniel Chapel," Nathaniel said.

"Your name's Nathaniel Elytharias Penn," she answered. "My name is Sarah Elytharias Penn, and you and I are two out of a set of three triplets. I have many more things to tell you about yourself, and I expect you have a lot to tell me, too, but first, can you get me out of here?"

The red-haired youth flung his arms skyward and sat, muttering to himself.

"Your trap," Nathaniel said. "Whatever it is that holds you burns me when I touch it."

"Silver," she said. "I guess this might be a surprise to you, but you're Firstborn."

"The wiindigoo told the truth."

"I don't know what a wiindigoo is," she said. "But you need to get someone in here who can open the silver door."

"Who?"

"The man imprisoning me is named Maltres Korinn." As the witch said the name, Nathaniel heard the man's image and voice. "I don't think he really wants to keep me locked up. Maybe you can persuade him."

Nathaniel nodded. "I'll try." Then a thought occurred to him. "The goddess whose chosen you hope to be . . . she's a serpent?"

Sarah stared. "She is *the* serpent, some would say. Why?"

"She's close. And she wants someone to come to her."

Sarah squinted at him. "Come *to* her? Where is she?"

Nathaniel considered. "She's on . . . the different hill. The one that doesn't point at the northern sky."

Sarah stood. "I know it."

The red-haired youth stared at her. ~*Sarah, what's goin' on?*~

"Shh!"

"The hill's broken," Nathaniel said. "It should be connected to the others, but it isn't. It needs something."

Sarah nodded. "Anything else?"

Nathaniel shrugged. "She's lonely."

Sarah looked sad. "She ain't the only one."

"And I... I'm attacked."

Sarah looked startled. "Here?"

Nathaniel laughed, wondering exactly what *here* meant in this conversation. "In Johnsland," he said. "In an old tobacco-curing barn that belongs to the earl. A Yankee wiindigoo and... dead people."

"Did you say a *Yankee* wiindigoo?"

"Yes."

"Is a wiindigoo another word for a wizard?"

"I don't know. I learned the word from a friend. It might be an Ojibwe word, like *moccasin*. Can you help?"

"Mebbe," Sarah said. "Yes, I think so. Now go! Get Maltres Korinn in here, quick as e'er you can!"

Nathaniel exited the prison-hill. He walked a short time among the hills, listening. He heard a wind full of the snarling of beasts, and another that clanked with the sound of metal coins, and a third that sang a sorrowful dirge of impossible love. Then he heard Korinn, and he followed the sound into another hill.

How much time was passing in the curing barn in the Johnsland hills as Nathaniel did this? He hoped his friends lived.

And if the wiindigoo broke into the barn before Nathaniel could return to his body, what then? Would his bear-self Makwa be able to keep him alive? Would Makwa defend Landon and the others?

Maltres Korinn stood with two other people over the sickbed of a fourth person. All four of them looked afflicted.

Maltres bore on his shoulders a yoke that bent him nearly double.

The woman standing beside him had an imp sitting on her shoulder, whispering into her ear.

The third standing figure was an old man, whose heart was laced with scars. As he shifted from one foot to another during the conversation, scars opened and bled, briefly.

The man lying on the bed was empty. A shell. Nathaniel looked at him and frowned, and then noticed that a cord exited one of his ears and fell to the floor. Following the string, he crossed the floor and then looked out the hill's window; the same man who lay on the sickbed an empty shell, with a cord flowing from his head, also stood outside the window, holding the far end of the same string.

~*I beg you to release her,*~ the woman said to Maltres Korinn. ~*This was a terrible mistake.*~

The imp on her shoulder, a knotted ball of cartilage with a wide, tooth-filled grin and a greasy forked tongue, frowned and hissed into her ear. She brushed at it, trying to knock it away, and missed.

~*The regent is correct,*~ the old man said to her. ~*This final night, and perhaps the goddess will choose a monarch for us again, and then that king or queen can decide what to do with Kyres's daughter.*~ A large scar on his heart split open and poured a stream of dark blood down his breast. ~*Perhaps that queen will be you.*~

The imp whispered and the woman smiled, pleased. Then she frowned. ~*Perhaps She'll choose Kyres's daughter as Her Beloved, and what then? The more I know of her, the more I see her father in her. She and I had... I wish you hadn't done this, Uris.*~

They were talking about his sister Sarah.

Nathaniel saw his way forward. Following the string back to its other end, he climbed inside the open mouth of the man lying on the bed. At his teeth Nathaniel met resistance, but he played a tattoo upon his drum and the horses carried him down the man's throat and into his heart.

Maltres Korinn shook his head. ~*Then I'll offer my queen my life.*~

Nathaniel found the bedridden man's voice, and the strings that worked his limbs. He sat up. "Listen to me, all of you."

The woman spun about, her mouth gaping. ~*Sherem!*~

Nathaniel shook his borrowed head. "My name is Makwa."

The old man balled his hands into fists. ~*What sorcery is this?*~

"I ride old paths," Nathaniel said. He caused his borrowed body to stand. "I don't have a name for them. I follow voices down the winds that blow between the stars. What sorcery would you call that?"

Maltres Korinn shook his head. ~*I have no name for that, either.*~

The old man looked pale and shocked. ~*What do you want, spirit?*~

"I come from your goddess," Nathaniel said. This was almost true. "She's trapped and lonely."

~She requires a Beloved,~ the woman said. ~She hasn't had one since Kyres Elytharias. Fifteen years.~

There was that name again, Elytharias. Sarah had said it was her own name, and that Nathaniel rightfully bore it as well.

He had much to learn.

~Fifteen years are the blink of an eye for a goddess,~ the old man said.

~And the blink of an eye is an eternity.~ The woman turned on the old man, fire in her stare. Her shoulder-imp nearly fell off, and clung to her hair with one yellow-nailed hand. ~Don't lecture me about the gods and their sense of time.~

"Your goddess won't choose a queen in Her prison," Nathaniel said. "Sarah Elytharias Penn can free Her."

Then he clapped his borrowed hands on Maltres Korinn's shoulders. His own hands slipped from the borrowed body and grabbed the yoke that Korinn couldn't see; in his own eyes, Nathaniel had four hands sprouting from two wrists.

He squeezed the ends of the yoke together. The wood in the middle bowed up.

Korinn gasped and stared, wide-eyed.

~What are you doing?~ the old man asked, leaning forward as if he might intervene.

The woman restrained him with a hand on his chest. ~Wait.~

~It hurts,~ Korinn gasped.

"Peace," Nathaniel whispered. "The pain ends now."

He roared and forced the two yoke-ends together. The yoke shattered into multiple pieces, and the force of the blow knocked Nathaniel right out of his borrowed body.

Like a discarded puppet, the body fell to the floor. Korinn dropped also, weeping.

Nathaniel sighed. He thought Korinn would free Sarah now, so Nathaniel's work was done. He turned to leave, and saw the man standing outside the window, holding the end of the string.

Nathaniel considered. Stooping, he reached inside the mouth of the man's empty body and dug around until he found the string end, a tangled knot pulled tight against one side of his skull. Gripping the knot tightly, he wound the string around his wrist to make it secure, and then began beating his drum.

He felt the power of his horses beneath him.

"Hold on tight," he said to the man standing outside the window. Then he galloped out of the hill.

As he passed, he snatched the imp from the woman's shoulder. It was a gristly knot, the size of a squirrel, and its eyes were jaundiced. The creature squealed in his hand and bit Nathaniel's finger. As his horses bore him outside and under the stars again, the string whipped through the head of the man lying on the floor, and the man standing outside the window was pulled inside. He hit the floor hard, both hands tightly gripping the string, and then was yanked back into his body through his ear.

Nathaniel slowed his horses, dropped the string, and returned to look through the window.

The man lying on the floor stood up. ~*What happened?*~ he asked.

Korinn, also standing, shook his head mutely.

~*You've been restored by the goddess,*~ the woman said. ~*She wants us to free Sarah Elytharias.*~

~*Can it be wise to do anything other than obey Her?*~ the healed man asked.

~*It can't,*~ Maltres Korinn said. ~*I go to free Elytharias now.*~

He strode purposefully from the hill.

The imp in his grip shrieked in wordless rage, biting Nathaniel again. Nathaniel hurled it to the earth and then trapped it under his heel.

The imp glared at him and howled one final time.

Nathaniel ground his heel back and forth until the imp was nothing but a knobby yellow paste.

At that moment, Nathaniel noticed a third version of the healed man. The third version was so faint Nathaniel could see through him, but he had stars shining in his eyes. He stood still outside the window, looking in. His hands were empty and his face was full of sorrow, so Nathaniel's healing of him was not complete. For that matter, there remained the old man with the bleeding heart. Nathaniel wanted to ease *his* sorrows as well . . . but *how*?

And Nathaniel worried he had already spent too much time here. Korinn would free Sarah, and she had said she would help him.

Perhaps the goddess would be her ally in that effort.

Nathaniel needed to return to his friends. He rode his horses back uphill to the windy plain under the upside-down stars. Again he crossed the gust bearing the beastly cries of raging animals, and the sheer will to destroy and cause pain that he heard in those voices made him shudder.

They also made him think of the earl.

Ma'iingan had said he would become a healer. Ma'iingan's manidoo had said the same thing, and now Nathaniel found himself indeed healing. Not physical wounds, but other sorts of scars and injuries.

Could he heal the earl?

He listened first for Ma'iingan's voice and heard it, shouting words Nathaniel didn't understand. Algonk war cries, perhaps, but Nathaniel heard strength and courage in the voice as well as fear.

He listened for the earl.

He heard the raptor's cries immediately and rode toward them.

He had found the slope down that he was sure led to the earl's manor when he was knocked from his horses.

Nathaniel rolled in the tall heavenly grass, smelling sweet nebula dust kicked up by his horses' hooves, and he managed to grab one of his beasts as it fled in panic. The horses pulled him and he sang to the beats of their hooves, gradually climbing back atop them and then reining them in and turning them back to face his attacker.

A man stood on the plain, and not on it. Beneath his feet was a pool of golden liquid that stank of putrefaction, a sea of corrupt pus. Faces floated in that sea—men's faces, women's, children's, the faces of beastkind, faces of beings Nathaniel couldn't identify. The faces bore expressions of fear and loss, and the man stood on their faces as one might stand on stones when crossing a shallow stream.

The man himself was as surreal and horrifying as the platform on which he stood. His feet were bare, with dead-white skin and long yellow nails—as long as a handspan, and the toenails dug into the faces of the beings trapped in the pool of rot and made them bleed. Tattered clothing clung to a wiry body whose pale skin showed in various tears and holes, and long nails extended also from china-white fingers. Long red curly hair spilled down over his shoulders, marking the black and white of his general appearance with a shocking, bloodlike accent. His face was also pale, long yellow teeth hanging from receded gums, but his eyes were white.

White and crawling with living things. As Nathaniel looked at the man's face, a worm dribbled out of his eye and down his cheek.

A faint cloud of sand swarmed about him, like a thousand screaming mosquitos.

"Out of my way, monster!" Nathaniel cried.

Thy words wound me. The man's lips didn't move, and his voice spoke directly into Nathaniel's mind. It sounded like crackling autumn leaves, or a fire built of wet pine branches. *I have come only to benefit thee, Serpentspawn.*

Nathaniel's head spun. Ma'iingan and his unnamed manidoo had brought Nathaniel to this wider, cosmic world, and yet in that world Nathaniel seemed to already have an identity.

An identity and enemies.

The long nails told Nathaniel what he was looking at. "Last warning, Lazar. Stand aside." He didn't feel as brave as his voice sounded.

Very good. The Lazar's smile was humorless. *Thou knowest thy fairy-stories.*

Nathaniel struck his drum and sang:

> *I ride upon four horses, I'll not be caged*
> *Not by murdering giants, nor Lazar mage*
> *My bones are made of iron of solid gauge*
> *I ride the land of spirits, through heaven I rage*

He charged the Lazar.

The dead man's face registered surprise. Nathaniel's horses sprang from the bank of the pool of death, scattering a cloud of star-spirit dust, and Nathaniel struck the dead man with his own shoulder, and then with the shoulder of each of his four horses.

The Lazar teetered and waved his arms, seeking his balance—

his long-nailed hand swiped at Nathaniel—

Nathaniel felt a burning sensation as his neck was scratched by three long nails. Then his horses landed on the far side of the pool and he galloped on.

He followed the earl's voice along a thin, biting wind. Looking over his shoulder, he saw the Lazar stabbing downward with his nails, apparently fighting the tortured faces within his own deathly arcane pool, and then the Lazar was out of sight.

Nathaniel found the ridge down to the Earl of Johnsland's manor and he followed it. The manor was a small home, more like one of the sod huts the earl's Irish workers built than like the brick palace Nathaniel knew, but he recognized it from the mold and rot that carpeted the roof and the walls. The same breeze that carried the earl's voice made his house tremble.

Nathaniel alighted, slinging his horses over his shoulder. He took a deep breath, then entered.

Within the cottage was but a single room, and in the center of the room a slat-backed wooden chair. On the chair sat the Earl of Johnsland, his old face riven with grief, his hands clutching a tiny wooden box—the same one he held in the physical world, or one that looked just like it.

On the back of the chair perched a vulture.

Crowding all around the earl were spirits. Nathaniel knew them for spirits—ghosts, perhaps—because he could see through them. They approached the earl in attitudes of supplication: some knelt, some lay on their faces on the floor, some pressed at the earl's feet. All of them raised their arms in begging gestures.

And to his surprise, Nathaniel knew one of the supplicants.

"Charles," he said. "Charles Lee."

Charles turned to look at him. He still bled from the wound in his forehead.

"It was my fault," Nathaniel said. "I'm sorry."

The ghostly Charles looked at his feet, then met Nathaniel's gaze. "I did my duty. I did what a man should do."

"No," Nathaniel said. "You did was a *good* man does. You're the truest gentleman I have known, Charles Lee. You're my hero."

"I wish my mother and father could have known," Charles said.

"You can still talk. Tell them yourself," Nathaniel pointed out.

"My mother is dead." Charles squinted at a horizon Nathaniel couldn't see. "I believe I can find her. But my father lives."

"I'll tell him."

"His name is Captain Sir William Johnston Lee." Charles looked at the earl. "And him? Can you help him?"

"I'll try."

Charles gripped Nathaniel's shoulder one last time. "You'll be your own hero now, Nathaniel. And a hero to many other people, I expect."

Nathaniel abruptly felt young, as if a century of aging had

been reversed in a single moment. "If I do, it'll be because of what I learned from you."

Charles grinned and took his arm back. Then his face dropped into the furrowed brow of uncertainty. "Do you think the pastors are right? Or the godar? Or both?"

"I know there are gods," Nathaniel said. "Or . . . powerful things, out of sight, that call themselves gods."

"And heaven?" Charles asked. "Is there a place where I can rest?"

"I don't know," Nathaniel said. "I'm learning that the universe is much bigger than I ever thought, and full of strange things. Maybe there is a heaven, where the just get to rest for all eternity. Though I heard someone say, just tonight, that an eternity and the blink of an eye are the same thing to the gods. Or maybe there's a heaven where the brave continue to be heroes."

Charles smiled again. "I like that."

Nathaniel pushed through the other ghosts as if they were a gauze curtain, until he came to the earl. Standing beside the man, he realized he was holding one of the ghosts' hands. The ghost looked a lot like the earl himself, and even more like George. Nathaniel thought he remembered this spirit's name.

"Richard," he said. "Richard Randolph Isham. This is your eldest son."

The earl and the ghost looked at Nathaniel with matched eyes. The raptor perched on the back of the earl's chair stared with the hatred and resentment of an animal defending its territory, or its rightful prey.

"Killed," Richard said.

~Killed,~ the earl echoed.

"Murdered?" Nathaniel asked.

"Killed in a fair fight, as far as that goes," Richard said. "Challenge offered and accepted, seconds present, and I chose the weapons. By Captain Sir William Johnston Lee."

~Killed, as far as that goes,~ the earl echoed. ~William.~

"Charles's father?"

Richard nodded and his eyes flashed. "But I was attempting to do my duty to the Emperor and my commander, Thomas Penn. And Lee killed me to stop me from my duty. He killed me to raise the banner of rebellion against his rightful lord."

~Rebellion, his rightful lord.~

"Why would he do that?" Nathaniel asked.

"As near as I can tell? Service to *his* lord and master, suh."

~*Tell his lord and master.*~

"You both acted with honor, then?"

"And yet I am dead."

The vulture reached forward to snap at Nathaniel, who danced out of reach.

Nathaniel considered. Then he took the earl's other hand in his own and stroked the back of it gently until the earl looked up and met his gaze. "My lord," he said.

~*Lord.*~ The earl's voice held within it a piercing raptor's cry, but also the mournfulness of the owl.

"William Lee killed your son Richard," Nathaniel said. "And your son Landon killed William's son Charles."

~*My son, Landon.*~ The earl nodded slowly. ~*Landon is my son. He does not replace Richard.*~

"And yet Landon lives. As does George."

~*George. Yes, George is my son, too.*~

"Can we not say that all have suffered grievously, and let there be an end to the killing, and a sharing of grief?"

The earl squeezed Nathaniel's hand. ~*But how?*~

Nathaniel turned, continuing to grip the earl's fingers. "Charles!" he called.

Charles came. "My Lord. Richard. Nathaniel."

"Richard and Charles," Nathaniel said. "The cosmos is large, and somewhere in it is Charles's mother. Richard—will you travel with Charles? You are both bold Cavaliers, and a traveler in a strange country needs a companion on whom he can rely."

The vulture above the earl's seat hissed and spat.

"My father needs me." Richard tightened his grip on the earl's other hand.

The earl looked uncertain.

"Your father will be well enough without you," Nathaniel said. "Landon and George are here."

~*Landon and George. My sons.*~

"Landon is a bastard," Richard hissed. "And George is a child."

"I will also be here," Nathaniel said. "Do you find me inadequate to the task?"

The vulture pecked, aiming for Nathaniel's head, but Nathaniel thumped his drum once and the horses leaped up to interpose themselves.

"My father needs me." Richard sounded less certain this time.

"Your father *needed* you," Nathaniel agreed. "You were here for him then. But he doesn't need you any longer."

"If you are certain." Richard looked to his father.

~*Certain.*~

"Father?"

The earl stood. With an angry squawk, the vulture leaped from its perch up into the air.

~*I am certain, my son. Go.*~

Richard released his father's hand and smiled at Charles. "Shall we find your mother, then?"

Then he and Charles were gone.

With an angry shriek, the vulture dove for the earl. Its neck extended and its beak opened, as if to snatch him up like a fleeing rabbit. The earl looked up at the incoming bird, eyes calm—

and Nathaniel's four horses leaped up to intercept the attack. With iron hooves, they kicked the vulture to the floor and then trampled it repeatedly. When they were finished, and returned into Nathaniel's drum, they left behind them a smear of red on the floor, marked with a few large feathers.

The earl sat again, burying his face in his hands, and wept.

Nathaniel rested his hand on the earl's shoulder.

~*I have lost so much!*~

"And yet you *have* so much."

The earl wept awhile yet, and when he looked up, his face beneath the glistening tears was calm. ~*I know you. You are Nathaniel.*~

"Nathaniel Chapel."

~*Nathaniel Elytharias Penn. Your mother was Hannah Penn, cunning, patient, iron-willed, and possessed of more charisma than any of the Penns since William. Your father was Kyres Elytharias.*~

"The mad rider of the Missouri."

~*The Lion of Missouri, dispenser of swift justice and protector of the weak. Hero of the Spanish War. The King of Cahokia, wooer of the far-famed Hannah, and my friend. Who was murdered by Thomas Penn, so when Kyres's man brought me the child to care for, I couldn't say no.*~

Nathaniel had a hard time grasping all the threads of this tapestry. "The Emperor Thomas murdered my mother? And you kept that a secret?"

~*I hid Thomas's guilt so I would not risk revealing my own glorious secret, that I concealed within my house the sapling in which Penn and Elytharias were grafted together!~* The earl looked down and shook his head woefully. *~But my son Richard learned the truth. Without consulting me, he confronted William Lee, and he died for it.~*

"And you kept me and Charles both about your household," Nathaniel said. "And when Charles's mother died, you gave her son a commission."

The earl shook his head. *~Yes, I gave her son his commission. I armed him at my expense and made him an officer, I kept that vow. I kept all my vows! When I die, they may say of me that I was a madman, but no one shall say I was an oathbreaker.~*

"You kept your vows." Nathaniel touched the earl's shoulder gently. "You cared for me and protected me when I was vulnerable, and an outcast. Thank you."

~For a short time I thought that Jackson would be able . . . but . . . Poor Jackson.~

Jackson?

"May I ask of you one final boon, My Lord?"

~You have but to name it. If not for the love I bore your mother, then for the love I bear you, I'll do what I can.~

"Though you may see me in your hall, I am elsewhere, and I'm being attacked. George and Landon are with me."

The earl stood. *~Tell me where, and my men will ride.~*

Nathaniel had no idea. "A tobacco-curing barn. Beside a narrow lane, surrounded by tobacco fields."

~There are fifty such places on my lands alone,~ the earl said. *~What more can you tell me?~*

Nathaniel's heart fell. "Little. Only that it burns."

~I will mobilize my men,~ the earl said. *~We will begin the search. You send word when you can. What sort of foe shall I advise my men to prepare for?~*

"Dead men who walk, and a sorcerer." Nathaniel considered. "Bring fire. And tobacco."

The earl strode from his hall without waiting for more. Nathaniel thumped a rhythm from his drum, leaping astride his horses as they came. He rode through the ghosts—were they fewer in number now, and less insistent?—then out of the hall and up the slope to the prairie of heaven.

As his horses' hooves struck the sandy soil of the sky, it

occurred to Nathaniel that the stars above him only moved in
their rotation. He had traveled, in some sense, from Johnsland
on the Atlantic coast to—he thought—Cahokia on the Mississippi, and the stars overhead had done nothing to shift other
than spin in their vast circle. Had he ridden the same distances
at the same speed on earth, he would have seen many stars rise
and sink above both the eastern and western horizons.

Did this have something to do with what the woman with
the imp on her shoulder had said about eternity and seconds?

Nathaniel's horses stumbled and he was thrown.

Instead of landing on the ground, he landed in a warm, wet
soup, a stinking cesspit of amber-orange color. He thrashed with
his arms—he was a poor swimmer, but strong enough to keep
himself afloat—and kept his head above the liquid long enough to
see that grass appeared to be growing across the top of the Lazar's
pool of sorrowful faces, and also that the grass was nothing more
than appearance. When he moved his hand, it passed through the
grass without encountering any resistance, and with no sensation.

A clump of real grass—grass from earth? That, too, seemed
strange. Floated in the center of the pool. Fueling the sorcerer's
work, maybe.

The Lazar strode casually up to the edge of the pool, and the
chorus of screaming came with him. *Who would have imagined
it would be so easy? But then, thou art young and inexperienced,
and likely no more clever than thy slattern sister.*

He placed his hands on his hips and laughed.

*My master will be well pleased. And when he devours thee, tell
thou him that it was his best servant Robert Hooke who sent him thee.*

Nathaniel's horses neighed and rolled out of his reach over
the top of the pool.

Then hands out of sight gripped him by the ankles and pulled
him down.

Mercifully, once he was inside the pool, he could no longer
smell it. He opened his eyes, and found he could see—but what
he saw gave him no comfort.

Orange light drifted down from somewhere above. Around
Nathaniel circled dead faces, mouths open and shrieking and eyes
staring blankly, and among and around the faces, hundreds of
hands. Hands of women and men, children's hands, the claws of
beasts. Hands that grasped at Nathaniel and dragged him down.

"I ain't a maniac."

———⟶•⟵———

CHAPTER TWENTY-SEVEN

The spirit-apparition had been her brother, Sarah was certain of it. And if *she* had magical gifts from her father, there was no reason to think that *he* might not *also* have unusual abilities.

And yet she was surprised when Maltres Korinn, counselor Uris, and Alzbieta Torias walked in through the door of her prison cell, accompanied by Yedera and Sherem.

Sherem was not only walking, but alert.

She stood. "You've seen the error of your ways."

Maltres Korinn said nothing. He unlocked the door to the cell, stepped aside, and bowed.

Cal stood too, and they exited the cell.

Uris handed Calvin his tomahawk. "I'm sorry, Calvin."

Cal grunted in return.

"My father's regalia?"

Maltres raised his face, eyes flashing. "They're the kingdom's regalia—" Then he mastered himself. "I gave the orb, the crown, and the plowshare into the keeping of the goddess. I left *your* staff where I found it."

Sarah looked up the chamber's airshaft at the dark sky. "It ain't yet dawn, Korinn, but it's gittin' there. I ain't got time for partial truths."

"I placed the regalia on the Serpent Throne."

"The Presentation," she guessed. "Your seven candidates are

getting ready to stand around the throne, and you thought maybe the regalia would add power to the ritual, or attract the goddess's attention, and make it more likely She would make the decision you've been waiting for so long."

Maltres Korinn nodded. "The candidates are standing there now."

"Six of the seven candidates," Alzbieta said.

Sarah took her cousin's hand and squeezed it. "Thank you."

Maltres bowed his head. "You see through my foolish machinations."

"Right now, I see the hour is late," Sarah said. "I've got a goddess to woo, two attackin' armies to repulse, and on top of everythin' else, a brother to rescue. I ain't got time to git my stuff."

"A brother?" Cal asked.

"I'll retrieve it," Korinn said instantly. "Where shall I meet you?"

"The Sunrise Mound. Calvin, I need to travel fast and light right now. Will you go with the Cahokians here, and see the job gits done right?"

Cal sighed and shook his head. "You know I will, Sarah."

Sarah took the time to stand on tip-toe and kiss Calvin's cheek. Without even looking to see his reaction, she raced up the stairs and into the night.

Her star-lore wasn't so good that she could tell much time remained before the dawn; the eastern sky was dark, but she thought sunrise must be close. The side of the city bordering the river seemed to be burning, and she forced herself not to think too much about that. Kneeling to wipe away an armful of snow and reveal a bare patch of frozen earth, she scrabbled to get dirt under her nails, then anointed her own eyelids with it.

"*Oculos obscuro*," she said, using one of the formulas she'd first heard from old Thalanes. She sighed, feeling his death—at her hands, though compelled by the Sorcerer Robert Hooke—as a fresh wound.

Unseen, she ran as fast as she could to Alzbieta's city home. The Imperial dragoon's coat she wore slowed her down, but the night was far too cold to seriously consider abandoning it. She stopped across the street from the Torias house to survey the scene: scruffy soldiers with mixed weaponry lay around the building with weapons pointed at it. Mixed among them were Cahokians, with their bowl-like helmets.

Sarah recognized some of the Cahokians—they had served

Sarah. They had served Alzbieta. Now they surrounded Alzbieta's home like an invading army. Alongside them were members of the Cahokian wardens, the city's watch, who wore their usual gray but now also carried firearms.

Were any of them wizards?

Sarah had to take the chance. Walking slowly so as to keep her steps quiet, she crossed the avenue. She was conscious of dozens of eyes looking past her, but no one said anything, and no one shot her.

Rather than open a door and risk notice, she walked to an open ground-floor window, cut deep into the earth of the mound. She climbed carefully over the sill, and stepped inside the building. Immediately, she was standing in deep shadow between Catherine Filmer and William Lee.

She stepped away from the window and let her spell drop. "Don't shoot."

"Beelzebub's bedpan!" Sir William made a choking sound, and then laughed. "I pray Your Majesty to forgive an old soldier. Also, to confirm that you're no apparition."

"You want to feel my hands and feet?" Sarah asked.

"She casts a shadow, Bill," Cathy said.

A shadow? From what sun? But then Sarah realized that the western fire threw a faint light on the eastern wall of the room, and she cast a shadow in that light.

She touched Bill's shoulder to alleviate any last doubts. "I can't stay. Everything is happening tonight, now. I've come for the slate, because I need to get a message to Jacob Hop, and then I must go to the Sunrise Mound."

Bill nodded, absorbing the information instantly.

"The Sunrise Mound?" Cathy looked intrigued. "The ancient grave on the edge of the city."

"I don't think it's a grave," Sarah said. "Or it's not *only* a grave. I think dawn will prove me right or wrong, one way or the other. Can you hold out until dawn?"

"For Your Majesty, we can find a way to hold out until doomsday. But would you not find it convenient for us to clear the path to the mound before you?"

"I can get around pretty well unseen myself," Sarah said. "What I would find convenient is for you to keep yourselves alive. Though, if you have the opportunity, I wouldn't mind seeing those Imperials cleared out of the city."

Bill nodded. "Understood."

Sarah left them and returned to her sleeping chamber, hoping nothing had happened to her enchanted writing slate, and that in her absence—or with the interposition of her prison cell's silver insulation—the magic hadn't faded.

The slate and chalk lay beneath her wooden bed, and when she picked them up, she felt the usual tingle. "*Verba transmitto.*"

Power left her as she cast the spell. She had more in her reserves, and the power she'd squirreled away in Thalanes's moon-brooch, but the experience of feeling the energy leave her reminded her what a boon the regalia were, with the Orb of Etyles's apparently infinite ability to channel energy from distant ley lines.

She chalked words onto the slate: MY BROTHER NATHANIEL NEEDS HELP. HE IS SURROUNDED BY UNDEAD.

She waited only seconds before her words disappeared, and were replaced by a message from her Dutchman: WHERE IS HE?

JOHNSLAND. THE EARL'S LANDS. WHERE ARE YOU?

CLOSE. HOW DO I FIND HIM?

Sarah wished she had the Orb, but she didn't. With her own fingernail, she scratched the back of her forearm, drawing blood. With the pad of her smallest and cleanest finger, she collected a drop of that blood—the same blood that flowed through the veins of her brother Nathaniel—and touched her witchy eye.

"*Fratrem quaeso.*"

She sent her vision to the Mississippi and then let the spell guide her. Seeing as through a veil of red, she watched the Mississippi and then the Ohio River and then a series of smaller rivers flow past, until she saw a tobacco-curing barn surrounded by bare fields. The barn was on fire, and shuffling corpses battered at its walls from outside. Sarah didn't see him, but she knew her brother was within. She pulled back, looking for landmarks, and saw a crossroads and a double bridge over a creek flowing through a deep ravine. On one side of the bridges was a thick grove of oaks.

TOBACCO-CURING BARN, ON FIRE, NEAR A FOUR-WAY CROSSROADS, A DOUBLE BRIDGE, AND AN OAK GROVE. BRING FIGHTING MEN, IF YOU CAN. THE ENEMY IS NUMEROUS.

BUT WE ARE FIGHTERS, Hop wrote. GOING NOW.

If she'd had more time, Sarah might have written words of encouragement. Instead, she hung the slate around her neck and pocketed the chalk.

Before leaving, she looked through her blood-borne vision one more time. At the edge of the orange firelight, she saw a presence she recognized—Ezekiel Angleton. She looked closer and saw the Yankee preacher's face; it was ghastly pale, and his teeth were longer than she remembered. His shoulders were wrapped in a ragged brown coat. He was chanting and cutting into the flesh of his own palm with a small knife. Sarah had to do something to help her brother survive until Jacob Hop arrived.

She touched Thalanes's brooch. *"Flammas amplifico."*

The effort to send power that far left her reeling, but the flames around the barn shot up and out. One of the corpses trying to pry a board from the wall caught fire, and shambled away with wordless shrieks.

Ezekiel looked around, as if sensing her presence.

She blinked hard, shutting off her vision. *"Oculos obscuro,"* she said again, and looked for another window to exit.

Calvin raced up the Great Mound. Despite his long legs and his many weeks of lung-strengthening and muscle-hardening travel since he and Sarah had left Nashville, he lagged behind Maltres Korinn and Yedera both. The regent ran like a man with three legs, springing off his black staff of office as well as his feet. The third contact with the ground give him an advantage especially on the long stretches where the steps were iced over. The Daughter of Podebradas blew up the steps like a storm, scale mail rattling and sheathed scimitar clutched in one hand.

Alzbieta, Uris, and Sherem followed. The priestess's slave bearers and palanquin stood at the bottom of the mound.

At the height of the stairs, Maltres came to a halt. Twelve men stood before shut doors. Under their short gray capes they wore gray tunics and trousers and curious sandals, which looked like they might be woven of straw or rope.

"Open up!" Maltres barked. "Now!"

One of the twelve had a helmet with a high crest of colorful plumes, and was armed only with a long sword, where the others leaned on spears. He held up a restraining hand.

"Captain," Maltres growled. "I said let me in or stand aside, now."

The captain smiled and nodded. "You say that now, but earlier you told me to open to no one."

Calvin hooked his thumb into his belt, near where his toma-hawk hung.

Korinn's face drained of color, from some combination of shock and rage. "I didn't mean don't open to *me*, you idiot."

"How do I know you're really the Regent-Minister? Maybe you're that witch in disguise."

Yedera whipped the scabbard from her scimitar, striking the captain with it across the face. Spinning forward with the bare steel in her other hand, she sank eighteen inches of her blade into the captain's neck.

The eleven other men stepped back, uncertain.

Yedera stepped on the dead man's forehead and pulled out her sword. She snapped it once to clear it of blood, flinging a scarlet arc down the stairs. "Your captain was bought," she said slowly to the soldiers. "Traitors meet a traitor's death."

"Open the doors," Korinn said again.

The soldiers obeyed, pushing the doors open wide, and Calvin heaved a sigh of relief.

Within was the scene he'd seen earlier, with the veil open. The difference now was that the lamp bowls on the Serpent Throne were lit, and six people he didn't know stood in a strange pattern across the floor. Squinting at it, he realized that their arrange-ment corresponded to the arrangement of the throne's lamps, and also put each of them standing on a point where lines in the floor's tiles intersected. The intersection points lay in the same arrangement with respect to each other as the lamp bowls, as if the Serpent Throne were casting a shadow forward into the floor tiles. Examining the pattern, he found the seventh spot, where Alzbieta Torias should be standing, and wasn't.

On the seat of the Serpent Throne rested Sarah's shoulder bag. Funny that Korinn hadn't taken the regalia out of the satchel; in time, would the shoulder bag that once carried Thalanes's cof-fee beans become part of Cahokia's regalia? Was that how these things happened?

The six had been facing the throne, but with the opening of the doors they turned to look behind them. One of them, a dark-skinned man out of place among the pale Eldritch, smiled. "You've brought Torias, I see."

Cal looked to his side, and found the slower members of the party catching up, panting.

A heavy woman wearing a leather cape frowned. "Only just in time. The night grows old."

A slender man, the youngest of the six, clapped his hands together. "And we've been having visions, have we not?"

A silver-haired woman frowned and shook her head.

A thin, pale man with receding hair shot a sour look at the young man. "Eërthes mocks us. Or if he's had visions, he's the only one, and he desecrates the very gift with his mockery."

"Come," Eërthes said. "Surely, of all beings in the cosmos, the goddess has a sense of humor."

Leather Cape growled. "Even a person with a sense of humor doesn't enjoy being the butt of every joke."

"We've been mistaken all along," Korinn said. "I don't have time to explain, but this isn't the place, and I believe . . . She won't choose any of you."

"Come," the black man said. "You wouldn't alienate your allies now. Surely, you must at least allow us to await the dawn."

Maltres hesitated, then nodded. "Yes," he agreed. "Await the sunrise, and perhaps it is I who am now mistaken. Perhaps the goddess will select one of you, and I'll return and abase myself as your servant."

"Excellent." Eërthes clapped his hands together as if finishing a performance. Cal wanted to punch him in the nose.

Korinn walked toward the throne.

The silver-haired woman hissed. The last of the six, a heavy woman with impressive facial scarring, who wore plain white tunic and trousers, stepped into Korinn's way.

"What are you doing?" the regent asked.

"What the Lady Alena is trying to tell you," the scarred woman said, "is that having begun a ritual in the sanctum, it would be foolish to now interrupt it."

"I agree that I'm a fool." Korinn stepped around the scarred woman.

"Desecration!" the silver-haired woman hissed. "Blasphemer!"

The other five candidates turned to stare at her.

"I reckon you ain't generally much of a talker." Cal had had enough of the ritual and the posturing. Lord hates a man as values empty performance over the true worship of the heart, he'd once heard Barton Stone himself say, and the true worship of Calvin's heart was to help Sarah. He started forward across the tile.

"Men!" Eërthes shouted.

Cal heard a scream behind him. He turned and saw counselor Uris, impaled on a spear and sinking to the floor. With his dying breath, the old man lurched forward, arms outstretched and reaching for the Serpent Throne. The eleven soldiers who had guarded the gate now advanced on Calvin and his friends.

The Cahokian wizard Sherem raised his hands and shouted something in a gibberish Cal didn't understand. Nothing happened, so he raised his hands and shouted again.

A spearman thrust at him—

and Yedera intervened, knocking the spear aside lightly and then slicing the attacker across his exposed throat.

"Mother of the unborn, fill me with blood!" She yelled and hurled herself upon the remaining ten soldiers.

Cal sprinted toward the far end of the sanctuary. To his left, Maltres began a parallel race, but he was immediately tackled by the scarred woman. The Lady Alena, if that was the woman with silver hair, sat on his sternum and pointed a dagger at his face.

The tall, very Eldritch-looking man wagged a finger of protest, but Calvin ignored him and ran past.

Eërthes moved into Calvin's path and tried to grab Calvin by his loose hunter's shirt. Cal pounded the young fellow in the nose with his fist. It was just one blow, but Cal was on the move and irritated, and he threw his whole body into the punch.

Eërthes went down.

Cal crossed to the center of the hall and stopped at the bottom of the stairs. He wasn't an especially spiritual man, but looking up at the Serpent Throne from its foot, he felt the presence of something.

Was it just the throne itself that awed him with its gleaming gold, its seven fires, and its fine craftsmanship?

Or was it the goddess?

He imagined himself fleeing. He imagined prostrating himself on the floor before the throne. He did neither.

He climbed.

In the space behind the veil, the feeling was stronger. His whole body hummed. He picked up Sarah's satchel and looked inside—the Orb of Etyles, the Sevenfold Crown, and the Heronplow were all there. He threw the bag over one shoulder.

Something hit the back of his skull.

Cal bounced off the hard throne and fell to the floor. He saw people running his way across the hall and climbing the stairs. He rolled over; standing above him was Eërthes. Blood poured from the young man's nose and he raised a spear high, preparing to impale Calvin.

Cal kicked his assailant's feet out from under him.

Eërthes fell sideways, landing on the seat of the Serpent Throne itself. Cal grabbed the arm of the throne and dragged himself up with one hand, freeing his tomahawk from his belt with the other. His vision blurred.

Face twisted in a knot of fury, Eërthes gripped the spear with both hands and stabbed—

Cal dropped to one knee, sliding under the blow—

and swung downward with the axe, splitting open Eërthes's skull.

The humming feeling Cal felt tripled in intensity. Blood spattered across the back of the throne and poured down over the seat and arms.

"Calvin!"

Cal turned, bloody axe in his hand. His head throbbed.

The spear-armed soldiers lay dead in a heap, surrounding Yedera. Her scale mail was bloody and so was her face but she stood, scimitar in her hands.

Uris was dead.

Maltres was on his feet—Sherem the Polite and Alzbieta stood beside him, having pulled off the Lady Alena and the scar-faced woman.

The black man, the woman in the leather cape, and the tall Ophidian all stood on the stairs leading up to the inner sanctum.

Everyone stared at Calvin.

Cal stared back. The feeling of holiness swelled to a feeling of dread, as if a thousand ghosts surrounded him and silently screamed. He swallowed hard. "I didn't want to kill him, he forced me to it. But I reckon now you can see I intend business. And iffen your goddess ain't struck me down, mebbe that means she's lookin' favorably on the business I'm about. Either way, now is the time to stand aside." He hefted his tomahawk.

The three Cahokians at the bottom of the stairs stood back.

"If the Presentation fails, Korinn," the silver-haired woman said, "it's your fault. You brought this Appalachee maniac in here." Her voice was scratchy, as if from long disuse.

"Your vows, Alena," Alzbieta Torias said.

"What do my vows matter now?" Alena snapped. "If I stand by and allow the goddess to be desecrated without objection in this manner, merely in order to keep a vow of silence, I am faithless!"

Cal descended the stairs, each step jarring new pain into his skull, and headed for the door. Sarah needed him.

"And what about when you allowed Eërthes to bribe the wardens to keep me out?" Maltres Korinn straightened his full height, holding his staff in front of him as if he were about to fight with it. "Wasn't that a desecration also? Or did you do more than merely *allow* him?"

"It wasn't you!" Alena screamed. "It was to stop the witch, and Alzbieta Torias, who betrayed us in favor of that Appalachee—"

"Enough of this!" the dark-skinned man said. "You're armed, Maltres. The Unborn Daughter of Podebradas and the Appalachee... what did you call him, Lady Alena? Maniac? The weapons are on your side, Korinn. Take the regalia and go. You must understand that if the goddess chooses one of us at dawn, you will suffer severe... repercussions."

"I ain't a maniac," Cal muttered. He met Yedera's gaze and they nodded respectfully at each other.

What was it she had said about herself? Something about not having to follow the rules. That sounded just fine to Calvin.

Korinn, Sherem, and Alzbieta Torias walked toward the door. Korinn stopped to answer the black man. "And you must understand, *poisoner*, that if the goddess chooses someone else as queen tonight, She will require your loyalty and cooperation just as surely as if She had been standing here among you. And as Duke of Na'avu, or in any other capacity in which I may serve, I'll do my utmost to serve the queen and the realm."

"You sound sure," the dark man said.

Stopping in the doorway, with Cal and the others already standing on the porch in front, Maltres shook his head. "What in life is certain? But I feel more confident than I have for a long, long time."

Cal offered Alzbieta Torias his arm and they headed down the steps of the mound.

Luman had stationed himself on the porch of the Basilica of St. Eve and St. Adam thinking that he'd turn aside Imperial

Ohio Company agents, and maybe even Company Regulars, if they came to loot the building. He was well-enough known to the various followers of Director Schmidt that they might take his instruction seriously and stand down. Exactly *why* he thought this was an important use of this time, he couldn't be certain.

Perhaps it was because Schmidt had dismissed him.

"Thank you, my Balaam," she'd said, as she and her agents marched to arrest the Penn pretender. "I have my letter from you, and that will be enough." She found him useful enough when he was needed for spying on reluctant Hansa agents or for defending the *Joe Duncan*, but his lack of real battle magic—"you know, lightning bolts and shields of fire?" was how she'd explained what she wanted—had been a disappointment, and she'd left him to his own devices at the start of the battle.

So maybe he wanted to thwart the Empire, even if only in some tiny, harmless way.

Or maybe he wanted to prove to her that he could do something worthwhile. Maybe he needed to redeem himself after his dramatic failure at summoning his own shadow.

Then again, there was something about the Cahokian church, with its peculiar concoction of star imagery, its male-female dualism, its heterogeneous theology, and its obsession with Eve, that attracted Luman. The Cahokian basilica was a building built by people who believed they had important secrets, and wanted to keep those secrets from outsiders and at the same moment reveal them to initiates.

Was that what Luman really wanted?

More than safety, more than power, did Luman Walters simply want to be *in the know*?

If so, that hardly made him the worst man in the world.

Maybe he felt he needed to atone for his crimes.

Perhaps in some recess of his heart he imagined himself heroically directing traffic away from the church to save it, and in response the clandestine coven of Firstborn mages-palatine bringing him into their innermost circle.

In any case, he hadn't counted on the beastkind.

Luman had sat through a quiet afternoon on the steep south-facing slope of the Basilica Mound. From the noise of the frequent desultory shots and the several full-scale assaults, he knew where the director had run her quarry to ground, and that her progress had then become slow. On the western Treewall, he watched waves of beastkind slam fruitlessly against the wall, repulsed by long spears and clouds of arrows and musket balls.

What magic traditions might he find among the beastkind? He'd heard tales of their wizardry, but never seen it. And to what lengths would he have to go to be invited into *those* fraternities?

He shuddered to think.

There was looting. Schmidt's skirmishers were loose in Cahokia, and Luman saw them ransack storehouses and libraries and barns, continuing the pillaging that had already driven the Ohio to the brink of starvation and over into revolt. Some Cahokians defended their buildings, but others stood aside and let the rapine continue. Perhaps they saw the Imperials as their only defense against the animal-headed horde. Perhaps they saw the Imperial blue and accepted it as a sign of legitimate authority.

Late in the afternoon, the gates of Cahokia on the north, south, and east all shut. The beastkind attackers hadn't become any better coordinated—they still consisted of little better than a ravening wave—but they had become so numerous that they threatened to surround the Treewall.

After dark, the director's shooting had become even more infrequent. Luman dozed, woke, dozed again.

And then woke to see fire.

At first, he'd thought the Treewall had been torched, but a quick glance showed him the dark, lightless line where the palisade still stood. But beastkind came snarling over the top of that wall and spilling into Cahokia as if over a ramp.

A ramp of what?

Luman didn't think beastkind had the discipline or the ingenuity to undertake earthworks.

Within the wall, defenders had built a ring of fire to try to contain the beastkind invaders. It was a complete failure—the beastkind had snatched flaming brands from that fire with their mouths and hands and hurled them into every thatched roof they could find.

Western Cahokia burned.

Luman assumed that the Imperial fighters would make short work of the beastkind. The Imperials, even the skirmishing militia, had pistols and muskets. They even had light field guns, though in limited number. What would a beastman berserker do, no matter how long his horns or heavy his shoulders, when a five-inch ball was fired into his chest?

An hour later, he saw the first beastkind at the bottom of the hill.

He'd brought two pistols and a very small pouch of shot, but they were small-bore pistols and he was not a practiced marksman. He checked his firing pans and found them primed.

When he looked up from the weapons, he faced a pack of beastkind charging up the hill.

They were led by a large man with a bison's head. Behind Bison Head came a fish with man's legs, a man with a gigantic rabbit's face and ears, and more. They snorted and howled, and their feet, claws, and hooves churned snow in all directions.

Luman raised one of the pistols, trying to show it clearly. A break in the clouded-over sky let through a gleam from a waxing gibbous moon, so the pistol—or even both pistols—ought to be visible.

If he weren't alone, he'd have fired a warning shot. But he had two loaded pistols, and no time to reload. Luman leveled the first pistol and fired into the charging mass.

Bang!

The fish-creature stumbled and fell. It continued to squeal and bubble, sliding down the hill as its fellows charged ahead. Luman slid the pistol into his deep coat pocket. The Homer lamella was supposed to provide protection against wild animals. Wild animals and demons. Would the himmelsbrief in his coat give any added defense? He'd seen it stop enemies, but... of a particular nature. Necromancers, walking dead, black magicians. He didn't think a heavenly letter would do anything against a charging bear, but maybe a bison-headed giant was closer to a devil than it was to a cow.

He took the second pistol into his right hand, aimed, and fired.

Bang!

None of the beastkind fell. Cursing, Luman pocketed his second pistol. His feet slipped in snow as he scooted away from the edge of the hill and groped under his own shirt for the lamella with Greek writing on it. His fingers were cold on his skin.

He found the amulet, gripped it, feeling it tremble to the touch, and said a quick braucher prayer. "*Hund, halt deinem Mund auf die Erden. Mich hat Gott erschaffen, dich hat er lassen warden.*"

At the same time, he squeezed the Homer amulet tightly

in his right fist and he made three crosses with his left hand in the air between himself and the beasts. It wasn't a spell for beastkind, but a spell for mad dogs, and as he finished his third cross, Luman was certain the spell would fail.

Stepping back, his heel slipped in the snow and he fell.

His tailbone felt the impact hard and he cried out; snow fell under his long wizard's coat at the collar, but he retained his grip on the iron lamella—

and the beastkind rushed past him, without looking twice.

With snuffling, yips, hisses, and roars, the beastmen rampaged to the front door, left unlocked, and entered the church. Screaming promptly erupted from the basilica, and refugees burst from the building's exits.

Luman stood slowly, his mind racing. The spells had worked, but he needed something bigger. He needed something that would flush the beastkind out... or put them all to sleep... or kill them.

Stopping to fumble powder and shot back into the pistols, and priming both firing pans, Luman considered and discarded one possibility after another. Then, with a gun in each hand, he went into the basilica.

Sarah arrived at the Sunrise Mound and released her invisibility spell. In the west, she heard shooting and animal screams. On the nearby south-facing wall of her father's city, she saw soldiers, Imperial and Cahokian alike, racing back and forth. Was the city under siege from beastkind, and the Imperials and Cahokians together defending? Was the city under siege from both Imperials and beastkind, and the Cahokians passively cooperating with the Imperials? Its leadership distracted with the Presentation, perhaps the Cahokians simply had no idea what they should be doing, and whom to fight.

The Sunrise Mound wasn't hidden, but it was low and inconspicuous, and the soldiers were looking for threats beyond the walls. The blanket of snow covering the mound was surprisingly thin. Now some of the pieces were coming together in Sarah's mind. The Sunrise Mound might or might not be the burial site of some primeval queen, but more importantly, it was the odd one out, of all the tall mounds, because of its placement with respect to the sky. The other mounds were oriented to the square, north-south and also east-west.

The Sunrise Mound was oriented at an angle.

What angle? Sarah was no astronomer, but she watched sunrises and sunsets like anyone else. As the winter progressed, the sun rose and set farther and farther south, until the day of the solstice—the day that was now about to dawn—when sunrise was at its most southerly. From then until the high peak of summer, sunrises and sunrises were progressively farther north each day.

At what position on the horizon would the sun rise when it came up in only an hour or so?

Sarah's guess was that the southeast side of the Sunrise Mound would point directly at the rising sun.

Tomb or not, if she was right, the Sunrise Mound was a temple. Older than the one on the Great Mound, no doubt. More sacred? Perhaps. Attached to the royal cult?

Sarah's bet was yes, all these things.

She hesitated at the edge of the mound, examining it through her witchy eye. She saw the seven stones—Eve-stones, Alzbieta Torias had called them, rather than Adam-stones. If Adam-stones marked the boundaries of land ownership and political control, what did Eve-stones denote? Four of the stones seemed to mark out four cardinal directions, not with respect to actual north and south, but with respect to the rectangular sides of the mound.

With a trembling foot, she stepped within the boundary of Eve-stones. She felt immediately a presence so close and so strong that she was surprised not to hear an actual voice.

But something was wrong.

She looked again with her witchy eye, and saw a veil of blue light. She hadn't seen it before, when looking at the mound. Was the veil visible because the solstice sun was about to rise? The veil surrounded the Sunrise Mound, and beyond it, Sarah saw . . .

Trees? A tree?

A woman?

A mighty serpent?

These were the accouterments of Wisdom. But they were trapped beyond the veil, or hidden behind it. How to supplicate the Goddess?

The trees and the serpent were also part of the iconography of Eden.

Something deep in Sarah's heart seemed about to come forth.

She stretched herself at full length on her belly, pointing her body along the cardinal lines: head toward where she expected the sun to rise, feet the opposite direction, arms extended to the square on either side. "Tell me, Mother," she whispered. "Tell me what you need me to know."

What had Alzbieta said about Eden? Something niggled at the back of Sarah's mind.

"I'm here, Mother. I'm yours."

Sarah heard running feet. She looked and saw faces she knew, with Calvin and Maltres Korinn in the lead. Calvin's face and hands were stained a vivid pink, as if he'd been bloodied, and then tried to wipe the blood off with snow. He wobbled on his feet, and on his shoulder he wore her satchel.

She rose, and remembered Alzbieta's comment. *Eden can only lie where the land is plowed.* She hadn't offered that as *her* opinion, but as one of *many* opinions about the location and meaning of Eden.

Eden can only lie where the land is plowed.

And what had Nathaniel said? That the hill was *broken.*

And again, Simon Sword, speaking of the Heronplow: *Your foundations will be solid, your boundaries known, your fields fruitful, and your people at peace with each other.*

Calvin grinned wide and stepped forward, crossing the line of Eve-stones—

howling, he staggered back—

something struck Sarah's consciousness as a hammer might hit her in the face. White light blinded her, a sharp pain filled her mind, and she heard a shrill scream.

The scream came from her.

"Cal!"

Blinded, Sarah stumbled forward until she reached what felt like a wall in front of her and stopped. She waited, panting, and her vision gradually cleared. She found herself standing at the edge of the Sunrise Mound, beside one of the Eve-stones.

She could go no further.

Behind Calvin and the regent came Sherem, running under his own power, and Yedera, the warrior Daughter of Podebradas, spattered with blood from head to foot, and finally Alzbieta Torias, carried by her bearers on a palanquin.

"What happened?" Sarah asked.

"The goddess has rejected Calvin," Alzbieta Torias said.

"Let us pray She accepts Sarah," Maltres Korinn murmured. Deep wrinkles around his mouth and dark circles under his eyes made him look as if he had aged ten years during the night.

"I don't understand," Sarah said.

Cal sighed. "I did what I had to do, Sarah. And I did it for you. And I got back the regalia. Only to git it, I had to kill a feller, and as it happens, I killed him in a pretty unlucky place."

"On the Serpent Throne." Alzbieta looked distraught.

"Where, as it also happens, certain old stories seem to suggest that we once sacrificed our kings and queens at the end of their reigns." Maltres cracked a wry smile. "So perhaps Eërthes got his way, after all. Maybe the goddess accepted him as king, and as king She slew him for a sacrifice."

"This whole bein' queen thing is soundin' less attractive every moment," Sarah said.

Alzbieta shook her head. "Only if She accepted Eërthes as a sacrifice, that would make Calvin a priest and sacrificer. And instead, She rejects him."

"There you go," Cal said glumly to Sarah. "That make you feel better?"

Sarah bowed her shoulders. "Cal," she said softly. "I love you. Now give me the satchel."

He opened his mouth, shut it, opened it again. With his jaw slack and an expression of shock on his face, he finally unshouldered the bag and tossed it to her.

She opened the satchel and considered the objects. Would it be presumption to wear the crown? Would it be neglectful not to? Hadn't Thalanes once told her that without the crown, there could be no monarch in Cahokia? Or had Sarah herself said that?

She sighed. It was all a guess.

But the goddess felt so close.

She settled the Sevenfold Crown on her head. It felt comfortable, despite the fact that her hair was still growing back in. Cradling the Heronplow against her side and clutching the Orb of Etyles in her hand, she tossed the bag back to Calvin.

"Thank you, Calvin Calhoun," she said. And then, just in case whatever was about to happen killed her, she added, "thank you for everything."

He looked into her eyes and nodded. "Anythin' for you, Sarah."

She took a deep breath, restraining tears. How was this supposed to work? The goddess was so close, She was beside Sarah, only there was a boundary between them. A boundary that ran around the base of the Sunrise Mound.

She knelt and nestled the Heronplow into the tall grass and the snow. The moon was past full, but still large, and the plow glinted a dull gold color in her natural eye. With her Second Sight, she saw it as green, like the Mississippi ley and the souls of the beastkind.

She rested one hand on the plow and breathed deeply.

A prayer? An incantation? Both?

With her other hand, she raised the Orb of Etyles and looked into it. In her Second Sight, deep within the orb, she saw the green glow of the Mississippi. Using the force of her will, she reached into the orb and drew that power into herself, then pushing back out the other arm and into the plow.

She stood slowly, focusing on the flow of power and maintaining it.

She wished she spoke the Ophidian languages, but she didn't, not yet, not beyond a few phrases. She'd have to make do with what she had.

"*Magna mater,*" she incanted, "*maxima mater. Rogo ut hoc aratrum pelleas.*"

She took another deep breath. She felt the plow beneath her fingers as if she were physically touching it, though she stood, and the plow bit into the cold soil.

From the other side of the veil, another hand took the plowshare and, together with Sarah, held it. The other hand was a woman's, long-fingered, and pale blue.

"Sarah, what's goin' on?" Cal called.

The Firstborn hushed him.

Sarah took a step forward, and the plow moved.

It wasn't effortless; moving the plow required great force. Sarah's heart beat wildly, and her breath was tight in her chest. Sweat broke out under the crown and poured down her face despite the chill of the night air. She walked slowly, and steadily, and the plow moved with her, chewing a single deep, even furrow around the base of the mound. It wove slightly out in order to encompass all the Eve-stones, and after several minutes of slow, consistent effort, Sarah had walked entirely around the Sunrise Mound and the plow found the beginning of its furrow again.

Sarah collapsed onto all fours, breathing hard.

When she looked up, she found herself in Eden.

"I think She also suggested I ain't gonna live very long."

———⊰•⊱———

CHAPTER TWENTY-EIGHT

Jacob Hop shuddered constantly.

It was exhaustion. Sleeplessness and strain. His legs felt like wood.

It might also be the coffee. He'd almost drunk the last of Sarah's brew.

Though it was an hour or more before day, lights shone from the earl's windows. Jacob turned onto the earl's lane from the highway and two mounted men in dark purple accosted him. One stepped into Jacob's path, and the other hailed him.

"Shine forth, O drinker of blood! Arise and kill, dreaded son!"

Jake shook his head.

"What's your business, stranger?"

"An urgent message for the Earl of Johnsland!" Jacob snapped, more fiercely than he really meant to. "From the Queen of Cahokia!"

"Cahokia has a queen?"

"Some have wondered whether Johnsland has an earl."

"Harsh words, but not false. But a new day is dawning in Johnsland, friend. Those who've sung of feathers and eggs will shut their mouths."

"A new day dawns in Cahokia, too."

The soldier nodded. "I expect the earl will be happy to hear your message later in the day."

"I did say *urgent*."

"The earl rides at any moment," said the guard standing in Jacob's path. "Since the sun is not yet up, you must guess that his errand, too, is urgent. Unless it has to do with the location of the earl's son, your message will have to wait."

"My queen is a lady of mighty gramarye. She woke me in the middle of the night to tell me the location of the earl's son," Jacob said. "He's surrounded by enemies. We must go to him now!"

The guards shot each other a questioning look.

"Come with me."

One guard led Jacob down the lane and around the back of the earl's house, where a posse comitatus of fifty men on horseback stood in a semicircle around the Earl of Johnsland. A few of the men wore Johnsland's purple, but most wore plain wool coats, undyed. The men of the posse were armed with rifles and knives, but they also carried bundles of firewood on their horses, and sacks whose sweet smell suggested they were packed full of cured tobacco.

Despite what Jacob had been led to think about the earl, he was dressed and mounted, with lucid eyes. He was unshaven, though, with ragged yellow nails, and his long white hair was patchy, with flakes of skin falling from his scalp. He looked as if he'd recently arisen from a long sickbed.

Or perhaps the grave. But for his eyes, he might have been a Lazar.

"Aaron, take your men up the Durham Pike." The earl was in the middle of giving directions. "James, I need you to rouse the constabulary in Raleigh."

"And the godar?"

"Feel free to shoot them if they intervene."

"I beg your pardon, My Lord," Jacob's guide said, "this man says he has information."

"My name is Jacob—" Jacob began.

"To the hells with your name," the earl spat. "Where is my son?"

"He's in a tobacco-curing barn," Jacob said. "The barn is on fire. It's near a four-way crossroad, a double bridge, and a stand of oaks."

The earl turned a cold eye on Jacob and frowned. "That is a queer way to describe a place, stranger. As if you'd seen it in a painting, but had no idea where to find the spot."

"My queen is a seer," Jacob said. "This is what she has seen."

The earl nodded. "You are Cahokian."

Jacob tried to keep surprise from showing on his face. "No. But my queen is."

"I know the spot, My Lord," one of the earl's men said.

"So do I, damn you!" the earl snarled, unexpectedly fierce. "Do you think in a *century* of sorrow I could forget the hills I grew up in, the land of my fathers? We ride!"

Whoops and hollers bounced off the earl's manor. The sound brought to Jake's memory the whoops and hollers of plundering hordes at whose head he'd once marched to war. He took a deep breath.

"My Lord," Jacob asked, "may I accompany you?"

"Take a horse and ride with me." The earl waited, staring into the darkness, as Jacob climbed painfully into the saddle, his legs shaking and uncooperative. Then they rode.

"Where are you from?" the earl asked. "You do not look Cahokian, but Dutch. Your voice sounds like a Pennslander. Are you Ohio German?"

"Nee," Jacob said, deliberately lapsing into a Hudson River accent. "I'm a Yonkerman."

"And well-traveled, as many of your people are." They rode up the earl's lane and turned onto the highway. Light from the torches behind them gave the road they traveled an uncertain and watery orange cast. "A merchant, then, who has fallen into the retinue of one of Hannah Penn's children."

Jacob was so astonished he nearly fell out of the saddle. "Yes, though I might have said 'ascended' rather than 'fallen.'" He hesitated. "Tell me how you guess that."

"We ride to find my sons," the earl said. "But also my foster son, who visited me in my grief and untangled the path before my feet. Whose true name is Nathaniel Elytharias Penn, though I hid him behind the foundling name of *Chapel*. I only tell you, of course, because of the mistress whom you serve."

Jacob blew a sigh of relief. "I'm so glad. I was afraid maybe I was tricking you into rescuing Nathaniel, when you thought you were rescuing your own son."

The earl laughed, a sound rich with age, knowledge, and loss. "You're a clever fellow. If your queen ever decides she has no further need of you, you're welcome in my hall."

"Thank you," Jacob said. "May I ask, My Lord...am I right to think your men are carrying sacks of tobacco?"

The earl nodded. "Nathaniel told me he was surrounded by walking dead. Draug. He urged me to bring fire, and tobacco."

That didn't answer Jacob's real question; did it suggest that tobacco repelled the walking dead? But it raised another one. "How did Nathaniel tell you this?" He imagined the earl and Sarah's brother, hunched over the two halves of a broken writing slate.

"I do not think it was a dream," the earl said. "But his coming to me was *like* a dream, and a pleasant dream that brought me relief, in a time when most of my dreams were nightmares."

They continued in silence for a bit.

The earl turned off the highway, into a steep valley with no visible track. "This way will save us miles. The farmer is my tenant, and won't begrudge us."

"I see no road, My Lord," Jacob said. "I only see a mountain I'd have hesitated to take even on foot."

"Have no care, Republican!" The earl laughed again. "Tonight, you are with men who ride!"

"I'm out!" Chikaak yelled over the smoke and the smell of blood.

Bang! Bang!

Cathy fired her last two shots.

"Chikaak!" Bill roared, loading three of his pistols. "Kindly escort the lady to the rooftop! We'll make a stand on the stairs!"

Cathy withdrew to the stairs, not waiting for the coyote-headed beastman to act. She knew where to step and which walls to hug to minimize the chance she could be seen from the outside; given the darkness within the building, the odds of being spotted were already slim.

Outside, the fire in the west grew.

And in the east, the first pale gray smudges of dawn had begun to appear.

Trapped between one growing light and another felt to Cathy like lying on the anvil and watching the slow downward swing of the hammer.

At the second story, Catherine pressed herself close to a window, in the shadow of a large cabinet full of scrolls. From hiding, she looked down on the mixed force of Imperial rabble and Cahokian Wardens. Behind them, protected by the earth wall of another building, she saw the heavy woman in command. She spoke with a stubble-faced paunchy man leaning on a long rifle like a staff. What was she telling him? What was she thinking? What did she want?

With Sarah's people trapped in the building, why didn't they simply burn it down? Did she want to capture them alive? Did she think Sarah was in the building, and want to capture *Sarah* alive? But then why not send a messenger with that demand?

Bang!

The first of Sir William's last three shots struck the paunchy man in his temple and dropped him cold.

Bang!

The second bullet, close on the heels of the first, tore a chunk of wood from the wall of the building only inches from the heavy woman's face. She drew back and out of sight, but not before Cathy saw her expression of surprise and fear.

Bang!

A buckskinner with a Brown Bess took the final bullet in the jaw and fell straight back.

On the floor below, Cathy heard Bill's running feet. She withdrew from the window and raced up to the rooftop, arriving through a hedge of beastkind with Bill immediately behind her.

The beastkind circled the stairs, pikes, bayonets, horns, and teeth bloodied and at the ready. From the street below came the shouted command, "attack!" Cathy heard the sound of charging feet.

Sir William eyed his troops. "In literary traditions, gentlemen, this is the moment in which I deliver a stirring speech about how we must hold out until our queen has had her triumph. I am not a literary man. For those of you who can understand my English, I will say this: defend the stairs."

Snuffling and the nodding of many animal heads. Chikaak thumped his breast once in a vaguely gladiatorial salute.

"For those of you who cannot, I shall say it another way." Bill raised the Heron King's hunting horn to his lips and blew three long notes.

Luman raced through his mental inventory. Among the spells of Jean d'Anastasi, the great recorder and transmitter of Mephite magic, he couldn't recall a single killing spell. Nor a wall, nor an explosion. Love philtres, dog-bite charms, the healing or causing of insomnia, the finding or losing of a path, yes.

But nothing useful to him now.

He leaned in the east-facing doorway of the church, watching the beastkind. They shattered sculptures, tore up pews, and defecated on the altar, roaring and hooting the entire time.

Barrett's famous grimoire *The Magus* offered him no possibilities. Perhaps if he'd had it in front of him to peruse, he'd have found something, but in his memory it was all seals for candles, the magical uses of stones, and acrostics. Useful, powerful even, when called for; of no avail when he wished to intervene in the desecration of a church. Perhaps Aggrippa's *Three Books of Occult Philosophy*, the source from which Barrett had infamously cribbed, might contain battle magic, but Luman had never so much as *seen* a copy of that tome.

Two of the beastkind, the one with the rabbit's head and one that looked like an octopus, broke into a storage chamber behind the altar and came out holding gold and silver plate: a pyx, a sacramental chalice, a tray. From a sheer destruction point of view, shattering the pews was more troublesome, but from the perspective of desecration and offensiveness, the theft was grievous.

Theft. Something itched at Luman's memory.

Theft. He knew a spell for thieves.

He thought it through, silently mouthing all the words to be certain he got it right. It was a braucher incantation—surely, such a spell could only work even *better* in the confines of a basilica.

But as he opened his mouth, he was struck by the vivid memory of the bat he'd killed in Parkersburg. Was his heart pure enough, did he have the faith to work effective braucherei?

He hesitated.

But his himmelsbriefe worked. And at this point, he had no better option.

"*O Petrus,*" he began. The charm invoked St. Peter the fisherman, but Peter Plowshare slipped into Luman's mind and stayed as he recited. "*Nimm vot Gott die Gewalt: Was ich binden werde mit dem Band der Christen-Hand, alle Diebe oder Diebinnen, sie mögen sein groß oder klein, jung oder alt, Mann oder Tier, so sollen sie von Gott gestellet sein, und keiner keinen Tritt mehr weder vor oder hinter sich gehen, bis ich sie mit meinen Augen sehe, und mit meiner Zunge Urlaub gebe, sie zählen mir den zuvor alle Stein', die zwischen Himmel und Erde sein, alle die Regentropfen, alle Laub und Gras. Dieses bitt' ich meinen Feinden zur Buss'.*"

Mann oder Tier, meaning *man or beast*, was his own addition.

It seemed appropriate in the circumstances, in a spell in which the thieves, male or female, old or young, were ensorcelled into motionlessness, by a magician who prayed they would repent.

Then he said the Lord's Prayer, crossing himself three times.

As he finished the third sign of the cross, the animal cacophony abruptly switched tone, becoming a colossal disconcerted wail. The beastkind thrashed their arms about, hurled the chalice and the pyx to the floor, tore at the surroundings—

but didn't move.

Their feet, paws, and hooves, were all rooted to the floor.

Luman felt like yelling in triumph, but he didn't. Of all moments, now he needed to be humble.

Cautiously, he walked from the door into the nave of the church, avoiding treading on the discarded blankets and food left by the refugees, as well as the wrecked pews. As the beastkind shrieked and howled at him, he surveyed the destruction; the structure itself seemed unharmed, but the furniture, the relics, the art, and the windows would require much repair and replacement.

"*You* did this." The accusation came from the bison-headed giant, who stood between the altar and the pews, frozen in the act of smashing the last of the rood screen with an enormous gnarled club.

"*God* did this," Luman said. Humility was essential for the successful practice of braucherei. "But I asked Him to."

"God." Bison Head snorted. "You mean the god who is eaten."

The beastkind shrieked and gibbered.

"Yes," Luman agreed. "But He isn't finished with you just yet."

The bison-headed beastman seemed unexpectedly upset at these words, snorting and beating his chest. "I could throw this club and smash your head to splinters."

Luman ignored the threat as well as the fidgeting and continued. "Here's one thing that can happen next: I can walk away. And in just a few minutes, the sun will rise. Those doors there face east, and so do those high windows, see up there? With the pictures of the Bridegroom and the Bride?"

"I see." Bison Head shook his club as if knocking the sun out of the sky. "The sun will rise and it will shine on me. I don't fear the sun."

"You should, though," Luman said. "If the sun shines on you this morning before I release you from this spell, it will kill you."

"You lie."

It wasn't a lie. Luman had never cast this spell before—he was more in the business of stealing than in the business of catching thieves—but he was repeating the lore about the spell as he'd learned it, and so far, the magic had worked. "If I'd told you before I worked this enchantment that it would stick your feet to the floor, would you have called that a lie as well?"

Bison Head said nothing.

Rabbit Head wailed.

"But the spell says that this is a penance. It prays that you will repent. *I* want you to repent."

"Repent?"

"Repent," Luman explained. "Change your mind, and stop being a thief and a rampager and a killer of men. So I can show you mercy."

Bison Head stared. "Mercy? Would this mercy be to kill us?" He shook his club again, this time at Luman.

Luman frowned. "No. I would release you alive. But you must repent."

"It's in my nature to be a rampager and a killer of men. Today it's the measure of my creation."

"It's also in your nature to die. But if today you can decide not to rampage and kill, then today you can live."

Luman in fact didn't want the beastman to declare himself penitent. He wanted the beastkind to refuse his offer, and fall over dead in the imminent sunrise. But the spell asked for repentance, and he thought if he didn't make the offer, he'd fail the moral test of braucherei, and the spell would end.

And then the beastkind would tear him to pieces.

And he'd never be able to write a potent himmelsbrief again.

Of course, if they declared themselves chastened, it could be a lie. And then he would release them, and they would tear him to pieces in any case.

"What sign do you want?" Bison Head asked.

Luman considered. "Swear. Swear by earth, and by your life, and by this holy city, and by the life of God, that you foreswear violence and theft."

"Which god?" Bison Head asked. "The God-Who-Is-Eaten, or the Heron King?"

"Both," Luman said.

"Is that all?"

"I'll release the others first," Luman said. "When they've reached the foot of this mound, then I'll release you."

"The sun rises very soon," Bison Head observed.

"Mercy is ready for you right now."

Bison Head roared, a sound that shook Luman's bones. Then he began to recite: "I swear by the earth, and by my life, and by this holy city, and by the life of both the God-Who-Is-Eaten and the God-Who-Is-His-Own-Son, that I foreswear all violence and theft."

The other beastkind followed along in the oathmaking, some saying the words in English, and others apparently rendering them in animal grunts and yips.

Luman nodded and gulped, trying not to look nervous.

"You, you, you, and you," he said, pointing at each of the beastkind in turn other than Bison Head. "In the name of St. Peter, go."

The beastkind raised their legs, free from the spell. They looked at each other sheepishly, and then Rabbit Head shrieked.

Bison Head answered with a bellow of rage that sent the rest of his pack scurrying out the church doors. Luman stepped aside to let them pass, then watched as they went down the hill. The sun disk must be only moments from breaching the eastern horizon, over the Cahokian Bottom.

"What's your name?" he asked.

"Kort," Bison Head said.

"Kort, in the name of St. Peter, go."

Kort stepped forward, freed.

But he didn't leave.

Luman forced himself to breathe calmly. He reached under his shirt and gripped his Homer amulet, just in case.

"You swore an oath," Luman reminded him.

"I know my oath," Kort said. "I came because I saw the token of the God-Who-Is Eaten and I wished to destroy his home. Instead, that god now sends me away, humbled. Tell me *your* name."

"Luman Walters."

"I will keep my oath, Luman Walters," Kort said. "And also this: as you have shown me mercy, I'll show mercy to others."

Luman nodded. "Go and do so, Kort."

Kort lumbered up the nave toward Luman, bending slightly to bow as he passed the magician, and then stepped out between the two stone columns into the first blinding rays of the morning sun.

Eden was a garden.

It was also a mountaintop.

And it was a palace.

It smelled of . . . something vaguely citrus, Sarah thought. A cleansing, crisp smell, like pine sap and oranges mixed together, with an undercurrent of cinnamon. And smelling it, she knew she had smelled it before.

When her staff had flowered, the blossoms had had the same odor, only fainter.

And thinking back, hadn't the tree that grew from her father's acorn on the Serpent Mound also had the same scent?

A ring of trees circled a meadow. The meadow was thick with jeweled flowers and the boughs of the trees hung low to the grass with juicy fruits, red, blue, white, and purple. Above the grass of the meadow flew bees and winged serpents; among the trees Sarah saw lions and antelopes. Beyond the trees lay rocky mountain crags, and one of them was familiar—it was a forested bluff, and at its peak a serpent-shaped mound, and at the head of the serpent, an oak tree glowing with a blue light.

Beyond the mountains lay a sky that burned so brilliantly azure that its brightness hurt Sarah's eyes to look at, and yet it was planted thick with stars.

In the center of the meadow stood a low, flat boulder. Runnels cut through its surface, and the runnels flowed with dark red fluid.

Beside the boulder stood a Woman. She was pale beyond the color white, but also blue, the faint blue of distant stars. She was beautiful beyond mortal reckoning, and Sarah found that the closer she looked at the woman, the less she could see. Was She fair, or was Her skin so dark it was almost black? Was Her hair golden and straight, or tightly curled and the color of mahogany? Were Her arms long or short? Were Her nails painted? Was She wearing a long red gown, or an apron of leaves, or an animal hide, or a dress of stardust, or nothing at all? Or was She in fact wrapped in the body of a living serpent?

Or *was* She a serpent?

Or a dove, or a gazelle? Or a tree?

Notwithstanding the shifting, unseeable appearance of the woman, Sarah knew Her. She was the presence Sarah had felt lying within the barrow of the Serpent Mound, at the junction of the Mississippi and Ohio rivers, the center of the great watershed basin of the entire continent.

At her feet squirmed lizards of pure fire.

"Thou hast come alone," the Woman said.

It wasn't a rebuke, but an observation. Still, Sarah knew she shouldn't have come by herself. "I should have brought witnesses."

"There are witnesses at the door. Invite thou them in."

"They aren't dressed," Sarah said.

"I shall dress them. As I have dressed thee."

Sarah looked down and found that she, too, wore a dress like a skein of spider's web sown with stars.

"How shall I think of Thee?" she asked the divine woman.

"I am the Woman," was the answer. "The Virgin and the Bride. The Daughter and the Queen. The Earth beneath your feet, the Moon with shifting face, and the Sun with Healing in Her Wings. I am the Serpent. I am Wisdom. I am the Hidden One, the Eternal. I am the Tree in the Garden, and the Tree that Rises into the Sky. I am the Mother of All Living."

Sarah felt very, very small. "The Mother of All Living... Eve. You're Eve? But isn't Eve different from Wisdom? Wasn't Wisdom the first of Adam's wives, and Eve the second?"

The Mother of All Living smiled. It was a kind smile, and within it were terror, chaos, and the unerring flow of all things, and as she smiled, so smiled the lions, the antelopes, the winged serpents, the bees, and the flaming reptiles. "Go thou, and bring thy witnesses."

Calvin stood with the four Firstborn, on the fringes of the mound, just outside the ragged ring of stones. Behind them he heard the steady breathing of Alzbieta Torias's bearers.

Cal saw blue streaks beginning to color the eastern sky and he worried Sarah might not have succeeded in time, but he doubted the Cahokians noticed; they stood at the foot of the small rectangular mound and stared.

Calvin didn't stare. He could barely bring himself to look.

Besides, he told himself, there was nothing to see. Sarah stood alone on the top of the low mound and stared at nothing, her lips moving but making no sound. Her face glowed, but that was likely just the light of the morning, or maybe it was because of some magic Sarah herself was doing. No point in staring at that, and Lord hates a man as makes a big deal outta nothin'.

But also, he was wounded. He had killed a man—his first—and he had done it for Sarah. And rather than thanking him, she and the other Firstborn had been treating him like a big sinner ever since.

He ached, inside and out.

His grandfather had sent him to take care of Sarah, and Iron Andy had said Cal must be ready to kill a man. Well, he'd gone and done it. Did that mean he'd done right? Was he now the hell of a fellow his grandpa wanted him to be?

He had learned the signs and tokens of Freemasonry, and he continued to use them, though they had done him no good.

He had cared for Sarah, protected her, risked for her, even killed for her. She knew how he felt about her . . . and yet she pushed him away.

Cal took a deep breath and sighed.

Sarah turned to face her friends and walked down to the edge of the mound. Her face still glowed. She stopped just inside the furrow the Heron King's plow had made around the mound.

"I need witnesses," she said.

Cal stepped forward, but Sarah held up a hand.

"Calvin Calhoun," she said. "It can't be you."

"The hell it can't," he said. "I got eyes as good as any man I e'er knew, and I'm honest as the day is long. You want me to witness somethin', I'll walk to Paris and spit in the eye of Nebuchadnezzar hisself to tell folks about it."

"True." Her eyes were sad. "And you've spilled blood on the Serpent Throne, Calvin. You're unclean, and you can't approach."

She might as well have struck him in the solar plexus with a rifle butt. Cal gasped for air, and his vision lost focus.

Yedera put a steadying hand on Calvin's shoulder. "I'll stay with you, Calhoun."

Cal barely heard the Daughter of Podebradas.

"I'll witness," Alzbieta Torias said.

"And I," Maltres Korinn added. "If I'm deemed worthy."

"And I," said Sherem.

"Come." Sarah held out her hand and Alzbieta took it. She in turn took Maltres by the hand, and he dropped his staff of office in the snow and gripped Sherem's wrist. Sarah pulled and they followed her within the plowed rectangle—

and as each stepped over the furrow, his or her face began to glow.

The three stared about them in wonder, as if they were having some mighty vision Cal couldn't see. Then they turned together, and all four of them faced away from Calvin, toward the east and the sun that was about to rise.

Sarah knelt.

The other three knelt behind her, and then all four touched their foreheads to the grass and snow.

"Dammit, I did everythin' right, Sarah," he said. "I did it all right."

"There is strength," Yedera said softly, "in being the one who stands part."

Calvin shook his head. "God damn it. God damn all of it."

He began to cry.

Kneeling in the presence of his Goddess, Maltres Korinn knew he was no longer mortal. He would become mortal again soon, and *that* knowledge pierced him like a spear, but for the moment, he was divine.

He was clothed in stars and he was one of the stars, one of the Sons of God.

He knelt in worship on the cosmic mountain, and below him cliffs fell away to distances unimaginable. Somewhere below, so far away he could not conceive of the distance, lay the mundane earth and all its concerns.

"Ye are come here to bear witness," She said, gazing over the head of Sarah, who knelt before her. She spoke to him and also to the Polite adept Sherem and the priestess Alzbieta, but the goddess looked deeply into Maltres Korinn's eyes, and into his eyes alone.

"Yes," he answered. He heard his fellow-witnesses accept at the same moment, a trio of acknowledgements in unison.

"My children have no need of a witness," the Goddess said. "Those who now dream, and those who are awake, shall all know at the rising of the sun what is about to take place here, now, everywhere, and forever. Ye are called rather to witness to the rest of the world. Are ye willing to stand always, and to bear a true witness?"

"Yes," said all three.

"Thou, Maltres Korinn?"

"Yes," he committed. He felt the obligation settle upon him like a heavy cloak, like a suit of mail. Should be confess his faithlessness, his doubts, his willingness to risk going against the goddess's Beloved?

But no.

She already knew.

"Thou, Alzbieta Torias?"

"Yes."

"Thou, Sherem, disciple of Pole?"

"Yes."

The goddess seemed satisfied. She turned her many faces—tree, dove, gazelle, serpent, woman, all at once, looking in all directions simultaneously and also focusing together with the intensity of a hurricano—down to look at Sarah.

"Behold ye, witnesses," She cried, in a voice like thunder and the crying of the dove, "and bear this message to all the earth. Let every king and counselor know, let the meek of the earth hear and rejoice. Let every prisoner hope, let every tyrant fear, let all the wounded know relief. This is my Beloved Daughter, in whom I am well-pleased."

She reached forward with both hands—or with six hands? or seven?—and placed them on Sarah's head.

"My Beloved," She said. "Thou art thou, and thou art I. I shall make my covenant with thee. For now, I give thee strength sufficient to all thy tasks, and cunning equal to every snare that shall beset thee. However short thy life may be, it shall be satisfying and glorious. Heal thou thy family, and consecrate our kingdom to bring it through the storm. Amen."

"Amen," Maltres whispered, and as he whispered it he heard the same word from a thousand other tongues, a million tongues, the tongues of angels that speak with fire. Looking up, he saw a choir of flashing stars, and as the echo of their Amen died, they began instead to sing, a long melody of unbearably sweet, lilting notes, that bore a single repeated phrase into the cosmos, over and over again.

Sarah Elytharias Penn, Beloved of the Goddess.

Calvin Calhoun heard a voice from heaven like many waters, saying:

This is my Beloved Daughter, in whom I am well-pleased.

"Sarah," he said softly, his cheeks still wet.

"Don't grieve for Sarah," Yedera urged him. "She's chosen. She's well."

The sky broke into song.

Chikaak's high-pitched yap sounded over the grunts, yells, and howls of Sarah's beastkind warriors.

The sun cracked over the eastern horizon. Bill noticed it in a bright yellow band that crossed Cathy Filmer's brow.

"Why, Miss Howard," he said, "you are wearing a crown, and it becomes you."

"Bill," she said pointedly, "there are more pressing matters at hand than flirtation."

"Hell's Bells," he grunted, turning to look back at his warriors and their fight. "You have the right of it. Only without powder and shot, I'm a useless old horse, fit for the knacker's yard."

To his surprise, the assault was falling back. It was the third such attack the Imperials and Cahokians had mounted from the floor below, and this one had begun with a charge of spearmen, and then been followed by skirmishers with firearms.

Bill recognized some of the spearmen. He was sad to see the ones he knew trampled and torn by his beastkind warriors, but he must do his duty.

But in the very moment when the sun rose, the stairwell roiled into a pit of confusion. It came from the Firstborn. They hesitated, as one man, as if they were all allergic to the sun and its sudden rise threw them out of their discipline. They hesitated, and on the faces Bill recognized, he saw remorse and fear.

After a moment's hesitation, the Firstborn began falling back to the floor below.

Shouting. Argument.

"What was the story the Lady Torias told?" Cathy asked.

Bill tried to remember. "About kingdoms sinking under water?"

"No, about Kyres and the moment when everyone knew he would be king."

"They just woke up and knew one day."

Cathy nodded fiercely. "They knew one morning. One day, with the dawn, they knew he was to be king."

Bill nodded. "I do not know the mechanism of it. I had known Kyres as prince, and then one day he became king, and

I assumed that the event followed the ordinary scheme of such things. Perhaps all the Cahokians dreamed the same dream."

Bill's beastkind, having driven their foes before them, fell back into position, awaiting the next attack rather than breaking formation to chase the enemy. Excellent discipline.

"It's happened, Bill," she said. "Whatever it was Sarah had to do. The Presentation, or whatever she did instead. It's happened. It happened with the dawn. The crown isn't mine, don't you see? It's Sarah's. The crown belongs to Sarah, and those Cahokian spearmen all know it. That's why they are falling back, out of surprise, confusion, loyalty, and fear."

"I see."

"Only what do we do about it?" she asked.

"That, my lady, is easy." Bill raised the Heron King's horn to his lips and blew the notes that signaled *attack*.

Eden was suddenly gone, and Sarah found herself kneeling in snow. The crown on her head and the iron sphere in her hands were both freezing cold to the touch, and she was exhausted.

Where was the Heronplow?

She cast about with her gaze and found it, resting in the seam by which it had stitched the mundane world to the world of Eden. She struggled to rise and couldn't—

but Maltres Korinn and Sherem seized her, each by an arm, and raised her up.

Alzbieta Torias descended the gentle slope and returned with the Heronplow in both hands. She held it reverently, gazing on it as an object of wonder.

"Is this, then, part of the regalia of your kingdom?" she asked.

"It ain't my kingdom yet," Sarah said. The goddess had described her as the *Beloved*, but Sarah didn't really know what that meant. Hadn't her father been the Beloved, too?

Did being the Beloved mean you automatically became queen? The story of Elhanan who was renamed David and later became king suggested that was the ordinary sequence. Could Sarah be the Beloved and someone else still be queen?

And what was the covenant the goddess had referred to?

Sarah's own lapse into Appalachee reminded her of Cal, and she looked around for him...

He was gone.

"Dammit," she muttered.

The Daughter of Podebradas stood patiently in the snow where Calvin had been. The look on her face suggested she felt whatever pain had driven Calvin away.

"Beloved?" Alzbieta asked.

"Ain't that...I mean, isn't that a priestly title?"

"Of course," Maltres Korinn said. "You're the Beloved, or the Beloved Daughter. The goddess herself told me so, and I swore to bear witness."

Sarah sighed. "I guess you'll tell me all about that. First, though, I need help getting to that gate over there."

The Treewall was only a long stone's throw away, but Sarah's legs felt like they had the solidity of warm butter. Leaning on Sherem and the regent, Sarah hobbled painstakingly toward the gate over frozen ground.

Lacking any other instruction, the palanquin bearers followed. Yedera came last, scimitar held high, guarding the rear.

"Beloved," Maltres said, "I must surrender my office, and throw myself upon your mercy—"

"Maltres Korinn," she snapped, "shut up!" She didn't raise her head as she spoke, staring at the snow-streaked grass in the morning light. "There'll be time for all the groveling and the hand-wringing later. Right now, I need my strength."

He fell silent. Together with the Polite, he virtually carried her to the gate. Alzbieta Torias walked beside them, leaving her sedan-bearers behind, looking at each other in puzzlement.

Above them, standing on the wooden branch-ramparts, leather-caped Imperial artillery watched beyond the walls. From within the city, on the western side, Sarah heard the cry of distress of her people, and the roar of the animals assaulting them.

She wasn't sure why she thought this would work, except that...the Treewall looked long-dead, and the Heronplow had long been in the possession of the Heron King. If it had once been in the possession of the Kings and Queens of Cahokia, might they not have used it as Sarah now intended to use it?

Moreover, if the rule of Peter Plowshare could render the beastkind docile and peaceable, might some of that magic be lodged inside his plow? Could Sarah turn Cahokia into a place of peace, using the plow?

Also, the goddess had told Sarah to consecrate the kingdom.

Wasn't that what Sarah had done with the Sunrise Mound? And hadn't she consecrated it with the Heronplow? Turned it, possibly, in a *holier place*, as Alzbieta said the Cahokians had been unable to do for a long term?

But she felt sick already, and unable to stand.

"Give me the plow," she said to Alzbieta.

Alzbieta looked at her feet. "If the Beloved will tell me where to place the plow—"

"Into my damn hands, like I said!" Sarah barked. Then, seeing the humiliated expression on Alzbieta's face, she softened. "I must seem weakened. I *am* weakened. But I can do this. I *can* do it, because I *must*."

"The Beloved looks quite vigorous," Maltres Korinn said.

"Strong," Sherem added.

"Liars."

"You look like you've lost half your size, Sarah," Alzbieta said.

"There it is." Sarah grinned and took the Heronplow from Alzbieta's hands. The weight nearly toppled her. "Leave it to family to tell the hard truth. Now, if I've lost half my beauty as well, I don't know what I'll do."

She didn't want to say that with Calvin's disappearance, she felt she'd lost half her heart.

But maybe he'd return.

Westward, several streets away, a pack of wolf-, boar-, and lizard-headed men emerged from a burning building. Seeing Sarah's party, they howled and charged.

"I cannot protect us," Sherem said. "I have lost my gift."

Yedera interposed herself between Sarah and the oncoming beastkind, sword in a low guard position.

Sarah knelt and placed the Heronplow at the base of the Treewall.

She took off the crown—her neck felt as though it might snap from the weight—and handed it to Korinn. "Regent-Minister, if you wouldn't mind."

Korinn bowed and took the crown in both hands.

Sarah wrapped her hands around the iron sphere of the Orb of Etyles. Through her witchy eye, she could see the Mississippi River within, but at the cusp of reaching into the sphere, she balked. She just hurt too much.

"You're the Beloved." Alzbieta put a hand on Sarah's forearm.

Sarah laughed drily. "I don't see as that makes me any more powerful. Though it might mean more people askin' me for things."

"They won't ask for more than you can give. The goddess promised that."

Sarah nodded. "I think She also suggested I ain't gonna live very long. Still, here we go."

Lacking any better words, she repeated her previous spell. "*Magna mater, maxima mater. Rogo ut hoc aratrum pelleas.*"

She willed the Heronplow forward and called the goddess to guide it. To her surprise, the golden plow turned into the gate, turned again, and pushed itself straight into the wood of the Treewall.

Sarah's three witnesses gasped as one.

Behind them, the slave bearers murmured.

The Treewall began to bloom.

While the Heronplow was close, Sarah saw the bulging wood as it passed through. Where the plow touched any tree of the wall, the tree turned green and blossomed immediately. Dead wood grew new bark, dead limbs filled with sap and dripped the excess into the snow. Leaves burst from the branches, thickening the defensive screen of the wall. Branches became supple, and knitted themselves together more tightly. Heat flowed from the Treewall, and the snow on the ground within twenty feet, waist-high in some places, quickly sank into the earth.

The moving Heronplow passed Yedera, who paid it no mind. It passed the charging beastkind and they leaped away, surprised. After a short and fierce exchange of grunts, they ran at Sarah again.

Men on the wall above her began to shout in astonishment. Some of them saw her and pointed, but she paid them no heed, focusing on her spell-prayer.

The beastkind howled.

Soon the plow was far enough away that Sarah could no longer see it. But she felt power flowing through her, her own body heating and drying out, and she saw the progress of the plow by the greening of the Treewall. The blooming spread all around the city faster than a galloping horse.

"Beloved," Maltres Korinn said.

The other two witnesses simply wept.

The beastkind were close enough that Sarah could see their

eyes. Yedera raised her blade and bellowed: "Mother Podebradas, give me victory or give me birth!"

The beastkind roared back.

When the Heronplow emerged against from the wood of the gate, opposite where it had entered, and found the beginning of its furrow, the beastkind stopped. They looked at each other with puzzlement, as if they were waking from a dream they couldn't understand.

Yedera hissed at them and shook her blade.

Without a sound, looking down at the ground as if embarrassed, the beastkind turned and walked away.

Sarah released the magic, dropped the Orb of Etyles, and fell onto wet grass.

"Sharing is not one of them."

———◆———

CHAPTER TWENTY-NINE

"The barn ceiling is about to fall in," George said.

Nathaniel hadn't awoken. He lay in the sweat lodge, mumbling and kicking his heels at the floor. Landon looked closer to death each time Ma'iingan checked on him.

And George was right: the ceiling was on the verge of collapse.

"I have a plan," Ma'iingan said. "If we each carry one of them over our shoulders and we run in opposite directions, maybe one of us will get away." It was a terrible plan. George Isham would drop Landon and run. Ma'iingan wouldn't drop Nathaniel, and therefore the wiindigoo would capture him. Everyone would certainly die except George, and he might not make it, either.

"I have wronged them both," George said. "I only wish I could carry one over each shoulder."

Or maybe George wouldn't drop Landon, and they'd all get taken.

"Let me try to create a little space we can work in," Ma'iingan said. It wasn't an escape plan, it was a scheme to buy a few more minutes. Maybe God-Has-Given would accomplish whatever it was he was attempting in those minutes. He handed his German rifle to the young Cavalier. "Shoot them if they come for me."

Axe in hand, he kicked the barn door, foot lashing out over flames. He'd intended to knock the door so it would swing open, but instead it fell completely off its hinges and toppled forward.

It hit the ground, but not flat—something, presumably one of the wiindigoo's walking dead, lay trapped beneath it, groaning and pushing.

Ma'iingan grabbed the burning frame of a drying rack by the only corner not covered in flame and dragged it behind him. He jumped deliberately on the yawing planks of the toppled door, taking his best guess at where the draugar's head was and hopping up and down on it with both feet.

Then he dragged the burning rack and pushed it against the barn wall, perpendicular, creating a corner protected on two sides by fire.

Bang!

A zaambi Ma'iingan hadn't seen fell to the ground, George's bullet in its kneecap. It groaned, and then it groaned even louder when Ma'iingan hacked off both its arms. With the second blow, Ma'iingan's axe stuck in the earth; he yanked, and it didn't come up.

With a groan and the sound of feet shuffling in the dirt, another zaambi came around the corner of the barn. Ma'iingan left the axe where it was. He unslung his bow and took three quick steps into the cold night. The draugar turned to enter the burning barn, raising its arms and reaching for George Isham, who was shoving the ramrod down the barrel of Ma'iingan's rifle.

Ma'iingan put an arrow through the draugar's head. The force of the blow knocked the creature staggering sideways and the arrowhead sank into the burning wall of the barn, trapping the zaambi in the flames. It continued to grope and to kick at the earth as its flesh charred and then ignited.

Ma'iingan watched while George carried Landon out, and then George stood guard. The Ojibwe knelt to grab Nathaniel by his shoulders, and saw a bear-shaped shadow crouched over him.

"Makwa," Ma'iingan said. "I do this to help the boy."

The bear-shadow emitted a plaintive whine.

What was happening to Nathaniel? Where was he?

Ma'iingan dragged Nathaniel into the terribly imperfect partial shelter. Immediately after Ma'iingan laid Nathaniel out and stood again, arming himself with his bow, the barn roof fell.

The blue pre-dawn light made the fire, which had been a towering protective wall, look like an orange carpet.

A tall black shadow approached, chanting in a nasal whine. Ma'iingan sank three arrows into the wiindigoo; they bristled from its chest like porcupine quills, and the wiindigoo drew a long, straight sword.

Ma'iingan grabbed a piece of timber from the fire. It burned at both ends, but along the middle it was solid piece of wood cut square, a finger's length to each side. He could barely grip it with his hands, but as the wiindigoo swung his sword at Ma'iingan's head, the Ojibwe brought up the timber and caught the blade. The wiindigoo was very strong and the blow knocked Ma'iingan back several steps.

Sparks showered around him.

"Hey, Zhaaganaashii," Ma'iingan grunted. "What do you want the boy for? We can share him, na?"

Behind the wiindigoo, several draug approached.

Bang! George fired at the shuffling dead and knocked one of them down.

"The Emperor Thomas Penn excels at many things." Again, Ma'iingan heard the nasal voice as a thought in his mind at the same moment he heard it with his ears. The wiindigoo swung his sword again and this time Ma'iingan stepped out of the way. *"Sharing is not one of them."*

Ma'iingan took a swipe with his timber, and the wiindigoo parried. Ma'iingan followed immediately by leaning in, shoving one flaming end of the timber into the wiindigoo's face.

The wiindigoo roared and stumbled back. Ma'iingan lost his balance, and suddenly the wiindigoo's sword was biting into his back.

He stepped through the attack and stumbled away, keeping hold of his timber. "Wiinuk," he muttered under his breath. He circled, barely avoiding the grasping hands of two more zaambi, and then squared off to face the wiindigoo again, fire at his back.

"I don't know your Zhaaganaashii emperor," he said. "But I only need the boy for a little while. Let him do a task for me, and then your Penn can have him." For a moment, as he said the words, he tempted himself.

"Waiting is also not one of Thomas's strengths." The wiindigoo swung his sword overhand and Ma'iingan blocked it. The force of the blow was much harder than Ma'iingan expected, knocking him to the ground and cracking the timber almost in two.

The wiindigoo stepped closer and stabbed.

Ma'iingan threw the timber and rolled away. The wiindigoo's

attack missed and the top of his sword sank several inches into the earth. The burning wood struck the wiindigoo in the center of his chest—

igniting his brown coat.

Ma'iingan rolled to his feet, pulling his stone-flake knife. Surely, this was the end of the wiindigoo.

But no. The wiindigoo laughed, a high-pitched sound like a shriek, and strode forward. His burning coat spread out behind him in the early morning air, throwing sparks and threads of flaming cotton in all directions.

It must be a trick of the uncertain light, but the coat seemed to reach forward, toward the barn, like a living, burning thing.

"Fire!" A voice shouted, and it sounded like George Isham, only different.

BANG! A disciplined volley of gunshots followed the cry immediately, the multiple guns firing with one voice that marked Zhaaganaashii shooting.

Not George Isham. The Earl of Johnsland, his father.

"Load!"

The wiindigoo retreated several steps, confusion and anger on his face. He tried to turn and look at the source of the shooting, but Ma'iingan wouldn't let him. The Ojibwe pressed his attack, darting in past the long sword to cut repeatedly at the sorcerer. It was a dangerous play, given the other man's longer reach and extraordinary strength, but the wiindigoo was distracted.

The flames of the burning barn leaped higher. The smell of asemaa grew more intense, as if someone had thrown a large bundle of the herb into the flames.

Bang!

This shot came from George, and the bullet struck the wiindigoo in the face. The tall man staggered and went down, and Ma'iingan leaped in for the kill—

but the wiindigoo batted him aside. It was just the sweep of one arm, but the wiindigoo's strength was such that Ma'iingan flew twenty feet to the side. He landed hard, feeling a knee give out beneath him as he landed and his skin scorched by the burning coat.

The wiindigoo leaped to his feet again, sword high, advancing on Nathaniel.

"Fire!"

Bang!

The wiindigoo fell, blood spurting from multiple wounds. Blood black as coal, black as the night sky around the Loon.

Two horses swept into Ma'iingan's view as he struggled wincing to his feet and looked for his knife; it had flown from his hand on impact. The riders were the earl and a short blond man Ma'iingan didn't know, and they placed themselves between the wiindigoo and God-Has-Given.

"Load!" the earl shouted.

The wiindigoo stood again, roaring in rage, and then the blond man dropped from his saddle and stepped toward the sorcerer. As the sun peeked over the horizon, its bright rays glinted on two blades in the blond man's hands, and Ma'iingan realized they weren't steel—they were silver.

He lurched forward to help.

The wiindigoo still had superior reach, and he charged the blond man, blood pouring from many wounds.

Bang! The earl fired a long pistol and struck the wiindigoo in the chest. The wiindigoo didn't slow its charge.

The blond man dodged a blow, and then another, looking for an opportunity to get within the long reach of his foe. The wiindigoo pulled his elbow back, preparing to stab—

and Ma'iingan caught the elbow with both hands.

The wiindigoo hissed in anger. With the sun behind his head, Ma'iingan would have sworn the wiindigoo's irises were pure black, and little black tendrils like capillaries of the night sky radiated outward from that pool of black, threatening to darken the entire eye.

The flames of the coat scorched him, but Ma'iingan thrust his knee into the wiindigoo's knee from behind, and dropped, pulling the wiindigoo on top of him.

Ma'iingan burned.

The wiindigoo howled.

The blond man dropped atop them both, stabbing with his silver knives.

The wiindigoo reacted with sudden energy, shrieking, hurling the blond man away, and leaping to his feet. He clawed at his chest, tearing the two silver knives from his body and dropping them to the ground. Smoke rose from the wounds and from the coat. Writhing, the wiindigoo squeezed out of the coat and hurled it to the snow.

The coat's flames blazed higher and its fabric twitched uncontrollably.

The wiindigoo spat a curse at the Earl of Johnsland, who stood tall in the saddle in front of Nathaniel. George Isham stood his ground beside the unconscious boy, Ma'iingan's German rifle raised to his shoulder.

With a wordless shriek of rage and hatred, the wiindigoo turned and fled. George fired, and at the earl's command, his men—a collection of purple-coated soldiers and others who looked like armed farmers—hurled another volley after the sorcerer, but whether they hit or not, the wiindigoo made it to the line of trees at the far end of the tobacco field and disappeared.

"Nathaniel!" Ma'iingan tottered in pain toward the boy. In addition to his throbbing knee, the torn flesh of his forearm, and the burns all over his body, his head and his lungs hurt—however sacred asemaa was, too much was still too much.

"He still sleeps," George Isham said, standing aside. "And he mutters."

The blond man rushed forward as Ma'iingan's side. "What does he mutter?"

"Hook, I think."

"Maybe he dreams of fishing." Ma'iingan couldn't help himself.

"Not a fishing hook." The blond man dug inside his coat and came out with a slate fragment and a lump of chalk. "Robert Hooke."

Ma'iingan coughed and shrugged. "Who's Robert Hooke?"

"Death. Or one of his minions, anyway." The blond man scooped up one of his silver knives—it looked like a sharpened letter opener—and pressed it against Nathaniel's neck. A welt appeared instantly and Nathaniel screamed, arching his back and kicking at the dirt beneath him.

But he didn't open his eyes.

"Hooke," he murmured. "Hooooooooke."

"Death has many minions," Ma'iingan said.

"More every day." The blond man began frantically writing on the slate with the chalk.

"Beloved," Maltres Korinn said, pointing. "What is that?"

"I ain't e'er gittin' used to *that* title, I tell you what." Sarah sat up with Korinn's help. At the touch of his goddess's Beloved, he felt an electric thrill, despite the sour Appalachee whine that rang in her voice when she was tired or distracted. "What you lookin' at?"

Korinn pointed again, at the slate that hung by a string around the Beloved's neck. "Words are appearing."

Sarah shuddered—fatigue, or pain?—and grabbed the slate with both hands. Maltres could see the words as they formed. They said: *NATHANIEL IS IN HOOKE'S GRASP. CAN YOU HELP HIM?*

"Dammit." Sarah's shoulders sagged. She looked ten pounds lighter to Korinn than she had just days earlier, positively bony. With a shock, he realized that tears were running down her cheeks and dripping onto the slate. "I got nothin'."

"Who is Nathaniel?" Korinn asked.

"My brother." Her voice sounded like an old woman's. "He's in . . . he's under attack by the Sorcerer Robert Hooke."

Korinn sucked in his breath. He knew the name.

"I would help." Sherem the Polite dropped to his knees and pressed his forehead down into the snow. "I would shield him. I would find him using your shared blood and ward him from the Sorcerer, but I have lost my gift. I can't do it."

Sarah touched Sherem's shoulder. "That's my fault, iffen it's anyone's." Her Appalachee accent softened. "Maybe Nathaniel can fight off Hooke himself." The shadow of an idea flitted across her face. "Or maybe . . ."

"Your Majesty?" Korinn prompted her.

"Get me the Heronplow."

Alzbieta Torias had already retrieved the plow from its furrow. Once Sarah had struggled onto her knees, written a few more words on the slate with a lump of chalk, and placed the slate on the ground a short distance in front of her, Alzbieta delivered the Heronplow. Sarah pushed the plow's blade into the earth before her, pointing at the slate.

She took a deep breath.

"*Magna mater,*" she said. "*Maxima mater. Rogo ut hoc aratrum pelleas.*"

It sounded like a prayer, and when she finished her words, she was sobbing. Then Sarah fell forward onto her hands and knees and spat blood into the snow.

The Heronplow shot forward and into the slate, cracking it into two—

and disappeared.

✧ ✧ ✧

PUT THE SLATE ON THE GROUND BY NATHANIEL, Sara's words appeared on Jacob Hop's slate, *AND STAND BACK.*

Jacob did exactly as he was told, and for good measure he tossed his two silver knives even farther away. Sarah must be about to work some magic through the slate, and he didn't want the silver to interfere.

"Get back!" he advised the others.

The slate snapped in half. Bursting through the dark gray stone at a running pace came a golden wedge; it took Jacob's mind a moment to recognize the wedge for what it was.

The Heronplow.

"Woden's missing eyeball!" The earl nearly fell from his horse, but George caught him and calmed the animal.

The plow raced forward toward Nathaniel, reached his ankle—and stopped.

It stood upright, biting into the earth, and trembling. It dipped from side to side, slid back several inches, and then lurched forward again.

Nathaniel gasped, his back arching again.

Jacob wanted to help, but he was afraid anything he might do to try to interfere with Hooke's magic could just as easily interfere with Sarah. He contented himself with crossing the fingers of both hands and giving encouraging smiles and nods to the Indian and the two Cavaliers who stood with him.

The plow staggered forward several more lengths. A long, slow, shuddering breath wheezed through Nathaniel Penn's lips.

"Kom, kom," Hop found himself whispering in Dutch. He bit his lip.

The plow emitted a shrill whine, and fell back a length. Then the whine rose in pitch and the plow shot ahead, riding all along Nathaniel's length, turning to enclose his head within the furrow it was plowing, and then turned again to descend his other side. The plow was picking up speed—

and then suddenly stopped.

Nathaniel screamed. Blood burst from both nostrils, spattering his chin and his shirt.

"Kom!" Jacob yelled out loud.

"Makwa!" the Indian shouted. "Makwa, wiiji'!"

It didn't sound like a spell, the Indian's cry sounded like the same sort of involuntary cheering that escaped Jacob's lips.

But suddenly, despite the bright morning sun, there was a dark shadow in the shape of a bear crouched over Nathaniel Penn.

Jacob staggered back.

"Makwa, wiiji'!" the Indian shouted again.

The bear hunkered down on Nathaniel's shoulder and gripped the Heronplow with its front paws and its teeth. Jacob Hop found he was holding his breath, and he sucked in cold air. Gripping the plow as if it were a bear pulling a salmon from a stream, the bear leaned forward with its shadow-bulk and pushed—

and the plow moved forward.

Nathaniel screamed, arching his back.

Something invisible resisted. The plow jiggled and quivered, and the blood flow from Nathaniel's nose increased. But the bear pushed...and pushed...and abruptly, the plow turned its final corner and found the furrow in which it had started.

The bear disappeared.

And Nathaniel collapsed.

For a moment, all was still and silent.

Then the plow turned and leaped again, back whence it came, shattering the slate into dozens of pieces and disappearing, as if the slate were a rabbit hole and the plow had entered it.

Jacob Hop took a deep breath.

"Now what?" George Isham asked. He had helped his father down from the horse, and the earl now leaned on his son's shoulder. Both men looked astonished.

Jacob *felt* astonished.

"Now we plant," the Indian said.

That didn't seem right to Jacob, but perhaps the Indian's words had been a spell after all, and the spell was not yet complete. "In the furrows? Plant what?"

The Indian shrugged. "Beans and corn and squash, I guess. My people aren't really planters. Our lakes give us wild rice without planting, and we hunt for meat."

"Plant? To what end?" Hop was puzzled. "And who...who are you?"

"That was a joke, German," the Indian said. "What do you do after you plow? You plant, I think. I'm Ma'iingan. If that name is too hard for you, you can call me *Ani*. I came here to rescue this boy."

He pointed at Nathaniel.

"I'm Dutch," Jacob said. "My name is Jacob Hop. And I came here to rescue him, too."

"Henh." Ma'iingan nodded. "I hope you're good at sharing."

Seven men in black and white rode up. Six were soldiers, in coats and riding cloaks, and armed with carbines. The seventh looked like a Wodenist godi, with black tunic and cloak, long black hair and beard, and a rune-carved spear in his hands. The priest wore a patch over one eye.

"We heard about the Isham boy," the godi said, dropping from his horse. Then his eyes widened. "Isham!" He looked about as if uncertain. "Isham, are you well? Do you know where you are?"

"I'm on my own land, godi," the earl said firmly, "where you are welcome…as a guest, and *no more than that*. And whether we are on my land or not, you may address me as *My Lord*."

"My…yes, My Lord."

George Isham gestured at the burning remnants of the curing barn. "See the last remnants of the Yule log we've burned this night, One Eye. Do you smell the burning branches of the tree of life? *I* do."

The earl laughed. "Perhaps you can find us a sheep to slaughter, godi, but I tell you this: the College is done officiating. My son and I rule this land."

Nathaniel opened his eyes, blinking repeatedly in the bright light.

The descent through Alzbieta Torias's city house was bloody mayhem, a hurricane of gore and death.

Not all the Firstborn participating in the siege on the side of the Imperials were Torias's men, who had trained with Bill on the ride north, but many were. When the sun rose, and the Firstborn, if Bill understood correctly, all suddenly realized that their goddess had chosen Sarah Elytharias Penn for Her own, and Bill had blown his horn, those Ophidians had responded as trained.

They had attacked.

Mostly, they had had the presence of mind to attack the Imperials. They were not in formation, but they attacked suddenly, and as if from ambush. Shouts of outrage, screaming, and gunfire, erupted from the floor beneath Bill.

Chikaak led the charge down the stairs. The Imperials at the bottom were distracted, having been suddenly attacked from behind by their former allies, and Sarah's beastkind fell on them without mercy.

As Bill descended, blowing again the signal to attack, some of the other Cahokians—the city's wardens—were switching sides as well. "The Serpent and the Throne!" an older man shouted, rallying pikemen and archers to him in the ruins of what had once been a part of Alzbieta's library.

Bill wasn't ready to regroup. He blew *attack* a third time, and charged into the fray himself, slipping between two hulking warriors of his own troop and snatching a brace of pistols from the hands of an Imperial skirmisher who had been trampled so thoroughly he'd split in half. The expression frozen into his facial features was one of mild surprise, as if he'd taken a bite of meat that had gone slightly off.

Bill fired at the retreating Imperials. He wanted to hit the heavyset woman who was their leader, but he found no sign of her. Instead, he shot a man who was reloading.

He charged out into the street, firing again, this time at a man about to stick his knife into Bill. In the street, he blew *regroup* and then *square*, and was grimly satisfied at the speed with which the beastkind formed into their column around him; he was even more satisfied as Alzbieta Torias's men fell into their places in the formation.

The other Cahokians had either fallen, or now formed up around the older soldier still shouting "the Serpent and the Throne!"

Bill surveyed the situation.

Ahead of them, the street was blocked with an array of Imperials. They were motley, some in uniform, some apparently traders, and some looking like leatherstockings or coureurs pressed into duty. They crouched behind barricades made of wagons, horse corpses, and furniture, pointing firearms at Bill and his fighters.

The woman who commanded them stood at the rear. She wasn't exactly taking cover, but she stood beside a heavy wagon stacked with lumber, within one step of shelter from bullets.

Behind Bill and to his side, similar groups of enemies blocked the other escape routes.

"Stop!" The woman had a voice like a bargeman, capable of ringing out over miles of foggy river. Her own men crouched, still aiming, and she directed her gaze at Bill.

Bill would take casualties. He eyed the ranks of the Imperials, trying to calculate how deep he could get into that mass and whether he could cut all the way through before his men were destroyed. He wasn't sure he could.

And dying here meant an end to service to Sarah, and to Kyres.

"Are you surrendering?" he called back.

The woman laughed. "I love a brave man. No! Rather, I'm doing you the courtesy of pointing out the true odds." She extended her arm to point at the nearest wall.

Bill looked. The cannons lining that stretch of wall, operated by leather-caped Imperial artillerists—the so-called Pitchers, famous once for *admitting* women and now for consisting *mostly* of women—had been turned around. They now pointed at Cahokia itself.

At Bill, or his general environment.

A snicker ran along the Imperial ranks.

Bill was supposed to be daunted. To hell with that.

He raised the Heron King's horn and blew *attack*.

A volley of musketfire and arrows erupted from Bill's men and struck the enemy ranks forward. Bill swiveled an eye back over his shoulder to see that similar volleys had struck the Imperials to the side and behind.

The answering volley was fierce, a hail of lead that swept across the front of the square, dropping every third beastkind warrior with serious wounds. The Firstborn behind were sheltered from the worst of it, as were the wardens.

In three directions at once, Bill's soldiers charged.

As tactics, it was a disaster waiting to happen. If any of the three assaults failed, Bill would have enemies at his rear. Bill was exposed to the cannons, and unless he closed immediately with the enemy so as to render cannonfire too dangerous, he would be mowed down by the big guns on the wall. The only things he had going for his maneuver were the desperation of his men, and a small element of surprise.

He rushed forward with his musketeers, behind charging pike- and bayonet-wielding warriors, slamming into the barricade and tangling with the Imperial soldiers on the other side.

Boom! Boom! Boom! The cannons began to fire.

Bill anticipated the Pitchers' attack and he gritted his teeth, expecting his men about him to be maimed and shredded, even if he himself managed somehow to avoid death. Instead, the first cannonball struck far back in the enemy ranks, plowing a bloody-soaked furrow of death through the Imperial fighters.

A bad miss?

But so did the second.

Bill looked back at the other pieces of the struggle and saw the same thing—the Imperial artillery was shooting at the Imperial militia.

Deliberately.

Could this be some work of Sarah's? He'd seen her redirect bullets before.

But…cannonballs? And so many?

Bill looked at the wall, and a heavy woman wearing a short leather cape waved at him.

He waved back.

Did he know any Pitchers?

It didn't matter. He blew *attack* again.

He found Cathy at his side, raising a Paget carbine to her shoulder. "We are not dead, my lady."

"Pray do not sound so disappointed," she said. *Bang!*

"Only surprised, Cathy," he told her. "Only surprised."

The heavyset Imperial woman had vanished. Bill hobbled forward with Sarah's charging troops. The warriors behind him having routed the skirmishers before them, they fell in around him and charged forward as well.

"To the Sunrise Mound?" Cathy asked.

"To the gates, Cathy. To the gates!"

At that moment, a musket ball struck him in the thigh.

Kimoni Machogu stood, addressing the gathered Electors and proxyholders. Elsewhere, Machogu would have been addressed as *Your Serene Highness*; here, among his peers, he was *Sir*, just as Thomas was merely *Mr. Emperor*.

To his friends, he might even be *Kimoni*.

The Assembly had convened that morning, easily meeting the quorum requirements; it could have convened even in the absence of proxyholders, would likely have been able to meet even absent the Electors Temple Franklin had strongarmed into appearing, tracking them down by their social appearances and extorting or physically coercing their participation. Probably, the high turnout was due to the facts Machogu was describing.

Machogu looked every bit the prince. He wore coattails and breeches of white, and black riding boots polished to a high shine. Heavy gold rings pierced his ears. He stood in the well of the Assembly Hall with his back straight, his shoulders back, and his feet apart, as if prepared to fight any attacker who might come at him. And this despite the pathos of his tale.

"This is no ordinary rampage," the prince, descended of pirate stock, said in peroration. "A rampage of feral beastkind is a matter for the town watch, or for the militia. This is something more. It's something worse."

The Assembly Hall rose steeply from its well on three sides, with seats and tables climbing in tight rows to accommodate all the Electors. There was little room for anything else, despite the hall's size. As dictated by the Compact, no paintings were allowed in the hall, not even of John Penn or Benjamin Franklin, and the only decoration other than the glittering glass chandeliers was the Imperial Seal, golden and enormous, that hung on the fourth wall. The Seal faced the Electors to remind them of their shared commitment as they debated.

Hatchet-faced Andrew Calhoun sat beside his neighbor and rival, toothless Charles Donelsen. Calhoun rapped the knuckles of his one hand on the table before him. "You say *something worse*. What are you thinking it is, Kimoni?"

Machogu hesitated, but didn't look away. "Some of my counselors advise me that it's the return of Simon Sword. My own father taught me not to believe in the bogey of the Missouri, but my mother taught me that there would be things in this world that surprised me. I cannot say what is causing this rampage beyond all rampages, but I won't say it isn't the Heron King."

"That's awful damn roundabout of you." When Calhoun spoke, he kept his Appalachee squeal but managed to sound something like a Pennslander.

Donelsen's accent, on the other hand, got the better of him. He was a thin man, but had a fat man's face and a wild tangle of black hair that looked as if it belonged on a man thirty years younger. More than anything, the flash of pink gums he showed every time he opened his mouth gave away his age. "You ain't sayin' it ain't the tooth fairy, neither."

"No," Machogu agreed. "But I *am* saying that my land and

my neighbors' lands are overwhelmed by refugees. I *am* saying that miles and miles of cropland has been burned or flooded. I *am* saying that a third of my soldiers are dead already, and the others are exhausted. I *am* saying that the tombs of my ancestors are threatened." This made it a serious matter; among the Bantu, only the noble dead were buried, and their rock tombs were of extreme worth. Other Bantu corpses were exposed to wild beasts.

"You sure turning to the Empire is the right answer?" Calhoun asked. "The Empire didn't help the Abbé de Talleyrand, and the only threat that poor bastard faced was France."

A low murmur ran about the room, almost rising to a *boo*.

"I don't know, Andy," Donelsen said, frowning. "I heard our neighbor the chevalier might have been involved in that one, too."

The murmur erupted into babble.

Thomas banged his gavel on the podium before him, reining in the outrage. He believed the rumors about the chevalier, naturally, since Le Moyne had been blackmailing Thomas for years. The news through Temple Franklin's network that the chevalier was entangled in some sort of fight to the death with the new Bishop of New Orleans was also welcome.

"Will you send me enough men to fight this scourge?" Machogu countered, gesturing to the two Appalachee Electors.

"I'll send as many as I can." Calhoun didn't look at Thomas, where he sat on the low dais in the back of the well, on a chair resembling the Shackamaxon Throne, though made of mere oak. From that chair and with his gavel, a key task of the Emperor (or his designate) was to preside over any duly-called meeting of the Electors. "I'd a sight rather send you men myself than ship money off to Philadelphia so that star-addled numbwit can grow his pile of cash."

"And the rest of you?" Machogu looked about the Hall. "Will all of you also send men?" Some of the Electors—Igbo, Appalachee, Ferdinandians, and Ohio Algonks—met his gaze and nodded. Others—Pennslanders and Covenant Tract men—looked away. Still others, like the Haudenosaunee and the Dutch, watched and made no sign. "And the Electors who aren't here? Chicago, who is burying his son? La Fayette and Champlain, who now argue who will fill the third seat in Acadia?"

Calhoun nodded sadly.

"You see?" Machogu asked. "I don't come of a people that

asks for help, and it pains me to be asking now. I'm warning you, if my lands are overrun, Louisiana will be next." Machogu sat.

The Memphite proxyholder stood, rings on all his fingers glittering. Memphis always sent a single proxy for all its Electors, since its god-kings and the other members of its incestuous court were too important, or too fragile, or too busy, to involve themselves in Imperial politics directly. It was too bad, really; Thomas enjoyed seeing the seven-foot-tall, red-haired members of the royal family looming over their neighbors. In a way, that image captured how Thomas felt about himself. The proxyholder was some court functionary with a title like *Sole Companion and Lector Priest*; he looked pure-blooded Amhara or Oromo, just a thin, dark-skinned man from the Mississippi's shores.

The Memphite cleared his throat. "Memphis supports a special levy."

"You mean a *one-time* levy." The lantern-jawed Bishop of Boston stood, one of that city's two Electors; the Lady Mayor, old John Hancock's niece, sat beside him at the shared table, scratching furious notes and glaring. The bishop dressed like a burgher, in a simple coat and white neckcloth, but Mayor Hancock dressed to dazzle, in a cocoon of gold thread and shining gold buttons. "Tell us what you have in mind, then. Shall we impose enough tax to send troops to Memphis and the Cotton Princedoms only? And then meet again, when more is required?"

"Hell, yes!" Charles Donelsen shouted.

"Memphis and Shreveport aren't the only cities in distress." Thomas rose. "I am but a poor star-addled numbwit," he paused to let a low chuckle ripple through the Electors and proxyholders, "but I find that I can hire reasonably good advice. And my advisors tell me that the Ohio suffers, as well."

"You want the Ohio to stop suffering, raise the Pacification!" Calhoun thumped his table again.

"That motion has already failed, Andy." Thomas deliberately used the intimate form of the man's name, raising an instant scowl on his craggy face. "There's too much concern for rebellion. The assassination attempt at the Walnut Street Theater—"

"Assassin himself dead, imagine that!" Charles Donelsen whooped. "No one to interrogate, how inconvenient!"

"It *is* inconvenient," Thomas agreed. "I would very much like to have learned which of the Ohio princelings sent him—"

"Twice wrong, Tommy!" Calhoun snapped. "We have no idea who sent that assassin! For all we know, it could have been you yourself who did it, and we certainly don't know he was on the errand of someone in the Ohio."

"He was Ophidian!" the Memphite proxyholder snapped. "I have seen the body. Do you think *Memphis* sent him?"

"You may always exhume the corpse," Thomas said mildly, "and if you're willing to undertake the necromancy, you may interrogate him yourself."

Calhoun stared at Thomas, fury in his eyes. "*I* have no truck with necromancers, as well you know."

The barb was pointed. Did Calhoun know something about William Penn's Presence in Shackamaxon Hall? Thomas frowned.

"Well, then!" The Memphite threw up his hands.

Calhoun was undaunted. "And second, the rulers of the Ohio are kings and queens. Their thrones are older than yours by centuries, which you know good and goddamn well."

Thomas shrugged, an open, inoffensive gesture that would only further enrage Calhoun. "I concede with all my heart the antiquity and dignity of the seven thrones of the Ohio. That doesn't justify their attempt to rise against Imperial order."

"'Imperial order'... is that what you call stealing all their food?"

"The Ohio Company doesn't steal anyone's food," Thomas said. "It operates efficient, safe markets throughout the Ohio, precisely to ensure that residents of the Ohio can still procure food even as Imperial troops—inadequate and ill-equipped though they may be—hunt down the rebellion."

The Ophidian proxyholders—none of the actual Electors dared participate in the Assembly, which was not, frankly, unreasonable—rolled their eyes or groaned in protest.

Adriaan Stuyvesant exploded from his seat, finger wagging fiercely even before he opened his mouth. "What you say about the Imperial Ohio Company is half a lie, at least! You know very well," the Dutchman's strong Vs made it sound as if he said *fairy* well, "that Imperial traders have forcibly excluded Dutch Ohio Company traders from markets, have sunk our people's boats, and have even killed them!"

"I know no such thing," Thomas lied smoothly. "I'm aware of your lawsuits, and once we can consolidate the two proceedings into one, we'll get to the bottom of the allegations!"

"The Dutch Ohio Company will never get a fair hearing in your Philadelphia court!" Stuyvesant was nearly spherical, and under his white perruque he had the cherubic pink complexion of a youth.

"Can the Imperial Ohio Company get a fair hearing on Wall Street?" Thomas returned. "But surely, you can see that any conflict in the Ohio is the result of the princes'—pardon me, the *kings'*—inability to keep order within their bounds, a fact I've been lamenting for years. Surely, the right answer is to approve the measure before us, to modestly increase Imperial tariffs and tolls, as well as troop recruitment. Once I can establish order in the Ohio, I'm sure your traders will bring you glowing reports and enormous annual surpluses."

Stuyvesant sputtered.

"Point of order," Donelsen cracked. "It ain't regular to say you've 'modestly' increased somethin' when it's been *tripled*."

"That's not a point of order," the Memphite proxyholder said. "Though it's a fair point of language. Or mathematics."

Thomas shrugged again. "The absolute amounts are small."

Stuyvesant found words again. "The forkedness of your tongue knows no bounds, Penn!"

"Mr. Emperor." Thomas smiled gently, never so happy for the timid form of address as in that moment.

Stuyvesant wagged his finger again. "You're telling me to give you money so that your right hand can have the resources to stop your left hand from choking me and picking my pocket."

"Another point of language," the Memphite said. "One hand cannot simultaneously choke a man and pick his pocket."

Stuyvesant threw up his arms in exasperation and snorted.

"I'm not asking anyone to give *me* money at *all*," Thomas said in his most placating voice. "I am inviting all the Electors—including the Electors of Pennsland, whose exaction I will pay out of my own revenues—to pay an increased contribution to the collective, in gold and in men. This contribution will defend His Highness Prince Machogu's lands, and Memphis, and Cahokia, and any other land in the Empire threatened by the current rampaging of the beastkind. Whether or not," he added, "the rampage has anything to do with the so-called Heron King."

"Which it clearly does," said the ambassador from Adena, holder of her king's proxy.

"You of all people should be happy I wish to send more troops."

The ambassador, a woman with short white hair and a deeply lined face, spoke without standing. Her face snarled in an expression of contempt. "You besiege us. Your Company burns our warehouses, and then sells weevil-infested flour to us at rates that amount to murder, and now you suggest we should be grateful to have more of the same. Your Martinite bigotry blinds your reason."

"You believe the Heron King is assaulting your lands, and you embrace him?" Thomas frowned.

The ambassador was unflappable. "I believe Peter Plowshare is dead, and I look elsewhere than to Philadelphia for aid."

"I don't invite you to look to Philadelphia," Thomas said. "Look rather to all the Electors. Look to the Empire, which is *us*, and the things we do *together*."

"Sophist."

"I call the question!" Stuyvesant yelled.

"Seconded," the ambassador from Adena said softly.

Thomas nodded his acquiescence. "The question has been called, and it is time for a vote. The Clerk of the Rolls shall call for a voice vote and shall report the result."

He had them. The Dutch would vote against him, and Ohio, and most of Appalachee, but others—the silent ones, the ones who were more afraid of assassins and beastkind and revolts than of Thomas—would give it to him.

And then the Ohio would be his.

*"Somewhere, there is a cotton cow,
who wonders what ghost it is who milks her."*

———◆———

CHAPTER THIRTY

"So you fellas don't like handlin' dead bodies, I guess."

Of the three Irishmen working within the stone mausoleum in Navarre Cemetery, not far from the Pontchartrain Sea, the speaker had the biggest head. Abd al-Wahid had the impression they were brothers, though they hadn't said so—they just looked similar, and they interacted like men who knew each other intimately.

The Irishmen spoke English. After their weeks here, Abd al-Wahid's men understood both English and French fairly well, though speaking the languages was still a challenge.

"Only dead bodies we make," al-Muhasib said.

"Heh heh, that's a good one. Eoin, did you hear the man? Dead bodies they themselves make."

"He's funny alright, Téodóir. Now get your crowbar under the lid there and let's lift." The Irishman in charge wore a leather coat that clanked as if it contained steel plates.

"Roibeard, don't you let Eoin lift, with his bad back and all." The joker with the big head, Téodóir, wedged the tip of his crowbar under the stone coffin lid and turned back to Abd al-Wahid. "It isn't often a resurrection man gets to work with so much light, is it?"

He meant the fire. New Orleans was burning, from three days of rioting, and light from the flames shone through the mausoleum's open door to illuminate the graverobbers' work. They'd brought a darklantern, but it sat unused in the corner.

The destruction of the cathedral had eased the chevalier's sickness somewhat. Now the mamelukes had come to excavate this tomb because the chevalier's pet witch told them that doing so might allow her to heal the chevalier completely.

"Thank the Lafittes," Eoin said. "The one's a pirate, the other's a blacksmith...fire comes natural to both trades, I s'pose."

"Fire comes natural to any rioter," Téodóir said. "A good riot is an invitation to arson and burglary, at the very least."

"Would that make you Jews, then?" Roibeard asked, beginning to lever up the lid. "I heard that Jews don't like to touch dead bodies."

"Nobody *likes* to touch dead bodies, Robby," Eoin said. "Some folk are just more willin' to do it than others, given the right circumstances."

"The poet says, what shall I say, O Muslims?" Abd al-Wahid smiled. "I know not myself, I am neither a Christian, nor a Jew, nor a Zoroastrian, nor a Muslim."

"Yes," Ravi said. He stood with Abd al-Wahid outside the mausoleum door, with the girl. "We're Jews."

Abd al-Wahid let the quip stand. What did it matter what some gutter-drinking Irish graverobbers thought of him?

"No," Téodóir said, "that's a joke, and they're not Jews. They've come from the Caliphate, Robby. They're great warriors from the Caliphate, everybody knows that, which might make them mamelukes. Except they've got that witch with them. You know what that makes these fellas, Robby?"

"Jews," Robby said stubbornly. "Jews plus a witch."

"No, lad. They're...mambolukes."

Téodóir stopped to laugh so hard at his own joke that he almost pulled the stone lid off the coffin and onto his foot.

"Ah, your witch was right," Eoin called. "Come on in and have a look, there's nothin' here that'll pollute you."

The leader of the three Irishmen picked up the darklantern, unshuttered it, and shone its beam down into the stone coffin.

"Would you look at that?" Téodóir said. "Someone's buried a dolly. Some little girl loved her dolly so much, she buried it in Navarre Cemetery."

Abd al-Wahid looked to the mambo, who stood shivering outside the tomb beside Ravi with a wool blanket wrapped around her like a cloak. The other mamelukes remained with the chevalier, protecting him against possible attacks from the bishop's men. Her face wore a stricken expression, and she looked at the stone angels and crosses about her as if she were seeing the spirits of the dead.

"Someone's gone to a lot of expense for just a dolly," Roibeard said. "Maybe it's a child."

"Too small. Besides, you don't go to the trouble of a full-sized coffin for a mere baby. And look, it's made of clay." Téodóir scratched his face. "Maybe it's meant to be a soldier. Someone's dressed it in Imperial blue and gold."

"No, Teddy," Eoin said. "That's not Imperial blue and gold, the Emperor uses horses and a ship and an eagle. That dolly's got a lily on its frock."

The mambo grabbed Abd al-Wahid by the wrist and nodded frantically. His shoulder, still bandaged and healing from the wound the houngan's man Armand had inflicted on him, ached.

"Ah, the chevalier. How did I miss that?" Téodóir grinned. "Some girl loved her gendarme dolly so much, when it was killed in the riots she gave it a proper burial. I wonder what drunk-arse priest she got to pray over a gendarme dolly. Bet he was Irish."

"Give me the doll," Abd al-Wahid said.

The Irishmen emerged from the tomb whistling, and Eoin handed the simulacrum to the mameluke. It was a simple clay figurine wrapped in a rough imitation of a gendarme's uniform... or the chevalier's own clothing.

The sky grew pale in the east, not from the fires, but from the arriving dawn.

Ravi laughed. "It's a golem, only without the names of God."

The mambo hissed. "God has nothing to do with this. It is a curse."

"We'll take the second half of our pay now," Eoin said.

"You were to be paid to dig up a corpse," Abd al-Wahid reminded him. "This isn't a corpse."

"We did the same amount of work." Eoin's smile was affable, dimly lit by the fires of New Orleans. "It's not my problem the tomb was as empty as Jesus'. Well, almost."

Abd al-Wahid handed the doll to Ravi, who examined it with interest. "Then you can consider my sparing your life as the second half of the payment." He rested his hand on the hilt of his scimitar.

"Just our lives?" Téodóir laughed. "Why, I have it on good authority those have *never* been worth shit."

Eoin nodded, his face bitter. He and his brothers retreated several steps. Finally, Eoin spat on the earth, and the Irishmen turned and trooped away behind the tombstones.

"This must be a curse on the chevalier," Ravi said. "What happens if we burn the doll?"

"The chevalier burns," the mambo said.

"And if we throw it in the river, he drowns? And if we take off its cloak, he's naked?" Ravi grinned. "What do we do with this, then?"

The mambo shuddered. "Give it to me. I will take it to the loa, and they will help me undo this hex."

"Will the chevalier heal?" Abd al-Wahid asked.

"If God wills it."

"No," Ravi said, "you were right the first time. God has nothing to do with this."

Luman found Director Schmidt in the middle of the morning. She sat under a tarpaulin stretched over four poles to make a pavilion, beside a brazier of embers, at a light table. Around her pavilion stood ammunition boxes covered with canvas to keep off the snow, stacked dried goods, water barrels, and various other supplies. She had set aside whatever papers she'd been reviewing to speak with a newcomer.

The new arrival was the red-headed Lazar.

The Company traders and militia gave Schmidt and her guest a wide berth. Men looked at the ground and signed themselves with the cross or clutched protective amulets rather than looking at the dead man.

Something had happened to the Lazar; the pale dead skin of his cheeks was scorched, and his red hair, fingernails, and toenails all looked as if they had been cut short, and were now regrowing.

Luman felt weary, even more fatigued than his night of sleeplessness ought to warrant. He deliberately circled the pavilion to enter from a side where he'd be visible to both Schmidt and the Lazar.

The Lazar turned to acknowledge him first. *Hedge-wizard.*

"Wizard enough to summon *you*." Luman straightened his coat, mostly to be sure he heard the reassuring crinkle of the new himmelsbrief inside the lining.

Not thine intent. Thou didst open a gate, and I found it convenient.

Luman nodded at the short nails, and the arms hanging at the Lazar's side. "You've had a rough night, Lazar."

The Lazar chuckled. *And also thou.*

"Not at all." *I saved a church,* Luman almost said, but then decided against it. "I was attacked by beastkind raiders, but you know how it is. A little hedge magic, and I was fine."

"Well done, my Balaam." Schmidt settled back into her chair. "I'm glad you're returning now. I require your professional opinion."

She pushed a canvas camp chair in Luman's direction, but he remained standing.

"Tell me how I can help, Madam Director."

"The Emperor sends no word yet of reinforcements. In the meantime, Mr. Hooke here has offered us a novel source of new troops."

"He promises to raise our dead men so they can fight again."

"You're not surprised, then?"

Luman shrugged. "This is Robert Hooke, Madam Director. What else would he offer you?"

"And here is where you tender me your professional opinion, my Balaam." The director smiled.

Luman felt tired. She had already accepted the Lazar's help. What did she really want from him? If he acknowledged that the Sorcerer Hooke was the better magician, would he end up subordinate to the walking corpse?

He might learn magic that way.

On the other hand, it had felt *good* to protect the basilica.

It had felt like a step in the right direction. He had offered the rampaging beastkind the chance to repent, and they had taken it.

Had *he* repented? Was he repenting *now*?

Maybe, with a few more such steps, he might convince Mother Hylia, or someone else like her, to open the door of Cahokian esoterica and invite him in.

"No, Madam Director," he said, "here is where I tender you my resignation. You only need one magician in camp, and Hooke is your man."

Schmidt didn't even look surprised, damn her. She rose to offer her hand, and Luman shook it. "And where will you go then, if you must be your own Balaam?"

Luman laughed, suddenly feeling relieved, as if a burden had fallen from him. "Some place where I can steal more magic, I suppose."

Hooke hissed, a sound that approximated laughter.

Luman didn't look at the Lazar as he walked away.

Ma'iingan rode the star-horse of Nathaniel Makwa down a steep hill. Suddenly, the inverted bowl of stars above him expanded through itself and then contracted again, becoming the stars he knew, in their correct places—

and he saw the camp of his people.

He knew he was back on the earth because his arm, bitten by the draugar and then sung over by Nathaniel Makwa, began to hurt again. So did his twisted knee. While crossing the plain of the stars he had felt uninjured.

He entered and found Waabigwan his wife, kneeling within their wiigiwaam beside a sick child. Giimoodaapi. The boy's breaths were labored and he sweated. He was ill with a fever.

"Are we too late?" Ma'iingan asked, turning to Nathaniel.

The Zhaaganaashii healer's eyes twinkled like stars. "You *will* be too late, if you don't become a little faster than that." Then God-Has-Given stooped, snatched up the boy in his arms, and sprinted out the wiigiwaam door.

Ma'iingan stared for a moment. He still saw Waabigwan tending their sick child—

out the wiigiwaam door, he saw Nathaniel running into the forest, holding the child—

and he knew what to do.

Hollering, Ma'iingan raced after the healer. The pain of his injuries fell instantly away. He ducked branches, and pans of flour and water—who was throwing those?—and chased Nathaniel three times around the camp, dodging among his own glum-faced people, who didn't seem to notice him.

The healer ran up a tree, light as any squirrel. Ma'iingan leaped—

and found, to his astonishment, that he too could run straight up the tree trunk. And when they had both reached the top of the tree, Ma'iingan chased the healer carrying his child across a river of stars he didn't know. At the end of the river, they passed through the open mouth of the earth and into broad caverns.

Here the stars shone, but up through pools of dark water on the floor. Ma'iingan chased Nathaniel among the pools, careful not to step into one, lest he fall into the night sky. Unseen creatures with skin dark as shadow grabbed at Ma'iingan and he squirmed aside.

Finally drawing close enough, Ma'iingan leaped—

snatched Giimoodaapi from the healer's arms and fell to the ground—

landing on the floor of his own wiigiwaam.

Nathaniel fell beside him, laughing.

Carefully, Ma'iingan placed the Giimoodaapi in his arms within the Giimoodaapi held by his wife. The two melted together, and the baby's breathing suddenly became regular. Waabigwan sighed with relief and clutched the baby to her breast.

Ma'iingan's knee and arm ached again. "You've done it," he said to the healer.

"No." Nathaniel shook his head. "*You* have done it. I think the baby will now be able to eat the food of the People. And what will you call the child?"

"Miigiwewin," Ma'iingan said.

"What does that mean?"

"It means 'gift.'" Ma'iingan smiled at his son, sleeping soundly. "He is a gift Gichi-Manidoo has given me. Also, the word sounds a little like midewiwin."

"And what does *that* mean?"

"The midewiwin are those among the People who bridge heaven and earth. They are the great medicine men and healers."

Miigiwewin, Waabigwan murmured.

Then she looked up, and it seemed to Ma'iingan that she saw him, and she smiled. *Ani?*

He smiled back.

Nathaniel clapped a hand on Ma'iingan's shoulder. "It's a good name, Ma'iingan. Now, are you ready to return with me to Johnsland? You have a long journey ahead of you to come back to this place, and the sooner you start, the sooner you will arrive."

"It's not a witchy eye, after all," the Beloved of the goddess said.

She stood before the Serpent Throne and looked down into it. Someone had removed poor Eërthes's body—Maltres wondered who had done that, in all the tumult—but his blood remained.

The three witnesses were alone in the temple with the Beloved. She stood leaning on Maltres for support, while the other two looked up from the nave. They had brought her here in Alzbieta Torias's palanquin because she had been too weak to stand. The eight bearers—who constituted a second kind of witness, Maltres thought—stood outside the Temple of the Sun. Torias herself had walked the entire way—did she feel released from her sacred prohibitions? Was that because of the presence of the Beloved? Or had she relinquished her priesthood, along with her claim to the Serpent Throne?

Maltres wasn't sure what Sarah meant by *witchy eye*, though she must be referring to her one exotically colored iris, the one that was nearly snow-white. "No?" he asked.

"It's the Eye of Eve."

Maltres nodded.

"You're Sarah Elytharias," Alzbieta said, as if reciting a poem. "Beloved of the Goddess and bearer of Her Eye."

"Sarah Elytharias Calhoun," the Beloved said, and then looked very tired. "I mean Penn."

"Of course," Sherem said. "We will file suit to vindicate your claims against Thomas."

Sarah laughed, a sound dry as a corn husk. "After all this, a lawsuit feels...mundane. But better a lawsuit than a war, I suppose."

"Better a lawsuit than a war," Maltres agreed. Then he knelt. He smelled Eërthes's blood, thick in his nostrils as he looked up at the Beloved, the future queen of Cahokia. "Beloved...My Lady... I plead for mercy."

Sarah swiveled the Eye of Eve and pinned it on Maltres. "What the...what are you talking about, Korinn?"

"I imprisoned you. It's within your power to kill me." Maltres spread his arms wide to embrace whatever fate she decided for him. "I beg you to show me mercy, take back the Earthshaker's Rod, and allow me to return home to Na'avu."

The Beloved stared at him. "I will *not* show you the mercy you seek," she finally said.

His heart sank, and he nodded. "I understand."

"You may not go home to Na'avu," she continued. "I need you here."

His heart fluttered; he wasn't going to die. "To...witness?"

"Yes," she said. "Also, I need someone to run this city, and for that matter the kingdom. 'Lord Mayor' doesn't quite feel right, that smacks of Pennsland or the Covenant Tract to me, but that's the job that needs doing. Lord Mayor for the whole kingdom."

"The Memphites call such a person the *vizier*, Beloved," Sherem said.

"Ah, yes." Sarah smiled, as if remembering something from years earlier. "That's right, the vizier. Very well, Maltres Korinn, Duke of Na'avu. I believe you're still regent-minister, since there is no queen."

"But that's a formality," Maltres protested.

"It's no formality," Alzbieta said sharply. "Enthronement is a trial, and more than one child of Wisdom has died attempting it."

Sarah waved them both to silence. "You're still regent-minister. Now you're also vizier. Keep the Earthshaker's Rod as your staff of office."

"That *does* require formalities," Korinn pointed out.

"We'll get to them later," Sarah said. "Right now, I need to eat a herd of horses and sleep for about a century."

"I've got no room," the keelboat man said. "I'm packed stem to stern with refugees, and they're all paying passengers."

"I can't pay, but I can pole," Cal shot back. "And iffen you need someone as can stay awake and sing so's the other boats hear us comin', I'm your man for that work, too. I got lungs like a blacksmith's bellows and I can go all night."

"You sound like a real hell of a fellow, and I see you've been on a keelboat before." The boatman, a dirty, unshaven man with big arms, one missing ear, and a slouch hat, grinned.

"I can shoot, hunt, trap, whate'er you need," Cal insisted. "Jest git me as far as Natchez-on-the-Trace, and I'll work all the way there."

He'd slipped out the gate of Cahokia before the whole wall turned into living trees—that just *had* to be Sarah's doing—and hiked south to a village on the river. Now it was mid-morning and he was trying to buy passage south. Only he had no money.

This was the third keelboat he'd approached; the first two had laughed him away.

He should have brought cash.

"I just don't need it, is all. What I need is a homeless Cahokian or Missourian, with specie in her wallet and a burning need to relocate to New Orleans. Better luck next time, friend."

Cal sighed. "Thanks, anyway."

On impulse, he passed the boatman a Masonic recognition token in the handshake.

As he then made to pull his hand back, the boatman shifted his own grip, grabbed Calvin's hand more firmly, and gave him back the same token.

"You, uh...you said you knew how to pole?" the man asked.

"I got strong arms," Cal said. "How hard can it be?"

"You'll have to sleep on the roof," the boatman said. "But I've got blankets. And if the Imperial Ohio Company makes trouble, it's possible we may have to do a little shooting."

"Hell." Cal grinned, relief flooding his chest. "I'm *used* to *that*."

It was Christmas day, and Chigozie was determined to celebrate. There was food—turnips, potatoes, and one pumpkin, all found in an intact root cellar behind a devastated farm and roasted together over the fire. And there would be music.

Ferpa had a reasonably melodious voice. Chigozie knew, because in prayer she became animated and loud, and although she had a tendency to break into something that sounded suspiciously like a *moo* in her most enthused moments, her words generally rolled forth in a rhythmic cadence that rang back from the snow-laden trees surrounding the farmstead in which they took shelter like a symphony.

She couldn't read, and after a few attempts, refused to try. So Chigozie had taught her words by repetition, and now they sang together.

> *Joy to the world! the Lady's come!*
> *Let earth receive her Queen*
> *Let every heart prepare Her room*
> *And heav'n and nature sing*

Something about the words as they came out didn't sound quite right. Still, he was thrilled to see Ferpa roll back and forth transported, and clap a hand over the cross burned into her breast. Heav'n and nature, indeed! Wasn't that the nature of the beastkind, heaven and nature mixed together? Wasn't that the nature of all mankind?

> *Joy to the earth! the Lady reigns!*
> *Let men their songs employ*
> *While fields and floods, rocks, hills, and plains*
> *Repeat the sounding joy*

There were no floods in sight, and Chigozie doubted their strains would reach all the way down to the Mississippi. But the rocks and hills sang back with sounding joy, and Chigozie fancied he heard beasts in the trees, rustling in a harmonious Christmas dance.

> *No more let sins and sorrows grow*
> *Nor thorns infest the ground*
> *She comes to make Her blessings flow*
> *Far as the curse is found*

"I have come."

Chigozie knew the guttural, rasping voice, and it stopped his song immediately. He opened his eyes, and after one more booming line, Ferpa also fell silent.

Kort, the bison-headed beastman, stood at the edge of the trees. His shaggy head was bowed, and he dragged his knotted club in the snow. Wounds now several days old pocked his body, and in his eyes, Chigozie saw something he hadn't seen before.

"You were right," Kort said. "I'm ready to ask for mercy."

Chigozie's heart beast faster, and he thought he heard the sky itself sing back to him the final verse of Watts's great hymn:

> *She rules the world with truth and grace*
> *And makes the nations prove*
> *The glories of Her righteousness*
> *And wonders of her love*

"Blessed are the merciful," were the only words he found to say.

Kort nodded heavily. The beastman knelt in snow and began to dig. He scratched at the hard soil with the butt of his club, and when he'd reached warmer earth beneath the frost, he used his hands. He dug for ten minutes with Chigozie and Ferpa watching, until blood ran from the torn nails of his hands. Finally, he'd made a pit large enough to bury a small man, and he tossed his weapon in, pushing snow and earth back over the top.

When he had finished, the beastman knelt over his buried club and pressed his bison's forehead into the snow.

"Yes," Chigozie said. "I think you are ready. I think we are both ready."

✧   ✧   ✧

"That one," Sir William said. "With the lizard's tail and the bear's head."

Sarah looked down from where she stood on the Treewall at the beastman the Cavalier had indicated. "He rages like the others. He is seized by a fury." She shivered slightly at the memory of a horse of such creatures, within her city's walls.

By her own choice, she had replaced her Appalachee clothing and the blue Imperial coat with a gray tunic, trousers, and cloak. When her hair had grown long enough, she intended to wear it bound behind her head, Cahokian-style.

"Yes, ma'am." Sir William rested all his weight on two crutches. Sarah and Cathy had done their best with his again-injured leg, but he couldn't stand unaided without pain, and maybe never would. "Only when he was within the Treewall, he was so calm I'd have called him civilized. Leaving the city has rendered him again feral."

"And our warriors?" Sarah asked.

"A few dead," Bill acknowledged. "A greater number injured. We will bury them as heroes."

"With Uris," Sarah said.

"Colonel Uris." Sir William straightened his back and stared into the distance. "We shall devise appropriate military honors for the man, with some combination of firearm salutes and unison roaring."

"It's the blessing of Peter Plowshare," Sherem said. The Polite did not raise his eyes as he spoke, had scarcely raised his eyes at all since witnessing the events on the Sunrise Mound. "This calming of the beastkind, it comes from him."

"No," Alzbieta Torias contradicted him. "It is the *wedding gift* of Peter Plowshare."

Sarah sighed. "Here we go again."

She missed Calvin. She had found him with her Eye of Eve, sailing downriver on a keelboat, but she hadn't tried to send for him. She understood his decision.

"If you would know the secrets of the Serpent Throne," Alzbieta said softly, "you can't flinch away when they don't please you. The goddess has chosen you."

All three of Sarah's witnesses nodded, as did Yedera. The oathbound Podebradan had said little since Cal's departure.

"It could have been someone else." Sarah wasn't sure that

was true, but she wanted it say it out loud to test the idea. "She could have chosen you. I merely stood in the right place, at the right time, with the right tools."

"You are the daughter of the king, Your Majesty," Bill said.

"Is that what did it?" Sarah pushed back. "Or was it the fact that I happened to have the Heronplow? Or was it the spells my dying father cast and the magical gifts he gave his children?"

The priestess snorted her disagreement, but bowed her head.

"When the poets write of this day," Sir William assured Sarah, "they will say that you were chosen, and the child of prophecy."

"You can only promise that if you write the poetry yourself, Sir William." Cathy Filmer kept Bill between herself and Alzbieta Torias; the events of the solstice seemed to have aggravated her distrust of the priestess. "This is a side of you with which I am unfamiliar."

"No, my lady," Sir William said, "there is another way. I intend to twist the poets' arms."

Cahokia was surrounded. Beastkind raged on the west, between the city and the river. North, south, and east, Imperial troops were camped, and their numbers grew daily. At night, creatures that had once been men shuffled in slow circuit around Cahokia, moaning without words and clawing at the Treewall.

At Sarah's orders, the gates had been shut, but she had distressingly few troops on the walls. The Imperial artillerists had defected to Cahokia, but otherwise Cahokia was defended by its wardens and by the private troops of a handful of its wealthier citizens.

Also, Cahokia had very little in the way of stores.

"Your Majesty," Cathy Filmer said, "have you considered that you might turn the plow to encircling the entire kingdom? Gift of Peter Plowshare or not, it would greatly relieve our current straits if every beastman on this side of the Mississippi were to calm down."

As if in answer, Sarah was taken by a coughing fit. It was short and furious, and she held herself up by leaning on the Elector's horse-headed staff. Finally, she gagged up a thin stream of thickened black blood.

Cathy didn't press her suggestion.

"I need to go back," Sarah said.

"To Nashville?" Sir William asked.

"To my father." She looked south. "I think he has things yet to tell me. But before that, I need to get a message to my brother."

"You've found him?" Cathy asked.

Sarah nodded. "I've found both of them."

La Verge Caníbal sailed into a fierce north wind that brought down with it a horde of refugees. They were no longer just Missouri farmers; Montse, clinging to the ropes or looking through a brass telescope from her tiny quarterdeck, saw Ohio Germans, Firstborn, and even a Memphite barge or two.

Something was breaking at the center of the continent.

Something was breaking inside Montse, too. Drawing back in her telescope, she leaned forward to cough and spit blood over the rail.

"I should make some crack about your sexual wiles," Josep said. He stood near her and also watched upriver. "Only I find I haven't the heart."

"It comes out the other end, too," Montse said. "You see, you may inherit *La Verge Caníbal* after all."

"You passed the coins?" Josep asked.

Montse nodded. "But I still hurt inside."

"We'll find a witch in Shreveport," Josep suggested. "Someone who can heal this wound."

Montse returned the telescope to her eye. "No, Josep, we won't stop to look for a witch. We'll go to Cahokia as fast as we can, and do everything we can to rescue Margarida. If I die, I die. But it turns out that the wound in my belly is nothing compared to the wound in my heart."

"I *do* know where they've gone," the boy said earnestly.

Kinta Jane held the draft horses' reins tight and chuckled softly. Old, tired, blinkered, and restrained, the animals didn't need the soothing, but it was part of the act, along with her broad-brimmed Pennslander hat, the stuffing in her shirt to make her look like a fat man, and the coal smudges on her face.

Temple Franklin, the Emperor's aide and confidant, looked down at the filthy ragamuffin standing before him and harrumphed. "Franklin's Players, you know who I mean?"

"Yes, sir. They're the ones who perform Jesus Born for Christmas, and Jesus Crucified for Easter."

"Precisely." Temple looked about the bustling market square over his spectacles. "Where are they?"

Wilkes, also in disguise, whistled and shoveled coal into a chute surrounded by cobblestones. The wagon stood in a small square only a few yards from the Lightning Cathedral—its tallest three spires, the east-facing ones, peeked over the bank facing Kinta Jane, their white stone hard to see against the white winter sky. The bishop's famous lightning crackled within enormous glass receptacles, big as barrels, in each of the three church-towers.

"Do you desire to see a mystery play, sir?" the boy asked innocently.

Franklin fixed a keen eye on the lad. "I see you've already decided your price. Philadelphia urchin today, Philadelphia lawyer tomorrow. Do you know what they say about Pennsland, boy?"

"That it's got a lot of trees."

Franklin snorted. "No, that's not it, true though it be. No, they say this: Pennsland is heaven for farmers, paradise for artisans, and hell for officials."

"And preachers," the boy added, as if reciting a catechism.

"You've been to school!"

The boy beamed, without losing his sly look. "Thanks to your grandfather, sir, I had to."

Franklin harrumphed again. "Well, you *should* thank him. I see you know who I am, anyway, and you know I'm not the wealthy man my grandfather was. How much will this information cost me?"

"A shilling," the boy said promptly. "Philadelphia."

"Go on, then," Franklin told him. "Where are they?"

The boy said nothing, but held out his hand, palm up.

"That's a lot of money you want," Franklin said.

The boy shrugged. "Don't pay me if you don't want to know."

Franklin growled but dug a silver coin from his purse. "Tell me."

The boy turned and pointed. "Out that gate there starts the Lancaster Pike."

"I know the road."

"Good. Take it and follow it straight."

Wilkes climbed aboard and Kinta Jane started the wagon forward.

Franklin adjusted his spectacles and frowned. "How far?"

The boy swung his head from side to side as if calculating. "About six hundred miles, I expect."

"Six hundred miles! But that would mean you want me to—"

"That's right!" The boy nodded, and then burst into a run, crossing the square and turning to yell back with hands cupped around his mouth. "You go to the Kentuck!"

Kinta Jane drove her wagon out of the market square. "Where to, coalman?" She was still unaccustomed to the use of her new tongue, and it still surprised her every time a barking dog fell silent in her presence.

"North, coalman," Isaiah Wilkes said. "Brother Onas is sleeping, so we must turn elsewhere for aid."

Ma'iingan arose early, offered asemaa to the four directions and to mother earth, and then sought the others to say his farewells.

Nathaniel and the Dutchman Jacob Hop stood inside the Earl of Johnsland's great hall. The healer wore his tricorner hat backward and his long coat inside-out, and carried his horse-drum slung over his shoulder.

Hop shuffled a warped and splitting deck of cards.

The tapestries were gone. The earl and his son George directed teams of Zhaaganaashii farmers who scrubbed the walls and floors in preparation for repainting. Landon Chapel moved slowly, directing men who replaced buckets of filthy water with clean water and lye soap. A carpenter removed windows in order to make way for new frames and glass, so the wind blowing through the hall was chill despite the bonfire at one end.

Ma'iingan arrived as the earl was handing a flat wooden box to Nathaniel.

Nathaniel inspected the box; there were no markings on it, and it was of simple workmanship. Ma'iingan recognized it as the box the earl had been clutching when he'd seen the man mad in his own hall, believing himself to be a bird. "What is this?"

The earl smiled, sorrow twinkling deep in his eyes. Having bathed and scrubbed away multiple layers of dead skin, grime, and the effluvia of illness, he looked like a much younger man. "When you came to me, you arrived with two things. I kept them both, expecting to give them to you someday. I found as I lost my grip on my own mind, I clutched these two things even tighter."

Nathaniel opened the box and took out the first item. It was a rag, a simple hand towel such as a scullery maid might use, gray with age.

"Squeeze it," the earl said. "Roll your hand down it, if you will forgive the vulgarity, as if you were pulling at a cow's teat."

Nathaniel frowned, but pulled down the rag. Though the cloth appeared dry, his action caused a stream of white liquid to jet from the rag to the floor. The healer almost dropped the rag, but then looked up at the earl with surprise. "What is that?"

"Milk." The earl shrugged. "Cow's milk, for all I can tell by the taste. I don't know where the milk comes from."

"Somewhere," Ma'iingan said, "there is a cotton cow, who wonders what ghost it is who milks her."

The earl guffawed. "Perhaps."

Nathaniel replaced the rag and drew the second item from the box. It was an acorn.

Old, plain, slightly cracked.

Then, as he and Ma'iingan and the others looked at it, words began to appear on the wood.

"We have a sister," Nathaniel read aloud as the words appeared, incised into the acorn. "The acorn will lead you to her."

"Who is we?" George Isham asked.

"Nathaniel and his sister," Hop explained. To answer the sudden raising of Cavalier eyebrows, he added, "the witch-queen of Cahokia."

"I hadn't heard," the earl said slowly, "but it makes my heart glad. Kyres's children rise, and almost, it is as if Kyres himself returns. And there is a third. Go with my blessing, Nathaniel. Find your sister."

"And you, My Lord Earl?" Jacob Hop asked.

"Evil news from Philadelphia." The earl's face darkened. "My proxyholder writes in a perfunctory way, perhaps believing me still mad, to inform me that he has voted to support the Emperor in pacifying the Ohio. He attaches the particulars, which greatly increase my taxes and also require me to furnish men for Imperial service. I must confer with my neighbors about what is to be done."

"And the Chief Godi?"

"I will confer with him as well. He is not my enemy, though he has meddled in my affairs beyond his writ. I understand his proxyholder voted similarly, but in his case, it may not have been against the Elector's preferences."

"I shall ride with my father," George said.

"And I shall make certain the manor is repainted before they return!" Landon cried from the corner of the long hall.

"And . . . Jenny?" Nathaniel asked softly.

"Jenny will stay here," George said. "Her child will be named Chapel, but I will acknowledge him, and Jenny will always have a place."

"And you will go home," Nathaniel said to Ma'iingan. The Ojibwe's arm still ached a bit, but after the healer's songs, his skin felt new and his lungs were clear.

"I could travel with you," Ma'iingan offered.

"You have opened the way for me," Nathaniel said. "I'm healed. It's enough, I think."

"Then I'll go home." Ma'iingan nodded. "And feed my son."

Belowdecks in the *Sint Michiel de Ruyter*, the mate fumbled with the keys. He did it quietly, not wanting to awaken the occupant of the tiny, timber-reinforced room. He froze at the soft *chink* of iron on iron, held his breath, and decided he hadn't been heard.

The ship rocked as it should, creaked as it should. Outside, an icy wind blew her northward toward her home port.

The mate slipped the key into the lock, which he'd had profusely oiled earlier in the day against this moment. In his other hand, he held a plate of biscuit and pork. Leaving the key in the lock, the mate eased open the door.

He took two steps in, carefully measured.

He set down the plate.

The room's occupant rose. This was the moment the mate feared, and he backed toward the door, murmuring placating things. "Er is geen problem, dit is een erg lekker diner."

The prisoner stepped forward, and in a shaft of light descending through a small crack in the planks above, the mate saw the thick tangle of curly hair on the prisoner's head rise and stand on end, as if she had been electrified.

"Helpen me!" he screamed.

He heard the splintering of the wood as the prisoner tore her chain from the wall, and then she swung the chain at the mate.

He threw himself on the floor, barely avoiding the attack. She swung again.

The last thing he heard was the cracking of his own skull.